I0760326

Island Escapes

Finding Cory

The Reluctant Billionaire

Her Fake Island Wedding

Slow Simmer

Fighting Fate

Crop It Like It's Hot

Better In Practice

Caitlyn Lynch

SHENANIGANS PRESS

shenanigans press.com/EN

For permission requests, please contact:

Shenanigans Press

PO Box 323, MORAYFIELD QLD 4506 AUSTRALIA

Email: cait@caitlynlynch.com

Contents

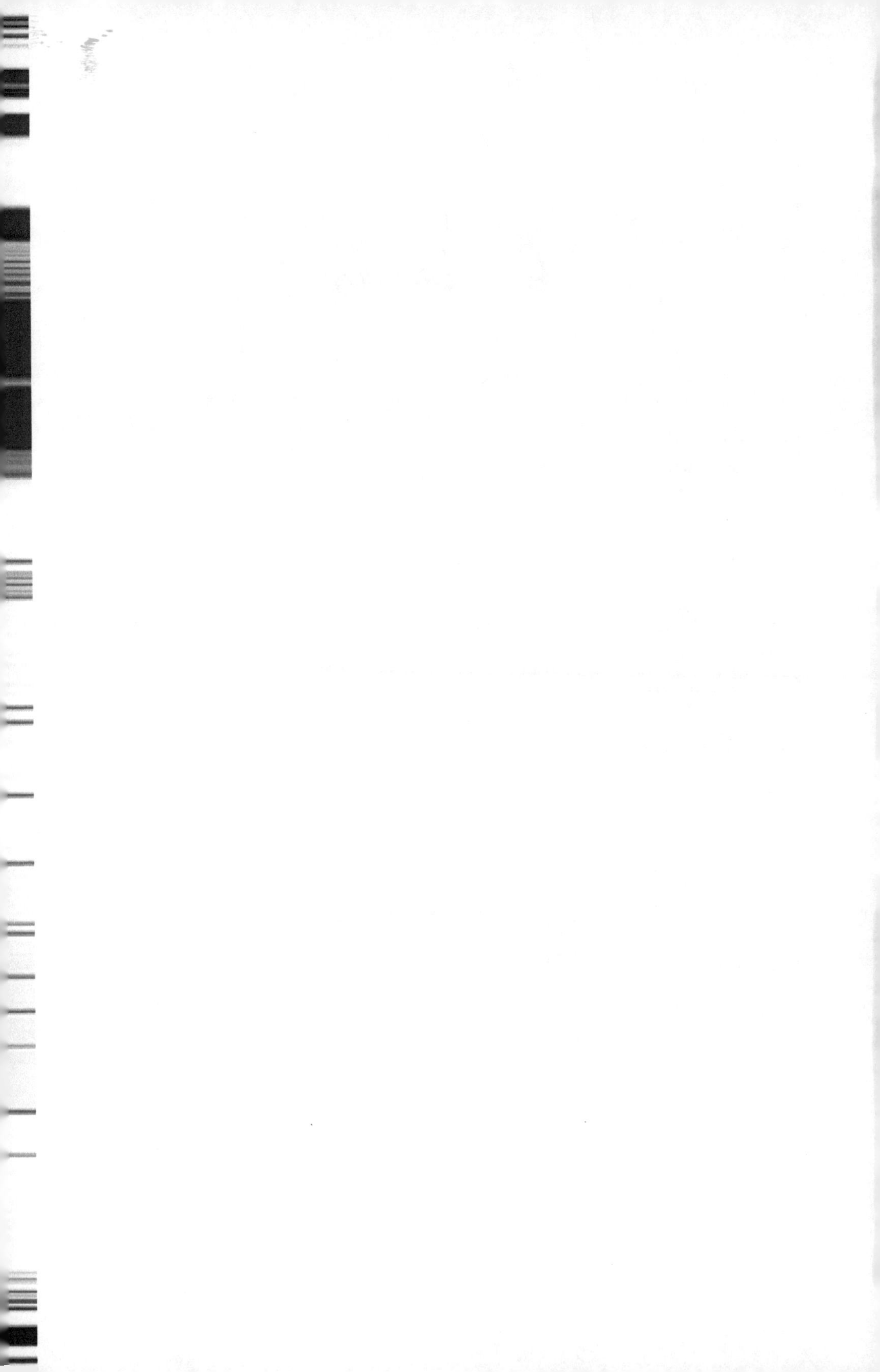

Finding Cory

Island Escapes
Book 1

Caitlyn Lynch

SHENANIGANS PRESS

shenaniganspress.com/EN

Contents

Chapter One

The cacophony of New York City seemed more intense than usual as Olivia Stratten manoeuvred her way through the crowded streets of Manhattan. Her cab driver seemed intent on making every red light, and the jerky stop-and-go motion did nothing to calm her nerves. She glanced out the window at the familiar sights of her home for the past decade, feeling a bittersweet mixture of nostalgia and relief. She was leaving this all behind—her high-powered job, her upscale apartment, and the scandal that had turned her life upside down.

The city seemed to pulse with an urgency she had never quite noticed before. Pedestrians hustled along the sidewalks, the air filled with the blaring of car horns, snippets of conversation, and the distant wail of sirens. Olivia's heart pounded in her chest, matching the frenetic energy of the city. She forced herself to take slow, deep breaths, trying to steady her nerves.

As the cab finally pulled up to John F. Kennedy International Airport, Olivia took a deep breath and stepped out, handing the driver a generous tip. The airport was buzzing with activity, a microcosm of the city she was leaving. People rushed by with luggage, announcements blared over the intercom, and the sheer volume of humanity moving through the terminal was overwhelming. Olivia checked in her luggage, going through the motions with the efficiency of a seasoned traveller.

The finality of her departure hit her as she passed through security and made her way to the gate. She was really doing this—leaving everything she knew for a new life on the other side of the world. As she boarded the plane, she couldn't help but reflect on the events that had led her here.

Brad Cochrane, her ex-fiancé, had been the architect of her downfall. His involvement in a massive financial scandal had dragged her name through the mud, even though she had been completely innocent. The advertising firm where she had worked tirelessly for years had unceremoniously let her go, and her reputation had been left in tatters. When the offer from Sunfish Island Resort came, it felt like a lifeline.

Olivia settled into her seat on the plane, staring out the window at the city she was leaving behind. She could still remember the shock and betrayal she had felt when the news about Brad broke. It had been a whirlwind of media frenzy, accusations, and investigations. She had been questioned by the authorities, her every move scrutinized, her personal life laid bare for all to see. The firm had distanced itself from her, and colleagues she had once considered friends had turned their backs.

Her thoughts drifted back to the day she received the call from Sunfish Island Resort.

John Hunter, the resort owner, had been impressed with a marketing campaign Olivia had pitched for his California winery. Despite the scandal, he had taken a chance on her, offering her the position of marketing manager at his newly refurbished resort in Australia. It was an opportunity she couldn't refuse—a chance to start over, far away from the judgmental eyes of everyone who knew her.

The flight from New York to Sydney was long and uneventful. Olivia tried to sleep but found herself tossing and turning, uncomfortable despite the plush business-class seat, her mind racing with thoughts of the unknown future. What would her new life be like? Would she be able to rebuild her career and reputation? She stared at the in-flight entertainment screen, barely registering the movie playing.

"Would you like a glass of wine, miss?"

She looked up to see a flight attendant smiling kindly down at her.

"Might help you get some rest," the woman said kindly.

"You know what, I will. A glass of red, please." *But just the one*, Olivia told herself firmly. She definitely didn't want to arrive in Australia drunk off her face!

The wine helped her relax, a little, and she put on an eye mask and did some calming breath exercises she'd learned in a yoga class. She didn't notice when the flight attendant silently plucked the empty wine glass from the tray in front of her, and the next thing she knew, the lights were coming up in the cabin and the smell of hot coffee was permeating the air.

***

When she finally arrived in Sydney, the warmth of the Australian spring was a stark contrast to the chilly autumn she had left behind. The air was filled with the scent of blooming flowers, and the vibrant greenery was a welcome sight after the concrete jungle of New York. Olivia felt a sense of hope stirring within her. Maybe this was the fresh start she needed.

The domestic flight from Sydney to North Queensland was shorter and more pleasant. Olivia gazed out the window at the breathtaking views of turquoise waters and lush green islands, feeling a flicker of excitement amidst her anxiety. As the plane descended, she took a deep breath, ready to embrace whatever lay ahead.

The incredible heat surprised Olivia as she stepped off the plane and walked down the steps to the tarmac. It was just like being slapped in the face with a hot, wet towel. She broke out in a sweat almost instantly and considered pausing to take off the jacket to her pantsuit, but the terminal was just a few steps away and the promise of air conditioning beckoned. Shouldering her laptop bag, she made rapidly for the doors.

Since she'd come in on a domestic flight from Sydney, she didn't have to clear international customs. After collecting her suitcase, she made her way to the greeting area and looked hopefully around. The airport was small and bustling, with a mix of tourists and locals milling about. Almost everyone who'd been on the flight with her were tourists, and they were making their way to several tour group and resort signs being held up around the area.

Olivia bit her lip, wondering if she should head for the brightly colored sign proclaiming the legend SUNFISH ISLAND RESORT with the tourists going in that direction, or if there was a different protocol for newly arrived staff. The vibrant sign stood out amidst a sea of others, its cheerful colors a stark contrast to the monochrome of her thoughts.

Not seeing anyone holding up a sign with her name, she shrugged mentally and headed on over. A pretty Chinese girl holding the sign and a clipboard smiled at her, though the smile turned quizzical as she took in Olivia's designer pantsuit and high-heeled pumps, a far cry from the comfortable holiday wear the tourists sported.

"Hi, I'm Jill! Your name, please?"

"Olivia Stratten."

Jill glanced down automatically at her clipboard before her head snapped back up. "Wait, you're the new marketing manager!"

"I am." Olivia smiled, trying to project confidence despite the sweat trickling down her back.

"Welcome, it's lovely to meet you!" Jill shoved her clipboard under her arm to pump Olivia's hand enthusiastically. "Sorry we didn't have a specific sign for you—well, we did, actually. Rosie was gonna hold it but it turns out that her boyfriend was the co-pilot on your flight and it's turning around and going back to Sydney in an hour so she went to try and see him for a few minutes."

Olivia blinked at the sudden gush of information delivered in a broad Australian accent. She'd only been in the country for a week and still struggled to pick up all the words when the locals talked quickly. She was pretty sure she'd gotten the gist, though, and nodded.

"That's alright. I hope she got some time with him."

Jill rolled her eyes. "Guy's a prick with a girl in every town. I keep trying to tell Rosie, but she's blinded by the whole airline-pilot-glamor thing."

"That's still a thing?"

"Considering how much pilots get paid, yeah," Jill said with a wry twist of her lips. "Here she is now."

Olivia turned to see another young woman hurrying toward them. She was a little taller than Jill and about Olivia's height, brown-haired, and very tanned. Her white teeth flashed in her brown face as she smiled.

"Hi, you must be Olivia! I'm Rosie, the staff manager at the resort. It's lovely to meet you!"

Charmed by the friendly, unaffected greetings from two women Olivia guessed were both around her own age of twenty-nine, Olivia smiled back at them. "It's lovely to be here. So different from New York." She'd left home in chilly, dark October, when the city seemed shrouded in gloom as winter approached. Sydney had been quite a shock to the system, warm and bright, green with spring growth. North Queensland was hot and far more humid. When she'd looked out of the plane window as it came into land, the view had been all turquoise water and sand-rimmed tropical islands.

"I reckon," Jill said with a laugh in her voice, giving Rosie a glance Olivia couldn't interpret before she turned away to see to the tourists awaiting her attention.

"Jill's our guest relations manager," Rosie said, gesturing for Olivia to follow her. Grasping her suitcase handle, Olivia obeyed, and Rosie led her out of the terminal to a golf cart parked outside and helped her hoist her case into the back.

"We'd go on the bus with the others, but it's full. We've got a lot coming in off this flight." Rosie hopped into the driver's seat. "So I borrowed this off a friend at the marina."

"Is that far from here?" Olivia hung onto the side of the golf cart as Rosie mashed the accelerator pedal flat to the floor and they took off at a surprisingly high speed.

"Not at all! Only a couple of minutes!" Rosie zoomed past another golf cart, narrowly missing an oncoming minibus. Olivia gave up and shut her eyes.

"Oh come on, you're used to New York traffic. My driving can't terrify you that much!" Rosie snickered.

"You'd make a very good cab driver," Olivia agreed, cracking an eye open as they slowed. Seeing boat masts in front of them, she relaxed, realizing they must be at the marina. "Which is all I ever took in New York. Generally, the subway is much faster anyway, so I mostly rode that."

"I think I'll take that as a backhanded compliment," Rosie snickered. "Well, you can drive next time, if I'm scaring you that much. Jill never lets me drive...."

"I can see why, but I don't have a lot of choice. I've never learned to drive."

"Really?" Rosie looked startled at that before casting her a cheeky grin. "Well. Technically you don't need a license to drive one of the resort golf carts. I won't tell if you don't."

Olivia had to laugh at that, getting out of the cart. "Is this the boat?" She looked at the catamaran yacht they'd parked behind.

"No, no. This belongs to my friend. Thanks, Matt!" Rosie yelled at the boat before heading around to the back of the cart to heft Olivia's suitcase out again. "We're just going along there."

"Oh." Olivia felt quite foolish. Lovely though the catamaran was, and obviously valuable, it looked minuscule compared to the magnificent motor-yacht at which Rosie had just pointed. "Wow."

"The resort has three of those; we use them for airport transfer, inter-island transfer, and our own dive-and-snorkelling tours," Rosie informed her. "They're brand-new. The new owners bought them after they finished the refurbishment last year."

"Impressive," Olivia said, taking in the boat as they walked closer. "Several million dollars, I'd say."

"No expense spared," Rosie agreed with a nod. "Everything on Sunfish Island is like that. You'll see. But the island was run-down for quite a few years before the new owners bought it and spent a fortune to do it up."

"Which is why you need me." Olivia nodded. She specialized in relaunching refurbished hotels. She'd originally applied for the job assuming she'd be based in New York, but the resort owners insisted she needed to be on-site. They'd hired her on a full-year contract and paid all travel expenses, and accommodation was included. It was the job of a lifetime.

"That's right." Rosie nodded. "Hey! Cory! Get down here and help carry Olivia's suitcase!"

"God, you're so bossy," a deep voice rumbled with a laugh, and Olivia looked up to see a tall figure silhouetted against the sun, standing on the boat's upper deck. She blinked, dazzled by the glare behind him.

"This is Cory Gillette, our activities manager," Rosie said as the man vaulted over the rail. He landed on the lower deck in front of them before walking down the short ramp separating the boat from the dock. "Cory, Olivia Stratten, our new marketing guru."

"Nice ta meetcha," he rumbled before bending and picking up her suitcase as though it weighed nothing.

Olivia could only stare speechlessly as Cory turned and walked back onto the boat. He looked as though he'd just stepped off an advertising billboard; tall, blond, and blue-eyed, he had a deep bronze tan and shoulders so broad they strained the seams of his polo shirt. Her gaze slid down his back involuntarily as he walked back up the ramp with her suitcase.

Cory's ass in tight khaki shorts was so spectacular she barely heard Rosie's "Come on, let's get aboard before the guests arrive."

"Ngh," Olivia said somewhat incoherently, still staring, but Rosie promptly cut off her view as she headed up the ramp in front of Olivia. Still thoroughly distracted and trying to peer around Rosie to get another look at that incredible back view, she followed Rosie up the ramp without watching her footing.

Which turned out to be an epically huge mistake.

The ramp was made of a pierced steel grating, and with Olivia's first full step onto it, her spiked high heel went straight through and jammed. Thrown completely off balance, she teetered, clutched for a nonexistent handrail, lost her balance completely, and toppled head-first into the murky waters of the harbour. The last thing she heard before the surprisingly warm waters of the harbour closed over her head was Rosie's shriek of horror.

She might never have learned to drive, but she had certainly learned to swim. After a brief panicky flail, she righted herself and kicked back up to the surface, clamping her lips tight and holding her breath. Her head broke the surface and she heard....

Not more shrieks of horror, but a deep guffaw of laughter.

Cory was leaning off the boat, extending a tanned hand in her direction, and absolutely laughing his ass off.

Cheeks flaming, utterly humiliated, Olivia accepted the offered hand. It wasn't as though she had much choice, after all. As far as she could see, she had no other way to get up to the boat.

Despite his chortles, Cory pulled her up as easily as he'd carried her suitcase, his other hand hooking around her waist when he'd raised her high enough to lift her aboard and set her on her feet. Her bare feet.

"I think this is yours," he said through his laughter, bending down to pull her shoe out of the ramp and offer it to her.

"Those were Jimmy Choos," Olivia said pathetically, accepting the shoe from his hand even as she mourned the loss of the other one, now no doubt sinking in the silt at the bottom of the harbour.

Cory laughed so hard he had to sit down on the deck.

"You're such an asshole," Rosie was at least trying to suppress her giggles, and making a fair job of it, as she dealt a slap to the back of Cory's head. "Are you alright, Olivia?"

She blew out her cheeks, looking down at her ruined two-thousand-dollar pantsuit, the single shoe nestled in her hand. And then she blinked. "Oh my God. My bag!"

"You had a bag... your laptop bag!" Rosie stared at her in horror.

They both peered down into the murky water.

"How deep is it?" Olivia asked.

"About eight feet." Cory finally managed to suppress his laughter. "And no, I am not diving down to look for it."

Olivia shot him a fulminating glare. "Don't put yourself out. I'll get it myself." Handing Rosie her shoe, stripping off her soaked suit jacket and tossing it aside, she dived neatly off the edge of the boat.

Chapter Two

"Now that I didn't expect," Cory admitted, peering down into the murky water after Olivia. His voice held a note of admiration mixed with concern. "D'you think I should go in?"

"I think she wouldn't have dived in if she wasn't quite confident she could do it," Rosie said thoughtfully. Her eyes followed the ripples where Olivia had disappeared. "And frankly I think you'd be better served here to pull her out again when she comes back up."

Cory started counting under his breath, though, deciding that if Olivia hadn't surfaced after sixty seconds, he was going in after her. He'd reached fifty-four when her head broke the surface again, her hair plastered to her face, and she gasped for breath.

"Did you get it?" Rosie called, her voice carrying a mixture of relief and curiosity. Gasping for breath, Olivia nodded, holding the strap up in triumph. Rosie grabbed the bag while Cory hauled Olivia out again, his hands strong and reassuring.

"There was no need for that," he chided gently, his eyes softening. "Seriously, all your electronics will be wrecked already."

"I know that." She cast him a scornful look, her breath still coming in gasps. "All my data is backed up to the cloud anyway. I just didn't want to lose my passport. It'd be an absolute pain to get a new one." Taking the bag from Rosie, she opened the front flap and pulled out a small, flat purse that contained her passport, credit cards, and some Australian cash. The money was plastic and would be perfectly usable once it dried out; the passport she was a little more concerned about, but it was worth trying to dry it out. The stamps and work visa were still readable, at least.

"Well, at least it'll be easier to get a replacement for a wrecked one than replace a lost one," Rosie said positively, and Olivia cast her a grateful look. "Plus, you've got about a thousand dollars there! I'd have dived into the harbour for that alone."

"Tell me you didn't drop your bag into the harbour and dive in after it," a laughing voice said behind them, and Olivia turned to see that Jill and her busload of guests had arrived.

"Nah, she got one of her snazzy heels caught in the ramp and took a header," Cory said, and it was more than evident that Jill wanted to fall about laughing as she pressed her lips together, eyes glinting with mirth. Instead, she shook her head and turned back to escorting the guests aboard.

They all got a guiding hand from Jill or the man who'd arrived with her, Olivia noticed a bit jealously. Letting a paying guest fall in the harbour would be bad for business, after all.

A light tug at her wrist made her turn back to Rosie. "It's a half-hour trip to the island. You'll be way more comfortable in dry clothes." Rosie pointed at her suitcase. "There's only a tiny bathroom, but at least you can change."

Grateful for the suggestion, Olivia nodded. She and Rosie retreated to the rear corner of the boat's main cabin while Cory and the other man pulled in the ramp and cast off the lines. Someone else must be upstairs driving the boat, Olivia surmised as huge engines started up and they slid away from the dock.

Another reason to be glad she'd decided to retrieve her bag, Olivia thought as she dug out the key for her luggage lock and opened her suitcase. She had a sinking feeling in the pit of her stomach that absolutely everything she'd brought with her was far too glamorous. Though this was a five-star, premium resort, even the guests were more casually dressed than the most casual outfit she owned.

"Wow," Rosie breathed in astonishment, staring into the case as Olivia took a couple of things off the top layer and set them aside. "You have really nice clothes."

"Nobody in New York takes you seriously if you're not wearing a designer label," Olivia said with perfect honesty. "I feel like I'm going to be very overdressed, though." She looked at Rosie's cotton shorts, resort-branded polo shirt, and rubber flip-flops. "I don't even own a pair of shoes without high heels."

That made Rosie laugh. "You'll be better off barefoot! Almost all the paths on the island are sand; you'd sink in." Lightly fingering the hem of a silk Mossimo dress, she said tentatively, "I have several spare pairs of thongs, and lots of casual gear. We're about the same size. You're welcome to borrow anything you like... if I could maybe borrow one of these gorgeous dresses to wear to the staff Christmas party?"

The Mossimo dress probably cost more than Rosie's entire wardrobe, Olivia knew, but the friendly overture was too kind to ignore. "You're on. But what are thongs? Because I don't think you mean what I understand by thongs...."

Rosie laughed and explained that thongs was Australian for flip-flops, as Olivia picked out the least dressy thing she could find, a Roberto Cavalli printed jersey dress. At least she had one pair of heels that weren't stilettos, she thought with relief as she dug out her favourite cream linen wedges. *Thank you, Kate Middleton, for making these an enduring fashion statement.*

There was nothing really to be done for her hair; she looked like a drowned rat and there were only paper towels to be found in the tiny bathroom. She washed her face and twisted her hair up into a wet knot atop her head; that would have to do. The light was too poor—and she had too little time—to do a lot about her makeup, but at least she could get rid of the raccoon-like circles under her eyes from her running eyeliner.

"Wow," Rosie breathed as Olivia returned a few minutes later. "How did you do that? You look like a million bucks again!"

Olivia smiled, warmed by the other girl's open friendliness and kind words. "Thanks, Rosie. I was feeling a bit like the Swamp Thing."

"Maybe the Creature from The Black Lagoon?" Cory sniped as he walked past. Rosie whacked at his legs, and he evaded her hand with a laugh.

Olivia glared at his retreating back. The guy might be gorgeous, but what an asshole!

"Don't mind Cory, he's a total troll," Rosie said, rolling her eyes.

"I think you're being insulting to trolls," Olivia quipped back, and they laughed. Despite the disaster of her unplanned dip in the harbour, Olivia relaxed. At least she'd have one friend at Sunfish Island Resort, she thought as Rosie leaned across her to point out the window and tell her that they were just about to round the southern tip of the island.

The island itself was breathtaking. As they approached, Olivia could see a lush canopy of greenery covering the hills, with pristine white beaches lining the shores. The water was a dazzling shade of turquoise, and she could spot colourful coral reefs just below the surface. She felt a thrill of excitement and anticipation as they drew closer to her new home.

Rosie held Olivia back until the guests had all disembarked. The other man took her suitcase with a friendly grin.

"Tell the porter to take it to 6B, please, Jack," Rosie told him.

"Sure thing." He gave Rosie a casual salute. "And welcome to Sunfish, Olivia."

At least everyone was very friendly, Olivia mused as she followed Rosie, who trailed after the last of the guests. Cory stood by the ramp, offering his hand to her in an exaggerated gesture, his blue eyes glinting with mirth.

She debated giving him a shove into the water. It was a very, very tempting thought... and it was also petty and beneath her. She swallowed the impulse and took his hand, letting him steady her as she crossed the ramp.

"Thanks," she muttered grudgingly.

"You're welcome. And... I'm sorry I wasn't there to help you before."

Startled, her gaze flew up to meet his. He looked quite sincere, and his hand was warm and strong as he held on to her for just a moment longer than necessary.

"Olivia Stratten," a voice said, thankfully obviating her need to think of something to say to Cory's unexpected remark. She let go of his hand and turned to see a handsome man in what she guessed was his early forties and actually wearing a business suit, albeit with an open-necked shirt and no tie.

"It's good to meet you. I'm Luke Collyer, the resort general manager." He took in her dripping hair with a curious glance but said nothing about it as he offered his hand for a friendly shake.

"It's very nice to meet you, Mr. Collyer." They'd communicated by email after the resort owners had hired her, and his ideas and incisive manner had impressed Olivia.

"Luke, please. We're not formal here at Sunfish."

She smiled in acknowledgment, following him along the shaded dock and into the hotel's main lobby.

"Wow." Olivia's head tipped up. The atrium was amazing, five stories high with a domed glass roof, and live palms growing in gigantic stone pots. Water trickled from stunning fountains and ran underneath shining plate-glass panels in the floor. There were fish in there, she realized, as one swam directly under her foot. It was hard to know where to put her eyes at any given moment.

"Pretty swish, huh?" Luke gave her a knowing smile. "It's very different to how it looked ten years ago, I can tell you. I was working here as assistant hotel manager at the time."

Most of the photographs available online had been of the old resort, so Olivia knew what he meant. She shook her head in wonderment.

"The owners really did spare no expense."

"This whole building is new." Luke gestured upward at the glass dome. "That even has cyclone shutters that can be closed over it. While we're required to evacuate all guests in the event of an oncoming cyclone because the island may be inundated during a storm surge, the upper floors of this building would actually be quite safe even under the most severe conditions."

"Impressive," Olivia said with a nod, wincing as a trickle of cool water ran down her neck from her soaked hair.

Luke tilted his head at her curiously. "Excuse me for asking, but why is your hair wet?"

She sighed and gave him a rueful smile. "I may as well 'fess up; I'm sure it'll be all over the resort within the hour. I fell off the ramp when boarding the boat."

"You what?" Luke looked startled.

"Entirely my own fault, I'm afraid. I was wearing spike heels and not looking where I was going."

Luke was clearly making an effort to hold back his laughter.

Olivia smiled at him cheekily. "Go on, you might as well laugh. I've seen the funny side now, anyway."

He permitted himself a few chortles before shaking his head. "I wish I'd seen it, though I'm sure you're glad I didn't. Well. I was going to ask if you wanted the full tour, but all things considered, I think maybe we'll postpone it to tomorrow morning and let you get settled in today instead. I've got meetings this afternoon, I'm afraid."

She smiled at him gratefully. "I admit I'm eager to get to work... but I'm even more eager to have a proper shower and wash the ocean out of my hair."

"Then let's make that happen." Luke turned to the left and swiped an access card through a slot beside a door marked STAFF ONLY. A short passageway led them outside and down a narrow path between high hedges. "This leads to the senior staff accommodation," he told her. "The cabins were actually part of the old resort; the owners decided to leave them for staff use when they built the new ones. You're in number six, which is a two-bedroom. You're sharing it with Suzannah, our executive chef; she's very nice but you probably won't see a lot of her. She's a workaholic."

Olivia nodded, looking with pleasure at the rustic timber cabins, set on low stumps, as they came upon them. Each had a small covered veranda at the front with a couple of comfortable-looking sun loungers; a brass number was screwed to the front railing on every cabin. It wasn't long before they arrived at number six, and Luke fished in a pocket to pull out a key and an access card, both of which he handed to her.

"The card gets you into all the staff areas of the resort. These cabins don't have electronic access like the newer ones, so you'll need to hang on to the key. It fits both doors to your room: the one that exits onto the veranda and the one into the living area of the cabin. Don't forget to lock both, and don't leave valuables lying around in the common area, because it's not secured; anyone can walk in."

Olivia nodded in understanding as Luke turned the door handle and opened the main cabin door. "This is lovely," she said in pleased surprise, looking around the simply furnished room. It had a tiny kitchenette at the other end, a large squashy couch facing a decent-sized flat-screen TV, and a small dining table with four chairs. The floor was tiled, and everything was immaculately clean.

"Maid service will go over the room once a week, on whatever is Housekeeping's quietest day that week. They can do your room and bathroom if you wish, but you need to let them in." Luke gestured to the door on the right-hand wall. "That's your room."

Her suitcase was already sitting by the door, Olivia noted. "Thanks," she said gratefully.

"I'll leave you to it. Suze will be in the middle of lunch prep, so you won't meet her until this afternoon. I'll get someone to come by and show you around a little bit, take you to the staff dining area—all your meals are included, of course."

"Of course," she echoed with a small smile. She'd never had an all-inclusive job before, but then you couldn't actually pay for much on Sunfish apart from drinks, she recalled from reading the existing marketing literature. Feeding the staff was pretty much required when they couldn't easily source their own supplies.

"I'll see you later. Get settled in," Luke left her with a friendly nod. Olivia sighed a little in relief as she was finally left alone, and the tension dropped from her shoulders.

Rising tension and nerves about making a good impression had twisted a tight knot in her stomach, making her unable to eat or drink anything since waking up – even the coffee had turned her stomach and she'd set the cup down after a single sip, shaking her head to the offered breakfast on the plane as nausea began to churn.

Feeling an intense thirst, she crossed to the kitchenette to take a look in the fridge. She found several cans of soda, some of brands she didn't recognize. They had to belong to the unknown roommate. Biting her lip, Olivia eventually shrugged and grabbed a cola. She could always replace it later.

Sipping on her purloined cola, she let herself into her room and dragged her suitcase in after her. The bedroom was just as well furnished as the shared living area, with a double bed, dressing table with large mirror, and to her surprised pleasure, a high-quality desk and office chair with a new-looking computer on the desk. It also had a generous-sized walk-in closet and a beautifully appointed ensuite bathroom.

Delighted by her new living quarters, Olivia decided everything else could wait until she'd showered. The drapes over the sliding door to the veranda were already closed, so she closed her door, stripped, and headed for the ensuite.

Chapter Three

Half an hour later, Olivia felt a good deal more human. She'd showered and washed her hair, put on the fluffy bathrobe she'd found hanging on the back of the bathroom door, and was now sorting through her suitcase rather despairingly, wondering what on earth she could wear. Everything she'd brought now looked far too formal, even though she'd selected the most "casual" items from her wardrobe before putting everything into storage back in New York.

A light tap on the door leading out to the veranda made her look up. She could only make out a vague shape through the sheer curtain. "Who is it?" she called.

"Rosie!"

Smiling, Olivia went to let her new friend in, her smile widening even further as she saw the armload of clothes Rosie was carrying. "Oh, you star. I was just wondering what to wear in order not to look completely overdressed."

Rosie smiled shyly back at her, piling the clothes on the bed. "I think you look great. Your clothes are just gorgeous."

"They are," Olivia agreed, "and they're perfect for New York City life, or even Sydney, but here on Sunfish I'll just look... I don't know. Like I think I'm better than everyone else. I want to fit in here, be part of this lovely staff-family vibe you all seem to have going on."

"You will! Everyone's really nice and welcoming. And... well, to be honest, probably falling in the harbour really helped, because now they all know a funny story about you and it'll be a good icebreaker for you to get to know everyone."

Olivia smiled wryly, choosing a pair of shorts and a flowered blouse from the pile Rosie had put down and taking them to the bathroom to dress. "And here I was thinking I'd made a disastrous first impression," she called back.

"Well"—Rosie looked at the laptop and tablet lying on a soggy towel on the desk—"I mean, it was a disaster in some ways, but in others it could be a blessing in disguise?" She looked up at Olivia as she returned from the bathroom.

"I've seen the funny side now, anyway." Olivia grinned back at her. "When Luke said he wished he'd seen it, I got a mind's-eye picture of how I must have looked and almost cracked up laughing on the spot."

"That's the spirit," Rosie said warmly. She took a pair of pink rubber flip-flops—*thongs*, Olivia remembered, sternly telling herself not to snicker—from the pile of clothes and held them out. "These ones are fairly new. Should last you awhile."

"I'm only borrowing these until I have a chance to go back over to Hamilton Island and go shopping," Olivia told her, accepting the shoes.

"Oh, don't. Everything there is really expensive because it's all brought in for tourists. Take the other boat over to Airlie Beach on the mainland—that one goes every day too. The supermarket is only a five-minute walk from the marina, and there are plenty of other shops too."

"That's good to know, thanks!" Olivia made a mental note to ask Luke which day she could do that. "And how about doing laundry?"

"I'll show you where the staff laundry is on the way to lunch. You ready?"

Olivia scooped her keys and access card off the desk. "I am now."

As they left the cabin, Rosie pointed to their right, away from the main resort building. "I'm in the next cabin, by the way, number 7. Jill and I share it. Suze, your roomie, is a close friend; she often comes over and hangs out with us. You're welcome too, anytime."

Olivia nodded. "Thank you," she said genuinely.

The girls turned to walk back toward the main resort, and a deep voice stopped them in their tracks.

"Well, well, it's the Little Mermaid! How's tricks, Ariel?"

Cory leaned on the veranda rail of the cabin next to her own, a broad grin on his face. Remembering the way he'd apologized to her as she left the boat, and thinking of Rosie's advice to look at the whole incident as a blessing in disguise, Olivia flipped him the bird with an answering grin. Cory laughed, vaulted easily over the rail, and fell into step beside them.

"Good to see you can laugh about it." He smiled down at Olivia. She had to fight not to be knocked sideways from the impact of his good looks again; that combined with an intoxicating, spicily masculine scent as he stood close to her made her head reel.

"I can laugh about it, but call me Ariel again and *you* won't be laughing," she said in a mock-menacing tone, narrowing her eyes at him.

Cory laughed again and nodded amiably.

Stop being nice, you're making it very hard for me to keep my mind out of your pants, Olivia thought with an internal sigh, and resolutely turned her eyes away from his chiseled, handsome features. She caught Rosie giving her a speculative look and did her best to smooth her face to neutrality.

"Cory's single, y'know," Rosie murmured as they stood in line for the lunch buffet in the staff dining room. Cory had peeled off to go speak to someone else and was thankfully out of earshot.

"Oh?" Olivia tried to keep her tone light and disinterested. "Why?" she had to ask. "I mean..."

"I know, and trust me, it's not like he doesn't get offers." Rosie gave her a conspiratorial grin. "Every week there's a few tourists trying to throw themselves at him, but Cory's not the sort to have flings." She handed Olivia a plate. "I've known him forever. We were in school together in Cairns as kids."

That explained how comfortable the pair of them seemed; they really were childhood friends. Olivia did her best to divert the subject, though. "You grew up in Cairns, so you're a North Queenslander?"

"Spent my whole life on or near the Reef," Rosie confirmed. "I'd never want to be anywhere else."

"Hear, hear," Cory affirmed, rejoining them and collecting his own plate. "It's 'beautiful one day, perfect the next,' don't y'know." He quoted the Queensland advertising slogan at Olivia.

"I haven't been here long enough to confirm the truth of that," she pointed out, "but I'm looking forward to finding out."

"You'll see." Cory sounded utterly confident. Looking at both him and Rosie, incredibly healthy-looking, tanned, and practically glowing compared to her pasty-pale self, Olivia could quite believe it. "Although you'll need to use some pretty heavy-duty sunblock," Cory continued, "or that lovely creamy skin will be lobster-red."

"I bought a bottle in Sydney," Olivia agreed, "and I'll get more when I go into Airlie Beach to shop Rosie's been kind enough to lend me a few things, but I'll need to make a trip."

"Thought I recognized that blouse." Cory grinned at Rosie as the three of them left the buffet and headed over to a table. "Looks better on Olivia, I'm afraid."

Rosie made a face at him, but she also gave Olivia a sideways glance and a surreptitious nudge in the ribs. Olivia rolled her eyes in return.

"We are not thirteen," she hissed in Rosie's ear as another man paused by their table, distracting Cory briefly. "Stop trying to matchmake!"

Rosie laughed but turned her attention to her food, which was well worth paying attention to, Olivia conceded. The buffet had a huge variety, everything beautifully presented and perfectly fresh. She scooped up a forkful of pasta salad and hummed with pleasure at the taste.

The other man who'd stopped to speak to Cory took the fourth seat at their table then, and Olivia swallowed hastily as Cory introduced him.

"Olivia, this is Bryce, the resort's dive master. Bryce, meet Olivia."

Bryce was younger than the other two; Olivia estimated him to be about twenty-three or twenty-four. His dark hair was buzzed close to his scalp, and his deep bronze tan set off grass-green eyes.

Involuntarily, Olivia wondered whether all Australian men were this attractive. Cory, Luke, and Bryce, the three she'd met on Sunfish Island so far, were all good-looking enough to be models... though if she were completely honest, Cory was the only one who'd sparked more in her than a mere aesthetic appreciation. She smiled at Bryce's cheerful greeting.

"Nice to meet you too."

"So when are you coming out for your first dive with me?" Bryce asked. Olivia blinked, another forkful of food on her way to her mouth.

"Uh, what?"

"No way can you effectively market this place without seeing its primary attraction. The Reef. And you can't really see the Reef without diving on it."

"Technically she already made her first dive," Cory said, grinning, and Olivia had absolutely no compunctions about kicking him in the shin under the table.

Bryce frowned with confusion, and Olivia realized that news of her plunge hadn't reached him yet. Prudently moving his shins out of her reach, Cory promptly filled Bryce in. Olivia settled for glaring at him, though the way Cory described her had her inwardly glowing. Or maybe not so inwardly, considering the way Rosie was smirking at her.

"You should have seen her. She dived off the boat like an Olympic champion," Cory concluded. "I half expected her to turn a double somersault on the way in. I'd give her a 9.9 for execution. She sure was a sight for sore eyes coming out too."

A little puzzled at that remark, Olivia frowned at him; at least until Rosie murmured in her ear, "Your blouse went transparent. Cory got quite the eyeful."

Olivia hoped the two men interpreted her flaming cheeks as being caused by Bryce's laughter. Picking up her water glass, she took a deep gulp. "I daresay people will be telling stories of my arrival for years," she said, "getting more exaggerated with each telling."

"It's a good enough story that we don't need to exaggerate." Cory grinned at her. She considered the position of his shins with a tilt of her head, making him chuckle. She picked a cherry tomato off her plate and flung it with deadly accuracy at his forehead instead.

"Now, now, children." Bryce caught the tomato as it bounced off Cory's skull, "settle down. You've got to work together."

"Quite," Olivia said. "You've had your fun at my expense," she told Cory directly. "Now can you just let it go—at least when I'm in earshot?"

"Fair enough." He shrugged amiably. "God knows I make an idiot of myself regularly enough that you'll soon have plenty of ammunition for return fire, anyway."

"I can certainly attest to that," Rosie agreed. "I have a million embarrassing stories about him from our schooldays I can share if he keeps being obnoxious, anyway."

Cory's blue eyes widened comically. "I'll behave," he said hurriedly.

Olivia had to laugh at his schoolboyish dismay. "You better." She pointed her fork at him.

"Yes, ma'am." He saluted her smartly. She didn't miss the warmth in his eyes as he looked back at her; a matching heat bloomed low in her belly. Pressing her knees together, Olivia looked away from those mesmerizing blue eyes and prodded at her lunch with her fork. Strangely enough, she no longer felt hungry.

Bryce and Rosie mercifully started talking, filling in the silence, and Olivia was content to just listen to their chatter. She glanced up at Cory through her lashes and found him pushing his food around his plate as well. He seemed to sense her eyes on him and looked up at her.

Their gazes caught and held.

She half expected him to make a quip or some sarcastic remark, but he just stared back at her, holding the fork still in his hand. For an endless moment they stared at each other, oblivious to the chatter and noise around them.

This is a terrible idea, Olivia thought. *I have to work with him.*

Cory smiled, the expression almost shy.

Oh, fuck it. Terrible idea or not, I'm not going to live like a nun for the next twelve months.

She smiled back.

***

Shortly afterwards, Rosie said apologetically that she had work to do, and Bryce left to take a new-divers class in one of the resort pools. They headed off leaving Olivia and Cory still staring at each other over the remains of their lunch.

"Do you have somewhere you need to be?" Olivia asked finally.

"Not until four thirty. Um. Luke actually asked me if I'd show you around a bit, but... if you'd rather someone else, I'm sure I can rustle someone up."

Time to make the call, Olivia.

"I wouldn't rather anyone else."

Cory's smile was slow and sure, warming through her. "Good," he said softly. "That's good. C'mon, then."

He offered a hand as she stood. Olivia debated taking it and decided she'd given the resort staff enough gossip for her first day. Besides, if she stepped a little closer, she could thread her hand through his arm instead and rest it on the pleasing bulge of his biceps. She got a few interested looks as she made her way out of the dining room on Cory's arm.

A row of golf buggies was parked behind the resort. Cory handed her into the passenger seat of one before going around to the driver's side.

"Please tell me that you don't drive like Rosie," Olivia thought to say suddenly, grabbing the dash as Cory started the engine.

He burst out laughing. "I promise I don't drive like Rosie. She's a maniac. Never has passed her driver's test; she can't drive anywhere except here or on Hamilton, with the golf buggies... and she's banned from driving one here too."

"That's a relief." Olivia took her hands off the dash before saying tentatively, "I've never learned to drive. It wasn't really necessary living in New York. The subway goes everywhere. Maybe you could teach me?"

"Sure," he said cheerfully, "want to start now?"

She laughed. "No, let me figure out my way around from the passenger seat first. I don't think I can concentrate on trying to drive while gaping like the tourist I am."

"Gotcha. Well, if you're the tourist, let me play tour guide." Cory slowed the golf cart as the path they were on intersected with another; he looked left and right before turning left. "First thing to note for when you do start driving: all our paths here are two-way and we drive on the *left* here in Oz."

"Noted," she agreed. "What's that?" She pointed off to the left at a small white building standing alone on a small rise.

"One of the wedding chapels. We have three, and an average of just under two weddings a day here. We have facilities for a lot more, and that's part of what Luke wants you to push in the marketing, I know... that this is one of the best wedding destinations in Australia."

"I can see why," Olivia agreed as Cory pulled the buggy off the path into a small parking area near the chapel. They got out and walked up to the small building. On closer inspection, she could see it was open on three sides, facing out over a small palm-fringed cove. The white sand and blue water were a stunning backdrop.

"Wow," she breathed, taking in the surroundings. "Just wow."

"Yeah." Cory placed his hands on the low railing at the side of the chapel, looking out over the water. "I see this view every day and I never get tired of it."

"I can imagine." Leaning into the railing as she stood beside him, Olivia gazed out at the ocean in wonder, taking in the colors in the water as the depth changed. "I've never seen anything like it. So many colors!"

"Beautiful," Cory agreed, but he was looking down at her now, not out at the water. Lifting one hand from the railing, he gently brushed a strand of curly, brown hair back behind her ear. "I was knocked sideways when I saw you walking down the dock today, Olivia," he said quietly, "and I feel like maybe you feel the same way, a bit."

She turned big dark brown eyes up to his but said nothing. He plowed on stubbornly. "Physical attraction is one thing, and I could put it to one side easily enough, but... everything about you has hit me for six. The way you dived back in to find your passport; the way you put me in my place for laughing at you. This might be crazy because we have to work together, but I'm seriously attracted to you. And I'd like to make that clear now, before we even get started. I don't want there to be any misunderstandings. If you're not interested, or if you want me to keep my distance because we're work colleagues, I can respect that, but I need you to set a boundary here. Because I don't want there to be *any* boundaries. I feel like you've been giving me some signals, but I need to make sure I'm not misinterpreting you."

He was being incredibly honest and direct, laying his soul bare to her with the heartfelt words. Olivia took a deep breath. "I think I might feel the same way. Except... what does 'hit for six' mean?"

Cory's serious expression dissolved and he let out a hearty chuckle. "It's a cricket term. Like... hitting a home run in baseball."

"You do know that hitting a home run has another meaning altogether, right?"

"I know." Slowly, giving her plenty of time to pull away, he put one arm around her, settling it lightly on her waist. "We can take this as slow or as fast as you like, Olivia."

She looked up at him and smiled coquettishly, turning to face him fully and lifting her hands to set them on his shoulders. "Slow's never been my style."

"I'm really glad you said that," Cory murmured, arm tightening around her to draw her close. He sank his free hand into her curly hair to hold her head still as he bent to kiss her.

Cory's mouth was hot and sweet-tasting as it moved over hers; gentle at first, at least until Olivia nipped his bottom lip. He let out a little growl at that and deepened the kiss, tongue sliding into her mouth possessively. She slid her fingers into his blond hair and gripped, nails scraping at his scalp, going up on tiptoe to push her body firmly against his, crush her breasts against the hardness of his chest.

They were both breathing raggedly when the kiss finally ended. Cory's hand shook as he brushed his knuckles over Olivia's cheek and traced a fingertip over her kiss-swollen lips.

Neither of them spoke; words would have ruined the moment, and they knew each other too little as yet to really know what to say. Instead Cory dropped his hand from Olivia's face reluctantly as she took a step back. He smiled as she slipped her hand into his.

"Why don't you give me the rest of the tour?"

Chapter Four

Sunfish Island was bigger than Olivia had realized. She'd studied the official literature, of course, and looked at photos and maps on the internet, but there so much of it had to be seen in person to be appreciated. Every turn in the path seemed to bring a new stunning view, another delightful residence or grouping of cabins.

"This place is just incredible," she said as Cory drove them into another part of the resort, where he pulled up within sight of a sparkling lagoon pool fringed with palm trees. "Just... I mean, I knew it was beautiful from the photos, but photos just don't do it justice."

"That's where you come in." Cory hopped out of the golf cart and gestured her to follow as he headed over to the thatched-roof bar beside the pool. "I personally think we need TV advertising. Sunfish Island had a reputation here in Australia as a cheap family place to go, back in the nineties and early two thousands. There's almost nothing now that was even here back then—a cyclone eight years ago put paid to most of the old buildings. The cabins we live in are among the few survivors."

"I see." Olivia slipped onto a stool beside Cory at the bar and waited as the bartender made drinks for a couple of guests. "So the existing reputation has it marketed to the wrong kind of clientele, because although Sunfish is family-friendly, it's five-star and certainly not cheap these days."

"Exactly. Plus, we need to get known outside of Australia. The Chinese, Japanese, Indian, and Russian tourist market is huge these days, and they're prepared to pay for top quality."

"Hey, Cory." The conversation was interrupted by the bartender, a petite, beautiful young woman with dark brown skin and long braids.

"This is Olivia, Nessa. She's our new marketing manager. Nessa is the best bartender on the island," Cory confided.

"Ahem!"

"Beg your pardon, in Queensland. In Australia! Probably the world!" Cory grinned and Nessa laughed.

"Better. Nice to meet you, Olivia." She leaned across the bar to shake hands.

"You're English," Olivia realized after hearing her accent.

"I certainly am. Been out here ten years and you'd have to drag me away kicking and screaming." She slid a coaster in front of each of them on the polished timber bar. "What can I get you?"

"I'm on duty later, so just a soda water for me, thanks," Cory said cheerfully. "Like a beer, Olivia? Or a cocktail?"

She'd dearly love a cold beer, and said so. Nessa set a bottle beaded with condensation on the counter beside a clean glass.

"One of our local lagers, give it a try."

One sip told Olivia that Nessa had made the right call; she took a long draught to soak the parched feeling in her throat and sighed with pleasure. "Lovely. Thank you."

"Welcome." Nessa gave her a bright smile and darted away to serve another customer who approached the bar, her long braids swinging.

"What's the policy regarding staff using the resort facilities?" Olivia asked as Cory take a long drink of his soda water, his throat working as he swallowed.

"Perfectly fine as long as you don't drink alcohol while you're working, are never inebriated on resort premises, and don't prevent a customer from using the facility. So if it's busy, find somewhere else to go, basically." Cory shrugged. "The resort is overstaffed and underoccupied at the moment, so it shouldn't be an issue." He lowered his voice. "We don't pay for soft drinks 'on tap' and you pay only cost price on other drinks, so it's a really good deal. We're very well looked after here." He nodded towards Nessa, who was expertly making a cocktail. "I prefer this bar because Nessa runs tabs for all of us on sight—she's much more relaxed about it than the other bartenders. Plus, it's only a five-minute walk from the staff accommodation."

"It is?" Olivia blinked, looking around. She'd gotten completely turned around on the tour, then. She could have sworn they were a long way from the main resort, but looking around now, she could just see the dome of the main building above the palm trees. "Oh, I see."

"I'll show you the path later. This is the closest swimming pool to the cabins too, and you can also swim at the beach down there." Cory pointed.

"It's safe?"

"Beach swimming? Yes, it's really shallow up to about a hundred meters out, and this isn't stinger season. No sharks, either. You should wear reef shoes, though, because there can be sharp coral and stonefish, which you do *not* want to step on."

"Venomous?"

"Yes. Spines on their backs. The pain is hideous, I'm told." Cory shuddered. "We've never had anyone stung here, but that doesn't mean you shouldn't be careful."

"I shall consider myself properly cautioned." Olivia smiled at him. "I did read up on Australia's wildlife before I accepted the job."

"And you weren't put off? Brave girl."

They both chuckled.

"Tell me about you, Olivia. I know enough about Hunter Enterprises to know the bosses would have hired the best. So why was the best willing to give up what was clearly a very lucrative and respected position in New York and fly halfway around the world to spend a year here? Because love this place though I do, it has to feel like the back of beyond to a sophisticated city girl like you."

His blue eyes were clear and calm as he watched her. Olivia took a deep breath, puffed her cheeks on the way out, and took another long sip of her beer.

"You're not starting with the easy questions, are you?" She smiled to take the sting from her words. "I guess we should start this off being honest with each other, though." Another long sip of beer, and she looked away from his clear blue eyes, which seemed to see right into her soul. "I *had* to get out."

He only listened, doing his best to be quiet and really pay attention to not just her words, but the emotions behind them, as she continued.

"I'd been in the rat race since my teens, since my parents enrolled me in an exclusive Manhattan prep school. There was this intense pressure to be the best, the smartest, the most popular. Some girls couldn't handle it; they cracked, took drugs, slept around. I thrived on it." Twirling her beer bottle in her fingers, she said, "I was always top of the pile. I was the one who got the internships, the scholarships, won the awards. Everything came so easily. Got picked up straight out of Stanford Business School to work at the top marketing firm in New York, made associate in two years, became the youngest partner in the firm's history on my twenty-sixth birthday."

Cory said nothing, just watched as Olivia talked. Her voice had no real pride in it as she talked about her achievements; she might have been reciting a grocery list for all the emotion she showed. Her eyes flicked back to his. "And with all the success came money, more of it than I really knew what to do with... and the perfect partner to share it all with."

He'd wondered if that would come up. There was no way a woman as beautiful and successful as Olivia hadn't had men falling at her feet.

"Brad Cochrane. Or as my friends dubbed him after the breakup, The Cockroach." She gave him a little half smile. "One of Wall Street's finest."

"Wait a minute," Cory suddenly put two and two together. "I know that name. Isn't he that guy who was recently convicted in the biggest money-laundering case in history? For the Mexican drug cartels?"

"Bingo." Olivia made finger guns and pointed them at him. "As his fiancée, I was suspect number two. Took me months to clear my name. Most of my assets are still sequestered, and almost all of my legitimate clients suddenly really wanted to work with other partners at the firm. I was asked to take a leave of absence... and then the contents of my desk got delivered to my apartment in a UPS box."

"Jeez, Olivia, that must have been absolute hell," Cory said quietly. He couldn't even imagine what she'd gone through, her professional reputation ruined by something that had absolutely nothing to do with her at the same time as her relationship collapsed under a tissue of lies. "I'm so sorry."

She drained the last of her beer and set the glass down on the bar. "I sued for wrongful dismissal... and lost. There was a clause in my contract about not bringing my good name into disrepute, and my name had been smeared all over the news in connection with Brad's. Even though I had nothing to do with his shit, I still lost everything. My job, my reputation... and after the lawsuit, there was no way any firm in New York would ever hire me again. All because I had the shitty taste to fall for a con artist."

There was really nothing Cory could say. What had happened to Olivia was deeply unfair. She gave him a wan little smile.

"So you see, I really didn't have all that many options when John Hunter called me. I'd just pitched a marketing campaign for his California winery when all the shit went down. He liked it, called to take me up on it, and was seriously unhappy when he found out I wouldn't be able to handle the campaign after all. He asked me to handle it privately, which I did... I had no idea when or if I'd ever get another job at all, and the lawsuit had eaten most of my savings. The launch went off really well despite everything, and he offered me this job. The rest, as they say, is history."

She shrugged, looking away at the ocean again. "You know, I don't regret it. It was killing me slowly, the constant pressure to dress the part, be seen in all the right places, be friends with all the right people. This"—she swept a hand around, indicating their peaceful surroundings—"maybe here I can find out who Olivia Stratten actually is when she's not under pressure to be perfect."

Cory bit his lip on the remark that almost spilled from him. Olivia turned to him, her eyes dancing with mirth.

"Maybe that's why I feel so comfortable with you already. You definitely don't know Perfect Olivia."

"I wasn't gonna say it." His grin broke out, though. "You did look like perfection walking down the dock. I was very intimidated."

"Until my clumsy ass fell in the harbour." She snickered, eyes alight.

On impulse he took her hand. "Olivia Stratten is someone who can laugh at herself, and that's the first trait I look for in a woman: a good sense of humour."

Laughing freely at that, Olivia squeezed his hand back. "Well. A couple of months ago, I'm pretty sure I wouldn't have seen the funny side, but I definitely do now."

***

Cory looked at his watch then and said with regret that he needed to get back. They waved to Nessa, who was just getting busy with the early evening cocktail hour, and hopped back in the golf cart. He pointed out the walking path, which was a shortcut to the cabins as they passed it.

"I have to go call the early evening bingo game," Cory said regretfully. "It's our regular bingo caller's day off."

Olivia laughed at the thought of Cory calling bingo numbers to a crowd of retirees. Because he was the activities director, she supposed he had to be able to cover for any of his team when required, though. Thinking that she needed to know more about the activities and events the resort offered, she questioned him about his job. Cory answered all her questions good-naturedly, clearly happy to talk about the job he obviously adored.

"Bryce was right when he said you really need to see the Reef, though," he said as he pulled the golf buggy back into the parking slot they'd taken it from. "Have you ever dived before?"

She shook her head. "Not proper diving with oxygen tanks, no. I'm a strong swimmer, though."

"That I already knew." He cast her a grin. "Well, you'd have to take a couple of Bryce's starter lessons in the pool to begin with, but I'm taking a group out snorkelling tomorrow, if you'd be interested?"

"I'd love to," Olivia said enthusiastically, before she thought to say, "I don't know if Luke will want me to start work here, though..."

"It's an early afternoon tour. You can catch up with him in the morning and see," Cory suggested. "I'm pretty sure he'll tell you to take a few days and familiarize yourself with everything the resort has to offer before you consider implementing anything, though."

That sounded like a sensible strategy. "Well, provided he's okay with it, yes, I'd love to come snorkelling."

"Excellent. Boat leaves the dock at one; we've got plenty of snorkelling gear, but make sure you bring your own sunscreen." He grinned down at her, and as they approached the door leading back into the main building, he drew her gently to a stop with his hand on her elbow. "There's nothing I'd like more than to spend the whole evening getting to know you, Olivia. I'm sorry I can't."

Cory's eyes were serious as he looked down at her. She smiled back at him, charmed again by his honesty and his straightforward, open approach.

"I'd like that too."

"I'm honoured by your trust in telling me about your ex and why you're here, and I promise you that nobody will hear a word of it from me."

She was already quite sure of that, but she nodded anyway, accepting his pledge. Cory bent his head slowly, allowing her time to move away if she wanted to, but she was more than happy to step in closer and accept the kiss he pressed against her lips.

"Tomorrow," he said, a low-voiced promise, before he swiped his access card and let them back into the building.

Olivia was sure the colour flags were flying high on her cheeks as she watched Cory bound up the spiral stairs in the atrium to the main lounge on the second floor where he had to call the bingo game. She caught herself admiring at the muscles bunching in his strong thighs as he took the steps three at a time, and laughed at herself. Cory was a whole lot more than just a handsome face and an attractive body.

"He's good-looking for sure, but Cory's a player," a voice said behind her, and Olivia turned to see Jill, the guest relations manager she'd met at the airport. "Don't get your heart broken."

Olivia wasn't entirely sure what made her ask, "Is that personal experience talking?" but the way Jill's face flushed told her that her shot in the dark was right on target. Jill didn't say another word, just turned and stalked away, outrage radiating from her in waves.

"I think I might have made an enemy," Olivia muttered regretfully. She couldn't do a lot about it, though; she guessed that the moment Jill so much as suspected chemistry between Olivia and Cory, her nose would have been out of joint. Thank God nobody had witnessed their kiss at the wedding chapel, or the quick embrace outside the door. Olivia's name would have been mud all over Sunfish Island before nightfall; no doubt she'd have been smeared as a slut who threw herself at Cory literally as soon as she arrived.

Wandering over to look at the tour-booking desk—currently unoccupied—and the large display of brochures for available trips, Olivia wondered if she *had* been slutty. She'd always had a policy of never getting involved with anyone she worked with. What was it about Cory that had made her forget that resolution within a couple of hours of meeting him? It wasn't just the way he looked. She'd worked with attractive men many times before and never felt remotely tempted. No, she felt a genuine connection with Cory, one that had been there from their first meeting, and every moment spent in his company since had only reinforced the impression that he was a man she could like and respect as well as lust after.

I'm not going to feel guilty for going after what I want, Olivia decided, squaring her shoulders and turning to look around the lobby. Whatever had happened between Jill and Cory was obviously in the past, and Jill's little display of jealousy only put Olivia on her guard. She couldn't trust anything Jill said about Cory now. Every instinct told her that Cory wasn't a "player" as Jill had described him—and wouldn't Rosie, who'd known Cory all her life, have dropped a gentle hint or two if he were, instead of eagerly matchmaking?

Chapter Five

Just as Olivia thought of Rosie, she came through a door on the other side of the lobby with Luke, the pair of them talking earnestly. They both spotted her and smiled at the same moment, coming over to join her.

"Hey, how are you settling in?" Luke asked cheerfully. "Better after the dunking?" His eyes twinkled.

"Much, thank you," Olivia said. "Rosie was kind enough to lend me some of her things, I'm afraid I vastly overestimated the dress code here at Sunfish. I think I'll need to go into Airlie Beach to shop one day, if that can be arranged?"

"Of course, the boat goes every day," Luke said with a shrug. "You can go anytime you like. As far as I'm concerned, you make your own schedule here, Olivia. The only instruction I have from Mr. Hunter is that I'm to see to it you have anything you need. Rosie mentioned your laptop and tablet took a dunking too."

"And my phone," she admitted. "Yes, I'll need to purchase replacements for those in Airlie as well."

"The resort has an account at the computer-and-electrical store. Put them on our tab." Luke's tone brooked no argument.

"Well... thank you," she accepted gracefully, secretly grateful. Replacing her electronics would have put a serious dent in her much-depleted savings. "That's very good of you."

He waved away her thanks. "There's a computer in your room, too, but that's mainly because I don't really have office space for you. You're welcome to work anywhere you like in the resort. Although you're on staff, you're not part of the guest relations side, and as such I don't mind if you want to act more as a guest here, to get the real guest experience, than as a staff member."

Startled, Olivia blinked at him. "Thank you! But I want to pull my weight around here too. If you need an extra pair of hands at any time, please just say so."

"Rosie will let you know." Luke gestured at Rosie, who hadn't said a word as she nodded along in agreement with what he was saying. "She's our staff manager."

"Well, there may be times when we do need extra pairs of hands, of course," Rosie said, "but I'll try not to shove you into anything you wouldn't be prepared for. I mean, I'm guessing you're going to spend a fair bit of time talking to guests anyway, asking them what they think are the best things about Sunfish for marketing purposes, so guest relations would probably be a handy spot for you. Which is Jill's department, of course."

"Of course," Olivia echoed, doing her level best not to let her feelings at the idea of having to work for Jill, even temporarily, show on her face.

She must have failed, though, because after dinner—eaten with Luke and Rosie, who both talked enthusiastically about how much they loved working at Sunfish—she was walking back to her cabin with Rosie when the other girl asked, "Um, Olivia, I hope you don't mind me asking this, but have you had a run-in with Jill?"

She missed a step, recovered. "I thought I wasn't that obvious."

"Jill has a way of rubbing people up the wrong way, sometimes."

"One would think that guest relations wouldn't be the best career for her, then," Olivia said dryly.

"You'd be surprised the shit she has to deal with," Rosie replied. "Guest relations manager is just a fancy title for 'troubleshooter.'"

"Hm." They'd reached her cabin, and Olivia stopped and turned to Rosie with a sigh. "I don't want to get off on the wrong foot, and I don't want to make any enemies, but I'm pretty sure Jill was predisposed to dislike me from the moment Cory started flirting with me."

"She was predisposed to dislike you from the moment she saw you in the airport and realized how pretty you are," Rosie said bluntly. "Because yes, as you've already figured out, Cory is a sore spot with Jill."

"Will you tell me about it?" Olivia pleaded. "I know Jill is your friend and I don't want to ask you to go behind her back, but I'm pretty sure I can't trust anything she says about Cory... and I'm pretty sure I *can* trust what *you* tell me about him, since you've known each other so long."

Rosie sighed and glanced at the lit window in her cabin next door. "Invite me in?"

"Sure."

They went into the lounge area and sat down. Rosie rubbed her hands together, looking as though she was thinking about what to say. Olivia waited in silence, not wanting to push. Jill and Rosie were obviously close, and she didn't want to force Rosie to betray her friend.

"Cory and Jill dated for a while when Jill got the job here in the middle of last year," Rosie said finally. "It lasted, maybe three or four months? I don't remember exactly."

"Why did they break up? I don't need all the gory details," Olivia said hurriedly, "but who dumped who would be good to know."

"Cory ended it, but Jill drove him to it. She was incredibly clingy and possessive. I'm sure you can imagine that with the way Cory looks, he literally can't help girls throwing themselves at him sometimes. There was this guest at the resort. She was here with her parents; she wouldn't leave him alone. She was all of seventeen, so Cory just treated her like a kid with a crush... which was exactly the right thing to do. He was polite but didn't encourage her, and he made damn sure she couldn't catch him alone anywhere. Which didn't stop Jill from getting wildly jealous every time Cory even glanced in her direction." Rosie sighed and leaned back in her chair. "Jill was being stupid, I told her so myself; told her Cory would never touch the girl."

"But she wouldn't listen," Olivia surmised.

"Yup, and in the end there was a really ugly scene where Jill confronted the girl and called her all sorts of demeaning names, told her to stay away from Cory. Honestly I think the only reason Jill didn't get fired for it was that the parents thought their daughter had been making a fool of herself and took *Jill's* side when the matter went up before Luke."

Olivia shook her head. "That... must have been pretty hard on the girl."

"Which was what Cory thought. The whole scene was just so unnecessary, and he told Jill that when he broke it off. She'd been jealous over nothing and he could see it inevitably happening again, every time he even so much as spoke to a pretty girl. He didn't want the drama."

And here I come with a history of nothing but *drama*, Olivia thought. "Thanks for telling me this, Rosie."

"You're welcome. I'd like to see Cory happy. I'd like to see Jill happy too, but the two of them just aren't suited for each other." Rosie shrugged, her irrepressible grin breaking out again. "I'm a natural matchmaker."

"What about you, anyone special in your life?" Olivia asked curiously.

A wistful look crossed Rosie's face briefly before she shook her head. "I'm afraid not."

"That look tells me that there's someone, though? Didn't Jill say you were seeing a pilot?" Olivia remembered the earlier conversation in the airport.

"Past tense, I'm afraid."

"I'm sorry to hear that," Olivia said genuinely.

"He was seeing multiple other girls"—Rosie's smile was wry—"and nice though he was—and honest about it, which was a big point in his favour—I'd like to be somebody's one and only."

Don't we all, Olivia thought. "Jill told me Cory was a player."

"Not in the least." Rosie shook her head vehemently. "Couldn't be further from the truth. Cory isn't one to start something unless he thinks it's going somewhere.

He was genuinely broken up about ending things with Jill, but her jealousy was just too much for the relationship to bear."

"So me even hinting that I might be jealous would be a big red flag," Olivia surmised. "I'll keep that in mind."

"You should. Because there are silly young girls who try to throw themselves at him every other week here, and Cory will be watching to see your reaction," Rosie warned. She covered a huge yawn and laughed at herself. "God, sorry. Been a long day. I'm gonna go crash."

"Thank you for telling me the truth."

"You're welcome." Rosie surprised Olivia with a hug, which Olivia returned tentatively. "Don't let Jill get to you. If I see or hear her starting any crap, I'll try and pull her up; she listens to me."

Olivia thanked her again, and Rosie took her leave with a cheerful wave, leaving Olivia alone with her thoughts.

***

Lost in thought, Olivia sat for a while in silence. She was startled when the cabin door opened and looked up to see a tall redheaded woman who was probably a couple of years her senior entering.

"Hi," she said uncertainly.

"'Allo, you must be Olivia! I have heard so much about you already! I'm Suzannah, your roommate."

"Oh." Getting to her feet, Olivia smiled in welcome. "Hi—nobody mentioned you were French!"

Suzannah laughed throatily, stepping forward and kissing Olivia enthusiastically on both cheeks. "Eh, we are a multinational crew here; nobody thinks much of it. As long as they can understand your accent, that is."

That made Olivia smile. She liked Suzannah immediately, admiring her poise and confident air. "I swiped one of your sodas from the fridge earlier," she confessed, figuring she'd best get that out of the way first. "I'll replace it, I promise."

Suzannah waved it off with another laugh, heading to the fridge herself. "Want another? I'm thirsty, been a busy night in the kitchen."

Olivia accepted the offer and they sat to introduce themselves to each other properly. Suzannah was more than happy to answer questions, talking about her training at Le Cordon Bleu in Paris and her past work in major hotels and famous restaurants. Olivia almost died of shock when Suzannah admitted to once having worked for Gordon Ramsey and having a glowing recommendation from the infamously critical chef on her résumé.

"Well, nothing I've ever done compares to that; you definitely win," Olivia said, very impressed, making Suzannah's throaty laugh ring out again. The French girl smothered a yawn then, admitting that she'd had a long day.

"Go sleep, we can talk more tomorrow. We've got plenty of time to get to know each other," Olivia insisted when Suzannah demurred, offering to keep her company. Left alone, she thought she should probably go on into her own room, in case she made noise in the lounge area and kept the weary chef awake.

At least the nightwear she'd brought was perfectly fine; she liked to be comfortable when she slept, so she just changed into a tank top and a pair of boyleg cotton shorts before slipping into bed and turning out the bedside light.

Sleep was nowhere to be found, though, and after a couple of hours tossing and turning, Olivia gave up. Getting out of bed, she went out onto her little veranda, sitting down on the chair and putting her feet up on the railing. It was blissfully cool outside now, whereas her room had been too warm; she sighed as the sea breeze washed over her and let her head tip back.

"Can't sleep either?" a low voice said, and she startled upright, yelping with shock as her feet fell to the floor.

"Sorry!"

"Who the hell is that?" Olivia pressed her hand to her pounding heart.

"Cory. Remember, I live next door?" There was a laugh in his voice.

"God damn it." She shut her eyes before opening them, laughing at herself and peering across the dark space between the two cabins. She could just about make him out in the dim moonlight, lying in... "Is that a hammock?"

"Sure is, and it's big enough to share. Wanna come join me?"

She hesitated only briefly before scrambling to her feet and heading over. "I've never been in a hammock before," she admitted, looking at Cory sprawled negligently in the net, one long leg hanging over the side. "How do you get into it gracefully?"

"Easier said than done," he chuckled, "but actually fairly easy when you have help..." He pushed at the floor with his foot, swung towards her, and scooped her easily off her feet to lie with her back against his chest.

Olivia flailed for a second before realizing she was actually making it more likely they'd both fall out, and relaxed back against Cory. "You could have warned me," she grumped.

"I could, but it wouldn't have been nearly as much fun." He nuzzled at her ear, making her shiver.

"Practical joker," she accused, but she couldn't repress the laughter in her voice and he knew it.

"It's a bad habit." He fell silent, and she did too, feeling oddly relaxed despite their intimately close position, despite having known him for barely twelve hours. Lying in the cradle of his thighs, head pillowed on his broad chest, Olivia felt more comfortable, more secure, than she had in a very long time. Than she could *ever* remember feeling, if she were completely honest with herself.

Cory's toe brushing the floor pushed off, set them swinging gently. The slow side-to-side motion soothed Olivia, and her eyes drifted closed.

"Are you asleep?" Cory asked quietly a few blissful minutes later.

"No." But she didn't bother to open her eyes.

"That's good." He hesitated before saying softly, "Because I'm actually a lot less sleepy than I was before you lay down on me."

She realized that the firm muscle pressed against her left ass cheek wasn't actually his thigh. It couldn't be, not unless he had three legs.

"Oh." Her eyes popped wide and her cheeks flushed with colour.

"You can get up, if you like." There was a definite *or* in Cory's tone, though he didn't say the word aloud.

"I think I'm perfectly fine here, thanks."

"Mm-hm." He moved slowly, though, his hand gliding gently across her stomach and up toward her breasts, making it obvious that she could grab it and push it off at any time. Far from doing so, Olivia closed her eyes and relaxed with a soft sigh as his hand cupped her breast through her top.

Cory's warm lips nibbled at her ear as his thumb rubbed small circles over her nipple, raising it quickly to a hard little point. It was Olivia who pulled up the hem of her top, though, taking his free hand in hers and bringing it under the thin fabric to cover her other breast.

Cory made a low, hungry sound deep in his chest, fingers tightening on her nipple. "So damn tempting," he rasped against Olivia's ear, hips grinding against hers, the hardness of his arousal pressing against her ass. "Come inside with me, Olivia..."

"I think I'd probably better not," she gasped reluctantly, arching up into his tugging fingers. "It's very soon..."

He growled wordlessly. "Okay, but I want you to know I'm gonna go jack off while thinking about you."

She smiled at that, turning her head to press kisses against his stubbled jaw. "Sounds hot. I'd like to watch you do that sometime."

"Mm. I'd like to watch you pleasure yourself too." He released her breasts and moved one hand slowly across her stomach and over her shorts before curving over her mound. "How do you like to do it... fingers, or toys?"

"Battery-operated boyfriend," Olivia moaned as his fingers crooked, pressing the thin fabric against her sensitive flesh. "I... I was nervous coming through Customs with it in my suitcase, actually. I had visions of the official pulling it out and waving it around in the middle of the terminal."

Cory laughed, the rumble in his chest shaking her whole body. "I'd have liked to have seen your face."

"That's because you have a low sense of humour and find amusement in watching me make a fool of myself," Olivia tried to say the words in a sniffy, offended tone, but Cory's long fingers had just insinuated themselves inside the crotch of her boyleg shorts, grazing gently over her folds. Her voice came out breathy and high instead.

"You look beautiful whether you're fully in control or taking an unexpected header into the water," Cory murmured hotly against her ear. "But I bet you're absolutely stunning when you come." One fingertip pressed firmly against her clit, rubbing a rapid circle. Olivia bit her lip to keep from screaming with ecstasy, acutely aware that they were outside. Yes, it was dark, but anyone walking on the path past the cabins would be able to see them if she made enough noise to attract attention.

"This okay?" Cory whispered, stroking faster. She nodded jerkily against his chest, as heat spiraled through her core, every nerve starting to tingle. His other hand had never left her breast as his fingertips carried on their teasing play with her nipple. He pinched lightly as his other hand slipped lower, fingers crooking up inside her as the heel of his hand rubbed firmly over her bud.

"Oh God, Cory, yes," Olivia gasped, her grasping his wrist with both hands and holding on to it so that she could grind herself against his hand to get just the pressure she needed. "Fuck, yes, there!"

"That's it, angel," he crooned in her ear. The hammock swayed and creaked below them as Olivia shuddered with completion, biting her tongue to keep from letting out loud cries of fulfillment.

Cory hummed with contentment, leaving his fingers right where they were until Olivia finally relaxed against him, her grip on his wrist falling lax. Gently he withdrew his hand and wrapped his arms around her to hold her close in a firm embrace.

"Thank you," Olivia murmured finally.

"Think you're relaxed enough to sleep now?" he asked with a soft chuckle.

Olivia laughed. "Mm. Yes, I rather think I am. How about you?" Deliberately she wiggled her ass, pushing it against the solid bar of his erection and grinning to herself at his heartfelt groan.

"I'm not relaxed at all, but I'll be fine. I can go cool off in the shower and take care of the problem."

"I could take care of it for you," she offered. His cock twitched against her ass, straining harder against her.

"Sounds good," Cory admitted, "but this isn't exactly the best position, or location, for that."

"True. Let's go inside, then."

"Thought you weren't ready for that?"

Olivia hesitated only a second before saying, "Not quite ready to hit a home run, no, but I'd like to get you off. Only fair."

"Oh, never let it be said I denied you the chance to even the score," Cory chuckled quietly before shifting under her, bracing them with his foot on the floor, and lifting quickly. Olivia found herself on her feet almost before she knew it, Cory standing up alongside her, taking her hand in his and leading her inside.

His room was a mirror image of hers, but a lot homelier, with just a small lamp beside the bed casting everything in a softly welcoming glow. Olivia smiled on spotting the vintage *Point Break* poster framed above the bed. Of course Cory would love that movie.

"No, here." She tugged back on his hand as he led her towards the bed. She pointed at the desk instead. "Take off your shorts and sit there." She grabbed the office chair and sat down, watching as he dropped his shorts quite unselfconsciously and stood nude and magnificently male before her before backing up to the desk and seating himself on the edge of it, knees spread apart.

Olivia stared her fill for a good minute before sighing. "Damn, you're gorgeous." He truly was, all golden skin over chiseled muscle, a scattering of dark blond hair on his broad chest narrowing down to the thin happy trail bisecting those perfect abs. His cock rose, thickly engorged from a nest of dark golden curls, swollen and flushed, a pearly drop of precum just beading at the tip.

Cory smiled at her. "That's my line."

"Hush and let me admire." Olivia scooted the chair closer, laying her hands on his strong thighs and pressing them a little farther apart so she could sit in between them. Leaning in, she breathed warm air over his cock and smiled as it twitched in response.

"Christ, Olivia." Cory's hands tightened where they curled around the edge of the desk, his knuckles whitening.

She smiled up at him, holding his gaze as her lips parted, tongue slipping out to moisten them before she licked a long, slow line up the length of his cock, swiping off the bead of precum and humming with pleasure at the salty-sweet taste on her tongue.

Cory's groan was heartfelt. Olivia laughed softly before licking her lips again and opening them wide, taking the flushed, swollen head of his cock into her mouth.

"Fuck, Olivia, I'm not gonna last."

Her mouth was too full to reply, but she let her actions speak for her, taking her hands off his thighs and wrapping one of them firmly around the base of his cock, the other rolling and caressing his balls between her fingers.

Cory cried out wordlessly, his cock jerking in her fingers an instant before the first spurt hit the back of her throat. Olivia took her time, slowly sucking up every last drop before licking him clean. His hand came up to slowly caress her hair, stroking through her thick curls.

"So good," Cory said quietly, looking down at Olivia as she finally moved back and smiled up at him. "Thank you."

She smiled slow and satisfied, like a cat licking cream from its whiskers. "You're welcome. I think maybe we'll both get a good night's sleep now, hmm?" Standing, she pressed a kiss on his lips before slipping away into the night.

Chapter Six

The bright, hot morning seemed unreal to Olivia as she woke up, the events of the previous day feeling dreamlike. She stretched and heard a knock on her door. Rosie stood there, already dressed and ready to go.

"Morning! Ready for your first full day?" Rosie asked, her enthusiasm infectious.

After quickly dressing, Olivia joined Rosie for breakfast. Rosie chattered about all the things Olivia should do on her first day, but Olivia had her own plan.

"I'm going snorkeling later," Olivia cut Rosie off, "but I'd really like to just take a walk around the resort this morning. Find my way around properly, really get familiar with the place."

"Absolutely." Rosie nodded her approval. "Reception has a good map of the island; stop there and grab one before you go. And don't forget a hat, and sunscreen!"

Olivia thanked Rosie for her advice, refraining from snapping that she already knew that. She hadn't seen Cory this morning, at his cabin or in the staff dining room, and butterflies were beginning to flutter in her stomach. What did she really know about Cory, anyway? She'd met him less than a day ago, yet the previous night they'd gotten extremely hot and heavy together.

Determined to forget about Cory for the time being and get to work, she grabbed one of the maps from Reception and headed back to her cabin to put on sunscreen and find her hat and sunglasses. Ten minutes later she set off, a bag slung over her shoulder containing a bottle of water, a notebook, and a pen. In the absence of being able to take photos and make notes on her phone as she normally did, the notebook would have to do.

She kept a close eye on the time during her walk, mindful that she needed to get back to her cabin in time to change and then meet the boat at the dock at one. Lunch wasn't in her plan, since she had no desire to humiliate herself yet again in front of Cory by getting seasick on the boat. The transfer from Hamilton Island had been short enough yesterday that she hadn't worried about it, but bobbing about on a smaller boat for a couple of hours could well be a different story.

Returning to her cabin with a stack of notes to consider, she swiped another of Suzannah's sodas, thinking guiltily that she must find out where to buy more, before finding her bikini. She'd brought three, sure there would be plenty of opportunity for swimming, but no swimming shirt. Chewing on her lip, she shrugged and grabbed one of Rosie's T-shirts, an elderly-looking one. Floating facedown in the water for an hour or two, she was likely to end up with a burned back if she didn't cover up. She made sure to thickly cover every exposed inch of skin with the waterproof, high-factor sunscreen she'd bought in Sydney before putting her hat and flip-flops back on and heading for the dock.

The boat was bigger than she'd expected; not one of the big handsome cruisers that transferred tourists to and from the island, but a generously sized motor-yacht. Cory stood on the deck, talking to a couple of tourists who'd just boarded. Both were attractive young women, who stood close and gazed at him with undisguised admiration.

Cory's eyes slid towards Olivia and he smiled but made no effort to break off his conversation. She nodded at him in greeting and boarded the boat, walking past him and finding a seat on which to put her bag containing her towel and water bottle. She absolutely refused to show jealousy; quite apart from the fact that it would put Cory off her completely, she was pretty sure she didn't have anything to worry about.

Her decision was vindicated a couple of minutes later as Cory came over to greet her properly, an arm sliding around her waist as he bent to kiss her cheek and nuzzle lightly against her neck.

"Hello, beautiful."

"Hello yourself." Olivia wiggled as his fingers slid against her ribs and he found a ticklish spot. Laughing as she squeaked and danced away, Cory pulled her back closer and ducked beneath the brim of her hat to claim a proper kiss.

His lips were warm and sweet; Olivia lost herself in the kiss briefly, in the slide of the heat of his body through the thin layers of their clothing as he pulled her close.

A wolf-whistle made them pull apart. Colour tinged Cory's cheeks as he made a face at the boat's driver. "Put a sock in it, Jodie."

The driver was an older woman with darkly tanned skin and white teeth flashing in her laughing face. Cory introduced Olivia, telling her, "Jodie's spent her whole life in the Whitsunday Islands. She knows all the best snorkel and dive spots, and nobody's better at finding the whales in whale-watching season."

"Which is when?" Olivia asked curiously.

"June to August is the best time. The whales give birth to their calves in the warm waters here; it's a natural nursery for them. We're not allowed to get too close, but sometimes they come close to us." Jodie smiled at her. "I've got some amazing photos and video we've taken off the boat; you can have whatever you like for marketing material."

"That's terrific!" Olivia said. Cory had remained at her side, his warm hand resting lightly on the small of her back. He moved away then with a murmured apology to go and greet some more tourists boarding the boat. Olivia barely noticed his departure, focused on her conversation with Jodie.

"That everyone, Cory?" Jodie called back after a couple of minutes. "Cast off, then!" she said when she got a reply in the affirmative.

"Do you need me to sit down?" Olivia asked uncertainly.

"No, you're fine there." Jodie expertly brought the boat's big engines up to a low rev, guiding the boat away from the dock with a deft touch. "You two look good together," she said unexpectedly.

"We only met yesterday," Olivia admitted, "but I feel like I'm falling head over heels."

"I've known that boy all his life." Jodie was wearing reflective sunglasses, so Olivia couldn't see her eyes, but her tone was friendly. "He's one of the few people I've ever met who's just as beautiful on the inside as the outside. Don't you break his heart, now."

"I'll try," Olivia promised, touched by Jodie's obvious fondness for Cory. Nobody seemed to have a bad word to say about him, except Jill who obviously had an ax to grind. "It'd be like kicking a puppy—how could you? I've got baggage, though. Maybe too much."

"Eh." Jodie shrugged, gunning the engines as they cleared the small harbour. "That's life for you. You'll do fine. You didn't look funny at him when those girls were all over him; that's the one thing Cory wouldn't be able to stand."

"Rosie warned me about that," Olivia admitted. They were having to speak more loudly to be heard over the engine noise, and she looked towards the back of the boat, hoping Cory wouldn't overhear. He was talking cheerfully to a young couple, though, helping them select snorkeling gear from a cabinet. "She told me about Jill."

"Did she now!" Jodie said nothing more, though, just concentrated on piloting the boat, and Olivia relaxed and turned her attention to the crystal blue waters they skimmed rapidly across.

"Hey." Cory came to join her a few minutes later, slipping into the empty seat beside her and putting his arm around her shoulders. "Want to come pick out some snorkeling gear? Everyone else has theirs."

"Sure." She followed him to the back of the boat, ignoring the two girls who'd been flirting with Cory and who were now staring at her and whispering to each other. They are no threat to me, she told herself and believed it. Even knowing

Cory as little as she did, she was quite certain the chance of him getting involved with one of the resort's guests was pretty much zero.

"How long does the boat trip take?" she called to Cory over the engine noise, which was even louder at the back of the boat.

"About twenty minutes," he called back, picking up a set of flippers and holding them close to her feet, nodding that he thought they were about the right size. She chose a mask and snorkel.

"This'll do."

"Got sunscreen on?"

"All over. I don't need a burn on my first full day."

"Damn."

She looked a query at him; he laughed, hooked an arm around her waist, and pulled her close. "I was hoping to be able to offer to help you apply it."

"Lecher," Olivia accused, laughing back up at him.

"You're mad if you think I'd pass up a chance to put my hands all over this gorgeous body of yours." He bent his head to bring his lips to hers, but Olivia let him claim only a brief kiss before pulling back.

"You're working, Cory. And so am I. I want to talk to some of the guests about what they like best about Sunfish Island. Get some idea of what draws people here in the first place." She gave him an apologetic smile, and he let her go with no sign of reluctance.

"Damn, I love smart women who are right all the time."

She gave him a pert smile for that remark before whirling away, snorkeling gear in hand, to go and get started on her job. It would be easy to get carried away in her romance with Cory, but that wasn't why she was here. She was being given a chance to repair her ruined professional reputation, a chance she'd never get anywhere else, and she had no intention of throwing that away.

Olivia was sitting and chatting with a friendly middle-aged couple when the engines slowed to a gentle throb. Looking out the window beside her, she saw they had drawn up to a small pontoon, which was obviously moored in place. Cory was standing on it and tied off a rope before he gave Jodie a thumbs-up and the engines died altogether.

The sudden silence was almost overwhelming. Cory and Jodie leaped into action, urging everyone off the boat and onto the pontoon, where Cory gave a quick talk about safety, warning everyone not to touch the coral and to stay within sight of the pontoon.

"We're in a bay with very little current, but if you get into any difficulty, turn over onto your back and raise your hand in the air, and I'll come get you," he concluded.

"Aren't you coming in, Cory?" one of his admirers asked.

"Afraid not. Jodie and I are your lifeguards. We're responsible for every one of you, so we'll be staying right here, watching over you. Now has everyone got their sunscreen on? Don't want any red lobsters coming back out of this water!"

There was a general chorus of agreement, then Cory gave them the go-ahead to enter the water. Olivia went in eagerly, keen to see the world-famous reef, although of course she was only seeing a tiny, tiny corner of the World Heritage Site here.

Almost instantly she found herself swimming through a school of tiny, brightly colored fish darting in and out of the coral. A manta ray lifted up from a patch of sand not far away and flew majestically through the turquoise water, wings sweeping slowly up and down.

She saw a new wonder everywhere she looked. She was a strong swimmer, so she had no problem staying under for a good amount of time, blowing bubbles and swimming with long, smooth kicks of her fins to propel herself through the water. It would be easy to lose track of time down here, she thought with a start when she surfaced to get a few deep breaths, checked the time, and found that almost an hour had passed already. She'd swum quite some distance from the pontoon; looking back at it, she found Cory peering towards her. He gave her a wave and she waved back before popping her mouthpiece back in and going facedown in the water again, heading back towards the pontoon this time.

"Enjoying yourself?" Cory said with a grin down at her as she surfaced near his feet.

"This is incredible," Olivia gave him a glowing, happy smile, pulling her mask off. "I mean, I've seen pictures, but I always assumed they were the exception—selected highlights, you know. Not the norm. But it's just as perfect down there as in every picture I've ever seen."

"You really have to go diving with Bryce. The outer reefs have even more variety." Cory reached for a large cooler he'd brought from the boat. "Want to hop out and have a drink of water? We've got about another half hour."

She accepted his offer of a hand out and sat on the edge of the pontoon, dangling her feet in the water as she drained the bottle of water he gave her.

"Hand me the bottle," Cory requested as she finished. "Gotta make sure we take all our rubbish back with us."

"Of course."

"Going back in?" He'd stayed standing beside her, but he wasn't looking at her, his eyes constantly scanning over the water checking on the other snorkelers instead. He took his job seriously, which Olivia genuinely appreciated. She wouldn't have wanted a man who flirted while he was supposed to be looking out for the safety of others.

She went back into the water for another swim and mainly floated along the surface this time, watching the schools of brightly colored fish darting among the coral and thinking that when she went into town to buy a new laptop, she'd have to have a look at waterproof cameras. An Instagram was just one of the ideas she planned to implement for Sunfish, and posting new photos from the Reef every day would be a big draw.

Returning to the boat, Olivia felt invigorated. The beauty of the reef had a calming, almost therapeutic effect on her. Back on the boat, Cory was organizing the snorkeling gear, and she took the opportunity to speak with more guests, gathering useful insights about what they loved about Sunfish Island.

As they docked back at the resort, Olivia felt a renewed sense of purpose. She was ready to tackle her new role with vigor. However, as she walked towards her cabin, she noticed Jill standing near the entrance, her expression unreadable.

"Olivia, can we talk?" Jill's tone was polite but firm.

"Sure," Olivia replied cautiously, curious about what Jill wanted to discuss.

"I've been thinking about how we got off on the wrong foot," Jill began. "I want to apologize for any tension I've caused. It's just... Cory and I have a history, and seeing him move on so quickly was difficult for me."

Olivia appreciated Jill's honesty. "I understand, Jill. It's never easy seeing someone you care about with someone new. But I hope we can find a way to work together professionally and maybe even become friends."

Jill nodded, the tension in her shoulders easing slightly. "I'd like that. And I know it's not fair to judge you based on my past with Cory. Let's start fresh."

"Agreed," Olivia said with a smile. "Fresh start."

As they parted ways, Olivia felt hopeful. Perhaps the conflicts that had seemed so daunting could be resolved with time and understanding. She returned to her cabin, ready to dive into her work and make the most of her new beginning on Sunfish Island.

Chapter Seven

The next morning, Olivia woke early, feeling a mixture of excitement and trepidation. Today, she would start on the significant project Luke had mentioned: an ambitious campaign to market Sunfish Island internationally. She dressed quickly and headed to the dining room for breakfast, eager to discuss her ideas with Luke and the rest of the team.

As she entered the dining room, she spotted Rosie and Cory already seated at a table, deep in conversation. Rosie waved her over enthusiastically.

"Morning, Olivia!" Rosie greeted her with a bright smile. "We were just talking about you. Cory has some ideas for the marketing campaign that he wanted to share."

Olivia smiled, feeling a flutter of excitement. "Great! I'd love to hear them."

Cory leaned forward, his blue eyes sparkling with enthusiasm. "I was thinking we should focus on the unique experiences Sunfish Island offers. The reef, of course, but also the cultural events, the local cuisine, and the sense of community. We want to attract tourists who are looking for more than just a beach vacation."

Olivia nodded thoughtfully. "I agree. We need to highlight what makes Sunfish Island special. Personal stories and testimonials from guests could be very powerful. Maybe even a series of short videos showcasing different aspects of the island."

Rosie clapped her hands together. "I love it! We could interview some of the long-time staff members too. People like Jodie, who have lived here their whole lives. Their stories would add authenticity."

Cory grinned. "Sounds like a plan. Let's run it by Luke and see what he thinks."

The three of them finished breakfast quickly and headed to Luke's office. He was already there, reviewing reports on his computer.

"Good morning," Luke greeted them, looking up from his screen. "What brings you here so early?"

Olivia took a deep breath and outlined their ideas for the marketing campaign. Luke listened attentively, occasionally nodding and making notes.

"I like it," he said finally. "It's fresh and engaging. Let's start working on the logistics. Olivia, you'll lead the project. Coordinate with the staff and gather the content. Cory and Rosie, I want you to assist her in any way you can."

Olivia felt a surge of confidence. "Thank you, Luke. We'll get started right away."

As they left Luke's office, Olivia couldn't help but feel a sense of accomplishment. This was her chance to prove herself and make a real impact on the resort's success.

The next few days were a whirlwind of activity. Olivia worked closely with the staff, interviewing them and gathering stories. She spent hours filming the breathtaking scenery and capturing candid moments with the guests. Cory and Rosie were invaluable, helping her with logistics and providing insights into the island's culture and history.

One afternoon, while Olivia was reviewing footage in her office, Jill knocked on the door and entered hesitantly.

"Hey, Olivia. Got a minute?" Jill asked, her tone tentative.

"Sure, come in," Olivia replied, motioning to a chair.

Jill sat down and took a deep breath. "I wanted to thank you for giving me a chance to start fresh. I know I've been difficult, but I appreciate your patience."

Olivia smiled warmly. "We're all in this together, Jill. Let's focus on making this campaign a success."

Jill nodded, looking relieved. "I actually have an idea for the campaign. What if we create a series of 'Day in the Life' segments, showing what a typical day looks like for different guests? We could follow a couple on their honeymoon, a family on vacation, and a solo traveler. It would give potential visitors a real sense of what to expect."

Olivia's eyes lit up. "That's a fantastic idea, Jill! It would add a personal touch and make the campaign more relatable. Let's work on it together."

As they discussed the details, Olivia felt a sense of camaraderie building between them.

Later that evening, Olivia and Cory met for dinner at one of the resort's finer restaurants, "The Coral Reef." The setting sun cast a golden glow over the water, creating a romantic ambiance that seemed almost too perfect. The soft murmur of the ocean waves provided a soothing backdrop to their conversation.

"You've been working so hard," Cory said, reaching across the table to take her hand. "I thought you deserved a break."

Olivia smiled, feeling a warm flush spread through her. "Thank you, Cory. It's been a busy few days, but I'm loving every moment of it."

As they enjoyed their meal, they talked about their day, sharing stories and laughter. Cory told her about an adventurous guest who had insisted on trying to surf despite the calm waters, and Olivia shared some of the more touching testimonials she had gathered from guests.

As the night wore on, the conversation turned more personal.

"Cory, can I ask you something?" Olivia said, her voice soft.

"Of course," he replied, his gaze steady.

"Why did you choose to stay on Sunfish Island? You could have gone anywhere, done anything. What keeps you here?"

Cory leaned back, considering her question. "I love this place. It's not just the beauty of the island, but the sense of community, the feeling of belonging. I've lived in big cities, but they never felt like home. Here, I feel like I can make a difference, be part of something meaningful."

Olivia nodded, understanding. "I think I'm starting to feel the same way. Sunfish Island is becoming my home too."

Cory smiled, squeezing her hand. "I'm glad to hear that, Olivia. You're already making a big impact here."

After dinner, Cory suggested a walk along the beach. The moonlight reflected off the calm ocean, casting a silvery path on the water. They walked hand in hand, the cool sand beneath their feet.

"I've never felt this way before," Cory said suddenly, his voice serious. "I know it's only been a short time, but I feel a deep connection with you, Olivia."

Olivia felt tears prickling at the corners of her eyes. "I feel the same way, Cory. You've become such an important part of my life."

Cory stopped walking and turned to face her, taking both her hands in his. "I want us to build a future together, Olivia. I know it's early, but I don't want to waste any more time."

Olivia's heart swelled with love and gratitude. "I want that too, Cory. Let's take this journey together."

As they kissed under the moonlight, Olivia felt a profound sense of happiness and contentment. She had found not only a new home but also a partner who believed in her and supported her dreams.

The following day, Olivia threw herself into her work with renewed energy. She coordinated with Jill to start filming the "Day in the Life" segments. They selected a few willing guests to participate, including a couple on their honeymoon, a family on vacation, and a solo traveler exploring the island.

The filming went smoothly, capturing candid moments of joy and relaxation. Olivia reviewed the footage later and felt a sense of pride in the work they were doing. This campaign was going to showcase the best of Sunfish Island and attract a whole new wave of visitors.

One afternoon, as Olivia was editing the footage, Luke walked into her office.

"Olivia, I've got some exciting news," Luke said, his eyes sparkling with enthusiasm. "We've been contacted by a major travel magazine. They want to feature Sunfish Island in a special edition about hidden gems. This could be huge for us."

Olivia's eyes widened in excitement. "That's amazing, Luke! When do they want to come?"

"They'll be here next week. I want you to handle the arrangements and make sure everything goes smoothly. This is a great opportunity to showcase our campaign as well," Luke said.

"I'll get right on it," Olivia replied, feeling a surge of adrenaline. This was a significant milestone in her marketing role, and she was determined to make the most of it.

The next few days were a blur of activity as Olivia prepared for the magazine's visit. She coordinated with the staff to ensure everything was perfect, from the accommodations to the planned activities. Cory and Rosie were by her side every step of the way, offering support and helping with the arrangements.

When the magazine representatives arrived, Olivia greeted them with a warm smile and a detailed itinerary. She took them on a tour of the resort, highlighting the unique experiences Sunfish Island offered. They watched as guests participated in snorkeling excursions, enjoyed spa treatments, and dined on gourmet meals prepared by Suzannah.

The representatives were impressed with the resort and the marketing campaign. They spent several days on the island, capturing stunning photos and interviewing staff and guests. Olivia felt a sense of accomplishment as she watched them work, knowing that their feature would bring significant attention to Sunfish Island.

As the magazine representatives prepared to leave, they thanked Olivia for her hospitality and professionalism.

"You've done an incredible job here, Olivia," one of them said. "We're excited to share Sunfish Island with our readers."

Olivia beamed with pride. "Thank you. We're thrilled to be featured in your magazine."

That evening, the staff gathered for a celebratory dinner. Luke raised a glass to toast Olivia and the team.

"I want to thank each and every one of you for your hard work and dedication," Luke said. "This campaign has brought Sunfish Island to new heights, and it's all thanks to you."

As they toasted to their success, Olivia felt a deep sense of belonging. She had found her place on Sunfish Island, but she knew this was just the beginning. There was still so much more to achieve and discover.

After the celebratory dinner, Olivia and Cory decided to take a walk on the beach. The night was clear, and the stars twinkled above them like scattered diamonds. They walked in comfortable silence, the sound of the waves gently lapping at the shore providing a soothing backdrop.

"It's amazing how quickly things can change," Olivia mused, breaking the silence.

Cory squeezed her hand. "Life has a way of surprising us when we least expect it. I'm just glad you're here, Olivia."

She leaned into him, feeling the warmth of his body. "Me too, Cory. Me too."

As they walked back to the resort, Olivia felt a renewed sense of purpose. She was ready to tackle whatever challenges lay ahead, knowing she had the support of the wonderful people she had met on Sunfish Island.

The next morning, Olivia woke up early, her mind buzzing with ideas for the marketing campaign. She quickly got dressed and headed to the dining room for breakfast, eager to start the day. As she entered, she saw Rosie and Jill already seated, deep in conversation. They waved her over with smiles.

"Morning, Olivia!" Rosie greeted her cheerfully. "Ready for another busy day?"

Olivia grinned. "Absolutely. We've got a lot to do, but I'm excited."

Jill nodded. "I've been thinking about some more ideas for the campaign. We could highlight some of the unique local traditions and events. It would really show off the culture and community here."

"That's a great idea, Jill," Olivia agreed. "Let's start planning out how we can incorporate that."

As they discussed their plans, Cory joined them, sliding into the seat next to Olivia. "Good morning, everyone. What's the plan for today?"

"We're going to start filming some of the local traditions and events," Olivia explained. "It will add a unique touch to the campaign and show off the culture here."

Cory nodded appreciatively. "Sounds like a plan. I'll help out with the logistics."

The team spent the next few days filming various events and traditions on the island. They captured the vibrant colors of a local festival, the intricate dances of a traditional performance, and the mouth-watering dishes prepared by the island's best chefs. Olivia felt a sense of pride as she watched the footage come together, showcasing the rich culture and community of Sunfish Island.

One evening, after a long day of filming, Olivia and Cory decided to relax by the pool. They lounged on deck chairs, sipping on cold drinks, and watching the sun set over the horizon.

"I can't believe how much we've accomplished in such a short time," Olivia said, feeling a sense of satisfaction.

Cory smiled. "You've done an amazing job, Olivia. The campaign is going to be a huge success."

She blushed at the compliment. "I couldn't have done it without all of you. It's been a team effort."

As they sat there, enjoying the peaceful evening, Olivia reflected on her journey. She had come a long way from the chaos and uncertainty of her life in New York. Here on Sunfish Island, she had found a sense of purpose and community. And with Cory by her side, she felt ready to face whatever challenges came her way.

The next day, Olivia received an email from the travel magazine. They were thrilled with the footage and interviews and wanted to publish the feature as a cover story in their print edition, with clips on social media. Olivia's heart raced with excitement as she read the email aloud to the team.

"This is incredible," Luke said, his eyes shining with pride. "A cover story will bring in so much attention and new visitors, and that magazine has a massive social media following. Well done, Olivia. This kind of result is exactly why John Hunter chose you."

The team celebrated their success, but Olivia knew there was still more work to be done. They needed to maintain the momentum and continue to promote Sunfish Island as a top destination.

Over the next few weeks, Olivia and her team continued to work hard on the campaign. They launched a series of social media posts, showcasing the beauty and unique experiences of the island. The response was overwhelmingly positive, with comments and messages pouring in from people all over the world.

One evening, as Olivia was reviewing the latest social media analytics, she felt a tap on her shoulder. She turned to see Cory, holding a small box.

"What's this?" she asked, curious.

Cory smiled. "Just a little something to celebrate our success."

Olivia opened the box to find a beautiful necklace with a delicate silver seashell pendant. "Cory, it's gorgeous. Thank you."

He leaned in and kissed her gently. "You deserve it, Olivia. You've worked so hard, and I wanted to give you something special."

She felt tears of happiness welling up in her eyes. "Thank you, Cory. This means so much to me."

As she put on the necklace, Olivia realized just how far she had come. She had faced challenges and overcome obstacles, but she had also found happiness and fulfillment. She had built a new life surrounded by people who cared about her and believed in her.

The following week, the travel magazine published their feature on Sunfish Island. The cover story was a stunning success, with breathtaking photos and glowing reviews. Olivia and her team watched as the resort's website traffic and booking inquiries skyrocketed.

Luke called another staff meeting to celebrate the success. As they gathered in the staff canteen, he raised a glass to toast the team.

"I want to thank each and every one of you for your hard work and dedication," Luke said. "This campaign has brought Sunfish Island to new heights, and it's all thanks to you."

As they toasted to their success, Olivia felt a deep sense of belonging. She had found her place on Sunfish Island, but she knew this was just the beginning. There were still challenges to face and goals to achieve, but with her newfound confidence and the support of her friends and colleagues, she felt ready for anything.

Chapter Eight

The morning began like any other, with the sun casting a golden glow over Sunfish Island. Olivia was in high spirits, ready to tackle another busy day. She had just finished her morning run along the beach, the salty breeze invigorating her senses. After a quick shower, she grabbed a light breakfast and headed to her office to review the latest social media analytics for their campaign.

As she settled into her desk, Rosie poked her head in the door, her expression unusually serious. "Olivia, Luke's called an urgent staff meeting. We need to go, now."

Olivia's heart skipped a beat. "What's going on?"

Rosie shrugged. "Not sure, but it sounds important."

Olivia hurriedly gathered her things and followed Rosie. The usual buzz of the resort felt muted, and staff members exchanged worried glances as they made their way to the staff canteen. When they arrived, they found Luke standing at the front, his expression grave.

"We've got a cyclone heading our way," Luke announced, his voice steady but serious. "It's expected to make landfall in about 48 hours. The Bureau of Meteorology is predicting the track way too close to Sunfish Island for my liking, and the storm is expected to reach Category 5."

Unsure exactly what that meant, the sharp intake of breath from multiple people around her told Olivia it wasn't good. Rosie's face was white when Olivia looked at her, and the seriousness of Luke's expression drove home the message.

"I believe we'll get the order to evacuate Sunfish sooner rather than later. Our priority is to ensure the safety of our guests and staff, and that will mean getting as many people off the island as we can. My secretary has started making calls to mainland evacuation centres who will prepare to receive our people. Boat captains; all leisure trips are cancelled for the immediate future. Get the boats fully fuelled and ready to begin evacuation runs to Airlie as soon as possible. I'll be making a general announcement to guests shortly and I expect some people will want to leave immediately."

Olivia glanced out the window at the clear blue sky, finding it hard to believe that a deadly cyclone was approaching. The serene beauty of the island seemed at odds with the urgency in Luke's voice. But the gravity of the situation quickly sank in as she looked around at the determined faces of her colleagues.

"Come on." Rosie grabbed Olivia's hand as the meeting dissolved. "Jill's going to need our help soothing disgruntled guests annoyed that an Act of God is about to wreck their holidays."

"How bad is a Category 5 cyclone?" Olivia asked.

Rosie slowed her fast walk to look at her. "As bad as it gets. There is no higher rating. The last direct hit Sunfish got from a Category 5 was when most of the island infrastructure had to be rebuilt."

"Oh. Wow." Suddenly, Olivia understood the fear she'd seen on other staff members' faces. "But I thought..."

"The new buildings are cyclone proof? Most of them, yes... theoretically, but they haven't been tested yet. There's a cyclone shelter under the main building, but it'll only hold a couple of dozen people. We need to get everyone we can off the island."

The radio on Rosie's belt crackled, and she tapped her earpiece. "Yep? Yes, hi Jill. I've got Olivia with me. Where do you want us?"

The team sprang into action, coordinating with local authorities and transportation services to evacuate the guests. Olivia found herself working tirelessly alongside Rose, grateful she wasn't fumbling through the work alone, guiding the guests to the boats and ensuring they had everything they needed for the journey.

The hours flew by in a blur of activity. As Luke had predicted, many guests - mostly the Australians who knew how dangerous a cyclone could be - wanted to get off the island as fast as possible. By the time the boats ceased running a little after dark on that first day, around half the island had already been evacuated, and Olivia felt ready to drop where she stood.

"Hey." She turned from watching the boat's running lights fade away into the dark and found Cory standing on the dock behind her, his face creased with concern. "You look wrecked. You okay?"

"Exhausted," she admitted. "It's been a long day."

"I know." He put his arm around her shoulders and guided her to a waiting golf buggy. "Pretty sure you and Rosie both skipped lunch, huh?"

"I haven't eaten since breakfast." She was almost too tired now to think of food, but knew it would be a bad idea to skip dinner. She stared as Cory drove up to the staff canteen - it was unrecognizable, with boards nailed over the windows.

"This is how we prep for a cyclone," Cory said wryly, seeing what she was looking at. "I've spent all day with a hammer in my hand here. It's how I knew you didn't come for lunch."

"Huh. You seem pretty calm, though?" He seemed completely unworried, Olivia thought, as they joined the line up of quiet, tired staff members getting food.

"I was born up here, remember? Cyclones are an annual occurrence. I've ridden out plenty, including Cyclone Yasi - the one that did all the damage here last time. It'll make a mess, but I'm not worried about my own safety, not in the new cyclone shelter."

"You're planning to stay?" Of course she should have realised Cory would stay, Olivia thought, as he nodded.

"Yes, Luke's staying, and Bryce, and most of the maintenance guys. We need to be here to switch off the power and water once the evacuation's complete, and then check the dock is safe for the boats to return once it's all over."

She didn't like the thought of Cory staying, putting himself in harm's way, but she recognised *he* wasn't concerned, which made her feel a little better about it. They sat down to eat together, and afterwards returned to her cabin, though afterwards Olivia was too tired to do more than fall asleep immediately in Cory's arms.

***

In the morning, the island was almost unrecognisable. The blue skies were gone, replaced by a slowly roiling mass of ominously dark grey clouds. The calm turquoise sea had turned dark and choppy, and even the guests who had been reluctant to leave the day before began to sense the urgency of the situation and started packing hastily, eager to get on the boats and leave before the waves became much bigger. Olivia found herself comforting a young American couple who were visibly shaken.

"Don't worry," she said, her voice soothing. "The mainland is well-prepared for this. You'll be safe there."

By mid afternoon, the last guests had cleared the island and Luke ordered all the staff who were going to report to the docks. Rosie gave Olivia a hug.

"I'll see you in a few days. Take care."

"Wait, you're staying?" Olivia asked, startled.

"Sure. I'm a North Queenslander too, remember. Cyclones don't scare me."

Olivia wasn't sure that was entirely true, not considering Rosie's pale face, but she didn't challenge her friend's bravado as Rosie pushed her towards the boat.

"This is the last boat, hon. Get on."

Jill and Nessa greeted Olivia as she walked up the ramp, making space for her to sit in between them, and Jodie grinned at her from the pilot's chair.

"Sea's getting rough, but I'll have you in Airlie safe in half an hour. Hang tight, girls."

"Got my barf bag ready," Nessa said cheerfully, waving a paper bag. "There's more in that box, Olivia, if you need one."

Olivia nodded, but her throat was tight as she watched Rosie and Cory stooping to cast off the lines.

Suddenly, she made a decision. She couldn't leave. She couldn't abandon her friends and colleagues.

"Wait, Jodie," she said as Jodie started to increase the throttle. "I'm getting off. I'm staying."

"Olivia, no!" Jill exclaimed, but Olivia shook her head, hurrying to the back of the boat and jumping the short distance to the dock. She almost overbalanced, and Cory caught her arms, steadying her.

"Olivia, what are you doing?" he asked, his voice a mix of worry and frustration.

"I couldn't leave you behind," she replied, looking up at him earnestly. "I want to help."

"Olivia..." Cory looked torn.

"Gotta go, Cory!" Jodie shouted. "Last chance, Olivia!"

"I'm staying. Go!" Olivia turned to wave Jodie off, and with a nod, Jodie goosed the throttle and gently eased the boat away from the dock, taking with it Olivia's last opportunity to leave.

"There. It's done!" She was scared, but she wasn't going to let Cory wrap her in cotton wool.

"You should go straight to the shelter," Cory sighed, but he was also smiling rather proudly at her. "You madwoman. Who wants to be in the heart of a Category 5 cyclone?"

"You and Rosie, apparently, and I'm not leaving you to it alone." Olivia stuck her chin out stubbornly. "Now stop fussing and let me help!"

He kissed her, long and slow, and as they stood there on the dock with the sound of the boat's engines fading into the crashing waves, the rain began to fall.

"What the hell..." Olivia broke the kiss and peered upwards incredulously. The rain had gone from zero to 100 in a matter of seconds; it was like having buckets of water tipped over her. She was almost instantly just as wet as she'd been on the day of her arrival, when she fell into the harbour.

"Welcome to the tropics!" Cory yelled over the sound of the hammering rain.

"Are you laughing?" Olivia shook her head, half laughing herself. "And you called me a madwoman!"

They made a dash for the golf buggy, but they were already soaked through. Cory paused to turn off the power and water at the docks before they made their way back to the resort.

"Stay with Rosie? Please? She knows how to handle herself in a cyclone and she'll know when you need to go to the shelter," Cory requested, as he dropped the two girls off at the main building. "I have to go make a circuit of the villas and shut off all the power individually, I'll be gone a few hours."

"Take care out there." Rosie tapped her radio meaningfully.

"You won't be alone, will you?" Olivia asked anxiously, thinking of the remoteness of some of the villas. If a tree fell across the pathway, Cory could be trapped and unable to get back to the resort.

"I'm taking Bryce with me," Cory promised, "and we'll call for help if anything goes wrong." He paused to give Olivia a quick kiss before jumping back in the buggy.

"He'll be fine," Rosie reassured, obviously seeing the anxiety on Olivia's face. "Come on. There's a lot of work to do."

"Do we need to put tape on the windows?" Olivia asked as Rosie led her down the path towards the staff quarters.

"No." Rosie laughed. "That's a myth, that taping an X on the windows can protect them. Most of them have storm shutters, and those that don't have hurricane film or are high-impact glass anyway, they won't shatter unless a tree falls into them. We're looking for anything loose. And I mean anything. Like that, see?" She pointed to one of the verandahs on the staff cabins, and a small table and chair. "That'll be two flying missiles if the wind hits at the wrong angle. Let's get them into the staff canteen."

Olivia was glad to have Rosie's company and experienced eye as they hurried around, securing everything they could, soaked to the skin in the pelting rain.

Late that afternoon, the winds began to pick up to terrifying levels, and Olivia was quite relieved when Luke's voice came over the radio, ordering everyone to the cyclone shelter under the main hotel. The cyclone shutters over the glass dome were closed, and the atrium was dark and gloomy as they hurried to the shelter. Olivia was glad to find Cory already there, stacking packs of bottled water with Bryce.

The shelter was simple but quite comfortable, with basic single beds and a group of comfortable chairs at one end. All the power had been switched off, but battery-powered lanterns provided a soft light, and a radio kept them connected to the outside world once Luke and Cory had closed the heavy steel door. The bathroom facilities were basic and the hot water limited, powered by a generator, but at least everyone was able to wash and put on dry clothes. The restaurant chefs had made a fantastic array of gourmet sandwiches and snacks before leaving, so at least they were well fed.

Olivia nestled in Cory's arms, listening to the reports on the radio and the howl of the winds outside. She noticed Rosie sitting close to Luke and watching him intently. A sudden thought struck her—did Rosie have feelings for Luke? She made a mental note of it, wondering if her friend's feelings were reciprocated.

The storm raged on outside, the wind howling like a living creature. It was too loud to sleep; the crew in the shelter ate and drank, played cards and Scrabble, talking quietly, trying to keep each others' spirits up through the interminably long night.

After what felt like an eternity, morning came and the winds began to die down. Luke checked his watch and announced, "We're in the eye of the storm. We'll have a brief respite, but it's not safe to go out."

Despite Luke's warning, he didn't heed it himself, and he and Cory decided to go outside to check on the situation. Olivia and Rosie waited anxiously, the minutes stretching into what felt like hours. The winds began to pick up again, and the two men had not returned. Even the other men in the shelter were beginning to look concerned.

Chapter Nine

"I can't stand this," Olivia said finally, after repeated efforts to contact Cory and Luke by radio had failed. "We need to go and look for them!"

Rosie seemed about to agree with her, but Bryce, the young dive instructor, stepped in front of the door and shook his head firmly. "Absolutely not. My life wouldn't be worth living if I let you go out there."

"Then come with me! Come on, they're your friends!" Undeterred, Olivia grabbed a raincoat.

Bryce hesitated, and Rosie picked up a coat too. "Well, if you're not going, I will. Come on, Olivia."

But they hadn't even reached the door when it creaked open and Cory and Luke stumbled in, soaked to the skin but unharmed.

"Were you two about to come out looking for us?" Luke asked, brows raising as he saw Olivia and Rosie wearing raincoats.

"Absolutely not," Rosie fibbed, straight-faced, and Luke narrowed his eyes, shaking his head at her.

"We're okay," Cory said, catching his breath. "But we need to stay put until the storm passes. It's a mess out there, but there's no major damage... so far."

The second half of the cyclone hit with renewed fury. The noise was deafening, and Olivia didn't think she would be able to sleep. But exhaustion eventually took over, and she fell asleep in Cory's arms, the sound of the storm fading into the background.

When she woke, the storm had passed. The shelter was quiet, though she could still hear rain falling outside. Olivia looked around and saw the tired but relieved faces of her friends and colleagues.

"Is it morning?" she asked, having lost all track of time.

Rosie shook her head. "Just after midnight. The cyclone's passed, but we need to stay put until morning. Too much debris outside to risk stumbling around in the dark."

They had made it through the storm. Now, it was time to see what was left of Sunfish Island.

As they emerged from the shelter once dawn had broken, the sight that greeted them was one of devastation. Fallen trees and debris were everywhere. But there was also huge relief, because none of the resort's buildings seemed to have sustained significant damage.

"Nobody touches anything until I've checked the power is safe to restore!" The resort's electrician held up a hand to warn them that the danger hadn't passed yet. "One building at a time. If you see anything you think looks suspect, let me know at once."

"You heard Darren. Let's get to it, folks."

As they stood together, surrounded by their friends and colleagues, Olivia felt a deep sense of fulfillment. The storm had tested them, but they had emerged stronger and more united than ever.

The initial devastation gave way to a sense of hope and renewal as the staff worked tirelessly to bring Sunfish Island back to its former glory. Each day began early and ended late, with everyone contributing to the massive cleanup effort. Olivia and Cory worked side by side, clearing debris, repairing damage, and ensuring the safety of the resort. The sense of camaraderie and shared purpose was palpable.

On the third morning after the cyclone's passing, as the team were clearing a fallen tree near the main path, Olivia noticed Jill returning with several other staff members who had evacuated to the mainland.

"Welcome back, Jill," Olivia said, smiling as she handed her a pair of work gloves. "We missed you."

Jill grinned, taking the gloves. "Missed you too. Let's get to work."

Jill was physically small, but she worked with a will, and she and Olivia set to hauling the large palm fronds to the wood chipper which would turn them into mulch for the gardens.

"Hey, Olivia," Jill said a little hesitantly. "I just wanted to say thank you for giving me a chance to start fresh. I know I've been difficult, but I appreciate your patience."

Olivia smiled warmly. "We're all in this together, Jill. And you've been doing an incredible job. I'm glad we're friends."

Jill looked relieved, her eyes shining with gratitude. "Me too, Olivia. Me too."

As the days turned into weeks, the island slowly began to recover. The cleanup efforts were arduous, but the sense of community and resilience was stronger than ever. Olivia and Cory's teamwork during the crisis had strengthened their bond, and they found solace in each other's support.

One evening, after a long day of work, Olivia and Cory decided to take a walk on the beach. The sun was setting, casting a golden glow over the water. They walked hand in hand, the sound of the waves a soothing backdrop.

"I'm so proud of what we've accomplished," Olivia said, looking out at the horizon. "Everyone's worked so hard. it'll be so nice to see guests returning in a few days!"

Cory squeezed her hand. "You've been amazing, Olivia. I have to admit I didn't think a former Manhattan city girl would have been able to get her hands dirty like you have."

She smiled, feeling a warm flush of happiness. "We've all been amazing. But I couldn't have done any of this without you, Cory."

They stopped walking, and Cory turned to face her, his eyes serious. "Olivia, there's something I need to tell you."

Her heart skipped a beat. "What is it?"

Cory took a deep breath. "I know we've only known each other for a short time, but I feel like I've known you forever. I can't imagine my life without you. I want to build a future with you here, on Sunfish Island."

Tears welled up in Olivia's eyes. "I feel the same way, Cory. This is home now, and you've become such an important part of my life. I want to build a future with you too."

They embraced, the warmth of their love enveloping them as the sun dipped below the horizon. Olivia felt a profound sense of happiness and contentment. She had found not only a new home but also a partner who believed in her and supported her dreams.

***

The story of the resort's recovery from the cyclone was a powerful narrative, and Olivia wasn't about to pass up the opportunity to use it in her marketing campaigns. Photographs of the mess they'd had to deal with in the aftermath contrasted with the resort's newly-pristine state, intriguing the public's interest, and new bookings came thick and fast.

The week after the resort reopened, the travel magazine finally published their feature on Sunfish Island. The cover story was a stunning success, with breathtaking photos and glowing reviews.

"This is amazing, Olivia." Luke put the magazine down on his desk and looked up at her, smiling from ear to ear. "John Hunter said you could work miracles, and he was right. We're booked out for the next three months, and it's not even high season yet."

Olivia found herself blushing. She hadn't blushed at praise for her work since she was an intern working through her summer break from Stanford, but, she thought, she'd never really done anything like this before. Oh, she'd handled work that was far more high-profile and broad in scope, but she'd never truly cared about the outcome. Never felt like she had a personal stake in the success of her projects. She'd taken pride in her work, but the monetary reward was the only real satisfaction she'd achieved from it.

Now, seeing the happiness of her friends as Sunfish Island came back to life, their joyous anticipation of having the resort being full of guests, Olivia felt like kicking her feet and giggling for joy. Walking out of the meeting with Luke, she headed down the stairs with a huge grin on her face, which only got wider as she met Cory on the way up.

"You look happy." He paused to slide his arms around her waist and leaned down to kiss her. "Good news?"

"Excellent news." She beamed at him. "The travel magazine spread is spectacular and bookings are soaring."

"All down to your brilliant work." He hugged her. "You done for the day?"

"Yes, I suppose so. Why? What did you have in mind?"

"An evening off... just the two of us."

"Sounds lovely!" She slipped her hand into his as they made their way down the steps. "Anywhere in particular? I have to tell you, I am hungry..."

"Ahead of you. I talked Suzannah into packing us a hamper of fabulous treats, and we're off for a picnic on the beach."

Cory led Olivia down to a secluded cove, where he had laid out a blanket and set up a small tabletop grill. As the sun dipped towards the horizon, he lit some tiki torches, bathing them in a warm, flickering glow.

"This is incredible," Olivia breathed, looking around at the thoughtfully prepared space.

Cory just smiled and pulled her close for a lingering kiss. "I wanted it to be perfect for you."

They sat and enjoyed the sumptuous picnic basket prepared by Suzannah. There were fresh seafood skewers to grill, along with salads, breads, fine cheeses and fruit. Cory had even managed to get a bottle of Olivia's favourite Napa Valley cabernet.

As they ate and sipped their wine, Cory and Olivia talked and laughed, reliving memories of their whirlwind romance. When the food was gone, Cory grabbed another bottle from the basket - a rich chocolate liqueur - and poured them each a snifter full.

Olivia hummed in appreciation at the first sip. "You've thought of everything."

"I wanted to celebrate you," Cory said huskily, setting his glass aside and pulling Olivia into his lap. "Celebrate this new life we've found together."

His lips found hers in a deep, passionate kiss. Olivia melted against him, the liqueur and the tropical night air going to her head. Cory's hands roamed her body as their kisses grew more heated and desperate.

Soon, clothes were being shed and strewn carelessly across the blanket. Olivia gasped as Cory's talented mouth blazed a trail down her neck and chest. When he took one taut nipple between his lips, she arched against him shamelessly.

Gently, Cory laid her back onto the blanket, his eyes burning with banked desire. "You're so beautiful," he rasped, hovering over her. "I want to worship every inch of you."

True to his word, Cory thoroughly explored Olivia's body with his lips, teeth and tongue until she was writhing and whimpering helplessly beneath him. Only when she was incoherent with need did he finally nudge her thighs apart and slide into her welcoming heat.

They made love slowly at first, savouring every stroke, every breathless gasp and moan. But eventually the rhythm built into a feverish pace, their cries of passion mingling with the crashing of the waves on the shore.

Olivia shattered first, her climax crashing over her again and again until Cory followed with a hoarse shout. He collapsed onto her, peppering her sweat-dampened skin with tender kisses as they gradually caught their breath.

Their lovemaking had been passionate yet tender, and Olivia felt utterly cherished as she basked in the afterglow, her head resting on Cory's chest. His fingers trailed lazily along her spine as they watched the stars blink to life in the velvety night sky.

"Did you ever imagine," Cory murmured, "when you first stepped off that boat onto the dock, looking like a drowned rat in your designer suit, that a few months later you'd be making love with me on this beach?"

Olivia giggled, swatting his chest lightly. "Absolutely not. I thought you were an arrogant jerk when you laughed at me falling in the harbour."

"Hey, I apologized for that!" He caught her hand and brought it to his lips to kiss her fingers. "Although I'm very glad you took the plunge that day. Otherwise, I might never have met you."

"Just imagine if I'd gone straight back to New York instead of staying," Olivia said, a note of wonder in her voice. The very idea seemed preposterous now.

Cory tightened his arms around her possessively. "I don't even want to think about that. You're mine now, Olivia Stratten. This island has claimed you."

"And this island man has claimed me right back," she replied, shifting to press a slow, smouldering kiss to his lips.

Soon, they were making love again, re-igniting the flames of desire. Olivia revelled in the freedom of making love under the starry sky, the ocean breeze caressing their entwined bodies. When they finally stilled once more, she felt like a newly emerged butterfly, radiant and reborn in Cory's arms.

Eventually, the tide began creeping higher up the beach. Laughing, they gathered their scattered belongings and the remains of the picnic. Still nude, they held hands and strolled back up the beach towards the staff cabins, splashing playfully in the shallows.

In the morning, Olivia would wake amazed all over again at the wondrous turn her life had taken. But for tonight, she surrendered herself completely to the magic of this island paradise and the man who had become her whole world.

As they snuggled together in Cory's bed, skin still tingling from their lovemaking, Olivia knew she had truly found her home - in Sunfish Island, in Cory's embrace, and in her own heart at last.

Chapter Ten

It was Christmas Eve, and Sunfish Island was a whirlwind of festive activity. The resort was at full capacity, visitors from around the world having flocked to the tropical paradise to celebrate the holidays in style.

Olivia was run off her feet, overseeing all the special events and activities the team had planned. From beach bonfire parties to gourmet feasts to snorkelling with Santa excursions, there was something to delight every guest. She'd barely had a moment to catch her breath, let alone spend quality time with Cory amidst the chaos.

But it was all worth it to see the joy and wonder on the faces of the guests as they experienced a Sunfish Island Christmas. This was exactly why she'd come here - to create magic and unforgettable memories.

She was just wrapping up a final coordinators meeting before the evening's activities when Rosie burst into the room, eyes wide.

"Olivia! We've got a VIP arriving, like, right now, and you won't believe who it is. Mitchell Van Horne himself!"

The name struck Olivia like a physical blow, all the air leaving her lungs in a rush. Mitchell Van Horne...her personal nightmare from New York. The sleek, polished advertising titan who had personally terminated her employment at Van Horne Partners in the brutal aftermath of the Brad Cochrane scandal. Whose high-powered lawyers had shot down her wrongful termination suit and drained her life savings in the process. Olivia had told Rosie the whole sorry saga over a bottle of wine one evening.

Her face must have drained of colour, because Rosie immediately looked contrite. "Oh god, I'm so sorry. I didn't mean to spring it on you like that..."

"No, no, it's alright." Olivia waved a trembling hand, struggling to regain her composure. She refused to have some knee-jerk panic attack, not when she'd worked so hard to build her new life and reputation here.

Jill would be handling the arrival, bless her. At least she didn't have to face Van Horne right away. She could gather herself first before she came face to face with him.

"Olivia?" Rosie's concerned voice broke through her anxious thoughts. "Are you okay? Do you need me to get Cory?"

"I'm fine." Olivia mustered a tight smile, knowing Rosie meant well. "Really, don't worry about it. I'll just...steer clear of the arrival area for now."

Squaring her shoulders, she gathered up her notes and followed Rosie out, splitting off in the opposite direction of the front entrance. Maybe she could sequester herself in her office and get a head start on the staff schedules for the next week.

Her steps slowed as she neared the open-air atrium, the sound of raised voices giving her pause. Surely not...not already?

But as she rounded the corner, the broad, immaculately dressed back was unmistakable. Mitchell Van Horne in the flesh, red-faced and obviously berating a staff member who could only be...

"Cory!" Panic lent wings to Olivia's feet as she hurried forward. Sure enough, there was Cory - her caring, wonderful Cory - standing stiffly with clenched fists as Van Horne dressed him down in that smooth, condescending tone she knew so well.

"Olivia Stratten!" Van Horne spotted her approach, his cold eyes locking on her with undisguised disdain. "Well, if it isn't the little slut who almost brought my company down with her philandering. I might have known we'd find you slumming it in some place like this."

Oh god, no...not in front of Cory, not like this! Olivia wanted to crumple with shame and humiliation. But she refused to let this bastard take anything else from her after he'd already stolen away her career and self-respect.

Lifting her chin, she met his enraged stare with one of flat defiance. "It's a pleasure to see you again...Mitchell. As always."

Van Horne sneered at her tone. "Don't get snotty with me, you ungrateful little bi—"

"That's enough." Cory's low, dangerous growl cut through, stopping Van Horne mid-insult. "I don't care who you are, mate. You don't get to speak to Olivia or any of our people like that."

For a moment, Van Horne looked almost comically nonplussed, clearly not used to being addressed in such a fashion. Then his face mottled a darker red and he puffed up like an angry bull.

"How dare you?! I'll have you fired, you insolent little—"

"You'll do no such thing." The quiet authority of Luke's voice sliced through the mounting tension. The resort manager stepped up beside Cory, clearly having witnessed the entire altercation.

"Sunfish Island does not stand for the mistreatment of its staff under any circumstances," Luke continued calmly. "Not even from VIP guests. If you cannot conduct yourself with basic decency and respect during your stay here, Mr. Van Horne, I'll be forced to ask you to leave."

For a long, charged moment, Van Horne could only sputter wordlessly, but true to form, he puffed out his chest and went straight back on the attack. "Do you even know who you have working here?" He pointed a thick finger in Olivia's direction.

"Ms. Stratten?" Luke responded. "Indeed; the best marketing manager Sunfish Island's ever had. John Hunter's personal pick for the position."

Olivia could have hugged Luke, but Van Horne only looked even more furious, turning to glare at Olivia. "You poached John Hunter's accounts from us! I should sue..."

"Mr. Hunter was extremely displeased with the alternative marketing proposal the firm presented to him when you told him I was no longer available," Olivia said, fighting to keep her voice steady. "It was your failure to satisfy that caused him to pull his accounts and come looking for me. And frankly, you had it coming. You wouldn't recognise a creative campaign if it bit you on the ass!"

Luke bit off a chuckle, and Cory openly laughed. Emboldened by their support, Olivia stepped closer to Van Horne, staring him straight in the eye.

"You've been riding on the coat-tails of your young, hard-working staff for decades. I worked eighty-hour weeks for you for little thanks and sod all recognition; you took credit for my work at every turn. Well, I don't have to answer to you any more. Don't have to suck up to your mistress-secretary in hopes of getting thrown some decent projects."

Mrs. van Horne, standing beside her husband, gasped.

"Surely you can't claim you didn't know!" Olivia had little sympathy for the arrogant woman, always consumed with her designer clothing and her social life. "They have a freaking kid together who started high school last year. Your husband's paying sixty grand a year for him to go to Dalton!"

"Mitchell? Is this true?" Mrs. Van Horne looked more furious than upset, and the tone of her voice threatened dire consequences.

"I... of course not! She's lying!" Van Horne blustered.

"Unlike you, Mitchell, I don't lie." Olivia stared him in the eye. "Nor does a DNA test," she noted to Mrs. Van Horne, who nodded, her mouth set in a grim line.

"Oh, we shall be addressing that, I assure you. Mitchell." She gripped her husband's arm. "Let's go."

"We just got here!" Van Horne didn't seem to know where to put himself.

"And we're going straight home, to get to the bottom of this matter. Thank you for the information, Ms. Stratten." Mrs. Van Horne nodded icily and marched out, dragging her husband along with her. Van Horne seemed deflated somehow, and watching him go, Olivia felt a sense of triumph. She might have lost the battle of her wrongful dismissal suit, but she'd won the war morally. She hadn't intended to unleash such devastating personal truths, but she'd be lying if she said there wasn't a part of her that relished seeing the arrogant bastard taken down a few pegs.

"You alright, love?"

Cory's concerned voice made her turn. He was studying her intently, blue eyes filled with a mixture of pride and apprehension. Olivia mustered up a reassuring smile for him.

"I'm fine. More than fine, actually." She blew out a breath. "God, did you see the look on his smug face when I called him out? Priceless."

Luke chuckled, clapping Olivia on the shoulder. "That was one hell of a pitch."

They all shared a laugh at Van Horne's expense. Only then did Olivia fully register the pride shining in Cory's eyes as he looked at her. She felt herself blushing, suddenly self-conscious under his admiring gaze.

"What?" She nudged him playfully. "You didn't think I had it in me to go toe-to-toe with an arrogant blowhard like that?"

"Oh, I knew you had it in you." Cory slung an arm around her shoulders, pulling her in for a quick kiss on the temple. "I just didn't expect you to literally verbally bitch-slap the wanker into the middle of next week. It was bloody brilliant."

Olivia giggled at his turn of phrase. She felt lighter than she had in years, as if a poisonous weight had finally been lifted off her shoulders. Van Horne and all his toxic negativity no longer had any power over her. Out here in this paradise, surrounded by people who valued her, she was free.

"Bloody brilliant isn't the half of it," Luke said dryly. "Although hopefully the Van Hornes won't trash us online."

Olivia's eyes widened with contrition. "Oh god, I didn't even think... Luke, I'm so sorry. I'll do whatever marketing is needed to do damage control, make this right."

But Luke was already waving off her concern with a casual flick of his wrist. "Please, it'll be a nice problem to have after all the positive publicity you've brought us lately. We can weather a few entitled rich snobs leaving angry TripAdvisor reviews."

His acceptance helped dissipate the last of Olivia's lingering tension. She couldn't remember the last time she'd felt so deliriously happy and at peace, or surrounded by people who so wholeheartedly had her back. This island, these people - they were her family now.

"Come on," Cory murmured in her ear. "Let's go celebrate you taking that prick down off his high horse. I'll crack open the best bottle I've got stashed and we can drink a toast to new beginnings."

Olivia beamed up at him, filled with love and gratitude. For this man who cherished her, for this new life that embraced her wholly. "I'd like that. Lead the way."

Hand-in-hand, Cory led Olivia away from the atrium and back towards the staff bungalows. The twilight had settled over the island in hues of burnt orange and deep crimson, painting the vibrant greenery of the landscaping in rich, warm tones. In the distance, they could hear the laughter and merrymaking of guests gathered for the evening's festivities.

It was a stark contrast to Olivia's bitter confrontation with Van Horne just minutes before. She felt worlds away from the negativity and stress of her former life in New York. This was her sanctuary now, her home, and Cory was the bright, shining centre of it all.

He glanced over at her with that lopsided grin she adored. "You look like the cat that got the cream, Ms. Stratten."

"Just feeling very satisfied with how that played out," she admitted with a shameless smile. "Like a weight has been lifted."

"You're free now, angel." His arm went around her shoulders, pulling her close. "Free to spread your wings and fly as high as you want without any wankers like Van Horne holding you back."

God, she loved this man's unwavering faith in her abilities. Resting her head against his shoulder, she let the tension of the day's events bleed out of her body. They walked in companionable silence until reaching Cory's bungalow.

He ushered her inside, turning on a few lamps to cast the comfortable living space in a warm glow. While Cory headed for the small kitchenette, Olivia wandered over to the entertainment centre, trailing her fingers over the framed photos. There were lots of shots of Cory with Rosie, Jill and the other staff members -- his island family.

Her gaze snagged on one photo in particular, a candid closeup of Cory laughing, head thrown back in unguarded joy. The image captured everything she loved most about him - his warmth, his playful spirit, the way he seemed to embrace life with such zest. Her heart felt full just looking at it. Below it was a photo of her, wearing one of the simple cotton dresses she'd picked up at the resort boutique, a hibiscus flower in her hair as she sat beside the pool.

"There's my favourite photo of you," Cory's voice was low in her ear. She turned to find him holding out a glass of deep red wine. "You looked so bloody gorgeous that day, love. Couldn't resist snapping a pic while you weren't looking."

"Flatterer," she accused lightly, accepting the glass and allowing him to guide her to the cosy loveseat. They settled in together, Olivia tucking her feet up and resting against Cory's side.

"To new beginnings," he said simply, clinking their glasses together. "And to the remarkable woman who will always be the brightest star in my sky."

Olivia had to blink back the tears that suddenly stung her eyes. This man's love and support was a precious gift, one she would never take for granted. Not after so many years of giving her heart to someone who never truly valued her.

Cradling Cory's stubbled jaw in her palm, she leaned in to brush her lips against his. The kiss started soft and tender but quickly banked into a slow-burning heat. Cory's free hand slid into her hair, angling her head for deeper exploration.

When they finally parted, breathless and flushed, Olivia found herself straddling his lap. She gazed down at him with heavy-lidded eyes, all thoughts of Van Horne and past hurts banished by the fire blazing between them.

"Make love to me, Cory," she whispered throatily. "Let me celebrate this new beginning with you over...and over...and over again."

The low, feral sound that rumbled from his chest sent delicious tremors cascading through her core. Then Cory's mouth was on hers once more, hot and demanding. His hands blazed scorching trails over her body as he divested her of her clothes with desperate urgency.

Soon, they were both bare, skin sliding sensuously against slick, heated skin. Olivia rocked against the rigid length of Cory's arousal, gasping into his hungry kisses. When he finally surged up into her welcoming depths, it felt like coming home.

Their lovemaking was fierce and possessive yet achingly tender. Cory worshipped her body with his lips and hands, overwhelming her senses until she trembled on the edge. Olivia clung to him, lost in the maelstrom of passion and love, spiralling higher and higher until her climax crashed over her in shattering waves.

Afterwards, they lay entwined amid the sumptuous disarray, bodies cooling yet sated. Olivia's head rested on Cory's chest, lulled by the steady beat of his heart. His fingers trailed in soothing strokes along her spine as he pressed idle kisses to her damp hair.

"Thank you," she murmured at last, tilting her face up to bestow a tender kiss on the underside of his jaw. "For giving this to me. For being you."

He cupped the back of her head, holding her close. "No, love. Thank you. For everything you are, everything you've brought into my life. I'm the lucky one."

And in that moment, Olivia was certain he was right. Her journey to this point might have been harrowing, but it had led her right where she was meant to be -- in the embrace of this incredible man on this slice of paradise they called home.

Wiggling closer, she allowed the rhythmic beating of Cory's heart and the gentle lap of the ocean waves outside to lull her into a deep, contented slumber. Tomorrow was Christmas on Sunfish Island, with all its magic still to unfold. But tonight, she had everything she could ever need or want already cradled in her arms.

Epilogue

The brilliant tropical sun had barely crested the horizon when Olivia awoke on Christmas morning, cocooned in Cory's arms. For a few blissful moments, she simply basked in the warmth and peace of lying beside him.

Eventually, though, she became aware of the muted sounds of celebration filtering in from outside. Laughter, cheerful voices calling out Christmas greetings. Reluctantly leaving the sanctuary of the bed, she padded over to the window and pulled back the gauzy curtain.

The view took her breath away, as it did every single morning. In the distance, glistening aquamarine waves rolled lazily towards the pristine white sand. Closer to the bungalows, the resort's lush grounds had been transformed into a festive wonderland.

Twinkling lights and bowers of bright tropical flowers festooned the wooden deck areas where groups of guests were gathering. Down on the beach, a massive bonfire pit had been dug into the sand, ringed by stacks of weathered timber ready to burn throughout the day. Nearby, long tables groaned under the weight of a mouthwatering Christmas feast that blended flavours from around the globe.

Everywhere Olivia looked, happy guests were embracing the holiday spirit. Some lounged on bright towels or blankets, working on impressive tans while kids frolicked in the surf, squealing with delight. Others congregated around the stacked buffet of international dishes and free-flowing drinks.

Scattered clusters of staff members wove through the merry throngs, distributing festively decorated leis or frosty beverages, always ready with a friendly word or helpful hand. At the centre of it all, a huge white canvas tent sheltered an elaborately decorated Christmas tree surrounded by mounds of gaily wrapped gifts.

As they made their way down the beach towards the hubbub, Olivia soaked in all the magical details. She could scarcely believe this was the same island she'd first set foot on just nine months ago. Though thankfully there were no plunges into the harbour this time.

"Merry Christmas, you two!" Rosie, looking suntanned and radiant in a vibrant red sundress, rushed over to meet them with big hugs.

"This is incredible, Rosie," Olivia said, looking around in wonder. "I never imagined this is what a Christmas in the tropics would look like!"

Rosie waved a dismissive hand. "Half the credit goes to you and that brilliant marketing campaign you put together! These are the highest guest bookings we've ever had over the holidays."

"Of which exactly none would have been possible without your top-notch resort operations," Olivia countered warmly. She adored the easy camaraderie between herself, Cory, Rosie and the rest of the Sunfish staff.

"Speaking of, I need to go take over Santa duties from Bryce," Cory interjected with a wry grin. He ducked down to brush his lips over Olivia's in a quick but searing kiss. "Try to behave yourself while I'm gone, yeah? I'll be back for dessert."

His blatant innuendo made her giggle and Rosie groan in mock disgust as he sauntered off, looking delectable in a hideous Christmas-patterned shirt and bright red board shorts. Trust Cory to make even garish resort wear look stylishly dishevelled and devastating.

"Y'know, half the female guests are going to be that much more reluctant to leave now that he'll be dressed as Santa," Rosie remarked dryly.

Olivia just laughed, relaxed and unbothered. The events of the previous night had banished any lingering spectre of jealousy or insecurity over Cory's status as somewhat of an island heartthrob. She felt buoyant, invincible, firmly rooted in the certainty of his unwavering devotion. After the trials they'd overcome to be together, some harmless, appreciative glances couldn't dent their unbreakable bond.

Throwing an arm around Rosie's shoulders, she allowed her friend to lead her further into the bustling Christmas festivities, and over to a table where Nessa, Jill and Suzannah were sitting, champagne bottles at the ready. Merrymaking, laughter and good cheer surrounded her from all sides as the radiant sun climbed towards its zenith. And somewhere amid the revelry, her one true love basked in the joy of playing Santa to the adoring masses.

For the first time in her life, Olivia felt like she was living in a real-life Christmas dream. One she never wanted to end.

***

The day seemed to stretch into a blissful eternity of sunlight, laughter, and tropical indulgence. Olivia floated through it all on a cloud of contentment, spending cherished moments with her beloved colleagues and the guests who had become temporary additions to their little island family.

As the hours melted away, the riotous celebrations gradually transitioned into more mellow festivities. The bonfire on the beach burned lower, ringed now by couples strolling hand-in-hand in the shadows. Lively music and raucous chatter gave way to softer acoustic melodies and intimate murmurings underneath a dazzling canopy of stars.

It was well into the starry night when Cory finally sought Olivia out again. She was cozied up with Rosie, Nessa and the others, sipping spiced cider and listening with sleepy smiles to Jill recounting an uproariously funny tale about her most recent dating misadventure.

Olivia felt Cory's presence like a warm caress over her senses even before he spoke. Turning, she found him regarding her with an intense yet tender expression that made her breath catch. He was gloriously rumpled after his long stint playing St. Nick, decorated shirt hanging open to reveal his tan chest, cherubic golden curls in disarray. Yet his eyes shone with resolution.

"There you are, beautiful," he murmured huskily. "I've been looking for you."

Rising fluidly to his feet, he extended one calloused hand in silent invitation. Olivia's heart stumbled in her chest as she accepted, allowing him to draw her up into the circle of his arms. Cory bent to brush his lips lingeringly against her knuckles before meeting her bewildered gaze.

"Come for a walk with me?"

She could only nod mutely, drunk on the look of adoration blazing in his eyes. Cory slanted her a secret smile before turning them towards the shoreline, his arm draped securely around her shoulders.

They strolled in comfortable silence for a few minutes, letting the gently lapping waves wash their bare feet, eventually reaching a secluded cove some distance from the main festivities. A private little paradise framed by towering palms and immaculate stretches of pale sand. When Cory finally halted their steps, it was to face Olivia directly, taking both her hands in his.

"This place..." he began in a voice hushed with reverence. "From the moment I first came here, it's felt like coming home. Even more than Cairns, where I grew up. Because for the first time in my life, I understood what it meant to be part of something bigger. This island, these people - it's where I finally found my purpose."

Olivia listened raptly, mesmerized by the unveiled earnestness in his expression.

"Then you arrived," Cory continued softly, "this gorgeous, brilliant, incredible woman from the other side of the world. And suddenly, it felt like the universe had shifted onto its proper axis. Like you were the missing piece of my soul that I'd been searching for my whole life without even realizing it."

Tears shimmered in Olivia's eyes as he brought one of her hands to his chest, cradling it against the steady thrum of his heartbeat.

"From that first moment, you became the single most important part of my world, Olivia. The woman I want to spend every morning and every night with for the rest of my life." His voice had gone deep and gravelly with intense emotion. "You're my home now, angel. And I can't imagine building a life in this paradise without you by my side as my partner, my teammate...my wife."

On the last word, Cory slowly sank down onto one knee in the silver-washed sand. Olivia's free hand flew to her mouth on a shocked exhale as he fumbled in his pocket and produced a ring box.

Reverently, he plucked out the stunning diamond solitaire cradled inside. It glittered in the starlight like a captured cosmic blaze as he looked up at her, blue eyes dark with solemn promise.

"Olivia Stratten, would you make me the luckiest man on this earth and in all the vast oceans? Marry me and build our forever with me here on Sunfish Island?"

Olivia could only nod wordlessly at first, overwhelmed by the maelstrom of love and joy detonating inside her. The tears she'd been valiantly holding back spilled over in hot streams as she finally gasped out a breathless, "Yes! Oh Cory, yes!"

His face split in a blinding grin as he surged back to his feet, pulling her hard against him. Olivia flung her arms around his neck, peppering his face with damp, rapturous kisses. The taste of his lips mingled with the salt tracks on her cheeks and the sultry tropical breezes swirling around them.

When Cory finally drew back just enough to capture her tear-stained face between his palms, Olivia felt herself falling endlessly into the warm, sparkling depths of his gaze. With hands that trembled ever so slightly, he slipped the glittering diamond onto her slender finger.

"My forever girl at last," he rasped. "My island bride."

Then his mouth crashed over hers in a searing, claiming kiss that sealed their unbreakable bond. There, amid the silver shadows and diamond-etched stardust, they became something new - infinite, unshakable, eternal. Two souls braided inextricably into one shared destiny written among these turquoise tides and golden shores.

~ The End ~

Read on to enjoy Nessa's story in ***The Reluctant Billionaire!***

Her Fake Island Wedding

Island Escapes Book 3

Caitlyn Lynch

SHENANIGANS PRESS

shenanigans press.com/EN

Contents

Chapter One

The warm wind blowing in Jace Hunter's face tasted of salt. Licking it off his lips, he closed his eyes and tilted his face up to soak in the sunlight beaming down on him. The heat felt good on his skin; he almost felt as though he was able to directly absorb the energy, like a plant. A small smile crossed his face at the whimsical thought.

"We're pulling in to the dock now," a voice announced through a speaker right above his head. Startled, his eyes snapped open and he glared at the offending machine. Not that it stopped the voice from continuing, "Welcome to Sunfish Island, folks!"

There were about a dozen other guests on the boat. Jace let them all depart first before pushing himself to his feet and shouldering his duffel bag. A deckhand was unloading suitcases onto the dock; Jace snagged his in passing and handed the young man a ten-dollar bill.

"Thanks, sir." The deckhand looked surprised to be given a tip. "American, are you?"

Jace shook his head. "No, but I've been living there for a while. Got in the habit of tipping. You've earned it, those cases look heavy." He nodded to the stack with his chin. "Have yourself a cold beer on me."

At the end of the dock, the guests were being greeted by resort staff, then directed to the main reception to check in and get their rooms assigned. A tall man looked in Jace's direction, started toward him, paused, and looked him up and down with a puzzled frown.

"Luke?" Jace offered a smile.

"It *is* you!" Puzzlement gave way to a wide grin. "I didn't recognize you!" Luke Collyer was Sunfish Island's general manager, an extremely competent, likable man. Jace had been involved in hiring him two years ago and the two men had taken to each other at once.

Jace shrugged wearily, shaking Luke's offered hand. "It's been a rough few weeks." That was an understatement. He'd been laid low by a nasty bout of the flu, but had tried to work through it, refusing to accept his own physical weakness. It wasn't until he'd collapsed in the middle of an important meeting, waking up in the hospital on oxygen, that he'd accepted he might not be at peak fitness.

The doctors had diagnosed pneumonia, kept him in hospital for a solid week, and finally let him go with a stern admonition to take a break. He'd fully intended to ignore them and go right back to work... except when Jace had walked in the door of his office on the top floor of Hunter Enterprises' New York skyscraper, his father had been sitting behind his desk.

John Hunter had built Hunter Enterprises from nothing to a multi-billion-dollar, diversified business empire. His devoted wife Maryann had been at his side the whole way, until her death from cancer five years earlier. Jace was their only son, the heir to everything. Living up to his father's expectations was something he'd spent his whole life doing, and John Hunter was a workaholic.

So it had come as quite a shock when John had stood up and said, "Get your ass out of this office, and don't you dare set foot in here again until you have your health back!"

Jace had laughed, but his father was deadly serious. "Your mother ignored her symptoms for too long. I won't see you sacrifice your health to this business, Jace. Get out of here. Go and smell the roses for a while."

His father had bulldozed over every argument Jace had tried to make, and truth to tell, Jace hadn't really tried all that hard. The Hunter Enterprises private jet had been on standby to take him anywhere he'd wanted to go. He hadn't been able to think of anywhere until his father had suggested the family's private villa on Sunfish Island, the resort island on Australia's Great Barrier Reef, which Hunter Enterprises had bought out and redeveloped a few years earlier. Jace had actually designed the villa as his graduation project for his architecture degree, but he'd never had the time to go and see the completed work.

"Your father said you'd been ill, but you look terrible," Luke said, jerking Jace from his reverie.

"Thanks," Jace said wryly, but he knew it was true. He'd lost a lot of weight during his illness. The tailored suits he customarily wore hung loosely on his frame; he'd left them behind in New York and brought shorts and T-shirts for his vacation. The dark blond hair he normally kept neatly trimmed had grown out long and shaggy, and he had several days' growth of beard on his face. He was unrecognizable from the high-powered businessman he'd been just a few weeks ago.

Which gave him an idea.

"Luke," he asked as they came to a parked golf cart and Luke hefted his case into the back, "who knows I'm here?"

Luke shot him a knowing look. "Only me. Your father called and asked me to have the villa opened up for you, but my staff don't know who's expected. You want me to keep it quiet?"

"I think it might be best. I don't particularly want the press getting wind that I'm here, Hunter Enterprises is privately owned so it's not like there's a stock price to crash, but still..."

"Jace, you don't need to give me a reason. It's all good." Luke handed him a plastic card. "Here."

"What's this?"

"It's a comp card. It means you don't pay for anything, anywhere, at any of the bars and restaurants. You own the place, after all." Luke's grin was cheerful. "It'd be a bit dumb to ask you to pay for anything. This way, you don't have to sign for anything; we're a cashless economy here, you'll recall?"

"Like a cruise ship." Jace nodded. "So, if I use this card, there's no need to use the villa's account, and no need to put my name on anything."

"And nobody to be alerted to your identity." Luke steered the golf cart along a paved path winding among groves of palm trees. "Housekeeping opened the villa up and stocked your kitchen, but I'll advise them that a family friend is using the place. If you want maid service, just let me know and I'll have somebody come in when you're out. Just one question, if I may?"

The sea glinted blue on their left as they ascended a slope, moving away from the main resort; Jace knew they were approaching the non-resort part of the island, where some two dozen exclusive private villas had been built. A couple of them were occupied by permanent residents, but the rest were holiday homes for the mega-rich. He wasn't likely to be afflicted with nosy neighbours.

"What's the question?" he asked, gazing at the glorious view of the sunlit Coral Sea opening up before them as they reached the top of the rise.

"How long are you staying? And do you need medical support while you're here?"

"That's two... but I'll answer. I shouldn't need any medical attention, no, and I expect to stay a couple of weeks, probably. Dad told me not to show my face at any Hunter Enterprises office again before two weeks is up."

"That doesn't include *my* office," Luke said with a grin. "Stop by anytime you want a chat, but I'll have no compunctions about telling you to butt out of resort business."

"Deal." Jace smiled back at Luke as the golf cart drew to a halt, thinking it would be nice to have a friend here he could talk to. Nice to have a friend to talk to at all, if he was being completely honest with himself. The cutthroat world of big business wasn't exactly conducive to close personal friendships.

***

Laying on the couch binge-watching Netflix was something he could only do for so long without going a little stir-crazy, Jace discovered after a couple of days. The scorching tropical sun made it unwise to spend too much time outside, though his winter-pale skin was already starting to develop a little golden colour.

He'd developed a routine: he swam in the villa's private pool every morning, lay in the sun for a little while to dry off, then went inside and made breakfast. The villa's kitchen was as well-stocked as Luke had promised; he had no need to go anywhere.

Bored after the first half-day, he'd tried to log onto his email and do some work... only to find a single message from his father, advising him the IT wizards had locked him out of all company business until further notice. He was restricted to entertaining himself with the villa's well-stocked supply of books or laying on the couch catching up on *House Of Cards*.

Switching the TV off, Jace got up to pace the room restlessly. His energy levels were starting to return, and the unaccustomed inactivity was beginning to chafe. He should have put a gym in the villa, he thought grumpily. Not that he was in any fit state for his usual five-mile run on the treadmill.

Well, if he couldn't run, he could at least get outside for some fresh air. He'd go for a walk, and if he found he had the energy, he might go all the way to the main resort building and catch up with Luke.

Decision made, it was only a few minutes before he was outside, hat on his head to shield him from the sun and running shoes on his feet. Someone had left a map of the island on the hall table, with the walking trails clearly marked. He grabbed it on the way out and checked the best route to take. Across the middle of the island into the southern end of the resort, he decided. The map's key indicated it should take about twenty minutes to hike the trail.

Ten minutes later, as he finally reached the top of the trail, he had to stop and lean against a tree for a while to rest. *Should have brought water,* he reproached himself. *Stupid thing to forget.* He should have known better, but it had been several years since he'd been on a hike and he'd been too eager to get out of the house.

Jace examined the resort below him. There was a cluster of private cabins at this end and a pool with a bar, one of several restaurants, a little further away. He could get a drink at the pool bar; he'd at least had enough sense to shove the comp card Luke had given him into his pocket. Wiping sweat from his brow with the hem of his shirt and cursing his physical weakness under his breath for the umpteenth time, he started down the slope.

"One dirty martini." Nessa set the drink down in front of her customer, swiped the card through her reader, and offered it for his signature. Over his shoulder, she spied a man emerging from the rarely-used trailhead beyond the pool; he looked hot and sweaty. Shaking her head, she turned to rinse out her cocktail shaker. *That guy was sure gonna need a drink.*

Turning back just as he sat down on a bar stool, she slid a coaster in front of him and said, "Good afternoon. What can I get you?"

Light blue eyes blinked at her, and the man said, "You're English!"

"I'm *from* England. I'm an Australian citizen," she gave her usual response. "Been here nearly ten years now."

"I guess the accent never really goes away."

She smiled tightly, knowing her accent gave her away as being from one of the seedier parts of East London. "Indeed." Slapping a cocktail menu down before him with perhaps a little more force than actually necessary, she turned away to serve another customer who'd just swum up to the pool side of the bar.

When she returned, the man asked for something long and cooling. Tempted to pour him some iced water, she asked instead, "Virgin?"

Jace blinked in surprise. "It's been a while, but no, I'm not."

The bartender threw her head back and laughed. She was pretty, Jace had noticed that right off: her skin a rich dark bronze with black hair falling to her waist in a mass of tiny braids. When she laughed, she was really beautiful, dimples appearing in her cheeks, light amber-brown eyes flashing with mirth.

"I was asking if you want a hard or a soft drink. Alcoholic, or not," she said through girlish giggles.

"Oh." Abashed, he felt colour coming to his face. "Sorry. Brain fog. I think I'm a bit overheated."

A tall glass of iced water was set in front of him. "Why don't you start with that, and then you can decide if you'd like something a bit stronger?" The dimples flashed again as she gave him a warm smile.

"Thank you... Nessa," he read the name tag on her blouse. "Short for Vanessa?"

"No."

"How interesting, your dimples disappear when your smile isn't genuine. Is it something embarrassing, then?"

Nessa's jaw dropped. "Are you always this direct?"

"I like to cut through the bullshit. Jace." He offered a hand across the bar. "Not short for anything. My mother just liked the name." Only after he'd already said it, did he think maybe he should have used a different first name. *Jace* wasn't exactly common, after all.

Nessa hesitated a minute, and then she took his hand, leaned forward, and whispered close to his ear, "Tennessee."

He grinned. "Nessa's better. Suits you. The other, I think I'd expect you to have a Southern drawl."

By now, Jace was the only one sitting at the bar. Nessa turned away from him, plucking a couple of bottles off the shelf. "No Southern drawl. I make a mean Georgia Peach, though."

She deftly poured peach schnapps, vodka, grenadine, and cranberry juice into a shaker with crushed ice, shook it up swiftly, and poured it into a tall glass, topping it off with lemonade and a maraschino cherry speared on a tiny plastic sword. "Give that a try."

His water glass was empty, Jace realized as she swept it from in front of him and replaced it with the cocktail. He didn't even remember draining it.

"Thanks." He took a sip, sighing with pleasure as the tart but sweet taste exploded over his tongue. "Ohhh. Oh, that's perfection."

Nessa smiled, turning to rinse her shaker out. "You're welcome. Got your card there?"

"Sure." He fished it out of his pocket, sliding it across the bar as she returned with a card reader.

Nessa swiped the card without looking at it, blinking as the reader immediately gave her a green light. "What--oh, this is a comp card." She handed it back with a curious look. "Are you staying at the main resort?"

"No, in one of the villas. It belongs to a friend." Jace took another long drink. "This really is exactly what I wanted. How did you know?"

"I'm psychic. Every good bartender is, don't ya know." Nessa flashed him a grin.

"I've heard that before. Half the ones I met in New York seemed to be studying psychiatry or psychology; they were pretty good mind-readers."

Nessa's smile was rather wry. "Psychiatry. Got my doctorate three years ago."

"Really?" He blinked at her. "Uh..."

"You're wondering why I'm still tending bar rather than earning a fortune in practice somewhere, right? I don't need to be a mind-reader to figure that one out. Almost everyone who knows I've got my doctorate has asked me the question at some point."

"Well, yeah." She was as sharp as she was beautiful, Jace found himself thinking, propping his elbows on the bar and listening in fascination as she spoke.

"I practiced for a year and realized I'd made a huge mistake." Nessa shrugged, leaning back against one of the low refrigerators behind her, arms folded over her chest. "Being responsible for other people's mental health is a massive burden, and one I was never really ready to take on."

"You lost a patient?" Jace guessed astutely.

"I lost a whole bunch of them. I was the junior staff psychiatrist at Wacol detention center in Brisbane. There was a prison riot." Nessa's eyes went dark and distant. "Four dead, all patients I'd seen in the previous month. Five more transferred to maximum security jails elsewhere."

"I'm sorry," Jace said quietly, knowing the sentiment was inadequate. Knowing she'd always blame herself, wonder if she could have seen it coming, could have done something to prevent it. "That must have been very difficult."

"As far as I was concerned, it was career-ending." Nessa picked up a clean glass and a cloth, and started polishing it unnecessarily. "I could have gone back, but I didn't want to. I tended bar throughout my degree and honestly I loved it. I went back to it permanently and decided to make it my career for good. Luke headhunted me for the resort about a year ago, and I never want to leave." She set the glass back into the rack of clean ones with a small smile. "So now I just dispense gentle advice and excellent drinks to people who are usually trying to relax anyway."

"I'll drink to that." Jace lifted his near-empty glass to her, thinking as he did so he almost envied Nessa her confidence, her surety she was now on the right path, even if it might not be the one she'd directed so much of her life to following. "Can I buy you one?" he offered on impulse.

"Thank you, but I don't drink on duty and I'm comped as much free soda as I can drink." Nessa shook her head at him with a smile, wondering as she did so why she'd told him so much of her story. She didn't usually open up to people this way on first meeting. There was something about Jace, though, something in his light blue eyes which made her think he would be a difficult person to lie to. "Another one of those?" She nodded at his glass.

"Better not, I haven't eaten for a few hours and I haven't had alcohol in a few weeks. I'll be all over the place."

"Drying out?"

"I've been ill, actually. Pneumonia."

Nessa nodded. She'd suspected something of the sort from the way his clothes hung a little on his frame, the gauntness of his cheeks, and the sallow tint to his skin. "Sunfish is a great place for recovery," she said. "Warm weather, great atmosphere. You staying long?"

Jace didn't detect any nosiness in the question; just natural curiosity. "Couple weeks, probably," he replied. "Maybe I'll see you around again."

"I'll be here." She tossed him a smile. "This is my bar. Eleven 'til seven, every day."

"You don't get any days off?" That didn't seem right. He'd have to speak to Luke about that; the staff needed personal time--

"Of course I do. It varies which ones, though. Depends on when I can get someone to cover."

"I see." He played with his empty glass, picking up the cherry and eating it before some impulse made him say, "Since you finish at seven, would you maybe care to have dinner with me?"

Nessa paused, her always-busy hands stilling on the glasses she'd been sorting. "Staff members aren't allowed to fraternize with resort guests."

"Fair enough, but I'm not technically a resort guest, am I? I'm staying in one of the villas."

She hesitated, then shook her head. "I have plans with some friends tonight."

Jace smiled, not taking offense. "Maybe another night."

"Maybe." She tipped her head noncommittally.

"It's been nice chatting with you, Nessa." He stood, stretched his arms up toward the sky with a sigh. "Oof, been too long since I did any exercise. I'm stiff just from that walk."

"Are you planning to walk back? Because it's gonna be dark soon, and we're up in the tropics here, we don't really get a twilight period. It goes from full light to pitch dark very fast."

"I've noticed that, watching the sunsets the last couple of days," Jace agreed with a nod.

"You don't want to be out on that trail in the dark. You won't be able to see your footing, might take a nasty fall..."

"You worried about me?" He gave her a cheeky smile. "Don't worry. I was planning on walking up to the main resort to see a friend who works there. I'll see if I can get him to give me a ride back in one of the golf carts."

"That sounds like a good plan." Nessa found herself watching as Jace stretched again, the hem of his T-shirt riding up to reveal a flat, toned stomach... was that actually a six-pack? He was an attractive man, she thought a little unwillingly, even with shaggy hair and a scruffy beard. She liked her men a little more clean-cut normally, but there was definitely something about Jace. Maybe it was those hypnotic light blue eyes. "See you again sometime."

"I certainly hope so." He gave her another broad smile before turning and heading off toward the main resort.

Nessa watched him until he was out of sight, wondering if she would indeed see him again. She didn't shake herself out of her reverie until a customer sat down at the bar and coughed politely to attract her attention.

Chapter Two

Jace ambled toward the main resort, taking his time to look at the beautiful surroundings, the immaculately tended gardens. The private cabins placed discreetly away from the path looked inviting; he thought he would rather enjoy one of those, maybe more so than the large, empty villa he was rattling around in at the moment. It hadn't exactly been designed for one person.

Smiling at his own foolishness, he strolled on, his mind back on the woman he'd just met. Nessa was an intriguing, beautiful puzzle; he found himself disappointed she'd declined his dinner invitation, and not just because he was lonely for any company. She interested him far more than the women he usually met, glossy, corporate ladder-climbers in New York who seemed more interested in his position and connections than in him as a human. Nessa seemed *real*; her honesty about her past only made him curious to know more.

Of course, her beauty didn't hurt either, he acknowledged to himself as he walked up the white marble steps into the main resort. Whatever genetic mixture had produced Nessa, it had gifted her with the kind of traffic-stopping looks which would probably have made her a successful catwalk model if she were about eight inches taller. Her face was imprinted in his memory: those wide, light-amber eyes, high cheekbones and delicately pointed chin, full soft lips curved into a knowing little smile.

"Shake it off," Jace told himself firmly. "She turned you down. She probably gets hit on twenty times a day, with a face like that." He'd stop by another afternoon and say hi, maybe gently repeat the offer, and if she said no again, he'd accept gracefully and shut his mouth. Pursuing a woman who didn't want to be chased was a dick move, and it wasn't like he ever lacked for feminine attention. With his looks and money...

Jace snorted, chuckling at himself. The last thing he wanted Nessa to be was the kind of woman who'd be interested in his money. How would she know he had any, besides? And as for looks... he raised his hand, ruefully running it over his scraggly beard. If he wanted to impress Nessa with those, he was going to need to clean up some.

Entering the main reception, he paused for a moment to admire the glass-domed atrium, the shimmering marble floor, and the huge tank of tropical fish opposite the reception desk. Hunter Enterprises had spent millions of dollars on Sunfish Island, and the money showed. The main building was magnificent, beautiful architecture and artistic design everywhere the eye settled.

Approaching the reception dress, he returned the friendly smile of the young man who greeted him. "I'm looking for Luke Collyer's office?"

"First floor, sir." The man pointed down the marble hall. "Just take the stairs and turn left at the top."

"Thank you." Jace followed the directions and found a glass-walled office with RESORT MANAGEMENT etched on the door. Inside, a young woman was shouldering her bag and heading out.

"Oh, hello!" She blinked in surprise as she almost collided with Jace. "Can I help you?"

"I was looking for Luke, but he probably already finished for the day. Never mind, I guess."

Blue eyes scanned his face, then the girl smiled. "You must be the friend Luke said might stop by. Jay, wasn't it? You can go on in. Maybe you can get him to finish work at a reasonable time, for once."

Jace didn't bother correcting her, just thanking her as she gestured him toward the inner office. Rapping on the door, he pushed it open and leaned in, grinning.

"Hey, your boss says you're working too hard."

Luke looked up from the computer screen he was frowning at, a smile coming to his face. "I was about to say that I'm the boss here, but technically I guess you do outrank me."

"I know I promised not to interfere in resort business," Jace said, moving fully into the room, "but it's come to my attention that my resort manager is working too hard, and you know what they say about someone who's all work and no play."

"You calling me dull?" Luke pushed his chair back, rose to his feet, and grinned broadly. "I'll show you dull. Come on. Time you sampled some of Sunfish Island's nightlife!"

"Be gentle with me," Jace begged laughingly as Luke slung his arm around Jace's shoulders and steered him out of the office. "I'm an invalid!"

They ended up in the resort's famous French restaurant. Recently awarded a Michelin star, the food was as good as anything Jace had eaten in the most expensive restaurants in New York. Luke called the sommelier over and ordered a bottle of an Australian white wine Jace hadn't heard of, which turned out to be so good Jace immediately decided to send his father a case.

"Damn," Jace said finally, sitting back in his seat and rubbing his stomach. "I don't think I'll have much trouble regaining the weight I've lost if I eat here regularly."

Luke chuckled, raising his glass to toast the sentiment. "I go running on the beach every morning to make sure I don't get tubby. The resort is extremely lucky to have Suzannah Monteil... I need to go through the budget and look at getting her another raise, actually, or she's gonna get poached from under our noses."

"I'll authorize it," Jace said immediately. "Pay her whatever you think fit. Word is going to get out pretty quickly and people will come to the resort just for the opportunity to eat here." He looked around the restaurant. He could only see one vacant table, a waitress already clearing and re-setting it to make it ready for occupation again. "It's already busy, but we could be completely booked out every night. A waiting list. Folks flying in by helicopter just to dine here."

"You sound like our marketing manager," Luke said with a grin. "I've already heard all this from her. I think she's got every major restaurant critic in the southern hemisphere lined up to visit us over the next month. That Michelin star has really put us on the map."

"Which is why you need to keep the chef no matter what." Jace nodded, his quick mind turning over the issue. "Is there any other incentive you want to offer her? Anything else she'd like?"

"I haven't really had the chance to sit down and talk with her about it." Luke shrugged. "Maybe you can meet with her yourself."

"I'll think about it, toward the end of my stay. I'd rather not talk to anyone in my official persona before that. Keep it quiet that I'm here, please."

Luke nodded. "Sure."

"You have my complete support in offering her whatever the hell she wants to get her to agree to stay, though," Jace offered. "Up to and including moving into the family villa once I've gone, if she'd care for more luxurious living quarters."

That made Luke laugh. "I'll keep that card up my sleeve just in case. I very much doubt she'd accept, though. Suzannah is... well, she's not the sort to be tempted by money or luxuries. Honestly, she'll probably demand the authority to order loads more exotic ingredients for the restaurant."

"Fine by me," Jace said, "she'll probably earn us another Michelin star with them, so authorize away." He toasted Luke with the last of the wine before draining it. "Hey, do I need to run the comp card?"

Luke waved him away. "It's all taken care of, don't worry. You had enough? Want a coffee?"

"Honestly, I'm fighting to keep my eyelids open," Jace confessed. "The rest of that nightlife you promised me might have to wait for another day."

"It's all good, mate." Luke gave him a warm smile. "You look pretty done in. Let me run you back home, eh? Get some rest. I don't want to be the cause of a relapse; your father would kill me!"

Jace found his head nodding as Luke drove the golf cart back to the villa. "Is it okay if I wander over again tomorrow?" he asked drowsily. "I could stop by and see Nessa again."

"Oh, you met Nessa?" Luke glanced at him as he pulled the cart to a stop. "She's something, isn't she? A real asset for the resort. I ran across her slinging drinks in a bar near the football ground in Brisbane; I'd never seen anyone make cocktails so fast."

The mental image made Jace smile as he got out of the cart and thanked Luke for the ride and his company at dinner. Luke sped off with a cheerful wave and Jace let himself into the villa, collapsing to lie on the couch. He fell asleep right there, worn out from the unaccustomed exercise, delicious food, and the alcohol he'd consumed.

***

Jace woke with a dry mouth, a sore head, and a desperate need to visit the bathroom. Attending to the last need first, he found some painkillers in his toiletries bag and washed them down with a large glass of water. A couple of slices of toast and three more glasses of water later, he started to feel a little more human. *No more drinking with Luke*, he concluded. The aftermath was no fun.

Refilling his glass again, he took it outside and sat by the villa's pool, dangling his feet in the sparkling blue water and gazing out over the pool's infinity edge at the ocean.

"I could live here," he said aloud, startling himself with the revelation. For years, his view had been the New York City skyline from his penthouse apartment; before that it was Sydney. Both cities with spectacular views available to anyone who cared to look. Still, this place had that one thing both places would never have: tranquility.

It was something Jace had never realized was missing from his life, until yesterday. The knowledge the phone wasn't going to ring, that nobody would bother him unless he actively went out and sought company, was eye-opening. For the first time he could remember, there were literally no demands on his time at all.

He'd thought the forced inactivity and solitude would drive him crazy with boredom. Instead, he seemed to have unlocked something which had been stagnant for too long: his creativity. Ideas for designs were beginning to surface in his head, as they hadn't since he gave up his dreams of being a full-time architect and joined Hunter Enterprises at his father's behest.

Nessa's story popped back into his head: the way she'd told him so emphatically she never wanted to leave Sunfish, despite her qualifications for a much more high-powered job. She'd consciously chosen a simpler life and found contentment. Perhaps it was her words which caused his introspection now, making him reconsider his own life choices. Kicking his feet absently in the water and watching the ripples spread out from the movement, Jace sighed. He couldn't walk away from his responsibilities, tempting though the idea seemed. His father had been grooming him for years to take over Hunter Enterprises, and Jace had excelled in every role he'd been given.

Capability did not equal enjoyment, however, and Jace hadn't enjoyed the work in a while. For the first time, he began to consider alternatives. Maybe he could speak to his father about other options, about looking at someone else being Chief Executive when his father decided to step down, because the idea of being responsible for the whole shebang seemed completely unpalatable.

The sun felt hot on his back, and he didn't have sunscreen on. Pushing himself up, Jace dried his legs off and headed back inside. Maybe he'd check in with his father. Just say hi. A quick calculation told him it was early evening in New York, a pretty good time to call. John would probably still be at the office.

Jace had to convince his own assistant to put him through. Nancy was a dragon, but a wonderful one; she managed every aspect of his life and mothered him unmercifully when he let her get away with it. She flatly refused to put him through to his father until he promised he wouldn't talk business, that it was just a social call.

"How's the sun, sea, and sand?" John Hunter boomed down the phone, making Jace grin. His father was always a larger-than-life character.

"I haven't actually been in the sea yet."

"Why not? It's not jellyfish season, is it?"

"No." Jace chuckled. "I just haven't got around to it, honestly. The villa's got almost everything I need, I haven't wanted to leave. I went over to the resort yesterday, had dinner with Luke. Don't worry, though, he told me straight up he'd kick me out if I even tried to talk business."

"I know."

"Of course you do," Jace realized. "You've been checking up on me."

"Actually, I called Luke to congratulate him on the restaurant getting a Michelin star. He told me he saw you yesterday, and that you seemed well but still kinda tired." John's voice softened, gentled. "And if I *was* checking up on you, Jace, it'd only be because I'm worried about you. You gave me a damn scare."

"I know. I'm sorry, Dad."

"I never wanted you to run yourself into the ground, son. You don't have to prove anything to me. I'm already proud of you."

A lump welled in Jace's throat; he took a moment to clear it before he simply said, "Thanks."

"Everything is fine here without you. Frankly, I think Nancy could run the place perfectly well without either of us."

Jace grinned at that. "I don't doubt it. Hey," he said as something occurred to him, "you should take a break here too, Dad. How long is it since you've been on vacation?"

"Flew up for Hamilton Race Week last year," John answered promptly. "Might come up this year too. It's only a few weeks away now, I've got several friends with yachts in the races. Maybe you'll still be there?"

"I hope not. I'll go stir-crazy by then with nothing to do!"

John laughed richly. "Go find some pretty girls to flirt with or something."

Unbidden, Jace's mind flew to Nessa. "Maybe," he said unguardedly, then changed the subject before his father could ask any awkward questions.

Hanging up the phone at last, Jace found he felt almost light, as though a weight had been taken off his shoulders. The news Hunter Enterprises was ticking along just fine without him should have been a cause for concern, a worry he was replaceable. Instead, the knowledge was strangely reassuring. Was it a sign, he wondered? A sign maybe his future really didn't lie in the company's executive offices?

Well, he didn't have to make the decision today, or tomorrow, or even next week. He had plenty of time to consider it, and where better than here, in this island paradise, with nothing else to distract the mind? Dropping the phone on the coffee table, he lay back on the couch, putting his feet up, and gazed up at the ceiling. The sunlight reflecting off the pool outside made little ripples of dappled rainbow light on the white paint. Gazing at them, Jace's eyes slowly drifted closed until he was sound asleep.

Chapter Three

Nessa hadn't expected to see Jace back at her bar, and certainly not so soon, but she was serving lunchtime drinks when he came ambling down off the hiking trail again. He looked a lot better today and better equipped as well, with a small pack slung over his shoulder. She guessed he had a water bottle in it. Too busy to do more than give him a quick nod in greeting as he slid onto a barstool, she took a few minutes to clear the order the waiter had just handed her for a dozen complicated cocktails.

"Hey," she slid a coaster in front of Jace and smiled. "You look better today. Got some colour in your cheeks."

He smiled back. "I totally had a grandpa nap after breakfast. It was fantastic."

That made Nessa laugh. "Good for you. What can I get you?"

"Haven't had lunch yet, so I'd better keep it virgin." He cocked his head at her. "Something long and cold. I brought water with me today, but it's still pretty hot walking."

She nodded and reached for a tall glass, shovelling ice into it before mixing orange, mango, and pineapple juices and topping it off with club soda.

"Looks great," Jace said enthusiastically as Nessa placed the glass in front of him with a flourish. He took a long drink, eyes closing with pleasure. "Ohhh. Beautiful."

"You're welcome." She set one of the food menus down beside his glass. "If you want to order lunch, I can put your order through here and the kitchen will send it out shortly."

"Oh, you do bar food here?" He picked up the menu and looked through it with interest, seeing a wide variety of dishes, from pizza and sandwiches to Asian dishes and Spanish tapas.

"One of the resort's restaurants is right over there," she gestured to a large hedge to one side of the pool. "The kitchen's just behind the bar. You can go in there for lunch, if you'd prefer."

"No, I think I'd like to eat here," Jace said thoughtfully. "Turkey and cheese focaccia with cranberry sauce sounds good, please."

Nessa put the order through, poured two more drinks as her waiter returned, and then found herself leaning with her elbows on the bar. "Have you been here on Sunfish long?"

"A few days, but I didn't really venture out until yesterday." He smiled at her. "I'm planning to remedy that, though, and do some exploring. This place really is like paradise."

Nessa smiled as she looked around, at the laughing patrons in the shimmering pool, the beautifully landscaped tropical gardens. "It really is. I get a bit blasé about it sometimes, but then someone like you comes along and makes me look at it through fresh eyes."

Jace nodded, taking another sip of his drink.

"Do you snorkel, or dive?" Nessa asked then. "If so, you should, while you're here. We're right in the middle of the World Heritage part of the Barrier Reef; there's no better diving anywhere in the world."

"I haven't for a long time, but I'd love to." He hesitated, remembering her quick refusal of his invitation the previous afternoon. "Do you get much chance to?"

"I haven't been in ages." She looked a bit wistful. "I really should. It's still fairly quiet this time of year, I could get a spot on one of the trips easily enough. In the high season, we're supposed to leave them for paying customers, obviously."

"Obviously," Jace agreed, nodding. It was a sensible policy. He fiddled with the straw in his drink for a moment. *Go on, bite the bullet. The worst she can say is no.* "I was thinking of maybe going up to the main resort and booking onto one of the trips. If you've got a day off coming up, maybe you'd like to come with me?"

He hadn't felt so shy asking a girl out in years. Nessa's light amber eyes were serious as she gazed at him, and then her dimpled smile broke out, wide and startlingly white in her brown face.

"I'd really like that. I've got the day off tomorrow, actually, if there are any spots available on one of the tours."

Jace had to suppress an inappropriate urge to punch the sky and whoop with victory. *Play it cool.* "Any preferences, snorkel or dive?"

"Snorkel. I've never been much of a diver, I admit. I get a bit claustrophobic."

He nodded, perfectly happy with that. "Sounds good. I'll walk over after lunch and check out what's available."

Nessa smiled and turned away to serve another customer. She couldn't keep her lips from quirking upward, she found; the thought of going snorkeling with Jace had a squirmy, excited feeling building in the pit of her stomach. *It's a date,* she thought, giving him a quick sideways glance under her lashes. His sandwich had just been delivered and he was thanking the waitress who'd brought it with a charming smile. The girl looked a bit dazed as she turned away; she caught Nessa's eye and grinned, miming fanning herself with a backward glance at Jace.

He's sexy enough to raise any girl's internal temperature, Nessa thought. Add his physical attractiveness, charm, and money–at least, she assumed he was reasonably well off. Enough to move in the rarefied circles where a friend owned a private villa on Sunfish Island, at any rate. Although she supposed it could be a friend with rich parents; there weren't many folks Jace's age who had that kind of money.

Everything about Jace added up to the kind of man women threw themselves at. And he'd chosen to ask her out, not once but twice, making a second attempt when she'd turned him down the first time. It was flattering as hell, Nessa acknowledged, glancing at him again, taking in his clean-cut, preppy good looks. He'd shaved since yesterday, removing the scraggly beard, and though he could still use a haircut, he looked even more handsome than she'd originally thought.

She was still busy serving customers when he finished eating and headed off, though he did catch her eye to give her a little wave. Her heart sank unaccountably, but leapt right back up again twenty minutes later when he ambled back to the bar, waving a slip of paper.

"We're booked on the all-day snorkel tour going out at eight-thirty," Jace said cheerfully as Nessa gave him one of her blinding smiles.

"Sounds terrific. I'll meet you at the dock?"

"Sure. They said the boat is equipped with everything we need, so all you need to bring is your beautiful self and your swim gear."

"You'd better wear a T-shirt." She pointed at him. "And we'll slather you in sunscreen, or that pasty skin of yours is gonna go lobster-red."

"Gotcha," Jace agreed. "Well, I'd better head on back. See you in the morning, then!"

"See you," Nessa said, and told herself not to be silly. It was ridiculous to be disappointed he hadn't repeated his dinner invitation. She'd be spending the whole day with him tomorrow. That'd be plenty of time to get to know him better.

***

Nessa woke early the following morning. Butterflies churned in her stomach. She told herself sternly not to be ridiculous; she was hardly a teenager on her first date with a boy she liked! Still, she couldn't quite tamp down the welling bubble of excitement as she headed to the staff cafeteria to get breakfast.

"Hey!" Her friend Olivia slid into the seat opposite her. "You're up and about early. Don't usually see you in here at this hour."

"I'm going out on a snorkeling trip today," Nessa explained. "Figured I should get in a good breakfast first; I'll need the energy."

Olivia shuddered dramatically. "You don't get seasick? I never dare eat if I'm going out on one of the boats, in case I wind up feeding the fish!"

"...Thanks for that image." Nessa looked down at the stack of waffles she'd selected, having second thoughts.

"Whoops, never mind me!" Olivia laughed, a blush staining her cheeks. "Shouldn't have mentioned it. You just have a good day!" Nessa couldn't keep the goofy grin off her face, and Olivia gave her a narrow-eyed look. "Why do I have the feeling this isn't just a fun day off for you? Wait. You met someone!"

"What are you, a mind-reader?" Nessa dug back into her waffles. "Yes, I met someone," she mumbled when Olivia prodded her.

"A resort guest?" Olivia's eyes widened.

"No! Come on, you know me better than that. He's staying at one of the private villas. It belongs to a friend of his."

"Oh, okay." Olivia nodded. "Is he cute?" Her grin widened cheekily.

"Well, I think so." Nessa grinned back. "But paws off. You're taken." She pointed her fork at Olivia sternly.

"Oh, don't worry, I'm more than satisfied with my catch." Olivia looked like a cat licking cream off her whiskers.

"And where is Cory this morning?" she asked, referring to the resort's activities manager.

"Oh, he's taking the snorkeling trip out. He already ate and went down to help prep the boat. So don't tell me, if you don't want to, but be warned I'll get all the juicy details out of Cory later. Can't escape the gossip network, darling."

Nessa wrinkled her nose with disgust and sighed. "Well, it's a first date. So there won't be much to tell."

"Apart from the fact that your date will no doubt be eating you up with his eyes. Are you wearing your red bikini? You'll knock his socks off."

She already had it on underneath her light sundress. Living on a tropical island, she owned half a dozen bikinis, but she never considered wearing any of the others when she opened the drawer this morning. The red bikini was a halter-neck, framing and lifting her breasts, the fiery colour a great contrast to her dark skin. Ties at the sides of the brief bikini bottoms were a wicked temptation, luring a man's attention to her hips, making him think about tugging on the ties to pull them free.

Nessa wanted that kind of attention from Jace. She'd done a fair bit of soul-searching after impulsively agreeing to go on the snorkeling date with him. She wasn't an impulsive person by nature, but in the end she'd had to conclude her subconscious had already decided. Jace was an attractive man. He wasn't the only one to show interest in her recently, but he was the only one in a long time who'd provoked a matching response from her. She'd spend the day with him and see how things panned out, but at the moment she provisionally intended on taking him back to her place that evening. Or going back to the villa where he was staying, if he invited her. She'd never been in any of the fancy private villas and found herself curious about what they'd be like.

"Earth to Nessa!"

She blinked, startled back to herself. She'd drifted off into a daydream thinking about Jace. About letting him pull the ties on her bikini. He had nice hands, she'd noticed when he was at the bar, with long, capable fingers. She'd had more than a few thoughts about those fingers caressing her skin, finding her most sensitive spots.

"Sorry, I was somewhere else."

"I could see that." Olivia smirked over the rim of her coffee cup. "You'd better get moving, sugar, or you're literally gonna miss that boat."

"Argh!" A quick glance at her watch and Nessa abandoned the remnants of her breakfast, scrabbling under her chair for the beach bag she'd brought with her.

"Have fun!" Olivia called after her as she hurried for the exit. Nessa waved hastily and set off for the boat dock at a fast trot.

Chapter Four

She wasn't coming. It was eight twenty-eight, and the boathand was preparing to cast off the lines. Jace bit down on his lip, wondering if he could ask them to wait five more minutes.

"We're one short," the tall blond man in resort-uniform polo shirt and shorts said, looking at the clipboard in his hand. "You're Jace Weller, right?"

He'd given his mother's maiden name as his surname when booking, not wanting anyone to clue in to his real identity. "That's right."

"And you booked for two?"

"Yeah, my friend should be here any minute--" He spied a figure hurrying along the path toward the dock. "Here she is now!"

"Hold off on that line, Ben." The man took a half a step back. "Whoa, Nessa?"

"Hey, Cory," Nessa grinned at him as she hurried up to the boat. "Hi, Jace." To his pleased surprise, she went up on tiptoes and brushed a kiss on his cheek.

"I... see." Cory blinked, looking from one to the other of them. "Okay, well, I guess that makes everyone, then." He made a final tick on his clipboard. "Take your seats, everyone."

There were several other guests on board and only a couple of seats vacant. Nessa sat down and Jace joined her; she dropped a bag at their feet and gave him a bright smile.

"You look beautiful," Jace said impulsively. She was wearing a light cotton sundress in a turquoise blue which looked utterly amazing against her deep brown skin. Her long black braids were hanging loose to her waist, brushing against his arm; he suppressed an inappropriate urge to take one in his fingers and play with it.

"Thank you!" Nessa held his gaze, her smile widening even further. "You're looking pretty good yourself. Like the threads." She flicked lightly at the lapel of the loud Hawaiian shirt he was wearing.

"It's not mine," Jace confessed, "I think it belongs to... the owner of the villa. I found it in the closet." He'd almost said *my father* then, but bit the words back just in time. He'd told Nessa the villa belonged to a friend. An uncomfortable feeling curled in the pit of his stomach; he didn't like misleading her. But then, he rationalized, he wanted her to get to know him without knowing who he was, about his wealth, his family name. It was very possible nothing would come of this, that they would go their separate ways in a few days and she would never even need to know.

Still, as he looked into her smiling, carefree face, Jace had the sinking feeling things weren't going to be quite so simple.

A heavy hand landed on his shoulder, making him jump. The boat had started moving, and he twisted around to find Cory had slipped into the seat behind them and was giving him the evil eye.

"Knock it off with the big brother act, Cory," Nessa said, shoving Cory's hand off Jace's shoulder. "I'm a big girl, y'know."

"Just making sure he knows there are folks looking out for you," Cory said, his tone perfectly amiable even if his eyes weren't.

"I had no doubt of it," Jace said with a friendly smile in return. "I'm sure Nessa's the kind of person who inspires intense loyalty in her friends."

Cory nodded, apparently satisfied with his answer. "Good. Well, in that case, have a good day!" He slid out of the seat again and strode up to the front of the boat, easily maintaining his footing against the sway, plucking up a microphone from the side of the pilot's chair. "G'day folks! Let me tell you about the awesome day we've got in store for you..."

Jace and Nessa both listened with interest as Cory talked, telling the group the itinerary for the day, including snorkeling at three different sites and lunch on the world-famous Whitehaven Beach.

"With any luck we'll see some humpback whales too, since they're passing through the area at the moment on their annual migration," Cory concluded, "so keep your eyes peeled."

The other tourists started chattering excitedly as soon as Cory put the microphone down. Nessa looked at Jace, her eyes shining. "I'm really looking forward to this. Thank you so much for inviting me."

"I'm looking forward to it too. The snorkeling... and your company."

Small fingers curled over his. Startled, Jace looked down at Nessa's hand, then up at her. She was still smiling at him. He turned his hand and laced his fingers with hers, feeling like a boy with his first crush finding out the girl he liked was interested in him, too.

They held hands the whole half-hour it took to get to the first snorkeling site, a secluded cove in the lee of one of the other islands in the chain. Cory informed them the island was completely uninhabited, a wildlife sanctuary, and they weren't permitted to swim ashore.

Jace had shoved his bag under the seat when he'd boarded. He pulled it out now and stripped off his Hawaiian shirt. Catching Nessa eying his chest, he grinned at her. He was picking up some colour to his skin after a few days relaxing by the villa's pool, and though he was still thinner than he'd been before his illness, it only threw his muscles into higher relief.

"I could leave the rash vest off if you want to admire the view," he offered, the stretchy swim shirt hanging from one hand.

Nessa laughed at him. "Put it on. I don't want to be distracted from the sights underwater." She rose to her feet, grasped the hem of her dress, and swept it up and over her head in one graceful movement.

Jace almost swallowed his tongue. "You think *you'll* get distracted?"

Nessa grinned, walking past him to scoop up a pair of flippers and a snorkel mask from the stack Cory had spread out on the deck. "Hurry up. No time to waste!"

Jace was all fingers and thumbs trying to get his rash vest on, then grabbing a mask and flippers. Cory laughed at him as he hopped on one foot, trying to wrestle a flipper on.

"She's right there, man. Wow, you've got it bad, huh?"

"Are you dead? Did you see her in that bikini?"

"Not dead, just very happily taken." Cory grinned at him before reverting to business mode. "Remember, don't touch any of the coral. You want to climb down the ladder?"

Jace shook his head. "I'm good. I'm a strong swimmer." Checking nobody was directly beneath him, he fitted his mask and snorkel before diving smoothly off the back of the boat.

Nessa wasn't far away, floating face-down on the surface of the water in a deadman's float position, obviously looking at something beneath the surface. Jace swam up beside her, swishing his flippers gently, peering into the clear blue water to see what she was looking at.

Nessa turned her head slightly to look at him without taking her face out of the water, reaching to touch his wrist lightly before pointing.

It took Jace a moment to see what she was gesturing at; she appeared to be telling him to look at a surprisingly plain patch of sand in the midst of some bright corals. Frowning, he peered closer, but then the sand shifted and he gasped, almost losing the rhythm of his breathing through the snorkel, as a stingray almost as long as he was lifted up out of the sand and sailed majestically off into the blue.

Jace looked at Nessa, eyes wide, sensing rather than seeing her amusement at his shock.

She touched his wrist again before swishing her flippers to move on.

They surfaced for a proper breath a few minutes later and Jace spat to clear his mouth of the salty water. "My God, that was incredible! Did you see the size of that stingray?"

"A spotted eagle ray, I think," Nessa said, laughing at his excited expression. "You'll have to meet our marine biologists sometime."

Jace nodded. A large part of the reason Hunter Enterprises had been allowed to redevelop Sunfish Island had been the huge marine biology research and education facility they'd agreed to build and permanently fund. One of the finest of its kind in the world, it had a team of four permanent research scientists and half a dozen assistants who came up on funded semester-long assignments from universities across Australia. Parts of the facility were open the the public; he'd been meaning to visit but hadn't had the opportunity yet. "I'd love to."

"I'll take you," Nessa said impulsively. "Laurie, one of the marine biologists, is a friend of mine. She'll take you on a behind-the-scenes tour if you're with me."

It was on the tip of his tongue to tell her it wasn't necessary, that Luke could arrange things, but he rethought the impulse. Nessa would want to know why Luke would be so willing to accommodate him, and that opened him up to questions he wasn't ready to answer. Besides, Nessa taking him to the facility would definitely be a second date.

"Thanks," he said, "that would be awesome."

"We could go early, before I start work. I'll catch up with her tomorrow and find out what day would suit." Nessa was bubbling with excitement, too. She pulled her snorkel down to her mouth again. "Come on. I want to see if we can spot any clown fish!"

Grinning, Jace popped his mouthpiece back in and dived after her.

The water was warm and buoyant, and in the sheltered cove there was no current to speak of. It was like swimming through a warm bath, relaxing and easy. Everywhere Jace looked, there was something new and amazing to see: brightly colored corals, invertebrates, and fish. Nessa pointed out a starfish of such an intense blue, even underwater, Jace could hardly believe it was real. He swam on at her side, head turning every which way as he tried to take it all in.

A sharp whistle cut the air as he surfaced briefly to get a deep breath. Surprised, Jace checked his dive watch. Cory had told them they'd have fifty minutes at this stop. Startled to see their time was up, he reached out and tapped Nessa's shoulder, then his watch.

She nodded and pulled her mouthpiece out. "That went quickly!"

"Certainly did," he agreed, as they turned and began swimming back to the boat. They weren't too far away; they'd been careful to reorient themselves on the boat each time they surfaced, swimming tracks parallel to their previous courses.

Cory leaned down to give them both a hand up. Jace waited for Nessa to go first, completely failing to keep his eyes off her beautiful butt as she climbed back aboard the boat. But then, it would have been most ungallant of him to make her wait in the water while he got out, and it would have taken a lot more discipline than he possessed not to look.

She looked over her shoulder at him and laughed.

He shrugged unapologetically. “I’m not dead.”

“Good thing, too.” Cory offered his hand but Jace waved him off, climbing the ladder back into the boat easily. Sitting back down beside Nessa, he accepted the bottle of water she handed him from the large cooler in the middle of the boat’s hull.

“You look a bit pale,” she noted, her eyes searching his face. “Are you feeling alright?”

“Yep.” He was grateful for the chance to sit down and rest, though, while the boat took them to their next location. Cursing the lingering weakness which still plagued his body after his illness, he cracked the top of the water and took a long drink.

“I brought snacks.” Nessa delved into the bag at her feet. “Healthy--” she held up a small bunch of ripe bananas, “--or not so healthy.” She waved a large bar of chocolate at him.

“Both?”

“Both is good. Fruit first?” Splitting a couple of bananas off the bunch, she handed one over. Jace peeled his and ate it with enjoyment, unable to keep his mind out of the gutter as he watched Nessa eat hers, her lips puckering around the fruit in an insanely erotic gesture. She knew exactly what she was doing to him, as well, her laughing eyes holding his as she ate.

Jace was glad his board shorts were loose.

***

Their second snorkeling location was at a platform anchored on an open-water coral reef. The water here was shallower than at the first site, so they just floated side by side, face down in the water, gazing with wonder at the natural beauties of the reef. Nessa got to see her clown fish and a couple of dozen other species besides.

“Next stop: Whitehaven Beach,” Cory said as they climbed back aboard once again. “You ever been there, Jace?”

He shook his head. “Looking forward to seeing it.”

“It’s one of the most beautiful beaches in the world. Sand so white it looks like snow.” Nessa sounded like a tourist brochure, not that he minded in the slightest. She practically glowed with happiness, her smile wide and white, her dark skin glimmering with salt water.

Tentatively, Jace slipped his arm around her waist as they sat back down, leaning over to kiss the point of her shoulder lightly.

Nessa’s breath drew in softly as she looked at him. He’d been the perfect gentleman so far, gallant and charming, though his eyes had told a different story as he'd watched her. His lips were warm against her skin, his eyes questioning as he lifted his head to look at her.

Leaning in, Nessa put her hand to Jace's cheek and brought her lips to his. He closed his eyes, she saw in the instant before she closed her own.

The first kiss was light, little more than a gentle press of lips. Jace didn't push, didn't try to pull her closer, and his reticence made Nessa want more. She kissed him with greater fervor, her lips parting, tongue flicking between them to trace over the seam of his. Then, at last, he kissed her back properly. His arm tightened around her waist as his tongue danced with hers, and Nessa slid her hand into his damp blond hair, grasping the wet locks.

"Ahem," Cory's not-at-all-subtle cough brought them back to awareness of their surroundings.

Probably a good thing too, Nessa realized ruefully. She'd been just about to climb astride Jace's lap and grab his hands and bring them to her breasts. Her nipples were aching inside her wet bikini top, wanting stimulation. With a reluctant sigh, she pulled back from the kiss, giving Cory a glare.

In response, he flicked his eyes at a couple of giggling teenagers on the other side of the boat.

Cory was right; they didn't need to be getting hot and heavy in public. But Jace's kiss had woken something deep inside of Nessa which she'd kept dormant for a long time. The end of the boat trip seemed very far away, and Nessa hoped she'd be able to hold out until they could finally be alone together.

"We're coming up to Whitehaven Beach now," Cory announced. "You can have a swim or whatever while we're setting up lunch; it'll be ready in about fifteen minutes. We've got an hour and a half total here, so make the most of it!"

Nessa hesitated, then asked Cory quietly, "Do you want any help getting lunch set up?"

He smiled down at her, touching her shoulder. "Nah, hon, you're all good. You're a paying guest today, courtesy of Jace here. You just have fun. I do this three or four times a week, got it down to a fine art."

She gave him a grateful smile.

"Damn, that sand really is white," Jace said in amazement, shielding his eyes from the sun's reflected glare. "Is it coarse sand, or fine?"

"Incredibly fine, ike powdered sugar," Nessa remembered from her previous visit. "It gets *everywhere*."

"At least we'll be swimming again afterward. And hey, if it gets in your bikini, I'll volunteer to help you get it out." Jace grinned wickedly.

She elbowed him lightly in the ribs, grinning back. "Behave, or our chaperone will be telling us off again."

They were both giggling like kids as they climbed off the back of the boat into the shallow water and walked hand-in-hand to the beach. The fine powdery sand promptly coated their wet legs, as Nessa had warned.

"This looks a nice spot," Nessa said as they reached a secluded section of the beach. "You okay to lie in the sun for a bit?"

"Sure, I'll just put some more sunscreen on."

They both spread out towels and lay down. Nessa pointed at her lower legs, laughing. "Look, my legs are nearly as white as yours!"

"Nessa!" Jace chuckled. "Never say that. Your skin is beautiful."

"Please say you're not going to call me cocoa or chocolate or anything like that?" She rolled to her front, shading her eyes with her hand to look at him.

"Come on! I'm an Aussie but I've been working in New York for five years now. I know how culturally insensitive it is to compare skin tones to food." He gave her a reproving look. "I'm not much for flowery similes as compliments, anyway. Blatant honesty is more my thing."

"Blatant honesty?" Nessa crinkled her eyebrows.

"You're incredibly beautiful. Your skin glows. Your eyes sparkle. I find it very hard to look anywhere else when I'm with you."

"...Okay, that's pretty blatant," Nessa said when she got her breath back. "Wow."

Jace grinned at her. "Just making sure you know how I feel. I could go on, if you like?"

"My head might get too swollen and explode. You're very good for my ego, though."

He reached across the small gap between their towels, fingers curling gently around hers. "I'd like to be good for a lot of things for you, Nessa. Sneaking off into the undergrowth to make out like a pair of horny teenagers is sounding mighty appealing right about now."

"If it wasn't for the wildlife, which would no doubt make that into a very dangerous endeavour." Nessa grinned back at him.

"Come on, I'm an Aussie. Snakes and spiders don't terrify me."

"I'm a Brit, and they do bloody well terrify me! Besides, it's the lizards you've got to worry about. Cory told me he saw a five foot long goanna here a couple of weeks ago."

"They're not gonna attack you." Jace chuckled at her expression of horror.

"Thanks, but I'm not prepared to risk my toes for the sake of a make out session with you. Tempting though that may be. You'll just have to wait until later."

"Later?" His fingers squeezed a little more firmly on hers.

Nessa smiled. "Later."

And with that answer, Jace had to be content, as Cory's sharp whistle called them up the beach for lunch.

Chapter Five

Nessa nudged Jace. "Wake up."

"Huh!" His eyes snapped open. "Whoa. I was pretty sound asleep, huh?" Yawning and stretching, he rubbed at the back of his head.

"I don't think the boat engine had even started before you were snoozing on my shoulder." She smiled at him. "You're still not fully recovered, huh?"

"Pneumonia really knocks the stuffing out of you," Jace admitted, "and it's been a pretty big day. Sorry. Didn't mean to drop off on you."

"It's fine!" She squeezed his hand lightly. "I wouldn't have woken you up, except we're almost home." She nodded forward, and he looked to see they were indeed slowing to move into Sunfish Island's dock.

"So we are." He hesitated a moment before saying, "Would you like to come back to the villa with me? I've got a fridge full of food, we can easily throw together something for dinner."

"Sounds lovely," Nessa said, enthusiasm clear in her tone.

Jace had taken the golf cart stored in the villa's small garage to get to the dock that morning. He gestured to it now as they disembarked and bid farewell to Cory. "I didn't think my legs would be up to walking back after a day spent swimming and snorkeling."

"My legs thank you for the consideration." Nessa tossed her bag into the back and settled into the plush leather passenger seat with a sigh of contentment. "And so does my butt; this is so much more comfy than those hard plastic seats on the boat!"

"Wait until you try out the showers at the villa." Jace grinned, getting in and starting the cart.

"Giant shower roses?"

"Yup, with super-high pressure. Not only that, they have adjustable jets coming at you from every direction."

Nessa moaned. "Drive faster."

"Yes, ma'am," Jace chuckled. "It's just up ahead."

"This one?" Nessa gaped as they approached and Jace pushed a button on the dash to open the garage door. "Wow, this is one of the best locations on the island!"

"Oh?" Jace said, deliberately obtuse.

"I've always loved the design of this house, too. Lucky you, to be friends with the owners," Nessa sighed enviously as they parked inside and got out of the golf cart. "Well, at least I get to be nosy and look around inside!"

"Poke your nose anywhere you like. I have free run of the place," Jace said, with absolute honesty.

Nessa gazed around admiringly as they entered the house proper, taking everything in: the high ceilings, the glass doors which slid all the way back to give an unobstructed view over the pool to the ocean, the imported Carrara marble tiles on the floor. Even the furniture looked architecturally designed, though still somehow temptingly comfortable. There were a few books and a laptop lying on the coffee table, but otherwise the place was very tidy and barely looked inhabited. Jace was obviously not a slob, she noted approvingly, as she glanced into the kitchen and saw no dirty dishes on the counter or in the sink.

"All the bedrooms have en suite bathrooms," Jace said. "There's one on this level and four upstairs."

Nessa didn't hesitate before saying, "Which one are you using?"

"The one on this level... too lazy to walk upstairs when I'm tired." He smiled self-deprecatingly. "You're welcome to use any of the others."

"Or I could share yours." Her eyes held his.

Jace drew a deep breath. "You're very welcome to share mine. Why don't you go have a shower while I quickly throw something together for dinner?"

"Sounds good," Nessa agreed, though she'd been rather hoping Jace might come shower with her. On the other hand, they were both sticky and sandy; a chance to wash up and eat first would be welcome.

"Right in here." He opened a door and showed her into a stunning bedroom suite, sharing the same magnificent views as the main room. The king-sized bed was made up with what Nessa guessed were silk sheets, in a stunning shade of turquoise blue. A door on the other side of the room opened into a lavishly appointed bathroom; plush towels in the same shade of turquoise hung on chrome towel racks on the wall. A third door led to a huge walk-in closet, with a few of Jace's things taking up scant space on the hangers and shelves.

"Wow," Nessa said, mouth open. She'd never seen a bedroom suite like this, and Jace had said the house had four more of them. "I guess this is how the other half live, huh?"

"Yeah." This was probably the most cheaply-appointed room Jace had occupied in the last five years; it was certainly nothing compared to his New York penthouse or the spectacular family mansion in Sydney's exclusive Point Piper. He was hardly going to mention that at the moment, though, so he took a step back. "I'll leave you to it. Make yourself comfortable."

She smiled at him as he backed out of the room, closing the door behind him.

Blowing out his cheeks, Jace headed for the kitchen. Pumping soap and washing his hands, he wondered what the hell he was doing. He didn't like misleading Nessa this way, pretending to be something he wasn't. On the other hand, he had the feeling Nessa would probably take off if she had any idea he took this kind of luxury for granted, that his family owned not only this house but the entire damned island.

With a sigh, he turned to the fridge. When Nessa came out, dressed again in her turquoise sundress, she found him chopping peppers and shallots, wielding an expensive chef's knife with flashing speed. He'd already grated cheese into a bowl and spread a couple of frozen pastry squares with tomato paste and crushed garlic.

"Pizza? Yum." She stole a piece of cheese and popped it into her mouth. He smiled without looking up from the chopping.

"I didn't ask if you have any allergies. And do you eat meat?"

"No and yes. Right now I think I could eat a horse."

"Haven't got one of those, sorry. How about some nuts?" He pushed a bowl of cashews in her direction before heading back to the fridge and pulling out a package of pepperoni. Nessa settled herself on a stool at the breakfast bar and watched him tear up the pepperoni before sprinkling the cheese, meat, and vegetables on the pizza.

"What would you like to drink? We're not quite as well-stocked as your bar, but there is some very nice wine."

"Sounds good," Nessa agreed. "Red, if you've got it."

"Sure." He pulled a bottle from a small wine cabinet set into the kitchen counter, opened it, and poured into what she was pretty sure was a Riedel crystal wine glass. Accepting the glass gingerly, frightened of breaking something which probably cost nearly as much as she made in a week, Nessa took a sip of the wine.

Her eyebrows flew up. "Please tell me you have permission to open this stuff."

"Free rein of everything in the house." Jace shrugged. In truth, the wine he'd opened for her was probably the least expensive one he had on hand. The wine cellar under the house had much more expensive ones stored in a climate-controlled vault.

"In that case, I shall appreciate every drop. Since it's probably my only chance ever to drink wine this good. It's Grange, right? What vintage?"

He put the bottle down in front of her silently, kicking himself for not having thought to pick up a cheaper bottle when he was at the resort. She was a professional bartender; of course she knew her wine. "Enjoy. I'm gonna go have a shower while the pizza cooks. It won't be long."

***

Jace was acting a little odd, Nessa thought as he left her alone. Picking up her wineglass, she headed over to the open doors leading out to the pool. Maybe he was a little nervous? She was pretty much a sure thing, after their scorching hot kiss earlier. Surely a guy who looked like Jace didn't lack for women throwing themselves at him, especially in New York. She hadn't asked what he did, but he had to be pretty successful if he ran in the same circles as people who could afford to own a holiday house like this.

With a little sigh, she propped one shoulder against the doorframe and sipped her wine, feeling the cool afternoon breeze blowing lightly over her warm skin. She wore nothing beneath her dress, and looked forward to shocking Jace with that fact.

"Hey," Jace's voice was soft as he approached her from behind.

Nessa smiled but didn't turn around, feeling his hands curve gently around her waist as he bent his head to kiss her bare shoulder. One thin spaghetti strap had slipped down onto her upper arm, and his fingers grazed her skin lightly as he lifted it back into place.

"Hey yourself." She set her glass down on the small table just inside the door and turned to look up at him. His shaggy blond hair was still wet, dampening the collar of the crisp white dress shirt he'd put on but not buttoned. A drop of water ran down the centre of his muscled chest, and she couldn't resist the impulse to lick it off.

Jace's hands came up, one to cradle the back of her head, the other under her chin to tilt her face up to him. His mouth slanted down over hers and this kiss was even better, even hotter, than the one they'd shared on the boat.

Nessa found herself pressed back against the doorframe, her arms coming up to wrap around Jace and hold him closer. One of his legs thrust between hers and she moaned into his mouth, grinding against his muscled thigh. Her nipples pebbled, pushing at his chest through the thin cotton of her dress. He brought one hand up to palm her breast, grazing his thumb over the aching bud.

Putting her hands beneath his shirt and stroking at his back, Nessa moaned into Jace's mouth when he pinched her nipple. Lifting one leg, she hooked it around his thigh to try and pull him closer still, not that there was the slightest space in between them. He lifted his mouth from hers only to kiss down her neck, nipping and licking at her throat, his tongue tracing hotly into the delicate hollows of her collarbones.

"Jace." Her voice was a husky rasp, a plea.

He took it for a request to stop, though, and moved back reluctantly, his hands falling away.

Nessa grasped at his shirt. "Take me to bed."

He looked down at her for a moment, a muscle in his jaw bunching and releasing, before nodding. "Let me turn the oven off."

It was a good thing he'd remembered, Nessa thought as he went into the kitchen and flicked a switch before returning to her side and offering his hand, or they'd probably have burned the house down instead of just burning up the sheets. At the very least, they would have stunk the kitchen up with burned pizza. She tangled her fingers with Jace's and let him lead her back to the bedroom, then draw her over to the beautiful bed with its silken sheets.

Nessa's long braids swung around her shoulders as she reached down to grasp the hem of her dress, drawing it up and over her head in one smooth movement, revealing she wore absolutely nothing underneath.

"Holy moly," Jace breathed, standing back to take her in. She stood unselfconsciously, comfortable in her nudity, aware of her own feminine power. Her breasts were high and full, tipped with plump nipples which were almost black on her dark brown skin. A narrow waist flared to gloriously curvaceous hips and down to juicy thighs, which he'd been thinking about having wrapped around his neck since he first saw her in her spectacular red bikini early that morning.

"You are stunning," he said reverently.

She smiled at him, chin lifted high and proud. "Get naked," she ordered, and he shrugged hastily out of his shirt, fumbled at the button of his shorts, watching lustfully as she turned her back on him and slid onto the bed, sighing luxuriantly as she lay down on the silk sheets. "Ohhh, this bed is even more comfortable than it looks."

Jace couldn't get out of his clothes fast enough, almost tripping as he kicked off his shorts. His cock stood up stiffly, leading him toward Nessa's lush body laid out on his bed, wanting to worship her.

She beckoned to him with a finger, smiling as he moved to the end of the bed and knelt at her feet, reaching to lightly grasp her ankles. "And what are you planning to do down there?" Nessa asked, hoping she already knew.

Jace's smile was lopsided, his eyes hooded with lust as he looked up the length of her body. "I'm gonna eat you all up, gorgeous." Slowly, he licked his lips before bending his head and pressing the first of many heated kisses on her leg. "So just lay back and relax."

Somehow, she didn't think she was going to be able to relax, not with Jace's warm, skilled fingers and his hot mouth working up the inside of her legs, switching from one to the other, nibbling and licking. He started sucking a love bite onto the tender skin of her inner thigh, and the first involuntary moan escaped Nessa's lips.

"If you don't like anything I'm doing, just say so. Or shove me off," Jace lifted his head long enough to say.

"Shut up and carry on," Nessa commanded, her eyes closed.

Jace laughed and obeyed, his fingers sliding further up her thighs. She had strong, muscled legs–he guessed she was on her feet at least eight hours a day in the bar, which required a certain degree of physical fitness even if she did no other exercise. She shivered as he edged higher, goose bumps springing up on her skin; he kissed them, nuzzling at the softness of her inner thighs, tasting her skin. He smelled the salty-sweet tang of her arousal and glimpsed the moisture welling below her neatly-waxed black bush.

As Jace moved higher, Nessa lifted her knees, spreading her thighs wider, giving him tacit permission to do what he liked. His arms slid beneath her thighs, pushing them up onto his shoulders, his hands reaching to grasp her waist.

"You better hold on tight, beautiful." His voice was lower than usual, a sensual rasp which scraped along her nerves, making her shiver in his hold. "I'm about to rock your world."

Nessa's teeth sank into her lower lip. Reaching down, she wrapped her hands around his wrists, holding on as he'd ordered. Jace made a low sound of approval, right before he pressed his tongue firmly against her clit.

Slim fingers clenched on his wrists and Nessa made a hissing noise between her teeth. Her clit was swollen, wet, under his tongue as he worked it over with slow, steady laps. He listened to her breathing quicken, feeling her thighs begin to tremble as they pressed on his shoulders. Patiently, he kept his pace slow, learning the exact pressure and movements to make her squirm and cry out, make her shudder and say his name in a low, husky voice which drove him wild. Grinding his hips against the bed in an effort to contain his own arousal, Jace kept at his self-appointed task until Nessa made a high, keening noise, her whole body tensing up, her hips lifting off the mattress to push herself harder against his face.

He sucked gently on her clit as she came, listening to her gasping breaths. He brought her down with care until she became too sensitive and let go of his wrist to push on the top of his head.

Leaning back and propping his chin on one hand, Jace grinned up at Nessa. "Feeling good?"

She made a vaguely incoherent noise and beckoned at him. "C'mere. Cuddle."

"Sure." He moved up to lie beside her, pulling her into his arms.

She sighed contentedly and reached to kiss him, not minding the taste of her own juices on his lips. Snuggling against him, she held on tightly for a little while. "You're really good at that," Nessa said finally.

"I aim to please."

She giggled at the tone he affected, planting a kiss on his collarbone. "I feel like there's something pressing I should remember, though."

"Yeah?" Jace laughed too. His cock was indeed pressing hard against her stomach, shoving urgently at her even though he wasn't moving.

She hadn't taken a good look yet, so she moved back a little to eye him up. "Mm, hello." He was long and thick, flushed with arousal, pre-cum beading at the tip. Reaching down to take him in hand, Nessa swiped her thumb over the creamy droplet, rubbed it gently into the head of his cock.

Jace made a hungry, eager little sound in his throat. Nessa looked up to meet his eyes and found them closed, his head thrown back. Blindly, he reached out to cup her breasts in his hands, tweaking her nipples, rubbing them between finger and thumb as she stroked his cock.

His attention to her breasts renewed Nessa's arousal, and she reached her free hand under the pillow to grab the condom she'd stashed there after her shower.

Jace opened his eyes as he heard the rip of the packet, smiling to see what she held. "I like a woman who thinks ahead."

She grinned, rolling the condom down over his straining arousal. "Always prepared, that's me."

"Isn't that the Boy Scouts' motto?"

"It's my motto. Call me a boy again and I won't jump your bones and make you scream my name."

Laughing, Jace rolled to his back, letting Nessa climb atop him, straddling his hips. "Trust me, beautiful, nobody could ever mistake you for a boy." His hands described an hourglass shape, tracing the air an inch away from her breasts and hips.

"Good." Grasping the root of his cock in her hand, she lowered herself onto him, guiding him into her wet channel. They both moaned simultaneously as they came together at last, Nessa's hips rolling to take Jace deep inside her body.

He grasped her hips in his hands, bracing her as she set up a rhythm, lifting up slow and then pushing down hard. Jace watched with something approaching awe as Nessa rode him, her head thrown back, long braids swinging around her, breasts bouncing as her strong thigh muscles worked, her body driving him hard and fast toward orgasm. He could feel it coming, the tingle of heat spreading from the base of his spine. Wanting Nessa to come with him, to share the ecstasy, he put a hand between them to rub his finger over her slippery-wet clit.

"Oh God, yes!" Nessa stuttered briefly in her rhythm, before resuming it again. She leaned forward to kiss Jace, sloppy and desperate as the tremors raced through her body, making her breasts tingle and her thighs shake. He held her close, working over her clit, his other hand cupping and squeezing her ass. Her nipples brushed against his chest, the final stimulation to push her over the edge, and she wailed his name against his lips.

Jace roared wordlessly as Nessa tightened around him, the hot wet clamp of her pussy sucking his climax from him. His eyes closed, his body shuddering as his seed jetted hotly deep inside her clutching, willing body. Stars burst behind his eyelids with the utter bliss of the release.

They clung together for several long minutes, breathing fast, skin damp with exertion. Finally, Nessa pulled back slowly and flopped down on the mattress beside Jace, moving closer to press her cheek against his side as he held an arm out toward her. He hugged her close, enjoying the way she fit against him.

It had been a long time since he'd felt so relaxed and comfortable. Tired from the day's exertions, he wanted to stay awake, to savor every moment of being with Nessa, but his eyelids felt incredibly heavy. *Just a few minutes*, he thought as they drifted closed.

Chapter Six

Nessa knew the exact moment Jace fell asleep. Already relaxed, his whole body went limp, his breathing slowing even further. Smiling, she stayed cuddled up to him for a little while, until her stomach rumbled loudly. So loudly, she feared she might wake him up.

Grinning, Nessa eased out from Jace's arm and climbed off the bed. Picking her dress up off the floor, she put it back on and headed for the kitchen to see if she could rescue the pizzas. They weren't fully cooked, so she took them out of the oven and switched it back on again before retrieving the glass of wine she'd abandoned. It was too good to waste. Sipping it as she waited for the oven to heat back up, she looked around the open-plan area with interest. The furniture was minimalist, glass and chrome, but looked expensive. The couch was white leather and a painting hanging above it looked vaguely familiar. Narrowing her eyes, Nessa stared at it for a long moment. It looked like a Georgia O'Keeffe. And she had a sneaking suspicion it was an original.

Well, the house had very clearly been built with no expense spared. The kitchen appliances were top of the line and she was pretty sure the gleaming tiles on the floor were Carrara marble. An O'Keeffe original just fit with everything else. Obviously Jace moved in some pretty exclusive circles.

Sipping her wine and walking around, Nessa peeked through an open door to see a lavishly equipped office, with three computer monitors on one desk. Stock market feeds scrolled silently across the screens.

She'd never asked what Jace actually did, she realized, but a stockbroker made total sense, all things considered. Some sort of commodities trader, maybe. He'd certainly have wealthy friends in that world and be accustomed to the finer things in life, like expensive wine. No wonder he hadn't blinked at opening a $500 bottle of Grange. He probably drank pricier wine every night in New York.

A photograph on the far wall caught her attention. She glanced around, feeling a little like an intruder, before taking a step into the office to look more closely. *The door was open*, she justified to herself.

The photograph was of a woman, slim and fair-haired, smiling into the camera. A baby was held in her arms, as fair and smiling as she was. From the fashion of the woman's clothes and the quality of the image, Nessa thought the picture was maybe thirty years old, but not much more than that. It was taken in Sydney, that much was clear; the distinctive shape of the Opera House was visible in the distance over the woman's left shoulder.

A ping from the kitchen startled her and she hurried back to find the oven was ready. The pizzas would only take a few minutes to finish off, so she figured she should wake Jace. He was tired, but he needed to eat to refill his energy reserves.

"Hey." Sitting on the bed beside him, she shook his shoulder gently. "Wake up, sleepyhead."

"No," he grumbled, an arm snaking around her waist to pull her back down beside him. "Don't wanna."

Laughing, she wiggled to get free, digging her fingertips into his ribs to tickle him. "Come on! Food's ready and now I'm really starving."

He groaned and let her up after stealing a kiss. "Alright, I'm coming!" Yawning, he stumbled after her into the kitchen and found himself pressed to sit down at the dining table while she dished up the food. "Hey, this isn't right. I invited you to dinner, why are you doing the work?"

"Because you fell asleep on me." She brushed a kiss against his temple before sitting down beside him and reaching for the salad she'd quickly thrown together.

Jace looked guilty. "Sorry about that..."

"I'm not offended." Nessa smiled at him to show him she meant it. "It's obvious you're not quite up to peak condition yet, Jace. I'd probably have fallen asleep myself after that spectacular sex, except my stomach was rumbling too loudly to let me!"

"You thought it was spectacular?" He looked almost shy, like he was desperate for her approval.

Putting down her fork, Nessa leaned over to kiss him, slow and sensual. "Damn right, and once we've eaten I'm fully planning to take you back to bed and find out just how good it can get."

"I am very much on board with that plan." Jace smiled at her as she pulled back and picked up her fork again.

"Eat up your vegetables like a good boy then, and I shall think of a suitable treat to give you afterward."

Shoving a deliberately large mouthful of salad into his mouth, he grinned around it as she laughed at him.

***

Nessa woke in the morning light, stretching luxuriantly. Every muscle in her body ached, but in the best possible way. Jace lay sprawled on his back beside her, the sheet tangled around his lean hips. A beam of sunlight slipped past the blinds to cross his chest, turning the brown hairs there to burnished gold. Fast asleep, stubble beginning to sprout on his cheeks, he was easily the most beautiful sight Nessa had ever awakened to.

Honestly, she'd like nothing more than to wake him up and carry on where they'd left off late last night, but the angle of the sun told her she'd already slept long past the time she needed to be up and moving. Slipping quietly from the bed without waking Jace, she found her clothes and pulled them on with a wrinkle of her nose; she'd have to move quickly to get back to her room and have a shower before she needed to get to work. Bending down, she brushed a light kiss over Jace's cheek, but he never even stirred. She crept out with a fond smile back at him. No doubt he'd stop by the bar later. Maybe she'd let him take her out to dinner this time.

***

The pool bar was busy that morning; a large group of new resort guests had arrived the previous day and set up camp. It was a wedding party, Nessa soon discovered, almost thirty young people who were close friends of the bride and groom. They kept her busy serving beer and cocktails from shortly after she opened the bar, too busy to dwell much on the events of the previous day other than feeling the pleasurable ache in her thighs and groin whenever she moved.

It was about two o'clock which she spied Jace arriving; he raised his eyebrows at the crowd around the bar, but found himself a stool at the far end in the shade and waited until she had a moment for him.

"Hey." Nessa dropped a coaster in front of him and smiled. "Sleep well?"

"Better than I have in a long while." Snagging her hand, he dropped a quick kiss on the back of it. "I can see you're busy, angel. Don't worry about me."

"'Kay. Get you a drink?"

"I wouldn't say no to a mojito."

She smiled and reached for the fresh mint stored in the cool box below the bar. "Coming right up."

Nessa had served Jace his drink and was busy making a pitcher of margaritas for the bride and her friends when, from the corner of her eye, she spied Luke walking up to the bar. She wasn't worried about the resort manager dropping by; Luke was a hands-on type and regularly did a walk-around of all the different facilities. She usually saw him at least once a week, and indeed when she was really busy he wasn't averse to rolling up his sleeves and helping serve drinks. He cocked an inquiring brow at her now.

"Need a hand?"

"I'm good, thanks." She gave him a cheerful smile, handing off the pitcher to the drinks waiter. "Get you anything?"

"I could go for a ginger ale," Luke grinned back at her, turning to survey the happy, noisy crowd around the pool as Nessa scooped ice into a glass and topped it off with the amber fluid and a lime wedge.

"Your wish is my command. Hey, I think we need another keg of Carlton Dry; could you do me a favour and have main stores send one down? I've been flat out since opening and I'm worried this one's about tapped out."

"I'll sort it for you." Luke pulled his phone from his pocket and tapped in a message before picking up his drink and toasting her. "Cheers." His gaze slid past her, and a broad grin spread across his face. "Hey, Jace!"

Surprised, Nessa turned to watch as Luke rounded the bar to greet the other man. The expression on Jace's face was oddly panicked.

"I didn't know you knew Luke," she said.

"This guy?" Luke jerked his thumb at Jace's chest. "I hope you've been taking good care of him, Ness. One word from him and even I would be out of a job."

"Don't be ridiculous," Jace said weakly.

"Sure, sure, you know you'd never find anyone as good as me to run this place for you. Trust me, you'll never find a better bartender than Nessa, but since you're drinking one of her creations, I guess you already figured that out." Luke chuckled, placing a friendly hand on Jace's shoulder.

Nessa's jaw had tightened, her lips thinning as she clamped them together. Obviously not trusting herself to speak, she turned away with a curt nod to pour more drinks as her server returned.

"Fuck." Jace shut his eyes and groaned.

"Why do I have the feeling that I just completely put my foot in it?" Luke asked, glancing from Jace to Nessa's turned back and the tightness of her shoulders. "She didn't know who you were?"

"No..."

"And that's a problem because..."

"We've kind of been seeing each other."

"Shit, Jace." Luke blew out his cheeks, shaking his head. "I'm sorry."

Jace shook his head too. "No, it's okay. I should have told her who I was. I knew no good was gonna come of keeping the secret, but it was hard to know what to say."

"Yeah, because 'I'm a billionaire and my family owns this whole island' is kind of a big thing to hit people with right off the bat." Luke's mouth twisted. "I really am sorry. Nessa–well, clearly you've already clued in that she's special. Would you like me to speak to her?"

"Oh hell no! I clean up my own messes, Luke. It wasn't your fault, you had no way to know I'd been misrepresenting myself. No hard feelings." Jace smiled to show Luke he meant it, but he never took his eyes off Nessa's turned back, her tightly controlled movements which spoke of her tension and upset. "I think I'd better give her some space."

"That's probably a good idea unless you want to get brained with a vodka bottle. Want to come for a walk with me?"

"Also probably a good idea." Getting up, Jace cast one more look at Nessa's turned back before following Luke. "So, where are we going?"

"Marine biology labs. They've got a rescued dolphin in the big pool and have been treating cuts on her fins after she tangled with the props on a fishing boat."

Jace couldn't help but think of the day before and Nessa telling him she'd like to take him to meet the marine biologists and view the facilities. It was more than possible that would never happen now.

"Sure," he said finally. "Lead the way."

Chapter Seven

Nessa tried to ignore Jace, but every fibre of her body was aware of him walking away with Luke, of the way he kept looking back at her until they were lost to sight behind the palm trees.

How in hell had she misread him so badly? How had she not picked up the fact he was hiding such a huge secret? Even more importantly, why was he hiding his real identity?

Thinking back, she realized Jace had never actually told her his surname. He'd never asked hers, either. *Could I need any more proof that I'm just a fling?* Disgusted with herself, she broke a glass washing it with unnecessary vigour. Swearing under her breath, she carefully cleaned up the shards and dumped them in the trash.

"Yeah, yeah, I'm coming," she told the waiter coming back to the bar and waving frantically at her. *No time for self-pity now, Nessa. You've got a job to do.*

The bar was busy until her seven o'clock closing, and she had a lot of work to do to clean up and close down. It was almost eight when she finally got to the staff dining room to find some dinner. Cory and Olivia waved her over to eat with them, but she shook her head, in no mood for company, finding a quiet table for one near the back of the room. She finished eating quickly and headed back to her cabin, just wanting to be alone.

There was a figure sitting on the steps leading up to her small veranda. Nessa stopped in her tracks.

"This is a staff-restricted area," she said, finally finding her voice. "Although I suppose that doesn't mean much if you own the entire fucking island."

Jace winced at the fury in her tone, then got to his feet. "Nessa..."

"You *lied* to me." Stepping closer, she jabbed a finger into his chest. "You told me the villa was owned by a friend."

"Well, technically it is--"

"Yeah, because you and your father are friends, right?" She shook her head. "Don't pull that on me, Jace. I can understand why you didn't blurt it out the first moment we met, but once you'd asked me out and I said yes? You should have come clean."

"I should've."

Nessa blinked, surprised at his calm agreement. "Why didn't you, then?" she demanded fiercely, still spoiling for a fight.

"Because you treated me like a normal person. Like just another guy who hit on you at the bar, and it was amazing."

"What? You get off on being shot down or something?"

"No, it's not that. I'm just... so used to being treated as one of *those* Hunters, looked at as some kind of meal ticket, that being treated as though I'm just another guy... it was unique, refreshing. As are you. I didn't want things to change, Nessa, and I knew you'd look at me differently if you knew I was rich."

"You're so dumb!" She shook her head at him. "I already knew you were rich; you run in circles with people who own private holiday villas worth tens of millions of dollars. I figured you for a Wall Street guy, the kind who gets seven or eight figure bonuses a couple of times a year. It makes no difference to me if you're a millionaire or a billionaire; I knew you'd be gone in a few days and I'd still be here, because I'm not the kind of girl who would ever be seen in society on your arm."

"Why not?" He sounded genuinely confused.

"Because I'm black and I'm from the East End of London, which is the wrong side of the tracks no matter how you cut it, and I don't want to be some sort of Pygmalion figure! I'm happy being who I am, Jace. I've made my choices and built myself a life I like; if I want to have a brief affair with some guy who will be gone in a few days, that's my choice too. You, though, you're not just any guy. Word gets out that Jace Hunter is on Sunfish Island dating some black chick and the next thing you know there'll be paparazzi lurking in the shrubbery outside my room trying to take nude photos through the goddamn window!"

He winced again, and Nessa shook her head. "I didn't sign up for that, Jace. When were you going to tell me? Were you ever, or were you just planning to leave and never let me know the truth?"

"I hadn't thought that far ahead. I just... fell for you." He stood still, hands hanging limply by his sides. "I never meant to lie to you. Certainly not to expose you to unwanted attention from the media or anything like that."

Nessa just stared silently at him for several long moments. "I can't do this right now," she said finally. "I'm sorry, Jace. I'm just... not in a place where I can deal with this right now." Walking past him, she unlocked her door.

"Can we at least talk about it?"

"About what?" Turning to look at him, she shook her head. "About the fact that I would never have said yes to a date with you if I'd known who you were? What the hell were you thinking, asking a girl like me out, anyway?"

"What do you mean, a girl like you?" Jace asked, baffled. "You're smart, beautiful, sassy; I'd have asked you out if I met you in a bar in New York instead of one here."

"Even if I was working behind it?" Nessa asked cynically.

"Yes! God damn it, Nessa, I'm not a snob. I don't care what background you came from, what matters is the person you are now."

"A bartender. The billionaire and the bartender, sounds like a Lifetime movie--"

"Stop putting yourself down!" He took two quick steps to stand right in front of her and reached up to grasp her shoulders. "You're not inferior to anyone, Nessa. Not because of your chosen profession or the color of your skin or any other damn thing. You'd slap me silly if I dared to imply that you were, so stop doing it to yourself, and while you're at it, don't treat me differently because of who I am. Money doesn't make anyone special, regardless of how some people seem to think it does."

"Don't be naive! You wouldn't even be back here if it weren't for the fact that you own the damn island!"

"I said it doesn't make me special, not that it doesn't buy me special treatment. I'm just a man, Nessa. The same man who made love to you last night."

His words stirred an instinctive reaction from her as her body remembered all the delicious things they'd done to each other the previous night. She looked away, unwilling to meet his eyes.

Jace's hands dropped from her shoulders. "I'm sorry I didn't tell you the truth," he said quietly. "I just... liked the way you looked at me. The way you talked to me. I didn't want that to change."

"It's changed now," she said, and regretted it immediately when he took a step back.

"Yeah. I guess it has."

There was silence between them for a tense, stinging minute, and then Jace said, "Look, I'm not gonna harass you. You know where to find me. Maybe you can sleep on it and we can talk tomorrow."

"Maybe," Nessa said finally. At least he was putting the ball in her court, giving her the choice; she was pretty sure he wouldn't turn up at her bar.

"Good night, Nessa." Jace's voice was soft, tender. She hardened herself against the impulse to tell him not to go, to grab his sleeve and drag him into her room, to her bed.

"Good night."

***

A knock on the villa's front door at nine o'clock the following evening had Jace falling over his own feet, desperate to get to the door. Yanking it open, he didn't bother to restrain his groan as he came face to face with Luke.

"Expecting someone else?" Luke asked dryly.

"Hoping. Not really expecting." Jace stepped back, gesturing for Luke to come inside. "Want some coffee?"

"Sure." Luke eyed Jace critically. "You look like you've been up all night."

Jace didn't answer, just leading the way to the kitchen and pouring a cup of coffee for Luke. "What brings you here?"

Accepting the cup, Luke leaned back against the kitchen counter and took a sip of the aromatic brew, eyeing Jace over the rim. "I had a visitor this morning, waiting for me when I got to my office. If it's any consolation, I don't think Nessa got any sleep either."

That didn't sound promising. Jace sighed. "She doesn't want to see me, does she?"

"She asked if she could take some holiday days," Luke said. "Girl hasn't taken a vacation since she got here. I said she could go as soon as I could rustle up a cover roster for her bar, which will probably take me until the end of the day. I'd say it's highly likely she'll be on the boat to Airlie tomorrow morning, so if you want to talk to her, today's your chance."

For a moment, he was tempted; he considered going straight for the door and rushing over to the resort to find Nessa. Reason won out, though.

"She's doing this to get away from me. Going to find her would be a pretty shitty thing to do when she's clearly trying to escape." The words burned like acid in his throat, but he made himself accept the truth. Nessa wanted to get away from him. He wasn't about to force himself on her, not now and not ever.

Luke studied him in silence for a minute before nodding and setting down his cup. "I'm sorry I dropped you in it," he said, "but you should have told her the truth from the beginning."

"I know."

"Good." Luke nodded curtly. "You might be my boss, but I can't have my staff harassed, Jace. Thank you for doing the right thing."

"No hard feelings," Jace said honestly. None of this was Luke's fault; indeed, he respected the other man more now, because Luke had obviously come here willing to stand up to him for Nessa's sake, even knowing Jace could fire him on a whim. "I'm glad she, and all your other staff, have someone who's willing to be in their corner." He offered his hand to shake. "And tell Nessa... well, tell her if she wants a holiday, that's great, but she doesn't need to leave because of me. Sunfish Island is her home and I don't want her to feel uncomfortable here. I'll stay a day or two longer, but I'm feeling a lot better now. It's time I got back to work."

Luke accepted his hand and smiled. "I'll let her know, but I'm gonna encourage her to take a few days. She could use a break. And let me know before you head out, yeah? It's been good getting to know you."

"You too." Jace was coming to think of Luke as a friend, he realized; even though Luke had known his identity from the beginning, he'd still treated him as 'normal'. Would Nessa have done the same, if he'd given her the chance?

He'd never know, now. Bleakly, Jace admitted to himself he'd absolutely blown it, as Luke took his leave and departed, the door closing behind him with a final-sounding thud. Nessa didn't want to see him, was even making plans to get away from Sunfish in order to avoid him. Whatever dreams he might have been harbouring for the two of them were now dead in the water.

Picking up the phone, he made a call, arranging for one of the Hunter Enterprises private jets to pick him up at Hamilton Island Airport the following morning. He might not head back to New York yet, but he was sure he'd find something to do at the Sydney offices to keep his mind off the broken, shattered pieces of his heart.

Chapter Eight

"What the hell do you think you're doing?"

Jace looked up in surprise at the yell and smiled at his father. "Working."

"You're supposed to be relaxing in the sunshine," John Hunter said gruffly, crossing the office and reaching to pull his son into a hug as Jace stood up. "You're still too damned thin, though at least you've got some colour back in your face. Why'd you leave Sunfish?"

"It was just time, Dad. I hadn't been to the Sydney offices in a while, figured I'd drop in and see how things are here." He smiled through the open door at the anxious PA hovering outside and waved her off before closing the door. While he'd left orders he wasn't to be disturbed, he hadn't expected his father to turn up. She could hardly have kept the company CEO from walking in.

"Humph." John scowled. "Why didn't you tell me?"

"Because you'd probably have ordered the pilots not to pick me up, and I'd have had to get a commercial flight. Which would be boring." Jace grinned.

"You're not too proud to fly commercial."

"No, but I didn't want to deal with anyone who recognized me asking why."

John grunted again, but Jace could tell he was already forgiven. "So talk to me about the island. How did you like it?" John grabbed a bottle of water from the refrigerator hidden in an antique wooden cabinet and took a seat.

"It's beautiful," Jace said, knowing the word was inadequate. "And the setup is magnificent. I met quite a few guests and nobody had a single gripe. The staff are absolutely on top of customer service, going above and beyond to make everybody happy. I was incredibly impressed with Luke Collyer."

"Good man, that." John nodded in agreement.

"It was really nice," Jace said, thinking it through for the first time, "to be in the middle of one of our businesses, for once. On the ground floor, seeing how the service gets delivered to customers. The staff at Sunfish, they're the heart and soul of that place. They're the face Hunter Enterprises shows to customers, and I gotta say they're doing a hell of a job."

John cocked his head curiously, listening to Jace's impassioned words. "You really liked being there, huh?"

"Yeah." More than liked, he'd loved it. He'd felt comfortable there, for the first time in a long time. The staff on Sunfish were down-to-earth, not afraid to get their hands dirty, hardworking people with a genuine love for what they did. They were far removed from the high-society crowd of New Yorkers who'd been Jace's social circle for the last few years. The mere thought of returning to that sterile, artificial life repulsed him now, and he knew he had to say something.

"Dad–even though I'm feeling better, I don't think I want to go back to the New York office. I... don't think I want to take over Hunter Enterprises from you. Ever."

To his complete astonishment, his father smiled broadly. "Took you long enough to figure that out."

Jace's jaw dropped open. "What?"

"Oh, you could do it, and you'd do it damned well, but you'd hate every minute of it. You're not ruthless enough, son. I love you more than I've ever been able to express, but you've got your mother's heart. God rest her soul."

Jace could hardly believe his ears. He'd always been afraid of disappointing his father, had always striven to be someone John could be proud of. "What will you do with the company?" he asked, almost afraid to hear the answer. "I don't want you to run yourself into the ground with it." It was a large part of the reason he'd worked so hard to be able to step up, knowing John wasn't getting any younger.

"I'm gonna privatize the company. The market's ripe for an IPO, we'll list forty per cent of the stock initially and see how things go. I'll put twenty percent in a trust for you and your heirs; Hunter Enterprises will always look after you, but it was my dream, not yours."

Jace was too choked up to speak.

John reached out to grab him into a tight hug. "I'm damned proud of you, son. Always will be. But you gotta find your own dreams to follow."

Father and son embraced for several long minutes, and John's voice was husky when he finally pulled back and said, "So what's your plan?"

"I don't know, yet." Except he rather thought he did. "I think I'd like to go back into architecture."

"You did graduate top of your class when you got your degree, and God knows Hunter Enterprises can always keep you in work even if you don't take on any other clients." John smiled a little mistily at him.

"I think I'd like to design houses rather than commercial premises, though." Spending time in the villa he'd designed as his graduation project had made him think more about the ergonomics of design, about marrying beautiful design with a home that was easy to live in and maintain.

"The only thing I have to ask you is that you keep everything on the down low until we've taken the initial stock offering to market." John gave him a serious look. "There are a fair number of our senior staff, folks who've been with us a long time, who have a stake in the company."

Jace knew most of the people his father was talking about. He'd grown up around them, called them uncles and aunts, absorbed the business of Hunter Enterprises by learning from their expertise.

"It's only right to do our best to make those shares worth as much as possible," Jace agreed. "Of course, Dad. You can count on me."

"I know." John clapped a strong hand on his shoulder. "We're taking Hunter Enterprises straight to the top of the Dow Jones."

"Just one thing," Jace said. "That twenty percent share you're putting into a trust? Could it maybe include complete ownership of Sunfish Island?"

"Of course." John looked at him curiously. "Sunfish is pretty special to you, eh?"

"It's a pretty special place." He wanted to make sure nobody else could ever come in and impose their own wishes on the island, sack staff and change the guest relations policies that gave the resort such a special atmosphere. Wanted to make sure no matter what, that Sunfish would always be Nessa's refuge.

"It's yours. Forever. I'll make sure of it," John promised, no further questions asked, for which Jace was grateful.

***

The news that Hunter Enterprises was going public sent shock waves through the staff at Sunfish Island. They all worried about what it might mean for their jobs, at least until John Hunter phoned Luke personally and told him Sunfish Island was being specifically excluded from the sale.

"Ownership of the island, the resort and everything to do with it has already been transferred into a trust, the sole beneficiary of which is Jace, at the present time, though any heirs of his will also be included at a later date."

After getting his breath back, Luke had to ask why.

A rich chuckle answered the question. "Seems he fell in love with the place, wanted to make sure no corporate types could come in and ruin it. He has ultimate say over anything that happens on the island now–and he asked me to let you know that he has full confidence in you." John paused to let that sink in. "You impressed him, Luke. He'll be in touch soon to let you know that himself, I'm sure, but we're both up to our eyes at the moment, as I'm sure you can imagine. He's in London right now."

Luke was still in a certain degree of shock. "This is so unexpected, Mr. Hunter, but thank you so much for calling to tell me in person. I really appreciate it."

"You're welcome. Don't know what magic you're working on that island but Jace came back a changed man, determined to follow his own dreams. If it was something you said to him, thank you."

"I... don't think it was me."

"No?" John asked curiously.

Luke said nothing.

There was a brief silence on the line, and then John said, "There was a girl, huh? Jace wouldn't talk about it, but I read between the lines."

Luke rubbed his forehead, wondered how much he should say. "He didn't tell her who he was. I accidentally dropped him in it, and she didn't take it well."

"Ahh," John said. "Well, whoever she is, she made him take a good hard look at himself, and he realized he didn't like the path he was on. I must ask you to keep this particular tidbit quiet, but after the stock goes to market, Jace is stepping back from his role here. Going back to architecture, and I have to tell you, I couldn't be happier for him."

Thanking John, Luke ended the call and sat dumbfounded in his office chair for several minutes, thinking through the implications of what he'd just learned. At last, a broad smile on his face, he pushed himself to his feet. The staff would all be relieved to know their jobs were safe, but there was one person he really should tell first.

***

Nessa had taken a few days off after she broke up with Jace, but knowing he'd left the island, she found herself returning sooner than she had originally planned. Dropping back into her usual routine, she still sometimes found herself looking at the seat he'd always taken at the end of the bar, wishing he was there, looking at her with those steady ice-blue eyes. She'd asked herself a thousand times if she'd done the right thing in ending their relationship. *We were ships that passed in the night,* she told herself. *Now I'm back in my safe harbour and he's off across the ocean somewhere.*

"Hey." It was Luke who slid onto the bar stool, smiling at her. "Got some news."

"You're not saving it for the staff meeting?" She wiped up a small puddle of spilled soda on the bar with a rag, but couldn't avoid meeting his eyes. It was quiet today, and she had no customers to tend to.

"Thought you might like to hear it first. Turns out Hunter Enterprises no longer owns Sunfish."

"What?" Nessa's jaw dropped. "It's already been sold–before the share offer? Who's the new owner?"

"Jace Hunter."

The cloth she'd been using to wipe the bar fell from nerveless fingers. "Jace?"

"Got the news from John Hunter himself. Jace apparently wanted to make sure Sunfish was safe from any corporate meddling. I've been assured he has complete faith in my ability to run the place... though I'm pretty sure there's one particular staff member I daren't fire."

Nessa found herself clinging to the edge of the bar to hold herself up because her legs felt too shaky to support her. "He did that for me?"

"Pretty sure you're a fairly large part of his motive, yeah." Luke eyed her sympathetically. "You know," he said in an apparent non sequitur, "Olivia still knows a hell of a lot of New York movers and shakers from her days as a marketing guru in the Big Apple."

Nessa eyed him curiously. "So?"

Luke grinned. "So, I have an idea."

Chapter Nine

Nessa smoothed her hands over the skirt of her tangerine silk dress once more, before stepping forward and handing the printed invitation she held to one of the PAs manning the door into the massive ballroom. Olivia's friend had assured her the invitation was completely legit, but Nessa still had the terrible feeling the PA, a beautiful blonde with a snooty expression on her face, would dismiss her as a fraud and probably have her arrested.

"Your name is Tennessee Williams?" The blonde gave her a sceptical look. Nessa cursed the last-minute rush which had meant Olivia had to email her friend a copy of Nessa's passport in order to get the invite organized in time for the event.

"Blame my mother, and please, please just call me Nessa," Nessa replied.

The blonde actually chuckled. "I know just how you feel. I'm Donna... but my real name is Chardonnay."

They exchanged conspiratorial grins, and Donna found Nessa's name on the list on her tablet and checked it off. "Have a good evening... Nessa."

"Thank you, Donna." Taking a deep breath, she tightened her grip on the fashionable little clutch Olivia's friend had provided, along with the designer dress and heels, before moving through the huge doorway into the ballroom.

Luke's brilliant idea had been for Nessa to fly to New York and use Olivia's old contacts to wrangle herself an invitation to the special Hunter Enterprises post-IPO party. Nessa still wasn't entirely sure how they'd managed to talk her into it, but here she was, wearing a dress worth more than a month's salary and a pair of shoes which probably cost as much as a new car, despite each apparently consisting of little more than a couple of flimsy straps, some rhinestones, and a sharp heel.

There had to be five hundred people here already and more arriving by the minute. How was she ever to even find Jace, never mind get close to him? She'd arrived in New York early that morning and spent the day being pampered in a ridiculously high-class beauty salon before coming here, but she'd taken the time to check the stock market. Wall Street was going crazy over the offering, the stock already soaring to almost five times its initial list price. Everyone here tonight looked to be celebrating pretty hard.

"Nessa?" a voice said behind her and she startled, spinning around and almost tripping over her heels. A slim Chinese woman in a designer business suit stood there; agelessly beautiful, her eyes told Nessa she wasn't nearly as young as she might be mistaken for.

Who the hell knows I'm here? "Um, yes, I'm Nessa."

"I thought you might be. I'm Nancy, Jace's assistant."

"He knows I'm here?" Nessa fought the urge to panic.

"Actually, he doesn't." Nancy reached out, giving her a gently reassuring pat on the arm. "Luke Collyer called Mr. Hunter–Mr. *John* Hunter, that is–and let him know you were coming. John asked me to be on the lookout for you."

"Oh." Nessa's shoulders relaxed a tiny bit.

They tensed right back up when Nancy said, "I can take you to Jace now, if you'd like?"

"I think maybe I need a drink first. Liquid courage and all that," Nessa admitted.

Nancy smiled, beckoning to a nearby waiter. "After the chaos this last week has been, I wouldn't say no myself. Champagne?" She scooped two crystal flutes off the waiter's proffered tray and handed one to Nessa. "Cheers."

"Bottoms up," Nessa said with a smile in return. The champagne was fabulous; Cristal, she was pretty sure, though the glasses were pre-filled and she couldn't see a bottle.

"Don't go anywhere," Nancy warned the waiter before draining her glass, handing back the empty and taking another one. "Come on, Nessa, keep up," she chided.

Laughing, she decided she rather liked Nancy. Nessa followed suit and claimed another glass. On an empty stomach, the bubbles went straight to her head, making her feel floaty and relaxed.

"Okay," she declared, "I think I can face him now."

"Marvellous." Nancy linked her free arm through Nessa's and drew her through the crowd. She seemed to know almost everyone there, greeting many people by name but forging an inexorable path onward until the last group of people melted aside and Nessa saw Jace.

Wearing a pale grey suit perfectly tailored to his tall, lean form, his brown hair immaculately cut, his jaw clean-shaven, he looked every inch the billionaire.

Right down to the famous supermodel on his arm, laughing as he spoke and leaning in to press a kiss on his cheek, dangerously close to his mouth, leaving a scarlet imprint of her lips behind. A camera flashed to capture the moment and the group surrounding Jace laughed, knowing what picture they'd see in the society pages of the papers tomorrow.

Nessa froze like a deer in headlights, staring as Jace turned his head to speak to the other woman. His gaze passed over her briefly, unseeingly. But that was enough. She yanked her arm from Nancy's and spun on her heel, rushing through the crowd as fast as she could manage in her narrow-skirted dress and ridiculously high heels, blinded by the tears running down her cheeks.

***

"Nessa?" It took a moment for Jace's weary brain to process what his eyes had just seen; his gaze snapped back to the woman he'd spotted in the crowd. She'd already pulled loose from Nancy and turned away, running through the crowd, long black braids swinging behind her.

Yanking his own arm free from the woman trying desperately to cling to him, Jace rushed forward. "Was that really Nessa?" he demanded of Nancy, waiting only for her nod before sprinting after Nessa's disappearing back.

She'd come. She'd come to him. Only to arrive just as some fortune-hungry attention-seeker tried to sink her claws into him. He could only imagine what Nessa must have thought of what she'd just seen.

The crowd slowed him down, stockbrokers high on champagne and success trying to catch onto him, shouting their congratulations, demanding to know where he was going in such a rush. He ignored them all.

"Nessa!" he yelled, losing sight of her briefly. Damn, she was quick even in a dress and heels; he pulled loose from the hands grabbing at him and raced after her. "Nessa!"

By the time he reached the doors, she'd disappeared. He looked frantically around, wondering which way she'd gone.

"Did you see a beautiful black girl in an orange dress run past?" he begged the PAs at the door, all staring at him as though he'd lost his mind.

"Nessa?" Donna, one of his junior assistants, asked. At his nod, she continued, "She went that way." She pointed to the hotel's main doors leading out onto Fifth Avenue.

"Bless you!" He followed at a dead run, but reached the exit just in time to see a cab pull away from the curb. "Damn, damn, damn!"

"Mr. Hunter?" Turning, he found Donna behind him, her expression anxious. "Is everything alright?"

He took a deep breath. "No."

He knew Nancy had trained the girl well when her expression smoothed to steely resolve, her chin lifting.

"Tell me what you need, sir."

***

The only good thing about her hasty dash home was when she'd boarded the flight still in her designer dress and heels, the check-in agent had taken one look at her outfit and given her a free first-class upgrade. The plane had been halfway across the Pacific when Nessa finally gave in and cried. A concerned flight attendant promptly descended on her with tissues, chocolate, and alcohol, which at least made the interminable flight seem to pass a little faster, even though she couldn't sleep.

At last, she stepped off the late afternoon boat from Hamilton Island and headed for her cabin, feet dragging with weariness. Falling face-down onto her bed still in her designer finery, she fell into blissful unconsciousness.

A loud rapping on her door woke her up. Groaning, Nessa pushed herself off the bed and headed for the door to open it.

"Oh. It's you," she said to Luke. Holding up a hand to forestall whatever he was about to say, she told him, "I don't want to talk about it. I just want to get back to work, okay?"

Luke shrugged after staring at her in silence for a moment. "Fine by me. It's nearly ten, though. Are you working today or is Eric covering the pool bar?"

She'd slept for almost sixteen hours! Startled, Nessa nodded. "I'm working." Looking down at herself, realizing she was still wearing the designer gown, she said, "I'll just take a shower and head on down there."

***

It felt good to step behind her bar again, even if her bottles were all in a muddle, she saw as she unlocked the grille covering them and pulled it back. Shaking her head, she started sorting them out. Why on earth was the Bacardi on the top shelf? She used it every five minutes making cocktails. Putting it back front and centre in its usual place on the lowest shelf, and beginning to sort the other bottles, she whirled around as a voice said, "Hey, Nessa."

It couldn't be... but it was, it was indeed Jace, leaning on the edge of the bar, wearing his old T-shirt with the sleeves ripped out, his sunglasses pushed up on top of his head, a good day's worth of stubble gracing his jaw.

The gin bottle Nessa was holding slid from nerveless fingers and hit the rubber mat at her feet, fortunately not smashing. She stood rooted to the spot, eyes on Jace, unable to believe what she was seeing.

"Don't be throwing the booze around, now." He straightened up and came around the bar, picking up the gin and putting it back on the shelf. Turning back to look down into Nessa's stunned face, he pleaded, "Say something, Nessa."

"What are you doing here?" she asked numbly.

"I'm home."

"What?"

"This is home, now. The villa is, anyway. I'm no longer working for Hunter Enterprises; I'm starting a private architecture consultancy and design business, based right here."

She couldn't make a sound come out, but her lips shaped the word, "Why?" and Jace understood.

"Because of you. You made me see that the life I was living was slowly killing me, that I had to make a change, find what I really wanted and go after it. This is what I really want to do, Nessa, and you," he lifted a shaking hand, tracing a finger gently down her cheek, "*you* are who I really want to be with. No high society lifestyle, just you and me and the things that make both of us happy."

"The girl I saw you with in New York...?"

"I'd just met her and she clamped on like a leech. I couldn't ditch her fast enough. I still can't believe you really came." He was still touching her, his hand curling around the back of her neck to draw her closer. "I barely got a glimpse of you, but you looked amazing."

Nessa laughed shakily. "I felt a fool. I didn't fit, there."

"You fit with me, and that's all I care about. We were both square pegs in round holes in our old lives, but put two square pegs together and you get... a really nice rectangle... okay, that analogy fell down a bit there."

"I like rectangles," she said nonsensically, but Jace's smile lit up as though she'd said three quite different words, and maybe in a way she had.

"I like rectangles too," he agreed, drawing her closer and bending his head until their lips met in a thoroughly satisfying kiss.

~ The End ~

*I hope you enjoyed reading **The Reluctant Billionaire**. I wanted to write a story where the hero discovers that all the money in the world can't buy him happiness. Sometimes, our path lies another way.*

*Read on for **Her Fake Island Wedding**, the next book in the **Island Escapes** series!*

Her Fake Island Wedding

Island Escapes Book 3

Caitlyn Lynch

SHENANIGANS PRESS

shenaniganspress.com/EN

Contents

Chapter One

"It's a disaster," Lucy declared melodramatically, sliding her lunch tray onto the table. It was lunchtime, and Sunfish Island Resort's staff cafeteria was busy, staff members hurrying in and out to grab a bite in between tasks.

Lucy had joined a large group of friends, and several of them looked up at her words.

"What's up, girlfriend?" Olivia, the resort's marketing manager, asked with an amused smile. Her American accent was just one of a dozen different accents in the room; although the majority of the resort's staff were Australian, there were plenty of other nationalities represented.

"You look as though someone stole your puppy," Nessa, the resort's best bartender and Lucy's fellow Englishwoman, put in.

"Worse," Lucy said dismally. "My mother's coming to visit next week."

That provoked laughter around the table. She scowled impartially at all of them.

"You've only been here a month," Olivia pointed out. "And why is she coming now? Did you warn her this is the hot season?"

"I did, and she says she's already booked her flights because she got them cheap. You don't understand what a disaster this is, guys. She'll spend the whole visit pestering to know whether I've found a man yet." Lucy poked at her salad with a fork miserably. Her mother had always been both overprotective and demanding with her only child, and now that Lucy had turned thirty, the insistence that she needed to hurry up and find a man to father her children before it was too late had only intensified.

At the same time, her mother liked to denigrate Lucy's judgement, always telling her that she had terrible taste in men and she mustn't rush things or she'd pick the wrong man and be literally left holding the baby.

It took everything Lucy had to not retort "Like you were?" every time her mother trotted out that particular criticism. Escape from her mother's constant nagging was just one of the reasons why she'd applied for the research position at Sunfish Island's marine biology centre, and actually being awarded the post was literally a dream come true.

"Is she really that bad?" Nessa asked sympathetically, and Lucy raised her eyes to meet the bartender's.

"You have *no idea*," she said dismally. "I knew she'd come out, especially when the contract actually included four weeks' free accommodation for visitors, but I really didn't think it'd be so soon."

The few blissful weeks she'd spent on Sunfish Island had been among the best of her life. From the day she arrived, she'd been warmly welcomed by her fellow marine biologists and the staff of the wider resort alike. Her job, studying the effects of coral replanting and regeneration on damaged parts of the magnificent Great Barrier Reef, was quite literally her dream and had been ever since she was a kid picking up shells and starfish on the beach near her childhood home at Dover.

"We'll help distract her," Olivia offered. "Won't we, Cory?"

Her boyfriend, Sunfish's activities director, looked up from his lunch with a nod and a smile. Cory Gillette was one of the best-looking men Lucy had ever met; tall, blond and athletic, he looked like a fourth Hemsworth brother. And he wasn't even the only one around the table who would fit right in with that famously attractive family.

"Does she dive?" Bryce was the resort's resident dive instructor, and had partnered with Lucy numerous times on her reef dives. "I can put her on the daily schedule, no charge... she'll be too tired to nag you."

Lucy smiled at him. If Bryce was only a few years older, she thought wistfully, she'd have made a serious pass at him, but he was only twenty-four and looked even younger. Blond, tanned and beautiful, she just had to appreciate him visually.

"Unfortunately, she's terrified of open water. Convinced there are sharks in it."

"Well, there are sharks in it," Bryce said equably. "Mostly only the little reef sharks around here, though."

"Somehow I don't think that would reassure her!"

Bryce grinned cheerfully at her, and Lucy found herself smiling back. It was difficult to stay down around Bryce for long; he was too relentlessly happy.

"We'll just have to put *you* on the dive schedule every day, then," he said.

"Then I'd be accused of avoiding her. No," she sighed. "There's no winning with my mother, not unless I produce a fiancé out of thin air and promise to start popping out babies nine months to the day after the wedding."

"That's the solution, then," Cory piped up, a wicked glint in his eyes. "We'll find you a fake fiancé!"

Chapter Two

"Wait, what?" Lucy blinked, startled.

"Fake fiancé," Cory smirked. "Just think how amazed your mother will be! She'd be completely thrown. Bet she wouldn't hassle you at all."

"Better yet," Bryce put in, eyes beginning to gleam in the way Lucy had already learned meant he was formulating some prank or other, "when she arrives, you should totally tell her that you have the best surprise ever for her - you're getting married while she's here! You were going to wait, but since she's here, the opportunity is just too good to miss!"

Everyone around the table, including Lucy, broke up laughing.

"Oh, man. Mum's expression would be *epic*," she said wistfully. "It'd all fall apart when I have neither a boyfriend nor a fiancé to present, though."

"Why not? I'll do it."

She gaped at him.

Bryce grinned. "Most epic prank ever! C'mon, it'll be fun. Mrs Heathers is a bit too stick-in-the mud to go for it, but Luke's a registered marriage celebrant as well, for when she has her days off. He'll totally play along, he could even fake up the registration and marriage certificates for you." He was referring to Luke Collyer, the resort's general manager.

"D'you know," Lucy said slowly, "I'm almost tempted to go along with you, just to shut Mum up." She looked thoughtfully at Bryce. They hadn't really spent a lot of time together, but she knew he had a wicked sense of humour and loved pranks. He was certainly good-looking enough to make any girl's heart flutter, with his height, bronzed tan and sparkling blue eyes, though his shaggy fair hair might need a tidy up. Or maybe not, she mused. It made him look even younger and more boyish, which would probably offend her mother even more.

"How old are you again?" she checked.

"Twenty-four," Bryce said easily. "I can be your toyboy!"

Cory was roaring with laughter, Olivia and Nessa giggling as well, egging her on and saying she should do it. Olivia offered one of her rarely-used designer dresses from her days as a New York marketing guru to use as a wedding gown, and suddenly Lucy was in.

"If Luke's up for it, I'll do it," she said decisively. "I'll owe you though, Bryce."

He grinned and gave her a cheeky wink. "I'll think of some way you can repay me!"

She couldn't help but laugh. No, she had no doubts about Bryce pulling off his part; he was a born actor and could easily have made his living on the stage or in front of the camera if he hadn't been so in love with the ocean. He'd play the besotted fiancé to the hilt, and all she would have to do was worry about containing her laughter and not giving the game away to her mother.

"Are you really going to do it?" Olivia asked.

"If Bryce is really up for dealing with my impossible mother, yes," Lucy declared.

"Charming impossible mothers is my speciality," Bryce claimed, making her laugh again.

"Right... well, if you are, I might be able to help with some of the stage setting," Olivia said. "We wanted to redo the weddings pages on the website anyway, and if you were agreeable to having all the photos used for that purpose, I could get you the photographer for free, and flowers. Might be able to talk Luke into giving you a table at *La Sirène*." She named the resort's Michelin-starred French restaurant.

Everything was moving a bit fast for Lucy, as Olivia pulled out her phone and started booking things into her diary. "Whoa," she protested. "I didn't even ask Luke if he'd go along with the fake-wedding plan yet!"

"Then you'd better go find him, hadn't you?" Olivia didn't even look up from her phone. "When does your mother arrive?"

Recognising Olivia was in full-on marketing guru mode, Lucy sighed and gave up the dates.

"Excellent, we don't have any weddings scheduled on the twentieth. I'll get Terry and Jerome on the case."

"Olivia, I really don't need wedding planners!" Lucy protested, starting to panic slightly.

Olivia looked up. "*You* might not, but if we're going to use this as a marketing opportunity, we're going to use every resource the resort has." She tilted her head, considering Bryce. "Including the hair salon... go book in for a haircut. I'll get hair and makeup for Lucy arranged on the morning of the wedding..."

"Last chance to back out," Bryce told Lucy jokingly.

"I think I should be saying that to you," she pointed out. "There's nothing in this for you but loads of hassle."

He smiled, showing the dimple in his tanned cheek. "Hey. It'll be fun. Come on, let's leave Olivia to her plotting and go find Luke. We should probably emphasise the marketing aspects rather more than the prank part..."

"You're not wrong," Lucy agreed, giving up on her lunch. She wasn't hungry any more anyway.

Olivia looked up from her texting to say "Stop by my place later and we'll look through my dresses... though I'm thinking I might just get some designer samples flown in from Sydney..."

"Run away, while you still can!" Nessa said laughingly, and Lucy and Bryce took to their heels.

"Are you quite sure about this?" Lucy asked Bryce as the pair of them headed for reception and the general manager's office located on the floor above. "I mean, you just volunteered for a fun prank and suddenly Olivia's turning it into a production of *Ben Hur*."

"Doesn't worry me," Bryce said with a shrug. "What about you? It's one thing to tell your mom about a fake fiancé but quite another to go through with a major production of a fake wedding."

"Yeah." Lucy chewed on her lower lip as they walked, unaware of Bryce staring at her mouth in fascination. "Frankly, I'm looking forward to it. I might not ever even tell her it was all a fake... I'll just tell her we changed our minds and got divorced."

"Oh, you never know," Bryce said. He put on an affected tone, making her grin at his light-hearted attitude. "You might find you like being married to me!"

Chuckling, Lucy aimed a light punch at his thick biceps muscle. "Sure, but being 'married' is gonna cramp *your* style!"

***

Lucy hadn't the faintest idea how crazy he was about her, Bryce realized ruefully. He'd thought Cory had given him away when his friend slyly suggested the fake fiancé idea while staring pointedly at Bryce, but Lucy seemed completely oblivious to the giant-sized crush Bryce had nursed ever since the beautiful, brilliant scientist arrived on the island.

Some days it seemed as though everyone but Lucy knew about his crush, too. Nessa had even made a teasing remark about it being a good thing the seat next to Bryce was vacant when Lucy entered the staff restaurant, else he'd probably have pushed someone out of the way in order to sit next to her.

He'd wanted to protest that he wasn't quite that much of a hormonal teenager, but Lucy caught his eye and gave her usual sunny smile, and the words died on his lips. Because where Lucy Manning was concerned, Bryce's hormones were indeed ruling his head.

Trying to keep his eyes off the perfect curve of her bottom in her thin shorts as she trotted up the stairs ahead of him, Bryce once again chastised himself for perving on her. Lucy had made it clear he was in the friend zone right from the beginning.

Pretending to be her fake fiancé was probably a recipe for disaster, but there was no way he could resist the opportunity to spend more time with her, maybe even romance her a little, get her to look at him as something other than her young friend she dived with sometimes.

"I'm not worried," he answered her comment about cramping his style. He hadn't had a date in months; the resort had a strict no-fraternisation policy between staff and guests, and the only staff member he'd felt any sort of romantic interest in was Lucy herself, Lucy of the fox-chestnut hair and the vivid blue eyes.

She wrinkled her pert, freckled little nose at him.

"Oh your own head be it, then. Just remember, you *volunteered*," she said in the English accent that always made his knees go weak, and opened the door to the general manager's outer office.

Luke's PA looked up from her computer and smiled at them both. "Can I help you?"

"Is Mr Collyer available?" Lucy asked politely.

"He's between meetings at the moment; I'll just check if he can see you. Please wait."

Within moments, though, they were being shown into Luke's office, large windows on two sides looking over the resort's main pool area and the exclusive beach bungalows beyond it. Luke rose from his desk, piled high with paperwork, to greet them.

"Hey, Bryce, uh... oh God, I'm so sorry, I've forgotten your name." He looked sheepish, which was a quite adorable expression on his handsome, tanned face, Lucy thought.

"Lucy Manning," she said with a smile, waving off his forgetfulness. "Hey, you've got several hundred staff of your own here, no reason why you should remember someone who doesn't even work directly for the resort!"

"I do know you're one of our marine biologists," Luke said, gesturing them both to chairs. "What can I do for the two of you, anyway? Some sort of diving issue?"

"Not at all," Lucy said, looking sideways at Bryce. Deliberately, he folded his arms and grinned at her. Watching her fumble her way through this promised to be highly entertaining. She narrowed her eyes at him, but he wasn't about to help out. It was her mother they were staging this whole show, after all. He was just along for the ride.

"We were wondering if you'd fake marry us," Lucy blurted, and Bryce almost choked at the expression of complete shock on Luke's face.

Chapter Three

"I'm sorry, *what*?" Luke said eventually, clearly finding himself unable to add up the pieces to make any sort of sensible explanation.

Lucy rushed into a babbled explanation about her mother coming to visit and Lucy's reasoning for producing a fake fiancé to get her mother off her back.

"I've heard worse plans for dealing with impossible parents, but actually going through with a fake wedding?" Luke looked sceptical.

"Well, that wasn't part of the original plan, except then Bryce suggested it and Olivia sort of took over. She says she has a plan to redo the weddings section of the website, and if we'll let you use the photos then you might be willing to go along and fake marry us." Lucy looked at him hopefully. "Although I'd have thought you might want to hire models or something..."

"You two are both good-looking enough to be models," Luke waved off that suggestion. "You look good together, actually." He tilted his head, considering them. "So... basically we stage it just like a real wedding, take a ton of photos we can use for publicity purposes, and this has the side effect of getting your mother off your case?"

Lucy smiled hopefully and nodded, and Luke looked at Bryce.

"And what's in this for you?"

"Helping out a friend... and pulling off a really epic hoax." Bryce grinned, knowing that the latter comment would be enough to convince Luke he had no ulterior motives. Except, Luke was general manager for a reason, and part of that included great insight into people.

"Hm," Luke said, his eyes narrowed, but he didn't ask Bryce any more questions.

***

Lucy held her breath as Luke looked at them thoughtfully, his gaze moving from her to Bryce and back again. Leaning back in his chair, he steepled his fingers and said nothing for a long moment, obviously considering the plan for flaws. "You could fill in the actual legal paperwork required by law to get married in Australia, and show your mother a copy," he suggested eventually. "It's the Notice Of Intended Marriage form, which has to be filed a minimum of one month before a wedding and is then valid for eighteen months, but it's not legally binding or anything."

"That works," Lucy looked at the calendar on his desk, counting days. "That would mean we could have the ceremony on the date Olivia suggested, the twentieth, two days before my mother leaves."

"The only flaw in the plan is that I have to register an actual marriage within fourteen days, and if your mother happened to look up the records later she wouldn't be able to find it. Though I presume you'll have admitted to the prank by then?" Luke raised his eyebrows at her interrogatively.

"Sure," Lucy agreed, though she hadn't really thought through when and how she might tell her mother. That was a problem for Future Lucy, and in the present she had a fake wedding to plan.

"As long as you don't sign the marriage register, it's not legal, then." Luke shrugged. "I can say all the usual words. I'm guessing you brought this to me rather than Mrs Heathers because you thought I'd be more amenable to the idea?"

"I don't know her," Lucy disclaimed, but Bryce chirped up again.

"It was my idea, and yes. She's a dear, and she's adapted really well to performing same-sex weddings now the law has changed, but I don't see her being party to any deception. She'd do the marketing part of it but she wouldn't agree to deceive Lucy's mum, I think."

"You're probably right. She hasn't had a break for a while... I might encourage her to take that whole week off," Luke said with a little glint in his eye. "Just to make sure there's no risk of anything slipping our which shouldn't."

He'd bought into the plan, Lucy thought with relief. "Thanks, Mr Collyer," she said gratefully.

"Call me Luke." He smiled warmly at her. "Just a moment and I'll print this form off... get it back to me before five today so I can scan and file it, please."

They waited while he clicked his mouse and tapped a few keys on the keyboard, and after a moment the printer whirred to life. Luke handed the still-warm pages over with a nod of dismissal, and they escaped his office with the papers clutched tightly in Lucy's sweating hand.

"God, that was nerve-wracking!" Lucy sagged against the wall once they'd retreated back to the staff quarters.

"Luke's very nice but I always get the feeling he can see right through me." Bryce stuck his hands in his pockets and grinned ruefully. "Pity you don't know him better. He'd probably be a lot more acceptable to your mum as a fiancé than I will be. Successful and all that, and I know girls think he's handsome."

"I s'pose," Lucy said doubtfully. "Can't say I noticed. I was too worried he was going to boot me out of his office with a flea in my ear. And my mum would never believe he was into me anyway; guys like that are never attracted to me."

"Like that?" Bryce cocked his head curiously.

"You know. Mature. Confident. Responsible." She grinned impishly. "I wouldn't last five minutes with a boyfriend like Luke. I'd be putting itching powder or something in his shorts, trying to get him to loosen up."

Bryce cracked up laughing.

"See! Even you recognise I'd drive him round the bend. No way would Mum buy someone like Luke was in love with me. I'm too dippy."

"You're not dippy." He shook his head at her, still laughing. "You don't get a doctorate in marine biology by being *dippy*. You just have a slightly eccentric sense of humour, that's all. It's adorable."

"And that's why Mum will believe in you where she wouldn't Luke. She'll think being six years younger than me, you won't care about my immature attitude."

"Hey, stop putting yourself down. You're not immature. You like to have fun; that's not a crime."

A little to her surprise, he held out a hand towards her. When she blinked uncertainly at it, he grinned. "Your mum definitely won't believe we're in a relationship if you can't even hold my hand to take a walk."

Lucy laughed and put her hand in his, feeling his long, strong fingers close around hers. "You got me there. Okay. Where are we walking to?"

"Don't you have to get back to the bio centre? Figured I'd walk you back. Presumably you'll need to let your colleagues there in on the prank as well so none of them let the cat out of the bag to your mother. I thought you might want me there to confirm that you're not pulling their collective legs."

"That's... really thoughtful of you. Thanks." Lucy hadn't really thought about telling her colleagues at the marine biology research centre about the plan, but she would certainly have to. "I guess I hadn't really thought of telling them this afternoon."

"Like it or not, you started a ball rolling, Lucy." Bryce's eyes were serious as he looked down at her. He was a full head taller than her five foot five, Lucy noticed inconsequentially, and his eyes were a beautiful shade of green, almost emerald. "By dinnertime the rumours will be all over the resort. Or hadn't you noticed the speed of gossip around here nearly approaches light speed?"

"I had," she admitted, "but somehow I hadn't thought anyone would care, because it's not like we're in an actual relationship."

"Are you kidding me? We need literally everyone on board to pull this one off. Everyone gets a chance to play a part. I reckon that's why Luke gave you the okay, actually; it's a fun project which will have all the staff on board and be great for morale."

"Wow," Lucy said when she caught her breath. "You... have thought this through way better than I have."

"Hey, you're too close to it. It's your mother you're trying to get off your back. Believe me, I know how that goes."

"Which is a good point, what about your parents? Won't it seem odd that they're not here?"

For the first time, she saw a shadow cross Bryce's open, cheerful face. "Not to me, no."

It was obviously a sore subject, but she was immediately dying of curiosity. Biting down on her tongue, she determined not to ask.

Bryce sighed and shook his head after a moment. "You should know, though. Because your mum is going to ask. I don't really talk with my folks. I'm a huge disappointment, you see."

"Why? You've got a good job doing something you love."

"Now I do, yeah. But I flunked school so badly, at sixteen the teachers told my parents there was nothing more they could do for me. I'm extremely dyslexic. For a few years there I honestly had no clue whether I'd ever be able to hold down any sort of job at all beyond manual labour on the road crews or something like that."

Lucy's mouth opened in a silent *oh*.

"My father is a cruise ship captain and my mother is an award-winning travel writer and photographer. They're both well-educated, erudite people who had no idea what to do with an idiot son."

"You're not an idiot!" Lucy said immediately, jumping to his defence. "You're a dive instructor, for God's sake; I don't even want to to think about how hard those exams must have been to pass with dyslexia!" A dive master herself, she knew the instructor's examinations were a great deal tougher, with written exams including equations and comprehensive knowledge as well as the practical tests.

Bryce grinned at her. "I studied for six months straight. Recorded everything onto an MP3 player and walked around like a zombie listening to my own voice reciting the nitrox tables until I was saying them in my sleep. Literally."

"You must have wanted it pretty badly."

"More than I'd ever wanted anything in my life," Bryce said simply. "We were in Thailand when I had my first dive; Dad was between ships and Mum was writing another book. I'd just been told not to bother going back to school and spent most of my time on the beach sulking... and panicking, if I'm being completely honest. It was quiet one day and I struck up a conversation with a couple of German backpackers who asked me if I wanted to go diving with them. I said yes on impulse, and after one dive I was hooked."

"But your parents weren't supportive?" Lucy queried.

He shrugged. "I don't think they saw a future in it. Not when they knew I'd eventually have to pass exams to reach a level where I could make a career out of it, anyway."

"And now?" She was honestly curious. Her mother might give her grief about her personal life, but she'd never been anything but supportive about Lucy's career, and had celebrated her winning the coveted position on Sunfish Island by proudly announcing it on Facebook and throwing her a going-away party.

"Eh, I think they're just glad they don't have to support me. We never had all that close a relationship. I spent school terms living with my grandmother mostly, because they were away so much, until I was old enough to go to boarding school. I was kind of a late-life accident for them anyway, I don't think they actually planned to have kids and didn't know what to do with me when I came along."

Lucy was pretty sure he didn't want pity, so she just nodded. "Would they even be available for the wedding?" she asked.

"Not on short notice. Dad's ship is in the Mediterranean and Mum's with him there. I suppose she could fly back, but... she'd probably find an excuse. All in all, better they just don't know about it. If they see pictures on the Internet I'll give them the truth... that they're being used for marketing purposes."

"That works," Lucy conceded. They'd arrived at the research centre now and she took a deep breath, squaring her shoulders before realising she was still holding Bryce's hand. It felt very natural, actually. Guiltily, she slipped her hand free and gave him a small smile. "Well. Better go recruit some more participants for the prank, then."

He laughed at her before opening the door and holding it gallantly for her to precede him inside. "Come on. I've got a beginner's diving class in the main pool at two. Let's get it over with."

Chapter Four

Walking away from the bio centre twenty minutes later, Bryce whistled tunelessly to himself. His skin still tingled from the feel of Lucy's small hand held in his. The scent of her apple shampoo still teased his nostrils from the unexpected hug she'd given him when he said he had to go. She was small and slight, but there was a surprising strength in her arms as she hugged on around his waist, and after a startled moment he'd folded his arms around her shoulders to hug her back.

"Thanks for everything, Bryce," she whispered. "You're a good friend."

Stuck in the friend zone. He hated himself for resenting the unpalatable fact; it was Lucy's absolute right to just want to be friends, and he really didn't want to be a petulant man-child about it. She didn't owe him anything, and he vowed to himself that he wasn't going to use the opportunity she'd given him to be a creeper. Whatever she asked him for, he would do, but he wasn't going to be pushy. Even asking her to hold his hand had felt as though he was coercing her into something she might not want, though she'd accepted willingly enough. He could still feel the soft warmth of her delicate fingers in his.

"Bryce!" a voice called his name, and he turned to see Rosie, the staff manager, hurrying towards him. The grin on her face confirmed that the gossip had already reached her. "Is it true? Are you and Lucy faking a romance to put the wind up her mother?"

"Not just a romance," he confirmed. "We're faking a full-on wedding."

"That's what Nessa gabbled at me before she ran off to start her shift, but I didn't quite believe it. Are you sure this is a good idea?" Rosie tilted her head and looked at him knowingly. "I wouldn't want you to get your heart broken."

"Does everyone but Lucy know about my crush?" Bryce asked despairingly.

"Hmm… I'd say yes, pretty much?" Rosie pretended to think before smirking at him. "You never know. She might realise for herself what a catch you are."

"In my dreams."

"Hey, that's not like you. Where's that positive attitude?" She nudged him lightly, and he smiled despite himself.

"I'm just thinking that Lucy's my friend, whether or not she ever wants anything more, and she needs this to feel better about herself and her relationship with her mum. That's what friends do, right? Help when you need something?"

"That's a good way to look at it," Rosie said encouragingly.

"Plus, Lucy's mother sounds like a bit of a bitch, and I know all about difficult, demanding parents. Maybe if mine come to visit, she'll return the favour and pretend to be my girlfriend… they'd be super impressed to see me with such a beautiful, smart woman." The more he thought about it, the more he liked the idea. His parents were probably due for a visit sometime this year; he was sure Lucy would happily help him out.

"Okay. Just… if there's anything you need a friendly ear for, I'm here, all right? And confidentiality applies. Lucy doesn't work for the resort anyway, so she doesn't fall under my authority. There's no conflict of interest."

"Thanks, Rosie," Bryce said, genuinely touched. Knowing how touchy-feel Rosie was, he stopped walking and extended his arms to invite a hug, which she happily dished out. "I promise I'll come to you if I'm getting out of my depth."

"Good." She patted his shoulder and let him go; with a quick glance at his dive watch, he broke into a jog. He'd need to hustle to get back to his cabin, get changed and get to the pool for the dive lesson on time. And he needed to start on time because when he finished, he'd have to hurry back to his cabin in order to have time to fill in the forms Luke had given him and Lucy to get back by the end of the business day at five. He should probably have asked Rosie for help with them, actually, she knew all about his dyslexia. Well, he'd just have to manage. He'd ask Luke to check it over anyway to make sure he hadn't made any egregious errors.

***

Throughout his beginners' lesson,, Bryce couldn't stop thinking about Lucy. Standing waist-deep in the pool explaining the proper usage of a regulator, he couldn't help but think about the first time he'd met her. She'd been on the island a couple of days and, as was standard procedure for the incoming marine biologists, had to go out on a dive with Bryce in order for him to sign her off as competent to operate without supervision with the island's equipment.

She'd almost danced her way onto the dive boat, wearing a bright red bikini which wasn't much more than a few triangles of cloth tied together with string. Bryce, turning to greet her, almost swallowed his tongue.

"Hi!" Lucy said brightly. "You must be Bryce! Excuse me not showing up in my wet suit but it's so damn hot I couldn't bear to put it on yet."

Somehow, he managed to find his voice, though he was pretty sure it came out an octave or two higher than normal as he returned her greeting and told her it was fine, they'd be taking a twenty-minute boat ride out to the dive site anyway.

Watching her wiggle and shimmy her way into the wet suit was one of the sexiest things he'd ever seen, though he was sure she wasn't doing it to give him a show intentionally. She was just utterly unaware of how gorgeous she was, he thought, as she turned back to him with another of those wide, cheerful grins. With the skin-tight suit only half-zipped up, his eyes were inevitably drawn to her breasts, and the way the suit almost popped them right out of that tiny red bikini.

Eyes on her eyes, Bryce told himself sternly, wondering why she affected him so strongly. He'd dived with plenty of beautiful women before, he lived on a tropical resort island where stunners in bikinis were pretty much everywhere, and yet somehow this small Englishwoman with the mouth that was slightly too wide, and a spatter of freckles across her nose that confirmed she wore not a scrap of makeup, had him completely off balance.

Lucy spent the whole boat ride to the dive site chattering away about how excited she was to dive on the Great Barrier Reef for the first time. "And the fact that I'm actually getting paid to be here, I can't believe I'm this lucky!" She turned shining eyes to Bryce who was just utterly enchanted. He didn't think he'd ever met anyone with such zest, such passion for life, and couldn't help wondering if she'd show a similar passion in bed.

Telling himself to stop being such a lecher, Bryce settled his eyes on Lucy's face and determined to keep them there. She was the kind of person who made even a sunny day seem dull in comparison, so it was hardly a hardship.

And that was where he'd kept them ever since, on her face and not her breasts, or that beautiful bottom, ridiculously curvaceous in her wet suit.

***

"Hey, Bryce. Bryce!"

A voice calling his name brought him back to his present reality, waist-deep in a swimming pool with four beginner divers who would be going on their first reef dive in the morning. Sternly castigating himself for losing focus, he smiled at the young woman who'd been trying to get his attention.

"Sorry, I was miles away. What's your question?"

She fluttered her eyelashes at him and edged closer. "Nothing about the diving - you covered everything very thoroughly. I just wondered if you were doing anything for dinner tonight? I have a table reserved at *La Sirène*."

Bryce didn't even know her name. She was pretty, and close to his own age, probably twenty-two or three, but her obvious advance left him completely cold. Even if resort policy hadn't forbidden fraternisation between guests and staff, he wouldn't have been tempted.

"Thanks for the invite, but I'll be having dinner with my fiancée," he said, suddenly inspired.

"Oh." The girl's face dropped visibly. "Well. Alright then. Does she work here?"

"She's with the marine biology research centre," Bryce said proudly, and that was the end of the conversation, as one of the other guests called to him with a question.

He made his escape quickly at the end of the lesson, hurrying back to his cabin and drying off before sitting down at the desk and looking at the form Luke had given him to fill in. As usual, the words swam and danced in front of his eyes, making him rub at his eyelids and pinch the bridge of his nose before he used his forearm to block out all but the first line and read the words slowly aloud.

A tap on the edge of the screen door made him scowl. "I'm busy!" he called out, hoping whoever it was would take the hint and go away.

"Looking at that form?" Lucy's English-accented voice said, and his head snapped around.

"Lucy!"

Bryce stood up so fast he knocked his chair over, though he managed to catch it before it hit the floor. "I thought you'd still be working - it's not five yet, is it?" Surely not, he'd only just sat down!

"No, I got the boss to let me go early. God knows I work plenty of unpaid overtime." She smiled up at him as he opened the screen door to admit her to his cabin. "I remembered what you said about being dyslexic and thought you might be having some issues with the form, so I figured I'd stop by and we could fill them in together before we take them back to Luke."

"That's a good idea," Bryce said, touched by her consideration.

"Also, I don't know your last name. I was about to write down *Hemsworth* when I realised it probably isn't."

Bryce blinked, bemused. "What? No, it's Seabrook. Hemsworth?"

"In joke." She plopped down to sit cross-legged on the end of his bed. "You and Cory both look like extra Hemsworth brothers. You know. Thor?"

He got it then, and grinned, shaking his head. "That's ridiculous."

"In case you hadn't noticed, I'm not exactly the most sensible person you'll ever meet."

"You're plenty sensible. You're here to help me fill in this damn form so we get it in on time, right?" Bryce sat down in his chair again and scowled at the offending piece of paper.

Lucy watched Bryce's face as he scowled at the form, obviously struggling to puzzle out the words, and melted inside. He looked utterly gorgeous sitting there in just a pair of board shorts, muscular bronzed torso on full display. *Is he even aware of how damn sexy he is?* she wondered. Particularly when he chewed on his full lower lip like that and stroked those long fingers over his chiselled jaw. She followed their path, mesmerised and suddenly aroused, thinking how his hands would feel on her body.

"Lucy?"

"Yes! Sorry, what?" Mentally kicking herself for being so distracted she hadn't paid attention to what he was saying, she focused determinedly as he asked the question again. "Yes, of course. Helping you with the form. That's why I'm here." Not that she would be of much use sitting on the end of the bed. Pushing herself up, she crossed to his desk and leaned over his shoulder. "All right, where are you up to?"

With her telling him what to write in each space, they were soon done, and Bryce rose to his feet, giving her a grateful smile. "Thanks, Luce. We'd better run these up to Luke's office." He picked up a T-shirt and pulled it on over his head; although the white fabric clung lovingly to his muscles and looked great against his tan, Lucy still spared a moment to silently mourn the loss of her spectacular view.

As she walked beside Bryce on their trip back to the main building, his hand brushed against her wrist lightly and almost automatically, Lucy took his hand.

Bryce's confident stride stuttered slightly, and he looked down at her hand before looking across at her face.

"This is okay, right?" she thought to check. "I mean... if we practice holding hands, it should seem natural by the time Mum arrives..."

"It's fine." His fingers curled more firmly around hers. "It was my idea, remember?"

And it was a good one. Also a bad one, because she could get to like holding Bryce's hand. A lot.

Chapter Five

Luke didn't appear to have moved since their earlier visit, though the piles of paper had migrated around his desk somewhat. He looked tired as he lifted his head and nodded to them to come in.

"Still set on this, then?"

"Yep." Lucy spoke for both of them, setting the completed forms down on Luke's desk. He looked at her thoughtfully, swinging back and forth a little on his office chair, before nodding and picking them up to feed into his scanner.

"I'll get them sent off straight away." He smirked a little. "And you should stop by and see Terry and Jerome. They're excited."

"Oh God, Olivia got to them already!" Lucy looked at Bryce with open dread. He chuckled at her.

"Come on, let's go see them now. Best start reining them in or you'll find they've planned the most elaborate wedding the island's ever seen and you'll have no choices in the matter at all."

The thought was so horrifying that she grabbed Bryce's hand again and half-dragged him out of the office without even saying goodbye to Luke. Hurrying along the hallway to the large office Terry and Jerome shared, her mind was full of enormous meringue-like wedding dresses and bridesmaids in a hideous shade of tangerine.

By the time they reached the wedding planners' office, she'd calmed down a little and remembered she didn't even *have* any bridesmaids. Which was something she'd need to arrange before her mother arrived. Maybe Olivia would agree to be a maid of honour.

Terry and Jerome were bent over the big planning table they used, arguing over something as they usually did. Lucy wasn't sure she'd ever seen the pair of them when they weren't bickering, though they were actually married. They'd been the very first same-sex couple married on the island when Australia legalised gay marriage, and their wedding photos were up on the website already.

"Lucy!" Jerome spied her first and straightened up, throwing his arms wide. "Darling girl! Come here, we have such plans for you!"

"Uh," Lucy said, "not too big, I hope. I've never had visions of an extravagant wedding."

"Told you not to get carried away," Terry said snarkily, folding his arms. "Classy and simple has to be the way to go."

Lucy shot him a grateful look and nodded. "That's what my mum will expect, anyway. Well. Simple, if not classy."

"Impossible mothers are a nightmare," Jerome said sympathetically. "We'll knock her socks off, Lucy. Don't you worry. You and Bryce make an absolutely beautiful couple - look at them holding hands, Terry!" He nudged his husband and Terry chuckled.

"Actually that's a point, we should make an effort to get some photos of you two together each day, so you're wearing different outfits and look like you're always in each other's company. Put them up on the resort's social media accounts so there's evidence for your mother to find if she goes looking..."

"You'd have been a terrifying criminal mastermind, darling," Jerome said. "But he's absolutely right. Tell everyone to take snaps of you regularly."

"There's just the slight problem that I hate having my photo taken and I always look like I have a weird fake smile," Lucy despaired.

"I'll tell everyone just to take candid shots. They're better anyway," Bryce said, surprising her. "It'll be good practice, looking at each other adoringly."

"That's the spirit," Terry said cheerfully. "Now, Lucy, Olivia said she originally suggested lending you one of her designer dresses but we can do better than that - there's a bridal shop in Airlie Beach we sometimes send customers to, and I've already spoken to their manager who would be delighted to dress you for free. Dress, shoes, accessories, it's all yours." He beamed at her. "And the jewellery shop right here in the resort will loan you an engagement ring until after the wedding, and two wedding bands to use at the ceremony."

They really did have everything under control, Lucy realised as Terry barrelled on, talking about hair and makeup, flowers and catering, photography and videography. After a couple of minutes she tuned out, looking up at Bryce and seeing him apparently listening intently.

God, he's so good-looking. Mum's never gonna believe he's in love with me.

As though sensing her scrutiny, he suddenly looked down at her and smiled. Holding her eyes, he lifted the hand still linked with hers and, to her intense surprise, pressed a gentle kiss to the back of her hand before lowering it again.

Lucy couldn't help but wonder what Bryce meant by the affectionate gesture. Was it just more 'practice' as far as he was concerned? She tried to tell herself not to read too much into it, but the soft warmth of his lips against her skin left a tingling feeling long after they'd left the wedding planners' office.

"Want to go get some dinner?" Bryce suggested as they headed back down the main staircase to Reception.

"Sounds good," Lucy agreed. "I was too distracted to eat much lunch."

"Yeah, I noticed."

"Did you really?" came out before Lucy could stop herself, and Bryce looked down at her with a slight smile.

"I notice everything about you, Lucy."

She hadn't the slightest idea what to say in response to that bombshell, but fortunately was saved from having to come up with a response when Cory came out of a side pathway to join them.

"Hey, you two! Having fun?" His smile was just slightly malicious.

"Your girlfriend's been the one having fun, I think," Bryce parried quickly.

Cory shrugged. "It's the low season. She's bored, and you basically dangled a fun project in front of her and gave her free rein to run with it."

"Honestly, I don't mind," Lucy said. "Quite the opposite - I'm grateful! There's no way I could pull off anything as convincing as what Terry and Jerome have been outlining to us, and Olivia's obviously the one who got them enthused."

"She does have a tendency to drag everyone along in her wake," Cory's grin was proud. "One minute you're carrying on as normal and the next Cyclone Olivia's blown through and everything looks wildly different."

It was more than obvious that Cory absolutely adored Olivia. His face lit up when he spoke about her, and Lucy found herself envious of the obviously tight and passionate relationship the two of them shared. She wanted that, wanted to feel that way about someone, a lover who'd talk about her with that joy and adoration clear on his face for all to see.

Would her mother believe she was marrying Bryce if Lucy didn't have that light in her eyes when she talked about him? Lucy had always been a romantic at heart, and her mother knew it.

Well, she'd just have to do her best, and spend the next couple of weeks getting to know every personal detail Bryce would share with her. She liked him, after all - perhaps a little too much - so spending time with him wasn't exactly going to be a hardship.

Chapter Six

"Breathe," Bryce nudged Lucy in the ribs lightly. "You've gone white as a sheet."

He was holding her hand, as usual these days, but this time she was clinging to it like a lifeline, because at any moment her mother was going to walk through the sliding doors from the airport's secure area and see them together, and the charade would begin in earnest.

The last two weeks had flown by; Lucy had a much greater sympathy for women who turned into bridezillas when things didn't go exactly to their plan now. On such short notice, Olivia, Terry and Jerome had pulled together an absolutely breathtaking plan for a wedding, but multiple things still had to be changed due to unavailability or expense. Lucy had just shrugged and rolled with the changes, but she could imagine how a girl who had her heart set on something could easily get upset and overwhelmed by it all in the run-up to the biggest day of her life. Especially if she had family who were bringing pressure to bear as well.

"Your mum's flight is starting to clear now," Rosie noted. Standing just in front of them, she was helping to greet the guests incoming to the resort along with Jill, the guest relations manager. Lucy didn't know Jill well, but the other girl had stepped up to do her part in the charade as well, upgrading Lucy's mother to a premium guest suite rather than a standard resort room and sending a request to Housekeeping to have a welcoming basket placed in the room. *Mother of the Bride*, the card tucked into the beautiful arrangement of fruit said, and there was champagne in the bar fridge too.

"Oh, God." Lucy's hands were cold and clammy, but Bryce didn't try to let go. He squeezed comfortingly on her numb fingers instead, trying to warm her.

"Easy. It's all gonna go fine. She won't see anything past that sparkler on your finger."

Which was yet another thing Lucy had to worry about. She'd tried to pick out a plain, simple ring at the resort jeweller. They'd had other ideas, and since their jewellery would feature prominently in the marketing photographs, she didn't really feel able to say no. Especially once they'd assured her their insurance would cover her in the case of loss or damage.

Consequently, she was wearing a spectacular princess-cut, two-carat diamond solitaire that would have cost Bryce about a quarter of his annual salary, if he'd been paying for it. She'd pointed that out, but Bryce had decided for reasons of his own to accompany her to the jeweller and he'd cut off her objections with a few simple words.

"I'd spend a lot more than that if I was lucky enough to find a woman as amazing as you who was willing to marry me."

The words had made her feel warm all over, especially combined with the sincerity in his eyes as he spoke them. Every time she saw the glint of the diamond, she remembered the way Bryce had called her amazing.

Taking a deep, calming breath, she looked up at him and smiled. He smiled back, and that warm glance between the two of them was the first thing Justine Manning saw as she walked through the sliding doors.

"Lucy!"

Her mother's welcoming call made Lucy startle and look away from Bryce, her cheeks flushing. "Mum," she said with a smile.

"Holy shit," Bryce said as she stepped forward, "*that's* your *mother*?"

Lucy knew exactly what he meant. Justine Manning would be fifty-three in a few months, but she looked to be in her mid-thirties at most, a stunning, model-tall, raven-haired beauty who turned every male head in a three-block radius. She looked like Lucy's taller, more glamorous older sister, perfectly made up with not a hair out of place even after flying halfway around the world.

"Darling, you look marvellous," Justine said in the plummy, upper-class accent Lucy had made a conscious decision never to sound like. "Love the tan! And who's this gorgeous young stud? Brought him along to carry the bags, have you?" She skimmed her eyes up and down Bryce's tall, muscled form in a blatantly sexual appraisal that made Lucy grit her teeth.

"Surprise," Lucy said with a grin. "This is Bryce. We're engaged." She waved her hand, making the diamond flash glints of multicoloured light.

For the first time in her entire life, Lucy saw her mother rendered absolutely speechless.

Bryce took that as his cue and stepped forward, extending a hand. "It's lovely to finally meet you, Mrs Manning. Lucy's told me so much about you."

"I wish I could say the same," Justine finally recovered enough to say, taking his hand. "Engaged? But why?"

Bryce blinked. "What?"

"Why are *you* engaged to *Lucy*? You gorgeous young thing, you could have anyone!"

Behind her, Lucy heard Jill and Rosie gasp in outraged unison. She had indeed told Bryce a lot about her mother, though, including a pretty accurate prediction of exactly what Justine might say when they dropped the bombshell. Bryce just raised his eyebrows and looked amused.

"That's a good one! I'm lucky Lucy bothered to look at me twice, Ms. Manning."

"You must call me Justine," she said after a brief pause. "Well. This is a surprise, but a pleasant one. When are you two planning to get married?" She gave the handle of her suitcase to Bryce as he gestured towards it.

"Well, that's the second surprise," Lucy said, taking a certain malicious delight in the way Justine's eyes narrowed, anticipating another bombshell. "It's a week on Friday."

Chapter Seven

"Are you okay?" Rosie asked in an undertone as Bryce helped Justine aboard the boat to Sunfish Island. "That was pretty extreme."

And publicly messy, Lucy thought but didn't say. Fortunately Jill had spirited the other incoming guests off to the bus, leaving Bryce, Rosie and Lucy to bring a stunned Justine along behind. By the time they arrived at the bus, Justine had progressed from "This has to be a prank" to "How *dare* you not tell me about this!"

At that point, Jill took charge, welcoming her to the resort as a VIP guest, which rather took the wind out of Justine's sails. The twenty-minute bus ride from the airport to the marina had been difficult, with Justine fairly shoving Lucy into a seat and hissing questions into her ear.

"It'll be okay," Lucy answered Rosie's question in an equally quiet voice. "To be honest, I'm quite enjoying seeing Mum this flustered."

Rosie's lips twitched with laughter. "It's pretty funny watching her with Bryce. She looks like she doesn't know whether she wants to ogle him or push him overboard."

"Don't give her ideas." Lucy couldn't help a giggle at the mental image, though.

Bryce returned to her side just then. "Come on, you two. You're the last ones to board; everyone's eager to get to Sunfish. Let's go." He slipped his arm around Lucy's waist, which startled her slightly. While she'd gotten used to holding his hand, this was slightly more intimate. She turned her face up to him in surprise.

"Your mother's watching," Bryce said softly, just before he pressed a light kiss on her lips and smiled broadly at her.

"Let's go, lovebirds," Rosie said loudly, striding up the ramp, and Lucy was grateful for Bryce's supportive arm around her waist as they followed, because that light brush of lips had rocked her to the core.

***

What the hell had possessed him, kissing Lucy like that? Bryce's lips were still tingling as he released her and moved to the front of the boat to help cast off the lines. Justine's denigration of Lucy had outraged him, though, and he was now determined to rub her nose in the fact that Lucy had proved her mother's predictions wrong. Kissing her had seemed like the most obvious thing to do, and he'd done his best to make it look natural.

The problem was that as soon as their lips met, he'd wanted more. It had taken everything he had not to drag her hard against him and kiss her senseless. His lips were still tingling, every sense on high alert, hyper-aware of Lucy's movements at all times. He was always aware of her, but right now he was pretty sure he could have closed his eyes and still known if she made the slightest move.

"Bryce," Jill's voice said behind him, and he jumped about a foot in the air, making her shriek with surprise.

"Sorry," he apologised. "I was miles away."

Hand to her heart, Jill stared at him wide-eyed. "I was just going to ask if you'd demonstrate putting on a life-vest while I do the safety briefing," she said.

"Of course." Embarrassed, Bryce followed her into the boat's main cabin, plastering on a broad smile for the benefit of the incoming guests. Justine was staring at him, even as a male guest probably fifteen years her junior shifted seats to sit beside her and make a hopeful pass. *Holy hell, she really was stunning*, he thought very privately. He hadn't actually asked Lucy how old her mother was, but Justine couldn't have been much out of her teens when Lucy was born, and she could easily pass for the same age as Lucy now.

That said, he'd always thought Lucy looked a lot younger than she actually was. Obviously, she'd inherited Justine's eternal-youth gene.

"Go away," Justine said coldly to the poor sap trying to hit on her, and the guy immediately moved away, crushed.

At least Lucy didn't inherit the bitch gene, Bryce thought, muscles along his jaw clenching. He'd been absolutely livid in the airport when Justine had put Lucy down by asking why on earth Bryce would be interested in her. What a dreadful thing to say about your own daughter!

More determined than ever to convince Justine that he was madly in love with Lucy and could hardly wait to marry her, Bryce smiled warmly in her direction several times during the safety demo, before going straight back out to the front of the boat where Lucy and Rosie were sitting.

"Hey." Taking a seat beside Lucy, he put his arm around her shoulders, deliberately leaned in close and planted a kiss on the side of her brow. "Your mother just shot down some poor fool who tried to hit on her."

Lucy smiled tightly. "No doubt there'll be plenty of that."

"She wouldn't be interested in anyone?" Rosie asked curiously, keeping her voice low.

"She hates men, and frankly she doesn't have a lot of time for women either." Lucy cast a glance at the open doorway, keeping her own voice low. "My father was married, promised he'd leave his wife for her. The usual. Didn't follow through. She had to fight him to get child support paid. I think she might actually have loved him until she realised he was lying his ass off."

Rosie winced; Bryce tightened his arm around Lucy instinctively, wanting to comfort her. She looked up at him with a small smile. "My mother is a bundle of neurotic contradictions, I'm afraid. Wants grandkids, but wants me to be married first, but is also convinced that no man is worth marrying."

"Frankly, you did well to turn out so normal," Rosie said, and Lucy chuckled.

"Who says I'm normal?"

"Beautifully, perfectly normal," Bryce said loudly, alerting the two girls to Justine's approach. He'd spotted her from the corner of his eye, approaching the door.

"Bit windy out here, isn't it?" Justine said, smoothing her hair as the wind whipped at it.

Silently, Lucy offered a spare hair tie from the several snapped around her wrist. Justine ignored the gesture, leaning in the doorway and looking at the three of them. Rosie promptly hopped up and offered her seat, and Justine accepted with a queenly grace, as though it was no more than her due. Bryce and Lucy both caught Rosie's eye-roll behind Justine's back and had to stifle chuckles.

"So how long will it take to get to the resort?" Justine asked.

"About another twenty minutes," Bryce answered her. "This is a fast hydrofoil boat; we're travelling at over thirty knots. You'll be able to see Sunfish Island shortly, once we pass through the channel between those two islands there."

"And you work there too, hm?" Justine queried.

"Yes, I'm the resort's diving instructor." *Here comes the interrogation*, he thought, and wasn't disappointed as Justine began to pepper him with questions.

"Justine," Lucy interrupted after a few minutes. "*Mum*. Leave it out."

"I'm just curious, darling! You haven't so much as whispered Bryce's name, one might almost think you were ashamed of him." Justine was wearing large designer sunglasses which completely covered her eyes and did a fair job of obscuring her facial expression, but Bryce was pretty sure her eyes were boring into him like lasers.

"Absolutely not," Lucy denied, and then she ducked her head. "To be honest... I've been having trouble believing that it's real. That I'm not just living in some fantastic dream."

Bryce saw Justine's mouth soften, and knew she was falling for it. It really was a spectacular bit of acting on Lucy's part, and completely believable considering Lucy's lack of self-confidence — *largely caused by Justine putting her down*, he thought.

"I'm the one who's living my dream, angel," he murmured, leaning in to press a kiss against her brow again.

"Well," Justine said after a moment of silence. "I can see the two of you are quite sickeningly in love."

She's genuinely falling for it, Bryce thought. He saw the corner of Lucy's mouth turn up, wondered if she was smiling on the other side too. She didn't say anything, though, so he stepped into the breach.

"Your daughter's an incredible woman, Justine. I know how lucky I am, believe me."

"Huh." Juliet shook her head slightly, and Bryce realized the only reason she was doubtful was her poor opinion of Lucy's charms.

"One look at her and I was slavering like a dingo in a drought," he said humorously, deliberately playing up his Australian twang, "but it was when I got to know her and realized how smart she was, I knew I was sunk."

Lucy pinched the outside of his leg lightly, a prearranged signal which meant '*you're overdoing things*'. Bryce disagreed.

"Girl of my dreams," he said, deliberately making his voice low and husky as he stroked Lucy's cheek lightly, pretending to forget Justine's presence entirely.

Lucy's eyes were very green and bright as she looked up at him. Perhaps she was trying to give him a stern glare, tell him to tone things down, but she'd pursed her lips to do it and suddenly all he could think about was kissing her again, more deeply than the brief peck he'd given her earlier. He forgot Justine's presence for real as Lucy's lips parted just slightly.

***

The way Bryce was looking at her made Lucy catch her breath. She was trying to glare him into silence, tell him he was overdoing things and Justine would smell a rat, but the husky tone in his voice and the heat in his eyes made it impossible to even think of being annoyed with him.

In fact, all she could think of was the way his lips had felt on hers. And of how much she wanted him to kiss her again.

Bryce's gaze dropped to her lips, and his own parted, the tip of his tongue darting out to moisten his upper lip. His head lowered towards hers, slowly, giving her time to back away if she wanted to. Lucy's eyelids drooped as she felt his warm breath against her mouth, already anticipating the heat of his kiss...

"Jeez, get a room, you two!" Justine said, laughing.

Lucy flinched back instinctively, her eyes flying wide and her face flushing red. "I, ah..."

"I see exactly how it is," Justine said dryly. "The two of you are so wrapped up in each other, you forgot I was even here."

"Yes," Bryce said, and he sounded a little puzzled. "Yes, that's exactly it."

Lucy sneaked a quick sideways glance at him, but he was rising to his feet and she missed seeing the expression on his face.

"We're coming around the point of the island now. The jetty's just ahead," Bryce told Justine as he headed to the prow of the boat and picked up one of the mooring lines, preparing to help dock the boat.

"I know there's a lovely suite reserved for you," Lucy told Justine brightly. "Jill pulled some strings to get you an upgrade."

"I assumed I'd be staying with you... but I suppose you and Bryce are living together anyway."

"The staff accommodations are pretty sparse," Lucy said, suddenly realising they hadn't thought of that. Of course her mother would want to see where she lived, and there wasn't a single thing in there to indicate it was occupied by two people.

Rosie had come back out of the boat's main cabin and caught the exchange; she locked eyes with Lucy now and gave her a reassuring smile. "I got it," she mouthed, and Lucy knew by the time she'd settled Justine in her suite, at least half of Bryce's belongings would have been relocated to her room and arranged to make it look as though he'd been living there for weeks.

"Welcome to Sunfish Island Resort!" Jill announced as Bryce leaped across to the dock to tie off the mooring lines. "If you'll follow me, we'll head up to Reception to get you all checked in so you can start enjoying your holiday straight away."

"Not you," Lucy said to Justine, "I already checked you in." She held up a key card with a smile. "No need to queue with the *hoi polloi*."

"Oh, that was thoughtful, darling. Thank you. Goodness me, it's hot!"

Now that the boat had stopped moving, the oppressive tropical heat descended on them. Lucy was slowly getting used to it, but particularly humid days still got to her, her skin feeling constantly damp and her hair frizzing heavily. She'd taken to braiding it and coiling it atop her head to keep the weight of it off her neck; a lot of the women on the staff kept their hair short but Lucy was a little vain about her hair and didn't want to cut it.

"There'll be a storm later this afternoon," she predicted. "We get them most days in the summer, but it doesn't really cool things down anyway. I did warn you that you were coming during the hot season. Apparently midwinter here is much nicer - like the really good bits of an English summer."

"Yes, but midwinter here is the same time as the English summer," Justine pointed out.

"Which is quite likely to be rainy and wet anyway," Lucy riposted. "Anyway, the heat takes some getting used to. You need to drink a *lot* of water — I had a permanent headache for the first couple of weeks until I figured out I was constantly a bit dehydrated. Now I carry a water bottle with me everywhere and refill it whenever I get the chance."

"Hm." Justine claimed her suitcase from the pile the deckhand was unloading onto the dock. "I was rather thinking I'd be drinking a lot of piña coladas and strawberry daiquiris, actually."

Lucy snickered. "Yeah, well, I set you up a bar tab for your room. You'll get staff rates on all food and drinks at the resort restaurants and bars."

"Such a considerate daughter!" Justine smiled warmly at her.

"Do let me get that for you, Justine," Bryce said cheerfully, gesturing at her suitcase as they came up alongside him on the dock.

"And such a nice considerate man you've found. Thank you, Bryce." Justine gave him the handle and she and Lucy followed him as he strode off towards the main resort.

"Well," Justine murmured, lowering her sunglasses to take a good look over them at Bryce's retreating back. "Now *that's* what I call an ass worth chasing."

Lucy choked.

Justine glanced sideways at her. "Oh come on, darling. I was beginning to wonder if you were interested in sex at all. Frankly, I'm relieved to discover your libido is alive and well, and that you not only have good taste, but the initiative to act on it once you see something you want. I'm not sure you need to marry him to get what you want, though."

"Is this some sort of strange reverse 'why buy the cow if you're getting the milk for free' speech?" Lucy asked after a moment of stunned silence. "Because my relationship with Bryce isn't just about sex." She'd almost said she wasn't even having sex with Bryce, but managed to stop herself in time.

Justine laughed. "An amusing role reversal, isn't it?" She said no more as they approached the main resort building, leaving Lucy silently fuming. Even when Justine gave a compliment, there would be a sting in the tail. She was like a jellyfish; beautiful but agonisingly painful if you got caught in its tendrils.

Chapter Eight

"Wow," Bryce said at last as he and Lucy stood facing each other outside the closed door to Justine's suite.

Lucy arched a cynical eyebrow at him. "Most men have that sort of reaction to Justine, strangely enough."

"That wasn't a good 'wow'." He reached for her hand and they walked back to the elevator together. "That was a 'wow, your mother is a real piece of work' wow."

"You think?" Lucy darted a sideways look at him, wondering what he meant. Men young and old tended to be so blinded by Justine's beauty they didn't notice her bitchiness.

"I don't mean to disrespect your mother, but she was an absolute bitch to you." Bryce looked furious on her behalf, and Lucy melted.

"Same shit, different day," she said with a shrug. "I was always a disappointment, from the day my father decided to deny paternity before I was even born. Maybe she could have overlooked that if I'd been the perfect little mini-me she wanted, but I wasn't... I was a sickly baby, demanding and difficult, and then I grew up far more interested in shells and starfish than clothes and makeup."

"I know about being a disappointment." Bryce's hand tightened on hers as the elevator doors opened and they stepped into the empty car. "Even so. Denigrating you right to your face, in front of your friends, that's pretty low."

"Suddenly my reasoning for wanting to present her with a fiancé seems quite sensible, huh?"

"Damn right it does." Turning to her, he took her other hand so that he held them both and looked earnestly into her eyes. "I've no doubt she's been putting you down your whole life, but please believe me, Lucy. You're brilliant and funny and just as beautiful as your mother; more so because you have a beautiful soul. I've never heard you say a truly unkind word about anyone, not even your mother, who certainly deserves it."

Her smile was a little bit wobbly as she gazed back up at him. "Believe me, sometimes Justine pushes me too far. I have no doubt I'll be venting in your ear at some point and tarnishing that image you have of my 'beautiful soul'."

"Never," Bryce said softly, and Lucy had the strangest impression that he was leaning down towards her, just a little bit. His gaze lowered slightly.

Is he looking at my lips? Instinctively she licked them, and Bryce leaned closer still.

"Lucy." It was a soft breath against her lips, and she angled her face up, eyes drifting closed.

He's going to kiss me...

Warm lips slanted down over hers, and she parted instinctively for him, breath coming quickly as the tip of his tongue traced lightly over her upper lip.

A loud *ping* shattered the moment, as the elevator doors slid open on the hotel lobby... and Jill's speculative expression.

Face burning, Lucy sprang back, yanking her hands from Bryce's grasp. "Thanks for helping Mum with her case," she gabbled quickly. "I'm just gonna get her a couple of water bottles to put in her fridge, make sure she drinks plenty. I'll see how she's doing with the jet lag, she might just want a room service dinner and an early night, but if she wants to eat out I'll text you and maybe you can join us?" Her words were falling all over each other, but Bryce just nodded, giving her a warm smile before stepping back and making his escape.

Jill was giving her a very knowing look, as she escorted two VIP clients into the elevator. "Deets later!" she hissed at Lucy just before the doors slid closed.

***

Bruce could still taste Lucy on his lips as he headed back to his cabin, where he found Rosie and Cory hastily shoving his belongings into bags.

"Uh, am I moving?" He arched a brow, leaning in the doorway to watch.

"Yes, because Lucy's mother is going to want to see where you two live, and it's going to be pretty damn obvious you're not living together if none of your shit is in her room." Rosie never slowed her speedy packing, and Cory didn't even look up.

Realising she was right, Bryce blew out his cheeks and went to join them. "So I'm moving in with her, am I?"

"Her cabin's nicer than yours," Cory said with a sideways grin at him. "She's got pictures up on the walls and everything."

Bryce supposed his room did look a bit bare. He'd never really thought of it as more than a place to lay his head when he needed to sleep, though, preferring to be outside or spending time with friends. His favourite place in the cabin was actually the hammock outside on the deck, which he paused to unhitch before following Rosie and Cory, laden with bags, off to Lucy's cabin.

The three of them spent a hasty half hour arranging things in Lucy's cabin, which Bryce had never seen, and had to admit it was a lot nicer than his, despite having the same basic layout. Lucy had several framed pictures of ocean life on the walls, soft cushions on her couch, a woven silk throw on the bed; all the little things that made it look like a home.

They'd just finished reorganising Lucy's wardrobe to have Bryce's clothes fit in alongside hers when his phone vibrated with an incoming text.

"It's Lucy," he said, checking it. *Mum wants a drink. Meet you at the pool bar?*

"Text her back, tell her to meet you here," Cory suggested.

"Good plan," Bryce agreed. He'd long since figured the easiest way for him to send texts was to use his phone's virtual assistant, so he quickly dictated a return message. *Cool. Swing by our room on your way down.*

Gotcha, followed by a smiley face emoji, came through a few seconds later, and he knew Lucy had received the message loud and clear.

"You two better scarper," he told Cory and Rosie. "Thanks for all the help."

"You're welcome!" he was told as they made themselves scarce.

Looking around, he couldn't see anything out of place. The cabin looked as though it was occupied by a couple; his toothbrush in a glass beside Lucy's in the bathroom, the nightstands beside the bed arranged into his and hers, with several books piled on her side and his dive computer on his. The only thing he had left to do was put up his hammock, and he hurried out onto the veranda to do that now, hoping the hooks on his were duplicated here.

They were, and he was laying at his ease, one foot brushing the floor pushing him in a gentle swing when Lucy and Justine came strolling down the path.

"Well, this looks very comfortable," Justine said, amused, as Bryce lifted his hand in a lazy wave.

"Hey, it's my day off," he said equably. "Wasn't technically on duty this morning, but I figured I might as well come in with Lucy to meet you. I'm taking out a night dive tonight." Pushing himself up to his feet, he stretched luxuriantly before bending to kiss Lucy. "I'll just grab my thongs."

"Thongs?" he heard Justine exclaim as he slid the screen door open to enter the cabin, and chuckled to himself.

"That's what Aussies call flip-flops," Lucy explained, following him in. "While they technically speak English, there are some weird colloquialisms that take a bit of getting used to."

Justine stood in the doorway, looking around, taking in the space. While the cabins were fairly generous for one person, they were cosy at best for two permanent residents. Bryce had deliberately left a discarded T-shirt draped over the bedpost, and Lucy picked it up, gave him an admonishing look and took it to the closet to put away.

"Sorry, sweetie," he said with a penitent smile, shoving his feet into his rubber thongs. "I'm still getting used to sharing my space," he told Justine. "I'd been living on my own for quite a while before Lucy swept me off my feet."

Lucy chuckled at that and nudged him in the ribs; he threw his arm around her shoulders to hug her close. "Don't deny it. You took one look and decided I was the one for you."

"He's full of it, isn't he?" Justine said, but she was laughing as she spoke, and Lucy laughed too.

"To be honest, he's not far wrong," she admitted. "I mean, look at him!"

Both women looked him up and down, making Bryce grin. "When you're done objectifying me, ladies, I can hear a cold beer calling my name," he said cheerfully. "And I'm sure I heard you say something about a piña colada, Justine - our bartender buddy Nessa makes the best one on the Reef. She's English too, a Londoner originally, though she emigrated out here when she was in her teens."

"Is she used to this heat yet?" Justine asked as they ambled from the cabin towards the pool bar, Bryce's arm still slung casually around Lucy's shoulders. "It's like walking around in a steam bath!"

"It's summertime, even the locals are feeling it," Bryce told her. "Hence, the desire for a cold beer. Just the one though, sadly, since I'm diving later."

They exited the staff accommodation area through a gate leading out onto the resort's main paths, and from there it was only a minute's walk to the pool bar where Nessa was shaking cocktails with eye-blurring speed.

"Hey!" the bartender called as they took seats at one side of the bar. Her long black braids swung as she replaced bottles on the shelf and almost danced over to them, teeth shining white in her dark face as she smiled widely. "You must be Lucy's mum. Delighted to meet you. What can I get for you?"

They ordered drinks, and watched Nessa mix the cocktails; she made it look like an art form, hands flashing as she deftly twirled bottles and blended ingredients. Pouring the cocktail into a tall frosted glass in front of Justine, she garnished it with a flourish; a piece of pineapple and a cherry on a skewer.

"Wow," Justine said, obviously impressed. Nessa grinned at her before setting a long necked bottle of beer in front of Lucy and another for Bryce.

"Glass?" Nessa checked, and Lucy nodded. Watching her from the corner of his eye, Bryce nodded as well. He'd seen Lucy drink from the bottle plenty of times, but perhaps Justine disapproved, in which case he'd make sure he minded his manners as well. Frankly, he didn't care either way. As long as the beer was cold.

"All right," Justine said when she was about halfway down her cocktail, "hit me with it. Why are you getting married in such a rush? Are you pregnant?"

Lucy snorted beer out her nose onto the bar. Bryce had to choke down his laughter, biting down hard on the inside of his cheek. He caught Nessa's eye as she came over and had to look away, seeing her fighting not to laugh as well. Justine's question had been quite loud.

"No!" Lucy gasped, grabbing the napkins Nessa swiftly deposited in front of her and wiping her nose with them. "Christ, Mum! Seriously?"

"Just asking, dear," Justine sipped at her cocktail, unperturbed. "I wouldn't be upset. You know I'm longing for grandchildren. Don't make me wait too long, dear," she turned to Bryce. "How are those swimmers? Nice and healthy? I hope diving doesn't affect sperm production. All those changes in pressure..."

He gave up the effort and burst out laughing.

"Just kill me now," Lucy groaned, face beet red.

Justine rolled her eyes. "Lucinda Marie Manning, I didn't raise you to be a prude. The two of you have clearly been banging on every available surface for some time. You're in your thirties now, after all; I just don't want you to waste time. Take it from me, have children while you're young, then you've still got plenty of life left to live once they've grown up and flown from the nest."

"Clearly you're a fine example of practising what you preach," Bryce said, since Lucy appeared to have swallowed her tongue.

"Of course. I'm glad Lucy waited longer than I did, but child-bearing years don't last forever. Nessa, darling, would you make me another one of those? It was absolutely marvellous."

"Coming right up." Nessa had given up any pretence of not eavesdropping after wiping Lucy's beer-snort off the bar. She made Justine's cocktail and delivered it with a flourish before quite blatantly hanging around to listen in.

Justine's eye was caught by light reflecting off something hanging around Nessa's neck. "I say, is that real?" She squinted at the diamond glittering blue fire from the ring on a thin gold chain.

"My engagement ring?" Nessa lifted her hand to lightly touch the ring. "Yes. I don't wear it working behind the bar, though. Too many glasses to scratch."

"Obviously your fiancé values you highly," Justine assessed the ring with an experienced eye, before glancing back down at Lucy's simpler, though still high-value, ring and wrinkling her nose slightly.

"I chose this," Lucy jumped to Bryce's defence. "I wanted something I *can* wear at work."

"Also, competing with Nessa's fiancé is a losing proposition," Bryce added, amused by Justine's attempted put-down. "She's marrying a billionaire, after all."

It was Justine's turn to choke on her drink. Nessa laughed out loud.

"Nessa's engaged to Jace Hunter. He owns the island," Lucy explained.

"And yes, I could give up working at the bar if I wanted, but I enjoy it," Nessa said when Justine gave her an incredulous look. "Jace is a very private person, but I like human contact. A few shifts a week here suits me fine."

"Well." Justine recovered her composure. "I'm sure you know your own mind. Congratulations," she added as an afterthought. "When's *your* wedding?"

Nessa shrugged. "When we get around to it. No rush." Her grin was absolutely wicked. "I'm a few years younger than Lucy, so I've got a couple extra child-bearing years up my sleeve."

"And to think, I thought you were my friend," Lucy said dryly, making Nessa laugh again.

Chapter Nine

Justine mellowed out after another cocktail, and somehow they managed to escape without directly answering the question about why they were in such a hurry to get married. Finally, Justine declared that the jet lag was catching up with her and she was going to go rest for a while before meeting them for dinner at the Italian restaurant in the main hotel building.

"And over dinner, you must tell me all about your family, Bryce!" Justine declared.

"Won't that be fun," Bryce muttered under his breath. Lucy squeezed his hand and he mustered up a smile.

"We'll walk back with you part of the way," Lucy said. "When we turn in through the staff gate, you just carry straight on into the main resort reception. You can't get lost."

Draining the last of his beer, Bryce set the glass down and thanked Nessa. She gave him a warm smile and a wink as she efficiently cleared away the empty glasses.

Lucy's hand slipped into his again as they walked away from the bar, and Bryce thought briefly about how natural it felt to hold her hand now. He knew he was still going to be reaching out to take her hand instinctively long after Justine had gone home, which was likely to lead to a few awkward moments.

"All right, I'll see you two lovebirds later," Justine said as they arrived at the staff gate. "No doubt you can think of something to do to fill in your afternoon!" She winked at Bryce.

She thinks we're going to have sex, Bryce realized, and told himself firmly not to blush. Lucy was already doing enough of that for both of them.

"Any time I get to spend with Lucy is a gift," he said, knowing it was a sappy line but sure Justine would eat it up. She gave him an amused look before turning on her heel and heading for the main resort building.

Lucy sagged against Bryce as soon as her mother was out of sight.

"Hey." Letting go of her hand, he put a bracing arm around her shoulders instead. "C'mon. You're doing great. She's fallen for it hook, line and sinker."

"She's been here for two hours," Lucy bemoaned as he opened the gate. "I've got to survive two *weeks* of this!"

"We'll survive it together." They reached her cabin and Bryce hesitated. "What do you want to do, here? Rosie basically moved me in with you."

Lucy chuckled, shaking her head. "Bless her. I thought she was just going to make it look good. On the other hand, Justine is the kind of person who would feel completely entitled to look in any drawer or cupboard she felt like, so maybe it's for the best."

"It's not going to be terribly convenient for you if I'm walking in every ten minutes to get a change of clothes or brush my teeth, though," Bryce pointed out.

"Well, you could just stay here," Lucy said, opening the cabin door and gesturing to him to enter.

A dead silence fell between them as Bryce stared at her.

"Uh, Lucy," he said hesitantly.

"Platonically! I mean, I'm not going to jump on you. It's a queen size bed!"

She was babbling. Bryce stared at her, wondering what the hell was going through her mind.

"I'm not going to jump on you either," he said slowly, "at least, not when I'm awake, but when I'm asleep... well, I don't think I'd jump on you then either, but how would you react if, for example, you woke up with me shoving my morning wood against your backside?"

Lucy's eyes widened, and then she let out a giggle of shock. "Bryce!"

"I'm sorry, but it's a natural thing. I wake up most mornings hard as a rock." He shrugged. "Nothing I can do about it... until after I've woken up."

Lucy's pale cheeks took on a deeper hue, and she dropped her gaze before murmuring "Well... maybe I could give you a hand with that."

She could not possibly mean what he almost desperately wanted to believe she did. Shocked, Bryce stared at her, not at all sure what to say. For a moment there was complete silence in the cabin, which suddenly seemed a lot smaller than it had before.

"Did you seriously just offer to give me a morning hand job?" he blurted out finally.

Lucy's lips twitched, and then she began to laugh, almost hysterically. Flopping down on the bed, she giggled madly, rolling up into a ball, grabbing her pillow to muffle her chuckles and snorts.

"Okay, I think today's been a bit much for you," Bryce said, realising she was overwrought. Gingerly, he sat down on the bed beside her, reached out to smooth his hand over her hair. She grabbed onto his hand and clutched it as though he'd thrown her a lifeline, still laughing but now with tears streaming down her cheeks. "Lucy. Take a breath, sweetheart. It's okay. Everything's going to be okay."

He ended up lying down with her in his arms, her small fists knotted in the fabric of his T-shirt, his hands stroking her back in a soothing, steady rhythm while she hiccoughed and giggled against his chest. Trying to calm her, he began to hum softly under his breath, after wracking his brain to think of something slow and gentle. Finally, Lucy's heaving breaths settled, her hiccoughs and giggles fading away.

"I'm sorry," she mumbled finally into Bryce's shirt.

"Don't be." He never slowed his gentle stroking of her back.

"Was that Simon and Garfunkel?"

He couldn't help but smile, though she wouldn't see it with her head tucked under his chin. "Only you, Lucy Manning, would retain enough presence of mind to identify a song while in the midst of a panic attack."

"It wasn't a panic attack. Just a... a minor breakdown."

"You're so full of shit. It's okay to admit your mother can drive you to panic attacks. How about we create some sort of signal we can use, which you can give me to let me know you need to get out and get some space to get yourself back together?"

She didn't say anything, but she did nod against his chest.

"A signal word?" Bryce pushed.

"How about '*Cecelia*'?" Lucy suggested after a moment.

"See, I knew you were a Simon and Garfunkel fan really."

Her tight grip on his shirt loosened enough for her to poke him in the ribs. "I just thought it'd be an easy word to work into conversation. Far as I know, there isn't a Cecelia on staff here, but Mum won't know that."

"Perfect," Bryce approved. He didn't loosen his firm hold on her, or slow his stroking of her back. Several long minutes of silence passed, but it didn't feel awkward. Lucy slowly relaxed against him, her hands spreading out to gently splay on his chest.

"Thanks," she said finally, though she didn't specify what for. Bryce figured 'for everything' would just about cover it.

"You're welcome," he responded. "Your mum's a piece of work, huh." He didn't make it a question.

"She was behaving quite well today, actually." Lucy tipped her head back to meet his eyes. "She does, when she has an audience of more than just me."

"Christ, Lucy." Instinctively, he tightened his hold, hugging her close. "Is it okay for me to say I don't want you to be alone with her?"

"That is very okay."

"I'll spread the word. I'm pretty sure Rosie, Nessa and the other girls will be happy to make sure you're always surrounded by a crowd." Lifting his hand to her face, he gently swept a lock of her dark brown hair back from her cheek, cupped it in his hand. "How can you look so like her and yet be so different? You're one of the sweetest, nicest people I've ever met, and Justine... is like a box jellyfish. Pretty to look at, but every tendril has a lethal sting."

"That might be the most accurate description of my mother I've ever heard." Laughter, true, genuine laughter, creased the corners of Lucy's eyes. "I've been wondering all day if I was mad to have gone ahead with this plan, but right now, you being here with me is the only thing that's making her visit bearable."

"I'm here, and I'm staying," Bryce promised, gazing into her eyes. He was sorely tempted to kiss her right then, but it would have been an utterly dick move. Instead, he hugged her closer, pressed his cheek against the top of her head. "Whatever you need, Lucy. I'm right here."

She didn't say anything, but her arm slipped around him and he felt her snuggle closer, turning her cheek against his head. After a few minutes, her breathing slowed, and he realized she'd fallen asleep. Carefully, he tried to disengage, leave her to rest, but even in her sleep she clung close, made a discontented sound.

Smiling, Bryce relaxed. If what Lucy needed was to sleep peacefully in his arms, that was what he would give her.

For as long as she needed, even if that was long after Justine had left the island, he'd give Lucy whatever she wanted.

Silently, as Lucy slept in his arms, Bryce admitted to himself that his feelings had gone far beyond a mere crush. While he'd admired Lucy before, spending all this time with her had only caused him to fall utterly, head over heels in love with the beautiful, brilliant, but above all kind and loving woman she was. Seeing her with Justine, the incredible contrast between two women so similar in looks but poles apart in personality, had only cemented his feelings.

Lucy Manning was the most incredible woman he'd ever met, and he was way, way in over his head.

Chapter Ten

Waking in Bryce's arms felt utterly natural and right. There was no surprise at finding the steady thump beneath her ear was his heartbeat, no concern at the warmth of his body against hers, the strength of his arms cradling her. Lucy sighed and stretched, humming a little with contentment.

"Feeling better?" Bryce asked, his voice rich with amusement.

"Nana naps are literally magic," Lucy sighed in response, looking up and grinning at him. "Thanks for not waking me."

"You needed the rest." Bryce took his sweet time letting go of her, but Lucy wished he hadn't bothered. Though the cabin was warm enough, her air con set to a warm twenty-four degrees Centigrade, she felt suddenly chilled with the loss of Bryce's heat. She rolled to her side and hugged a pillow, watching as he hesitated in front of the wardrobe doors.

"I should get changed before we go to meet your mum for dinner." Gesturing down at his board shorts and T-shirt, he smiled self-deprecatingly. "This might have been okay to meet her at the airport, but she won't think much of me if I don't bother to change. Would you mind if I wash up and change?"

Lucy's brow furrowed until she realised he was asking if he could use her bathroom. "Of course," she said at once. "Yes. If we're going to share the room, Bryce, you don't even have to ask!"

"Unless you need to use it first?"

"Nah, I'm good here for a few minutes. I like to wake up slowly and stretch a bit."

"Noted." He smiled at her before gathering some clean clothes and heading into the bathroom. The door closed, but she didn't hear the lock snick.

The fact of the unlocked door held Lucy's eyes riveted to the handle. She could hear the water running, could imagine Bryce's tall, strong form slicked with water as he took a shower, the droplets running over the contours of his muscles. Following a path she couldn't help thinking about tracing with her tongue.

Why hadn't he locked the door? Her hands twitched with holding them back; she wanted desperately to go and turn the handle, ease the door open just a tiny way. See if she could spy his reflection in the mirror on the opposite wall, if it hadn't fogged from the heat of the water.

Oh my God. I'm turning into a voyeur. With a tiny shriek, Lucy forced herself off the bed and over to the wardrobe, grabbing randomly for a dress to wear. She'd bought a dozen or so lightweight cotton dresses since arriving and spent most of her off-duty hours in one. Selecting a navy-blue one with bright fuchsia and gold tropical flowers printed on it, she hesitated, looking at Bryce's clothes hanging alongside hers.

I should feel like my space is being invaded... shouldn't I? Instead, there was a feeling of comfort and domesticity about the scene. Reaching out, she lightly touched the sleeve of one of his few formal shirts, feeling the crisp fabric under her fingertips.

"Bathroom's free," Bryce said behind her, and she jumped about a foot in the air, letting out a startled shriek. "Hell, I'm sorry! I wasn't trying to be quiet — I assumed you heard the bathroom door open!"

Closing her eyes, Lucy pressed one hand against the wall to steady herself. "I was miles away," she admitted, unable to look at him and confess she'd been fantasising about the two of them living in cosy domesticity forever and ever.

"Obviously!"

She heard his footsteps, even though he was barefoot, as he crossed the tile floor, coming to stand right in front of her. Opening her eyes, she peeked up at him.

God, he's beautiful.

Blond hair darkened with water, tawny stubble just beginning to coarsen his chiselled jaw, Bryce looked down at her with a slight frown. "Are you feeling okay, Lucy?"

No. My eyes feel gritty from sleep and my hair is all over the place, and I desperately need a shower... Out loud, she said "I'm fine. Or I will be, once I've had a shower."

"All right." He didn't step aside, though, to clear her path to the bathroom, just stood there looking down at her.

Is he looking at my mouth? Unconsciously, Lucy licked her lips, and saw, to her fascination, Bryce's pupils flare wide.

"We didn't talk about that kiss earlier," Bryce said, his voice lower and huskier than it had been a moment earlier.

"Which one?"

"Any of them, frankly. They were all..." he seemed to be searching for the right word. "Unexpected."

Not the worst choice of word, she supposed. She knew he didn't mean he hadn't been expecting the kisses, only that he'd been surprised by his own reaction to them. Which at least answered the burning question of whether he'd been as affected as she.

"It's kind of difficult to talk about," Lucy admitted, "because all I can think about it how much I want to kiss you again."

"Yeah?" He didn't miss a beat, just took a step closer. "I haven't stopped thinking about it either."

The dress she was still holding slithered to the floor unnoticed as Lucy reached out, and Bryce met her halfway. In a moment they were clinging tightly to each other, mouths fused together, the kisses almost frantic as they both released the emotions they'd been bottling up all afternoon.

Lucy jumped up and hooked her legs around Bryce's waist, unable to get close enough with the height difference between them. He groaned against her mouth, one hand sliding under her butt to support her, and then turned to carry her over to the bed.

He was hard, she discovered with delight as he came down on top of her, knees between hers. Lucy ground against him with a low moan in her throat, her groin tilted against his, the heat and pressure of his arousal blissful through the thin layers of their clothes.

"*Lucy.*" His growl of her name as he temporarily abandoned her mouth to start kissing down her neck brought her back to reality, much though she'd have preferred to stay floating in her blissfully sensual haze. It took every bit of willpower she could muster to push feebly against his shoulders and say,

"Bryce, stop."

Bryce groaned against her throat, his rocking hips stilling. "Please tell me you didn't just say that."

"We gotta."

"Ugh!" Rolling off her and collapsing to his back, he flung a forearm up to cover his eyes.

"Bryce, I'm sorry," Lucy said desperately. "But we're supposed to meet Justine in fifteen minutes, and if we don't show she's totally going to come looking for us."

"It wouldn't reinforce our story if she happened to catch us going at it, then?" He cracked a smile, though he didn't uncover his eyes to look at her. "Go take a shower, Luce. I'm just gonna lie here and think about ice water baths for a while."

He needed to. She couldn't resist a look as she rolled off the bed and headed for the bathroom; his erection was tenting the lightweight fabric of his khakis.

If only we had time... "Then what?" Lucy asked herself aloud as she stepped under the shower spray. She deliberately hadn't waited for it to warm back up. Her overheated body needed cooling down as well.

Were we really on the verge of having sex? It wasn't as though Bryce could fake his body's reaction. He'd most definitely been up for it, and considering the way he'd groaned her name, very much aware of where he was and who with.

Oh God, I need to stop thinking about it. She was wet between her legs, and thinking about how hard and hot Bryce had felt against her, the delicious friction she'd found rocking against his thick erection, really wasn't helping the situation. Grabbing the mixer tap, she turned the temperature lower again and reached for the soap. She just wished she could wash her dirty mind as easily as her body.

***

Bryce wasn't in the room when she left the bathroom. Stepping into her shoes, Lucy opened the sliding door, guessing she might find him in his hammock outside. She'd walked past his cabin many times and seen him relaxing there.

He looked up at her as she stepped outside. One foot on the floor pushed him back and forth in an idle swinging motion, the hammock creaking quietly.

"Hey."

"Hey," Lucy said in return, feeling suddenly awkward. Unsure exactly what to say to him now, she stood nibbling on a hangnail.

"Hungry?" Bryce stilled, before pushing to his feet in a single graceful movement. "Because I'm starved." He reached for her hand as though it was the most natural thing in the world, and Lucy let him take it.

"Yeah, I'm hungry," she agreed. "I was too nervous to eat at lunch."

"I noticed," Bryce said, with a gentle squeeze to her fingers. "Probably why two cocktails put you right to sleep."

"That, and the fact that I haven't slept much the last three nights," Lucy said dryly as they made their way to the main resort building.

"Don't let her get under your skin, Lucy," Bryce told her. "Listen to me. You're a beautiful, brilliant woman. You've got a good job in an idyllic location and," he slid her a cheeky grin, "a hot younger man just dying to fulfil your every sexual fantasy."

Lucy chuckled, as he'd obviously meant her to. "I guess, when you put it that way."

"You've got nothing to be ashamed of. Quite the opposite. So lift your head up and *own* it, girl. Justine ain't got nothin' on you."

"When you look at me like that," Lucy said softly, "I almost believe it."

He stopped walking right outside the restaurant entrance, framed her face between his big hands, and kissed her.

"Believe it."

Lips still tingling from the kiss, Lucy let Bryce lead her inside. Justine wasn't there yet, which didn't surprise her. Justine always loved to make an entrance.

One of seven restaurants on the island, this was one of the largest, with an Italian-themed buffet every night. She didn't know the waitress who came up to them with a cheerful smile, but Bryce obviously did.

"Hey, Nina."

"Hi, Bryce! Eating here instead of the staff dining room?" She gave him a puzzled look. Though they received a discount, staff had to pay to eat in the resort's public restaurants, whereas the staff dining room was always free.

"Lucy's mother arrived today," Bryce said.

"Ahh." Nina's tone made it clear she knew all about their wedding deception. She gave Lucy a slightly disparaging look up and down, though her tone was friendly enough. "I'll give you one of the booths and bring her over when she arrives."

"Thanks, hon."

"Anything to drink?" Nina checked as she seated them.

"Not for me, I'm heading out for the night dive in an hour," Bryce said.

"Justine will probably want wine, so I'll share a bottle with her, but I'll wait and let her choose it," Lucy said.

"Well, wave me down if you change your mind, or if there's anything else you want." Nina's smile at Bryce was boldly inviting, and Lucy found herself clenching her fists under the table. The other girl was perfectly entitled to flirt, she tried to tell herself. After all, as far as Nina knew, Bryce was just helping her out while her mother was visiting. He was single, and therefore fair game.

Lucy still wanted to scratch her eyes out.

Chapter Eleven

Justine certainly knew how to make an entrance, Bryce thought. She timed it perfectly, waiting until the sauce between the buffet and the door was clear before stepping forward and pausing, looking around as though she couldn't find them even though they were almost directly opposite her.

One poor guy at the buffet dropped his plate, which shattered into a thousand pieces and broke the sudden startled silence which had fallen. Nina and another waitress at once hurried over to clean up, the man hastily retreating, tripping over a chair as he gazed open-mouthed at Justine.

All around the restaurant men — and not a few women — were staring. Justine had dressed to kill in a slinky dress of pale silver satin, cut diagonally off one shoulder and slit well up her thigh on the opposite side.

"Holy shit, that's Justine Manning," a man said in the booth beside them, his tone awed, and Bryce saw Lucy wince.

It was at that moment he realised he'd never asked what her mother did for a living.

"She's an actress," Lucy muttered, when he leaned across to quietly murmur the question in her ear. "She plays a *femme fatale* on one of the longest-running British soaps."

That explained quite a lot, including why Justine looked so impeccably groomed. Her black hair shone, falling just past her shoulders in glossy waves, pinned up on one side with a deep red flower. Lips painted the same colour as the flower, she smiled as several people approached her to ask if they might have autographs or selfies.

"I'm here visiting my daughter," Justine said loudly as one fan asked eagerly why she was on the island. "She's one of the resident marine biologists. Come over here, Lucy darling!"

Bryce followed as Lucy got up, the look on her face making it clear she was reluctant to enter the limelight.

"I had no idea you had a daughter!" the woman talking to Justine gushed as Lucy approached. "No — this can't *possibly* be your daughter! You're not old enough!"

"You're so sweet." Justine's laugh was like little silver bells... or tinkling razor shards, Bryce thought. Lucy seemed to shrink into herself as Justine wrapped an arm around her shoulders. "I'm very proud of Lucy. She's terribly smart... and she's getting married next week, which is why I'm here, of course!"

"Of course, they had to get married during a break in filming," the woman nodded, looking from Lucy to Bryce with a smile. "Congratulations."

"Thank you," Lucy muttered.

Somehow, Justine had managed to make a wedding she hadn't even known about that morning all about her, Bryce thought with an exasperated shake of his head. She was certainly comfortable in the limelight, expertly handling the fans who came up, excusing herself after a few minutes with a tinkling little laugh.

"I'm starving, my dears! I'm staying for two weeks, no doubt you'll see me around."

As though by magic, the little crowd of British tourists who'd gathered around her dissipated, and Justine sashayed over to the booth where Lucy and Bryce had retreated.

"Sorry about that, darling." She glanced at the empty seat opposite them with a little pout of her lips, but then seemed to accept she couldn't really ask Lucy to move so she could sit beside Bryce. Taking her seat, she looked at their water glasses.

"Not drinking?"

"I've got to take out a night dive," Bryce explained. "I'll have a quick dinner with you, but then I'm afraid I'll have to excuse myself."

"Oh, what a shame. What about you, Lucy?"

"I was waiting for you. Thought you'd like to choose some wine," Lucy explained, and Justine seemed pleased by her thoughtfulness.

Dinner passed pleasantly enough. Justine, like Lucy, had a healthy appetite, though Bryce noted she watched Lucy's plate and made sure to eat just a little less. Even in this, she was competing with her daughter.

To Bryce, despite Justine's show-stopping appearance, there was no comparison. One was all show, and the other had the substance. This close, he could see how Justine's artfully applied makeup enhanced her features... and it occurred to him that at least some of her incredibly youthful appearance might be due to Botox or plastic surgery. She looked too smooth, almost plastic, especially compared to Lucy's fresh, natural appearance. He'd never seen Lucy wear any other makeup than lip gloss. She really didn't need it, her lightly tanned skin flawlessly smooth, her lashes long and dark, soft lips kissably pink, drawing his gaze inevitably and making him think about their earlier kisses again.

He could see Lucy didn't feel she came off well in comparisons to her mother, though, and vowed to do his best to reassure her later. He hated to leave the two of them alone, certain Justine would be much more bitchy to Lucy once she had her on her own than she would in front of him.

So he was very grateful when Luke entered the restaurant about five minutes before Bryce would have to leave, coming up to their table with a broad smile.

"Hey Lucy, Bryce. And this must be our newest celebrity guest."

Justine preened as Luke turned his considerable charm on her. Standing up, she let him take her hand, bowing over it gallantly.

"Lucy didn't mention you were *the* Justine Manning. I just found out from the resort's Instagram feed going crazy," Luke said wryly, and Bryce was suddenly quite certain Luke hadn't a clue who she was. He'd probably Googled her hastily before coming to the restaurant.

"Well... it's not like I'm here to perform." Justine flicked her eyes towards Lucy, who hastily rose and made the introductions, presenting Luke as the resort's general manager.

"Luke's also officiating at our wedding," Bryce put in, thinking that was worth mentioning. "Though Sunfish has a full-time celebrant, she's away next week, so Luke agreed to stand in for us."

"Happy to do it," Luke said heartily, putting a hand on Bryce's shoulder. "I've never seen a couple so in love, have you?" he asked Justine.

"They can't keep their hands off each other, that's for sure," Justine said with her tinkling little laugh, and Bryce was suddenly struck by a flash of inspiration.

"Are you busy, Luke? Because I'm about to head out with the night dive, and I'd appreciate it if you'd stand in for me and keep Justine and Lucy company for a while."

"I'd be delighted," Luke said warmly, and Justine brightened.

"Do sit down," she slid over and patted the vacated seat beside her. The look she skimmed over Luke was positively acquisitive, and Bryce felt briefly sorry for his boss. But then, Luke was a grown man and could look after himself.

"I'll walk out with you," Lucy said as Bryce made his apologies. Her hand felt cold as her fingers curled around his, and he held onto them firmly as they left the restaurant.

"You okay?" he asked quietly once they were out of earshot.

"Yeah. I forgot how difficult it is to go out with her in public." Lucy grimaced slightly. "That was only a fraction of the attention she gets in England, of course."

"I can imagine." He could also see how Justine basked in it, manipulating the limelight to push Lucy ever further into her shadow. With a quick glance over his shoulder to check they were still visible from the booth where Justine and Luke now sat, Bryce drew Lucy to a halt. "You've managed her awesomely so far, and Luke's smart enough to spot the signals if you need to let him know you don't want to be alone with Justine."

"You've been so amazing," Lucy said earnestly, staring up at him. "Thank you so much."

Bryce ducked his head a little bashfully. "It's nothing." He flicked another glance back at the booth, saw Justine watching them. "And since she's watching, I think we should give her something to stare at. I'm gonna kiss you now, okay?"

***

"Uh," Lucy said intelligently. "Uh, yeah. That's okay."

Bryce's arm curled around her waist and he bent his head slowly, obviously giving her time to back off if she changed her mind. Not that Lucy could imagine any reason she might ever want to *not* kiss Bryce. Even if he hadn't already proven himself to be an exceptional kisser, he was, well, *Bryce*. She tilted her face up, eyes drifting closed and lips parting instinctively.

"Fuck, you're beautiful," Bryce muttered gruffly, and Lucy's eyes flew open again briefly just as he kissed her.

Did he really mean that? Growing up in her mother's shadow, Lucy had always been the ugly duckling, Intellectually she knew she was passably pretty at least, but the way Bryce looked at her, the way he kissed her, made her *feel* beautiful for the first time in her life. She swayed towards him as he broke the kiss, wanting more, wanting to feel that way again, and Bryce muttered a curse under his breath.

"I'll see you later," he said before kissing her again, a little rougher this time, a little deeper.

Lucy's lips were tingling as she returned to the dinner table, flags of scarlet colour flying high on her cheeks. Justine had already looked away, was focusing all her attention on Luke. Lucy wondered if she'd have to warn him off — Luke was far too nice to get caught in Justine's web — but decided he could take care of himself when he shot her a surreptitious wink at one point. They were all playing their parts, and Justine, the professional actress, hadn't the slightest idea.

Oh, the delicious irony.

The sensation of victory carried Lucy through the rest of the dinner, and thankfully immediately afterwards Justine admitted jet lag was making her tired.

"Get some sleep, Mum. I'll meet you in the morning, take you on a tour of the island. Say nine o'clock? Give you time to have some breakfast first. I'll meet you in the main lobby, by the information desk."

"Sounds lovely, darling." Justine air-kissed both her cheeks. "Good night."

"Lovely to meet you, Justine." Luke gave her a warm smile. "See you again soon, I hope."

"You can count on it." She gave him a sultry look before turning on her heel and heading for the elevators.

Luke blew out his cheeks as he watched her go before shooting Lucy a wry look. "If I hadn't been forewarned that your mother was a difficult type, I might be trailing along behind her with my tongue hanging out right about now."

"Please don't fall for her," Lucy begged earnestly. "You're much, much too nice."

"No fear, hon. I'm married to my job." Luke smiled, the corners of his eyes crinkling. "Besides, I can hardly have a strict policy of no involvement between staff and guests if I don't follow it myself, can I?"

"Great leaders lead by example," Lucy murmured.

"Since you don't actually work for me, I'll take that as the compliment it is." Luke nodded his head to her gravely. "We're here for you, Lucy. I wondered when you first came to me why you were doing this, but I think I understand a little better now. Don't let Justine get under your skin, huh? It's only two weeks, and you'll have plenty to distract her with."

"You mean Bryce, and the wedding."

Luke's grin was wicked. "Sic Terry and Jerome on her. And Olivia. No doubt Olivia will know how to put a good PR spin on one of Britain's biggest soap stars holidaying here."

Lucy wrinkled her nose. "Undoubtedly. I just know Justine will want to make our wedding all about her."

Luke looked at her oddly. "Your fake wedding."

"Hm?"

"Your *fake* wedding, Lucy. You're not really getting married, remember?"

"Oh." Feeling a scalding blush start crawling up her cheeks, Lucy started babbling. "Well, of course I hadn't forgotten. It's just so easy to get lost in all the little details, even though Terry and Jerome are absolute stars at organising things, all they do is show me ideas for approval. This is the most wonderful practice for if I ever do get married."

Luke's expression was decidedly cynical as he looked at her, but he nodded and said nothing, a small smile lifting the corners of his lips. "Well. You can count on my support, whatever you need."

"Thank you so much," Lucy said again as he smiled and left her. It was a shame Luke didn't have a romantic interest of his own, she thought. Not that she would wish Justine on anyone, much less a man she liked so much!

Chapter Twelve

It was well after midnight when Bryce walked wearily back into the staff area and hesitated at a fork in the path. Going back to his cabin seemed pointless since there was almost nothing of his there, not even his toothbrush, but going to Lucy's felt kind of presumptuous. She was probably asleep, anyway, and he definitely didn't want to wake her. The way she'd fallen asleep on him that afternoon spoke of nights she'd spent awake worrying.

He'd go by her cabin and see, he decided after a moment. If she was awake, he could just grab his toothbrush and a change of clothes, and then go back to his place to sleep.

There were no lights on in Lucy's cabin, and Bryce's shoulders sagged. Well... he could still get a shower and just sleep in the nude, he supposed. They hadn't stripped his old bed, at least. He was turning to walk away when a voice said his name softly.

"Lucy?" He turned back, squinting.

"Here."

She was in his hammock, he realised as she lifted a hand, a tiny citronella candle burning on the rail beside her to keep the mosquitoes at bay.

"You should be resting." Walking up alongside her, he looked down, trying to make out her expression. She was on the wrong side of the cabin for the bright moonlight to illuminate her features, and the candle's glow was too small to be helpful.

"Couldn't sleep. How was the dive?"

"Nothing out of the ordinary. How was your evening, after I left? Did Luke stay?"

"He did, and he was wonderful." She sat up, lurching to try and get out of the hammock, giggling as it swung wildly. Bryce chuckled along with her, leaning down to grab her and lift her to her feet. She clung to his shoulders, gripping the snug material of his T-shirt, clinging to slightly damp skin.

"I came to pick up my toothbrush and some clean clothes," Bryce said after a moment of tense, singing silence.

"You have to sleep here," Lucy blurted, and he raised his eyebrows.

"Excuse me?"

"Justine went to bed early. Jet lag. She's quite likely to be up at the crack of dawn and perfectly selfish enough to come looking for me. If she finds you not sleeping here, well… all the hard work we put in today would be wasted, wouldn't it?"

"Lucy." He stopped after the single word, stalling out. Then restarted again. "After earlier, is that a good idea?"

"Earlier?"

"Yes, earlier, when we damn near ripped each others' clothes off!"

"Oh. That."

They were almost nose to nose. Bryce's hands shook with the effort of not reaching for her, not grabbing her and dragging her hard against him.

"I want you," he said raggedly. "I've spent damn near every minute since that kiss here earlier thinking about it, thinking about you. About how much I *didn't* want to stop."

The silence seemed to go on forever. Bryce died a little inside as Lucy just stared at him, wide-eyed. And then she said;

"So this time, let's not stop."

This is going to complicate things, Bryce thought as Lucy's arms wrapped around his neck and she pulled his head down. But then her soft lips pressed against his and he stopped thinking about anything except the way she tasted.

***

For an awful moment, Lucy thought Bryce wasn't going to kiss her back. Then he made a rough noise in his throat, arms wrapping around her tightly to lift her off her feet. She felt him step back, kicking the screen door open before he carried her into the cabin and lowered her to the bed, lips still fused with hers as they drank each other in.

She wanted to feel his skin against hers, tore frantically at his T-shirt until he reared back off her and ripped it off. The moonlight pouring into the room limned his lean, strong torso in a silvery halo, brightening his blond hair. He looked almost like an angel there above her, but no angel would be cupping her breasts through her dress, thumbs teasing her nipples to hard, aching peaks.

Bryce was kneeling on her dress; frustrated beyond measure, Lucy shoved at him. "Off," she demanded.

"What?" He froze, hands still on her breasts.

"Get off! I need to get my dress off!"

His chuckle was relieved as he rolled to the side, reaching down to help pull her dress up and off over her head. Hurling it aside, Lucy almost flung herself against Bryce's chest, moaning with pleasure as the warmth of his skin soaked into hers.

"Christ, Lucy." Bryce sounded as affected as she felt, his voice hoarse. His hands stroked down her back, hesitated at the clasp of her bra.

"Take it off," Lucy begged.

Still he hesitated, before asking in a low voice "Do you have protection, Lucy?"

"I'm on the Pill, but yes. Condoms." She waved a hand vaguely at the nightstand. "Top drawer."

She wasn't going to mention that she'd bought them at the hotel's small shop before returning to her cabin after dinner, in the hope this very scenario might occur. Bryce probably wouldn't care that she'd premeditated his seduction, but she still didn't plan to mention it.

"Good," Bryce mumbled, unfastening the snap of her bra before rolling back to reach for the nightstand. "I was going to get some from the shop, but they'd closed by the time the dive boat got back."

Lucy laughed out loud, but shook her head when he turned to give her a quizzical look. "Nothing. Never mind. You found them?"

"Right here." He held up the box. "You sure about this, Lucy?"

"Never been more sure of anything in my life," she said with complete honesty, and he nodded.

"Me, too."

Bryce was down to just a pair of thin board shorts now, the lacing coming undone easily as Lucy tugged at it. His cock strained towards her through the opening, thick and long, hard steel covered with velvet-soft skin. She wrapped her fingers around him, testing his size, catching a droplet of thick cream on the end of her thumb and smearing it back into the head.

"Fffuuucckkk," Bryce husked out, hands shaking as he reached to cup her breasts again. "Easy there, Luce..."

She smiled, sliding her hand along his thick length, adding a sharp little twist as she brought it back up again. "Something the matter?"

"Yeah, I'm not gonna last long enough to get inside you if you keep that up." Bryce's words were almost hissed out through clenched teeth. He gave her nipples a sharp little tug, making Lucy gasp in response. Her grip slackened, and a moment later Bryce was pushing her down to her back, mouth seeking her breasts as one big hand skimmed down over her stomach.

She was still wearing her panties, but she knew very well they were soaked with the evidence of her lust. Bryce seemed to stall out as his fingers encountered the damp patch over her crotch, but only briefly before his fingers were nudging the fabric aside.

"Christ, you're so wet," he murmured, pulling off her nipple to look up at her. "Lucy..."

"Sh," she ordered, spearing her fingers into his thick, shaggy golden hair and urging him back to her breast. They could talk later about how she'd been lusting after him almost since they met. Or not, preferably. His fingers were working sheer magic, grazing lightly at first over her clit and then making rougher circles, finding the exact pressure to make her hips buck up off the bed and small cries erupt from her lips. His mouth stayed busy too, suckling first one nipple then the other, each tug of his firm lips sending further bolts of pleasurable sensation through her.

***

Lucy seemed almost delirious, unintelligible cries and moans spilling from her as Bryce coaxed her up towards orgasm. Her nails scored his scalp, fingers tugging on his hair. The small pressure only increased his own arousal, making him grind his hips against the mattress in a desperate search for relief.

"Bryce, please!" Lucy cried out finally. "I want you — want you inside me — please!"

It would have taken a much stronger man than Bryce Seabrook to deny her. With a groan of need, he lifted his head and reached for the box of condoms he'd dropped on the edge of the bed. By the time his fingers closed around it, Lucy had wriggled out of her knickers with a very distracting shimmy of her hips and was lying back, a come-hither look in her eyes.

In the heated dreams from which he'd awakened far too often, he hadn't rushed. He'd taken his time to explore every inch of Lucy, find all the trigger spots which made her moan and gasp, but in real life, that exploration would have to come later. She was in no mood to wait and he honestly thought he might explode if he tried to hold out any longer. Easing to kneel between Lucy's spread thighs, he guided his sheathed cock to her soaked entrance.

Lucy's moan as he pressed inside her almost set him off. He had to pause, grip tightly around the base of his cock for a moment and breathe deeply to keep control. Her hands came up to settle on his shoulders, slender legs winding around his hips as she tried to pull him deeper, and he groaned.

"Easy, babe, easy. Gimme a second."

She whined his name, tugging on him frantically, and he was lost. With a fierce thrust of his hips he plunged fully inside Lucy, revelling in her shriek of pleasure, working his hand in between them to find her clit and rub it almost frantically, bringing her up to the peak as he flew there himself. His own groans and shouts mingled with hers as they chased ecstasy together, until Lucy's nails dug into his shoulders, body bowing up against his as she climaxed for a second time.

She was so beautiful in the throes of her pleasure, long slender neck arched back, her dark hair thrashing around her on the white pillow as she flung her head from side to side, writhing sinuously underneath him.

With a desperate moan of relief Bryce let go, feeling his balls tighten and pull up hard against his body as seed spurted in hot jets into the condom.

"Oh God, Luce," Bryce mumbled against her hair. He was shaking, slight tremors running through him with the incredible intensity of the release, as he reared back and lifted his hand to touch her cheek, kiss her lips. "God, that was..." He didn't have words, could only gaze at her in wonderment.

She smiled up at him, her hands stroking lightly over his shoulders. "It was, wasn't it?"

Bryce could only nod, grunting slightly as he eased back. Lucy made a small sound of protest as he slipped from her and clambered off the bed to go to the bathroom, and when he returned after cleaning up and brushing his teeth to find she'd crawled under the sheet, she lifted one edge of it invitingly.

"You okay with me sleeping here?" he checked, sliding into bed beside her.

"Sure. I'm not a cuddly sleeper, though," she warned.

"Thank God for that. It's way too hot in Queensland to be cuddling up to a hot body in your sleep."

***

Lucy giggled as Bryce defused what could have been a slightly tense moment with his trademark humour. He was right, of course, it was far too hot to cuddle anyway. She was hot and sweating after even the quickie they'd just had, even though the air conditioner was on low, keeping the room cooler than the hot, humid night outside.

Rolling on her side to look at him, she smiled. The moonlight pouring into the cabin through the big windows — she rarely drew her curtains — meant she could see his face clearly, although her own would probably be in shadow. He looked relaxed, a satisfied smile curving his mouth. As she lay there admiring the perfect symmetry of his face, his high cheekbones, broad brow and sharp blade of a nose, he reached out and traced the end of his thumb lightly over her lower lip before placing his hand gently over hers where it rested on the mattress between them.

"You okay?" he asked softly.

"Oh hell yes!" Lucy opened her eyes wide. "That was *fantastic*."

"Really? I thought it was terrible. Not the sex, I mean, not *you*. Me. *I* was terrible."

She laughed in disbelief. "Are you kidding?" Turning her hand under his to interlace their fingers, she squeezed gently. "Yes, it was quick, but that was just what I wanted — what I needed. There's a time for slow and languid and there's a time to bang and get it out of your system."

Bryce flinched back slightly, and it was Lucy's turn to hastily restate her meaning.

"Not that you're out of my system!"

"I'm not?"

"If you're still here when I wake up in the morning, I'm gonna pounce on you," she warned, and he laughed.

"I'm not going anywhere, angel. Trust me on that." Bringing her hand to his lips, he kissed the back of it gently before laying it down again. "And if I wasn't so damn exhausted, I'd be encouraging you to jump on me now."

Lucy knew just what he meant. Her whole body was still humming with pleasure, but she was so tired she was fighting to keep her eyelids open. Letting them drift closed, she listened to the soft sound of Bryce's slow, even breathing for less than a minute before sleep claimed her.

Chapter Thirteen

"Yoo-hoo, darling! Lucy!"

"Fuck!" Lucy sat bolt upright, clutching the sheet to her bare breasts. Despite making the excuse to Bryce the previous night to convince him to stay, she hadn't really thought her mother would come looking for her at some unearthly hour.

Glancing at the clock by the bed, though, she groaned. It wasn't early; it was ten past nine, and she'd told Justine she'd meet her at nine in the lobby to take her on a tour of the island.

"Hm?" Beside her, Bryce rolled closer, an arm curling around her waist and pulling her towards him. "Is it morning already? Good, I can ravish you again..."

She spared a few seconds to appreciate how he looked, all rumpled in the warm light of morning, his hair shining gold, blue eyes peering up at her as he tried to pull her down for a kiss.

"My mother's here!" she hissed.

"Don't want to walk in on anything, darling," Justine said loudly from outside the door. "Did you oversleep or did that gorgeous man of yours just not let you out of bed on time?"

"Sorry, Justine," Bryce called back after a moment as Lucy fled for the bathroom. "My fault. Lost track of the time. I kept her up late, too."

"Naughty boy," Justine said playfully, and slid the door open. Bryce made sure the sheet was covering his hips before lying back and putting his hands behind his head, feigning a casualness he didn't feel. Justine just stood and surveyed him for a moment, a smile on her perfectly painted lips. Even this early in the morning, she was fully made up, large designer sunglasses perched atop her glossy hair, wearing a white silk blouse with large pink flowers printed on it and white designer Capri pants. And white high-heeled sandals, Bryce noted, willing himself not to laugh at how ridiculously overdressed she looked. She could have just stepped off a film set or a yacht in St. Tropez.

"Hey, Mum." The bathroom door slid open and Lucy emerged, putting the final couple of twists in her simple braid before wrapping a tie around the end. "Be right with you, I just need to put sunscreen on."

The contrast couldn't be more extreme between mother and daughter. Lucy looked surprisingly fresh — Bryce suspected she'd just splashed cold water on her face — her eyes sparkling, cheeks glowing. She wore a strappy pale blue cotton sundress, and stepped into a pair of old rubber flip-flops as he watched.

"Are you wearing sunscreen?" Lucy checked as she grabbed the bottle sitting on the dresser and squeezed some onto her hands. "Otherwise you're going to fry."

"My moisturiser is SPF 30, darling," Justine dismissed.

"That probably won't be enough. I'll bring the bottle." With a glance at Bryce, Lucy said brightly "Will you put some on my back?"

"Of course." He patted the bed between his thighs, accepted the bottle as she sat down. Took his time massaging the thick sunscreen into her shoulders and upper back, ignoring Justine entirely. "There," he murmured at last, leaning forward to nibble her ear. "Enjoy your morning. I'll catch up with you for lunch? Got an afternoon dive leaving at two."

"Lunch sounds good." Lucy turned her head to kiss him, smiling at him gratefully. Though after the previous night, Bryce had no idea why she might think he wouldn't go along with anything she wanted. He craved her again now, wanted to tell Justine to get lost and pull Lucy back into the bed, spend the whole morning exploring her body, the softness of her skin, the sounds she made as he made love to her.

As she capped the sunscreen and got off the bed, he had to shift a knee up to hide the fact that he was tenting the sheet. Justine was pointedly ignoring the pair of them, picking up and putting down things on Lucy's dresser.

"Cheap moisturiser, darling, really?" She held up a bottle and shook her head. "I thought I taught you better than that."

"You tried to raise me with expensive tastes, yeah," Lucy said dryly. "Considering how much of the stuff I go through in this heat, I'd be broke in a few weeks if I tried to use high-end stuff. That's been working for me."

Justine pursed her lips and shook her head. Bryce sensed this was a regular battle between the two, and one Lucy had long since won by simply ignoring her mother's recommendations and demands.

He heard Justine start up again as the two of them left, Lucy with a final wistful glance over her shoulder at Bryce still in her bed. He gave her a warm smile and she returned it before closing the door behind them.

Still tired, Bryce only gave brief thought to trying to go back to sleep. Sleeping in Lucy's bed without her felt too intrusive, somehow. Pushing himself up with a regretful sigh, he headed for the shower. He'd clean up, get some food, and go prepare for the afternoon dive class. At least that would keep him busy until he could see Lucy again.

Chapter Fourteen

Lucy had spent most of her free time in the last few weeks planning activities to keep Justine as busy and engaged — and therefore, out of Lucy's hair — as possible. The tour of the resort in a golf buggy, pointing out all the beauties the island possessed, was just the start, and occupied the rest of the morning. They caught up with Bryce for lunch at another of the resort's restaurants, this one an Asian noodle bar overlooking the beach and coral lagoon beyond.

"I thought you might want a rest this afternoon, so I've scheduled to go into work for a few hours," Lucy told Justine as they ate their lunch. "If you don't want to sleep, you could relax by the pool, though."

Justine looked dissatisfied, and turned to Bryce. "What about you, Bryce dear? Are you busy?"

"Taking out a dive at two," he said cheerfully. "I'd say come along, except you shouldn't dive for forty-eight hours after a long flight."

"No, thank you anyway." Justine shuddered slightly. "I don't care for being underwater. I'm proud of what Lucy does, but I'll have to settle for admiring her work from above the waterline."

"Well, there's plenty to see at the marine biology centre anyway. The stingray feedings are my favourite."

Justine looked a little uncertain. Lucy chimed in again with another suggestion.

"Or there's always the spa. You've got a VIP account which means you can jump the queue for spa bookings, or even have a therapist come to your suite, if you want. Watch a movie on TV and get your nails done, maybe?"

"Now *that's* a good idea," Justine said with an approving nod. "Then if I want a snooze, I don't even have to move! Clever girl."

Bryce really didn't care for her patronising tone, and from the corner of his eye he saw Lucy's jaw clench. Silently, he reached under the table and took her hand in his, feeling the tension in her stiff fingers. Gently, he massaged her palm with his fingertips until she relaxed again.

***

Lucy thanked her lucky stars, as she carefully loaded a batch of newly-grown corals into a transport tray, that her work wasn't something she could just walk away from completely for too long. For at least a couple of hours a day, she could escape Justine and lose herself in doing something which mattered to her, and today she had almost a whole day's escape. A large batch of corals was ready for replanting and she was going out with several other staff from the marine biology centre on a dive to replant them on a depleted part of the Reef. Pioneered in the Caribbean, the program was already showing great promise after only a couple of months here. Of course, the team had been growing the corals in the 'nursery' for months before she arrived, but Lucy still felt as though every one was her 'baby' as she directed the replanting program.

The other especially good thing about today, apart from a full day's respite from her mother, was that Bryce was assisting on the dive. She'd only climbed out of their bed an hour ago, and here he was again now, smiling down at her as he helped her load the transport trays onto the boat.

"I'm really looking forward to today," he voiced exactly what she was thinking, and she smiled back at him happily.

"Me too." She'd even fished out her best bikini for the occasion — Bryce had made a remark to Justine the day before about Lucy wearing a red bikini the first time they met. Surprised he'd remembered such a small detail, she nonetheless dug it out of a drawer and put it on before donning her usual work uniform of blue T-shirt and khaki shorts. No sooner had the boat pulled away from the dock, everyone settling down for the hour-long trip to the replanting site, than she pulled her shirt off and cast Bryce an inviting look.

"Want to rub in some sunscreen for me?"

"Temptress," he said with a laugh, pushing his sunglasses up on top of his head and taking the bottle from her hand. "You're lucky there's nowhere private on this boat except for a very small toilet, or you'd be about to get ravished."

"Yeah?"

"Damn right. That bikini shouldn't be legal." His eyes were locked on her breasts, though they did drop lower as she removed her shorts too with a shimmy of her hips. "Hot damn, Luce. You trying to give me a heart attack?"

From any other man, such a display of blatant lust would have given Lucy the creeps. But this was Bryce, Bryce who told her he admired her brain just as frequently as he remarked on her looks, Bryce the most considerate man she knew. Even as he rubbed in the sunscreen, warm hands massaging her skin sensuously, he took the time to warm the cream in his hands first before putting it on her skin.

"You shouldn't be allowed to be brilliant *and* beautiful," he murmured in her ear, nibbling on her earlobe, making her shiver in sensual delight. "Makes the rest of us feel inadequate."

"Same as you shouldn't be allowed to be sexy and charming," she riposted, but her voice was high and breathy. She'd made a tactical error, she realised; she felt hot and needy, her nipples jutting hard against the thin fabric of her bikini, dampness welling between her legs.

"When we get back to the cabin," Bryce murmured in her ear, hands sliding down to massage her upper thighs and up to the high edge of the bikini bottoms, "I'm gonna bend you over the bed and fuck you until you scream my name."

Lucy had honestly never realised just how sexy being talked dirty to could be. When Bryce did it, her knees trembled and her pulse raced, her breath coming faster.

"Since you can't get a room right now," Jodie the boat pilot called to them then, "take your hands off her before I make a citizen's arrest for indecent behaviour, Bryce Seabrook!"

Laughing, he lifted his hands and took a reluctant step back. "Later," he told Lucy with a dark look full of promise before he turned and headed aft to check on the oxygen cylinders.

"I can't wait," she muttered hoarsely to his retreating back, before turning with a sigh to pull her wetsuit from her dive bag. With hours to go before they returned to the island, she was going to have to concentrate on her work, or the time would drag interminably.

They couldn't even bolt straight off the boat once they docked, of course. Lucy had to help her team get the empty trays back to the research centre, and Bryce had to take all the oxygen cylinders back to the dive hut for test and refilling. By the time everything was done, it was almost six o'clock, and they'd agreed to meet Justine for dinner at seven. Lucy should really be washing out her salty hair in the shower and deciding what to wear, but instead she was lying on the bed, wearing nothing but her red bikini, waiting for Bryce to get back.

At last, the screen door slid open and he brushed aside the curtain hanging over it with a puzzled look, since Lucy rarely bothered to draw it.

"Ah," he said, seeing her on the bed, and turned to close the door and replace the curtain. "You waited for me, I see." He grinned broadly as he approached the bed, yanking his shirt off over his head and discarding it onto the floor. Lucy didn't even care just then, watching avidly as his shorts went the same way and he paused to open the nightstand drawer, grab out a condom.

"You made me a promise." She licked her lips as she watched him roll the condom onto his jutting, swollen cock.

"I did, and I've been thinking about it all damn day. Get over here. And gorgeous though you look in that bikini, it's going to have to come off."

"Take it off then." She crawled to the edge of the bed obediently. The bikini was ridiculously easy to remove, with shoelace ties at the sides of the bottoms and in between her breasts. One yank of Bryce's strong fingers and her breasts sprang free, nipples peaked and hard, anticipating his touch.

"Christ, Lucy," he said hoarsely, and looking up at his face, she caught her breath at the intensity of the passion she saw there.

"Don't just stand there," she said when he just gazed at her for a moment. Reaching down, she tugged loose the laces which held her bikini bottoms together. "Don't make me wait."

"Never," Bryce promised, and then he was going to his knees beside the bed, cupping her breasts in his hands before his mouth closed over one nipple, hot tongue laving the stiff peak until she shuddered and gasped his name, her fingers running into his thick blond hair to hold him close.

Desperate for more, Lucy grabbed his hand, pulling it between her legs. She felt Bryce smile against her breast before he curved his fingers, crooking two of them up into her already wet passage, his thumb gliding over her clit.

She made a low, hungry sound in her throat, hips rolling against his hand, seeking more stimulation. His teeth grazed her nipple, making her jump slightly. Bryce pulled back briefly, looking up at her.

"Tell me if I'm being too rough," he said. "My control... I lose it when I'm with you, Lucy, I want..."

"I want, too," she said throatily, leaning forward to kiss him.

"Turn over, then." He slipped his fingers out and stood, towering over her. Shaking a little with excitement, Lucy turned over and went to her hands and knees on the bed, looking back over her shoulder and chewing on her lower lip as she watched Bryce with wide eyes.

"You're so bloody beautiful," he said, his accent thickening. "Fuck me, I'm a lucky bugger."

"No, fuck *me*," Lucy demanded with a giggle, waggling her bottom at him deliberately.

"An' you're a cheeky sheila." He grasped her bottom firmly in both big hands, pushing his hips forward so his cock slid between her thighs, glancing over her clit and making her moan. "Something you want?"

"You," she half-sobbed as he repeated the motion, teasing her almost beyond bearing. "Please, Bryce!"

He didn't make her wait, thrusting to the hilt on one swift, hard motion with a grunt of effort, drowned out by Lucy's ecstatic shriek. She writhed on the deep impalement, her eyelids fluttering closed, brow dropping to rest on the bed between her hands.

"No," Bryce gritted out. "Head up. Look."

His hand in her hair at the nape of her neck made her lift her head and now she saw what he was seeing; they were right opposite the open bathroom door, looking into the big mirror over the sink. Bryce loomed large and solid behind her, and she — well she looked almost wild, her hair a tangled mane of dark curls, her eyes large and lucent, pupils blown wide with lust, her mouth open as she gasped for breath.

"So fucking sexy," Bryce said raggedly. "Watch yourself, Lucy — see what I see when I make love to you. How beautiful you are when you come."

His hips flexed as he began to pump, one hand on her hip and one on her shoulder holding her steady for him. His cock shuttled in and out of her faster and faster, slamming deep with every thrust, rubbing right over the sensitive little bundle of nerves deep inside her body.

What he was doing alone would have been enough to push Lucy up to the edge of orgasm pretty damn quickly, but combined with the sight of their reflection in the mirror, Bryce's expression tight with lust as he fucked her roughly, her breasts bouncing with the jolting of their bodies together... Lucy lost it within seconds, struggling to keep her eyes open to watch, seeing the expression on her own face go slack as the climax washed over her.

When she was able to focus properly again, she watched Bryce, admiring the way the muscles of his arms and chest rippled with his movements, his whole body working as he chased his own release. His eyes met hers in the mirror and he grinned, almost feral.

"You like this, huh?"

She could only nod, unable to speak, utterly overwhelmed with sensation. She hadn't really come back down from the climax, was just coasting along on the crest of the wave, waiting for him to join her. "Please," she managed to whimper out, and Bryce groaned, his face tightening, teeth sinking into his lower lip.

She felt the pulse of heat deep inside her even as he stilled at last, hips thrust right forward, his fingers tightening on her hip until she suspected she might have fingerprint bruises there tomorrow. Not that she cared, not in the least.

Bryce's grip slackened, and he leaned forward to kiss her spine gently before easing back and withdrawing from her. Collapsing face-first onto the bed, Lucy turned her head to the side and watched him walk to the bathroom on legs which looked as rubbery as hers felt.

After a moment, she heard the shower start up, and groaned loudly. "Do we have to?" she called mournfully.

Bryce laughed, coming back to stand over her. "Well, I'm pretty sure Justine would actually understand if you told her you're too fucked out to move. But can you bring yourself to tell her, that's the question?"

"Oh, shut up." She swatted in his general direction, then squeaked as he caught her hand and hauled her up off the bed and over his shoulder in one easy motion. "What are you doing? Put me down!"

"I'm taking you to the shower, dirty girl." He patted her ass. She patted his in return, making him roar with laughter as he carried her into the bathroom and straight into the shower stall. "Stop that, woman. Or we'll be late!"

The shower stall was way too small for two. Even so, Lucy could be inventive, when she wanted to be.

They were *very* late.

Chapter Fifteen

Lucy floated through the next few days on a dreamlike cloud of happiness. Even Justine's constant critical scrutiny and regular barbed comments couldn't pierce her bubble. Bryce was by her side every moment they could possibly contrive; nobody would have doubted that they were utterly in love. Or at least, in lust.

It should probably have bothered her more than it did that the wedding was starting to feel real. She began to feel invested in the plans Terry and Jerome were making, in Olivia's marketing plans, in every little detail of the big day. She almost got into a row with Justine over the menu for the wedding luncheon, at least until Bryce drew her aside and murmured quietly in her ear;

"You've loved everything Suzannah has ever cooked. Trust her to make it perfect."

Just hearing his voice in her ear calmed her, grounded her. She let him take her hand, drew in a deep breath, and nodded. "You're right, of course. Stop that, it's annoying."

The corners of Bryce's eyes crinkled up in the way she was coming to love as he smiled. "Just trying to be the voice of reason for my bridezilla."

"Ugh, am I really?" She wrinkled her nose.

"Little bit." He held up a hand, forefinger and thumb an inch or so apart. "It's totally turning me on, though. Can we sneak off and you can use that bossy voice to order me around in bed?"

He could always make her laugh. She almost fell into his arms, feeling his warmth and strength as they closed around her.

"I couldn't do this without you," she mumbled against his chest.

"You don't have to. Just a couple more days, angel." He kissed her forehead. "Hang in there."

***

Lucy had lost weight in the last two weeks, Bryce thought as he hugged her close. Justine was getting to her. She never said anything about Lucy's weight, but she always made a point of only taking a small amount of food, eating about half of it, then watching Lucy with raised eyebrows if she kept eating. The subtle psychological pressure was clearly taking a toll. Bryce could hardly wait for Justine to leave, for the tiny stress lines around Lucy's mouth to relax, for her to eat a full meal without eyeing her plate suspiciously.

Glancing across at where Justine was immersed in discussions of flower arrangements with the two wedding planners, Bryce guided Lucy outside and around the corner, out of sight. She didn't seem to want to let go of him, hanging on tightly around his waist. Fortunately, there was a couch there, positioned to allow guests a quiet space if required, so he pulled her to sit down with him, not particularly surprised when she wiggled onto his lap and tucked her face into his neck. Lucy wasn't cuddly in her sleep, but she most certainly was while awake.

"Only a couple more days, and one of those is the wedding," he murmured soothingly against her hair. "And if Justine dares be bitchy to you on our wedding day, I swear I'll throw her off the dock."

He felt her shoulders shake as she laughed silently. Then she pulled back and looked up at him, whispering softly "It's not really our wedding day, though."

Bryce didn't say anything. The wedding had begun to seem real to him; sharing Lucy's bed and her life felt so utterly right and natural, being married to her was just one more logical step. They hadn't even talked about what they would do once Justine had gone home, though, and adding to Lucy's stress by pressing her on the matter was unthinkable at the moment. Instead he nodded, kissed her forehead, and pulled her to lie against him again.

"Tomorrow's your girls' spa day," he murmured, "and our friends will all be there for you. Olivia and Nessa and the others have Justine's measure, so relax and let yourself be pampered."

"I'm looking forward to it, actually. Except the part about the photographer following us around."

"Well, she's female as well, and you already covered with her what you do and don't want shown. Just go with the flow and enjoy the day, angel." He nuzzled her hair. "The girls in the spa are good, but they can't improve on perfection anyway."

"You really are very good for my ego." He could feel Lucy smiling against his throat as she spoke. "You make me feel beautiful... for the first time in my life."

"You *are* beautiful. I could strangle your mother, for what she's done to your self-confidence." He tightened his hold. "I'm gonna keep telling you until you believe it. You're beautiful. The most beautiful woman I know."

***

"If I didn't know better, I'd say you two were a loving couple just about to get married." Luke's dry remark made them both startle up. He stood looking down at them, hands in the pockets of his grey suit trousers, shirt sleeves rolled up to his elbows, tie loose in his open collar.

"Uh," Lucy looked quickly to the door of the wedding planners' office.

"Don't worry, I'm not gonna give you away. Terry and Jerome have her well in hand; Justine's met her match at last, I think. Just wondering what exactly is going on with the pair of you. It's not like you were putting on a show for anyone in particular just then." Luke kept his voice low.

"Was that a question?" Bryce asked, sure his cheeks were on fire with embarrassment.

"I wasn't asking a question, no. Probably about time the two of you asked each other a few, though." With a firm nod, Luke strode past them and along the hallway to his own office.

"He might be right," Lucy mumbled after a moment of awkward silence. She couldn't look directly at him, Bryce noted, and her face was as red as his felt.

"It can wait," he said quietly. "You've got enough on your plate, Luce. Once Justine's gone home, you and I can sit down and figure out what we're doing here." Lightly, he touched her chin, encouraging her to meet his eyes, and once she did, he told her "Just in case you're in any doubt, I don't want this — *us* — to end once she leaves."

Lucy's smile was shy, but blinding. "Me neither. But you're okay with not talking it over until after the weddi... until after Mum's gone home?"

"Perfectly fine with it. No pressure even then, angel. We'll talk when you're ready."

Lucy had to bite on her lips to just keep from blurting out '*I love you. How's that for talk?*'

Instead, she sighed and pushed herself up off the couch. "We better get back in there before Terry and Jerome decide they've had enough and strangle her."

"If she changes one more thing about the plans, I might just help them," Bryce muttered, but he stood up too and took her hand.

"Once more into the breach, huh?"

"As many more times as you need me to, angel."

She almost said it then. Instead, she tightened her fingers around his, thinking that some way, some how, once Justine was gone, she was going to do everything she possibly could to build a real relationship with Bryce. The five years age difference between them seemed utterly irrelevant now. He clearly couldn't care less about it, so why should she? If the difference was reversed, nobody would even think twice about it.

Chapter Sixteen

Lying in bed beside Lucy in the warm morning light on the day before their wedding, Bryce studied her sleeping face. With her hair splayed around her face like a dark halo, lips parted slightly as she breathed in the slow rhythm of sleep, she looked like an angel to his dazzled eyes. He only hoped the spa day helped relax her rather than stress her out; several of her friends had arranged their schedules to have at least part of the day with her. He'd impressed on Olivia the need never to leave Lucy alone with Justine, and Olivia had promised to stick to Lucy's side like glue.

Several of the girls who worked at the spa were friends of his. They all knew about the situation as well and had taken pains to assure Bryce they'd make sure Lucy had a good day, and they'd keep Justine too busy to needle or harass her daughter.

Checking his watch, he grimaced slightly. He'd have to wake her shortly, and then he wouldn't see her until the actual ceremony tomorrow. Luke had put one of the premium resort cabins at their disposal for a couple of days as a wedding gift, and an extra suite in the main resort for Lucy to sleep in tonight, both of which they felt slightly guilty about but had no compunctions about accepting. Not when they'd had the photographer snapping candid shots of them both constantly for the last couple of days too, right down to Bryce getting his hair cut yesterday morning.

Lucy sighed and shifted a little in her sleep, the sheet slipping further down her body and revealing her breasts to his gaze.

Well, Bryce thought with a grin, *at least he could make sure her day started pleasurably*. Easing down the bed, he closed his mouth on one rose-pink nipple, licking and tonguing gently until it peaked in his mouth.

"Don't stop," Lucy murmured after a minute or so, and her hand slid into his newly-shorn hair to hold him close.

"Not stopping," he mumbled, moving across to the other breast to suck that nipple to a pouting point as well. His hand eased between her thighs, which Lucy willingly parted for him, her breath hitching as his fingers burrowed gently.

"Best way to wake up," she mumbled as his thumb started swiping circles over her clit.

Bryce hummed in wordless agreement, sliding down between her thighs and tracing his tongue over the path his thumb had just taken. Lucy's thighs lifted over his shoulders, her heels pressing into the solid muscles of his back, urging him on.

He had no intention of stopping, working his tongue over her clit until she was sobbing his name and tugging his hair, her body quivering as she came, soaked pussy clenching on his fingers.

"My turn," Lucy said when she got her breath and her strength back, pushing Bryce down to his back. He lay back with a grin as she reached for a condom, reaching up to tease her nipples as she mounted him, sinking slowly down on his rigidly erect cock.

"Christ, you feel so good, angel," he gasped as she seated herself fully.

"Mm hm," Lucy agreed breathlessly. She tipped her head back, her dark hair rippling over her shoulders as she flexed her thighs to lift herself up and lower down again. To Bryce's dazzled eyes, she was a goddess, his Aphrodite riding the waves of passion along with him until they both found completion, gasping and straining against each other in mutual climax.

As she lay on his chest afterwards, both of them damp with sweat and breathing heavily, Bryce stroked her hair and tried to come up with the words to express how he felt. "That was magical," he whispered finally, and felt Lucy smile against his chest.

"For a dyslexic, you've got a good way with words."

"If only," he mumbled. Maybe then he'd be able to find the ones he needed to tell Lucy he was hopelessly in love with her and praying she didn't drop him like a hot potato once Justine left the island.

"Thanks for the stress reliever." Lucy patted his chest before climbing off him. "I gotta shower before I go to the spa, or I'll stink of sex."

The bathroom door clicked shut, leaving Bryce staring at it. *Thanks for the stress reliever?*

Hopefully, Lucy was just even worse with words than he was.

***

"That may have been the worst post-coital line in the history of the world," Lucy groaned, leaning her forehead against the shower wall and wishing the water could wash away her idiocy. "I might just as well have said *wham bam thank you man.*" And after Bryce had woken her up so delightfully, too! When would she ever learn to just keep her mouth shut?

Mind you, it would have been much, much worse to blurt out what she'd actually been thinking. Telling Bryce she loved him would probably have him running for the hills.

With a sigh, she reached for the shampoo and started washing her hair. Their relationship was getting stranger by the day, trapped in the weird situation she'd put them in with her own chicken-shit inability to stand up to her mother. What the hell were they going to do once Justine left? Would they just go back to being friends? Would Bryce move back to his own cabin?

Closing her eyes against the sting as she rinsed the shampoo out, Lucy blew water droplets out with frustration. She was too scared to talk to Bryce about their relationship until after Justine left, not that she thought he'd bail on her at this stage. They just had to stick it out a couple more days, get through the wedding day and then they could talk. Really talk.

She felt sick with anxiety at the mere thought.

***

Bryce was gone when she left the bathroom, the bed neatly made. He was heading out on a full-day dive today, Lucy knew, and that evening had been invited to Jace's villa with some of his friends among the male staff for a small bachelor party.

"Ready?" A knock on the door made Lucy look up to see Olivia standing there with Gemma, the resort photographer who had been documenting the lead-up to the wedding.

"Yeah," Lucy said, dry-mouthed. "Sure."

Gemma had her camera in hand, but lowered it to look closely at Lucy as she walked past to leave the cabin. "Are you okay, sweetie? You look a bit frazzled."

"That's what the spa day is supposed to be for, right?" Lucy's laugh sounded fake to her own ears. "Relax the bridal jitters?"

Gemma and Olivia looked at each other, and Lucy could practically hear the unspoken words. *But you're not actually getting married.*

"Just don't leave me alone with my mother," she carried on quickly.

"On top of it," Olivia said comfortingly. "We've got you booked in for private sessions with Shae all day, and your mom with Eleanora. You'll only see her at lunchtime, when we'll all be together."

Lucy took a few deep breaths as they walked up to the spa, a series of luxurious timber cabins set apart from the rest of the resort, overlooking a crystal blue lagoon. She was going to relax and enjoy today, she was determined. She would never treat herself to this sort of thing normally, and she wasn't even paying. All she had to do was let Gemma take a few pictures for publicity use, and Gemma had even promised to let Lucy see them before they were published, too.

"Good morning, darling!" Justine was already sitting in the waiting area, leafing through a glossy magazine.

"Morning, Mum. Looking forward to the spa?"

"Why, yes; it's been a while since I treated myself. You're the one who needs it though, darling. You look positively peaky."

And that's why every time I never really even get started on feeling guilty about deceiving her, Lucy thought, grindting her teeth. *Every time I even think about it, she says something like that.*

"Ready to get started, ladies?" a sweet voice said, and Lucy looked around to see a petite, beautiful woman with a cap of short black curls framing her face standing by the reception desk, a white beautician's smock wrapped around her slim form. "I'm Shae and I'll be taking care of the bride."

"That's me," Lucy said, raising her hand, and Shae gave her a warm smile.

"Come along with me then. Eleanora will be out in just a few moments for you," she told Justine.

Lucy hadn't encountered Shae before, but took to the other girl immediately. Shae's quiet, gentle manner was extremely reassuring, and she didn't chatter while she began Lucy's first treatment, a seaweed wrap over her whole body. Instead, she quietly checked Lucy was comfortable being photographed mid-treatment before calling Gemma in to take a few pictures.

It felt odd lying on the table naked except for being wrapped in warm seaweed, but surprisingly relaxing. Lucy closed her eyes and put on a small smile as Gemma snapped a few pictures.

"Come back in an hour for the massage," Shae suggested. "Will you be okay with that, Lucy? You'll be naked, but the shots have to be non-sexual anyway, Gemma can just take a pic of my hands on your back or shoulders..."

"I trust you girls," Lucy mumbled drowsily. She could already feel tense muscles letting go, was really looking forward to the massage now, as well as whatever else Shae had planned.

She heard Shae laugh, say something to Gemma, and then a door closed.

The next thing she knew, Shae was waking her up, telling her it was time to take the seaweed wrap off and wash down.

"Wow," Lucy mumbled, blinking to clear her eyes. "I must've been more tired than I thought."

"It's a stressful time, leading up to your wedding," Shae said sympathetically. "You can snooze off again during your massage, I promise I won't mind. It's for relaxation rather than therapeutic, so you shouldn't feel any discomfort unless you've got really stiff muscles somewhere."

"Nothing in particular," Lucy shook her head as Shae gently washed her off with a warm, wet cloth. "Are you married, Shae?" she asked, feeling a little awkward about being naked on the table in front of the other girl, despite Shae's calmly impersonal manner.

"No," Shae said, a little flatly, and then "I almost was, once."

"How close is almost?" Lucy couldn't resist asking.

"We were standing in front of the altar when he decided he didn't want to go through with it." Shae's smile was a little tight. "Apparently, it was just me, though. He got married to someone else five months later."

"Oh, that's harsh. I'm so sorry," Lucy said sympathetically.

"Thanks. I'm over it, though. Better to find out he wasn't Mr Right before we said the vows than after."

"Truer words never spoken," Lucy agreed.

"Though I shouldn't be telling you my sob story. You're the one who's getting married to your gorgeous sweetheart tomorrow. I'm jealous; Bryce is a darling!"

Shae didn't know the wedding wasn't real, Lucy realised as the therapist poured a warm, sweetly scented oil into her hands and began the massage at the soles of Lucy's feet. It only took a minute for her to forget all about that, though, as Shae's talented hands found pressure points and muscles she didn't even know were tense began to relax.

"Oh God, that's wonderful," she mumbled, hearing Shae's quiet chuckle as she continued her work.

"Relax, Lucy. Let it all go. I'm gonna massage all this stress out of you. Stop thinking about tomorrow and just focus on right now."

Chapter Seventeen

Bryce spent all day worrying about how Lucy was getting on. Once the boat was out on the Reef, he had no phone signal so couldn't text Olivia or Rosie to check in on her. He considered asking Jodie, the boat captain, to radio in, but she gave him a very old-fashioned look when he hinted about it, so he shut his mouth.

"You just concentrate on doing your job, sonny," Jodie said dryly. "I'm about ninety-five per cent certain Lucy will still be on the island when you get back."

"Only ninety-five?" Anxiety sent a crawling tension up Bryce's spine. "Why wouldn't she be? Have you heard something?"

"Did I say ninety-five? I meant a hundred. Oh look, that guy's putting his fins on too early, what a dick." Jodie deflected him smartly, grinning behind his back as he turned to check on the rookie diver automatically. They were almost up on the dive site and Bryce would be kept busy buddy-checking everyone's tanks, hoses, connectors and regulators until they were in the water, then keeping an overall eye out once they were down. Hopefully, keeping busy would keep his mind off his wedding jitters.

Bryce could tell Jodie was trying to distract him, and he wasn't ungrateful. Every minute today seemed to be dragging endlessly; whenever he looked at his watch the numbers on the digital display had barely increased at all.The dive group were barely competent and sorely trying his patience, too. He felt an intense relief when Jodie finally called time and the boat started back to the island.

"Bloody sit still, will you? You're distracting me." Jodie never took her eyes off the horizon or her hands off the wheel as she spoke.

Bryce stilled his bouncing leg and tried to take calm, slow breaths. "Sorry." After a few minutes of desperately trying to stay still, he asked "Have you ever been married, Jode?"

The older woman shot an amused glance at him before returning her gaze to the sea. "Twice," she replied eventually. "First time, I was young and stupid, got married right out of high school. We were separated before I turned twenty."

"And the second time?"

"Married a Navy man." A smile touched her lips. "The sea's always been the third party in our marriage. Works just fine."

"You're still married?" Startled, Bryce looked at her left hand. He'd never seen Jodie wearing any rings, or heard her mention a husband.

"Twenty-seven years, just passed. He's the captain on the HMAS *Wangaratta*. Coming up on retirement next year, and wondering what to do with himself. I'm trying to convince him to join me out here."

"You must have spent a lot of time apart, over the years," Bryce commented thoughtfully.

"More apart than together, really." Jodie shot a sideways glance at him. "Don't let anyone tell you marriage is all sunshine and roses, son. It takes hard work and a shit ton of patience, but at the end of the day, the rewards are worth having. Callum and I might not have a conventional marriage where we sit down to dinner together every night, but it works for us because we both have the will, and put in the effort, to *make* it work."

"You do know Lucy and I aren't actually getting married, right?" Bryce checked.

"The way I heard it, all you have to do is ask Luke to file the paperwork within a month and you *will* be legally married." Jodie shrugged, not looking at him. "Guess you've got a month to convince Lucy being married to you is all she ever wanted, huh?"

Bryce opened his mouth, but no words came out. Finally, he nodded his head, and Jodie let out a quiet chuckle.

"Trust me, everyone can see how perfect the two of you are together. Oh, and Lucy's just as head over heels for you as you are about her, if you were worried about it."

"She is? Has she talked to you?"

Jodie shook her head, laughing more loudly. "No. She didn't have to. Anyone with eyes can see it... except you, obviously. Have a little faith, Bryce."

***

Without being able to see and talk to Lucy, all Bryce could do was stew on Jodie's words all the way back to the island and all evening. He got a good deal of good-natured joshing from his friends as they sat around drinking excellent wine and eating pizza at Jace's stunning villa, watching the sun go down over the ocean.

It occurred to him, about halfway down a bottle of wine, that none of this friends were acting as though the wedding was anything but real, even though they all knew very well the whole thing had at least started as a prank.

"Cory," he grabbed at his friend's arm as Cory came to sit back down, pizza slice in hand, "why's everyone acting like this is a real wedding?"

Cory, rather the worse for wear on wine himself, had to consider that a while before shrugging. "Well, it pretty much is, isn't it? Luke said all you have to do is file the paperwork."

"Why's he going around telling everyone that?" Bryce demanded plaintively.

"Why don't you ask him yourself?" Cory responded with impeccable logic. "He's sitting right over there."

"Well, he and Jace are talking. I didn't want to interrupt."

Cory chuckled. "They're not talking business. Go on, head over there!"

Easy for Cory to say, Bryce thought, but he got to his feet as Cory nudged him. Cory was one of the senior resort personnel as Activities Manager, after all, despite his relative youth. Bryce was just a dive instructor, senior to the others who held the position only by virtue of having been employed at the resort longer.

"Here's the groom!" Jace toasted him as he approached, smiling broadly, and Bryce gave the billionaire a tentative smile. Jace just didn't look or act like he'd been born with the proverbial silver spoon in his mouth, he thought privately. Right now he was slouched on a poolside deck chair with an almost-empty glass of red in his hand, wearing cargo shorts, a faded rock band T-shirt, and rubber thongs on his feet. "Are the wedding nerves kicking in, or is the wine helping take the edge off?"

"The wine is definitely helping. Thank you, by the way. I'm not all that knowledgeable but I can tell this is the good stuff." Bryce lifted his glass.

Jace waved off his thanks with a grin. "Can't have you waking up with a hangover tomorrow. I haven't met your bride but I don't want to get off on the wrong foot by delivering a horribly hung-over bridegroom from a bucks' party I hosted."

And that was why Jace was different from other billionaires, Bryce was pretty sure. He'd met a few very wealthy men, since Sunfish Island was a playground for the well-heeled, and he couldn't imagine any of those self-centred characters would give a shit what a woman they hadn't even met might think of them.

"About tomorrow," Bryce said hesitantly.

Luke lowered the glass he'd been about to take a sip from. "You crying off?"

"No!" The refutation was swift and emphatic. "I'd never do that to Lucy!"

Luke tilted his head to give him a thoughtful look, opened his hand in a gesture for Bryce to continue.

"I was wondering, uh, you told Lucy and I that it would basically be a real wedding, we just wouldn't file the official paperwork."

"That's correct." Luke nodded. "You have thirty days to file it if you change your minds and want to make it official, though."

"Yeah. And um. I've been wondering why you've been telling everyone else about that?"

There was a distinct smirk on Luke's lips as he took a sip of wine before answering. Jace was looking interestedly between the two of them, spoke to fill in the silence.

"Is the gossip I heard true... that you and Lucy were just friends when this started off but now you're hooking up?"

Bryce winced. *Hooking up* seemed like such a crude way to put it. Lucy wasn't just a hookup. She was far, far more than that. "We're together. Yes."

"Fake romance turning real, it's a cute story." Jace offered him a friendly smile.

Luke spoke up again, finally. "And if you want to make it really real, all you have to do is ask me to file that marriage certificate. I don't deny I've mentioned it to a few other people, but I haven't instigated the conversations. I think you underestimate the amount of interest your friends have in your future happiness, Bryce. Yours and Lucy's."

Bryce frowned and shook his head, not understanding.

"They want to see you happy. Both of you," Luke clarified. "And it's obvious to anyone with eyes that you make *each other* happy. Putting the thought in your minds that maybe actually getting married could be the best thing that you can do for your mutual future happiness?" He shrugged. "I'm not surprised they're all but hitting you over the head with the idea."

"Oh." Startled, Bryce sat back and considered that. "Do you know if anyone's mentioned it to Lucy?" he asked hesitantly.

Luke and Jace both laughed at that.

"Really?" Jace snickered. "The girls have spent all day getting their toenails painted and their legs waxed and God only knows what else together, and you think they haven't been talking about it?"

"How could they? Her mother's there, and Justine doesn't know this is all a hoax."

"Women always find a way. Hell, Nessa's been filling my ear with how romantic it would be if you two really got married." Jace finished his wine, seemed to consider going to get some more, and slumped down in his chair. "Nah, I've had enough," he muttered.

"Maybe you and Lucy should just talk to *each other* about it," Luke said pointedly.

Bryce had to laugh. "Yeah, you're right. I mean... I knew we needed to talk, but I think we've both been putting it off until after Justine leaves. Put on a united face until then, you know? That woman." He shook his head slowly. "I honestly find it hard to believe someone like her managed to raise a daughter as kind and loving and compassionate as Lucy."

"You're making me glad I haven't yet had the pleasure," Jace commented. "Luke filled me in on who she is, obviously."

"She's a viper."

Bryce blinked at Luke in surprise. He didn't think he'd ever heard the resort manager say anything so harsh about anyone before. "Took the word right out of my mouth," he murmured.

"She's very good at pouring on the charm when she wants to, but I like to think I'm pretty good at reading people. Justine Manning has the coldest eyes I've ever seen. There's nothing but cold calculation behind them." Luke shook his head. "Every interaction, she's thinking what benefit there might be to her. She's been posting photos on her Instagram and tagging the resort, we've had a distinct upsurge in bookings from the UK since she started, and she mentioned her activity to me yesterday and hinted heavily that she'd like another couple of weeks comped to her later in the year in exchange."

"Please tell me you said no!" Bryce gaped in horror.

"I pretended to be extremely dense and not get the hint. If she wants to return, she can pay like everyone else. We're booked up months in advance these days anyway; all those UK bookings are coming towards the end of this year and into next year, when we have vacancies. It's not really like we'd lose out if she hadn't done her little bit of promotion, and there's no direct evidence that's what caused the uptick anyway." Luke smirked before finishing his wine and getting to his feet. "If looks could kill, you'd be looking for a new general manager by now, Jace. More wine?"

"What the hell." Jace held out his empty glass. "Hit me up."

"Bryce?"

"I've probably had enough." He smiled apologetically. "Please don't force any more down me. I'm really gonna need my wits about me tomorrow."

Luke's smile was wry. "Stick here with us, then. We might be the 'less fun' corner, but at least nobody will make you do shots over here."

"Are you calling me old and boring?" Jace objected.

"Well, I didn't use those words specifically," Luke attempted to backtrack, but Jace cut him off with laughter.

"It's perfectly fine. Hey, I'm so boring I retired from being a New York playboy billionaire!"

"Retired you may be, but you're definitely not boring," Bryce put in. "Believe me, I'm more than happy to hang out with you guys." He toasted Jace with his glass, and Luke, returning with a fresh bottle, topped it up in passing.

"Sip on that. We'll wrap it up in an hour or so anyway, Jace can kick everyone out."

"I'm totally useless as a bouncer," Jace protested, making both of them laugh. Bryce relaxed back into his chair, feeling a lot more comfortable now. Luke and Jace were his bosses, yes, but they were also both incredibly approachable and friendly. He could definitely see why Nessa, easily the best judge of character he knew, had fallen for Jace.

"So," Jace said now, "I've never learned to dive and Luke tells me it's the only way to see some of the best bits of the Reef. How about some private lessons?"

"Any time you like," Bryce said. "After the wedding, of course!"

"I'll be knocking on your day bright and early the day after tomorrow, then?" Jace teased.

"I wouldn't advise it, to be honest. It might be only a fake wedding, but Lucy and I have planned some real days off, starting with a lie-in the day after. Knocking on my door early will mean you get to face an irate Lucy, and I wouldn't recommend that. Not unless you'd like your balls rearranged, anyway."

Jace roared with laughter and leaned over to tap his glass against Bryce's. "To feisty women," he said, still laughing. "May they never change."

"Amen to that!" Bryce agreed.

Chapter Eighteen

"Rise and shine, princess bride!"

"Hurgh!" Lucy shot upright, disorientated at first to find herself not in her own bed. Nessa was standing over her, a broad grin on her face. Through the doorway behind her, she could see Rosie, Jill and Olivia already bustling around, and she was sure she could hear a male voice amidst the feminine chatter.

"It's nine o'clock, sugar. Didn't sleep well?"

"Appalling," Lucy confessed, rubbing at her eyes. "I kept waking up because I couldn't hear Bryce breathing." She'd had trouble going to sleep even after a few glasses of champagne, and then kept waking up every few minutes.

Nessa's smile was sympathetic. "I know exactly what you mean. Even though Jace was snoring like a chainsaw when I crawled in next to him last night, I still slept better than I did while he was away."

"Bryce doesn't snore."

"Nor does Jace, usually, but considering the number of empty wine bottles in the kitchen I think it was quite a party."

"Ha." Rolling her head around on her neck, Lucy stretched her arms out to the sides. "Despite the crappy sleep, I feel good. Shae loosened out knots I didn't even know I had."

"She's good. And she's here to help you with your hair and makeup, so get your ass out of that bed and have a shower. Ten minutes or I'll sic Terry and Jerome on you. You'll mess up their carefully planned timetable if you take any longer." Nessa gave her a laughing wink before closing the bedroom door and leaving Lucy alone again.

Quite sure Nessa would carry through on her threat, Lucy scrambled out of bed and ran for the bathroom. Her hair had been washed and styled the day before, so she stuffed it hastily into a shower cap to keep it from getting wet while she washed.

When she emerged, wrapped in a fluffy towelling robe, Shae was waiting with her gentle smile and quiet manner, a case of makeup ready on the dresser beside a croissant and a cup of coffee.

"I'm not big on a lot of makeup," Lucy eyed the big case doubtfully as she sat down at Shae's wordless gesture and reached for her breakfast. "Um. If I wear a lot of makeup, I... look more like my mother than I'm comfortable with."

"I'll keep it light and natural," Shae promised. "It's going to be hot today anyway, you don't need it all melting off to leave marks on your dress."

Gemma slid into the room to take pictures as Shae used a delicate, skillful touch to just touch up Lucy's natural beauty. They'd already agreed Lucy would wear her hair half up, half down, with some intricate braids pulling the top section away from her face before Shae arranged the rest in an artful tumble of soft waves falling forward over her left shoulder. A strand of pearls on loan from the resort jewellery shop held the arrangement in place, more pearls in her earlobes and a single teardrop-shaped one hanging from a gold chain at the hollow of her throat completing a simple, classical look.

"You look stunning," Gemma sighed, kneeling on the floor to get an upwards shot of Lucy looking in the mirror. "You'll knock Bryce's socks off. Have you seen the response we've been getting on the Big Wedding series on Instagram and Facebook? The bookings for weddings are going cray-cray. Terry and Jerome have been hitting up Luke to hire them another assistant to handle all the details they don't have time for."

That was good. Creating good publicity for the resort at least assuaged a little of Lucy's guilt over having so much effort expended on something which wasn't even real.

"You're a miracle worker, Shae," she said, hardly recognising the woman in the mirror. That woman looked a good deal younger than Lucy's thirty years, fresh-faced and bright-eyed, her hair elegantly arranged.

Shae laughed. "No miracles required when I've got such a wonderful canvas to work with. All we need now is the dress."

Gemma set the camera down. "Let me help? Please? No shots until you're in it, I promise."

"Of course. It's hanging up in the wardrobe right there." Lucy gestured.

The only thing she was planning to wear under the dress was a pair of white silk panties and a blue silk garter Olivia had given her. Strapless, the boned corset of the dress lifted and supported her breasts perfectly when Shae laced it up for her, multiple layers of chiffon silk skirts falling just to her ankles. Lucy had flatly refused to wear the stiletto heels Olivia had tried to talk her into, preferring flats, especially since she knew she'd have to walk on sand to take the sunset photos on the beach which were part of the day's plan. In the end they'd compromised on wedges with a one-inch heel, comfortable enough to walk all day in if she needed to.

While she didn't officially have bridesmaids, the bridal shop who had provided her dress had outfitted Olivia, Nessa, Rosie and Jill with four silk sheath dresses in four different colours, with shoes to match. They looked like a garden of exotic tropical flowers as Lucy stepped hesitantly into the suite's living area, bright and beautiful in turquoise, golden-yellow, emerald and fuchsia.

"Oh, you all look spectacular," Lucy said, delighted. "Gemma, take some photos..."

They all laughed at her. "You're the bride, darling!" Olivia took her arm, gently urged her into the middle of the group. "And you outshine us by miles, I must say. You'll knock Bryce's socks off."

Gemma's camera clicked rapidly as the friends embraced. Shae stood back, smiling a little wistfully, until Terry entered to tell them it was time to go.

"You look fabulous, darlings, but I don't have time to pay you flowery compliments. Jerome's babysitting Bryce and reports he's in a bit of a panic." Terry grinned at Lucy. "So let's get you there on time, hm? I've got golf carts and drivers waiting downstairs. Move it, move it, ladies!" He clapped his hands together, chivying them from the room.

Of course, it wasn't so simple. They had to pause everywhere, in the lobby so other guests could gawk at Lucy and Gemma could snap some more photos, at the golf cart where Shae helped arrange her skirt and tweaked her hair one last time.

Lucy felt as though she was about to burst with frustration by the time the procession finally got going, hers the last cart to roll away. Terry was driving her himself, Shae sitting beside him in case any last-minute adjustments were required to Lucy's appearance, Gemma in the cart in front, even now hanging out the back to take more pictures.

"Are you okay?" Shae turned to ask as they drove slowly up the paved path to the scenic pavilion overlooking the sea where the ceremony was to be held. "You're not wearing enough makeup to cover the fact that you've gone kinda pale."

"I just want this to be over," Lucy confessed.

Shae's smile was sympathetic. "Just relax and let yourself enjoy the day," she advised. "Look at the sky; not a cloud in sight, it's the most perfect shade of blue. Listen to the birds, smell the sea air and the tropical flowers. Just take it all one minute at a time. Close your eyes for a moment and take deep breaths. I'll count for you. Breathe *in*, two, three, four, *hold*, two, three, four, breathe *out*, two, three, four, *hold*, two, three, four..."

Breathing deeply in time with Shae's quiet chanting, Lucy felt the tightness in her chest easing. She felt the cool breeze against her cheeks as the cart coasted along the track, heard parrots squawking in the trees as they passed, smelled the heady hibiscus mixed with salt in the air.

"Better?" Shae asked quietly.

"Yeah." Lucy kept her eyes closed, though, maintaining the steady rhythm of her breathing.

"That's good, because we're here and Terry's about to stop the cart. Keep up that breathing, sweetie."

Lucy opened her eyes. They were just slowing down, Terry bringing the cart into line with the others waiting behind the pavilion. Her four 'bridesmaids' were waiting for her, smiling broadly, and behind them she could see quite a little crowd seated in front of the pavilion.

At the front of the crowd, Bryce was standing between Luke and Cory, his eyes fixed on her as Terry helped her out of the cart. Seeing him there, standing tall and straight, his fair hair cut neatly short, his face clean-shaven, wearing a silver-grey waistcoat over an open-collared white shirt and light grey formal pants, he looked so handsome the unreality of the situation struck Lucy forcibly.

Of course this wedding wasn't real. No way would she be walking up the aisle to marry a man who looked like that. She was just ordinary, by her own choice, and guys like Bryce didn't marry *ordinary*.

Lucy didn't even see her mother in the front row pretending to cry, as she walked through the crowd to Bryce. He was gazing at her, lips slightly parted as though about to speak, an expression she couldn't really define on his handsome face. She had to remind herself to walk slow, not to just run to him and cling on tight. It seemed to take an eternity to traverse the short distance which separated them, reminding herself to keep her smile in place with every step.

***

Bryce stared in awe as Lucy walked towards him. She looked like a princess in that dress, a single white lily clasped in her hands the perfect finishing touch to complete the illusion of classic perfection. A soft smile illuminated her face as she approached, and he reached out to take her hand instinctively.

"You look *incredible*," he said sincerely, causing a little ripple of laughter among their audience and Lucy's smile to widen.

"I was thinking the same," she said saucily, letting her eyes drop and come back up again in a blatant once-over.

I love you, he almost blurted, but managed to close his lips over the words, squeezing Lucy's hand lightly instead before turning to face Luke, who was grinning broadly at both of them.

"Welcome," Luke began, "to the wedding of Bryce Seabrook and Lucinda Marie Manning..."

Chapter Nineteen

Lucy struggled to pay attention as Luke spoke. She and Bryce had opted to go with the simplest, shortest version of the marriage ceremony and standard vows. Bryce's look of horror when Luke asked if they were going to write their own had been enough for Lucy to immediately veto the idea.

"I do," she said at the appropriate moment, surprised by how clear and definite her voice sounded. Her gaze locked with Bryce's, she felt strong and confident, somehow certain she was exactly where she was supposed to be.

Suddenly, it was all over and Luke was pronouncing them to be man and wife.

"Kiss the bride, mate!" Cory yelled loudly, and Bryce laughed, slipping his arm around Lucy's waist and dipping her backwards. She found herself giggling too, reaching up to hook her arms round his neck and hold on tight as his mouth came down on hers.

"Save that for later," Luke said in a gently reproachful tone about a minute later, amid loud cheers and shouts of;

"Get a room!"

Lucy was laughing as Bryce lifted her back upright, her eyes sparkling with joy, and he very nearly kissed her again right then. They were being swarmed by their friends, though, separated and both hugged and congratulated loudly. Accepting a surprisingly tearful embrace from Olivia, Bryce spotted from the corner of his eye Justine edging in to embrace Lucy.

"Danger incoming," he muttered in Olivia's ear, and she promptly released him, in time for him to get back to Lucy as Justine spoke.

"You look beautiful, my darling," Justine gushed, "although..."

Bryce spoke loudly, before Justine could make whatever backhanded compliments or outright criticisms she'd undoubtedly spent the whole ceremony thinking up. "Doesn't she, though? I've always known you were the most beautiful woman I'd ever met," he spoke directly to Lucy, "but today... well, you take my breath away."

High colour staining Lucy's cheeks, she ducked her head a little and laughed shyly. "It's the dress."

"It's a pretty dress, but it's the woman wearing it I can't stop staring at." Very conscious of Justine standing by, lips pursed as though she'd just sucked on a lemon, Bryce tucked his arm around Lucy's waist, holding her possessively close.

"Could I get a photo of you as the mother of the bride, Justine?" Gemma asked at that moment. "Love that hat, by the way!"

Justine preened, lifting a hand to touch the brim of the angled, super-fashionable scarlet hat she wore, a stunning foil for her designer white silk gown printed all over with huge red poppies. "I took a trip over to Hamilton Island to get it. There are some quite nice shops there."

Bryce saw Lucy roll her eyes, grinned. '*Quite nice*' was a very understated description for the upmarket boutiques Justine had spent a day touring. She'd had to buy an extra suitcase to take all her new purchases back to England in.

Luke touched his arm then, drew them both aside to sign the wedding certificate and the resort's wedding register. Then it was time for Lucy to have some pictures with her 'bridesmaids', and Terry and Jerome became Gemma's willing assistants, chivying everyone into the perfect positions for photos.

Lunch was booked for the party at *La Sirène*, the resort's Michelin-starred restaurant, and even Justine could find no fault with the incredible food served to them by unobtrusive staff, nor the superb wine Jace had provided from his private cellar.

Anticipating that Justine would, given the opportunity, stand up and say any number of unkind things about Lucy in the guise of reminiscing about her childhood, Bryce had already put his foot down and declared there weren't going to be any speeches, because he quite simply didn't want to give one. Cory presented a toast to the bridesmaids, grinning besottedly at Olivia as he did so, and then Luke proposed one to the bride and groom, and that was the sum total of the formalities at the meal.

Bryce was pretty sure Justine was gritting her teeth to keep her smile firmly fixed in place, but he'd deliberately asked Terry and Jerome to seat her in between Luke and Jace, so she could hardly complain she wasn't given a place of honour. Bryce just had no intention of allowing her to belittle Lucy on their wedding day.

Once again, he had to remind himself the wedding wasn't real. Lucy would have a real wedding one day, to some lucky bastard Bryce already hated without knowing a thing about him. The mere thought of her walking down the aisle to some other man, her eyes glowing with love for someone who wasn't him, made him feel sick to his stomach.

After the luncheon was when Bryce and Lucy really had to earn their keep, or at least earn back the cost of putting on the wedding, by letting Gemma photograph them at every scenic spot on the island, including in the honeymoon cabin they were getting for the night, complete with a beautiful feast of cold foods laid on for them, before another quick trip out for sunset photos on the beach. Lucy blessed the speedy tropical sunsets as darkness finally fell and Gemma regretfully lowered her camera at last.

"That's all, folks," she said with a smile. "You can drop the glued-on smiles now."

"Good, because my face feels like it's about to crack," Lucy joked, sagging against Bryce.

"You've been a trooper," Bryce praised, putting his arm around her. "We done, Gemma?"

"Consider your dues paid. I'm off to lock myself in my office and spend the next few days buried in Photoshop and Instagram." Gemma grinned wickedly at them and said teasingly "I'll let you know if we need any reshoots."

That prompted Lucy to flip her the bird, which made Gemma burst out laughing before she hopped in her golf cart and headed back to the resort. Bryce had long since commandeered one to drive himself and Lucy around, and he helped her back in now before getting into the driver's seat.

"Do you want to check in with everyone else?" he asked.

"Absolutely not."

He grinned at her definitive answer. "Leaving them to their own amusements it is, then. Let's go see if there's any of our feast left."

"Gemma said a staffer was coming in to put everything in the fridge, so we can just help ourselves." Lucy leaned her head against his shoulder as he put the golf cart in drive. "I'm so tired, Bryce." She smothered a massive yawn in her hand.

"Me too. No idea how people have the energy for wedding nights after doing this for real, plus an evening reception," Bryce joked.

"Can't imagine." Lucy yawned again. "Maybe I'll perk up once I've gotten out of this dress and had something to eat."

"It's spectacular, but I've been wondering all day how you were breathing in it. Your waist looks so tiny." The golf cart only needed one hand to drive, so Bryce slid his free arm around said tiny waist. Lucy chuckled quietly against his shoulder.

"Breathing's not too bad. It's eating and drinking which is the problem, or rather the aftereffects of. Going to the bathroom is a bit of a production - I was glad Gemma wasn't there taking photos while Olivia and Shae were both helping hold the skirt above my head so I could pee!"

Bryce broke up laughing at the mental image her words invoked, and Lucy giggled along with him.

"This has been a really awesome day," Bruce said impulsively.

"It has, hasn't it?" Lucy agreed. "Honestly, it's been the most perfect wedding day. I couldn't have wished for anything more."

Say something, a little inner voice yelled at Bryce, but they were pulling up outside the honeymoon cabin now and he shut off the motor, getting out of the golf cart and offering Lucy his hand. She took it with a bright smile up at him.

"You look so beautiful," he managed to get out as he led her inside. "The, uh, the pearls in your hair really... really look amazing. And the dress, and... everything."

"You scrub up pretty well yourself." Lucy flicked at the edge of his waistcoat with a polished fingernail.

Closing the door behind them, Bryce glanced around the cabin to check they were really alone. "Lucy," he began, but she was already tugging her hand out of his, kicking her shoes off and walking away towards the bedroom.

"Please come help me out of this dress," she begged. "It'd be really nice to take a deep breath."

Swallowing the words, he followed her.

She stopped beside the bed and glanced over her shoulder at him. "The laces untie here," putting one hand to the small of her back, she plucked at the ribbon bow tied there. "Then loosen them upwards. You shouldn't need to unthread them all the way, just loose enough to slide down."

"Okay." He felt all thumbs as he took the thin silk ribbons in his fingers and picked clumsily at the knot, silently cursing whoever had tied a double knot in the bow. "Did you have to hold onto the bedpost to get laced into this?" He tried to make small talk as he worked.

Lucy chuckled softly. "Like Kate Winslet in *Titanic*? Have you seen that?"

"I confess I have. I like movies, and we do get free access to the resort's movies-on-demand channel." Finally the knot came loose in his fingers.

"Not exactly like that. I didn't need to get laced into a nineteen-inch waist or whatever it was. I was holding the front up while Shae laced the back, actually." As the laces came loose, Lucy sagged a little bit, taking in a deep breath and letting it out. "Phew. I understand now why all the pictures of ladies from the old days show them with perfect posture, though. You don't have much choice."

The bodice came loose and Lucy made no attempt to catch it as the whole dress slid to the floor, leaving her nude but for her thong and the blue garter around her thigh. Bryce almost swallowed his tongue.

"Fuck, that's all you've been wearing under this dress all day?" he asked, his voice hoarse.

Lucy turned to him, smiling, and reached to put her arms around his neck. "Bet you can't get out of your clothes that fast."

"Bet I can give it a red-hot go!"

She'd only managed to remove her earrings and necklace before he'd shed everything and was on her, pulling her down to the bed with him, both of them laughing wildly.

"Wait, wait, I gotta get these pearls out of my hair," Lucy begged through her giggles. "If I break the strand I'll be in so much trouble."

Bryce sighed exaggeratedly, but helped her unpin the arrangement which held up the top part of her hair. The pearls fell free and he discarded them to the bedside table, running his fingers through her silky dark locks.

"Lucy." He put all the depth of emotion he felt for her into the single word, and her laughter died, her eyes wide as she looked up at him.

"Bryce?" Her voice was small and soft, questioning.

"You have to know how I feel about you." The words burst out of him, too fast, tangling on his tongue, but he knew she understood by the way she went stiff against him, pupils blowing wide with shock. "I'm in love with you, Lucy, I have been since the first time I saw you, I think, and today has been like the culmination of every dream I ever had, but... but I can't do this. Not if you don't feel the same way. I can pretend until your mother goes home, but..."

"Bryce." Tears started in Lucy's eyes, and she reached up, placed one finger against his lips to still his babble. "I love you."

Chapter Twenty

"I love you." Lucy said it again when Bryce said nothing in response, just stared at her, a frown furrowing his brow. "Today's been like a crazy wonderful dream for me, too. That, plus everyone's been telling me I gotta hang onto you, that now we're together we should stay in it for the long haul, that we should ask Luke to file that marriage certificate before the thirty-day deadline."

"I've been hearing that too," Bryce said finally. "It's almost like we've got our own little fandom frantically shipping us together." The corner of his mouth quirked up, a glint of amusement entering his eyes. "I'm pretty sure there was a betting pool on when we'd first sleep together. From her smirk the day after, I think Nessa won it."

Lucy bit back a laugh. "Yeah, she confessed as much to me yesterday. I asked how they all knew. Apparently, uh, sound carries quite well at night and Rosie heard us that night when she was walking back to her cabin. Plus, I had shocking stubble rash the following day and you were, to quote Cory, 'strutting around smirking like that cat who got the cream'."

"Sounds legit," Bryce admitted sheepishly. "Look, Lucy... there are a lot of different ways we could take this from here. We could take it back a step once your mother leaves, I could move back to my cabin and we can 'date' for a while, take things slower."

Lucy was already shaking her head. "What would be the point? I already know I like living with you, like waking up next to you. We've spent the last two weeks as much in each other's pockets as we're ever going to get, considering the amount of time we've both had off work, in a pretty stressful situation given Mum's presence and the whole wedding thing. I say we go forward from here." Chewing on her lip, she awaited his answer anxiously.

"That'd be my vote as well," Bryce agreed, and Lucy let out an audible sigh of relief. "I doubt I'd end up sleeping in my own bed more than once in a blue moon anyway. If we make this official, we can apply for one of the 'couples' cabins, too, which are bigger."

Lucy hadn't even thought of that, but he was quite correct. Justine didn't know about the policy, so they hadn't bothered, but once two staff members completed paperwork to declare they were in an official relationship they were able to put themselves on the list to get one of the bigger cabins, when one became available. Though she didn't mind sharing her space with Bryce, she couldn't deny it was decidedly cosy for two people to live there full-time.

"Good idea," she agreed. "And, uh... the other thing?"

"The other thing?"

She chewed on her lip again before mumbling "The paperwork thing," while avoiding his eyes.

"Lucy." Bryce touched her cheek gently. "Look at me."

Taking a deep breath, she looked up into his blue eyes, once again marvelling at how handsome he was.

"I just told you that today was a dream come true for me. Being married to you would be living in that dreamland, full-time, every day. I can't imagine ever not wanting to be married to you. So as far as I'm concerned, let's take a walk up to Luke's office and ask him to file those papers, first thing tomorrow. I'm all in with you, Lucy. All the way."

"Oh," she gulped, tears welling again. "Oh damn, I'm gonna cry."

"Please don't!" He leaned down to kiss her trembling lips, pulling her close against him and stroking her back until she stopped trembling, made a protesting little noise against his mouth. "Sorry." He pulled back and smiled down at her ruefully. "Seeing you cry just breaks me. Can't deal, I'm afraid."

"Your fault." She sniffed back more impending tears valiantly. "You're making me too happy."

"Is that a yes?" Cautious delight dawned.

"Was there a question?" she teased.

"Do I need to go down on one knee? Okay then," when she shook her head. "Will you, ah, make our marriage official, my darling, beautiful, brilliant almost-wife?"

She didn't hesitate a moment before saying "Yes!"

~ *The End* ~

I hope you enjoyed reading Bryce and Lucy's story!

Read on to enjoy ***Slow Simmer****, when two warring chefs turn up the heat at La Sirène!*

Slow Simmer

Island Escapes
Book 4

Caitlyn Lynch

SHENANIGANS PRESS
shenanigranspress.com/EN

Contents

Author Note

Michelin do not produce an Australian version of their famous guide, and hence there are no Australian restaurants with Michelin stars, a fact of which I was unaware when I wrote *Finding Cory* and gave the resort's top restaurant a Michelin star.

That said, who's to say they might not produce one, one day? And it's not like they'd give restaurants advance warning they were assessing them for ratings. Could happen any time. Any time at all...

Chapter One

Suzannah Monteil could speak four languages fluently, and swear like a sailor in half a dozen more. It was the latter skill she utilised as she stared at the disaster on her serving counter. Her long, capable fingers slashed at the air as she expressed her extreme displeasure with the sagging mess masquerading as a wedding cake her cringing pastry chef was trying to pretend had nothing to do with her.

"Suzannah!"

A shout finally broke into her tirade and she whirled on the heels of her sensible shoes, green eyes afire with fury. She didn't calm down in the slightest even as she came face to face with her boss, resort manager Luke Collyer.

"Look at it!" she shouted, pointing a trembling finger at the lopsided cake. "*Look* at it, Luke! I cannot send that out of my kitchen, not tomorrow, not ever!"

Summoned by the maître d'hotel who'd merely informed him that his temperamental chef was in a taking again, Luke surveyed the cake and bit his lip, wincing. Suzannah might have lost her temper, but she certainly had cause this time.

"That's... not a good-looking cake," he said finally. "Is that supposed to be the wedding cake for the big wedding tomorrow?"

Being chosen as the venue for the wedding of a movie star and a supermodel was a major coup for Sunfish Island, and Luke was well aware it was in large part because of *La Sirène*, the restaurant Suzannah ran with an iron fist. One of the first restaurants in Australia to be awarded a Michelin star, *La Sirène* was one of the resort's major attractions. And there was no way in hell that travesty of a cake could be served up to the two hundred guests attending tomorrow's ceremony, many of them celebrities with huge social media followings.

"What's your plan?" he asked calmly as Suzannah trembled with rage. He knew his executive chef; she'd already solved the problem in her head, but she needed to vent.

"I can fix it," the hapless pastry chef said.

"*I* will fix it," Suzannah said testily. "By starting again, from scratch. The cake has collapsed because it is not well made, which means just stripping the icing off and re-decorating is unacceptable. Undoubtedly I will be up all night." She glowered, and Luke winced again. It was nearing midnight already, and the wedding was at eleven in the morning, a lunchtime reception to follow.

"Thank you," he said inadequately.

"It is my reputation on the line, is it not?" She shrugged in a very Gallic way. "Unless we want this idiot's creation to end up on CakeWrecks dot com, I *have* to fix it."

Luke choked at the mere idea. Suzannah shot him a wry smile before turning to point at the pastry chef.

"Vicky." She swivelled her finger towards the door. "Get out. You're fired."

"But..." Vicky looked at Luke for support.

"Nope. You're fired. You've got twenty-four hours to gather your stuff and get off the island." Suzannah was well within her rights to fire the woman for a disaster of this magnitude, and Luke had no intention of undermining her authority in the restaurant. Even though Vicky was several years older than Suzannah, she didn't have a tenth of Suzannah's talents.

"Bitch!" Vicky hissed at Suzannah. "Good luck finding someone to replace me - nobody wants to work for a control freak like you!"

"That's enough," Luke said sharply. "Get your things. You're on the first boat to Airlie in the morning, and if you want any kind of reference from us at all you'll be spending the rest of the night packing and preparing to leave quietly."

"Thank you," Suzannah said with a sigh as Vicky stormed out, shooting vindictive glares at everyone who even glanced in her direction. Unbuttoning her white chef's coat, stained after a long evening cooking, Suzannah shrugged out of it and stretched briefly before tossing it in a waiting laundry hamper and reaching for a fresh one. "Well, I'd better get started on this cake."

"Can I get you any extra help?" Luke asked. "I know your staff are all about to clock off for the night but I can authorise some overtime if you need, I'm sure some of them would be willing to stay and help you get the cake done quicker."

Suzannah shook her head. "I will be faster working alone, without any of them to distract me. Don't worry, Luke. Nobody will ever know *that* even existed." She shook her head over the awful cake.

"You're a superstar, Suzannah."

"I know." She smiled at him before turning away, picking up the offending cake and tossing it straight into the food waste disposal bin. "Now leave me alone to cook. And for God's sake, find me a decent pastry chef. If *La Sirène* is going to be the first Australian restaurant outside Melbourne or Sydney with two Michelin stars, I need the best."

"Well, we can advertise the position, shortlist some people for interview..."

"*Non!*" Suzannah reverted to her native French briefly, waving her arms for emphasis. "I do not have time for all that nonsense. You and Jace promised me I should have whatever I wanted; well, I want the best. Find me the best."

Luke watched as Suzannah turned away, headed over to the huge industrial refrigerators to pull out eggs, milk and butter. He had every confidence that she would pull off a spectacular cake by tomorrow, and it would be the crowning highlight to an incredible meal for the two hundred guests which would be raved about and end up extending the already-long waiting list for a table at *La Sirène* even further.

Suzannah Monteil had put Sunfish Island on the foodies' map by winning that Michelin star, and Luke, with the approval of Jace Hunter, the resort's billionaire owner, had indeed promised her anything she wanted. Despite her temperamental attitude, this was the first thing she'd asked him to deal with for her, so he figured he'd better come up with the goods.

He hoped Jace had some ideas, because he honestly had no idea where to start looking. Being a billionaire, Jace must have eaten in a lot of fancy restaurants. Maybe he'd have contacts who could suggest someone.

***

Twenty-four hours later, Suzannah finally collapsed into her bed.

It had been one of the longest days of her life, even for a professional chef used to early mornings and late nights. She'd slaved all night to create the spectacular, three-tiered wedding cake decorated in the bride's signature pale pink and white checks, then supervised her staff as they prepared the all-organic speciality local produce menu the bridal couple insisted upon. With almost twenty-five per cent of the serves being further specialised, of course. Gluten-free, nut-free, seafood-free, lactose-free and vegan food had all been prepared and served to their guests, and many images of the beautifully prepared and presented dishes had been uploaded to Instagram and Twitter accounts with followers numbering in the millions.

Tables at *La Sirène* were booked out three months in advance now. Suzannah smiled wearily into her pillow, a smile of genuine satisfaction. By any measure, the day had been a huge success, even though she'd worked herself to exhaustion making it as perfect as she could.

Until Luke found her a new pastry chef, she'd have to take over the pastry kitchen herself and supervise her sous-chefs in the main kitchen, and she groaned at the thought of the extra hours she'd have to put in. With any luck, they'd hire a replacement who was up to her exacting standards within a few weeks.

Suzannah's tired, stinging eyes finally closed. She had to be up in five hours to select the fish from the fresh catch for the following evening's menu, and while normally she might catch a couple more hours sleep after that, there were two more big weddings coming up that week with speciality cakes to prepare. She might as well get started tomorrow, to avoid having to pull another all-nighter.

She fell asleep with visions of wedding cakes dancing in her head, and woke just before her alarm from a nightmare of being featured on Cake Wrecks. Shaking her head to clear the last vestiges of the bad dream, she shuddered with the memory. Her career would be over if something like that ever happened. It was every chef's nightmare to end up on a foodie disasters blog, or to be named and shamed in a harsh review in a major publication. She'd known several who ended up retiring in disgrace from *haute cuisine.* You just never knew when a mystery diner might end up at one of your tables.

Nobody in Australian fine dining circles had any idea Michelin were expanding their critic program to include Australia for the first time, after all, until the first Michelin Australia guide was published and *La Sirène's* phone started ringing off the hook.

***

The buzzing of her alarm roused Suzannah from a sound sleep and she reached out to silence it with a groan, immediately pushing herself upright. She was far too experienced to allow her eyes to close again. That way lay blissful oblivion... and being hopelessly late. Which in her job, meant she didn't get first pick of the fish from the boat which pulled in to the island's dock at five o'clock every morning.

For the last three weeks, she'd been running both the pastry kitchen and the main restaurant kitchen, and the pressure was beginning to take a toll. She hadn't managed more than five hours of sleep a night since summarily firing Vicky, and though she'd do exactly the same thing again, she was really hoping Luke and Jace came up with a replacement soon. Jace had taken off in his private jet for Europe a few days ago, and she had her fingers crossed he might have her new pastry chef with him on his return.

And also, that whoever he hired was competent at the least. She was in no mood to clean up any more of other people's messes.

The dinner hour rush was just beginning when Suzannah heard her name called and looked up to see Luke standing at the doorway between the two kitchens. Handing her blowtorch and the task of caramelising brown sugar on the top of individual crème brûlées over to an assistant, she made her way over to him.

"What?" she said brusquely.

There was a man standing behind Luke, she registered, just on the other side of the doorway. There was something familiar about the way he stood, lounging comfortably with one hip against the counter, ankles crossed, arms folded. Her eyes flew to his face and she took in the designer stubble, the chiselled cheekbones, the amused gleam in honey-gold eyes.

"Oh, *no*," she said.

"Meet your new pastry chef!" Luke sounded really quite excited. "We have our very own celebrity now, Suzannah... Carlo Gianetti!"

"I know who he is." Suzannah kept her tone flat. "And he's not staying."

"Can't take the competition?"

Carlo's voice sounded exactly as she remembered, a sensual, husky rasp which still made goosebumps raise up on her skin. Suzannah narrowed her eyes at him.

"There is no competition. This is my kitchen, and you don't belong in it. Get out."

"Now just a minute," Luke cut in. Glancing around, he saw every eye on them. "Outside, the two of you. I don't think this conversation requires an audience."

Suzannah glanced around, and immediately everyone's attention was back on their appointed tasks. She sniffed audibly, letting her staff know she wasn't fooled for a moment and she wouldn't tolerate any inferior dishes being served from her kitchen, before following Luke and Carlo out of the restaurant's rear door.

Chapter Two

Seeing Suzannah in the flesh again had left Carlo speechless for several moments. In his memory, she was still the gangly girl still in her teens who'd been the first woman he fell in love with.

For a full year, they'd worked side by side at the famous *Le Cordon Bleu* chef school in Paris, competing to each be the best in their class. It was the night after their final presentation exam, before they knew whether they'd passed or not, when they drank far too much wine in a seedy bar and somehow ended up in bed together.

That night, Carlo finally understood just why Suzannah got under his skin so much. Why he could take competition from everyone else, male or female, and laugh it off, but why every sniping comment from her made him edgy.

They were both young enough not to recognise sexual tension for what it really was. But that night in Suzannah's narrow bed in her tiny garret apartment, they practically blew the roof off with passion.

He remembered waking after a brief doze, finding Suzannah's red hair tumbled on the pillow, his face buried in the fragrant curls, before taking her in his arms again. Her smile was like the sun coming up.

She'd changed in the nine years since he'd last seen her. Grown into those gangly legs, developed curves even the stiff chef's coat couldn't disguise. Her face had matured too, losing the last vestiges of her teenage youthfulness and becoming fine-boned, serene as she worked, drawn in tight lines of anger now as she faced him and Luke, her arms folded defensively across her body.

Only her hair was unchanged, a thick mass of copper curls. Pinned up atop her head and severely restrained at the moment, Carlo knew when she let it down the curls would fall almost to her waist.

This was a mistake, he found himself thinking, because he'd barely set eyes on her again and he wanted to kiss her, wanted to unpin her hair and fist both his hands in its thick weight, kiss her until she melted into him the way she had all those years ago.

He shouldn't have come.

"I'm sorry you've had a wasted trip," Suzannah said, not sounding sorry at all as the kitchen door closed behind them, giving them some semblance of privacy, "but this obviously isn't going to work out. I'm sure Jace can arrange for your return to Milan."

Even though he was already thinking coming had been a mistake, Carlo's hackles rose at her flat dismissal of him before they'd even had a chance to talk. He didn't even have to speak up, though; Luke was already doing that.

"Now just a minute." Luke looked between the two of them. "Do I take it you two already know each other?"

"We were at culinary school at the same time in Paris." Carlo waved a dismissive hand, as though to say the past was of no importance. "It was a long time ago."

Green eyes flashed as Suzannah glared at him. "What are you even doing here?" she hissed, ignoring Luke completely. "Aren't you happy with your family business in Milan and your status as the hottest celebrity chef on YouTube?"

"If you watched my program, which obviously you don't," Carlo said, trying to appear unruffled, "you'd know my younger sister and her husband have taken over the business. My dessert offerings have always been my speciality, and I felt it was for the best they take over general operations and leave me free to do my own thing. Working for a Michelin-starred restaurant as a specialist pastry chef was too good an opportunity to pass up."

Not that he'd have accepted a similar offer from any other restaurant. He'd kept track of Suzannah over the years, knew very well where she worked, so when Jace Hunter contacted him out of the blue and asked if he'd be interested in the position at *La Sirène*, he'd said yes before he even really thought about what he was getting into.

Which was, apparently, Suzannah's bad books, as she paced up and down beside the rubbish bins gesturing rudely and swearing to herself in French.

"You do realise I understand every word?" Carlo said in the same language.

"Yes, but Luke doesn't." Suzannah stopped in her pacing and shot him a ferocious look. "This isn't going to work, Carlo. It can't. I can't work with you."

"Why not?" he asked, and heard the echoes of long-ago hurt in his voice as he added "You're the one who left *me*, remember?"

He couldn't see the colour of Suzannah's eyes in the dim light behind the restaurant, but he knew them by heart, could imagine the emerald in them brightening as she stared at him in wide-eyed silence.

"If we could return to English for a moment," Luke said dryly, and both of them snapped their heads around guiltily to look at him.

"My apologies," Carlo said guiltily. He was always very conscious of his manners, and he did answer to Luke, after all. Or would, if Suzannah could be convinced to let him stay.

"Suzannah," Luke nodded briefly at Carlo before turning his attention to his executive chef. "Do I take it that whatever issues you have with Carlo have nothing to do with his ability in the kitchen?"

"No," Suzannah said sulkily after a pause.

"I'm sorry," Luke addressed the remark to Carlo, "but I have to ask her this. Suzannah, has Carlo ever assaulted, threatened or intimidated you?"

"No!" She looked shocked at the idea. "No, Luke, it's nothing like that. We... have a history, that's all."

"We were rivals in culinary school and then we were lovers," Carlo said baldly, seeing no reason to hide the truth.

"I see," Luke said after a brief moment of shocked silence.

Suzannah flushed to the roots of her hair, the darkening cast of her skin visible to the two men even in the bad light. "It didn't end well," she said, almost inaudibly.

For a moment, the three of them stood in silence, and then Luke sighed and ran a hand through his hair. "I don't think you're being fair," he told Suzannah finally. "How long ago was all this?"

"Nine years," Suzannah said immediately, making Carlo blink. He could name the exact day and time he last saw her, but hadn't thought she would have the information on the tip of her tongue like that.

"And you don't think you've both grown up enough to work together?"

Ouch. The biting remark found its target, Carlo saw, as Suzannah's spine stiffened.

"Give me an opportunity," he said quickly, before she could lose her temper and say something she might regret. "I'm sure you've learned a lot in nine years; so have I. Let me make you a dessert dégustation menu, for lunchtime tomorrow. If you're not completely sold on everything I make, I'll go."

He was careful to keep his tone completely reasonable. Luke nodded approvingly at him, and they both looked at Suzannah to see her reaction.

Carlo knew her well enough to guess she wanted to reject his suggestion on the spot, but doing so would look unreasonable at best, maybe even petty and vindictive, and she really wasn't an unreasonable person. She had high expectations of herself and held others around her to the same standards, both in the quality of her cooking and in her personal life.

"*D'accord,*" she said grudgingly at last, then translated for Luke's sake. "All right."

"Excellent," Luke said, and Carlo could tell he was being deliberately hearty. "I'll come down, and bring Olivia over. She's our marketing manager," he advised Carlo. "Once you're confirmed in the post, she'll be the one plastering it all over social media. I understand you have almost a million subscribers on You Tube, and Jace agreed with you that you can continue to film here as long as it doesn't affect the day-to-day operations of *La Sirène*?"

"That's right," Carlo nodded. "I haven't made any announcement yet, of course."

He was pretty sure Suzannah was grinding her teeth. They needed to talk, privately, but she didn't seem inclined to give him even a moment.

"I have to get back," she said abruptly, turning to open the kitchen door. "The pastry kitchen will be open to you tomorrow morning," she threw over her shoulder to Carlo. "Don't be late getting in... and don't distract my staff. They have a lot of work to do."

"Yes, ma'am," he said to the closing door.

"That did not go the way I expected," Luke said after a long minute of awkward silence. "Would you mind filling me in on the details of '*it didn't end well*', please?"

Suddenly, Carlo felt absolutely exhausted. He'd spent most of the last thirty-six hours on a plane, and thinking about being face to face with Suzannah again for the first time in almost a decade had kept him from getting any sleep, even though Jace Hunter's private jet was sinfully comfortable. His body clock was completely out of sync, and he had to get up in just a few hours ready to cook the best desserts he'd ever made in his life.

Yet, he couldn't refuse to explain.

"Sure," he said wearily. "Would you mind if we talked about it over a stiff drink, though? I'm feeling very much in need of one right now... and then a hot shower and a few hours of sleep before I get in the kitchen to impress Madam Picky."

Luke laughed, and put a companionable hand on Carlo's shoulder. "Of course, mate. Right this way. I've got a bottle of Scotch in my cabin, and it's just a couple of doors down from yours. You can go to bed and crash out right after we've talked."

"Sounds like a plan." A glass of Scotch sounded heavenly, almost as good as a bed. Carlo followed as Luke set off through the resort, wending his way through palm-tree lined paths with confidence despite a lack of signs and limited lighting. It seemed like a maze to Carlo's overtired mind, but he was sure he'd get used to it, just like the heat. Even after dark had fallen, the air was hot and muggy, the humidity much higher than he was used to. He just hoped his room was air-conditioned, or sleeping would be difficult no matter how tired he was.

"This one's yours," Luke paused outside a small cabin. It looked pretty luxurious for staff accommodation, and with his brain filter compromised by exhaustion, Carlo said so. Luke laughed.

"They used to be guest accommodations, actually. After a hurricane a few years ago damaged much of the existing infrastructure, the Hunters bought the island and did a complete rebuild. Left the existing cabins for staff. Only senior staff get these nice ones, but you definitely merit one, considering your celebrity status and how much we expect you to enhance the reputation of *La Sirène*, and by extension the whole resort."

Carlo wasn't too tired to understand the warning in Luke's tone and the implication that if he didn't enhance the resort's reputation, they'd have no hesitation in replacing him. He nodded in understanding, and they moved on, walking a couple of cabins further along the row. Luke gestured him to take a seat on the small veranda, going inside and returning a couple of minutes later with a bottle and two glasses.

Luke let him savour the first couple of sips, the welcome burn going down his throat, before speaking.

"So, you and Suzannah had a thing going on. Tell me about it... and tell me why you didn't let Jace know the pair of you had a history when he offered you the job, please. I'm quite certain you already knew she was here when you accepted."

Carlo winced. "I know how good she is," he answered the last part of the request first, "and I know you wouldn't want to risk displeasing her, in case she walked out on you. I wanted to see her again, though, and please believe me that I genuinely want the job, and I'll do it to the best of my ability."

Luke inclined his head in acknowledgement of the promise. "And the rest?" he asked, not unkindly. "I don't like surprises, Carlo. If this is going to come back to bite me, I'd like the full story."

"I wish I had it," Carlo said, surprising himself with the bitterness which came into his tone, "but I still don't know why she left me."

Unwillingly, he found his mind ranging back over the years, to when he was young and hopelessly in love with a fiery redhead who cooked like a dream.

Chapter Three

Suzannah couldn't settle to anything once Carlo and Luke had left. She managed to curdle a sauce for the first time in years, burned her wrist on the edge of a hot pan and for the final straw somehow tripped over her own feet and dropped a carton of eggs as she carried them from the cold room to her workstation. Staring down at the oozy, sticky mess running all over her shoes, the cardboard container and the floor, she heaved a deep sigh and closed her eyes.

"Suzannah?" a voice said behind her, and then asked in her native French "Are you all right?"

Opening her eyes she looked around and found a smile for Edouard, the restaurant sommelier. A charming, handsome Frenchman some ten years her senior, she guessed the rest of her staff had probably recruited him to approach her, and with any luck get her out from underfoot before she did something disastrous.

"I think I'm having an off night, Edouard," she replied in the same tongue.

"So I see." He cast an amused glance down at her feet. "Dinner is almost completed. Why don't you call it a night? I'm sure your sous-chefs can handle whatever is left."

She knew they could. She'd trained them to her own exacting standards, after all. Looking around the kitchen, she saw a hive of ordered industry, everyone very studiously paying attention to their assigned tasks and not watching her at all.

"You might be right," she said. "It's been a long few weeks. I haven't had a night off since I sacked Vicky."

"You haven't had a morning off, either," Edouard pointed out dryly, taking a clean towel from a rack and dropping it on the floor behind her. "Here. Step on that and clean your shoes off. Angelica," he snapped his fingers at one of the apprentices, who dropped what she was doing and rushed over at once. "Clean this up, please."

"Yes, sir!" The girl practically genuflected, hurrying to get cloths as Suzannah stepped onto the towel and wiped the egg white off her shoes. They needed cleaning properly, but she didn't want to remove them in the kitchen.

"We've got this, boss," Julie, her senior assistant chef, called across the kitchen. "Go have an early night. God knows you deserve one."

"All right, all right." Suzannah surrendered to the inevitable. "Julie, you're in charge."

"I won't let you down, boss!" Julie's look of determination made Suzannah smile. The other woman would be a hell of an executive chef one day, and a lot sooner than she realised.

"Just a moment," Edouard said, heading for the door, and when he returned he had a bottle of wine in hand. "Here. Take this with you and have a glass or two to help you relax."

The wine had been opened and re-corked, Suzannah saw as she accepted the bottle. Her eyebrows rose as she read the label and she looked a question at Edouard.

"A customer last night ordered and paid for it, but only drank half, and said he didn't want to take it with him." Edouard gave her a very Gallic shrug, and a wink. "It's too good to give it to you heathens to cook with."

Suzannah laughed, and tucked the bottle under her arm. "Thank you, Edouard." She put a friendly hand on his arm. "I'll enjoy it."

Edouard smiled warmly back at her, urging her towards the rear door. "Go. Get some rest. I'll see you tomorrow."

***

Outside in the warm, jasmine-scented darkness, Suzannah slipped her sticky shoes off and stuffed her socks into them. There was grass alongside the paths which led back to her cabin, and she revelled in the soft coolness under her tired feet as she walked slowly through the night.

Crickets chirped in the bushes, and the soft strains of a piano being played at one of the resort's bars drifted to her on the soft ocean breeze. It was an absolutely beautiful night, fragrant and serene. A night for lovers, Suzannah found herself thinking as she walked, and snorted aloud.

It was Carlo's surprise arrival which had her thinking about lovers, of course. While he wasn't the last man she'd shared her bed with, he was the last - indeed, the only - who'd left a lasting impression. The only serious relationship she'd ever had, in those long-ago days of first love she'd daydreamed of the two of them getting married and running a restaurant together someday. To her at age twenty, that had seemed the pinnacle of ambition.

Carlo, however, came from a very different background to Suzannah. She was the daughter of a working-class single father from one of the poorer districts of Paris, learning to cook when she wanted better than the simple meals which were all her weary papa could make when he arrived home tired from work. She got her first job aged thirteen at a cafe near their small apartment, and graduated from waiting tables to working in the kitchen a year later.

School had never been something she particularly enjoyed, but in the hum of a busy kitchen, Suzannah found her place in the world. The cafe owner saw the passion in her work and encouraged her to become a professional chef, setting up a savings plan for her and matching her savings when she was offered a place at *Le Cordon Bleu*.

Suzannah came from a working-class, hardscrabble background, and at just eighteen was thrust suddenly into a world she'd never realized existed. Most of the kids at the prestigious culinary school were from wealthy, even aristocratic backgrounds. Few of them had the ambition, drive or talent which propelled Suzannah to the head of the class almost immediately. Out of all her classmates, only Carlo could match her... and that was only because of his background, as the son of a wealthy Milanese family with an already-famous restaurant, one whose kitchen Carlo had literally grown up in.

She'd watched him with fascination, this assured Italian man - for even at nineteen, Carlo was definitely not a boy - whose hands were as confident as his attitude. Handsome, cockily sure of himself and his place in the world, Carlo never seemed to have doubts about anything he did, whereas Suzannah was constantly questioning and second-guessing everything from whether she had put too much pepper in the soup to whether she belonged among the well-heeled, wealthy crowd she was thrust into.

There were always girls hanging off Carlo, from the school and from other places, attracted by both his looks and the charisma he exuded as effortlessly as breathing. Invisible - or so she thought - Suzannah watched with both fascination and envy as the parade of beautiful, designer-dressed girls never seemed to end.

She hadn't thought Carlo was even aware of her existence, such was her own inability to blend in with her classmates, until he looked across at her cooking station one day, catching her surreptitiously watching him, winked and said "You'll want to watch that sauce, Red. I can smell burning." He sniffed theatrically.

"It's not mine," she snapped back instantly, though she did take a moment to check. "I never burn things!"

"I know. I'm envious."

To her surprise, Carlo smiled at her. Flustered, she said sharply "Maybe if you paid more attention to your cooking and less to chasing skirts, you wouldn't burn things either."

"Ouch!" Flamboyantly, he clapped a hand over his heart. "A hit direct, Red! Jealous, are you?"

"In your dreams," Suzannah sneered. Narrowing her eyes, she added "And my name is Suzannah, not Red."

She hadn't waited for him to respond, had turned her back and bent to check the soufflé rising in her oven.

Of course, after that Carlo seemed to be underfoot everywhere, calling her Red and casting smoldering, smirking looks in her direction even when he had another girl - or two! - in tow. Suzannah did her best to ignore him completely, even though she was all too well aware her body had different ideas. The prickles of awareness which chased up and down her spine whenever Carlo was near warned her to stay as far away as she could get.

Unfortunately, as the school's star students they were constantly thrown together, being challenged and pushed to compete with each other by the professional chefs who saw their potential and wanted to get the best out of them.

It was in their final weeks when things came to a head. Too busy with the practical examinations they were undergoing almost daily to prove their fitness for graduation to keep up his usual flirtations, Carlo turned his attentions to the nearest available female - Suzannah. She'd tried hard to stay unmoved, but failed dismally. Particularly as she got to know him better and realised he wasn't the spoiled rich kid she'd thought him; yes, he came from a much more affluent background than she did and had been given every advantage, but he was also truly dedicated to the arts of fine cuisine and talented as hell, especially with the delicate flavours and artistic presentation of desserts.

Eventually, one night after their final exams were over, she let him take her out to a wine bar and they both drank far too much. Unable to resist his blandishments, Suzannah invited him back to her place... and discovered that her few sexual experiences up to that point in no way prepared her for the incredible way Carlo could make her feel.

She'd wondered aloud, afterwards, just how much practice it took to get that good at sex, and he'd rolled over to lean over her, give her that intense dark stare of his.

"If that was just sex for you..." He shook his head, ran his hand through his hair. "That was *life-changing*. I don't have the words to describe how incredible that was, Suzannah... and how much I desperately want to do it again."

He wasn't lying about being eager for an encore, Suzannah discovered as his erect cock nudged her thigh. Truth be told, right then she couldn't think of anything she wanted more, either.

They'd spent almost an entire week in bed, surfacing only to get food and drink, and by the end of it Carlo finally had Suzannah convinced he didn't view her as just another notch on his bedpost. When the phone call came to let Suzannah know she'd graduated top of her class, Carlo had been quite plainly overjoyed for her.

"You deserve it," he'd said, hugging her tightly. "You deserve every bit of success and acclaim. You're going to be a superstar, Suzannah; we all knew it from the first day."

Carlo had been a close second in the rankings, of course, and as the two top graduates they had their pick of positions. Both offered a one-year graduate position as sous-chefs at Alain Ducasse's legendary *Benoit* bistro, for months they lived and worked together in perfect harmony. Suzannah was honestly surprised at how well they managed to get along; she'd spent so long sniping at Carlo and being envious of the ease with which he managed social situations, she'd never realised just how easy he was to get along with.

Lying in her bed, staring sleeplessly at the ceiling despite her exhaustion, Suzannah smiled bitterly at the thought of herself as a young girl utterly smitten by Carlo Gianetti.

What a naive idiot she'd been, to think she could ever belong in his world.

They'd been living and working together for almost eight months when his parents turned up in Paris, irritated by Carlo's failure to go back to the family restaurant in Milan. Their obvious shock at discovering he was living with a girlfriend spoke volumes; Carlo had never even mentioned Suzannah's existence to them.

The Gianettis were even more wealthy and well-connected than Suzannah had ever realised. The 'family restaurant' turned out to be not just a restaurant, but a castle converted into a premium five-star hotel, the Michelin-starred restaurant ensuring bookings were always sought-after. Carlo was a scion of a long line of Italian nobility tracing their descent from the infamous Borgias, his father still holding the title of *Comte*.

Their disapproval of Suzannah, a girl from the lower end of Paris' working-class, could not have been more obvious. Carlo was quite sharp with his parents over it, flatly refusing to accept their decree that he should return to Italy at once.

She'd loved him for that. Loved him more when his parents finally left, frustrated, and he turned to take her in his arms, telling her he would choose her over them every time. That they'd spent his whole life controlling him, grooming him for something which was never his dream.

"I want to travel. To work in amazing restaurants all over the world, learn different cuisines, incorporate them into my own style... and I want to do it with *you*."

It was the happiest day of Suzannah's life.

The end of their apprenticeship year at *Benoit* came quickly, and Ducasse wrote both of them glowing references. The job offers started coming in quickly, mostly at restaurants and hotels in Paris and other cities in France, a few in London. An intriguing offer for Carlo in Geneva. Another for Carlo in Barcelona. One for Suzannah in Dubai she rejected out of hand; while the money would be excellent, the Middle East was one place she did not particularly want to work.

After a few days, Suzannah began to see a disturbing pattern. The offers for her, while reasonably compensated and high enough profile to interest her, weren't in the same league as those Carlo was getting.

The day he got the offer from *Le Bernardin* in New York, Suzannah finally understood. A restaurant with three Michelin stars making an offer to a chef Carlo's age, without so much as an audition or an interview? Somebody was pulling strings behind the scenes, and she had a pretty good idea who.

She also knew the offer was too good for Carlo to turn down. And sure, she could follow him to New York, find work somewhere decent enough, work her way up the ladder. Watching him be fast-tracked to the top when she knew her skill at least equalled his would eat away at her, though, and she knew it would destroy them.

Her pride would not allow it to come to pass. She refused to trail after Carlo like some lovesick puppy, and she most certainly would not allow him to reject such an opportunity for her sake; that would be the height of foolishness and ever-practical Suzannah could not abide that. No, she would take the best of the offers she had received and go to London, make her own way to the top of her profession.

She was already packed when Carlo arrived home from his shift at work. Handing him the offer letter from *Le Bernardin*, she said simply "I've accepted an offer in London. Take care and good luck, Carlo," before wheeling her suitcases out the door.

He followed her all the way down to the street, demanding she talk to him, tell him why she was leaving. When she hailed a taxi, he jumped in the other side. Indeed, they were at the railway station and Suzannah was perilously close to tears when he finally realised he could not dissuade her from leaving. He'd watched silently as she presented her ticket and boarded the Eurostar train which would take her to London, his expression one of stricken grief.

Suzannah had done her best, over the years, to forget that look on Carlo's face, the last sight she had of him as the train pulled out of the station and she was finally free to let the tears flow.

She'd never managed to put him out of her mind entirely, though. Seeing him again tonight had been a shock to the system, particularly when her body responded with traitorous arousal to his closeness and she realised she wasn't over him.

She'd probably never be over him.

Carlo Gianetti wasn't the kind of man you could ever forget.

Chapter Four

Carlo had never seen a kitchen quite like the one which was now his domain. *La Sirène*'s pastry kitchen was separated from the main kitchen by an open doorway, both of them equipped with every top of the line industrial appliance any chef could ever dream of wanting. This was Suzannah's doing, he knew. Jace Hunter was a billionaire, and he knew the value of having a chef of Suzannah's calibre. Carlo was willing to bet after the restaurant was awarded a Michelin star, Jace and Luke had offered Suzannah anything she wanted... and she, never remotely interested in material wealth, had used their offer to make her restaurant kitchen into something the world's top chefs would envy.

And now, the pastry kitchen was Carlo's. It was four in the morning and at the main bread kitchen not far away, the bakers were working on fresh breads and pastries for breakfast, but right here and now, *La Sirène* was all his.

Smiling, he set to exploring his new kingdom.

By the time the fresh fish arrived from the docks at just before six, he was in full swing, singing along with music from his phone he'd synced with the Bluetooth speaker. Several of the big ovens were fired up and there were mixing bowls everywhere, flour and sugar dusting formerly shining clean steel surfaces, a pile of eggshells in a bowl, macarons resting on a counter before crisping...

In short, it was a mess. And it was just the way Carlo, who thrived on disorder, loved it. He hadn't had such a good time cooking in ages, always either on camera or in the tighter confines of the kitchen in Castillo Gianetti where he wasn't even able to devote all his time to the sweet desserts which had always been his greatest creations.

He'd never seen such fine ingredients as *La Sirène's* pantries and refrigerated storage room were stocked with, either; the fresh tropical fruits and locally produced chocolate, coffee, cheeses and cane sugar.

Quite frankly, Carlo Gianetti was as happy as a pig in mud, and it showed as he serenaded the empty kitchen at the top of his voice, singing along to Ricky Martin and shaking his (if he said so himself) very fine bon-bon along with the music.

Unfortunately, it didn't seem Suzannah appreciated either his bon-bon or his singing, as her shriek of rage cut through his consciousness. The music snapped off as she slapped her hand down on the speaker's power button, and Carlo spun around, almost dropping the bowl of melted dark chocolate, beaten egg whites and whipped cream he was carefully folding together to make a decadent chocolate mousse.

Carlo was quite impressed as Suzannah set out on one of her epic rants, shaking her finger at him and spitting swear words in several languages. Her curse vocabulary had definitely expanded in the last few years. He wasn't even sure what some of the words meant.

"*Buongiorno, mia bella*," he said cheerfully when she paused to take a breath. "Looking forward to our little dégustation this afternoon?"

"I'm looking forward to kicking your ass out of my kitchen," she snapped back, green eyes flashing with rage, her red hair almost seeming to bristle as she stalked towards him. "Look at this godawful mess!"

"You always were a neat freak, *mia ragazza*," he said fondly. She had raging OCD, a typical trait in a top chef, and one he did not share unless one counted his rigid requirements about the perfection of the food which was sent out of his kitchen. Indeed, he was messy in his habits whenever he could get away with it, and in this beautiful, dedicated pastry kitchen with all the space he could possibly desire, he would most definitely be able to get away with it.

As long as Suzannah didn't murder him, anyway. Good thing all the sharp knives were in the other kitchen and out of her reach at that precise moment, Carlo thought as she eyed him, teeth grinding quite audibly.

"Don't call me that," she snapped. "You'll refer to me as Chef Monteil, thank you. And don't you dare get in the way of my staff. Lunch and dinner still have to be served today; if you've used the ingredients they'll need for today's desserts, I don't care how good your cooking is, you're fired. This is an island and we can't just run into town for fresh ingredients; you have to order them and they come on tomorrow morning's supply boat."

"I'm a professional, *cara*," Carlo said, somewhat insulted. "I read through your menu and made sure you'll have what you need for a couple days' worth of desserts, not just one."

She humphed at him, her expression telegraphing disbelief.

"Why the hell do you have such a problem with me being here anyway?" He set down the bowl before he got agitated and over-mixed the mousse. "You're the one who left me without a word of explanation, remember?"

"That was years ago, it's nothing to do with why I don't want you here now!" Suzannah protested, but he knew her well enough, knew her minute shifts in body language and the way her green eyes flickered away from his, to know she wasn't telling the whole truth.

"If you wanted to work in London so much, why didn't you say so? I had plenty of options, we could have carried on working together, but you made it more than clear you didn't want me to follow you. Still, I'd have thought you'd have gotten over that by now."

"There was nothing to get over!" She clenched her fists by her sides.

"Then why do you have a problem with me?" Carlo folded his arms and tried to look casual, but the truth was, he wanted an answer. He'd wanted an answer ever since he stood on the platform in Paris watching the train disappear into the distance, wondering how and why his whole life had just come crashing down around his ears.

"Because you're more concerned with your status as a celebrity than with good food." Suzannah's answer startled him, and he dropped his hands to his sides, starting forward.

"I'm *what*?"

Colour blazed in her cheeks as she continued. "I've seen some of your YouTube footage. You take shortcuts, use ingredients you know to be inferior..."

"What?" He honestly had no idea what she was talking about.

"Vanilla essence out of a *bottle*?"

He began to laugh. Her scandalised expression was just too funny as she spat out the words, as though they were the rudest of epithets. She looked even angrier at his laughter, turning on her heel to storm out. Somehow stifling the laughter, Carlo reached out to touch her shoulder, not wanting to grab her, but needing to stop her leaving. He had to explain.

"Suzannah, you've been watching my introductory shows, haven't you? The short, ten-minute ones."

"I don't have the time or inclination to sit through hours of your nonsense!" she snapped back at him, her cheeks still red. She didn't like admitting she'd watched any of his shows, he recognised.

"Those shows are designed for beginner cooks, and people who don't have the *time or inclination*," he threw her own words back at her, "to spend an hour making a dessert. Of course I suggest they use time-saving ingredients. I also tell them in the video that it's only a substitute and using fresh vanilla extracted from vanilla pods is best. I'm not there misleading them into thinking what they use it to make will be as good as what you'd get at a gourmet restaurant. Nor would I serve it at my own restaurant. Everything I cook during filming gets devoured by friends and staff, people who don't pay a penny for it."

"Oh." Suzannah's mouth hung open and her face somehow reddened further.

"You've never done any TV work, have you?"

"No," she admitted.

He'd have known if she did. While he wouldn't exactly say he'd stalked her, he'd definitely paid attention to her career. If she'd ever been on TV, he'd have known about it. Even when she worked for Gordon Ramsay, she'd avoided the cameras in the celebrity chef's kitchens.

"The camera would love you," Carlo suggested it gently. "Part of my agreement with the resort is that I can film episodes for my channel here and I'd love to have you feature..."

"Let's see if I allow you to stay first," she snarked, turning on her heel and stalking out, but not before he saw the flare of interest in her eyes. Her curiosity was piqued, he hoped. She really would be amazing on camera, her beauty and animation lighting up the screen, but her culinary skills would be the real ratings winner.

Smiling at her retreating back, Carlo picked up his mixing bowl and returned to work. He still had to impress her this afternoon, not to mention Luke and Jace, and he had a lot of work to get done first. The staff would be coming in to begin work on the lunch menu shortly and he really was going to have to tidy up a bit first. Still, that would only take a few minutes, and it was time for the macarons to go in the oven. Then he had two varieties of ice cream to make, figs to roast in maple syrup, strawberries to poach in balsamic vinegar, his speciality lemon and mint souffle to make...

The music had been silenced, but that didn't stop Carlo. He burst into song again as he whirled around the kitchen.

***

Hidden from view behind the separating wall which divided the two kitchens, Suzannah found herself smiling. Carlo had always been unapologetic in his fondness for American pop songs. Somehow, she wasn't in the least surprised to find him singing along to Ricky Martin as he cooked. Tempted to peek and see if he still danced along to the music, lean hips swaying to the beat, she sternly restrained herself. If he caught her peeking, he'd be even more insufferable.

Stiffening her spine, she walked out into the bright, humid morning, squinting wearily as the morning son seared her eyes. She hadn't had enough sleep last night. Carlo had occupied her mind into the small hours despite her exhaustion, and her alarm had woken her far too soon. She was going back to bed for a few hours.

Even if the sound of his rich singing voice would probably be stuck in her head for days.

Chapter Five

The rest of the kitchen staff started arriving at about ten, by which time Carlo had cleaned up the worst of the mess he'd made. Or at least, piled all the dirty bowls and tools he'd used in one of the giant industrial sinks in the washing area. A junior walked in and sighed before making a start on the mountain, shooting Carlo an irritated glance. Well, there was one staff member he'd have to win over, Carlo thought guiltily. No doubt the kid was used to it, though, assuming Suzannah still went on her occasional all-night cooking benders trialling new recipes.

A slight, almost delicate-looking girl came to stand in the doorway between the two kitchens, smiling as she caught his eye.

"Hi, I'm Julie," she said cheerfully, her accent telling him she was Australian.

"Carlo," he said affably.

"I know who you are. I love your show."

She was trying not to gush, he thought. He offered a warm smile. "Well, perhaps you can appear on future episodes."

"Really?" Her eyes went very wide. Charming girl, Carlo thought privately, though he had no intention of encouraging her hero-worship of him.

"Indeed, as long as you are good at your job, and since you are employed in Suzannah's kitchen I have no doubt of that. Tell me, what's your position here?"

"Senior assistant to Chef Monteil." Julie looked proud of that, as well she should. Carlo knew all too well that Suzannah was exceedingly picky about who she worked with, and Julie certainly wouldn't be her trusted right hand if she wasn't more than just competent.

"I'm preparing a dégustation dessert menu for this afternoon," Carlo said, nodding at the crust he was just pressing into a row of miniature springform pans.

"So I hear. What's that for?" Julie sounded like she was dying to ask questions, but also worried about prying. Carlo took pity on her.

"It's a macadamia and pistachio crust for a cappuccino cheesecake. I'll be serving it with a black cherry drizzle."

"Wow." She looked at the processor behind him, currently beating the cream cheese and sugar together, and the two ice cream machines churning beyond that, before a smile crossed her clever, narrow face. "Well... no doubt we'll have plenty of opportunity to work together. I'd better get cracking. Catch you later!" Waggling her fingers at him, she withdrew, and as though her exit was a sign of approval, the other staff all began to chatter at once, asking him questions, telling him how much they enjoyed his show and how excited they were to work with him.

Carlo answered their questions as best he could, though he steered deftly clear of any which touched on Suzannah. Laughingly, he declined offers of help, saying the dégustation needed to be all his own work.

"Stick with your own jobs," he advised. "I don't want Chef Monteil angry with me on my first day, if your work doesn't get done!"

They were certainly well trained, he observed, as the mere mention of Suzannah's name had them scurrying to their work stations. Clearly, they respected their boss, and he would never for a moment undermine that.

He heard Suzannah come into the other kitchen; the tempo of work picked up and spread to the pastry kitchen, the young chef next to him suddenly paying much closer attention to the meringue swirls he was piping onto a baking sheet.

"Good morning once again, Chef Monteil," he said, keeping his tone respectful, though he didn't turn around from the sauce he was stirring. The hairs on his arms prickled as she came to stand behind him, glancing over his shoulder.

"Now, now," Carlo said teasingly. "You must wait for your surprises, Chef."

Suzannah sniffed audibly. "I don't like waiting."

"So I recall," he said softly, and she stepped back hastily.

"There will be six for the dégustation," she said quite loudly. "Please be ready to begin by two-thirty."

"As you wish, Chef," Carlo said deferentially, but he grinned to himself as she moved away. She'd asked for that... and he remembered all too well that she was an eager lover, always impatient to tear his clothes off and fall into bed. No, patience wasn't really Suzannah's strong point... except when it came to her cooking, of course.

He wanted to watch her, but forced himself to concentrate on his own work. He had to be faultless today, everything so perfect even Suzannah couldn't find a single flaw.

Knowing Luke and Jace would be at the dégustation, and recalling Luke had said something about the marketing manager attending, Carlo had to wonder who the other two would be. Who had Suzannah invited to sample his desserts?

Someone who would back her judgement, he guessed, and therefore he wasn't surprised in the least when he went out to the restaurant at two-thirty and Suzannah introduced him to the sommelier, Edouard, who was sitting at the table beside her.

"A pleasure to meet you," Carlo said affably, offering his hand to shake. "And I'm so glad Suzannah asked you to sit in; tasting my desserts will of course be invaluable when you select dessert wines to pair with them."

"Indeed." Edouard offered a limp handshake, not bothering to stand, and then completely ignoring Carlo, turning back to Suzannah. "As I was saying, the Montrachet is a perfect partner for that wagyu beef..."

Carlo blinked, surprised, but didn't really have time to remark before they were joined by Luke and Jace, accompanied by two young women.

"Hi again, Carlo," Jace shook his hand with a warm smile. "Good to see you here. How are you settling in?"

"Loving the kitchen," Carlo said with perfect honesty. "It's an amazing setup you have here. I've never seen better."

"We're blessed with space and the money to do it right, and Ms. Monteil's expertise to tell us how," Jace disclaimed, but he still looked pleased. "This is Nessa, my fiancée," he indicated the short, stunning black woman at his side, her long hair in tightly woven braids reaching almost to her waist, a pretty aqua sundress setting off her glorious dark brown skin. "As soon as I mentioned sampling lots of desserts, she invited herself along."

Carlo laughed, shaking Nessa's hand as she offered it. "Well, I hope you won't be disappointed."

"I'm sure I won't be," she flashed dimples in her cheeks as she smiled back at him. "As long as there's chocolate?"

"There's chocolate," he affirmed, and she chuckled, stepping back to allow Luke to introduce the other woman, a lovely brunette wearing what Carlo was pretty sure was a designer sheath dress and high heels.

"Olivia Stratten, the resort's marketing manager," Luke presented.

"So pleased to meet you!" Olivia pumped his hand, showing very white teeth in a broad smile. She was American, Carlo realised. "Really looking forward to using your celebrity status to enhance the resort. And to tasting your cooking, of course."

"Of course." Liking her at once, Carlo smiled back warmly. "Whatever I can do to assist. I'll be making my announcement on my YouTube channel in a day or so, perhaps we can get together and you could help me script it?"

"I'd be delighted to."

"Ahem," Suzannah cleared her throat imperiously, gesturing everyone to their seats. Carlo was amused to see even Luke and Jace obeyed her directions, though less so to see that Edouard kept his seat beside Suzannah, even moving a little closer. The sommelier's body language was decidedly proprietary, angled in towards Suzannah, regularly touching her arm and leaning in to murmur quietly in her ear… in French, which Carlo spoke perfectly, but he was sure not everyone at the table did.

Rude.

Well, two could play at that game.

"The first dish I have for you," he said, taking the cover off a large silver domed dish on the next table over, "is a macaron with strawberries poached in balsamic glaze."

There was more than one audible gasp at the table as he placed a small plate before each of them, the delicate pale pink macaron angled jauntily against a pair of strawberries, the dark balsamic glaze drizzled artistically over the arrangement.

"Damn, that almost looks too good to eat," Nessa said in an awed tone, making Carlo chuckle.

"But indeed, you must eat. I promise, it tastes even better than it looks. Enjoy, and I will return shortly with another course for you."

He gave them five minutes before returning with a second covered dish. Clearing the plates deftly, he served the second course, a macadamia and mango ice cream in a chocolate wafer shell.

Luke, Jace, Olivia and Nessa were vocal in their praise as the courses progressed. Olivia proclaimed his cappuccino cheesecake on a macadamia and pistachio crust with black cherry drizzle to be the best thing she'd ever tasted, and Nessa swooned over the rum-soaked chocolate cake with orange Chantilly cream.

Edouard's nostrils were looking decidedly pinched as Nessa started discussing dessert wines with him. Eavesdropping, Carlo discovered Nessa was a professional bartender, and Edouard clearly wanted to dismiss her suggestions but didn't dare, not with her billionaire fiancé sitting right beside her nodding along with every word.

Carlo fought back a grin as he set another plate in front of Suzannah, his signature dish. He'd spent years perfecting his lemon and mint souffle. She'd been remarkably poker-faced thus far, but surely, surely she couldn't hold out against perfection?

Chapter Six

Suzannah wanted, so badly, to find something wrong with Carlo's cooking. He'd never lacked for skill, though, and his artistic presentation was even better than hers. Every plate he set before her contained a tiny masterpiece of culinary art which looked, as Nessa had said, almost too good to eat.

But when one did taste it, ah, that was when the true magic was revealed. Delicate yet intense flavours exploded on the taste buds, everything precisely calculated to deliver the maximum gastronomic pleasure.

She could find no flaw. The macarons, downfall of many an experienced chef, were perfectly risen, crisp on the outside, chewy inside. The soufflé was a perfect little puff of sweet delight.

When he rounded out the dégustation with a trio of deep-fried chocolate wontons, filled with dark, milk and white chocolate, she couldn't take it any more. Luke was looking at her with an expression which said there was no bloody way she was firing Carlo, and the truth was she really couldn't without looking ridiculously petty. He'd always been good, and the years he'd spent in Italy running Castillo Gianetti had obviously given him the opportunity to perfect his skills.

Quite simply, he was the best dessert chef they were ever going to be able to attract. Better than she was in this area of the craft, she admitted very privately to herself. She had the technical skill but not the artistic flair for sweets which Carlo did.

Saying so stuck in her throat, though, and she finally flung her napkin down on the table, rose to her feet and walked out, ignoring Edouard's sharp inquiry as to whether she was all right.

"I take it I'm staying, then, since she didn't dismiss me?" she heard Carlo drawl behind her, and gritted her teeth. Bloody, *bloody* man.

"Of course you are, Carlo!" Jace said enthusiastically, but anything else which was said was mercifully cut off as the automatic glass sliding doors closed behind her.

"Suzannah!"

Who the hell had been stupid enough to follow her when she was in this mood? She turned with a scowl, and Edouard almost ran right into her.

"Pardon me," he apologised at once. "Are you all right, Suzannah? Did something make you feel sick? That's a perfectly good reason to refuse Gianetti's appointment..."

Suzannah's scowl deepened. Why would *Edouard* not want Carlo to stay? She had a personal reason not to want him on the island, but Edouard must surely recognise his skill.

"Not at all," she disclaimed. "I'm just annoyed. His recipes are so good, surely you must see that the entire dessert menu must be redone? And we only just did it! That means another round of training for the pastry kitchen staff, and it will be at least two, three weeks before we can put the new menu online. A great deal of interruption to the routine, just as we are coming into the busy season!"

Edouard looked at her uncertainly. "Surely we could wait to implement the changes," he suggested, but she shook her head.

"No. No, it would be a waste, limiting Carlo to what a chef of lesser skill has created." Steeling herself, she lifted her chin.

Never let it be said Suzannah Monteil backed down from a challenge. She started walking back to the restaurant at a steady pace. There was a great deal of work to be done. *Work, that was how she was going to get through this. Keep everything on a professional level.*

She did her best to ignore the little voice in the back of her head which usually whispered words of reason when she was being foolish. Because at the moment, all she could hear was cynical laughter.

***

Back in the restaurant, all was quiet, the others obviously having finished up and left while she was storming around the garden in a rage. The table they'd used had been cleared and laid with a fresh tablecloth, set again with cutlery and glassware for dinner, no sign that they'd been there at all.

She could still taste the faint, sweet aftertaste of the dark chocolate wonton on her tongue, though. Damn Carlo, he'd served those deliberately. They'd been a staple on the menu at *Benoit* back when they worked there together, and had always been her favourite.

Standing in the middle of her kitchen, she closed her eyes and took several slow, deep breaths. In and out. In and out. Repeat, until she felt calmer.

When she opened her eyes, Carlo was leaning in the doorway between the two kitchens, ankles crossed and arms folded in his signature pose. He looked as though he'd stepped straight out of a glossy magazine, too handsome to be real.

For a moment, they stared at each other in silence, and then Suzannah shrugged. "You knew all along I couldn't refuse to have you here after they'd tasted your cooking. There's no need to gloat."

"I'm not gloating, Suzannah." He unfolded his arms and straightened up, taking a couple of steps towards her. "We need to work together, here. Friction between us isn't going to be helpful."

"Why are you here?" burst out of her, the demand fuelled by frustration. "You have the world at your feet, you could work anywhere if you don't want to run Castillo Gianetti any more. Why *here*?"

"Why are *you* here?" Carlo turned the question back on her.

Suzannah blinked. "Creative freedom," she said finally. "When Luke offered me the job, he gave me total free rein, said I could take the restaurant in whatever direction I wanted because it was completely new. There was no established theme I had to follow. They even built the kitchens to my specification and, until you, have given me total authority to pick my own staff."

"The way I heard it, you told Luke to just find you someone good," Carlo raised a brow, and Suzannah looked down, a little shame-faced.

"I didn't have the time. And I do trust his judgement. He knows my standards."

"When he contacted me to offer me the position, he told me the restaurant was aiming for another Michelin star and needed a superstar dessert chef to make it happen. He also told me that he was happy, keen even, for me to continue with my YouTube filming because it will be good for the resort profile, and would be happy for me to accept other TV work should it arise for the same reason. I understand there are several TV shows scheduled to shoot on the island over the next couple of years, and at least one movie which will use the resort as a base for its staff, as well as any number of high-profile celebrities planning their weddings here. This is an amazing opportunity for me too, Suzannah."

She nodded. She could understand that. There was still one question she was burning to know the answer to, though.

"Did you already know I was working here before you accepted?"

Carlo hesitated. "Yes," he said finally, "and I'd have considered a lot longer before accepting the opportunity if you hadn't been here, but I do think I'd have accepted it anyway. As I said, it's too good to pass up. The salary Jace offered, on top of free accommodation, didn't hurt either."

Well, at least he was being honest about it. Respecting that, Suzannah nodded.

"I don't dispute your talent or ability to do the job," she said. "I just feel it could be awkward, us working together."

"We're both adults. I'm a professional and I'm here to do a job. I've never let my personal life interfere with my work, and I'm not about to start now."

She never had either. At last, she nodded. "Fine. We'll give it a go... but remember, Carlo. This is *my* restaurant. You disrespect me in my kitchen, or undermine me with my staff, or take credit for my work, you're gone."

The injured look he gave her made her feel about two centimetres tall. She stamped ruthlessly on her immediate urge to apologise; she'd meant every word of it, and although the Carlo she'd known years ago would never have done any of those things, he might have changed. Celebrity status in particular could do strange things to people.

"No problem," Carlo said, and he offered her his hand. "Boss."

That made the corners of her mouth try to twitch upwards, but she suppressed that urge as well and shook his hand.

"Welcome to *La Sirène*, Chef Gianetti."

"Thank you, Chef Monteil," he said, equally formally, and then his mouth broadened in that irrepressible grin she remembered far too well. "So what did you think of my soufflé?"

"It was sublime, as you well know. We need to rethink the menu, and soon. Come into my office and we can sit down and start working out the plan to retrain the pastry kitchen staff... and I can give you the folder for upcoming wedding cakes." She was more than a little relieved to be handing that particular job over. She'd woken more than once in a cold sweat after dreaming one of her cakes had ended up featured on Cake Wrecks.

Carlo, on the other hand, looked delighted.

"One of the junior bakers has shown a lot of skill with icing and decorating. Perhaps you might take her on as something of an apprentice?" Suzannah suggested as she handed the wedding folder over. "She's got a real artist's touch, made these stunning sugar roses for this one last week."

"Oh, lovely," Carlo said in appreciation as she brought up a photo on her computer screen. "Yes, that's definitely a talent who needs nurturing. Her name?"

"Samira." Suzannah reached for the printed roster hanging beside her desk, a larger version of which was pinned to the kitchen wall. "She's due on again tomorrow morning, and you've three cakes to do this week. Details for the first two are in the folder, the third bride arrives today and I've an appointment with her scheduled at ten tomorrow. I'll sit in because I've already spoken with her, but as far as I'm concerned, it's in your hands now."

"Thank you, Suzannah," Carlo said quietly, and she looked up to meet his eyes, finding him giving her an intent, serious look. "I appreciate this."

She didn't ask exactly what. Her cooperation, she assumed. Well, if he could be professional, so could she.

Even though the traitorous little voice in her hind brain was loudly wondering if Carlo still looked just as good naked as she remembered.

Chapter Seven

"Hey," Nessa said in surprise as Suzannah slid onto a stool at the pool bar. "Don't often see you here."

"It's my day off," Suzannah said, a little crossly. "Why shouldn't I be here?"

"No reason." Nessa shrugged. "Just that I haven't seen you down here in a couple months. And I know I'm working fewer days now, but even so. You used to come down in the quiet hour after lunch quite often, grab a cool drink and shoot the breeze before heading back to start dinner prep."

"A cool drink sounds good, I'll take a fruit punch," Suzannah said pointedly, making Nessa laugh.

"Whatever the reason, it's good to see you." She set the tall glass in front of Suzannah and leaned on the bar, smiling at her warmly.

Suzannah's cross mood evaporated, and she smiled back. "You, too." She took a long sip of her drink before admitting "I've been run off my feet lately, but being able to hand over the pastry kitchen has made a huge difference. I don't know what to do with all this extra time I've suddenly got!"

"Talking of your new pastry chef," a voice said, and Suzannah turned her head to see her friend Jill taking the seat beside her, "holy macaroni, he's *hot*."

A pretty Chinese-Australian woman a couple of years older than Suzannah, Jill had the tricky job of guest relations manager, which she always said with a dry smile meant 'troubleshooter and general kicker of asses'. She spoke fluent Mandarin and Japanese and enough to get by in half a dozen other languages, including Suzannah's native French, which she often asked if she could practice with her.

"You know he's Italian, right? He'll probably give you language coaching if you ask," Nessa suggested, pouring Jill a drink too.

"He can coach me in anything he likes," Jill sighed dreamily, staring past Suzannah with something a lot like naked lust on her face. "Just *look* at those abs!"

Slowly, almost dreading what she knew she would find, Suzannah turned to look.

Carlo stood beside the pool, clearly having just emerged from a swim. His dark hair sleek with water, droplets slid down his chest and shoulders, tracing a path down to navy blue board shorts which clung to him like a second skin. He was talking to two teenage girls who were clearly hanging on his every word, staring at him raptly.

He was well worth a few stares, Suzannah admitted to herself privately. Her memory hadn't done him justice, or maybe it was just that he'd filled out some with muscle in the years since she last saw him. Naturally olive-skinned due to his Italian heritage, he was all lean muscle under smooth skin, strong and defined.

She wanted to trace the path of the water droplets over his pecs and abs with her tongue.

Shocked and angry at herself, Suzannah twisted back around to the bar and grabbed up her drink, draining it quickly and setting the glass down again. Nessa was watching her with knowing dark eyes.

"He's seriously sexy, Suzannah. You two have some history? He can't take his eyes off you, you know."

"Nonsense," Suzannah said far too quickly. "Rubbish. That's ridiculous."

Nessa was laughing at her, and Jill said teasingly "Methinks the lady doth protest too much. You won't mind if I have a crack at him, then?"

For a moment, Suzannah saw red. She had to take a deep breath to make herself say "Have at it," and even to her own ears she sounded utterly unconvincing.

Jill began to laugh too. "Even if I believed for a second you meant that," she got out through her giggles, "I'd be wasting my time."

"There's always a lot of competition for Carlo's attention, but you're more than pretty enough to catch his eye," Suzannah disagreed, not wanting Jill to put herself down even if the thought of the two of them together did make her feel sick with jealousy.

Nessa laughed harder. Jill sobered, shaking her head, and reached out to put her hand on Suzannah's arm.

"That's really kind of you to say, honey, but what I meant was, it wouldn't matter if I looked like Margot Robbie. He'd still be staring at you."

"He's not..." Suzannah trailed off. Jill was giving her a very pointed stare, and then she tilted her head very slightly to the left.

Suzannah's head turned almost against her will. Carlo was approaching at a quick walk, eyes fixed on her, a smile on his handsome face.

"Hey," he said cheerfully, slipping onto the vacant stool on her other side.

"What are you doing here?" As soon as the words slipped out, Suzannah wanted to take them back.

Carlo's brows went up, and his cheerful smile slipped slightly. "Taking a break after the lunch rush," he said. "Samira is doing some very delicate hand-painting work on the cake for tomorrow's wedding, and everything is well in hand for tonight's menu. Is there something you needed me to look after in the main kitchen?"

Well aware she'd been ungracious, Suzannah shook her head. "No, no. I was just surprised to see you here, that's all."

"It didn't take me long to discover Nessa's the best bartender on the island. Oh, hi Jill." Carlo's eyes finally slid past her to Jill, but cut almost instantly back to Suzannah again. "It's a surprise to see *you* here, actually." His gaze dropped only briefly, but she knew he'd taken in every detail of her swimsuit, a very modest black one-piece which revealed less skin than any other woman at the poolside except Nessa, who wore her work polo shirt and shorts.

She didn't even own a bikini, and suddenly she was wondering if she could find one she liked in the resort boutiques. Giving herself a stern mental shake, she frowned at Carlo.

"I've been busy."

"Well, you know what they say. All work and no play makes Suzannah a workaholic."

"I am not a workaholic!" she denied hotly, and was shocked to hear Jill and Nessa chorus in unison;

"Yes, you are."

"What?" She whipped her head round, giving each of them in turn a betrayed look. "You two are supposed to be my friends!"

"And friends point out when friends are working too hard," Jill said dryly. "When was the last time you left the island, Suzannah?"

She had to stop and think about it. After a moment she snapped her fingers triumphantly. "I went to that new winery opening in the Barossa Valley last month!"

"That was *three* months ago," Nessa said, "and Edouard, Luke and I were there too. It was a work trip. We visited three wineries, a boutique brewery, and two organic fruit farms. All in two days, and all because you wanted to check out their produce for the island." She raised her eyebrows at Suzannah. "We never stopped working. You even selected the restaurants we ate at to check out the competition."

Suzannah frowned. "Three months? Really?"

"Really, and it doesn't count as a break." Nessa leaned her elbows on the bar and looked Suzannah in the eye. "Friend to friend, I'm telling you, you've been working too hard, and it started long before you fired Vicky."

She didn't like hearing it, and she especially didn't like knowing Carlo was sitting beside her listening to every word. "Noted," she said crisply. "Now could you please stop lecturing me and pour me another drink? And since it's my day off, you could put a shot of rum in the next one."

"Done." Satisfied that Suzannah had heeded her intervention, Nessa turned away and within moments was setting down a tall, frosted glass before her. "Enjoy. One for you too, Carlo?"

"Yes, but make mine a virgin. Unlike Suzannah, I've got to go back to the kitchen." Carlo smiled warmly.

Jill sighed from Suzannah's other side. "Sadly, I'm back on duty in an hour. We've got a conference starting tomorrow and most of the delegates are coming in on a charter flight to Hamilton this afternoon." Setting her empty glass down on the bar, she rose to her feet. "Catch you guys later!"

"Later," Suzannah said, watching Jill walk away. She glanced quickly at Carlo, fully expecting him to be appreciating Jill's neat figure from the back, especially in the hot-pink bikini Jill was sporting, but Carlo's eyes were firmly fixed on her. "What?" she asked, a little uncomfortable under his scrutiny.

"You're happy here."

It was a statement, not a question. Not quite understanding his meaning, Suzannah frowned. "Yes, I'm happy. I've been here almost three years now, made *La Sirène* into the restaurant of my dreams..."

"I'm not talking about the restaurant. Stop thinking about work for just a moment, will you?" He smiled to take the sting from the words. "I'm talking about you. You were never much for friendships back when we lived in Paris, your home town no less, but here, you seem to have a lot of people you're close with. Everyone smiles when they talk about you."

"They do?"

"Indeed. Your staff are in awe of you, of course - Julie might actually believe you can walk on water."

Suzannah smiled a bit at that. "She's going to be a superstar one day. We're lucky to have her."

Carlo nodded in agreement. "It's outside the restaurant staff where your friends are, though. Nessa thinks the world of you." He tilted his head towards the diminutive bartender, currently shaking a cocktail for a customer at the other end of the bar with her distinctive flair. "Olivia told me you were her roomie when she first arrived on the island, and how kind and supportive you were. Lucy, that sweet marine biologist who's married to the dive instructor, said you went out of your way to make her wedding cake yourself - even though you *had* a competent pastry chef then - and..."

"Stop." Suzannah held up her hand. "You'd have done exactly the same thing."

"Without pay for the hours you put in?"

"She and Bryce are my friends." As far as Suzannah was concerned, that was all that needed to be said.

"That's my point, exactly! You and I were at school together for a year and lived together for another, and in all that time, I don't think I could name one person who you'd really considered a friend. Yet here, you have so many! This place is good for you, Suzannah." He looked earnest as he leaned towards her. "You might be working too hard, but it's still good to see you looking so well and happy, and with friends who obviously care about you."

She didn't know what to say. Carlo seemed absolutely sincere, his eyes intent on her face. Finally she nodded. "This feels more like home to me than Paris ever was," she admitted. "Though it can get pretty unbearably hot when summer comes, I don't think I'd ever want to go back to living in a cold climate. I haven't seen snow in five years and you have no idea how happy that makes me!"

She tried to make a joke of it, and Carlo chuckled, the low, sensuous sound that still made goosebumps pop up on her arms, all these years later. Moving quickly, hoping he didn't notice her reaction, she jumped up to her feet.

"Anyway, I came down here for a swim and I haven't had one yet. See you later!"

Chapter Eight

Carlo watched Suzannah hurry away, appreciating the sight of her tall, shapely body in the simple one-piece she probably thought demurely covered her up. He didn't need to see her stomach to admire her, though. After all, he could see every inch of her spectacular legs.

At almost six foot in her bare feet, Suzannah was only an inch shorter than Carlo himself, and he was a self-confessed legs man. On her feet all day, moving fast around a busy kitchen, she was fit and lean, and those long legs were slender and toned.

"You're drooling," an amused voice said behind him, and he wrinkled his nose before turning back to smile ruefully at Nessa.

"It's her legs, I'm afraid. My baser instincts overcome me when I see those legs. My brains just dribble right out of my head."

"What a revolting image!" She was laughing at him. "Everyone's dying to know what's the deal with you two, you know. My money's on a youthful affair which ended badly."

"You're a perceptive woman, Nessa." Carlo lifted his glass to her in a toast. "I'm afraid Suzannah walked out on me, and my ego never quite recovered from the blow."

"Why? Were you running around on her?"

"I've no idea, and *hell* no! I was crazy about her." Something about Nessa's calm manner inspired him to share confidences, and he probably shouldn't, Carlo realised. At the same time, he didn't want to antagonise Suzannah's friends. "We were both working crazy hours; I wouldn't have had the time, even if I'd been inclined to look at another girl!"

"Good to know," Nessa nodded. "So... she just broke up with you?"

"She just left. Packed her suitcases and took the Eurostar from Paris to London. If I hadn't come home as she was leaving and insisted on going with her to the station, I wouldn't even have known that much."

"Jeez." Nessa looked startled. "That seems pretty drastic."

"At the time, I thought it was the end of the world." His heart still ached when he thought of that day; Carlo put a hand over it and looked towards the pool, where Suzannah was swimming casual breaststroke laps, weaving around playing children with amused looks. "Looking back, I suppose she just didn't know how to tell me it was over. We were both little more than kids, barely out of our teens, and I guess she didn't want to settle down. I had all these plans - I'd just introduced her to my parents, for God's sake!"

"She really broke your heart, didn't she?" Nessa said sympathetically.

"She did." Carlo smiled ruefully. "I've long since forgiven her, but I'd be lying if I said I didn't take this job at least in part because of her."

"Hoping she might give you a second chance?"

"I guess so." He shrugged. "She doesn't seem that way inclined, though."

"You might be surprised," Nessa said cryptically. "Give her some time."

"Eh, I've got plenty of that." Finishing his drink, Carlo set the glass back down on the bar. "Thanks, Nessa. I'd better get back to work."

"Catch you later." Nessa collected his glass with a nod and a friendly smile, and Carlo headed back to his room to shower and change into work clothes. He couldn't stop thinking about what Nessa had said; did the bartender know something he didn't about Suzannah's feelings towards him?

"Don't get your hopes up," he told himself aloud as the shower beat hot water down on him. "She'd still much prefer it if you weren't here at all."

***

It was the first evening Suzannah hadn't been in the kitchen since Carlo's arrival, and he was a little shocked by just how quickly things went sideways without her commanding presence. Julie knew her stuff as a chef, but as a people manager she just didn't have the confidence to snap out orders to her underlings. Four times Carlo ended up leaving the pastry kitchen for the main kitchen to sort out issues, drawn by the sound of raised voices.

"Enough," he said sharply to one of the waitresses, picking up two plates from the counter and shoving them into her hands. "Your business is out there, not in here. Go. When you return, the other two plates for your table will be ready."

Julie looked almost ready to cry, but she was also swiftly preparing the second round of plates. "Thank you, Chef Gianetti," she mumbled.

"You're welcome." Leaning in across the counter towards her, he said quietly "You're in charge in Chef Monteil's absence. Don't forget that. You're letting them walk all over you."

He didn't have time to stay, but he did Julie a favour by shooting glowering looks at several of the people around her. They all looked away, shame-faced, and he muttered under his breath before returning to his own domain.

None of them had any idea whether, on any given day, a customer sitting at one of their tables might actually be a restaurant critic. These days, everyone *was* a critic, thanks to TripAdvisor and other online rating sites. One bad night in the kitchen could cost them a great deal, especially since they hadn't the faintest idea when another Michelin judge might visit. Nobody had even known Michelin was planning an Australia guide until the first was published, after all!

All Carlo could do was keep a lid on things for tonight. At least he could make sure patrons left the restaurant after a dessert course to remember. The staff in the pastry kitchen were getting up to speed with some of his new recipes by running them as nightly specials, and feedback so far was everything he might have hoped.

The only blight on the horizon was Edouard the sommelier, who seemed to find fault with everything Carlo did. The Frenchman rarely said anything directly, but his disapproving glances and his immediate disparaging of Carlo's suggestions for possible dessert wines to pair with his creations made it clear Carlo was an unwelcome intruder.

Was there something going on between Edouard and Suzannah? Carlo really couldn't be sure. They were certainly close, Edouard almost possessive of her attention, and Suzannah didn't seem uncomfortable with it. Both of them were professional enough to keep any personal relationship outside the restaurant, but Carlo suspected considering they all lived on a literal island, a secret like that couldn't be kept. Someone would have been seen sneaking about in the night and the gossip would fly.

No, the pair weren't in an active relationship, he thought... but it wasn't for lack of Edouard wanting to. The mere thought of the two of them together kept Carlo awake at nights, despite his tiredness. Every time Edouard was in the kitchen at the same time as Suzannah, Carlo's focus was utterly shot; he couldn't concentrate on what he was doing, always straining to try and overhear their conversation. When Suzannah laughed at something Edouard said, Carlo ground his teeth.

It was at lunchtime the following day when he finally snapped. The lunch rush had passed, the main kitchen in cleanup mode now and the pastry kitchen sending out the last few desserts. Edouard came in and was leaning on the counter, Suzannah laughing at something he said.

"You should be concentrating on your staff's performance, not flirting with the sommelier," Carlo said in rapid-fire French as he set two plates on the counter for one of the wait staff to take out. He was pretty sure nobody else in the kitchen except the two in front of him spoke French well enough to follow what he'd just said.

Suzannah's cheeks flamed red. Edouard, the coward, retreated back through the doors into the main restaurant as she whirled to face Carlo.

"*What* did you say?"

"You heard me. It was a shit show in here last night. They can't function without you cracking the whip over them, which means you've fucked up, Chef." Carlo was spoiling for an argument. He continued speaking French, though, not wanting the rest of the staff to know what he was saying.

"My office, *now*." Her eyes flashed emerald fire as she jabbed a finger at the door leading to her shoebox of an office.

Carlo waited only until the door closed behind them before speaking again. "Your tendency to over-control is coming back to bite you in the ass. It's not that you don't *want* time off, but you can't have it, isn't that right? You don't trust them to maintain your standards without you here, and guess what, your lack of trust is a self-fulfilling prophecy, because now they don't trust *themselves*."

Suzannah had been about to go off like a rocket, Carlo was pretty sure, but as he finished speaking she paused, arrested by what he'd just told her.

"What? What happened last night?" She looked almost ready to snatch the office door open and barge out into the kitchen again. Carlo reached to put a hand on her sleeve, stop her doing anything dramatic.

"It wasn't a disaster, but it was very obvious your staff are used to having you on top of everything, all of the time. Without you there to hold their hands and wipe their noses, they were all over the place."

A frown settled on Suzannah's face, her brows drawing together. Reaching up, she pulled off her cap, letting her thick red curls tumble free, and took a step back to perch a hip on the edge of her desk. "Julie's perfectly capable of managing the menu."

"She is, but Julie doesn't have it in her to manage the *staff*, not right now. You've taught her well as regards her skills with food, and she obviously idolises you, but she doesn't have your strength of character. She might never have it. You had more command in your little finger at eighteen than she does at what, twenty-five?" He stepped forward, unable to resist getting closer to her, reached out to touch her cheek lightly. "It's innate, in you. She'll have to learn it the hard way."

"I don't understand what you mean." Suzannah shook her head. She still looked tired, Carlo thought, as though her day off hadn't refreshed her much at all. Surprisingly, she wasn't slapping his hand off her face, though, so he left it there, stroking her cheek very lightly with the back of his finger, savouring the softness of her skin.

"I'd call it charisma. Even as a girl, you had it in spades; the way you spoke, the way you held yourself. You had a complete and total confidence in your abilities I could only envy."

"You?" She laughed, sounding as though she didn't believe him. "Come off it. I was the girl from the slums, the one nobody asked to parties or on dates."

"Nobody asked you anywhere because you intimidated the hell out of them. Believe me, I had no idea about your background until you told me about it yourself, after we started dating."

"Really?" She looked surprised by that, before shaking her head. "We aren't talking about me, we're talking about Julie. I don't know how to help her, if it's confidence she has a problem with."

"Because it's never been your problem." Her hair had fallen against his hand as she shook her head, and he tangled his fingers in a couple of the long silken curls now, stroking slowly. "Maybe it's *because* of that hardscrabble upbringing. You had to learn to be tough from an early age, and eventually it just became part of who you are. Makes sense that you don't know how to teach someone else how to do it."

She put a hand up slowly and her fingers touched his, held on. Startled, Carlo wasn't about to let go.

"How do I help her, then?"

She was asking for his advice. Carlo blinked a couple of times, genuinely astonished, and Suzannah smiled wryly.

"I've done some growing up in the last nine years, Carlo. Enough to learn that when I don't have the skills to do something, it's time to ask for help. You recognised a problem I didn't even know I had. Maybe you've got some idea how to fix it."

"I could work with her," he said slowly. "If you were okay with that. I know she's your protegée."

"She is, but I'm not so arrogant as to think she can't learn useful skills from someone else!" Her fingers tightened on his and she straightened up, looking him straight in the eye. "If you're willing to help her, I'd very much appreciate it."

Chapter Nine

Carlo looked almost shell-shocked, Suzannah thought as he nodded assent. He really hadn't expected her to accept his advice, to listen to him, but when someone was right, they were right, and a wise woman or man listened and learned.

She wasn't sure when he'd taken her hand and started touching her hair, but she liked it far too much. She must be touch-starved, she decided as she tried to tell herself she should let go of his hand, move back.

Somehow, she couldn't stop looking at his lips, those beautifully shaped, masculine lips. Her traitorous memory supplied a perfect recall of how they tasted, how they felt exploring every inch of her body as he teased her to impossible pitches of ecstasy.

"Maybe I can teach you something, too," Carlo said softly, his dark eyes gazing steadily into hers. "Help you let go some of that tight control, hm?"

Unable to speak, she swallowed to try and get some moisture into her dry mouth. He was so close, she could feel his breath on her mouth. Her eyelids drooped, her eyes wanting to drift shut. He was going to kiss her...

"This really can't happen," came out of her mouth.

Somewhere deep in her mind, her libido gave up with a roll of its eyes and slinked off to sulk in a corner.

"You pick your moments, don't you?" Carlo let go of her hand and took a step back.

Suzannah took a deep breath, shaking her head to clear it of the lingering sensual fog his mere presence seemed to cause in her. "You know I'm right. Whether or not Julie can learn to manage the staff effectively, I *have* to retain their respect. Nobody knows about our past relationship, and I need to keep it that way."

"Or what?" he asked dryly, folding his arms and cocking an eyebrow. "Or they might notice you're a sexy as hell, red blooded woman? Half your staff are sleeping with each other anyway, and the other half are involved with other members of the resort staff."

"They are?" Suzannah blinked in surprise.

"You really don't notice anything that doesn't have to do with food, do you?"

The question annoyed her, mainly because as usual with Carlo, his jab was right on target. Her jaw clenched, but she consciously ordered herself to relax it.

He's been on the island a week and it's clear he knows more about my staff than I do. Which means he's right and I've stuffed up.

Lowering her head so she didn't have to look at him, she took a deep breath before speaking.

"Thanks for bringing the problem to my attention, Chef Gianetti."

Carlo laughed, and she looked up again to meet his eyes. He was leaning back against the office door, a wicked grin on his handsome face. "You do realise everyone's going to assume we were making out in here anyway, don't you?"

"Are you trying to say we might as well?"

He shrugged, the maddening grin still in place, and she reached behind her without looking, picked up a pen off the desk and threw it at him. "Get out of here."

Her lips were twitching, though, giving away her desire to smile, and Carlo laughed, batting the pen away. "Another time, *cara*." He winked at her before exiting.

The door closed behind him and Suzannah sagged, rounding her desk to collapse into her office chair.

Her hands were shaking, she noticed dimly, blood roaring in her ears from her racing pulse. She'd fought hard to conceal her physical reactions from Carlo, but was pretty sure she'd failed. How she'd found the willpower to tell him not to kiss her, she hadn't the faintest idea. She'd wanted him to so badly she could almost taste it.

Sighing, she picked her cap up and starting cramming her hair back into a bun at the back of her head. The night wasn't over yet, and she needed to make sure everything finished up smoothly. Tomorrow, she'd figure out what to do about her own failings with her staff... maybe she'd go see her friend Rosie, the resort's staff manager. If anyone could advise her, it would be Rosie.

***

At lunchtime the following day, Suzannah strode back into the restaurant armed with new confidence in herself and a plan. Rosie had listened to her anxious outpouring and given her some actionable first steps to take… first among them being "Listen to Carlo. He's a smart cookie if he's got all this figured out after only a week, and while he could have been more tactful approaching you with it, I'd say he only wants to help."

Therefore, her first move once she entered the kitchens was to step into the pastry kitchen, where Carlo was hard at work piping small spirals of melted chocolate onto baking paper, presumably to form decorations on whatever fabulous concoction he planned to serve up that evening.

"Morning," she said cheerfully.

Carlo glanced up and smiled. "Good morning, Chef Monteil," he said very properly.

Suzannah could almost feel the tension of the staff working around them, all talk silenced and ears on stalks as everyone surreptitiously watched. They were all wondering just what had transpired in her office last night, Suzannah was quite sure, and firmly ordered herself not to blush as she thought about Carlo's remarks. No doubt there would indeed be speculation, but she didn't intend to fuel it.

"I don't see your dessert special for tonight on the board, what are you planning?"

"Mandarin chocolate bombe, which is a flourless chocolate sponge inside a spherical chocolate shell stuffed with dark chocolate mousse, finished with mandarin cream and slices of mandarin for garnish."

"Very good." She nodded approval and tried not to salivate, because it sounded absolutely fantastic. "I look forward to sampling it."

"Should be ready shortly, the chocolate shells are just setting." He cocked an eyebrow at her, silently asking if there was something else she needed.

"After lunch is finished, would you sit down with Julie and I in my office?" she requested, hoping he'd work out why without her needing to spell it out in front of the rest of the staff.

"Of course. I'm at your disposal, Chef." His expression was calmly attentive, his tone respectful, but she could see the glint of amusement in his eyes.

She gave him a crisp nod and withdrew, returning to her own domain and Julie, who looked at her with anxious eyes.

"Is something wrong, Chef Monteil?"

"Not at all. I just want your input as we finalise the new menu."

"You do?" Julie looked startled.

"Absolutely. You'll be just as responsible for implementing it, after all. We're not only changing the dessert menu; I have several ideas for the main menu and for some new specials I'd like to try, and I'll need your help training the staff. Plus you'll be in charge whenever I have a night off, of course! I want to make sure you're comfortable with what we're putting in place."

Startled but obviously gratified to be consulted, Julie thanked her and returned to work with a smile on her face, long knife flashing as she expertly filleted and sliced a huge fish, a whole fresh barramundi, ready for char-grilling and serving over a sweet potato mash with a green curry infused coconut cream sauce.

Ordinarily, Suzannah would have picked up some utensils and set to work herself, but today she paused and looked around the kitchen, making herself slow down and take in everything, observing more than just the food preparation going on.

Her staff were cheerful, talking to each other as knives chopped, blenders whirred and pots were stirred. The occasional quiet laugh sounded out as they chatted, the atmosphere of the kitchen at a fairly low intensity in this brief lull before the first orders started coming in at noon.

What did Carlo see when he looked around? Nibbling on the edge of her lip, Suzannah let her gaze sweep over the staff again, this time looking at more than just expressions, at the body language and silent signals she'd been missing before.

There, by the big stainless steel sinks, Nita was washing broccoli and trading decidedly flirtatious glances with Ramon. Beyond them, Joel and Richard's shoulders were touching as they peeled prawns, the two of them trading looks which were definitely more than fond. Suzannah hadn't even realised the pair were gay, not that it made the slightest difference to her... except she should watch out for anyone *else* treating them differently, it occurred to her.

Homophobia would definitely not be tolerated in her kitchen, any more than racism or sexism. Or any other -ism, including ableism; she paused to smile at Lydia, an Australian Army veteran who had lost her left arm below the elbow during overseas service. She had an advanced prosthesis but her dream of being a chef had taken quite a few hits before she applied for a job at *La Sirène*. Right now, she was preparing scallops for appetisers, her prosthesis actually an advantage as she was less at risk of cuts from the sharp shell edges.

And Lydia was exchanging heated glances with Geordie, a burly Scotsman who was one of the most recently arrived staff members, as Geordie deftly tossed a big skillet of mushrooms in hot butter.

Was everyone in her kitchen getting it on except her? Suzannah wondered. She glanced sideways at Julie, now preparing a second barramundi. She'd been working with the other girl for eighteen months and knew almost nothing personal about her, she realised with a pang of guilt. Yes, getting overly friendly with your underlings wasn't the best idea, but she should have made more of an effort. Maybe it wasn't too late to start.

"You're rostered off tomorrow. Got any plans?" she asked in a cheerful tone as she took her place beside Julie at the long stainless steel counter.

Julie looked around in surprise for a moment, obviously wondering if Suzannah was talking to someone else, before blushing slightly and returning to her work. "Going over to Airlie with my boyfriend," she said. "I fancy doing a bit of shopping."

"Didn't know you were dating anyone," Susannah kept her tone light as she deftly mixed flour, salt, sugar, ground chili and ground cumin in a bowl for her spicy tempura batter base. "Does he work here too?" Collecting the chilled sparkling water from a nearby refrigerator, she measured it and poured it carefully into the well she'd made in the dry mixture.

"He's a landscape gardener," Julie answered. "Though he's technically employed by the resort, he spends most of his time working on the gardens at the private villas. They contract with the resort for services."

"Sounds intriguing, if you like gardening!" Suzannah remarked. "Is he involved with our herb garden?" The resort actually grew a large amount of their own fresh herbs and had a small grove of tropical fruit trees as well, all of the produce supplied to the resort restaurants.

Julie's blush deepened. "That's how we met, actually. I went down to the fruit grove to see if we had any passionfruit coming ripe and Pete was up a coconut tree. He almost dropped a coconut on my head."

Suzannah laughed delightedly. "But that's adorable!"

Julie giggled too, her eyes shining as she looked up. "Pete says it'll be a great story to tell our grandchildren. I keep saying he's getting ahead of himself... but I really do think he's the one."

"How lovely, and I hope you're right," Suzannah said, and she meant it. Julie was a sweet girl with a bright future as a chef, and she deserved to find love and happiness.

"What about you, Chef?" Julie asked, her tone a little tentative. "Is there anyone special in your life?"

Slapping her down for being too familiar was absolutely the wrong thing to do at that moment, Suzannah knew it, despite it being her first instinct. Instead she pasted on a small smile and shook her head. "I'm married to *La Sirène*," she said in a teasing tone.

Julie smiled in response to the joke, but then she glanced around, as though checking nobody was close enough to overhear, before asking in a quiet voice "What about Carlo?"

Suzannah made herself stop whisking the tempura before she overdid it. "What about him?" Her voice had gone a bit squeaky, she registered too late.

"Well, he certainly looks at you as though *he's* interested. And, I mean... he's lovely, isn't he? So handsome, and really nice with it. If I didn't have Pete, I think I'd probably be totally losing my head over him, like a teenage fangirl!"

There was nothing to dispute about Julie's statement, Suzannah thought a little dismally. Indeed, she'd once lost her head over Carlo entirely. Instinctively she glanced towards the pastry kitchen, but he wasn't visible from where she stood at that moment.

Which was good. The last thing she needed was the opportunity to moon over his too-handsome face instead of focusing on her work.

Chapter Ten

Carlo plated up one of his mandarin chocolate bombe specials to put in the dessert showcase at the front of the restaurant before dinner that evening, and another one to take to Suzannah for sampling. She gave him an amused look, but set aside the lamb racks she was dressing and washed her hands.

"This did sound fantastic when you told me about it earlier," she said, accepting the offered plate and inspecting the glossy chocolate sphere nestled amid piped creamy waves, thin lines of mandarin syrup criss-crossed underneath and three carefully prepared mandarin slices arranged symmetrically around the whole. "And it looks stunning."

The chocolate shell, about the size of a tennis ball, cracked and splintered at the slightest tap of her fork, and Suzannah dug in to scoop out a forkful of decadent chocolate mousse and sponge cake.

"Talk about spoiling my dinner." Gathering a little of the mandarin cream up too, she put the fork into her mouth.

The moan she let out would have made a dead man sit up and take notice, and Carlo was very far from dead. His cock leaped instantly to attention, pushing hard against the fly of his pants, and he spared a moment to be grateful for the long chef's coat which maintained his modesty.

Although if Suzannah moaned like that again, he was going to lose it and kiss her right here in the kitchen in front of all the staff, and to hell with the ensuing gossip.

Suzannah had closed her eyes as she tasted the decadent treat, and she opened them now to reveal their emerald colour glimmering through her long lashes.

"Christ, Carlo, that's absolutely *sinful*," she said, her voice a little huskier than usual.

"That's the general idea." He could barely speak. The sight of Suzannah licking chocolate off her lips nearly sent him to his knees. Her eyes held his, and slowly, tantalisingly, she scooped up another mouthful.

She was doing it deliberately this time, and everything in Carlo wanted to respond to the challenge her eloquent look sent him.

You're working, he told himself sternly, though it was hard to hear the voice of his conscience over the blood pounding in his ears. Suzannah was challenging him to maintain his professionalism in the face of temptation.

It was one of the hardest things he'd ever had to do, but he made himself turn away and say "Enjoy your dessert, Chef," over his shoulder as he headed back to the pastry kitchen.

Behind him, he heard Julie say "That looks fantastic, Chef, could I have a taste?"

Suzannah's throaty chuckle reached his ears, followed by "Bugger off and get your own."

He had to laugh. At least she appreciated his cooking. And later, after the restaurant closed down for the night, he was going to find out if that inviting look she'd given him was a limited-time offer or not.

***

Carlo didn't have a great deal to do that evening; the chocolate bombes had all been made earlier that day and only needed their presentation plates finishing before sending out to the diners. Keeping a weather eye on the staff taking care of the rest of the standard desserts from the menu, he allowed himself to relax a little.

Which, of course, was when a yell of "Fire!" went up in the main kitchen.

Carlo reacted fast, sprinting through the doorway in time to see a sheet of flame whooshing upwards above an open grill. Suzannah was only a couple of steps away, turning with a startled look on her face.

It all happened so fast, it didn't occur to him to wonder until much later why the automatic fire suppressant system hadn't come on. He reacted by instinct, leaping forward and slapping his hand down on the manual release.

Fire suppressant rained down from the hood above the grill, extinguishing the flames almost instantly. Greasy black smoke billowed upwards instead.

"Shit!" Suzannah yelled. "Don't let the doors open!" She pointed to the doors leading out to the dining area, and staff who'd stood frozen during the emergency rushed to hold them closed.

"Get all the extraction hoods running at max," Carlo ordered sharply, and within a couple of minutes the pall of smoke was clearing.

Suzannah looked shell-shocked, unable to understand how the fire had started, but there was no time now to investigate. Diners were waiting for their meals, the grill had to be cleared and cleaned and fresh food cooked. Carlo set to with a will, scraping the grill off while Suzannah moved to prepare the dishes again. Between them they had the mishap corrected in ten minutes flat, a short enough time nobody outside the kitchen would ever guess there had been a problem in the first place.

***

Rolling his head from side to side to stretch out tight neck muscles, Carlo glanced around the pastry kitchen. The last plate had gone out about a quarter hour before and all activity was centred around cleanup now. He'd been briefly panicked they might run out of the chocolate bombe specials, but there were still three left in the refrigerator after the final order came in.

"I'm gonna call it a night," he told Samira, the young chef with a talent for cake decoration. She was in her own corner of the kitchen, making tiny sugar roses for a wedding cake. Glancing up, she nodded, the corners of her eyes crinkling.

"I'll finish these off and turn in myself. I can supervise the washing-up, Chef Gianetti, I promise."

"I know you can." He could still see Julie in the main kitchen, anyway, and she wouldn't leave until the kitchen was resorted to the pristine state Suzannah required. "Good night, and don't stay up too late. Those could wait until tomorrow morning."

"They could, but I'm having fun." Samara smiled shyly, and he laughed before bidding her a good night again and taking his leave.

Carlo debated going to Suzannah's cabin, but he was tired and sweaty, and he probably stank of smoke from the incident earlier. He'd take a shower first, wander by and see if there was a light on. If she hadn't left a light on, well, he'd assume she'd just been testing him earlier on to see if he could stay professional in the face of extreme provocation.

And if she had left a light on, well...

His train of thought stuttered to a halt as he approached his own cabin and a tall, slim figure stood up from the chair on the tiny veranda outside. Red hair haloed by moonlight, Suzannah was there waiting for him.

He hadn't thought she'd follow through, Carlo realised as shock rooted his feet to the ground. He'd fully expected to go by Suzannah's cabin, find it dark and silent, and spend yet another night tossing and turning as sleep eluded him.

"This is a terrible idea," Suzannah said.

"And yet, you're here." He made no move towards her. If she wanted to leave, he wouldn't try and stop her.

She said something under her breath very fast in French, and stepped forward rapidly, grabbing at him, one hand on his shoulder and the other curving behind his head to grasp onto his hair as she brought their mouths roughly together.

She'd brushed her teeth and smelled delicious, clean and fresh. She'd showered before coming to him, Carlo registered, thinking only vaguely of his own less-than-pristine state as Suzannah kissed him, the urgency of her desire very evident. He wrapped his arms around her and kissed her back hungrily, letting her know his need very much matched her own.

"Inside," Suzannah pulled back from the kiss at last. "Please, Carlo..."

"I need to wash up," he said regretfully, even as he let her pull him towards the cabin. "I'm..."

"I don't care," she said. "I can't wait. I need you."

That was the end of any thought of delay from Carlo. His hands shook as he scrabbled in his pants pocket for his key, somehow managed to get the door unlocked and pull Suzannah inside, grateful he'd thought to program the air-conditioner to come on in the late evening, making his room blissfully cool now. A small lamp glowed beside the bed, bathing the room in a soft golden light as he turned to pull the curtains quickly closed.

Suzannah had put on a dress after her shower, the first one he'd seen her wear here on the island, where she seemed to live in her work uniform. Reaching down to grasp the hem of the simple cotton garment, she pulled it up and over her head in one easy sweep, revealing to a dazzled Carlo that she wasn't wearing anything underneath it.

His tongue seemed to be stuck to the roof of his mouth as he stared, eyes almost out on stalks. The last nine years had been very kind to Suzannah Monteil; he already knew that from having seen her in her swimsuit, but naked she was absolutely spectacular.

At twenty, she'd still not quite grown into her height, all gangling legs and slight curves. Today, she was sleek and strong but all woman, her breasts a juicy handful, the flare of her hips a sensual lure it would have taken a far stronger man than Carlo to resist.

With a groan deep in his throat, he reached for her, hands settling gently on that rich curve of her waist. Suzannah made a soft sound, her emerald gaze holding his steadily, though he saw her lick her lips and suspected she wasn't as confident as she pretended to be.

"You are so beautiful, *cara*," he told her, his voice a husky, lustful rasp. "Glorious."

A little smile curved the corners of her lips up, and she tilted her proud head slightly to one side before purring "Show me."

He was absolutely delighted to oblige, drawing her over to his bed, thankful for his tidy habits as he'd made it before leaving for work. Guiding her to sit down, he paused to yank his T-shirt off over his head, making a face as he tossed the damp, not-too-sweet smelling fabric aside.

"You sure you don't want to wait for me to take a shower?"

She grinned, unexpectedly wicked. "You'd only get all sweaty again. Maybe we'll take one together. Afterwards." Reaching for his belt, she pulled the tail free from the loop on his pants, released the buckle. Carlo knew his need for her was pretty obvious, his erection pushing against the thin fabric of his pants, but she showed no hesitation, freeing the button and easing his fly down carefully.

Plainly, Suzannah didn't intend to waste time... and Carlo had no intention of slowing things down. He stepped out of his shoes, helped Suzannah pull down his pants and jockey shorts, took them off along with his socks, and finally stood proud and naked before her.

"Lie back," he requested. "I've been thinking about this for a long, long time. Want to make sure I get it right."

Chapter Eleven

Suzannah raised her eyebrows at Carlo's request, but she was willing to oblige... as long as he didn't make her wait too long, anyway. Lying back against the pillows, she watched as he left her briefly, going into the bathroom and returning with a box of condoms still sealed in cellophane. Opening the box, he extracted a foil packet and set it on the nightstand.

She frowned when he didn't immediately open the condom. He was certainly aroused, his cock jutting proudly towards her as he knelt beside her on the bed.

"Carlo..." she began, wanting to tell him she was ready, more than ready. He reached down and gently laid a finger against her lips.

"Let me touch you," he begged softly. "Please."

Desperate though she was for satiation, she stilled and nodded, allowing him his way. For now.

Carlo began with the lightest of touches, skimming his fingertips down the centre of her throat and across her collarbones, before leaning in to claim her mouth again. She arched into his kiss, moaning in her throat as those clever fingers just tapped a peaked, aching nipple before moving on again.

"Please." It was her turn to beg when he broke the kiss, but he only smiled.

"Patience, *cara*," he whispered, moving down over her, and then his mouth settled on her nipple and she forgave the delay immediately.

He'd always known exactly how to touch her to drive her completely out of her mind, and as his hot mouth and knowing hands worked their magic, Suzannah dissolved into a mindless, needy wreck, grasping at him desperately and begging him to *hurry, please, just fuck me, now.*

She rather thought he'd intended more, but when his fingers dipped between her legs and found her soaked, he let out a groan.

"Oh, *cara*. You're so ready." He stroked gently over her clit, slick with her juices, and she gave up on asking. Reaching for the nightstand, she grabbed the condom packet and slapped it against his chest.

"Now!"

He laughed at her demand, but he took the condom from her fingers and ripped the foil, sitting back on his haunches to roll it on. "You haven't learned patience, I see."

"And you haven't learned when to just shut up and fuck." She mock-glowered at him, making grabby hands towards his torso. Truthfully, she didn't mind that he was quite chatty during sex, only that he expected her to be able to respond coherently, and it was somewhat embarrassing when she couldn't get out complete sentences. Or any words at all.

As for his maddening patience during foreplay... well, she'd take that over a man who didn't bother with foreplay at all. It was just the effect Carlo had on her, that she was always at fever pitch so quickly, desperate to feel him inside her. Having to wait when he was right there, hard and ready, seemed so ridiculous.

At least he wasn't arguing or insisting on waiting longer, moving to kneel between her thighs with a look of hungry anticipation on his handsome face.

"I'm so tempted to duck down and eat you out," he said, and she shook her head, even though the thought of his hot tongue on her sensitive clit made heat twist in her belly.

"Later, if you still want to. Please, Carlo. I need you."

"I need you too, *cara*," he confessed gruffly, reaching out to link his hands with hers, leaning down to kiss her. The tip of his cock nudged into the entrance of her vagina, and Suzannah lost her breath.

Every sensation seemed magnified as Carlo rocked his hips in a slow, easy rhythm, driving a little deeper with each stroke. She could feel the rasp of his stubble against her chin as his tongue played a teasing game of tag with hers, the crispness of his chest hair tickling against her aching nipples. His pulse was racing, she could feel it where their wrists pressed together, or maybe that was hers.

Lifting her legs to ease his passage, Suzannah curled them around his hips and tugged, impatient for the deep, full penetration she knew Carlo had given her. He'd anticipated the move, though, and resisted, laughing softly against her mouth.

"Easy, *cara*. Let me savour you. I promise, you'll come so hard and so often tonight you'll be hard pressed to walk in the morning." Pressing his forehead against hers, he growled the words softly against her mouth. Suzannah shuddered as he shifted, tilting his hips to change the angle.

"Please." It was a thin whimper. She should hate herself for sounding so needy, so pathetic, but she could feel the fine trembling in Carlo's muscles, knew it was costing him to hold back. A thin sheen of sweat was breaking out on his back.

"Soon. I can't hold out against you, you feel too good." Closing his eyes, he held still for a long moment before opening them and smiling down at her. "All right, you beautiful, impatient woman."

Suzannah moaned with ecstasy as Carlo straightened up, sitting back on his heels and letting go of her hands to curl his under her butt, lifting her almost into his lap. The angle he created was sublimely perfect, the tip of his cock just glancing that little spot high on her inner walls as he finally thrust to full depth.

"Oh, God!" Suzannah cried as he pulled back and then thrust again, harder.

"No, *cara*," he said, "just your Carlo," and thrust again.

She'd forgotten how good it was, or maybe it was even better now they were both older, more experienced. Carlo knew exactly what he was doing, setting up the perfect rhythm to drive them both insane, guttural sounds spilling from his lips as he pounded deep into Suzannah. She could feel herself tightening, feel the dizzying spiral beginning, and dug her fingernails into the mattress beneath her, trying to find an anchor, but there was none to be had there.

"*Carlo!*" It was a scream of his name as fireworks went off behind her closed eyelids, her brain playing tricks on her in the moment of extremity.

She only vaguely felt his last few thrusts into her clenching passage before he gasped "Oh, *cara*," and went still. Heat bloomed inside her and Carlo toppled forward, bracing himself on shaking arms and pressing kisses against her cheek and lips.

Suzannah reached up and looped her arms around his neck languidly, returning the slow, sensual kisses and revelling in the humming pleasure still infusing her body. Carlo felt heavy and solid above her, reassuringly anchoring her to earth when she felt as though she might float away at any moment. She sighed with displeasure when he lifted up to pull out of her, but let him go.

"Now I really need to shower," Carlo said quietly. "Will you still be here when I come out, *cara*?"

She was too tired, too comfortable in a bed which smelled reassuringly like Carlo, to even consider why he might be worrying about her leaving. "Not going anywhere," she mumbled, snuggling down against his pillow. "Hurry back."

"I will." He kissed her shoulder before leaving the bed, flipped a cover over her considerately. Eyes closed, she smiled.

Suzannah fell asleep to the sound of the running water and Carlo singing in the shower, a smile of absolute contentment on her face.

***

It was still dark when she woke up spooned against Carlo's body, one of his strong arms curled laxly around her waist, and almost immediately Suzannah developed a serious case of morning-after regret. It wasn't a situation she should be finding herself in, she chastised herself silently while wondering if she'd be able to make her escape without waking him up. He slept lightly, though, and if he caught her in the middle of sneaking out, it would be so much more mortifying than just facing him and behaving like a grown-up.

"I can practically hear the gears whirring in your brain," Carlo murmured in her ear, his stubble scratchy on the back of her neck as his jaw moved. "Stop thinking so hard, Suzannah."

"Can't help it," she admitted, even as her body quivered in involuntary delight at the way his arm tightened, pulling her closer against his body and the morning wood she quickly discovered he was sporting. "We really shouldn't be doing this."

"Says who? I read the staff code of conduct. The only people we're not allowed to get involved with are resort guests. This isn't the military, where relationships within the chain of command are strictly prohibited." His breath tickled her ear, even as his hand slid stealthily upward to cup her breast. "I'm not going to undermine you, Suzannah, quite the opposite; I'll back you up any way you need. *You* earned that Michelin star. *La Sirène* is *your* restaurant. I'm just your pastry chef, and believe me, I have no designs on your job. Just your body."

She smiled, as he'd intended her to, she guessed. "I know you wouldn't undermine me." The thought had never even crossed her mind. "Not intentionally. I just worry about keeping the respect of the staff, if they know I'm sleeping with you..."

Carlo snorted. "Have you *met* you? Disrespect, my ass. You'd singe their ears if they dared, and not with a brulée torch, either!"

That made her laugh, and she twisted over to face him, tossing the mass of her hair out of the way when he lifted his head off it. She didn't really know how to put into words the questions she really wanted to ask - *are you staying? Where is this going?* - and Carlo seemed to read her uncertainty in her eyes.

Gently, he placed his forefinger against her lips. "Hush," he said quietly. "There'll be time to work out exactly what this is, what *we* are, later. Right now, I need to make love to you again."

"I should really get down to the dock," Suzannah muttered half-heartedly. "Pick out the best fish..."

"You're paranoid. They wouldn't dare to give you any less than the best, for fear you'd show up tomorrow morning and flay them with that wicked tongue of yours."

He was almost certainly right. She'd placed the order via email the day before, anyway, and the boat captain knew her well. He'd make sure everything she ordered was taken up to the kitchens, whether she was there or not.

She was totally justifying the decision to stay in bed with Carlo, she recognised that. And she didn't care in the slightest. Laughing as he eased his body over hers again, she wrapped her arms around his neck and pulled him down for a heated kiss.

Chapter Twelve

Carlo made it to the kitchen before Suzannah, who left his cabin to go shower and change in her own. Sauntering in whistling cheerfully, the notes died on his lips as he found Luke in the kitchen talking to Samira and admiring the just-finished wedding cake covered in delicate sugar roses.

"Morning, Carlo. Isn't this spectacular?" Luke gestured to the cake.

"It is, Samira's very talented. Did you even go to bed, or did you sleep here?" he teased the young baker, who ducked her head shyly.

"I got plenty of sleep, Chef," she said quietly.

"If you say so. You've done an incredible job with this." Carlo moved around to the other side of the counter to inspect the cake from all angles. "You'll have your own wedding cake business soon enough, mark my words."

"I'm more than happy here learning from you, Chef!" Samira gave him a devoted look. "I know there's a lot more to being a pastry chef than a knack for making pretty flowers."

"You're not wrong, but you're well on the way there. Anyway, what can I do for you this morning, Luke?"

"I stopped in to see Suzannah, actually, but she's not in yet. Came in here to look at the cake when I caught a glimpse through the door." Luke gestured at the doorway between the two kitchens. "How are things going, with two senior chefs working here? I know there was a little friction at the beginning..."

"Not from my side," Carlo said quickly, wanting to nip that rumour in the bud. "I think Chef Monteil was just a little miffed she was presented with a *fait accompli,* rather than getting a shortlist to choose her own candidate from. Everything's flowing smoothly."

"The restaurant's certainly getting rave reviews. Have you looked at the latest?"

Carlo had to admit he hadn't. He'd been too busy. Luke rolled his eyes, looking amused.

"Take it from me, the new desserts you've been trialling are going over very well indeed."

"Considering the one he gave me to try last night, I'm not surprised," a voice drawled, and Suzannah stepped into the pastry kitchen. She looked fresh and bright, her auburn curls drawn up in a knot on top of her head, no sign on her face that she'd been awake half the night having wild, passionate sex.

"Morning, Suzannah." Luke smiled at her broadly, and Suzannah returned the smile.

"It's always a pleasure to see you, Luke, but I know you wouldn't be in my kitchen unless there's something you need to discuss with me. Step into my office?"

"Of course. Carlo, would you join us? There's something I need to discuss with you both, as it happens."

Luke didn't look particularly serious, so Carlo assumed it wasn't anything grim. When the three of them were squeezed into Suzannah's tiny office, Suzannah in her chair, Luke in the one visitor's chair and Carlo propping up the wall at the side, Luke filled them in.

"Have you heard of B-Rex?"

Suzannah looked blank, but Carlo nodded. "He's an American rap musician. Won one of those big talent quests a few years ago and has gone on to make it pretty big."

"Very good. Culture points for Carlo." Luke grinned at him. "And please tell me you both know who Myst is?"

Even Suzannah nodded at that. Myst was a breakout Australian pop star; you couldn't switch on a radio without hearing one of her epic ballads at the moment.

"They're doing a duet which Myst hopes to use to break into the American market. B-Rex is over here on tour and the song has already been recorded; they only have a limited window to shoot the video, though, and the production company have reached out. Myst's manager owns one of the private villas on the island and they're going to use that and a couple of our locations to shoot."

"Wow," Carlo said, properly impressed. "That's massive."

"Next week."

Suzannah's mouth opened in a silent O and she traded a quick glance with Carlo. "Riiiiight," she said finally, drawing out the word. "And you're telling us this because...?"

"Because the production company have specifically requested that *La Sirène* provide catering for the stars, for the three days they'll be here on the island, including provision of dishes which may or may not appear in the final cut of the video." Luke smiled tightly as he explained. "The figure they offered made even my eyes pop. So I said yes."

"Could be worse," Suzannah said after a moment, "you could have told them you'd make restaurant tables available, when we're booked out six months in advance and have an absolute policy of no bumping."

"If they'd asked, I'd have said no. However, this is a different thing, and if you two pull this off, I'll see that fifty per cent of the fee we're being paid for the catering services goes to you. Directly."

Suzannah waved a hand, dismissing that. "The money isn't important."

"Speak for yourself," Carlo drawled, and she shot him a suppressing glance.

"Do they have specific things they're asking us to do? Or will they be selecting from our menu?"

"Unknown," Luke spread his hands. "I wish I could tell you. The production assistant I've been talking to says B-Rex will arrive on the island on Tuesday, Myst and the director on Wednesday. There's a whole entourage coming along with them, as you can imagine. I'll leave a message that you'd like to consult with someone who can make decisions on that as soon as possible."

"Possibly forward a copy of the menu through to them?" Carlo suggested, and Luke agreed that was a sensible idea.

"I realise you two will basically have to neglect responsibilities here for a couple of days to fuss over a pair of spoilt celebrities," he said wryly, "but... I have to ask you to do exactly that. It's important for the resort as a whole, and I swear it'll be worth your while."

It wasn't as though they had an awful lot of choice, but they would both relish the challenge. Luke nodded and said he'd keep them in the loop and get them any information he could, as it came in.

"Anything you need, it's yours," he said in parting. "Up to and including express airfreighting produce from wherever you need it. Just say the word."

Suzannah thanked him, and he nodded as he rose to his feet.

"I'll leave you to work."

The door closed behind him, and Suzannah and Carlo looked at each other.

"Won't this be *fun?*" Carlo said after a moment.

"Thanks for the sarcasm," Suzannah said, giving him a cynical look. "Come on." She got to her feet. "The only thing we can do right now is get lunch on track. After lunch, though, we need to sit down and work the roster out and plan for how we're going to arrange things. Everything will have to be prepared here, transported and made up on site in the villa, which means either you or I will have to be on site at all times to make sure the presentation is spot on. I just hope it's got a usable kitchen or we'll be trying to cook on a barbecue or something."

"We'll worry about that when we know the layout, and the menu," Carlo said. "Hey, maybe we'll get lucky and it'll be close to Jace's villa. I'm sure he'd let us stage out of his kitchen if we need to."

Suzannah brightened. "And we can probably find that out, at least. Luke will know which villa it is. I'll drop him a line." Reaching for her computer, she started typing rapidly.

Back to business it was, then. Tempted to lean down and snatch a kiss, Carlo decided not to push his luck.

"I'll get to work," he said, keeping his tone light.

Suzannah didn't look up. "Tell Julie I won't be long, please," she requested. "I'll fill her in on what we'll need to do... and Edouard, too, he'll probably have to select wine..."

Mention of Edouard set Carlo's teeth on edge instantly. He was pretty sure it wasn't going to go over well with the sommelier when he found out Carlo and Suzannah were sleeping together; Carlo wouldn't put it past him to try to break them up somehow, or rat them out to Luke. Although Carlo was pretty sure Luke wouldn't care in the least as long as it didn't affect their work.

Heading out into the kitchen, he left Suzannah's office door open and paused to speak to Julie briefly, just letting her know that there was a special event coming up which would require some extra effort and Suzannah was working on details. Taking it in her stride, Julie nodded, her confidence that he and Suzannah would manage everything and just tell her what her role would be was obvious... and heart-warming.

Back in the pastry kitchen, Carlo got to work, putting the imminent disruption out of his mind. He was planning to film for his YouTube show later that afternoon; Gemma the resort photographer was coming in to do the camera work. He needed to have all the dinner prep and whatever Suzannah needed him to do finished before three so they could have a clear couple of hours before the staff came back in for dinner.

He was rapidly cracking and separating eggs when a shriek of utmost horror had him dropping everything and sprinting for the cold room.

Samira stood in one corner, hands to her cheeks. As Carlo rushed to her side, she turned to him with an utterly devastated look on her face before bursting into tears and throwing herself into his arms.

Looking over the head of the stricken young chef, Carlo's eyes widened. In the corner of the cold room, carefully sheltered from accidental knocks, was the wedding cake he had made and Samira had slaved so long and hard over decorating. Every one of her delicate sugar roses had been crushed and mangled, and the formerly perfect pink and white cake was streaked with ugly dark green smears and drips. Carlo could only surmise an entire bottle of food colouring had been poured over it.

"What the *hell*?"

Carlo turned his head to find Suzannah glaring at him and Samira, sobbing heartbrokenly against his chest.

"Someone's sabotaged the cake for today's wedding," he said flatly, hardly able to believe it had happened.

"*What?*" Her expression morphed from angry jealousy to shock. "No... it must have been an accident."

"A bottle of green food colouring isn't an accident," Carlo said grimly.

Shock turned to disbelief and then to rage as he moved Samira gently aside to give Suzannah a good look at the damage, and then she let rip with swear words in half a dozen languages, practically turning the air blue with her fury. Abruptly, she turned on her heel and stormed back out into the main kitchen.

He'd have to trust her to find out who would do such a thing. There were no surveillance cameras in the cold room, and literally every staff member would have been in and out multiple times in the last couple of hours. With the cake not in open view unless someone walked to the very back corner and looked behind the stack of egg boxes, any of them could have done it at any time.

Right now, he couldn't even think about it. He had a disaster to salvage, and he wasn't even sure he could calm Samira down enough to help.

"Hey. Hey! You can fall apart later," he said, Grasping her shoulders in his hands and giving her a gentle shake. "This is horrible, but trust Chef Monteil to get to the bottom of it and deal with whoever did it. You and I have a cake to fix. Now, I'm gonna strip off this icing and start fresh... how many sugar flowers do you reckon you can make in the next three hours?"

Samira gulped down a sob. "Twelve," she said in a shaky voice after a moment's consideration. "Maybe a couple more, if we can spare someone to help dry them."

"We'll find someone." Filming his You Tube show would have to wait, but Gemma was a helpful sort. Once he filled her in, he had no doubt the photographer would be more than willing to stand by Samira and transfer sugar petals in and out of the dehydrators. "I can probably get another five or six done once I've re-iced. That'll have to do."

There had been over thirty originally. Maybe once the lunch rush was finished - and Suzannah was going to have to cover the jobs both he and Samira would normally be doing - they'd be able to get another couple of hands in. It wasn't Suzannah's forte, but she was absolutely capable of making the flowers too.

There was no time to waste. With another gentle squeeze on Samira's shoulders, Carlo let her go and stepped forward to pick up the cake. "Thank God they didn't just smash something heavy down on it. We'd be screwed."

"It would have made too much mess." Samira sniffed. "Oh... look!"

Now Carlo had picked the cake up, they could see what lay behind it; a discarded, empty bottle of food colouring and a pair of food handling gloves, green stains marking the fingers.

"I bet they wore those to crush the flowers, and then poured the colouring over it. What assholes! Who would do this? *Why?*" Samira's cry was plaintive.

"I don't know," Carlo said grimly, "but I wouldn't want to be in their shoes when Suzannah catches up with them."

Chapter Thirteen

The rest of the day was a blur of rushed activity. Carlo and Samira worked frantically to salvage the cake and Suzannah stood in the centre of the kitchens, somehow managing everything so that lunch ran as smoothly as usual even with two crucially important staff members unable to assist. Nobody had come forward to admit guilt, of course, and nobody had seen anything amiss in the cold room until Samira found the cake.

Suzannah didn't have time to investigate right now, but there was no way she was going to let something like this drop. It was sabotage, plain and simple, and she needed to know who and why, and then get them the hell out of her kitchen so nothing like it could ever happen again.

All of the staff in the pastry kitchen seemed shocked and horrified, working extra hard to take up the slack, none of them leaving until everything which could possibly be done to prepare the desserts for dinner was taken care of. At that point, Suzannah dismissed them all, telling them to take a break before coming back at five.

Carlo and Samira were shoulder to shoulder at the bench, dehydrators humming away in front of them drying sugar flowers as the two chefs worked at breakneck speed to prepare more. The resort photographer was watching with wide eyes, occasionally lifting her camera for a sneaky shot but mostly waiting for them to snap an instruction, telling her what to do next.

"Are any of these salvageable?" Suzannah asked, moving to where the icing and crushed flowers removed from the cake lay in a mess of green, pink and white crumbs.

"Didn't really have time to look," Carlo admitted without looking up. "There might be some buds and a leaf or two, but a lot of them had green dye on them and I figured it was probably quicker just to start fresh."

"Maybe for you two, but I'm not as quick at making them. I'll have a poke through, see if I can salvage anything." Carefully, she began sifting through the mess, kicking a rubbish bin over to the foot of the bench and dumping everything which was definitely too ruined to use. Ten minutes later she had quite a pile of usable petals and buds, enough to make up a couple of flowers at least, and transferred them carefully to the bench beside Carlo.

"Brilliant!" He shot a quick glance at her. "We're gonna pull this off, I think. Sorry to wreck your planning session, though."

"Don't be ridiculous." Fixing the cake was the most urgent priority. The wedding couple weren't high profile, but they'd paid a hefty price to have the cake they wanted and their reception hosted in *La Sirène's* private dining room, and Suzannah would have moved mountains to avoid letting them down. Fortunately, she didn't have to. She had her very own miracle workers right in front of her.

***

At five o'clock, Carlo called time on their work. The cake didn't look quite as incredible as it had originally, but even the most critical eye wouldn't be able to find fault with it. The wedding guests would begin arriving shortly for pre-dinner drinks, though, and the cake was supposed to be on display when they did. Carefully, Carlo picked up the display board and headed out to put the cake on the stand all ready for it, Gemma hurrying ahead of him to open doors and clear the way.

"Take the evening off," Suzannah told Samira as the young chef sagged wearily against the workbench.

"Oh, but I'm on the roster." Samira straightened up. "I'm fine, really, Chef."

"You've done a terrific job. You've earned the evening off, whether you're tired or not. Go. Relax. That's an order." Suzannah smiled to take the sting from her words, and Samira smiled shyly back.

"My back's pretty stiff," she admitted.

"Why not give the spa a call, see if they've got any evening massage appointments? Ask for Shae, and tell her I said it's on me. You've saved our bacon this afternoon, Samira," Suzannah raised a hand to quiet her as the younger woman protested. "I won't forget it."

"Thank you, Chef," Samira said sensibly, obviously realising continuing to argue with Suzannah would get her nowhere.

"Thank *you*," Suzannah replied, watching as Samira took the time to tidy her workspace before leaving the kitchen, bidding a cheerful good evening to her co-workers as she went.

"She's a terrific young chef," Carlo said as he returned to the pastry kitchen.

"My office," Suzannah said abruptly, and he raised an eyebrow but followed her into the small room, watching as she closed the door and turned to lean on it.

"What's wrong?"

"Are you sure Samira didn't sabotage the cake herself?"

Carlo's eyebrows shot up, but he appeared to give her question due consideration. "I suppose she'd have had the opportunity, same as anyone else on the staff," he said slowly, "but... why on earth would she? She's had to work like a slave all afternoon, and she was fully prepared to keep going until midnight. It's not like she'll get paid any extra for it, either."

"Except by gaining your trust."

"She already has it!" Carlo gave her an incredulous look, shaking his head. "She was devastated, Suzannah. No, I can't believe it was Samira. Why would you suspect her?"

"I can't count anyone out. I wondered, last week, after that incident with the fire when the automatic fire suppressant system didn't come on, and now I'm certain. Someone's trying to sabotage us." Suzannah took a deep breath, hoping she wasn't misplacing her trust in Carlo, but she made herself carry on and tell him the rest. "That's not all, either. Twice in the last month - before you got here - there've been things which could have gone seriously wrong and created a major incident if I hadn't been quick enough to spot them. There could have been a mass food poisoning in the restaurant on the last occasion. Then there was that fire last week, and I still haven't figured out how that started. Now this."

Carlo stared at her before slowly sinking into the chair in front of her desk. "*Why?*" he said finally. "It doesn't make sense. It's not like there are rival restaurateurs here trying to shut you down."

"It started after I fired your predecessor," Suzannah admitted, taking her own seat, letting her shoulders slump with weariness as she shared the burden she'd been labouring under at last. "I can only think someone was upset she got fired and is trying to get revenge."

"Who would want to do that? I can tell you Samira doesn't speak highly of her," Carlo noted. "She wouldn't let Samira do any of the wedding cake stuff. Samira said she told Vicky on the day she got fired that the supports she was using weren't going to cut it, by the way."

Suzannah grimaced. "Shows how much I notice. I thought the two of them were quite close, which is why I suspected her."

"Oh, Suzannah."

She must have looked quite pitiful, because Carlo got up and rounded the desk, leaning down to pull her to her feet and then into his arms for a hug. He smelled good, Suzannah noted as she buried her face in his neck, like sugar and vanilla and almonds. Sweet and delicious.

"We'll find out who's doing this," Carlo vowed, holding onto her tightly, one hand stroking down her spine soothingly. "And then I'll kick their ass."

"I can't trust anyone, and it's a horrible feeling," Suzannah mumbled, feeling tears prick at the back of her eyes. "Except you... because the sabotage started before you came."

"I hope you'd know you can trust me even if it hadn't," Carlo said, but he understood Suzannah's paranoia. There were so many ways to wreck a restaurant's reputation by accident, never mind the mischief someone actively trying to sabotage them could get up to. Thinking about it, he frowned. "Have you told Luke?"

Suzannah nodded against his shoulder. "He's arranging to have a couple more cameras installed, discreetly. The work will be done after midnight, when the kitchen is closed, so nobody knows about it."

"Good plan." She didn't seem inclined to pull away, so Carlo kept on holding her, enjoying the way she was leaning trustingly against him. Tall and sturdy, she felt wonderful in his arms as her body curved into his embrace. His cock swelled to attention, and Carlo eyed Suzannah's desk thoughtfully for a moment before regretfully putting the thought from his mind. They still had dinner to get through.

"We'd better get back to work," Suzannah said, her tone reluctant as she echoed his thoughts.

"I know, but don't for a moment think I don't want to keep you in here and ravish you on your desk." Deliberately, he made his tone light and teasing, and it had the desired result. Suzannah laughed, pulling back to look at him.

"Maybe later," she said archly.

"Promises, promises." Reluctantly letting her go, Carlo turned to the door, about to open it when her voice stopped him.

"I'm glad you're here, Carlo."

He turned to look back at her. Expression serious, she gazed at him steadily, but he saw the way her long, capable fingers twisted together. She was nervous about his answer.

"I am, too," he said.

Chapter Fourteen

The following day brought news from Luke that the additional surveillance cameras had been discreetly installed the previous night, and emails from the producers of the music video for B-Rex and Myst.

"A nondisclosure agreement?" Suzannah crooked an eyebrow as she read through the document.

"Looks pretty standard," Carlo said. He'd worked with celebrities a few times before, for his YouTube show. "They just don't want the media turning it into a circus." He borrowed a pen from Suzannah's desk and scribbled his name at the bottom of his copy. He, Luke and Suzannah were back in her office again, the lunch hour over.

"Fine." Suzannah signed her copy too, and they both handed the papers back to Luke, who slipped them into a folder before bringing out some more papers.

"Now you've signed those, I can show you these. The 'script' for the music video calls for B-Rex to 'cook' a romantic dinner for himself and Myst and serve it on the villa's back deck overlooking the ocean as the sun sets."

"Cliché, but I'm sure it will look charming," Suzannah murmured, flicking through the script.

"Indeed. The speedy sunsets up here in the tropics mean they'll probably only get one or two takes to get it right, though, so everything will have to be ready perfectly to the minute."

"How many days will they be filming for?" Carlo asked.

"They're planning on two. Good thing the weather's predictably excellent at this time of year, isn't it?"

"Here's hoping we don't get any afternoon tropical storms rolling in," Suzannah murmured. She was scanning through the stapled sheets Luke had just handed her. "There's nothing on here about what food they want B-Rex to 'cook', though."

"Still waiting on that. There's a list of what they want for the film crew, who will be based in the Jacaranda conference suites."

Carlo nodded. That set of conference suites was located on the side of the resort closest to the private villas, only a few minutes' walk or maybe two minutes in one of the complimentary golf carts. With rooms ranging in quality from the resort's basic standard - which would be considered luxury in any other resort on the Reef - to seriously opulent on the upper floors, it made sense to put the crew up there, away from the regular holidaymakers who might be tempted to post on social media if they knew celebrities were on the island.

"Are we supplying all this?" Suzannah cast a faintly appalled eye over the long list appended to the document.

"No! We'll open up the conference room kitchen and have it catered there using supplementary staff from the other restaurants."

"Good." She breathed an obvious sigh of relief, and Carlo had to cover his mouth with his hand to suppress an amused grin. Suzannah would have made it happen if Luke had asked, but catering for seventy people in addition to *La Sirène*'s daily operations and making special screen-worthy dishes to appear in the video itself would likely have taxed even her abilities.

"I'm afraid you'll have to wait until B-Rex or his people get back to us," Luke said apologetically. "I did send the menus through to them."

"Whatever they want, we'll make it happen," Carlo said, smiling at Suzannah. She smiled back at him, her beautiful green eyes locking with his for a long moment before she looked quickly away.

She'd taken him to her cabin the previous night, saying she wanted to sleep in her own bed. Despite their mutual exhaustion, they'd still found the energy to make love again before drifting off in each other's arms.

He'd woken in the early hours of the morning to find her already gone, returning to her self-appointed duty to inspect the fishing catch. She'd slipped back in beside him not long after, though, sun-warmed and laughing, her clever fingers dancing down his body to bring him to instant, roaring arousal.

Luke left them a few minutes later and Carlo took a quick look around the kitchen outside the office, noting that the place was completely empty, before closing the door again, grabbing the chair Luke had just vacated and wedging it under the handle.

"What are you doing?" Suzannah asked, puzzled.

"No lock on the door." Carlo gestured at the chair. "Just making sure nobody's going to walk in on us."

Suzannah's mouth opened in a startled O before she grinned. "You're insatiable."

"Damn right," he agreed, striding around the desk and dropping to his knees in front of her chair. "And I've been thinking about having you on this desk for days now, so take pity on me before I expire from thwarted lust."

"So dramatic." She rolled her green eyes at him, but she was still smiling, and she reached up to unbutton her blouse as she spoke. "I hope you brought a condom, because I definitely don't keep them in my desk."

"Maybe you should start," he suggested, producing one from his back pocket with the air of a magician pulling a rabbit from a hat. "Because this definitely isn't going to be the last time."

***

"Tell me to shut it if I'm out of line, Chef," Julie said as the two of them worked side by side plating dishes at lunch the following day, "but you seem particularly happy today."

"Do I?" Suzannah spared a glance at her assistant. "Why do you say that?" She was trying to present her usual professional aspect to her staff, even though she definitely felt different. Sore, to start with... it had been quite some time since she'd engaged in any bedroom activities, and she and Carlo had been very enthusiastic over the last couple of days.

"You were humming."

"I was?"

"Sounded like Beyoncé." There was a definite little smirk on Julie's face.

She'd been singing *Crazy In Love*, Suzannah realised, and felt extremely relieved that the flush on her cheeks could be put down to the heat in the kitchen. Carlo had been shooting her promising looks every time he crossed her line of sight for the last hour, and she was looking forward to him barricading them in her office again that afternoon.

Unfortunately, just as Carlo was entering her office with an anticipatory grin on his face, Suzannah clicked on the email from Luke marked URGENT.

"B-Rex and his manager will be available for the next hour for a video call," she said, holding a hand up to stall Carlo. "We really need to talk to them and see what they want."

Carlo sighed, but he reached for the spare chair and pulled it up beside her, smiling as she fussed a little with her hair before reaching for the computer again.

"You look stunning. Don't flirt with B-Rex or I'll be jealous," he said, his tone teasing.

"Don't be ridiculous." As if a famous musician would look at her! He probably spent his days surrounded by beautiful models and actresses just dying for his attention.

She'd also been under the impression that B-Rex was black, like most famous rappers, so it was a surprise when a young man with a lot of tattoos under very white skin, peered out of the screen and gave her a toothy smile. A slightly older man in a suit, who Suzannah assumed was the rapper's manager, sat beside him.

"Good afternoon," Suzannah said politely. "I'm Suzannah Monteil from the *La Sirène* restaurant and this is Carlo Gianetti, our pastry chef."

"Hey, gorgeous," B-Rex said. "This my homeboy Joey."

Suzannah ignored the inappropriate compliment and forged on with the question she had pre-planned.

"Have you had the chance to look over the menus we sent through to you, Mr... ah... B-Rex?"

"Yah," B-Rex nodded. "And that stuff, it's all way too fancy. Just do some hot dogs and fries, yah?"

Suzannah's jaw dropped. She had absolutely no idea what to say, and when she glanced across at Carlo, she saw he looked just as flummoxed - and not a little bit outraged.

"With respect," Suzannah gathered herself to say finally, "if you want hot dogs and fries, why is the production company willing to pay a premium for two highly-trained chefs to prepare it for you?"

"I dunno, babe." B-Rex heaved a sigh, leaned back in his chair and looked at his smart watch. "I ain't even read the script for this shoot. Why so much fuss about what I gotta eat?"

Helpless, Suzannah looked at Joey, who seemed to finally realise some intervention would be needed.

"You supposed to be cooking a fancy romantic dinner for Myst, man," he told his client.

"Yeah? But I can't cook."

"That's not the point," Carlo said, obviously seeing that Suzannah was beyond words. "We'll do all the cooking behind the scenes. You'll just have to drop a bit of garnish on the top and carry the plates to the table."

"Cool, cool," B-Rex nodded several times, still looking at his smart watch. "Whatever you think best, my dude. Find out what Myst likes to eat. I'd look a dipshit if I served her steak and she's some paleo keto vegan or something, yah?"

That was a sensible statement, at least. Suzannah nodded. "We'll try and find out. What about you, is there anything you don't eat?"

"Lots of shit, yah," B-Rex grinned toothily at her. "But I don't actually have to eat it, do I?"

Carlo grinned. "No. But if you did, and liked it, you could tell all your friends and Instagram followers how awesome we are."

B-Rex laughed and pointed finger guns at the camera. "I like you, dude. I'll do that. Just make me look like Masterchef, yah?"

"You got it." Carlo made finger guns back, B-Rex got up and walked off, and Joey promptly followed him.

Suzannah made sure the computer was definitely switched off, and turned the webcam around as a precaution, before giving into laughter and collapsing on the desk.

Carlo just shook his head, a grin on his face. "Suzannah, it wasn't that funny. What an ass! He had no respect for you at all, completely dismissed you!"

She wiped tears of laughter from her eyes, still chuckling. "Oh, I don't care. Ignorance isn't the same as deliberate disrespect." She went off into a stronger fit of giggles again, choking out "Hot dogs!" when Carlo looked at her quizzically.

He had to laugh along with her. The rapper asking Suzannah to prepare hot dogs was just so ridiculous. She was taking it better than he'd expected, certainly better than she would have years ago, when her prickly dignity wouldn't have allowed such a demeaning request to pass without losing her temper.

A knock on the office door startled them both, and Suzannah glanced guiltily at Carlo, both well aware they'd have been having sex on her desk by now if they hadn't had to make contact with B-Rex.

"Come in," she called, and the door opened to reveal the sommelier, Edouard.

"Good afternoon, Suzannah," he said, as always speaking in French and completely ignoring Carlo's presence. "I was just speaking with Luke, who said you would be contacting the client this afternoon."

"Yes," Suzannah had successfully quelled her laughter. "Yes, we just spoke to B-Rex and his manager."

Annoyed by Edouard's attitude, Carlo folded his arms and leaned against the wall by Suzannah's desk, deliberately remaining close to her.

"And did the client mention anything about what wine he would like?" Edouard enquired.

Carlo suppressed a snicker. "Probably Budweiser," he said. "To go with the hot dogs."

Suzannah lost her hard-won composure and collapsed into another fit of the giggles.

Edouard looked completely horror-struck. "I *beg* your pardon?"

"B-Rex isn't exactly a gourmand. He asked for hot dogs."

Carlo honestly though Edouard might faint. The sommelier groped for the edge of the desk, leaned on it heavily as though afraid he might fall down.

"*Hot dogs?*" he gasped in tones of purest disgust before putting his nose in the air as Carlo started laughing too. "I'll wait for further information from the producers, then," he said, turned on his heel and left them alone.

"You're gonna throw up if you keep laughing that hard," Carlo told Suzannah. She'd now progressed to snorts and cackles, clutching at her stomach.

"*Hot dogs,*" she said on a final snort. "Oh, God. I'll never be able to hear that again without laughing."

"I don't think Edouard shared your amusement," Carlo said dryly. She waved off his concern, plucking a tissue from the box on her desk and wiping her eyes.

"He's far too stuffy. A good laugh never heard anyone."

"It's good to hear you laugh," Carlo said softly, reaching out to touch her hair lightly. She looked up at him and smiled.

"Go wedge that door shut," Suzannah ordered, grinning, "and you'll hear me make a lot more happy noises."

Chapter Fifteen

Myst, or at least her management, were much more helpful than B-Rex, providing the information that Myst rarely consumed red meat and had an allergy to shellfish by email within an hour of being sent the query. Carlo and Suzannah discussed possible options while lying in bed that night and sent through some suggestions via email the following morning, along with a couple of wine suggestions to appease Edouard.

"Looks like Myst makes her mind up quickly," Suzannah looked up from her computer as Carlo entered her office that afternoon. "She's chosen the chicken and pesto tagliatelle, and your mandarin chocolate bombe for dessert."

"Clearly a lady of discerning tastes," Carlo said cheerfully. "And, bonus, the bombes can be made ahead."

"So can the pesto if we need to, and the tagliatelle will just come from the fresh pasta stock for the day. I won't have a lot of cooking to do, it's just the presentation." Leaning back in her chair, Suzannah read the email over again. "She wants Australian sparkling wine rather than French champagne, but we're not allowed to show any labels according to the record producer. The wine will be poured into glasses on the table."

"Sounds suspiciously simple. Undoubtedly something will happen to stuff it up." They shared a wry glance, all too aware of how even the best-laid plans could go awry, especially when celebrities prone to diva-like behaviour were involved.

"Especially if our saboteur chips in," Suzannah voiced her fear. "You or I need to be the only ones who touch anything going to be served to Myst and B-Rex, and we need to be sure nobody else can get to it, at all times."

"Good point." Carlo considered. "I could make the bombes the previous day and take them down to Jace's villa, to store in his fridge. Along with the pesto, if you want to make that ahead too."

Suzannah nodded in agreement. "We'll take everything we plan to use down the previous day, I think. Don't give anyone the opportunity to tamper. It's easy enough for me to whip up a quick batch of pasta down there."

Putting their heads together, they started making a list of everything they'd need to check Jace had in his villa, or take over themselves. Suzannah threw up her hands about ten minutes in and suggested they just go over to Jace's and have a look.

"Good plan. You got his number?" Carlo asked.

"No, but I have Nessa's." Fishing out her phone, Suzannah sent a quick text, and a moment later a *ping* announced a return message.

"She's invited us to come over. She and Jace are there now," Suzannah said.

"Do we walk? I don't know where it is."

"I do, and no, it's way too far to walk on a hot afternoon like this! We'll grab a golf cart... and I'm driving."

Carlo shrugged, not having a problem with that in the least. He didn't even know where they were going, hadn't been over to the half of the island where the luxurious private villas were located. He was more than happy to let Suzannah lead the way.

"Holy wow," he said about ten minutes later, staring open-mouthed up at the large, architecturally-designed villa Suzannah had just parked outside.

"You do recall Jace is a billionaire?" Suzannah said teasingly. "Besides, it doesn't compare to having your own castle."

"I suppose." He gave her a quizzical look as they left the buggy and walked up to the villa's smoked-glass front doors. "What makes you say that?"

Suzannah's expression was incredulous. "Are you joking? You've got Castillo Gianetti to go back to any time you like!"

"It's hardly mine, though!"

"Semantics! You'll be the *Comte* once your father dies, won't you?"

"Wherever did you get that idea?" Carlo blinked at her, astonished. "I have an older brother, who has two sons of his own. I'm well down the line of succession to the title, thank God."

"*What?*" Suzannah's jaw dropped, and she was gaping at him in complete astonishment when the door swung open.

"Hey," Nessa said cheerfully. Taking in the couple standing on the doorstep staring at each other with mutually shocked expressions, she wrinkled her nose. "Is my timing shitty? Do you guys need to talk whatever that's about over before you come in?"

"No," Suzannah said after a moment, tearing her gaze from Carlo's. "Sorry, Nessa. I was just... surprised by something Carlo told me."

"Okay." Nessa shrugged amiably. She looked charming, Carlo thought, wearing a soft white cotton dress which left her shoulders and most of her slim legs bare, the colour a stunning contrast to her deep brown skin. Her long black braids, each secured with a tiny bead at the very end, swung around her as she turned to lead them into the house. "Jace is just on the phone with a client," she said over her shoulder as she led them into the magnificent kitchen. "He'll be along in a minute, but he said have at it. Check out everything, see what you might need."

Carlo stared around, impressed. He'd seen a few high-end private kitchens, but honestly never one so well-designed and fitted out as this. The appliances alone would cost more than his very generous annual salary.

"Wow," he mouthed, turning in a slow circle, staring as Nessa opened a tall cupboard door which proved not to be a cupboard at all, but the entrance to a butler's pantry.

"Over the top, isn't it?" Nessa said cheerfully. "Jace actually thought you might like to borrow it to film your YouTube shows, if you have any issues scheduling it in the restaurant kitchen. There's always so much going on there."

"That would be incredible," Carlo said, astonished at the offer but not about to turn it down. He looked around, taking in the wonderful natural light and the spacious room. "Is the villa they're filming the music video in like this? I can see why they chose it, if so."

"They're all different, but I believe it's about the same size," Nessa said, opening a massive stainless steel refrigerator and taking out a covered dish of fruit salad. "You guys want some of this? I'm starving today. Can't stop eating."

"I wouldn't mind, actually," Suzannah said, and Carlo nodded. Nessa brought out some bowls and served some for all three of them while they checked out the butler's pantry, adding yogurt and setting a spoon beside each bowl. They took them to the marble breakfast bar at one side of the kitchen to eat, and were still sitting there talking when Jace came in.

"Hey," Jace smiled in welcome, walking up behind Nessa and putting his arms around her waist. She leaned back against him comfortably, placing her hands over his. "Do we have everything you'll need?"

"I think so." Suzannah nodded. "You've got a pasta making attachment for your kitchen machine, which is the only thing I'd need on the day to make some fresh tagliatelle."

"Yum," Nessa said. "Don't suppose I could convince you to make enough for us too?"

Suzannah laughed. "I'm used to catering for a couple of hundred, Nessa. I'm not sure I *could* make a small enough batch of pasta to do just a couple of plates!"

"Awesome, we can be your taste-testers," Jace said with a cheeky grin.

"The least we can do to say thanks for taking over your kitchen for the day is feed you," Carlo put in. "I'll make sure there are a couple extra of my mandarin chocolate bombes set aside for you."

"And that's why you're my second favourite guy on this island." Nessa gave him the thumbs-up. "Better watch your step, darling," she said teasingly to Jace. "I might throw you over for Carlo if you don't keep me happy."

Jace laughed, obviously not in the least threatened. “Nessa is the lowest-maintenance woman I’ve ever met,” he said, nuzzling at his fiancée’s ear. “I can’t even spoil her because there’s nothing she really wants.”

“Doesn’t stop you trying,” Nessa said dryly. Lifting one slim leg, she pointed at her ankle. “He gave me that the other day. A six-month anniversary present.”

Suzannah was pretty sure the anklet glimmering bright against Nessa’s dark skin was platinum and real diamonds. She made suitably impressed noises, but Nessa wasn’t really listening, just gazing up at Jace, both of them perfectly in tune with each other to the point they’d obviously forgotten Carlo and Suzannah were even present.

We were like that once. Suzannah sneaked a glance at Carlo, who was looking down into his empty bowl, a frown furrowing his brow. *Until I left*.

She was still reeling from the bombshell revelation that Carlo wasn’t the eldest son, wasn’t the heir. He’d never really talked about his family, and she’d assumed it was because he didn’t want to rub her nose in the vast gulf between their social stations. When his parents turned up in Paris, they’d done the job for him.

“I think we should leave the two lovebirds alone,” Carlo leaned towards her to murmur, and Suzannah nodded. They’d seen what they needed to.

“We’ll get out of your way,” she said, getting up, and both Jace and Nessa startled.

“Sorry,” Jace said, but he looked unrepentant. “I’d invite you to stay, but the reality is I totally want you to leave so I can take Nessa back to bed.”

Nessa burst out laughing, and Suzannah blushed. Carlo was grinning, reaching out to shake Jace’s hand.

“Say no more. We’ve got work to do, anyway. Thanks for letting us take a look around, and for letting us stage out of your kitchen, of course.”

Jace waved a hand dismissively. “It’s nothing. It all benefits the resort, anyway. Just let me know if there’s anything else you need.”

They thanked him again and took their leave. Getting back into the golf buggy outside, Suzannah started driving back to the main resort, but as they passed a side track, suddenly swerved onto it.

“Where does this go?” Carlo asked.

“Somewhere we can talk.”

“Sounds like a good plan,” he said dryly. “Long overdue, if you ask me. I have some questions I’d like answered.”

Suzannah winced. She could guess what at least one of them might be, and she wasn’t sure she had an answer for him, not one which would make sense in hindsight, anyway. Her walkout all those years ago seemed like the action of a petulant child when she thought about it now.

The track ended behind a low sand dune, and they left the cart to climb over the dune and down onto the secluded beach below, a small cove fringed with rocky outcroppings on either side. There was nobody else in sight.

Removing her shoes, Suzannah sighed with pleasure as her feet sank into the fine, powdery sand, so pale it was almost white. Warm in the late afternoon sun, it clung to her skin as she walked towards the shade cast by several large palm trees nodding over the beach. Carlo followed her silently, sitting down beside her when she stopped walking and cast herself down on the sand.

"Nice spot," he said, looking out at the water, aqua close to the shore, a deeper blue further out where the reef fell away to deeper waters.

"I come here to think, sometimes," Suzannah admitted. "It's very tranquil. Quiet."

The only sounds were the rhythmic rush of small waves on the shore and the occasional squawk of a tropical bird in the trees, the breeze brushing the palm fronds against each other making a soft shushing sound.

"Did you ever think about me?" Carlo asked. "Did I ever cross your mind after you boarded that train?"

"Every day for about five years," she confessed after a long moment. "After that... maybe every other."

"*Why?*"

There was so much loaded into the one-word question. He didn't have to elaborate, didn't have to specify what exactly he was asking. She knew.

"Because if I didn't leave then, I'd never have been able to do it, and it was the right thing for me to do at the time."

"You broke my heart, Suzannah, so I hope you'll forgive me when I say that's not enough of a goddamn answer!"

She dared a glance at him. He looked furious, hands white-knuckled as he gripped them together, tanned skin drawn tight across his high cheekbones.

"We were from different worlds," she said finally. "It was clear to me that I didn't belong in yours."

"Is this about that visit from my parents? What did they say to you? And how in hell did you get the impression I was the eldest son and heir?"

"Why didn't you tell me you weren't?" she snapped back. "You never even mentioned your family. I assumed you didn't want me to know about them, and then when your parents turned up I realised why - you never had any intention of inviting me into that world. You were just slumming it with me!"

"Don't you ever dare say that about yourself again!" He almost shouted it at her, dark amber eyes flashing with rage. "I never talked about my family because you never talked about yours; you made it clear you had tragedy in your background and I didn't want to rub your nose in the fact that I had a large, loving family who would do literally anything for me!"

"They disapproved of me," Suzannah said flatly.

"They thought I was too young to settle down," Carlo replied. "I told them I wanted to marry you."

Her jaw dropped, and she tore off her sunglasses to stare at him in utter shock. "You *what*?"

"All our plans to travel the world together, learn new cuisines and cultures, it would all have been much easier if we came as a husband and wife team," he pointed out. "My parents tried to convince me to wait, see if we could put up with each other on our travels, but I didn't want to. I was hopelessly, head over heels in love with you, and I didn't care who knew."

Chapter Sixteen

Suzannah looked as though someone had just hit her on the head with a brick. Carlo didn't think he'd ever seen her look so stunned. She shook her head slowly, as though unable to take in what he was telling her.

"It wasn't just your parents," she said finally. "It was everything... the whole world we were living in. You must have noticed the differences in the job offers we were getting. That offer from *Le Bourdain* was the final straw."

"An offer I had no interest in taking!" Carlo threw up his hands. "I honestly didn't care where I worked, so long as I was with you. Is that why you left, because you were... what, *jealous*?"

Her jaw jutted, and he was sure she ground her teeth before she snapped out "Yes, all right? I *was* jealous. I smashed headlong into the glass ceiling while you sailed through it like it didn't even exist, because of your gender and your family and your charm and... *everything*. I had to work my guts out to prove myself in every position I ever held, while you just had it all handed to you on a platter!"

Carlo opened his mouth to snap back at her, and then he closed it again. Finally, he said "You were always more ambitious than me, Suzannah. Maybe that's because of where you came from, and yeah, maybe I got opportunities you didn't because of male privilege and the advantages of my background. Ones I'm only just beginning to recognise now, if I'm completely honest, as I see how hard you've had to work to get to where you are. Particularly considering that you are without question the most gifted chef I've ever worked with."

Suzannah blinked at that, startled by the compliment, and Carlo nodded.

"I'm not just saying that. Hell, I was practically raised in the kitchen of one of Italy's best restaurants, and I wasn't within spitting distance of you when we were in training. I think you're the only person who even thought there was a competition. Everyone was so intimidated by your talent, not to mention your work ethic."

"Huh," she said, looking pole-axed. "Really?"

"Really." He reached out to touch one dangling red curl, wind it gently around his finger. "I had the biggest crush on you, *cara*. This magnificent red-haired goddess who cooked like an angel and gave anyone who had the temerity to speak to her a terrifying glare. Took me the longest time to figure out you were shy."

"I didn't know how to talk to any of you," Suzannah confessed. "Everyone was so socially adept, and you... well, there were always girls hanging all over you. I didn't want to be just another one of your groupies."

"Suzannah Monteil." He half-laughed, shaking his head with disbelief. "You could never be *just* anything. You were exceptional at nineteen; now, you're extraordinary."

Her emerald eyes were wide and soft as she gazed at him, and he wondered what she was thinking. She was too beautiful not to kiss, though, and Carlo was only a man, after all.

Their lips clung, Suzannah's arms curling up around his neck, her hands running into his hair as she kissed him back. It would have been so easy for him to lose himself, but he still didn't have an answer to his question.

"Why did you leave me?" He pulled back only far enough to ask.

"Because I was young and insecure," Suzannah answered finally. "We came from different worlds and we were headed in different directions. I didn't want to hang on your coat-tails in New York or anywhere else, didn't want to be the girl from the wrong side of the tracks who was the dark blemish in your glittering life. I had to find my own way, don't you see?"

"I do, and I see that you've succeeded without hanging on anyone's coat," Carlo said dryly. "Despite that glass ceiling and being from 'the wrong side of the tracks' as you call it. You're the youngest chef in Australia running a Michelin-starred restaurant and nobody can ever say you got an easy ride."

She nodded in agreement, a hint of pride entering her expression.

"So can we please put forever behind us any suggestion that you might somehow be not good enough for me? If anything, it's the other way around. I'm the one who's coasted through, had everything easy in life. I'm the hanger-on here."

"No," Suzannah protested, but Carlo reached up and touched his finger to her lips gently.

"I'm just hitching my wagon to your Michelin star."

She laughed at his joke, as he'd hoped she would, and she put her hand up to curl her fingers around his, her eyes soft. "This time, I'm not running, Carlo. I've found my place in the world and I'm putting down roots. If you want me, this is where we stay."

He kissed her again before gesturing around them, at the spectacularly beautiful beach, the lapping waves. “So much hardship, you ask me to endure! Such suffering!”

Suzannah giggled, and then her expression turned mischievous and she slid her hands up inside his T-shirt. “Take it off.”

He couldn’t help a look around.

“Yes, this is technically a public part of the island. But in three years living here, I’ve never run across anyone else in this particular spot.”

“On your head be it if we get caught mid coitus,” Carlo said with a grin, but he shucked his shirt readily enough and leaned back, taking his weight off Suzannah to help her remove her shirt too. She wasn’t wearing a bra underneath, her breasts spilling free to fill his hands, nipples already peaked with desire. He was about to close his mouth over one when a thought struck him.

“I don’t have a condom with me.”

Suzannah gave an overly-dramatic sigh, wiggled until she could put a hand into her back pocket, and pulled out a foil packet. “Do I have to think of everything?” she teased.

Carlo smiled, accepting it from her as she wiggled out of her trousers and underwear, lying spectacularly naked before him.

“Come on, catch up,” Suzannah demanded when he just stared at her in awestruck silence.

“Hey, steady on. If I rush we’re both liable to get sand in places where it’d be inconvenient, not to mention painful,” Carlo joked gently, spreading his T-shirt out under her hips. Suzannah chuckled and nodded to acknowledge his point, before making grabby hands at him as he took off the rest of his clothes. He was already hard, cock jutting eagerly towards her as he freed himself and rolled the condom on, careful not to get any sand on it.

Neither of them wanted foreplay. Suzannah hooked her legs around Carlo’s hips and pulled him to her, moaning with satisfaction as he sank deep into her welcoming core. He gasped to find her soaking, hot and slick enough for him to push in to the hilt with a single thrust.

“Yes,” Suzannah cried, arching up against him, hands reaching around to grab onto his butt and hold him hard against her. “Oh, yes, Carlo!”

“Fuck,” he gritted out through clenched teeth, bracing himself on his elbows and closing his eyes for a moment, pressing his brow to hers. He was too close to the edge, the novelty of making love out in the open, in broad daylight, on a beach where anyone could discover them, adding a spice to their lovemaking. One hand sank into warm, powdery sand; the other into Suzannah’s thick hair, holding onto her as he sought for a little control. “You feel so damn good.”

“You, too,” she whispered against his lips, her hips rocking against him in a delicious, slow movement which only shifted him in and out an inch or so each time, but felt good enough he knew he’d be seeing stars in short order.

"Too close," Carlo gasped against her mouth, but she shook her head, straining against him, a high-pitched whine in her throat telling him she was just as close, just as desperate. "Oh God... *Suzannah...*"

She sobbed his name in response, short nails digging into his buttocks as climax drew her body up into a taut arch. Relieved she'd found her release, Carlo allowed his own, closing his eyes and letting the pleasure wash over him.

"I love you," he whispered against Suzannah's mouth a few minutes later, and felt her smile against his lips. "Don't run out on me again. I couldn't take it a second time."

Her arms were tight around him. "I'm not going anywhere. You want out of this, you're going to have to leave... with me trying to drag you back the whole time."

The laugh which bubbled up out of him was pure relief, and he opened his eyes to see Suzannah smiling up at him, love clear in her emerald-green eyes.

"I'm sorry," she said, and he blinked.

"What for?"

"Running out on you all those years ago. I was a coward, I should have stayed and fought for you..."

Carlo shook his head quickly. "I don't blame you at all. In your shoes, I might well have run too. And hey... we were both young and naive. We might have hated each other in six months."

"True," her mouth quirked in a sad little smile. "I can't help feeling like we wasted too much time, though."

"We just took the time to grow up and come back to each other, that's all." He smoothed a red curl back from her brow. "Just promise me one thing?"

Smart woman, she asked "What?" rather than just saying she'd do anything.

"Promise me you'll *talk* to me about stuff that worries you in the future? I know you're used to being independent and not relying on anyone, but I can't correct any misapprehensions you're labouring under if you won't talk to me about them. Like me being the eldest son and somehow required to return to Italy and become the head of the family." He cocked an eyebrow at her and shook his head, wondering where she'd managed to get that idea. His own fault, he supposed. He hadn't talked much about his family, not wanting to rake up old wounds about Suzannah's lack of one.

Suzannah giggled at his wry comment. "I promise I'll talk to you before leaping to conclusions," she said through her laughter. "And I already do talk to you about problems - I trusted you enough to tell you about the saboteur, didn't I?"

"You certainly did." Carlo kissed her for that, and for the promise. "And we're gonna deal with whoever it is. Together. As well as B-Rex and his hot dogs."

"Do not talk to me about hot dogs!" She started laughing again as she poked his shoulder, and he grinned, stealing one more kiss before easing carefully back from her.

"C'mon. We've played hooky long enough. Let's get back and make sure nobody's burned down the kitchen in our absence."

"Don't joke about it!" Suzannah paused in shaking the sand out of her shirt to give him a reproachful look.

"You don't think they'd go that far, surely?" Carlo stared at her. "I mean, that fire, it was inconvenient but not life-threatening."

"Who knows what they'd do? I don't even know *why*," Suzannah said glumly.

"We'll figure it out." He reached for her hand. "You and me. Together."

Chapter Seventeen

Either word had gone round somehow about the new cameras being installed, or the saboteur was just biding their time, but nothing out of the ordinary happened over the next few days. *La Sirène* was busy as always, and with several big weddings to stage Carlo was kept too busy to even think about the problem, though he knew it was always on Suzannah's mind.

There was a very awkward conversation the day before the music stars were due to arrive, when Luke barged into Suzannah's office one afternoon and caught Carlo and Suzannah kissing, Suzannah on Carlo's lap in her office chair with her blouse half undone. She blushed fierily, Carlo said a lot of swear words in Italian, and Luke's eyebrows just about hit his hairline.

"I thought you two didn't like each other? No, never mind, I don't need the full story." Luke held his hands up in front of him. "Just don't let it affect your work."

"Never!" Suzannah promised immediately, Carlo only a breath behind her, and Luke nodded.

"You're both adults, and both professionals. I'll trust you to manage your own personal lives." He looked pointedly away as Suzannah rebuttoned her blouse.

"Thank you. Uh... did you want something?" Carlo asked as Luke turned to leave.

"Just Edouard out of my ear," Luke said over his shoulder. "He's been in my office three times in the last week whinging about Carlo sexually harassing you, Suzannah. I just wanted to make sure it was mutual." The door closed behind him, and they were left alone staring at each other in shock.

"What the..." Carlo paled with fury, fists clenching. "How *dare* he!"

"Easy," Suzannah patted his shoulders soothingly. "He's just looking out for me, Carlo - Edouard's been like an older brother to me. Though I'm not sure how he could have misconstrued anything you've done as sexual harassment." She frowned, puzzled. "You've never been anything but totally respectful in public."

"And yet he's gone to Luke three times with complaints?" Carlo snapped. "He wants me gone, Suzannah. You can't put any other spin on making complaints like that."

Concerned, Suzannah chewed on her lower lip. "Let me talk to him," she said quietly. "I'll explain we're together... it's probably time we came out in the open anyway. Someone's going to spot you sneaking into or out of my cabin one of these nights."

"I'm getting tired of that too, but if you think they don't all know already, you're kidding yourself. Julie thanked me today, and when I asked what for, she said 'putting the boss in such a good mood' and winked."

"Oh, God," Suzannah had to laugh. "How do you think they figured it out?"

"Like you said, somebody probably saw us. Or possibly heard us in here, one time. Or maybe just saw the way you're constantly undressing me with your eyes." He grinned teasingly, dark eyes alight with amusement.

"I do not!" She poked him in the ribs, still laughing. "Well, not *all* the time, anyway."

"Edouard totally got things the wrong way round. If anything, *I'm* the one getting harassed and objectified. I've seen Julie nudging you and teasing you that you should 'get a piece of that Italian stallion'."

"Stop it." He was obviously teasing, and she couldn't stop laughing. "I'll talk to Edouard. I promise. Cut this nonsense down before it goes any further. And yes... tonight we'll tell everyone. Together. Now cut it out, we need to head over to Jace's with the stuff we've got prepared for tomorrow."

***

Suzannah didn't get an opportunity to talk to Edouard that day. It was his evening off and he'd switched off his phone. Mindful that she'd promised Carlo they would bring their relationship into the open, though, she stood with her hand in his as the last plates were cleared from the dinner tables in the restaurant and told the staff that they were in a relationship.

Wolf-whistles erupted from the largely female staff.

"Go get it, Chef!" Julie hollered from the back of the room. Suzannah flipped her the bird, making Julie laugh loudly, and then several people were offering congratulations and saying how good they looked together. Samira, Carlo's shy cake decorator, gave Suzannah a very surprising hug and told her how happy Carlo seemed and that she was so pleased for them both.

"Take an early night, Chef." Julie made her way through the throng. "I can handle cleanup and prep for tomorrow. Go take that gorgeous stud to bed." She winked at Carlo, who laughed and kissed her cheek.

"You're outrageous." The assistant chef had grown enormously in confidence since Suzannah expressed her clear faith in Julie's abilities and pushed her to take on more responsibility. A fun, bubbly personality was surfacing, along with a boundless store of jokes which kept her co-workers in stitches.

"Just saying what all the other girls are thinking - that they wish they were getting to sample that hot Italian salami too!" Laughing, she embraced Suzannah before trotting back off across the kitchen to her workstation.

"Come on." Carlo's arm slid around Suzannah's waist and he tugged her towards the door. "Let's get out of here."

Smiling, she let him tug her outside, a chorus of well-wishes and crude suggestions following them. The staff would all have settled down by tomorrow, she knew; they were just letting off steam.

***

Suzannah and Carlo slept in the following morning. Knowing it was likely to be a very full couple of days, they'd done as much as they could the previous day. All ingredients and as much as could be prepared in advance were at Jace's house, safe from potential sabotage, and Suzannah would spend the day down there, leaving *La Sirène* for Carlo and Julie to manage.

As usual, the restaurant was fully booked out, plus there was a twenty-person sixtieth birthday party for a wealthy guest in the private dining room at lunchtime and a fifty-person wedding dinner that evening. They quite simply couldn't afford the time for anything to go wrong.

"Good luck with B-Rex and Myst," Carlo said as the two of them parted outside Suzannah's cabin. "I'll come down after lunch is finished and see how things are going. Don't stress about *La Sirène*. I'll look after your baby."

"I know you will." Suzannah kissed him and set off to collect a golf cart, her mind already on the day ahead. She'd never worked with a film crew before and had no idea what to expect; even though she wouldn't be on camera, she'd still be jumping to the director's cues.

Luke was at Jace's house when Suzannah arrived, greeting her warmly. "They've already started filming," he told her as she headed for the kitchen. "The director will call me when they're ready for us. You'll get half an hour to walk B-Rex through what he has to do to complete the dishes."

"It won't take that long," Suzannah said, and then rethought. She could show a trainee chef in about five minutes, but B-Rex had seemed pretty clueless.

"This is Myst's partner, George Dennis," Luke said, gesturing as a tall man unfolded himself from a chair at the kitchen table. "Like us, he's rather in the way next door so Jace invited him over here."

"Hey," George said with an awkward wave. Suzannah tried not to gape at him, because she knew exactly who he was. Captain of the Australian international rugby union team, she'd had no idea he was dating the pop star. "Uh, Myst and I aren't publicly together yet..."

"My lips are sealed." She mimed locking them and throwing away the key, making George smile. Waving him to sit down again, Suzannah opened the refrigerator. "All right, I'm going to get started on making the pasta. I made lots of the sauce, I've lost the ability to cater for small parties, I'm afraid, so we'll all have to have some for lunch. Use it up and make sure it's okay for Myst to eat, hm?"

George nodded enthusiastically at that. Suzannah smiled to herself as she set up the kitchen machine and started weighing her ingredients. She'd fed plenty of sports stars in the restaurant, and they all enjoyed their food. Keeping George happy would be simple, and hopefully his appreciation would influence Myst too.

"Where are Nessa and Jace?" she asked Luke quietly as George returned his attention to a tablet on the table in front of him.

"Gone on an all-day dive trip," Luke said. "They figured you didn't need them underfoot as well."

That was incredibly thoughtful of Nessa and Jace, and Suzannah felt a surge of affection for the pair. She would make sure to leave some special treats in the fridge for them, she thought.

"I don't need you hovering, either," she said teasingly to Luke. "Go sit down with your laptop or something. I don't need any extra hands, trust me; I *can* still cook without an entire kitchen full of assistants!"

"I wouldn't doubt it for a moment." Luke grinned broadly. "But I did plan to offer to do your washing-up."

"Oh stop it, you're being adorable." She waved him off, and he left her with a grin, going to join George at the table and opening his laptop.

Suzannah got to work, tuning out the two men as she set the mixer going on the pasta, prepared a dough and left it to rise for the herb and garlic damper she'd serve alongside the pasta, and pulled out the ingredients for the fresh pesto sauce she intended to make. Although she'd considered preparing it the day before, she did prefer to have everything as fresh as possible. Julie's boyfriend had delivered a box of fresh herbs to Jace's that morning by special request, and Suzannah hummed happily as she washed the fragrant basil, parsley and oregano.

It wasn't until George started humming along with her that Suzannah realised she was singing Ricky Martin. Laughing to herself even as she never stilled the movements of her hands, she mused on just how easily Carlo had slotted into her life. It was just so darn comfortable having him around; from knowing she had someone in her corner she could trust absolutely and confide in, to the way he made her take time out to relax and enjoy herself outside of work.

Her phone vibrated in her pocket, but only briefly, indicating the arrival of a text message. In no hurry to answer it, she finished what she was doing and washed her hands before fishing it out.

Everything under control here. Love you.

"That's a seriously goofy grin," Luke commented, making Suzannah look up with a start. She blushed and shoved her phone back into her pocket. Luke smiled, not unkindly. "Suits you."

"Thanks," she mumbled a bit sheepishly, and then jumped as a phone rang. It wasn't hers, though. Luke snatched his phone up off the table, frowned as he glanced at the display, then answered it.

"Luke speaking. Okay... yes, put him through." He looked across at Suzannah with a slight frown, then turned his back and strode over to the huge sliding doors leading out to the pool area, opening one of them slightly to step outside. "Go ahead," Suzannah heard him say before he closed the door again.

Shrugging, she returned to work. Less than a minute later, though, Luke came back inside, looking a little pale under his tan.

"Something urgent's come up," he said hurriedly. "I have to get back to the resort for a while. I'll come back as soon as I can."

"Don't worry," Suzannah told him. "I've got everything under control here." He looked concerned, she thought, if not a little shocked; obviously he desperately needed to be somewhere else. She waved a hand towards the front door. "Go, Luke. I've got this."

Luke nodded and was gone without another word.

"Sounds like a crisis," George observed from his seat at the table. "I suppose you get a lot of that in this industry. Difficult customers and stuff?"

"I could tell you some stories," Suzannah said with a laugh, hoping to distract him from wondering what was bothering Luke. "Anonymously, of course!"

"I bet." The big rugby player grinned wryly. "I'm getting a fascinating insight into the entertainment industry dating Myst, I can tell you. Did you know B-Rex's real name is Brian?"

Chapter Eighteen

The kitchen seemed somehow empty without Suzannah, Carlo thought. Julie had really stepped up, though. Obviously determined to justify her boss's faith in her, the assistant chef was crisply issuing orders and keeping everyone on their toes, her eyes everywhere. Samira and the others in the pastry kitchen seemed determined to show what they could do as well, and with half an hour to go before lunch would start to be served Carlo found himself at a loose end.

Not wanting to hang about and put the staff off their groove, he decided to take himself off to Suzannah's office for a little while and work on her computer. He knew the new surveillance cameras Luke had installed could be accessed from there; he might as well pass a little time and look to see if he could spot anything suspicious.

Taking a seat at Suzannah's desk, he tapped keys to wake up her computer, thinking he should really warn her to password-protect it. It was another target for potential sabotage, after all.

As he rolled the cold room surveillance camera backwards at high speed, going through the last two hours' worth of footage in ten minutes, he pulled out his phone and sent her a text, not expecting a reply. Nothing out of the ordinary was happening on the tape, the usual staff members zooming in and out in comically jerky, swift motions, before he reached what was obviously the start of the morning shift and the movement in the cold room stopped.

Not inclined to sit through a lot of boring nothingness, Carlo reached for the mouse to increase the speed for a while; he'd go back to about eleven the previous evening, when the last things from dinner would have been cleared up.

A flash of colour on the screen arrested his attention just before he clicked, and Carlo frowned. What had he just seen? He paused the camera instead of increasing the rewind speed, played forward again.

"What the *hell*?" he said aloud as he watched someone who had no business in the cold room at all entering. And then he stiffened, eyes opening wide with horror.

Snatching up the phone on the desk, he hit the speed-dial button for Luke's office, asked his secretary to connect Luke immediately.

"Go ahead," Luke's voice said a few moments later.

"Are you with Suzannah right now?"

"I'm outside, and I'm wondering why you're calling me instead of her."

"I've found the saboteur, and I need you back here right now before I confront them. Without telling Suzannah, because she needs her head in the game there."

"Is there an imminent threat to health and safety if you wait?" Luke asked after a moment of shocked silence.

"No."

"I'll be there in ten minutes. Sit tight."

"Will do." Carlo hung up as the line went dead, clicked the mouse and dragged it back to watch the thirty seconds of damning footage he'd found over again.

The sommelier Edouard entered the cold room, glancing over his shoulder. His royal-blue formal jacket was the flash of colour which had caught Carlo's eye, as Edouard walked quickly along the cold room, withdrawing a syringe from his pocket. He stopped right in front of the cake stand at the end of the room before taking off the protective dome and plunging the syringe into the birthday cake prepared for that afternoon's celebration. Just seconds later, he was dropping the syringe back into his pocket and walking back the way he'd come.

"Un-fucking-believable," Carlo said softly, and then he paused the camera feed and hurried out of Suzannah's office, returning to the pastry kitchen and pulling Samira aside. She looked at him with wide eyes.

"Is something the matter, Chef Gianetti?"

"The birthday cake's been sabotaged," he said very quietly. "I know who did it; I'm waiting for Mr Collyer to get here so we can confront them. I need you to quickly and quietly prepare a replacement cake. Fortunately the birthday guest may be wealthy, but he has simple tastes; he just wanted a chocolate fudge cake. You've got a couple hours to get it done."

Samira's eyes narrowed angrily as he spoke, her jaw setting stubbornly. "I won't let you down, Chef," she promised, keeping her voice low as he had done.

"Good. No matter what happens, that cake has to be ready, okay?"

"It will be." She looked both proud and determined, and he was certain he could leave the cake in her capable hands. With a quick glance around to check all was in order, he went back into the main kitchen and intercepted Julie.

"Mr Collyer's on his way in to address a problem. I'll be meeting with him in Suzannah's office; unless the restaurant is literally on fire, nobody is to disturb us, okay?"

Julie looked startled, but she nodded. "Anything I should know about?" she queried.

"You'll know all about it shortly." Seeing the anxiety in her expression, Carlo lowered his voice. "You're not in trouble, Julie. Just hold the fort a little while longer, okay? And make sure nobody disturbs Samira. She's got a special job to do for me."

"You got it, Chef."

He saw the same pride and determination come into her expression as he'd seen in Samira's, and nodded. "Thank you."

Julie nodded in return before returning to her work with renewed vigour, and Carlo headed back to Suzannah's office. He brought up a second window on the computer and found the current surveillance feed from the main restaurant. Edouard was clearly visible, moving about between tables as customers began placing their drinks orders, heading for the wine pantry and returning with bottles.

It was possible Edouard had sabotaged something else, but Carlo didn't think so. The sommelier was deliberately targeting desserts for a reason, and Carlo had a pretty fair guess as to what it might be. Obviously, he was hoping to get away with it, and sabotaging something else would make it twice as likely he'd be caught.

A rap on the door had him glancing up and calling "Come in!"

Luke entered, an uncharacteristic frown on his face. "I was honestly hoping this was all some sort of series of unfortunate coincidences," he said as he closed the door. "I didn't want to believe anyone here would deliberately try to sabotage the restaurant."

"You're really not going to like this, then." Carlo stood and gestured for Luke to take his seat.

Luke looked almost sick, but he sat down and set his jaw, watching as Carlo brought up the short piece of damning surveillance footage.

"No *way!*" Luke's jaw dropped as he watched. "*Edouard?*" He looked up at Carlo. "You don't seem surprised?"

"I'm not, really. He's wanted me gone from the moment I got here."

"But the sabotage started before you arrived," Luke pointed out. "After Vicky was fired."

They stared at each other in speculation before Luke shook his head. "We're not getting anywhere just guessing. I don't want to do this here, either. I'm going to go out into the restaurant and ask Edouard to accompany me to my office. I'll imply I've uncovered some evidence about his claims of you harassing Suzannah, if that's what it takes to get him to come with me. You go and meet us there." Picking up the desk phone, he tapped a key to speed-dial his own office.

"Put me through to the police station at Airlie," he requested, "and then get the helicopter on standby. They're going to need to bring officers over here."

Carlo pursed his lips in a silent whistle, but he met Luke's eyes and nodded. Edouard would have to be held to account for what he'd done. And the cake was evidence; they didn't even know what the substance was Edouard had injected. It could even be lethal.

With that thought, Carlo headed for the cold room with a roll of tape he'd picked up from Suzannah's desk drawer. He took a couple of minutes to tape the cover dome down over the cake stand and securely taped on a note which said DO NOT TOUCH, with his signature at the bottom. Hopefully, that and the surveillance tapes would satisfy the police that the cake hadn't been tampered with by anyone except Edouard.

Ten minutes later, he arrived at Luke's office and was waved in by Luke's secretary. He was quite relieved to see Cory, the resort's activities director, sitting in the waiting room leafing through a magazine, apparently just killing time. A big, well-muscled guy, Cory glanced up to catch Carlo's eye and gave him a slight nod.

Not that Carlo thought he and Luke couldn't handle Edouard if the sommelier should by any chance turn violent, but having large, intimidating backup on hand until the police arrived was always useful.

Edouard looked positively smug as Carlo entered, and he had to wonder what Luke had said to get the sommelier looking like that. Edouard probably believed he was about to witness Carlo getting his marching orders.

"I have some surveillance footage here I'd like you to look at," Luke said, after inviting Carlo to take a seat. "I believe you'll find it pretty damning."

Edouard still looked insufferably smug. Carlo wondered what he thought he was about to see, but it certainly wasn't the footage from the new hidden camera in the cold room which Luke played for them on his large desktop screen.

The silence in the room was almost deafening until Luke said quietly "I should advise you that this meeting is being recorded, by the way, and will be turned over to the police when they arrive, along with the footage I've just shown you, and the cake which Carlo has taken steps to secure as evidence."

Pale-faced, Edouard seemed almost to have shrunk into his seat. He just shook his head and said nothing.

"Was it poison?" Carlo had to ask. "Would someone have died?"

"No!" The sommelier flinched. He didn't seem inclined to say any more, though, not even when Luke slammed his hand down on the desk.

"Why? Tell me that! What reason could you possibly have for doing this?"

Luke was furious, Carlo realised, barely holding his temper in. Edouard didn't answer the question, however, and Luke audibly ground his teeth together.

"Maybe he'll be more inclined to talk to the police," Carlo said. "I think I hear the helicopter now."

"Good," Luke ground out, "because the sooner this madman is off the island, the happier I'll be!"

***

Carlo and Luke saw Edouard handcuffed and escorted onto the helicopter by one police officer, to be returned to the mainland and taken into custody there, while the other accompanied them back to the restaurant to take the cake into evidence. They found the used syringe hidden in the wine pantry, and the police officer sniffed as she carefully bagged and labelled it.

"Nasty business. Good thing you spotted him on the cameras."

They'd handed her a USB key with copies of the incriminating surveillance footage, too, and she told them the lab would prioritise identifying the contents of the syringe. Her partner would hold off questioning Edouard until she returned to the police station, and she promised to keep Luke updated if he decided to talk. All he'd said as he was placed under arrest was "I want a lawyer", so it was doubtful they'd have any answers quickly.

"I'm going to head down and see Suzannah," Carlo said as Luke and the police officer prepared to leave the restaurant.

"Break the news?"

"I'll have to." He wasn't looking forward to it. Suzannah would be devastated at the betrayal of her trust; he knew she'd considered Edouard as like an older brother. Still, he wouldn't have her hear it from anyone else.

Chapter Nineteen

Luke had only been gone a couple of minutes when a harried production assistant came in and asked Suzannah to go to the other house, where the video crew wanted to talk to her about what she'd be doing. George tagged along behind, and Suzannah watched in amusement as he and Myst practically fell on each other. It was obviously a very new romance, she thought - well, it had to be if they were still worried about keeping it quiet from the press.

Myst, as petite and beautiful in real life as she was on the screen, looked tiny in George's burly arms. The menacing-looking rugby player was clearly besotted, and the pop star just as evidently returned the feeling, despite George's battered face. Suzannah felt warm just looking at them.

"It's the ginger babe!" a voice exclaimed, and she sighed as B-Rex approached, grinning.

"Nice to meet you at last... Brian," she said, and B-Rex laughed good-naturedly.

"Aw, you discovered my dirty secret. It kinda destroys my mystique when you know about it, yah?"

He was actually a sweetheart, Suzannah decided. "You destroyed your mystique when you asked a haute cuisine chef for hot dogs, I'm afraid," she told him.

"Hot dogs?" another voice interjected, horrified. "That's not what we ordered, is it? B-Rex, what did you do?"

"Your secret's safe with me," Suzannah whispered as B-Rex looked briefly panic-stricken, and then she stepped past him to offer her hand to the older man she assumed was the producer, or director or whatever they called it. "Just a joke, sir."

"Good, good." The director looked relieved. "Okay, come through this way and we'll do a walk-through. You can explain to me what food you have and what B-Rex will have to do on screen, and then we'll do a dry run."

There was an awful lot of standing about involved in shooting a music video, Suzannah soon discovered, and going over the same thing over and over again until they had everything precisely cued to the music. Which meant she had to coach B-Rex through serving the pasta onto two plates, sprinkling pine nuts over the top with artistic flair and carrying them to the table, in the space of exactly nineteen seconds.

While she was working through that, trying not to get exasperated with the musician's fumbling, the camera crew were out on the beach with Myst, filming her walking in the edge of the water, lip-syncing along with the music being pumped from a large speaker.

"Like this," Suzannah said, taking the serving tongs from B-Rex and showing him the deft little twist of her wrist which swirled the tagliatelle into a perfect little cone.

The rapper sighed, but he took the tongs again as she tipped the pasta back into the pan. "I wonder if we could cut the scene from me lifting the pasta from the pan, to putting the plates on the table?" he said. "You could do the presentation bit, that way."

"I'm more than happy to, but I don't think that's part of the director's vision. So let's see if you can't get it right. You nearly had it last time," Suzannah encouraged.

"It smells fantastic. Can't I have a taste?" B-Rex wheedled.

"Of course you can." She opened a drawer and found a fork, handed it over. "Have you had lunch yet?"

On discovering they hadn't eaten since an early breakfast, Suzannah insisted B-Rex sit down and eat a plate of the pasta with a hearty chunk of damper on the side. George had already wolfed down a huge helping and pronounced it fantastic, and Suzannah watched with pleasure as B-Rex took a mouthful and his eyes lit up.

"Shit. This is your hot cuisine?"

"*Haute* cuisine," she corrected him, smiling. "It means high - it's French."

"Don't think I'd appreciate it as much if I was high," B-Rex said quite seriously, and she had to cover her mouth to stifle a laugh.

Myst came in from the beach then, flushed and warm, and George immediately rushed to get her a glass of iced water. The producer wanted to take her straight back outside but George wasn't having any of it, insisting Myst needed to eat.

The director looked all set to argue until George stood directly in front of him and scowled. The rugby player looked intimidating as hell, at which point the director decided he'd quite like some lunch himself, actually.

It was as good as watching a comedy on TV, Suzannah decided, once again having to stifle her laughter. She was having fun, she realised, even out of her element as she was. She was dying to tell Carlo about all of this later.

As though her thoughts had summoned him, he arrived at that moment, escorted by the harried production assistant. He smiled as B-Rex got up to shake his hand and greeted George and Myst politely when they were introduced, but Suzannah thought he looked worried about something. When everyone's attention was returned to what they'd been doing before, he came up quietly beside Suzannah and put his arm around her waist.

"Everything okay, *cara*?"

"It's been fun, actually. B-Rex is getting the hang of the presentation."

"Good."

"Everything okay at the restaurant?" Carlo seemed distracted, and that got Suzannah worrying. When he hesitated, she frowned and said "Excuse us a moment," to the room at large before grabbing his hand and almost dragging him outside.

"Spit it out," she demanded. "What's happened?"

"I'm so sorry," Carlo said, his eyes anguished. "I'm so sorry, *cara*... we caught the saboteur."

"Carlo, you're frightening me! What's happened? Is anyone hurt?"

He shook his head quickly. "No, it was on Luke's new surveillance camera in the cold room. He was injecting something into the birthday cake for Mr Hodges' party. Suzannah - it was Edouard."

Suzannah stared at him incredulously. "No," she said after a minute of shocked silence. "No, you can't... no. Not Edouard."

"I'm so sorry," Carlo said again, reaching out his arms towards her, and she collapsed against him, feeling suddenly cold and sick.

"*Why?*" she gasped, anguished.

"He wouldn't say." Carlo smoothed his hands down her back soothingly. "Luke and I confronted him, but all he said was that he wanted a lawyer. He's been taken into police custody. They'll let us know if he decides to talk."

Wounded to the core by the betrayal of someone she had trusted, Suzannah groaned against Carlo's shoulder. He tightened his arms around her, just held her for long moments as she came to terms with it and slowly pulled herself back together.

"What do you want to do?" Carlo asked, and she loved him for offering her the choice. "If you need some time, I can take over here, and Julie has the restaurant safely in hand. Or you could head back there and reassure yourself everything is okay, or carry on here... whatever you need, we'll make it work."

For a long moment, she held tightly to his solid strength, trying to absorb his calm into herself, and then she lifted her head.

"We carry on as we planned. I'll stay here until they wrap filming for the day and then come on over to the restaurant. The director said they'll wrap right after sunset, so I'll be over there by the time dinner really gets going."

He didn't ask if she was sure, just put his arm around her and accompanied her back into the house. "I can stay an hour, *cara*," he said, and she nodded, grateful for his steadying presence.

She was especially grateful when, a couple of minutes after they walked back into the kitchen area, Myst leapt up from where she'd been sitting at the table talking with the director after eating and bolted outside to throw up at the foot of a large palm tree.

"*Merde!*" Suzannah bolted right after her, panicking. Had Edouard somehow managed to sabotage her ingredients before she brought them over here? But others had eaten the pasta, George ate a whole bowl of it, and hadn't been ill...

Myst held out a hand to hold Suzannah at bay, giving her a weak smile. "Morning sickness," she whispered. "Shh."

George was right on Suzannah's heels, gathering Myst's long hair in his big hand and holding it back from her face, wrapping his other arm around her supportively. Realising she was both incorrect in her assumptions and unwanted on the scene, Suzannah retreated hastily.

Carlo was hanging onto the edge of the kitchen bench, looking almost as queasy and panicked as Suzannah had felt a moment earlier. She met his eyes and shook her head, smiling.

"Nothing to do with us, she's pregnant," she said, speaking in rapid French, and Carlo immediately looked relieved.

"Thank God," he said. "For a moment there, I panicked."

"Me too." Suzannah let him draw her into a close embrace. B-Rex and the director were the only other people in the room, the crew on a short break, and the two men were obviously already aware of Myst's condition. B-Rex was eating his pasta unconcernedly and the director rose to approach Suzannah and Carlo, expression wary.

"Obviously, with Myst and George's relationship not yet public, her condition has to remain a secret as well," he began, and Suzannah at once held up her hand to stop him.

"As far as we're concerned, the confidentiality agreement we signed regarding the video shoot covers everything which happens on site," she said firmly.

The director looked relieved. "What happens on Sunfish Island, stays on Sunfish Island?" he joked.

"Stays in this room. You don't want to know what the island gossip network is like," Carlo said dryly. "Please believe, nobody will hear of this from us."

"Thank you," it was Myst's voice, a little thin and weak, as George solicitously let her back inside and over to the luxurious designer couch in the living area. "I'm so sorry I threw up your wonderful pasta, Suzannah - I promise, it was nothing you did." The pop star grimaced as she sat down. "I've barely been able to keep anything down for the last week. Whoever called it *morning* sickness was a bloody liar."

Suzannah lost no time in going over and crouching before Myst, reaching to touch her hand. "Is there anything we can get for you? It's no trouble to make anything. Anything you want, we've got the ingredients. I hear ginger's good for morning sickness, I had a friend who couldn't keep down anything but ginger oatmeal biscuits and ginger ale for a couple of weeks in her early pregnancy.

Still, it was more calories than none." She was babbling, she realised, but she was genuinely concerned, and George was giving her a grateful look, obviously appreciative of her kindness.

"That... actually sounds not totally unappealing," Myst said after a few moments of consideration. "I can't promise I'll keep it down, but at least the *thought* doesn't make me want to hurl."

Suzannah turned to look at Carlo, but he was already heading for the door. "I'll see if Jace has what I need," he called over his shoulder on the way out. "If not, I'll run back to *La Sirène* and make a batch!"

"Thank you so much," George said gratefully.

"As I said, it's no trouble at all," Suzannah said. "We're here to provide anything you need."

"In that case," B-Rex put in behind her, "about those hot dogs?"

Chapter Twenty

Carlo was rather surprised when Suzannah came to join him in Jace's kitchen shortly afterwards, wiping tears of laughter from her eyes. He was just sliding the first batch of cookies into the oven.

"Good thing this kitchen's so well stocked," he said, "though I had to use ground ginger. I'll go back to *La Sirène* and make some for her with fresh after, but the poor girl can't have eaten much in days. No wonder she looks like a breath of wind could blow her away."

"Oh, no, she's so stunning," Suzannah said wistfully. "And did you see the way George looked at her?"

Carlo looked at her strangely as he closed the oven door, and then he straightened up and came over to her. "Like a man hopelessly in love, terrified the woman in his arms might turn out to be just a beautiful dream he can't hold onto?" he asked.

"Yes," Suzannah said in surprise. "Yes, exactly like that."

"Do you realise that's how I look at you?" His strong, capable hands settled at her waist and he looked earnestly into her eyes. "*Cara*, to me, you're far lovelier than any waifish pop princess. You're a strong, beautiful, confident woman, the most talented chef I've ever known, and I've been hopelessly in love with you since I was nineteen."

"Really?" Suzannah's green eyes went very wide, and Carlo shook his head, laughing softly.

"How do you not *know* this, Suzannah? Have I not made it obvious? I've barely noticed another woman since I was a teenager, because none of them could even hold a candle to you. I came here hoping, praying you'd give me a second chance that whatever took you away from me back then was no longer an issue. That I'd grown up to be worthy of you." Carlo hardly dared to blink as he spoke, baring his soul to her. Praying she wouldn't reject him again.

"*You*, not worthy?" She gaped at him. "But it was always *me*..."

"Only in your own head." Carlo refused to hear it any more. "This is the twenty-first century. Nobody cares what sort of family you came from or what suburb you grew up in, Suzannah. They respect you for what you've made of yourself, and I respect you *more* knowing that you did come from humble beginnings and have ascended to the very top."

"You do?"

Carlo shook his head, half-laughing, and then he took his hands off her waist and reached up to frame her face with them. "I love you," he told her, as plain and clear as he could, and then he repeated it in French, Italian and Spanish for good measure.

Suzannah's beautiful smile dawned as he stumbled through the words in German, and she giggled when he attempted Mandarin. "Stop. Stop! I believe you!"

"Oh good," Carlo said gratefully. "I was all set to try Japanese and Russian too, but Takeshi said my accent was so bad he didn't even understand me."

"You idiot." She leaned in and pressed her lips to his. "You only needed to say it once. I love you, too."

"Good." He kissed her back, lingeringly, and they lost themselves in each other until the oven timer Carlo had the foresight to set began beeping.

"The cookies!" they both cried in unison, and Carlo dived for the oven.

They returned next door with a plate of warm ginger oatmeal cookies, both uncaring of how they looked, Suzannah's lips kiss-swollen and her chin and reddened from Carlo's stubble, his hair standing up every which way from Suzannah running her fingers through it. Myst and George were oblivious, focused on each other, but B-Rex gave them a decidedly amused look.

"Didn't know 'baking cookies' could be so much fun," he drawled. Suzannah stuffed a cookie in his mouth as she passed, grinning at him. He chuckled and took a hearty bite.

Suzannah was fairly sure George was going to end up eating more of the cookies than Myst, but the diminutive pop star was nibbling on one at least, and colour seemed to be coming back into her cheeks. They'd undertake to keep her supplied with as many as she wanted while she was on the island, and Carlo had already decided he'd be sending a large care packet with her when she left.

Luke arrived shortly afterwards, just in time for them all to be kicked out again so the dinner-serving scene could be filmed at sunset.

"The police called," he said succinctly. "Edouard's lawyer took one look at the surveillance footage and advised Edouard to make a full confession immediately. Turns out he was having a secret affair with Vicky and was furious you sacked her Suzannah. It was as simple as that."

"So simple, and yet he could have ruined everything." Suzannah shook her head and sighed sadly. "What will happen to him now?"

"That'll depend on what deal his lawyer can negotiate with the prosecutor." Luke shrugged. "If he's lucky, he'll avoid jail time - but almost certainly his visa will be revoked. He'll have to go back to France and try to find work there."

Suzannah spared a few moments to regret the end of a friendship she had genuinely valued, but it was clear Edouard had never been who she'd thought. "Thanks for letting us know," she said quietly to Luke, who nodded and gave her a sympathetic smile before his phone rang yet again and he excused himself to take the call.

"I'd better get back to the restaurant," Carlo said regretfully. He hadn't let go of Suzannah's hand for more than a few seconds since the cookies came out of the oven, and she seemed just as reluctant as he to let go now, pulling closer to him for a few moments and nestling her face into the curve of his neck. He put his arms around her and held on tight.

"I'll be back as soon as I can," she promised, before turning her face up to his and smiling. "And Carlo?"

"Yes, *cara*?" He couldn't resist stealing a kiss, as close as she was.

"I'm not running out on you this time. Not ever again." Emerald eyes were bright and very earnest as she gazed on him. "And if you dare run out on me, I'll chase you down until I catch you."

"Wild horses couldn't drag me away, *cara*." Carlo knew, for certain, he was in for the long haul. He and Suzannah were going to earn another Michelin star, maybe even two, and he was going to get her in front of a TV camera if it was the last thing he did. Suzannah Monteil was born to be a star, even if she was too modest to realise it.

***

Five months later

"Hey, sit down." Luke rose to greet them as Suzannah and Carlo entered his office. He was smiling broadly, so they knew they hadn't done anything wrong; it was likely good news he'd called them in to deliver. But the new Michelin guide wasn't due for a couple of months, so it couldn't be that. Glancing at each other speculatively, they took the indicated seats in front of Luke's desk.

"You look like the cat who just ate a canary," Carlo remarked. "I can practically still see the yellow feathers twitching."

Luke grinned. "Tweet, tweet. I never really thought this day would come."

"What day?" Suzannah demanded, impatient as ever.

For answer, Luke set a magazine down on the desk, *Australian Gourmet Dining*. "It's the annual Best Restaurants issue," he said. "Page twenty. Take a look."

Suzannah's fingers shook as she fumbled through the glossy pages, Carlo's head tilted close to hers as they both peered at the magazine. Finally it fell open to the right page, and they stared at the half-page, glossy photo of the two of them, one taken from the resort's website publicity pages.

"Best restaurant in Queensland?" Suzannah read the caption underneath the photo incredulously, before her head snapped up and she stared at Luke. "Is this real?"

"It certainly is." Luke's grin widened even further. "Not only that, you're fifth in the entire *country*."

Suzannah's eyes filled with tears, but Carlo knew they were happy ones. It was an incredible achievement for a restaurant in its first five years of operation to make that list, and it was largely down to Suzannah's talent and hard work. He put his arms around her and kissed her brow as she tilted her head down to put her face into her hands, crying happy tears into them.

They both knew what it meant; that second star was all but in the bag. All of the top ten restaurants in the country in the previous year's edition of the magazine had earned at least two stars.

"You earned this," Carlo said fiercely into Suzannah's ear. "Every bit of this is down to you; it should be your picture alone in there. Not me stealing your glory."

She shook her head, pulling her hands away and frowning at him. "No, Carlo. Look." She stabbed her finger at the facing page of the magazine, where several photos of dishes served at La Sirène accompanied the article. "That's your lemon and mint souffle, and your bush honey and macadamia cheesecake. We're a *team*."

Carlo stared at her, at the pride and determination in her expression, and he'd never loved her more than right at that moment.

"Will you marry me?"

The words came out without conscious thought, but he knew as soon as he said them it was the right time, the perfect moment.

"Ahem," Luke said, and they both looked at him, startled. "Clearly you've forgotten I'm here, so I'll just, ah, not be here. Take as long as you like. Bye. And if it's not too premature, congratulations!" He practically ran from the room, closing the door firmly behind him.

Suzannah couldn't help it; she started to laugh. "Oh, Carlo. You just made poor Luke flee his own office in embarrassment!"

He grinned. "I've been trying to scare other men away from you for years; it finally worked!"

It took several minutes for both of them to stop laughing, but finally Suzannah clasped his hands in hers and leaned in to kiss him, giggles still intermittently bursting out of her.

"Yes," she said. "Of course, Carlo. I'd love to. I love *you*."

~ The End ~

Thank you for taking the time to read Suzannah and Carlo's story!

Read on for ***Fighting Fate,*** *Rosie's story, as she finds herself falling for a former MMA fighter recuperating from serious injury on the island!*

And if you enjoyed reading about George and Myst and would like to learn how the rugby player and the pop star fell in love, you can find their story in Star Rucked Lovers!

Fighting Fate

Island Escapes Book 5

Caitlyn Lynch

SHENANIGANS PRESS

shenaniganspress.com/EN

Contents

Chapter One

"You look *incredible*, Rosie!"

Turning to admire her reflection in the mirror, Rosie smiled. "I do, don't I?"

Privately, she thought she'd never looked so good. Wearing one of her glamorous friend Olivia's designer gowns from her New York days, Rosie's slightly-too-plump figure looked nothing short of fabulous, curves in all the right places. Her beauty therapist friend Shae had done her hair and makeup without asking why it was that Rosie wanted to look particularly special tonight, and she looked naturally fresh and beautiful, yet somehow sultry and sexy at the same time.

"It's like magic," Rosie mused, "clothes and makeup really can turn an ugly duckling into a swan."

"Tell me you didn't just call yourself an ugly duckling!" Her best friend Jill pushed off the door frame where she'd been leaning, admiring how Rosie looked, and came over to grab her shoulders. "You're gorgeous, girl. Not just tonight, but every day. I keep telling you, I'd give anything for your cleavage."

"You'd look ridiculous with my cleavage. Like a Barbie," Rosie pointed out practically, and Jill laughed, not offended in the least. Chinese-Australian, Jill was slight of frame, almost Rosie's polar opposite.

"Well, some of your cleavage, anyway." Jill gave Rosie's bosom, well-displayed by the clinging fabric of the dress, an envious gaze. "You'll have all eyes on it tonight!"

Rosie didn't care about all eyes, just one particular set, but that was a secret she held very close to her heart.

"Any particular set of eyes you're hoping to catch?" Jill pressed lightly.

Rosie gave her a quelling look in the mirror.

"Fair enough, I won't pry." Jill held her hands up in surrender, backing towards the bathroom door. "I'll just say good luck, eh? Have a good night!"

"Thanks," Rosie said softly, but Jill was already gone. Rosie returned to checking her reflection, fluffing the soft waves Shae had coaxed her normally straight brown hair into, still amazed by her own transformation into the siren she saw in the mirror.

It doesn't matter what I think, what anyone else thinks. Only what Luke thinks.

With a determined sigh, Rosie squared her shoulders and turned to exit the bathroom. She'd forgotten the spiky heels she was wearing, though, and skidded, having to catch herself against the door.

Phew, that was almost a disastrous start to the evening! She refused to take it as a bad omen, though, stepping more carefully as she exited her bedroom into the small living area of the cabin she and Jill shared in the private staff area of Sunfish Island Resort.

On duty that evening, Jill was already gone. Rosie left the cabin into the warm, fragrantly scented evening, pausing to pick a beautiful hot-pink frangipani flower from a tree and place it carefully behind her right ear, with a private little smile for the symbolism. *Behind the right ear if seeking a relationship, behind the left ear if taken*. It came from Hawaiian culture originally, and she wondered if Luke knew its meaning.

Probably, she thought as she walked the path towards one of the sprawling resort's conference centres. She was pretty sure Luke Collyer, Sunfish Island's general manager, had done a stint on Hawaii at some point in his career in hotel management. Maybe she'd ask him tonight, ask if he understood the symbolism of the flower. Could be a good way to lead up to what she'd been wanting to ask him for years now.

She could hear the music coming from the conference centre already, quickened her step. Tonight was the second of two staff parties for the Sunfish Island staff; because the resort never shut down, the party was split over two nights to ensure everyone was able to attend at least one of them, their role covered by other staff members for the evening.

There was a buffet and tables in one half of the big conference room, a disco going on in the other half. Rosie laughed as her friend Bryce the dive instructor waved her over to dance, and mimed eating first, pointing at the buffet. Bryce nodded with a grin and returned to dancing with his wife Lucy, a pretty marine biologist who worked at the resort's environmental research centre.

Starving hungry since she'd skipped lunch, Rosie headed for the buffet and loaded a plate with finger food. Getting a glass of wine from the bar to go with it, she balanced it in one hand with her plate and paused at the side of the room, scanning the dance floor.

No Luke yet, she concluded. Undoubtedly he'd be making sure all was running smoothly around the resort before coming to the party. With a staff of several hundred and between two and five thousand guests on the island at any given time, Luke was never really off duty.

He works too hard. He needs someone to take care of him while he watches out for the rest of us. Rosie had worked at the resort almost four years now, and while she'd had a crush on Luke from day one, working in close proximity with him had only deepened her affection.

Nibbling on a tiny, delicious quiche filled with spinach and ricotta, Rosie watched the dancers and daydreamed of her boss, the way he looked in a suit, though more often than not he could be found with jacket and tie discarded, shirtsleeves rolled up as he dived in to assist his staff with whatever tasks needed doing.

"Looks good," a voice said behind her, and Rosie choked on a crumb. Cross-eyed briefly, she coughed it discreetly into a napkin before turning and smiling.

"Hi, Luke."

"Hey, sorry, didn't mean to sneak up on you." Luke smiled down at her, perfect teeth gleaming white in his tanned face, not a hair out of place. "You look nice, Rosie."

"Thanks," she said, but he'd already looked away after giving her little more than a cursory glance.

"Looks like everyone's having a good time." Luke nodded approvingly, taking a sip from the glass in his hand - which looked depressingly like sparkling water, Rosie thought gloomily. No chance of him loosening up with alcohol, then.

In which case, no time like the present.

"Hey Luke, I've been wondering," she said.

"Yes?" He turned back to her with his ready smile, attentive to whatever she was going to say, and she steeled her courage.

"Have you ever worked in Hawaii?" Deliberately, she reached up to finger the frangipani behind her ear.

"I have, actually. I was on Oahu for a few months years ago, at a small private hotel up on the North Shore. Catered almost exclusively to surfers." Luke's gaze snagged on the flower, a furrowed line deepening between his brows.

"You'll know what this means, then?" She couldn't back down now. "Behind the right ear, that is?"

"Yes, I know what it means." The furrow deepened further. "Rosie..."

"I know there's a no-fraternisation between staff and resort guests rule, of course," she said. "And as staff manager, most of the staff work for me, which makes it an ethical consideration..."

"I know that. I'm under the same constraints." Luke moved back very slightly.

"But you and me, we wouldn't be..."

"Rosie." His tone was sharp. "I think you shouldn't say any more."

She hesitated, but only for a moment, telling herself she could talk down his objections. "Luke, you and I could..."

"Rosie." He cut her off again, tone gentler this time, and he reached out and took one of her hands in his, squeezing it gently. "I'm very fond of you, but I think of you as a sister. That's all."

She stared into his blue eyes, saw kindness in them, affection, even sadness for the pain he was causing her, but nothing more.

"I just made a complete fool of myself, didn't I?" Her voice came out high and squeaky, far too close to a wail for comfort.

"No, Rosie." Luke squeezed her hand again. "I'm flattered, really. It's just not something I could ever see happening."

"Right." Pulling her hand from his, she tried to smile, but the muscles of her face resisted and it ended up more of a grimace. "Excuse me, please."

She knew Luke was watching her with a worried frown as she turned on her ridiculous spiky heels and walked out, but if she didn't get away she was going to start crying and that would just be the last straw.

"Rosie," she heard him call after her, but she kept walking, quickened her pace when she heard him call again.

He might come after me. I can't face him.

The tears were already starting to flow down her cheeks. Anyone who saw her would stop her, ask if she was okay, and she just couldn't bear it. Turning in the opposite direction to the staff area, she hurried blindly along a path leading she cared not where.

She stumbled and almost fell as her ankle twisted under her. Cursing under her breath, she stopped just long enough to take her heels off before running on, faster now, determined to get well away from where anybody might see her.

I can't even go back to the cabin. Jill will wonder why I'm back so early, want to know what happened.

There was no way she was ready to talk about it. She was sure Luke would never tell anyone what had transpired, and nobody had been close enough to hear their conversation, but any number of people must have seen her flee and not come back, plus Luke going after her and calling her name.

No doubt gossip would be flying already. Tomorrow, everyone would be coming up and asking her what happened, was she okay, what did she and Luke argue about? Should they be concerned? Was anyone getting fired?

To ease their minds, she would have no choice but to admit the truth; it was personal. She'd propositioned Luke and he'd turned her down.

With a despairing groan, Rosie sank down on a lounger, drawn back to the edge of the beach for the night. Nobody would come by here until morning; she was safe from interruption. Safe to think.

I've wasted four years of my life mooning after a man who hasn't the slightest interest in me, was the only conclusion she could come to. Oh, she'd dated in the meantime; most recently an airline pilot who lived up to the reputation of having a girl in every city.

In truth, she hadn't minded not being Dustin's one and only. If she had been, the relationship might have become serious, and the depth of her crush on Luke hadn't allowed for her to feel that way about anyone else.

What am I going to do now?

That was the million-dollar question. Staying and facing everyone who knew how spectacularly she'd crashed and burned, not to mention having to be around Luke continuously with this awkwardness in between them would just...

Well, Rosie didn't have the words to describe how soul-crushing having to face every day with this hanging over her would be.

There was only one logical conclusion to all her problems, both her complete lack of a love life and the disastrous hole she'd dug for herself in her workplace. Which was also her home.

There was no escape.

Unless she left.

The thought was so terrifying Rosie felt short of breath. Pressing her hands to her chest, she tried to take deep breaths, but the thought pressed in on her until it was the only thing on her mind, an unpalatable but inescapable truth.

If I stay here, I'm never going to find love.

Not to mention I'll spend every day dying of embarrassment because everybody knows what an epic disaster I made of propositioning Luke.

But leaving Sunfish Island...

She felt sick at the mere idea. Her friends were here, the closest thing she really had to family, her home. Leaving and starting again somewhere else was terrifying to contemplate... but it was the only answer to her predicament.

Drawing her knees up and hugging them, Rosie gave in to her misery and began to cry.

Chapter Two

Dawn was just beginning to turn the eastern sky over the Pacific Ocean a spectacular shade of rose gold when Adam Gillespie began his morning jog. He admired the colours as he began with a few stretches before starting a slow jog along the broad track leading down towards the beach on the island's eastern side. By the time he hit the sand he'd picked up speed, and enjoyed the way the fine sand sucked at his feet, making him work hard for every step.

Nothing like running barefoot in soft white sand, still cool from the night, he thought as he pounded through the sand, feeling the strain in his calves and hamstrings with every stride. He'd missed being able to run barefoot, the way he'd grown up.

Adam had almost half a mile of beach to run on, and he planned to run the full length and back at least three times before heading back to his villa to do the weight-training part of his daily routine. As he neared the far end where the main resort was, though, a sound which wasn't softly lapping waves or birdsong reached his ears and made him slow his pace.

There was a woman on one of the lounge chairs pulled back under the palm trees, curled forward over her knees and absolutely sobbing her heart out.

Adam didn't hesitate, diverting immediately to run over and fall to his knees at her side.

"Hey, are you all right? Are you hurt?"

The woman flinched back from him, her head coming up and red-rimmed brown eyes meeting his. To his surprise, Adam recognised her; he'd seen her several times since his arrival a couple of weeks ago, wearing the resort uniform of turquoise polo shirt and khaki shorts, striding around the resort with a tablet in her hand, always busy, always with a smile on her face.

He was pretty sure she was in Human Resources or whatever the resort called that department, since she always seemed to be interacting with staff members rather than guests. Certainly she'd never even given him a glance, though he'd looked at her, attracted by her curvaceous figure and that ready smile.

She was wearing what he suspected was a designer dress, a pair of high heels thrown in the sand beside the chair, her brown hair tumbling in softly messy waves around her shoulders, mascara streaked under her eyes.

"Are you okay?" he tried again when she just stared at him. "Only, I saw you crying, and I'm a bit of a sucker for damsels in distress." Aware he could appear slightly terrifying to those who didn't know him, he smiled gently, sitting back on his heels and trying to look as friendly and harmless as he could manage.

***

Stunned by the sudden appearance of a concerned stranger, Rosie took a moment to try and gulp back her sobs. She'd been sitting on the lounger all night, trying to come up with a way out of her predicament which didn't involve handing in her notice and leaving the island, and unable to come up with one. Really, she should have run out of tears hours ago, but it seemed the beauty of the sunrise had the power to set her off again, as she wondered despairingly how many more island sunrises she'd get to enjoy.

"I'm, I'm fine," she gulped out, shaking her head.

"You don't look all that fine," the stranger said bluntly. "Has someone hurt you?"

"Not physically." Her heart was another story, but she couldn't blame Luke, not really. He'd never given even the slightest indication that he might be interested in her romantically, nothing that could even be misinterpreted. Rosie was honest enough with herself to admit she'd just hoped he was hiding his feelings and would admit he felt the same way about her once she made the first move.

"Ah. Broken heart?" The stranger gave her a sympathetic smile and she rubbed at her eyes with a pained wince, taking a good look at him for the first time.

He was absolutely massive, was her first impression. Even sitting back on his heels in the sand, she had to look up to meet his eyes, which were a very dark brown, in a dark brown face. Symmetrical, strong features with deep-set eyes, a squarish nose and a firm mouth made her think he was probably Aboriginal rather than African or African-American, as did the distinctly Australian accent.

Her eyes slid downwards, snagging on a tattoo which began on the left side of his neck and curled downwards in dots and lines, bands of red, green, yellow and blue making up the shape of a magnificent serpent. The snake curled down across his torso from left to right, ending on the lower right side of his abdomen in a flicking tail.

Fascinated by the incredible detail of the tattoo, Rosie forgot herself and stared. A kangaroo bounded across sharply defined abdominal muscles; there was a goanna climbing his left pectoral, a bright green frog on his shoulder, all contained within the serpent's massive body.

She'd genuinely never seen anything like it; it was a remarkable, unique work of art.

"I'm sorry," she said after a moment, managing to drag her eyes back up to his face. "I'm staring."

"It's okay."He had a seriously gorgeous smile, Rosie couldn't help but notice, broad and cheerful, teeth white against his dark skin. "It's meant to be eye-catching." A big hand swept up his torso, touching the head of the serpent on his neck. "Still, I didn't stop for you to admire my tatt. I've been running here all week and you're the first lady I've found bawling her eyes out, so." Huge shoulders lifted and fell in a shrug. "Maybe I could offer a sympathetic ear, if there's nobody who needs punching out for you? I'm Adam Gillespie, by the way. Just so you're not spilling your guts to a complete stranger, if that's what you feel like doing."

Pushing himself up and back, he seated himself on the next lounger over from Rosie's and looked at her quizzically.

"Eh." Rosie wrapped her arms around her calves and rested her cheek on her knee, looking at him sideways. "I brought it on myself, by being a blind idiot."

"Yeah?"

The way he said it seemed to invite confidence, and he relaxed back onto the lounger as though he had nothing better to do than sit and watch the sunrise and listen. Emboldened, Rosie carried on.

"I've had this massive crush on my boss for ages, and last night was the staff Christmas party. I borrowed this fancy dress off a friend, got all dolled up and had a couple of drinks to get my courage up, and I hit on him. He turned me down flat."

"Yowch!" Adam winced.

"Oh, it gets ever so much worse. Half the staff witnessed me bolting with my tail between my legs, and I'm going to get bombarded with questions about why I was so upset and who's going to get fired. I'm the staff manager for the resort," she explained. "So to reassure them, I've got to tell them the truth... that it was personal."

Adam whistled between his teeth, his expression sympathetic. "Salt in the wound, huh?"

"Yeah." With a sigh, Rosie looked away and out at the sunrise, the sun rising over the Coral Sea in a glorious ball of fiery orange. "I'm thirty-three," she said after a couple of minutes of surprisingly comfortable silence, "and I've never been in love, but I want to be. I want to find a nice guy and get married and have kids one day."

"Sounds like a perfectly reasonable thing to want," Adam agreed. "I'm thirty-seven and at that point in my life where I'm starting to think along those lines too - and hoping one day isn't too far away."

"It's not unreasonable, is it? At least, I've never thought so. But I've come to the unhappy conclusion that with Luke unable to return my feelings about him, I'm gonna have to leave the island and go work somewhere else. Somewhere with a bigger dating pool."

"You must meet a lot of people, though!"

Adam sounded genuinely surprised, and Rosie flicked a glance at him. "I do," she agreed, "but the resort has a strict non-fraternisation policy between staff and guests. And while I could technically date another staff member, they all report directly to me, except Luke, so that's just ethically not something I could contemplate."

"Well, Luke's your boss, right? I guess that's how he feels about you," Adam pointed out, and Rosie laughed darkly.

"Yeah. Maybe. Or maybe he just doesn't fancy me. That's more likely. I've seen him look admiringly at other women; he likes tall, willowy girls, not short chubby ones like me. I'm too fat. Even a designer dress can't change that."

"Bollocks!" Adam said the single word sharp and succinct, startling Rosie, who jerked her head up to stare at him.

"What?"

"Forgive me, but I've seen you around the resort the last few days, and I noticed you even in a polo shirt and shorts. You've got a great figure, and you look fit and healthy. Unsurprisingly, considering the amount of walking you seem to do on a daily basis. You're not fat in the slightest."

Startled, and more than a little flattered, Rosie blinked at Adam in surprise, not at all sure what to say. He grinned at her shocked expression.

"Hey, I'm a red-blooded guy, and I'm not blind. I notice pretty girls. I swear I didn't mean to be a creeper, though!"

Rosie laughed, a little shakily. "It's okay. I'm flattered, I suppose. I'm not really the kind of girl who catches the eye all that much..."

"You stop that right now." He waggled a stern finger at her.

"But I'm not! My friend Olivia who I borrowed this dress off, she looks like a fashion model, the dress only fits me because I'm half a foot shorter than she is so it stretches sideways..."

"Bet she doesn't fill it out like you." Adam let his eyes drop just for a moment before he returned them to her face, but Rosie blushed as she realised he'd just given her cleavage a pointed look.

"It was all wasted effort anyway," she said with a sigh. "Luke didn't even look at me twice, and I spent forever getting ready, even got a friend to help with my hair and makeup."

Adam looked more thoughtful than pitying as he considered her. "It does seem a shame to waste all that effort," he said. "Why don't you come out to dinner with me tonight instead, and I promise to treat you like the beautiful woman you are? No strings, no expectations. Just a well-deserved confidence boost."

Chapter Three

Rosie hesitated for a long moment, considering Adam. He was really a very good-looking guy, she thought, taking a moment to give him a more thorough look over. Her gaze snagged on the slim black and gold watch on his left wrist.

That's a Piaget Altiplano. And I think it's a real one.

Which meant Adam was well-off, and the way he looked, surely he had no shortage of women vying for his attention.

Conclusion; probably not an axe murderer rapist who pickles up tragic lonely fat girls to victimise.

He actually seems really nice.

After all, he'd interrupted his run on the beach when he heard her crying, had come over to check if she was alright, even said he'd beat someone up for her.

A nice, good-looking, apparently well-off guy just asked me out to dinner.

"Yes," Rosie was a little surprised to hear herself say. "I'd really like that. If you mean it?"

"I definitely mean it." His eyes crinkled at the corners in a surprisingly cute way as he smiled at her. "You just name the place and the time, and I'll... um, well, I probably can't do the pumpkin coach and shit, but I can definitely play Prince Charming to your Cinderella for the evening."

Rosie laughed. "You're a really nice guy, huh?"

"Well, hopefully you'll still think so this evening."

"Hamilton Island," she said, and he blinked.

"Excuse me?"

"I'd rather not have dinner at any of the island's restaurants," she said apologetically. "Literally everyone knows me and the gossip... I'm sure you understand. We can get the last boat back this evening, it doesn't leave until ten."

"Works for me. Would you like me to book somewhere?"

Rosie shook her head. "It's fine, I can get us a table anywhere. Meet me at the dock at five-thirty?"

"I'll be there," Adam promised. "You sure you're going to be alright today?"

"I'll be fine, thank you. I've got a day off rostered anyway." She smiled thinly. "I'd hoped to be spending it in bed with Luke, but I guess I'll just catch up on the sleep I've missed."

"Sounds like a plan." Adam rose to his feet, held out his hand. She put hers in it and let him help her to her feet.

"Thanks for stopping, and listening," she said, feeling it needed to be said.

"Any time." He let go of her hand, stooped and picked up her shoes to hand them to her. "Only thing is, I still don't know your name."

"Oh!" Startled, she realized she hadn't told him. "It's Rosie. Rosie Brown."

He was even bigger standing up; she had to tip her head way back to meet those dark brown eyes. Six foot five at least, she estimated, and the muscles practically screamed *professional sportsman*. She was going to have to Google once she got back to her room.

"Can I walk you anywhere?" Adam asked, and Rosie shook her head.

"No, I'm good, thanks. It's not far back to the staff quarters. You carry on with your run."

He nodded, mouth twisting thoughtfully as he gazed at her, and then he said "Alright. I'll see you later."

She watched as he turned to stride back down the beach, going almost to the water's edge before breaking into a loping run which carried that huge frame with deceptive efficiency and speed. He was a tiny figure in the distance within mere moments, or so it seemed, and Rosie sighed and turned to head back to the resort, praying she wouldn't run into anyone she knew. It looked a lot like she was doing a walk of shame, after all. Maybe the early hour would save her.

Only a couple of the garden staff were about, thank goodness, and they were both focused on their work and didn't pay any attention to her tiptoeing past, probably thinking she was a resort guest.

Rosie practically held her breath as she let herself back into her cabin, praying she didn't wake Jill. There was a note pinned to her bedroom door.

I WANT DETAILS, was all it said, and Rosie winced. Jill would be sympathetic, but she was also very forthright and would probably have some pithy comments to make about Rosie's reckless decision to leap in feet-first and proposition Luke publicly.

In hindsight, it was a dumbass decision, but she'd got caught up in the romance of having an ugly-duckling makeover, convincing herself it was all she needed to make Luke really see her as a woman for once.

Adam made me feel more feminine in ten minutes than Luke has in four years.

Although she couldn't imagine why, as she caught sight of herself in the mirror and stifled a yelp, cramming her hands against her mouth. She looked terrible, her makeup smeared all over her face and her hair a disastrous mess instead of the elegant arrangement of glamorously tousled waves she'd been sporting the previous evening. Her tears had made black raccoon circles under her swollen, red eyes, and there was sand stuck to one of her cheeks.

Honestly, she couldn't recall ever looking worse.

And yet Adam still looked at me as though I was attractive.

It was a puzzle she couldn't make out, and after a night of no sleep and more tears than she ever wanted to cry again, she wasn't going to solve it any time soon. Switching on the shower, she eased out of Olivia's dress, wincing at the state of it. Despite what Adam had suggested, there was no way she'd be wearing it to dinner with him. She'd drop it at the resort dry-cleaner and wear something of her own.

She stood under the shower for a long time, letting the stream of warm water rinse away the misery of the night before, the let-down and disappointment. She couldn't blame Luke at all; he'd never given her any reason to think he might have any kind of feelings for her other than friendship.

I built it up into a castle of dreams and now it's all crashed down.

Oddly, the thought of leaving the island and her friends hurt far more than the idea of never seeing Luke again. Which was confirmation, if she needed any, that the love she'd convinced herself she felt for Luke wasn't real. It was all in her own head.

"Rosie!"

The hammering on the bathroom door made Rosie wince. "Be right out!" she called, shutting off the shower.

"Time to face the music," she whispered, looking at herself in the mirror as she wrapped a towel around herself. With her face scrubbed clean, her hair wet and slicked to her scalp, the redness of her eyes was all too obvious.

Jill was lurking right outside the bedroom door, a broad grin on her face. "You naughty girl, Rosie, who did you... oh my God. What happened?" She stared at Rosie, her expression changing from mischievous glee to horror in an instant as she took in her best friend's appearance.

"I made the world's biggest fool of myself," Rosie said wearily, "and I'd really rather not talk about it."

"Oh, *Rosie.*" Jill shook her head, sitting down on the end of Rosie's bed. "Just tell me one thing."

"Okay?" Rosie said cautiously.

"Was it public, and therefore am I going to be fending off questions about it all day?"

"Oh God." It had been, and therefore she wasn't being fair to Jill leaving her in the dark. Throwing herself face first on the bed, Rosie dragged a pillow over her head. "This is the most humiliating thing that's ever happened to me," she said, muffled.

"Worse than when you ran over that wallaby with a golf cart on Hamilton Island in front of a bunch of horrified Japanese tourists?"

Rosie pulled the pillow off her head and fixed Jill with a death glare. "You promised never to mention that again!"

"I figured it was a special occasion. Come on. Whatever happened can't be that bad. Are any wallabies dead this time?" Jill's eyes danced with amusement.

Despite herself, Rosie's lips twitched. Jill was always good at pulling her out of a funk.

"The only thing dead is my pride. It's just waiting for decent burial now," she said with a sigh, rolling over and plumping up her pillows to lean back against them before pouring her heart out to her best friend.

***

"Oh my God. *Luke*?" Jill said incredulously.

"And that's why it was an unmitigated disaster. He was just as surprised as you are."

"Probably more, because I at least knew you had a crush on him, whereas I'm pretty sure he was happily oblivious."

"Ugh." Rosie considered trying to smother herself with the pillow again. "It was *awful*. He was so clearly wishing for the earth to open up and swallow him so he didn't have to listen to me."

"Oh, Rosie." Jill gave her a sympathetic look. "I'm sorry."

"Thanks." Rosie was honestly grateful; she knew Jill was more than capable of giving her a lecture, but obviously she could see how deeply Rosie was affected and had decided to be kind.

"Where were you all night, then? I assumed when your bed hadn't been slept in that you'd hooked up with someone?"

"Nah. I ended up on the beach feeling sorry for myself, crying most of the night." Rosie hugged her knees. "And then the weirdest thing happened."

"Yeah?" Pulling her legs up onto the bed, Jill sprawled out comfortably and fixed Rosie with an interrogative stare. "Spill all, then."

"This guy - this really, really *hot* guy - was running on the beach and he must have heard me crying. Came over to see if I was alright. I ended up spilling my guts to him and then he asked me out to dinner."

Jill's eyebrows flew almost up to her hairline. "Say *what*?"

"And I said yes."

"*Rosanna Brown!*"

She smiled guiltily. "I'm meeting him at the dock later, we're going to get the boat over to Hamilton Island and eat there."

Jill whistled between her teeth. "Wow, when you decide to jump out of your comfort zone you don't do things by half measures, do you?"

"C'mon, I'll be perfectly safe. I'm going to book us in to that nice pizza place by the harbour, and I'll tell the boat pilot if I'm not on the last boat back, to raise the alarm."

"Still, a complete stranger? And a resort guest to boot?" Jill shook her head. "You know I won't tell on you, but..."

"Even if someone does see me and tattle to Luke, I'm pretty sure he'll be inclined to cut me a fair bit of slack at the moment," Rosie pointed out dryly. "Quite apart from the fact that I intend to hand in my notice as soon as I've found another job elsewhere."

Jill's jaw dropped, and she stared in silence for a long moment, obviously putting two and two together to make five. "Oh, Rosie," she said at last, the words soft. "Really?"

"It's a catch-22, and you know it. How many times have we both bemoaned the limited dating pool here? And I'm even more constrained than you because almost every staff member on the island reports directly to me. If I want any chance at a serious relationship, I need to get out of my comfort zone long term, get out there and *look*."

Huffing out a breath, Jill shook her head, but her expression was understanding. "It's a big step," she said finally. "Maybe I should leave too."

"If you're doing it for your own reasons, fair enough, but don't you dare do it because you think I need a babysitter!" Rosie waggled a finger at her best friend, and Jill laughed.

"I'll think about it," she said. "Where are you going to look? Elsewhere on the Reef?"

"Any other island resort would put me back in the exact same situation," Rosie shook her head. "Port Douglas or Cairns, maybe. Brisbane. Sydney."

"Big city living? Can't see you enjoying that."

"Won't know until I've tried it. And hey, if I meet the right guy, we could end up back on the Reef in a few years."

In her heart of hearts, Rosie knew she'd never be truly happy anywhere but the tropical north of Australia, where she'd spent her whole life. Still, she was willing to give other places a try.

"Might even give Hawaii a go, if I could get a working visa for the States," she mused.

"Or a cruise ship?" Jill suggested.

"Maybe." That had possibilities, too. She'd contact a firm she often used in Brisbane to headhunt staff in the hospitality and tourism industries for the resort, ask them to keep an eye out for some likely positions for herself. "Right now I want to get some sleep before I go out with Adam this evening, so if you wouldn't mind buggering off, that'd be awesome."

"Adam, is that your hot stranger's name?" Jill gave her an inquisitive eyebrow waggle, and Rosie poked her with a foot.

"Yes, it is. I'll fill you in more tomorrow, I promise."

"I'll hold you to that," Jill warned before scrambling over to give her an unexpected hug. "I'm sorry it didn't work out the way you hoped with Luke, hon," she said into Rosie's ear.

Rosie hung on tight for a moment, her eyes stinging again. "I'm sure it's all for the best," she made herself say.

"You hang onto that thought." Jill pulled back, tucked a strand of wet hair behind Rosie's ear, sharp eyes searching her face. "You deserve to be happy, hon. You really do, and I'm sure Mr Right isn't too far away. He's out there searching for you too, promise."

"Well, I hope he hurries the hell up," Rosie grumbled. "He's late!"

Chapter Four

Adam more than half-thought Rosie might not show up. He stood on the dock looking at the fast catamaran which made an hourly return trip to Hamilton Island, hands shoved in his pockets, occasionally pulling one out to glance at his watch.

"You boarding?" the young deckhand at the gangway asked him finally. "It's twenty-five past."

"Just waiting to see if my date shows." Adam gave him a rueful grin, and the deckhand laughed.

"Alright, mate. I can give you another two minutes. That her coming now?"

Adam looked in the direction of the man's gaze, smiling as he saw Rosie hurrying down onto the floating dock. "That's her," he said, relieved.

"*Rosie?*"

The deckhand was staring at him in disbelief. Adam frowned at him before turning his attention back to Rosie, admiring her outfit. She was wearing a different dress, a soft floaty thing of white cotton printed with tiny blue flowers, blue ballet flats on her feet, her brown hair a mass of softly tumbling waves.

"You look beautiful," he said warmly, and with complete honesty, delighted to see her blush a little.

"Thank you. I'm so sorry I'm late. Got caught up with a problem on my way here." She grimaced. "We'd better board. Evening, Mal."

"Uh, hi, Rosie," the deckhand stammered as she practically skipped past him up the gangway. Adam followed, grinning at the obviously flabbergasted teenager.

"She showed," he said cheerfully.

"Of course I showed! Did you think I'd stand you up?" Rosie turned to face him at the doorway to the boat's interior.

"I thought you might have had second thoughts." Adam shoved his hands back in his pockets and shrugged awkwardly. "We didn't exactly meet under the best of circumstances, and you really don't know me."

"No," Rosie agreed, and then she smiled, a smile which transformed her from merely pretty to strikingly beautiful, "but I think I'd like to."

He was so transfixed by that smile he almost forgot to duck entering the boat and brained himself on a bulkhead. At the last moment he spotted it and ducked down lower than necessary, so he entered the cabin in an awkward half-crouch.

The cabin was nearly full, day trippers returning to Hamilton Island, he guessed, so he followed Rosie to a bench seat over on the other side and took a seat beside her, sitting on the edge to avoid crowding her.

"So," he said as the boat engines began a deep roar behind them and the boat slid slowly away from the dock, "did you Google me?"

"I didn't, actually. I slept longer than I expected and then woke up starving. And by the time I'd eaten and then sorted out the snakes' nest my hair had turned into because I slept on it wet," Rosie fingered one wavy brown strand and grinned, "I barely had time to rush down here and not stand you up completely by accident."

"I'd have been just as devastated if you stood me up accidentally or on purpose," Adam said, straight-faced.

Rosie chuckled, her expression shifting to curiosity. "What would I have found if I did get a minute to Google you?" she asked.

Adam took a moment to choose his words. "I just retired," he led out with, "but you'd have found a lot of footage of me fighting inside an octagonal cage."

"Octagonal... wait. You mean MMA? You were an MMA fighter?" She gawped at him.

"I *told* you it was him!" a teenage boy sitting on the bench seat behind them nudged his father. "Excuse me, you *are* Adam Gillespie, right?" The kid leaned forward eagerly. "Could I maybe get a selfie with you?"

The father looked quite keen to get in on the action as well, so Adam smiled obligingly and took a selfie with them both. He even pretended to punch the father in the head for the son to take a photo, to the boy's immense delight.

"But are you really retired?" the boy asked as they sat down again. "Really, really? Like, no comeback in a year or so?"

"Yeah, you've still got plenty of good years in you," the father chipped in.

Adam shook his head. "The heart is willing but the flesh is weak, I'm afraid. In the case of my left elbow, literally. After the third tendon repair, my surgeon told me I was done."

"Oh man, that's rough. Sorry to hear that. Conrad here loved watching you fight, made us stay up until four in the morning that time you fought Mossman in Vegas."

"That was a good one. Always nice to meet a fan," Adam said with a smile at the boy.

Rosie had her phone out as he sat down, stared at him with huge eyes.

He gave her a rueful grin. "Still got signal, huh?"

"Enough to be impressed!" She put the phone down. "You're an actual *superstar.*"

"Former," he corrected.

"I don't think you get to retire from being famous and having fans all over the world," Rosie pointed out dryly, tilting her head back to indicate the boy still gazing at him with obvious hero-worship.

"Maybe not," Adam conceded, "but I'm out of the public eye now and happier for it, believe me. It's exhausting to have your every move scrutinised by press who are paid to chase every bit of gossip in your specific sport. That's why the most recent reports about my retirement include the full text of my surgeon's report." He nodded at Rosie's phone. "I didn't want there to be any question about whether I was going to make a comeback or not, at least in professional circles."

"I see." She looked down at the phone in her hand before turning it off and slipping it back into her purse.

"Anything else you want to ask?" Adam asked softly.

Rosie flicked a quick glance at him, then at the father and son seated behind them. "Nothing that can't wait," she said, by which he understood she'd rather they had a bit more privacy to talk. He couldn't think of anything she might ask he didn't mind saying publicly, but he didn't mind waiting, either. It wasn't exactly a long boat trip, anyway.

***

"So I've never been out to dinner with a celebrity before," Rosie began as they walked side by side along the Hamilton Island marina. "Are there any unwritten rules I should be aware of?"

"Probably depends on who you're with," Adam said, looking down at her with a wry smile. "I'm pretty cool about autographs and selfies unless I'm literally in the middle of eating, in which case I usually ask if they'd mind waiting until I've finished. Most people do wait until I've stopped eating anyway. If it gets too intense, which isn't really all that likely here, I usually say I'll give fifteen minutes and that's all folks."

"Fair enough." She stopped outside the pizza restaurant. "Here we are. Hope you like pizza?"

"Love it, especially these days when I don't have to micro-analyse every bite of food I eat."

Rosie considered that as they were shown to a table and took their seats. With a tendency to carry a few more pounds than she'd really have preferred, she was a bit of a yo-yo dieter. It took impressive discipline to do what Adam had described, day in day out for what must have been years on end, while maintaining what she could only imagine was a gruelling exercise regime.

"Hi, here's the drinks menu," a bubbly blonde waitress placed a folder on the table. "Can I get you anything to start?"

"Iced water for me, please," Adam said affably. "Rosie, would you like a cocktail or anything?"

"You know what, I would. Could I have a mojito, please?"

"Coming right up. I'll leave you to look over the menus; our specials board is just up there. Gimme a shout if you have any questions!"

Rosie watched Adam's eyes as the waitress bounced away, but he didn't watch the pretty blonde go. He was looking at her instead, a smile on his firm lips.

"What?" she asked when he kept looking at her.

"Just admiring." He tipped his head slightly. "Been a while since I got to take a beautiful woman out to dinner."

"I don't believe that for a minute. There must have been, I don't know, do you call them groupies on the MMA circuit? The girls who walk around the ring with those cards, too..."

"Ring girls." Adam smiled. "Professional models, for the most part. And very nice, I'm sure, but as a professional, you get to fight maybe three, four times a year when you get to the top level. The rest of the time, you spend in a gym smelling of old socks."

"The gym, or you?" Rosie grinned teasingly at him.

"Both, once I'd been in there long enough."

The waitress returned with their drinks, and Adam toasted Rosie with his iced water.

"To the guy who turned you down. His bad taste is my good fortune."

She took a sip of her mojito while she considered that. It was a nice sentiment, really. *And I do believe that all things happen for a reason.*

"If I didn't say it before," she said, "thank you so much for stopping on your run to talk to me this morning. I was having a massive wallow in self-pity and you helped me snap out of it."

"We all need a wallow sometimes." Adam's gaze was direct and honest. "I spent a couple months taking way more pain pills than I needed after my surgeon gave me the final verdict on my elbow."

"Wow," Rosie said after a moment of shocked silence. "That puts a one-night crying jag in perspective, huh."

"I'm not diminishing your pain, here! Just saying you actually dealt with it in a much healthier way than I did. If I wasn't trying to be such a big tough strong guy, maybe I'd actually have let my emotions out and mourned what I was losing properly rather than trying to bury it all in prescription drugs." Adam shrugged massive shoulders. "It's why I'm here. Getting away from temptation."

Rosie sipped her drink and considered him. "I think that's plenty brave of you. You could have gone to rehab, seen psychotherapists..."

"Did a bit of both," he admitted, "but in the end I decided getting away entirely was the best course of action."

"Coming home? I'm presuming you lived in the US during your fight career."

He nodded. "In LA, which is not reality as the rest of us know it. I'm from Arnhem Land originally, but my family are in either Katherine or Darwin now. Staying with them would be plunging into a different kind of chaos, and I needed the space to figure out who I am now, what I'm going to do with the rest of my life."

The waitress returned then to see if they were ready to order, and Rosie quickly apologised, since neither of them had even looked at the menu yet.

"No worries, I'll stop back in a few."

Rosie squinted up at the specials board, trying to make out the wording.

"Do you need glasses?" Adam asked, obviously noticing her squint.

"Well, sometimes," she admitted, not wanting to admit that she had them in her purse but didn't want to put them on, in case he was put off by her nerdy look.

"Me too," he startled her by saying, fishing a slim case from his pants pocket. "At least to read the small writing on this menu. Would it kill them to print it in a font size bigger than twelve point?"

Rosie started laughing, making Adam look up at her in surprise. "What?" he said.

"You keep surprising me!"

"Is that good or bad?" He flashed her a grin, a surprisingly shy one, she thought.

"It is." Taking out her glasses, she perched them on her nose and read the specials board in comfort.

"Would you like wine?" Adam asked when she closed her menu and laid it down on the table. "Or are you happy with cocktails?"

"I could go some wine, as long as I'm not trying to get through a bottle on my own. Do you drink alcohol?" She glanced at his ice water.

"I don't, no. Family issues." His smile was a little bitter. "Habit, too. Alcohol was always empty calories I couldn't afford."

"I'll just get another cocktail when the meal comes, then," Rosie decided.

The waitress returned then for their orders, and Rosie made her selection; a small seafood pizza with a side salad.

"That's all you're having?" Adam checked.

"It'll be plenty." Amused, she watched his brow furrow. "You have no idea how much an average person eats, do you?"

"Not really," he admitted. "Do you mind if I get a starter? You could have a bit..."

"Go for it."

He shot her a grateful glance before turning back to the waitress and ordering garlic bread, stuffed mushrooms, a large house special pizza with so many toppings Rosie guessed it would probably be an inch thick, and a large Caesar salad.

"You're right," Adam told Rosie as the waitress departed, "I've spent the last few years living in a bubble."

"I wouldn't go quite that far," she disclaimed.

"It's true, though. Since I moved to LA, the only people I spent time with were my training partners and my trainers, all of whom are former career fighters themselves. It's not just that I wouldn't know how much an average person eats, I wouldn't know *what* they eat on a daily basis. Hell, we had a chef who prepared all our meals for us; we rarely ate out because we couldn't know the precise portion sizes or ingredients we were consuming."

"It sounds very regimented," Rosie said thoughtfully, resting her chin on her hand to gaze at him.

"That's a really good word for it." He nodded in agreement. "Every day was the same; get up early, train, eat, train some more, eat, rest, train..."

"It doesn't sound all that different to a routine most folks with a regular job get into, though," Rosie pointed out. "They get up at the same time, take the same transport to work, and a lot of people have to do the same repetitive tasks when they get there, too!"

"I suppose. Not you though, right? I'd guess your job's changing all the time."

"Why it keeps me interested," Rosie told him. "Yes, there's a certain amount of repetition, but dealing with the challenges of keeping so many staff happy, managing turnover, interviewing, fitting new people into an established hierarchy - it keeps me busy."

***

Adam admired Rosie as she talked about her work. She obviously enjoyed the challenges of her job, her eyes bright, hands moving expressively, her laugh cheerful as she told him an amusing anecdote about a temporary American staff member who refused to go outside the main resort building because of the Australian wildlife she was convinced was just waiting to murder her.

"What about you?" Rosie surprised him by asking then. "What are your long-term plans now you've retired?"

"I don't know," he had to admit. "I'm still trying to think that through. I earned enough money in my career I could buy myself a nice place somewhere and just play golf for the rest of my life."

"I'm sure you could," Rosie agreed, "but would that make you happy?"

Adam grimaced, thinking he'd probably be bored out of his head within the first week or so. At least at the moment, he was thinking, planning, considering options and researching possibilities. If he settled for such a passive existence, he suspected he'd drive himself around the bend. "Probably not."

The garlic bread and stuffed mushrooms arrived just then, and Rosie accepted a small portion of each at his urging. Conversation paused for a little while as he ate, starving; he'd been eating his own rather plain cooking for the last fortnight and the rich scents and flavours were a feast for the senses. He savoured every bite, nodding his thanks to Rosie as she signalled the waitress over to refill his empty water glass.

The pizza place was obviously a popular place to eat, filled with families for the most part, the occasional small group of adults. Adam was fairly sure he and Rosie were the only couple in there on their own, and thought wistfully that she'd obviously chosen the least romantic restaurant she could think of. His first date in over a year and his date was keeping him at arms' length, for which he couldn't really blame her, he supposed.

Rosie drank her cocktail quite slowly, he observed, and as she'd said she would, she ordered a second when their main meals arrived. She preferred to stay in control of her senses, he thought, which again was only prudent when out with a stranger, though he was pretty sure the restaurant manager actually knew her. The woman had paused by their table as though to greet Rosie, but moved on at a quick head shake.

Ensuring her own safety, Adam thought. *Smart as well as pretty.* Not that he needed the confirmation; Rosie's conversation made it more than clear she was intelligent, her quick mind seizing on any topic he brought up and considering it from all angles.

He'd made up his mind long before they finished the meal to ask her for a second date. Even though she was probably on the rebound from her crush rejecting her, Adam liked Rosie way too much to give up easily. He had time on his side, could give her whatever time and space she needed until she could consider him on his own merits.

"Since I invited you out for dinner, would you allow me to get the bill?" he asked as he finally pushed aside his empty plate. "Also since I ate six times as much food as you did."

"I had cocktails, though," Rosie argued.

"You did. How about this; you can pick up the tab next time?" he suggested, feeling suddenly as nervous as he ever had before a big fight. Heart in his mouth, he waited for her answer.

Chapter Five

Rosie blinked at Adam, sure she couldn't have heard him correctly. "Next time?" she echoed.

"I'm hoping there'll be a next time, anyway." He ducked his head and smiled at her almost shyly. "I've really enjoyed tonight, Rosie."

"So have I," she said, realising to her surprise that it was true. Adam was really easy to talk to, not only comfortable opening up about himself but also asking questions and listening when she talked. Which was a very rare trait in a man, at least in her experience.

"How about it then? We could call this date zero if you like, and then next time would be date number one?"

Adam seemed to be genuinely in earnest. Rosie sipped the last of her cocktail and considered him, thinking she'd be mad to turn him down. Not only was he the first man in quite a while to show romantic interest in her, he was also sexy as hell, obviously comfortably off, and a genuinely nice person.

Still, some part of her hesitated, the part which had convinced her Luke was her only chance of happiness.

"It's fine if you want to say no, or if you'd like to think about it for a while," Adam said, and his easy acceptance of whatever she wanted to decide helped make Rosie's mind up for her.

"I'd love to go on another date with you," she said, "so yes, I will let you buy this one on the understanding that next time, I'm picking up the tab."

Adam's grin was wide and white; he didn't hide his emotions, Rosie thought, and he seemed honestly delighted by her response. Signalling to the waitress, he asked politely if she could bring them the bill.

Rosie watched as he picked up the pen and added a generous tip to the bottom of the check when the waitress brought it, handing his credit card over with a "Thank you, that was a delicious meal and your service was excellent."

The pretty blonde blushed and gave him a rather starry-eyed look, which Rosie had to admit was justified. At least she wasn't ill-mannered enough to try and slip Adam her number with Rosie sitting right there, though she did give Rosie a look of pure envy.

Which made Rosie once again question just why Adam was there with *her*. And why he'd asked her for another date, too. He must have women throwing themselves at him. *Why would a man like Adam pick me, a girl who's average in just about every way?*

"Finished?" Adam said, nodding towards her glass.

"Sure," she agreed, wondering why he was in such a hurry to get out of there. They could have had another drink. Though when she stood up and turned around, she saw what he'd obviously already seen; a queue of people outside the pizza place waiting for tables.

"Busy place," Adam noted as he led the way outside, holding the door open for Rosie to come out. "Though considering how good the pizza was, I'm not surprised. Thanks for suggesting the place."

"You're welcome." Pointing across the road, she said "That's a really good Bavarian brew house and restaurant. We could go there next time."

"Great idea! Can we go look at the menu?"

"Sure," Rosie agreed, and as they stepped down from the raised pavement to cross the road, a huge hand folded gently around hers.

Surprised, Rosie looked down at her hand, and then up at Adam. He wasn't holding on tight, though, she could easily pull her hand away if she wanted to, and his hand felt really nice on hers, strong and warm but not sweaty, so she left it there.

They stood hand in hand to check out the menu, Rosie shaking her head at the host who came to ask them if they wanted a table.

"Looks great," Adam said after a few minutes. "I want to order half the menu, even when I'm full of pizza."

Rosie chuckled, and he looked down at her with a grin. "Not really. But maybe tomorrow night? Or whatever night you're free next to play hooky with me?"

"Probably not tomorrow," she admitted. "I won't get away by a reasonable time. Maybe the following night, though, I can let you know?"

"Suits me," he agreed amiably.

"That said, we don't need to get the boat back for another hour. Want to take a walk?" Rosie suggested.

"Love to! Which way?"

She pointed to their left, along the marina past the ranks of yachts moored at floating slips. "Down that way to the yacht club? Otherwise it's a fairly steep hike over the middle of the island, and though I'm sure you wouldn't even break a sweat, I'd probably expire before I got to the top." Pretending to consider, she said "Actually, it'd probably be easier for you to give me a piggyback."

Adam snorted with laughter. "I'd happily give you a piggyback if you needed one. But since there's an alternative, let's both maintain our dignity and walk to the yacht club, huh?"

"Smart man. I knew there was a reason I liked you apart from those stunning good looks."

Adam actually stumbled, fingers tightening around hers for a moment. "You think I'm good-looking?"

"Are you kidding?" Rosie stopped in her tracks. "I didn't have time to Google you properly but I'm a hundred per cent sure I'd have found glamour type shots of you posing for some Men's Health sort of magazine. Probably in black and white."

"Well." Adam frowned. "I was world champion for three years. Of course I did features like that, there's a certain amount of media attention which goes with it..."

"You have to be joking!" Rosie spluttered. "You really don't have any idea how you look?"

He looked down at her with furrowed brow, and she shook her head and resumed walking, perforce tugging him along with her since he was still holding her hand.

"You really have spent the last few years isolated in a gym smelling of sweaty socks, huh," Rosie said after they'd walked for a few minutes.

"Yes?" Adam looked even more puzzled, and she smiled.

"I guess that makes me the lucky one."

"Isn't that what I said to you about your crush not recognising what an amazing woman you are and grabbing on with both hands?"

"Every cloud has a silver lining, I guess," Rosie mused. After all, if Luke hadn't turned her down, there was no way she'd be here with Adam, and she had to say, she'd had an absolutely delightful evening so far. Strolling along with him hand in hand on a warm summer night, the air scented with delicious wafts of garlic and herbs from a restaurant they were passing overlaid on the salt-water scents of the marina, she struggled to recall a time she'd felt as simply *content* as she did right at that moment.

They strolled past the moored rows of boats and down the road towards the yacht club; Adam turned towards the villas beyond it, but Rosie tugged on his hand.

"No, this way. There's a beach."

"Another beach?" He glanced down at her with a grin. "I've even got a handkerchief in my pocket to offer you this time, if you feel like having another crying jag."

"Ho, ho." She nudged his arm lightly with her shoulder. "I refuse to cry another tear over a man who, as you said, doesn't recognise how awesome I am."

"That's the spirit," Adam encouraged.

"Because damn it, I deserve a man who sees *me*," Rosie warmed to her theme. "I deserve to be admired and treasured."

"You definitely do." They'd reached the edge of the sand and Rosie paused to take her shoes off; Adam let go of her hand to do the same, stuffing his socks into them, before they walked down across the still-warm sand towards the edge of the sea, quiet now with soft wavelets just lapping at the sand.

"The water's still warm!" Adam discovered as he got his toes wet. Rosie chuckled, hanging back.

"Well, yes. The sea temperature doesn't really change day to night here, since it's so shallow. I'd stay out of it, though. It's stinger season."

Adam sighed a little wistfully, but he left the water and came back to where Rosie was just sitting down on the sand, sitting down next to her before surprising her by suddenly flopping down on his back and resting his head on his hands.

"Stars are bright tonight," he observed. "I'm loving seeing the stars again. There was way too much light pollution in LA."

"I don't remember when I last just lay back and looked at the stars," Rosie said, suddenly finding that quite sad.

"Here. Put your head on my shoulder so you don't get sand in your hair." Adam put his hand on her arm lightly, and without even thinking about it, she shifted to lie at a slight angle to him and lay back, resting her head on his thickly muscled shoulder.

"Wow," she whispered, awestruck. Even though they were just a short walk from lit buildings, Hamilton Island didn't have enough light pollution to really affect the stars. The sky looked like an upturned bowl of midnight blue speckled thickly with bright white.

"Amazing, huh?" Adam's voice rumbled through his chest, a deep vibration through her ear, and she was suddenly very aware of him as a man, of a warm, slightly spicy scent enveloping her as she lay on him.

Honestly not quite sure what to do with her sudden awareness, Rosie just lay quietly and gazed at the stars, listening to the music coming from the yacht club and Adam's steady breathing, until her phone beeped in her purse.

"What's that?" Adam asked as she sat up to fish it out.

"Time to head back to catch the boat, or we'll be sleeping on this beach tonight." Tucking her phone away, she pushed herself up to her feet and dusted at her sandy legs, sighing as the fine sand clung to her. "Ugh, the sand on these beaches is beautiful, but so sticky!"

"Like powdered sugar," Adam agreed, getting up with a grace remarkable in such a big man. He didn't seem too worried about it, though, just wiping his hands on his pants and giving them and his shirt a light shake. "Don't think I'll bother putting my shoes back on, though. I don't like sand in my socks."

Rosie didn't put hers back on either, just carrying them in one hand, and as they walked back up the beach, Adam's strong fingers curled around hers again.

This time, she turned her hand and threaded her fingers with his. He glanced down at her once, a smile curving the edges of his lips upwards, before looking forward again.

Despite the height difference between them - he towered a clear foot above her, maybe even a little more - he moderated his pace to walk comfortably beside her.

The pavement scraped Rosie's feet as they crossed back over from the sand, but she ignored the slight discomfort. She spent plenty of time padding about barefoot anyway, all her off-duty hours. She had tough feet, and she guessed Adam's were probably a lot tougher. *Don't MMA fighters fight barefoot?*

"Is that the boat?" Adam asked, and she looked up and nodded before seeing the large crowd of people on the dock and saying;

"Oh, crap."

"Is there a problem?"

"No, I just forgot there was a charter flight due in tonight. About a hundred guests are due to go over and check into the resort."

"Will there be room for us on board?" Adam queried.

"Yeah." Rosie wrinkled her nose regretfully. "Unfortunately there will also be several of my colleagues."

"Ah. Do you need to pretend you don't know me? That deckhand kid did see us together earlier..."

"Yeah, but he's too scared of me to gossip." Rosie flashed him a quick grin. "It might be best if we board separately."

"Got it. You go first, then. I'll come along in a minute."

"Thanks," Rosie said sincerely, before leaving him lurking beside a building and hurrying down the gangplank.

Jill was on the dock, of course, smile firmly in place as she greeted guests and ushered them aboard the boat. The smile slipped as she saw Rosie, her eyes widening, before she made a frantic gesture to one of her assistants to take over and grabbed Rosie's wrist.

"Your date!" she hissed, almost dragging Rosie over to the far side of the transom. "Are you on your way back? Where is he?"

"Coming in a minute so it's not blatantly obvious we're together. Keep your voice down?" Rosie pleaded, and Jill nodded at once.

"I won't give you away, but I'm dying to know what he looks like! Point him out?"

"Oh, you can't miss him," Rosie said dryly, watching Adam ambling along the dock, joining the arriving holidaymakers. He pulled his boat transfer ticket from his pocket to show Jill's assistant, who waved him on board.

Jill looked right past Adam, Rosie noticed with amusement.

"Where?" Jill demanded eagerly.

"He literally just walked right past you and had to duck his head to avoid hitting it on the door," Rosie told her.

Jill turned to stare at Adam, just making his way towards the front of the boat, and then back to Rosie with an expression of pure disbelief on her face. It was so comical Rosie started laughing.

"*That.* That... gorgeous hunk of beef is your rebound date?" Jill finally said, and Rosie couldn't stop laughing long enough to answer, so she just nodded helplessly.

"Holy shit, girl," Jill breathed. "Fuck what anyone says. Who's gonna report you, anyway? You go get some. You earned it." And she shoved Rosie firmly in the back, urging her after Adam.

Adam looked up in surprise as Rosie slipped into the vacant seat beside him. "Hey," he said with a broad smile. "Change of plans?"

"Change of attitude," Rosie corrected.

"Yeah?"

"Yeah. Fuck 'em all."

Chapter Six

Startled when Rosie declared her change of heart, Adam nonetheless gave her an approving nod.

"That's the spirit. Don't let the bastards get you down, eh?"

"Yup." She took his hand this time, threading her small fingers into his and then leaning her head against his shoulder.

Surprised but encouraged, Adam turned his head down towards hers, breathing in the fragrance of her brown curls. Salt air, he thought, clean and fresh, and coconut, and a tang of something a little sharper he couldn't place. Complicated and surprising, like Rosie herself.

He wanted to kiss her, quite a lot in fact, but the chattering crowd of tourists excited to be heading to the resort for the start of their holidays stopped him, that and the suspicion it might be a step too far for Rosie.

Instead, he settled back into the seat for the ride back to the island, listening with half an ear to the excited chatter all around them, hearing the calm instructions from the young woman who walked to the front of the boat and asked everyone to take their seats in a clear, carrying voice before conducting a succinct safety briefing.

The pretty Chinese woman grinned at Rosie once she'd finished, giving Adam a thorough look-over and a nod before taking herself off to the back of the boat.

Rosie had flushed pink, he saw when he glanced over at her. "Good friend of yours?" he asked quietly. The two young women had to be about the same age.

"My roomie, Jill," Rosie said. "My best friend," she admitted after a couple of beats.

And confidant, Adam interpreted silently. "You share a room?" he asked out loud, thinking that had to be tough to maintain any privacy.

"A cabin. Two bedrooms, one bath, a kitchenette and living area. It's cozy but nice. We don't work the same hours, so we're not in each other's pockets," Rosie added. "Jill's the guest relations manager, and I'm staff manager, so we have quite different spheres of responsibility."

"I'd think you're both in senior enough roles to merit private living quarters," Adam commented.

"I'm sure we could if we really wanted, but there are only a limited quantity of private staff cabins. We tend to leave them for the couples, and we've been sharing a long time." She thought about it. "Must be nearly seven years, wow, that's a long time! We were both only assistants when we started."

"That's very humble of you." Adam thought back to his early fight days, to sharing a room with another young fighter-in-training, and how Earl had demanded his own place once he'd won his first fight. Adam hadn't cared, really. He was so exhausted by the time he fell into bed he wouldn't have noticed if he'd shared a room with a herd of elephants, but then, there were always those for whom even a taste of fame and power went to their heads.

Earl had won his first two fights, lost his next five, and disappeared off the scene one day. Last Adam heard, he was in Thailand taking part in the weekly money bouts there, where he could get a regular paycheck and live cheaply. There were worse ways to live, he supposed, but he wondered what sort of savings Earl had, what he'd do when getting kicked in by ferocious Thai kids got too much for his aging body.

Hell, I don't even know what I'm *going to do, even though I don't have any money worries!* He'd lived frugally even in LA, neither accustomed to nor desiring luxuries, and he'd been very well compensated for his stellar fighting career. The villa he was borrowing on Sunfish Island was as opulent as any Vegas hotel suite he'd been comped for championship bouts.

"You look deep in thought." Rosie nudged him lightly, and he turned back to her with an apologetic smile.

"Sorry, just contemplating the rest of my life. Retirement's... strange."

"In what way?"

She looked interested, so he tried to explain. "I used to wake up every day knowing when my next fight would be and against whom, training towards a very specific goal. Six to eight hours of training a day, and then another couple watching my opponent's fights, analysing every one of his moves, working out both counters to them and potential plans of attack."

"Wow." Rosie looked impressed. "I never thought about it, but I suppose there's a lot of strategy involved."

"My coach always said it's all in the mind. Win the mental game and you'll beat even an opponent who's physically superior to you."

"I can't imagine you'd meet too many physically superior fighters." She surprised him by giving him a blatant once-over, lingering on the thick muscles of his biceps swelling the short sleeves of his shirt.

"You'd be surprised," Adam managed to get out despite the spike of lust currently kicking him hard in the guts. "Not many bigger, or who hit harder, but definitely some who were quicker or had moves I couldn't match."

"I have the feeling you're being modest and I *really* need to Google you." Rosie narrowed her eyes at him. "How many fights did you lose in your professional career?"

Damn, she can read me like an open book. He wasn't willing to lie to her, and the question she'd asked left little wiggle room for prevarication. *I suppose she's used to asking pointed questions when she interviews prospective employees - and probably picking out the lies better than any lie detector.*

"One," he finally admitted.

"*One?*" Rosie jaw dropped.

"The last one." To a brilliant fighter ten years his junior, a man who truly deserved the titles he'd won by defeating Adam. "I was offered an insane amount of money to take a rematch, more than the man who beat me, in fact."

"Were you tempted?"

"That kind of money would tempt anyone, but reality slapped me in the face pretty hard. My arm needed surgery, and my surgeon was very clear about possible outcomes if I fought again. Those possibilities would have been in my head the whole time, and I wouldn't have done the fight justice, so it was time to call it quits."

Rosie considered his words for a long time, and he wondered what she was thinking. The question she finally asked surprised him.

"Did you want to fight again? Even if the money hadn't been on offer?"

"Yes." The answer came quickly. "If I'd been fit, I'd have fought for free. It was the only thing I've ever been really good at. Those moments of pure adrenaline in the cage, they made all the hard months of training worth it."

"It was never about the money." Rosie said it quite confidently, not a question at all.

"As long as I'd earned a living wage, that would have been enough." Adam shrugged again. "I earned enough to help set my whole family up comfortably, and then more besides."

Rosie was gnawing on her lower lip, and he finally had to ask.

"What are you thinking?"

"Oh." Her smile was wry. "Just about my own dumb choices. A few hours and time to think has given me clarity about my own situation, and I'm coming to realise my crush on Luke was way more about me being able to stay in my own comfort zone than about him. Talk about a day late and a dollar short."

"I don't follow?"

Rosie took a deep breath, shaking her head and making her soft brown curls bounce around her shoulders. "It doesn't matter any more. Making a wrong move has just made me realise it's time to make the *right* move, not hang around hoping for things to fall into my lap."

"Sometimes you gotta make the wrong move to figure out what the right move is," Adam agreed, though he still wasn't sure what she was getting at. "Sometimes it takes a catastrophe to put you on a new path. There were days when I thought the end of my fight career was just the end."

"Those days with the prescription painkillers?" Rosie asked, though her expression was understanding rather than judgemental. "I gotta admit, if I hadn't met you, I'd probably be spending the night drowning my sorrows rather than looking past them."

"It's very easy to go looking for crutches rather than solutions." He squeezed her hand gently. "The right answers might not become clear all at once, but that shouldn't stop you moving forward."

"Once more unto the breach, dear friends," she murmured.

"Stiffen the sinews, summon up the blood, disguise fair nature with hard-favour'd rage," he quoted right back at her, and saw her mouth fall open with shock. "Yes, I can quote Shakespeare, and more than just rousing battle speeches, too."

"On the other hand," Rosie said cryptically, "maybe some things just do fall into your lap, after all," and she shocked Adam by reaching up to put her arms around his neck, tugging him down towards her and kissing him full on the mouth.

***

Adam didn't respond for the longest moment, which made Rosie panic and wonder if she'd read him completely wrong, if she'd just been imagining the appreciative way he'd been looking at her all evening. She was just pulling away, face flaming with humiliation, which his lips moved against hers and one powerful arm slipped around her waist, drawing her closer against him.

From tense and embarrassed, Rosie found herself melting as Adam kissed her back. It was a slow, measured sort of kiss, the tip of his tongue tracing her lips, dancing lightly with hers.

Rosie's eyes drifted closed as she leaned into Adam. He was warm and incredibly firm; it was like leaning against a heated wall. He smelled good too, like salt air and a tinge of something woodsy and masculine she suspected was probably expensive aftershave. His jaw was smooth, and she was pretty sure he'd shaved especially for their date.

Someone cleared their throat loudly close by, and Rosie jerked back, looking around to see a mother with two young children in the seat behind frowning disapprovingly at her. Blushing, she glanced up at Adam through her lashes, finding him smiling down at her. He said nothing, but his hand found hers again, fingers interlacing, his thumb drawing delicate circles on the back of her hand.

Jill was giving her an enthusiastic thumbs-up from the other side of the boat, Rosie spotted, a broad grin on her friend's face encouraging her to say the words which spilled out next, spoken in a low voice to avoid offending the woman behind them any further.

"Come to my cabin, once we get back to the island."

Adam's eyebrows went up, and she noticed for the first time a thin scar bisecting one of them, a darker brown than the rest of his skin, wondered if he had other scars from his years in the fight game.

"How intoxicated are you?" he asked, and Rosie gave him an expressive look.

"Hardly at all. I had two mojitos, with food, and we left the restaurant well over an hour ago. I'm fully capable of making an informed decision, I promise."

"Then yes," Adam said with a slow smile, making things clench up low in Rosie's belly. "I'd love to come to your cabin."

Chapter Seven

Rosie jumped to her feet as the boat came in, ignoring the safety instruction to remain seated until the boat was docked. Adam followed her to the rear of the boat, laughing as she jumped to the dock before the gangplank was even lowered.

"Come on!" she beckoned to him, and he jumped the gap easily, grasping her hand in his.

"Easy." Dark brown eyes twinkled down at her. "I'm not going to change my mind. Or are you rushing into this because *you're* having second thoughts?"

"Definitely not." She tugged him after her, up off the dock and across the grounds to the staff-only area of the resort, ducking down a narrow, unlit path the guests wouldn't even notice as they disembarked the boat. Adam kept up easily, his long strides eating up the ground as Rosie scurried along, only pausing to punch in the code at the locked gate.

On the little veranda outside her cabin, Adam drew her to a stop and pulled her into his arms to kiss her again, but he was too much taller than she. Rosie groped behind her for the door handle, fumbling it open and almost falling through, one arm around Adam's neck to drag him with her.

"Over here," she panted, pulling him towards her bedroom. "Please, Adam..."

"I got you," he said in a husky rumble before suddenly sweeping her off her feet and carrying her, bridal-style, into her room.

Delighted, Rosie clung to him, though his strength was such that she never feared for a moment that he'd drop her. She did think to check "Your elbow?" as he laid her gently on the bed.

"More than up to carrying you, beautiful," he told her, reaching out and fumbling for the switch to turn on the lamp beside the bed. "Before we start, though, you got protection?"

She grinned and waved her purse, the strap still hooked around her wrist, at him. There was a still-sealed packet in there, and she refused to think about the fact she'd bought them hoping to get lucky with Luke. She was with Adam, here and now, and he deserved her full attention.

"Excellent," Adam said with a decidedly wolfish grin, and he straightened up and began to unbutton his shirt.

Rosie watched with unabashed appreciation as he slipped it off, twisting at the waist to toss the shirt onto her dresser. "Just don't move for a moment," she begged. "Let me get a really good look."

Adam laughed and stood still, arms hanging loose at his sides. "Want me to turn around for you?" he asked, teasing.

"In a minute, I'm enjoying the front view." She most definitely was. Of course, Adam was shirtless when they met on the beach that morning, but she'd been in no fit state to appreciate him, in a distressed state of mind and with red, sore eyes from crying all night.

He stood patiently while she gazed her fill, a small grin quirking his mouth. "Just give me the word when you've had enough staring and want to try touching, hm?" he said after a couple of minutes of silence.

"Sorry, I'm just stunned to silence by how gorgeous you are," Rosie admitted. "I mean, seriously, you look like you just wandered off the set of a superhero movie, took a wrong turning and found yourself lost in my bedroom."

"It was a right turning, and I'm not lost."

"But you're not denying the superhero movie?"

"I may potentially have had a walk-on part as 'muscled bodyguard' in one, once," Adam confessed, and Rosie shook her head.

"Of course you did. I don't know why I'm even the slightest bit surprised."

Setting one knee on the bed, he paused until she realised he was waiting for her invitation. Crooking a finger to beckon him closer, she hooked her arms around his neck as he moved over her and dragged him down for a kiss.

"Not only hot as hell, but a real gentleman," Rosie sighed blissfully as Adam broke the kiss and began trailing his lips down her throat. "I really lucked out this time, huh?"

"I'm the lucky one," he mumbled gruffly, warm breath tickling over her collarbones.

"We're going to have to agree to disagree on that." Even as she said it, Rosie thought it was the only thing they'd disagreed on so far. For a man who'd made his living by beating up other men, Adam was incredibly chill and easy to talk to.

Not that she wanted to talk any more, her breath catching in her throat as one huge hand curved underneath her breast, cupping it lightly, thumb skating over her nipple as it hardened beneath the thin fabric.

Adam made a low sound in his throat, a hungry sort of sound, and looked up at her with glint in his dark brown eyes. "Rosie, stop me any time, okay?"

"No," she said breathlessly.

"No?"

"No, I'm not going to stop you. In fact, don't you dare stop." Grabbing his wrist, she pulled his hand more firmly against her breast, or tried to. It was a bit like pulling on a building. He scrutinised her face for a moment before letting her move his hand, a slow smile dawning before he bent his head to kiss her again.

Rosie sighed into Adam's mouth as he took his time kissing her this time around, a slow, leisurely exploration of her reactions, his tongue licking lightly into her mouth, duelling with hers and drawing back, luring her into chasing after it. Hungry for more, she reached up to run her hands into his hair, enjoying the crisp, dense texture under her fingers.

His hand was a warm weight on her breast, the only thing moving his thumb as he teased her nipple to an aching point. Arching up into his touch, Rosie whimpered, trying to hook her ankle over his leg, pull him closer. He gave her what she was asking for, shifting his lower body over her, though she was dimly aware he was leaning on one elbow, not allowing his much larger mass to crush her. It felt really good, the heavy weight of his legs and lower torso anchoring her, giving her something to cling to as his hand on her breast sent her practically into orbit with lust.

Adam didn't seem in any particular hurry, taking his time to kiss Rosie into a state of utter mindlessness. His steadying weight, his apparent patience, made her urgency subside a little, and she was able to slow down and live in the moment, enjoy the slow, languid kisses and take her time to explore his chest and shoulders with her hands. He was chiselled to perfection, thick muscles rippling under smooth, hot skin, and from his reactions he was enjoying their makeout session just as much as she was.

She could feel his cock against her thigh, thickly engorged inside his close-fitting pants, and wondered how that could possibly be comfortable. Running a hand down his back, she tugged on his belt, encouraging him to move off her.

"Problem?" Adam lifted his head to inquire.

"Too many clothes," Rosie declared.

His chest rumbled with a low chuckle. "You think?"

"I know." She tugged at his belt. "Off. All of it. Please?"

"You didn't even have to say please, but I do like that you asked nicely. Means I can ask nicely if I can take this pretty dress off."

She laughed up at him as he did a push-up above her, muscles rippling in his shoulders in a way which made her heart pound and her breath come quicker. It was pure reflex, feminine instincts responding to the display of male strength and prowess.

"Sure, you can take it off. It's pretty easy, no zips or buttons, just comes off over my head."

"Think I can handle that." He sat back on his haunches, reached to gather the hem in his big hands and draw it upwards. She lifted to help him, first knees, then her hips, then a half-sit up before lifting her hands above her head.

"Lovely," Adam murmured, gazing his fill as Rosie lay back down.

She looked away, not meeting his eyes. While she didn't hate her shape, she doubted she stacked up all that well against women he might have encountered in his career, ring girl models and professional athletes. At least she was wearing her absolute best underwear, a brand-new satin balconette bra and bikini knickers set she'd splurged on during a recent trip to Brisbane, white with a print of tiny blue flowers.

"Really like this." Adam trailed a finger down her cleavage, touched the delicate blue bow at the centre of the bra. "Lovely."

"I like pretty underwear," she admitted. "My workday clothes are utterly practical, so it's sort of the one way I can express myself, even if nobody else usually gets to see it."

"Lucky me, then." He skated fingertips lightly over the smooth satin, the sensation barely registering through to Rosie's skin. His gentleness, the delicacy of his touch, seemed so incongruous with his sheer size and power. Her sense of urgency was returning, an impatience, a wish for Adam to *use* some of that strength and nail her into the mattress.

"Too many clothes," she said again, reaching for her purse, lying close to her hand on the bed. "And get one of these on."

"You're a bossy little thing, aren't you?" Adam said with a grin, but he reached down to unfasten his belt, push his trousers down, taking his boxers with them.

Rosie's eyes widened and her fingers froze mid-fumble with the condom packet.

"Impressive," she said finally, her mouth dry. He definitely was, his cock both long and thick, standing proudly out towards her.

"Proportional," he replied with a grin, but he didn't move any closer to her until she'd gotten past her momentary surprise. Then he eased to lie down beside her, propping himself up on an elbow, free hand skimming over her breasts lightly until she moaned and pushed against his hand, urging him to use more pressure, give more stimulation.

"May I?" he murmured low, hand sliding around to her back, fingering the hooks of the bra.

"Please do," she panted, desperately wanting *more*. Her hands traced over the thick muscles of his torso, outlined his abs, before slipping lower. She curled one gently around the root of his cock, her breath catching as she realised her finger and thumb wouldn't meet around his girth.

Adam made a strangled little sound in his throat, fingers stalling and fumbling, but finally he managed to pop her bra catches undone, eased the straps down her shoulders. Oddly, his fumbling made her feel more confident, believing that she wasn't just the latest in a long line of conquests for him, because surely if he was, he'd have been smoother, more deft. Not shuddering against her, her name a soft gasp from his lips as he searched for her mouth to kiss her thirstily.

"Fuck, Rosie, I... fuck." He pulled away from her quickly, shifting down the bed so she could no longer reach his cock, pressing his face between her breasts and laughing softly. "I feel like a horny teenager, about to cream his shorts. Gimme a minute, huh?"

"How about you give *me* a minute?" she suggested instead, curving her hand around the back of his head and urging his mouth to her nipple.

"Oh yeah," was all he said before he latched on obediently, sucking in rhythmic deep pulls that had her hips rocking instinctively against him, hungry, needy sounds spilling from her lips.

Thick fingers traced over the triangle of damp satin covering her mound and she parted her legs for him immediately, desperate suddenly for fulfilment, for release. He was still gentle, tentative, and she reached to grab his wrist and urge his hand more firmly against her, making him chuckle against her breast.

"I got you, angel. Here. Like this?" and he rubbed a fingertip over her clit, quick and hard.

"Yes," Rosie said on a strangled gasp, "don't stop!"

He didn't, setting up a fast, firm flicker over her clit which tipped her over the edge in moments. Rosie's body bucked, stars flaring behind her eyelids as she cried out, the orgasm searing in its intensity.

***

Adam gentled his touch, but he kept stroking, teasing lightly until Rosie's eyes opened again. She hummed softly, her hand flexing lightly on his wrist.

"Okay?" he asked softly.

"Hmmm." Her smile was satisfied, a woman who was well pleasured. "How 'bout you?"

"I'm in no hurry." It was a lie; his cock was aching, throbbing with need, but he wasn't about to rush her.

The corners of her mouth tipped up further, and she rolled her head towards him, meeting his eyes. "You're full of it."

"I'm full of something," he admitted, laughing at the direct way she called him on the white lie. "No rush, though. Really. If you're good there, we can leave it..."

"I'm not that much of a cock-tease." Her hand curled around his cock.

He liked her directness, her honest and blunt way of speaking. And he very much liked the way her hand felt on him. There was no way he was going to last long enough to get inside her; he managed to say as much between gasps and gulps for breath.

"Next time then," she murmured, her other hand slipping down to cup his balls, knead them in her fingers, and he lost it completely, jerking and shuddering, hissed oaths spilling between his lips as he came, thick jets of cum spraying across her hand and his clenching abdominal muscles.

Soft lips pressed against his shoulder and Rosie murmured words of praise he barely heard over his own loud, panting breaths.

"Fuck," he said finally. "Fuck."

"Well no, but almost." She laughed quietly before getting up and moving away; he heard water running in the bathroom before she returned with a cloth in her hand.

"I got it," he mumbled, taking the cloth from her as she leaned over to wipe at his stomach. "God. Sorry." She'd run warm water on it, he discovered as he wiped with still-shaking hands at the sticky mess.

"You're apologising for giving me a fantastic orgasm?" Rosie flopped onto the bed beside him and grinned, eyebrows arched. "You're forgiven."

He started laughing, dropping the soiled cloth to the floor beside the bed, before rolling over and reaching to kiss her. "You are so funny! God, Rosie, I'm so glad I met you today."

"I'm glad I met you too," she said softly, before her jaw cracked on a massive yawn.

"Do you want me to go?" he asked immediately. "You're tired."

"I'm tired, yeah, but don't go. I'm happy for you to stay and sleep here. Maybe we can revisit this in the morning?" She'd scooped up the unused condom packet, waved it at him before putting it on her nightstand.

"I'm very much up for that plan," he agreed, and Rosie smiled before another yawn overtook her.

"Gonna go clean my teeth," she mumbled before pushing herself off the bed and stumbling to the bathroom. "Hey, I have a new toothbrush here," she called back, "still in the packet, you're welcome to it."

He waited for her to finish, raising his eyebrows slightly when she returned wrapped in a bathrobe but saying nothing. Instead he scooped the cloth from the floor and headed for the bathroom, washing the sticky cloth out under the tap and hanging it up to dry before cleaning his teeth.

Rosie had exchanged the robe for a nightgown, he saw when he returned to bed; a simple sleeveless long T-shirt in black with a picture of a ghost on the front and the legend I BOO WHAT I WANT. Amused, he grinned down at her before easing back into bed on the other side.

"You are too cute," he murmured, leaning across to kiss the side of her brow. She made a nonsensical little mumbling sound, and he realised she was already half asleep. One hand pillowed under her cheek, her hair tumbling about her face in rumpled waves, she looked soft and lovely. The kind of sight any man would dream of coming home to.

Gently, he brushed away a lock of hair which had drifted across her face and was dangling against her upper lip. She did a vague slow blink and half-smiled at him before her eyelids closed.

Grinning, Adam reached out to switch off the lamp before easing himself down against the pillows. Rosie's bed wasn't as large or comfortable as the one he'd been using at his friend's luxury villa, but it was in his estimation a hundred times better, because of the soft, sweet, warm woman asleep in it. Sleep hadn't been coming easily of late as he tried to puzzle out his future path, but listening to Rosie's quiet, even breathing, he drifted into oblivion within minutes.

Chapter Eight

Rosie woke up much as she always did, curled on her side with one arm tucked under her pillow and half asleep. Wrinkling her nose, she tugged her arm out, rolled to her back and stretched.

Her hand encountered warm, hard flesh and her eyes flew wide as suddenly, she was fully awake. Shooting to sit upright, she stared at Adam, who looked back at her from amused eyes.

He was wide awake, she realised, and wondered how long he'd been awake for. Considering the training regimen he'd given up not long ago at all, he was probably used to getting up at some ungodly hour to start training.

"Good morning," he rumbled, and Rosie felt the colour flood into her cheeks.

"Hi," she said, feeling gauche and foolish.

A smile curved his lips, and he rolled to his side, propping himself up on an elbow. Just that seemingly casual movement made muscles ripple in a way which looked almost pornographic, even though the sheet covered him to a perfectly decent level.

She was staring, Rosie realised, and dragged her gaze back to his face. "I have to get to work," she mumbled.

"No worries," he said cheerfully. "I'll get dressed and get out of your hair." He rolled to his other side away from her, leaned off the bed to retrieve clothes, and within moments was pulling them on.

Rosie quite realised she probably shouldn't be watching him, but she just couldn't look away. The play of muscles rippling under dark brown skin was almost hypnotising.

Adam glanced over his shoulder, caught her watching, and winked. Blushing, Rosie ducked down to hide her face behind the sheet, heard his low laugh.

The bed moved as he got up, and she heard him shuffling his shoes on, before a hand plucked lightly at the sheet, pulling it down to her chin.

"You are absolutely adorable," he murmured softly. "Have dinner with me again tonight?"

She opened her mouth to say yes, but they'd have to go over to Hamilton again because she could get fired for fraternising with a resort guest otherwise, when the next thing he said took the wind right out of her sails.

"You could come to the villa, if you like. I'm not a bad cook."

"Wait," Rosie said, arrested. "What villa?"

Adam's brow furrowed. "Didn't I mention it? I'm staying in one of the private villas on the west side of the island. A friend of mine owns it."

Rosie's jaw dropped. There were less than twenty of the private villas, all valued in the multi-million dollars. Jace Hunter, the island's owner, lived in one of them, and the others were all owned by similarly high-profile and extremely wealthy individuals.

"What friend?" she asked, stunned.

"Tad O'Dell," Adam said with a shrug, naming an Irish billionaire entrepreneur Rosie had certainly heard of. "He owns a share in the UFC. Really nice guy."

"He... lent you his house?"

"One of them. I think he's got a couple dozen." Adam's glance was quizzical. "Everything okay, Rosie?"

"Yes," she said vaguely, still astounded by the revelation that he wasn't a resort guest at all. That her little rebellion, her act of defiance in getting involved with him, was nothing of the sort. "I'm... fine."

"So," he said, still gazing at her with an eyebrow raised curiously, "dinner?"

"Why not." Rosie smiled at him, and his expression cleared. "What time?"

"Seven? Would you like me to pick you up? I have a golf cart, though I'm sure you have access to one too..."

"Actually, I don't." Rosie blushed. "I'm banned from driving on the island."

A grin broke slowly across Adam's face. "That sounds like a ban with a story behind it. Possibly more than one. Maybe you'll tell me tonight?"

"Maybe," she said, blush deepening. "Pick me up at main reception at seven?"

"Will do." He leaned forward and kissed her lightly, just a soft brush of lips against hers, before smiling and moving back. "Looking forward to it."

"Me too," Rosie said quietly to his retreating back, as he slipped out of her room almost soundlessly, his grace astounding for such a big man. "Me, too."

***

Spending the evening - and then the night - with Adam, had almost made Rosie forget her self-created scandal. Right up until she walked into the staff dining-room to get some breakfast and every eye turned to her.

"Oh, crap." She froze mid-step.

"Keep on walking." An arm linked through hers and she was almost dragged to a table.

Turning her head, she saw her friend Olivia, the resort's marketing manager. "Hi," Rosie said weakly, "could you just bury me right here? Might be easiest."

"Don't let them see you sweat." Olivia's pretty face was set in a smooth, expressionless mask, and suddenly Rosie remembered that Olivia had come to Sunfish Island after her New York career collapsed around her ears when her then-boyfriend was exposed as a major white-collar criminal.

"You ran away to the far side of the world after your scandal," Rosie objected as she took a seat at Olivia's urging.

"After I spent several months trying to brazen it out," Olivia said with a wry smile. "I only left because I literally couldn't get another job anywhere else after I got fired. But I assure you, nobody ever saw me crack publicly. The sharks would have eaten me alive."

Rosie could almost feel the weight of the avid stares on her. Gritting her teeth, she forced a smile when Olivia's boyfriend Cory put his tray down on the table and gave her a sympathetic nod.

"Want me to fix you a plate?" he asked.

"Oh God, yes please." Standing up to walk to the buffet with everyone staring at her was beyond Rosie just now. She wasn't sure she'd be able to manage to eat, even, but at least she could try. "Just some yogurt and granola would be great. And coffee. Lots of coffee."

"Same for me too, if you're playing waiter," Olivia said, and Rosie felt hopelessly grateful that Olivia obviously didn't plan to leave her alone.

"I suppose Jill filled you in?" Rosie asked dismally, trying to sink lower in her chair.

"She did." Olivia's expression was deeply sympathetic. "I wish you'd said something to one of us before you took the leap, Rosie."

"I do too, because it's obvious you'd all have correctly told me I was massively wasting my time."

"I'm sorry," Olivia said kindly. "Luke's a great guy and I can completely see why anyone would have a crush on him, if that helps at all, but yeah... I'd have told you it was one-sided and not to set yourself up for failure. Especially not publicly."

Rosie winced, but one reason she valued Olivia's friendship so much was the American girl's straight-talking attitude. "I fucked up, but it might be for the best, in the long run," she said as Cory set two bowls on the table and took off again to get their coffees.

"Why do you say that?" Olivia picked up her spoon and dug into her granola.

Rosie fiddled with hers, stomach still churning uncomfortably, though people were finding other things to talk about and look at now; she was no longer the centre of everyone's attention. "Because it's going to force me out of my comfort zone," she said finally, had to laugh at Olivia's exaggeratedly raised eyebrows. "Yes, I am indeed extremely uncomfortable right now and it's all my own fault, but that's not what I mean." She nodded thanks to Cory as he set her coffee in front of her before taking his own seat. "What I mean is... if I had indeed... with Luke... it would have been so *easy*, right? Everything all neat and tidy."

"Ah." Olivia got it, Rosie could tell. "But since you didn't..."

"I need to look for another job."

Cory paused with a forkful of scrambled eggs halfway to his mouth. "Away from *Sunfish*?"

Rosie gave Cory a fond look. They'd been friends since their school days, both growing up in the same suburb of Cairns, had been delighted to find each other again when they both came to work at Sunfish a few years earlier. "We can't all be lucky enough to have the love of our life fall off a boat right in front of us, Cory. I'm just facing up to the unhappy truth that I'm going to have to go looking for mine."

"Oh jeez, Rosie." Cory put his fork down, his face full of sympathy. "What can we do?"

"I'm not in a panic. I want a job to go to before I hand in my notice, so I'm planning to update my resumé and have a quiet chat to a headhunter I know... but if either of you have any contacts who know of a position which might suit me, I'd appreciate a heads-up."

They both nodded in understanding. Olivia tilted her head. "In America?"

"Maybe. I was thinking about Hawaii. Or a cruise ship, perhaps... new horizons."

"I know a few people. Got a college sorority sister who works for Disney in Florida... I can ask around. Let me have a copy of your resumé."

"Will do." Buoyed by their support, Rosie finished her breakfast and walked out with her head held high, deciding to go to her office and go through some staffing requirements she needed to work out. She'd have a good reason to be calling the headhunting agency then, and could just slip in her own available status at the end of the call.

She got sidelong glances in the Personnel office, of course. The two clerks who handled payroll giggled behind their hands and wouldn't meet her eyes. Her second-in-command, Nadiya, cast her sympathetic glances but was too busy to stop to chat, occupied in settling a dispute that had arisen over rostering in the resort's laundry. Rosie buried herself in work and tried to pretend the whole disaster with Luke had never happened... which turned out to be surprisingly easy, since her mind kept drifting instead to Adam.

Skimming through applications and emailing candidates to set up interviews, she was working pretty much on autopilot. Which left a good proportion of her mind free to drift, reminiscing back on the previous evening. How charming Adam had been, how much of a good time she'd had... especially once they got back to her cabin. Even though they hadn't actually ended up going all the way and having sex.

Rosie blushed just thinking about it, excitement welling in the pit of her stomach as she thought about spending another evening with Adam.

"Hey," Nadiya popped her head into Rosie's office, startling her. She never closed the door unless she was in an interview, so Nadiya hadn't had to knock. "I'm flat out today, going to grab some sandwiches from the canteen and eat at my desk. Want me to bring you some?"

"Yes, please." Rosie didn't have to think about it. She definitely didn't want to run the gauntlet of all those curious, speculative glances again today.

"You look flushed. Are you all right?" Nadiya gave her a curious look.

"Of course! Why wouldn't I be?" Rosie realised it was a stupid thing to say even as Nadiya looked astounded.

Coming into the office fully, Nadiya shut the door behind her. "Rosie," she began, but Rosie held up a hand to stop her.

"Whatever you might have heard, it's almost certainly wildly exaggerated."

"Jill told me that you had a few drinks, hit on Luke and he turned you down, and you were pretty upset about it. It didn't sound all that far off the mark considering I've suspected for a while you had a massive crush on him." Nadiya folded her arms and raised her eyebrows. "So I'm going to ask again. Are you all right?"

Rosie winced at the blunt summing up, but then she nodded. "I'm fine. It was a moment of madness; if I'd been thinking straight I'd have known very well he'd never have taken me up on the offer." She smiled. "Apart from the embarrassment of everyone knowing I made a dick of myself, I'm over it. And everyone will find some new piece of gossip to obsess over soon enough."

Nadiya gazed at her thoughtfully for a few minutes before nodding. "All right, if you say so. I know you've got close friends you can talk to, but if you want to talk to me confidentially... you can, you know. If work's uncomfortable... I know you're my boss, but there might be times you'd rather I took on certain things..."

"Like talking to Luke?" Rosie smiled wryly. "No. It's okay, seriously. I'm an adult, and a professional. If anyone gives me shit about it directly, I might let you handle it so I wouldn't be seen to be retaliating, but I can handle side-eye and a bit of embarrassment. Call it my penance for being a dumbass."

"Gotcha." Nadiya nodded, accepting her word for it. "So. Sandwiches?"

"Please. And a cola as well, if you wouldn't mind. I need the caffeine!"

"You got it, boss." Nadiya gave her a thumbs-up and a wink before disappearing.

Nadiya would be able to step up into my job no problem, Rosie thought, leaning back in her office chair and swinging gently from side to side as she mused. *Luke wouldn't even need to recruit to replace me. Just promote Nadiya and let her find her own assistant.* She certainly didn't need to feel guilty about leaving anyone in the lurch; even if she quit tomorrow and walked away, she was confident Nadiya and the rest of the personnel team would manage. Not that she was planning to, of course; she'd find a new job and then hand in her notice and work out the required period.

With that thought, she reached for her keyboard again, and logged into her personal cloud storage. It had been a few years since she last updated her resumé, she'd been promoted since and taken on all kinds of new responsibilities. Time to make sure she looked as appealing as possible to her prospective new employers.

Chapter Nine

Busy with work, Rosie completely lost track of time. It wasn't until she found herself squinting in low light to read the text on a printed form that she looked around and realised the sun was almost below the horizon, the light coming in through the window beside her desk fading fast.

Which meant it was already after six, she thought, and she needed to pack it in, go have a shower and get ready for Adam to pick her up.

A ball of excitement knotted in her stomach at the thought, and she reached to shut down her computer with slightly unsteady fingers.

Nadiya was just picking up her things at her desk as Rosie left her office, and everyone else had already gone for the day. They walked out together, Rosie checking that the locks engaged automatically behind them. The Personnel offices were swipe-card access only, restricted to the staff who worked in them because of the confidential records kept there.

"Want to go get some dinner?" Nadiya suggested as they made their way downstairs. They'd have to pass by the staff dining room to return to the staff quarters, so Rosie supposed it made sense that they could eat before going back.

"I'm meeting someone, actually," she said.

Nadiya gave her a quizzical sideways glance. "A man? A *date*?"

"Yeah," Rosie admitted. "You don't know him," when Nadiya made a *gimme* gesture, inviting her to continue. "And no, he's not a resort guest. Staying in one of the private villas."

"Well." Nadiya grinned at her. "You move on fast, huh? Well, have a good time!"

"I intend to!" Rosie gave her a quick wave and sped up her steps, hurrying down the path to the staff cabins. She needed to hurry or she wouldn't really have time for more than a speedy shower.

Jill was in the small living room they shared, and immediately demanded details of the previous evening's date.

"I'm meeting him at seven outside reception," Rosie cut her off. "He's not a resort guest, either. He's staying in one of the villas."

"Really!" Jill followed Rosie into her room. "Come on, you can fill me in while you have a shower and get ready," she said, when Rosie tried to shoo her out. "Let me pick out something for you to wear."

Rosie gave up and headed for the bathroom. As she washed off hastily, she called out answers to Jill's rapid-fire questions as best she could, filling her friend in on everything she knew about Adam. She'd resisted the temptation to do more research on him, knowing well that what was on the internet might be a long way from reality, considering his celebrity status. Her innate sense of fairness just wouldn't let her do it, anyway, knowing that he couldn't do similar research on her. They'd just have to get to know each other the old-fashioned way.

Wrapping a towel around herself, Rosie went back into the bedroom to find Jill had emptied half her wardrobe onto the bed.

"You're putting all this back when I've gone," Rosie warned.

"You should be putting most of it in the donation bag for the charity shop, or tearing it up for rags!" Jill held up a cotton dress so old it was almost shapeless, the hem half down, the fabric worn thin and nearly transparent. "What is *this*?"

Laughing sheepishly, Rosie grabbed the dress off the hanger, balled it up and shoved it in the bin. "All right, all right, I do need to have a wardrobe clean out. But not right now, okay? I've got to be outside front reception in fifteen minutes."

"You'd better do your face, then. And put this on." Jill shoved a hanger at her, and Rosie frowned.

"That one? I don't know..." It was a dress she'd been given, a turquoise silk sheath she'd worn at her friend Lucy's wedding a few months ago.

"You were absolutely stunning in it, and you haven't worn it since. Put it on." Jill pulled a pair of strappy tan sandals from the bottom of the closet and waved those at her. "And these."

"You're so bossy," Rosie said, without any heat in it, as Jill set the shoes down and started poking through her makeup. With a sigh, Rosie started digging through her underwear drawer to find the bra she needed to wear with the dress, secretly not unhappy to be wearing the pretty pale blue silk plunge.

"I'm just confident in my decision-making," Jill said airily, moving around Rosie to pull up her zip. "Here, give me your eyeliner. I'll be quicker than you."

"You've also got a much heavier hand than me. No thanks." Rosie held onto the pencil. "Why don't you start hanging my stuff back up while I do this?"

Jill sighed as though put-upon, but did start picking up the mess she'd made after Rosie gave her a pointed look. "Will you be coming back tonight?" she asked, apparently casually.

"I don't know," Rosie admitted. "Don't wait up."

"I'm not your mother," Jill laughed at that. "But that said... just in case I need to send out a search party..."

"I don't know exactly which villa number it is, but it's the one owned by Tad O'Dell. Shouldn't be too hard for you to track down if you need to."

"Tad O'Dell? The Irish tech entrepreneur?" Jill closed the closet door and turned to give her a surprised look. "He owns a villa here? I didn't know."

"Me either, but apparently he owns a share in the UFC too, which is how Adam knows him."

"He's hot as hell."

"I know," Rosie sighed, reaching for her lipstick.

"I meant O'Dell... but your big muscly bloke isn't bad either." Jill chuckled at her. "Hey, want me to stuff a couple of things in an overnight bag for you?"

"That feels kind of presumptuous." Rosie thought about it. "Maybe just... toothbrush and some clean underwear in my bag."

"And condoms?"

The box was still sitting on her bedside table, the foil packet they hadn't got around to using sitting beside it. Blushing, Rosie nodded, but Jill just took it in her stride, putting them into Rosie's handbag before going to fetch her toothbrush.

"And now you'd better go, because it's right on the dot of seven and while you don't want to be eagerly waiting for him, you don't want to keep him waiting too long either."

Rosie wouldn't have minded if Adam had arrived to find her waiting, but she didn't argue with Jill, just taking her bag and giving her friend a quick hug and air kiss to the cheek. "Thanks for your help."

"Have a good time!" Jill called after her as Rosie hurried out.

I'm sure I will. Hurrying up the path, she was aware that she attracted a few looks, friends among the staff obviously wondering where she was off to all dressed up. She ignored them all, walking through reception without even glancing at the front desk and out the front, where a silver golf buggy was waiting.

"Of course it's a Bentley golf buggy," she said with a laugh.

"Would a billionaire have anything else in his holiday home?" Adam responded with a dry grin. "Good evening. You look gorgeous."

"Thank you." Rosie felt a blush coming to her cheeks again as she hopped into the front seat, sinking into the buttery leather.

"Busy day?" He turned the key and sent the cart whizzing off, the electric engine so quiet it was almost inaudible.

"Buried in paperwork," Rosie admitted with a grimace. "We'll be coming out of the low season in a few weeks so it's time to think about taking on some more staff. We advertised openings last week and my inbox is three hundred resumes deep."

"Yikes! Rather you than me." Adam shot her a sympathetic look. "I can see why, though. Who wouldn't want to work here? It's basically paradise."

"It is, and we pay well compared to pretty much everywhere else similar. Which means positions here are sought after. Helps to be backed by a billionaire who's carrying no debt, means the resort isn't operating on the razor-thin margins a lot are."

"I can imagine," Adam said thoughtfully. "Jace Hunter actually lives here, doesn't he? How involved is he in running the place?"

"Hardly at all, he's very hands-off." Rosie sighed with pleasure as the golf cart hummed up a low rise and they got a spectacular view of the last moments of the sunset, the western sky briefly ablaze with incredible smears of neon purple, hot pink and brilliant orange. Adam pulled the cart over to the side of the path and they just sat in silence and watched the colours flare until they faded to deep, midnight blue and the sky was suddenly awash with stars. "Oh. That was a good one," Rosie said softly at last, breaking the silence.

***

"Every single sunset since I've been here has been spectacular," Adam said, starting the cart up again. "And yet every night it's different. Just incredible. I never saw anything like that in LA. And the stars!" He looked up briefly, shook his head. "I'd forgotten."

Sunfish's isolated location and low-light pollution buildings did make for spectacular star-gazing conditions. The sky looked like an upturned, dark blue bowl absolutely full of blazing points of light. Rosie leaned to the side of the cart to look up, hanging onto the side bar; Adam glanced over at her, thinking how lovely she looked with her soft curls blowing in the breeze and that fabulous dress clinging to her in all the right places. He'd almost swallowed his tongue as she came sashaying down the steps in it, and suddenly felt very underdressed in his shorts and polo shirt.

He was so busy staring at her he managed to miss the fork in the path which led to the villa, and had to back up a little way. Rosie didn't say anything, though, for which he was grateful, and it was only a short distance from there before he turned onto the driveway and pushed the dash button to raise the garage door.

He'd left the outside floodlights on before he left to pick up Rosie, glanced across at her to see her reaction. Her lips pursed in a soundless whistle, which was pretty much the same thing Adam had done on first seeing the house. Tad O'Dell had made a billion dollars investing in small tech companies with brilliant ideas and not enough capital to see them take off, pouring in resources and then reaping the profits when the inevitable massive success occurred. He had access to cutting-edge technology the general public would never even see, and he'd had much of it built into his state-of-the-art holiday home.

Rosie confined herself to a single "Snazzy place," as Adam escorted her through the house to the kitchen, where he pulled a platter of sliced vegetable sticks from the fridge and set them on the marble breakfast bar.

"It's way over the top," Adam said, "but beggars can't be choosers. I needed somewhere to hide out and Tad offered. I'm grateful."

"Is he likely to turn up himself?" Rosie nodded as he plucked a wine bottle from a fridge built under the counter and offered it to her. "My friend Jill is nursing a massive crush on him; she'd love to meet him."

"Don't know, to be honest." Adam poured wine into a glass for her, put the bottle away and took out a sparkling mineral water for himself. "He's pretty busy, understandably. And no offence to Jill, but Tad does tend to only date supermodels, so unless she's taking time out here between Paris Fashion Week and the Victoria's Secret show..."

Rosie laughed, taking a sip of her wine. "I'll make sure she hasn't any expectations - even if he ever turns up! Mm, these look good." She selected a cucumber spear, held it over the triad of bowls he'd set beside the plate. "So, what are the dips?"

"Beetroot and ricotta hummus, roasted eggplant, spinach and artichoke, and this one's cashew, lime and herb. And yes, I made them." He grinned at her raised eyebrows. "When you have a specialty diet, you either spend a lot of money getting professionals to prep stuff for you, or you get pretty good at figuring out novel and tasty ways to eat the healthy stuff you need to eat."

He suspected she was hiding trepidation as she dipped the cucumber spear in the beetroot dip, but her eyebrows flew up after she crunched down.

"Good?" He helped himself to a piece of capsicum, scooped some of the cashew dip, his personal favourite.

"Really good!" Rosie tried the other two, hummed thoughtfully and finally proclaimed the beetroot dip her favourite. "Suzannah would love to try these. If you're willing to share the recipes, of course."

"Sure," he shrugged obligingly. "Is she vegan? I have a variant for the beetroot one that's vegan, if she is..."

"No, she's a chef. At *La Sirène*."

"Wait, the Michelin-starred chef?" Adam blinked, startled.

"Yes, but she's not at all pretentious and she loves trying out new flavours and recipes. These are as good as anything that comes out of *La Sirène's* kitchen, believe me. Well," Rosie considered. "Maybe they don't quite measure up to the deep-fried chocolate wontons."

"Those sound *sinful*." Adam almost groaned at the mere idea. He could barely even remember what chocolate tasted like, outside of protein shakes, which could really only be called chocolate if you were in a particularly charitable mood.

"I could probably bribe Carlo - he's the pastry chef - to put some aside for you, if you want to try them. I'd say get a reservation, but they're booked out months in advance."

Adam was about to thank her for the offer but decline, when it occurred to him that he could just say yes. He didn't have to exert iron control over every single thing he ate any more.

"I would love that," he said. "And I'd be happy to make up some sample pots of the dips and write out the recipes, if you really think Suzannah would like to try them."

He'd made a chicken and pumpkin risotto for the main course, which Rosie enthusiastically proclaimed as delicious too. Watching her eat, gesturing with her fork in between bites as she chatted, her face animated, he could hardly stand it. His mind wouldn't get out of the gutter; all he wanted to do was sweep the plates off the table, lay her down on the smooth glass surface and just feast on her sweetly curvaceous body until she was screaming for him.

"You're very quiet," Rosie noted eventually. "Am I not letting you get a word in edgewise? Sorry."

"I'm enjoying listening to you," he said, quite truthfully. "You're very funny."

She'd been telling him an amusing anecdote about some of her co-workers, without names, obviously thoughtful of their privacy even though he wouldn't have a clue who they were even if she had supplied the names, and she really was funny, with impeccable comic timing as she delivered the punchlines.

Rosie looked pleased by the remark, a soft pink flush rising on her cheeks. "I'm still talking too much."

"I'm not sure I'd make much sense if I tried to talk," he confessed. "I'm too distracted by how attractive I find you!"

"Really!" Her eyes flashed with delight, and then she set her fork down beside her plate, rose to her feet and walked around the table to him.

Adam pushed back his chair, preparing to stand up instinctively, but Rosie put her hands on his shoulders, pressing lightly, encouraging him to stay down, before twisting slightly and sitting down sideways across his lap, putting her arms around his neck. She wasn't a tiny woman, a hearty lapful of curves he couldn't help but fold his arms about.

"Maybe you should do something about that, then," Rosie murmured, her voice soft and sultry.

Adam suspected she wasn't nearly as confident as she was trying to appear; he could see the pulse beating in her throat, frantically fast, feel her quick, shallow, nervous breaths.

"What did you have in mind?" he asked, nuzzling lightly against her throat, mouth open to taste her skin, breathing in the warm, sweet, summery scent of her.

"I think you should take me to bed," she murmured on a soft sigh, tilting her head to offer him better access to her neck.

Chapter Ten

Rosie knew she wasn't a lightweight, but Adam made her feel like one, standing up and carrying her easily with no signs of strain, out of the kitchen, through a luxuriously decorated lounge room and into a vast bedroom. There was an honest-to-goodness four-poster bed, king size at least and maybe even bigger, sheer white drapes fluttering in the light breeze blowing in through the open mesh-screened windows overlooking the pool and the sea beyond. A diffuse light glowed from a small lamp beside the bed, casting the whole room in a soft, romantic glow as Adam laid her gently on the plush mattress.

Rosie was hyper aware of everything; the softness of the high-thread-count sheets beneath her skin, silky smooth and cool against her bare arms and calves. The heat of Adam's hands as they slid away from her body only to curl around her feet, huge, thick fingers deft as he unfastened the strap around each shoe and removed them. The gust of warmth from his breath, puffing out against her knees as he leaned forward and pressed a kiss to each kneecap, making her laugh quietly.

"Really? That's where you choose to kiss?"

"You have pretty knees," he said gruffly, eyes very dark as he looked up at her. "I'm planning to kiss every inch of you, though, if that's alright with you."

Her breath caught in her throat, and she couldn't make a sound come out. She nodded instead, enthusiastically enough she thought briefly that she probably looked like one of those ridiculous bobble-headed dolls, but Adam only smiled.

"Good."

His voice was a low purr against her leg, his hands curving around the outside of her thighs and pushing her skirt up, big body nudging her legs apart so he could like down between them.

It felt really good. Little sparks of sensation rippled from wherever his fingers or lips touched, and Rosie decided to just relax and savour the feeling. Closing her eyes, she rested her head back against the pillows, surrendering herself entirely to Adam. Completely confident that she was safe in his hands, and not only that, about to have one of the best nights of her life, one she'd look back on with amazement in the years to come. That she, plain and ordinary Rosie Brown, once upon a time, made love with an MMA superstar in a billionaire's bed.

"I like that smile on your face," Adam murmured, "and I'm aiming to make it bigger, but you're going to need to tell me how the hell this dress comes off."

She laughed without opening her eyes, reached across her body and jiggled the zip fastener under one arm. "Pull this, then it goes off downwards."

He zipper hissed down, then he was touching her shoulders, sliding the straps off gently before smoothly easing the silky fabric off under her body, deftly lifting her hips before sweeping it right off over her legs.

Rosie grinned to herself. "No way could I have taken that off in any kind of graceful manner while lying down, so thanks for that."

Opening her eyes, she looked up at him, admiring again how incredibly handsome he was. He sat back on his haunches and peeled his shirt off over his head, giving her the opportunity once again to ogle his frankly delicious chest.

She crooked a finger to beckon him down to her, suddenly wanting him to kiss her again, and he came willingly, leaning on one elbow to keep from crushing her with his weight.

His mouth was so incredibly hot, and Rosie could feel herself getting wet between her legs. Adam kissed unhurriedly, as though he had all the time in the world to savour her mouth and meant to do so thoroughly, hot tongue licking and exploring. Rosie, on the other hand, felt as though she was about to explode. She couldn't keep still, running her hands up his tightly muscled back and over his broad shoulders, her hips shifting restlessly, pushing up against him until he shifted, letting her grind against his thigh, seeking the friction she so desperately needed.

"*Fuck*, Rosie," Adam gritted out against her throat, and she let out a sigh of relief, that he was just as affected as she was; she'd been starting to think she was the only one going out of her mind with lust. The desperate hunger in his voice, the way his fingers shook and fumbled as he tried to undo the catch of her bra, told her that he was going just as wild as her.

Rosie hooked her knee up over his hip, gasping as his hand slid down to grasp her thigh and pull her harder against him, before easing under, thick thumb glancing over her crotch.

"You're wet," Adam groaned, kissing downwards to her breasts. "Fuck, Rosie..."

"Yes," she agreed, mindless with need. "Yes indeed, let us fuck. Wait. Damn."

"What?" he lifted his head immediately.

"Left my purse in the kitchen. Condoms?"

"Yes." He rolled away from her, pressed on the front of the silver futuristic cube which passed for a nightstand. A drawer slid silently out and Adam felt inside, coming back with a handful of foil packets and a triumphant grin. "Stocked up at the resort shop," he admitted, "more in hope than expectation."

"I'm glad you did." Plucking one of the packets from his hand, Rosie grinned back. "You're overdressed right now, though. How about you fix that?"

Adam wasted no time in yanking his clothes off, flinging them across the room without care for where they landed. He was obviously eager, making Rosie feel warm and wanted, more desirable than she had in a long time. Down to just her knickers, she didn't feel self-conscious at all about her body, too busy staring in awe at his. His chiselled physique really was a work of art.

"I want," he said, "to eat you out."

Rosie finally managed to drag her gaze off the perfection of his abs and up to his face. "You won't hear me complaining. Screaming, possibly, but not complaining."

"Pretty sure nobody lives close enough to hear you no matter how loud you scream." He paused, one knee on the bed. "Wow. That sounded horribly serial-killer-ish. Let me rephrase..."

She burst out laughing, reaching up to grasp his shoulders and pull him down to her. "Less talking, more kissing!" she demanded, and he seemed more than happy to oblige.

His hands were warm and strong, but gentle, roaming down her body as he shifted to lie beside her and hold her close, one thick arm curved under her waist with his hand on her back, the other hand cupping her breast. He teased her nipple with a light, taunting touch, circling and flicking until Rosie tore her mouth from his and made a frustrated, desperate sound, grabbing at his hand and squeezing his fingers.

"I won't break!" He was being too cautious, too tentative, and while she wasn't into rough stuff, she was going to need more stimulation than what he was giving her.

Adam rumbled a soft laugh. "Greedy. I'm trying to take this slowly. We've got all night."

"Yes," Rosie agreed, "but I want to come *now*, and I want you inside me when I do."

His eyes flared wide, breath suddenly coming faster. "Rosie."

She wiggled back, squirming her hands down the narrow space between them she created, wrapping them around his cock where it butted hard against her stomach, thick and twitching slightly at her touch.

Adam made a gruff sound deep in his chest, eyes drifting closed for only a moment before he shook his head. "No, damn it. I already lost it with just your hand on me last night."

"Uh, ditto, in case you forgot," Rosie pointed out, but he was already pulling back, crawling down the bed, thick thumbs hooking into the sides of her knickers and taking them down with him as he nudged her onto her back.

"Two minutes," he suggested, edging her knees apart. "Let me eat you out for two minutes, and then you can put that condom on me and we'll bang however you want to do it. I just need to know you're wet first."

That was not only reasonable, but considerate. Rosie was pretty sure she was already more than wet enough just from anticipation, but she was certainly not averse to the idea of Adam going down on her. He lifted her thighs over his shoulders, dark eyes glinting as he looked up the length of her body before reaching up to cup her breasts.

"Best view in the world," he murmured, before diving deep, tongue going straight to work on her clit, circling and swiping, lips sucking, teeth grazing lightly over the sensitive bud until Rosie was squirming and panting, feeling that odd tingle starting to race up her spine.

"Stop," she gasped finally, grabbing at his head and pushing feebly. He responded instantly, though, moving back and lifting his hands off her as well. Rosie scrabbled for the packet she'd dropped in the sheets, tearing it open with fingers that shook slightly before pushing herself to a half-sitting position and reaching for him.

Adam groaned, head tipping back as she rolled the condom on. "How do you want it?" he queried softly. "Like this? Or would you like to be on top?"

"Next time," she said, "next time I'll go on top. Right now..." she lay back and beckoned, trying to look confident and sex-kittenish, even though a part of her brain was laughing in disbelief, whispering that she was making a fool of herself.

Adam didn't seem to think she was foolish. The look on his face was all the confidence boost she needed, as he leaned down, bracing his arms either side of her before leaning on one elbow and putting the other down to his cock, guiding the tip to her entrance.

Rosie made a slightly strangled noise as he leaned in, pressing in slow but insistent. He was a big guy, built proportional and she... well, it had been a while, and even then the guy hadn't measured up to Adam.

He paused, checking in with her, which was just so damn sexy, she thought, digging her nails lightly into his shoulders to encourage him on. He was incredibly considerate, asking what she wanted, waiting for her explicit consent before he did anything, and just that sheer thoughtfulness was such a turn-on. Especially from a guy who looked so big and rough and brutish.

Adam groaned out loud, his breath coming faster, hot against her throat. Sweat was breaking out on his shoulders, and considering how fit she knew he had to be, and that the room was comfortably cool from the air conditioning, Rosie knew he wasn't sweating from exertion. He was enjoying their lovemaking just as much as she was.

He hit a certain spot inside her and Rosie's brain just flat-out stopped functioning. She bucked her hips up frantically, chasing that sensation again, and found it.

"More," she said, voice high and desperate.

Adam grunted wordlessly in reply, his hands curling around her hips as he shifted back, drawing a wail of protest from her as he partially withdrew - before he sat back on his haunches and dragged her up on him, chest to chest, nose to nose.

"Oh God." This angle was even *better*.

"Just me." Adam grinned, and then he kissed her, his hips starting to pump, and Rosie lost her mind.

She was pretty sure she screamed the roof down, thinking afterwards it was a good thing they were at his place and not hers. In the moment, though, she absolutely didn't care, and neither did Adam, deep-throated roars of pleasure from him joining her shrieks of ecstasy as they drove each other absolutely wild.

Chapter Eleven

Rosie was fast asleep when Adam woke, in the warm light shortly after dawn. He looked at her sprawled in his bed, flopped on her stomach with one knee crooked, cheek resting on one hand, her brown curls a tangled tumble on his pillow. She wasn't a graceful sleeper, her mouth a little wide open, the sheets kicked into a tangle around her knees.

Adam thought she was the most beautiful sight he'd ever woken up to. He reached out instinctively to touch her, hand hovering over her hip, when he caught himself. Tempting though it was to snuggle into all those soft curves and hope she'd help him take care of his morning wood, she was asleep and he wasn't about to take her consent for granted. It was still ridiculously early, besides, and he'd kept her awake late... not to mention she'd expended quite a bit of energy last night!

Easing out of bed as quietly as he could, he slipped into the bathroom and then into the closet, collecting clean running clothes before sneaking silently out of the bedroom with his running shoes in hand. He'd go for a run and see if Rosie was awake by the time he got back.

Slipping back into the house forty minutes later, his nose twitched. Was that... *bacon*?

Rosie looked up from the stove as he walked into the kitchen and smiled at him. "Morning."

"Bacon."

Her smile broadened. "Single-track there? Okay. It's nearly done. Well. Depends how you like your bacon. I'm personally a big fan of super crispy very nearly burned bacon, but if you like it still flexible, it's probably about ready..."

He honestly wasn't that picky. It had been a long time since he'd had bacon. Rosie must have found it in the freezer, along with the sourdough loaf she'd carved slices off and was now picking out of the toaster.

The first bite of the bacon sandwich, with real butter on the toast and barbecue sauce oozing out of the edges, was very nearly as good as sex with Rosie the night before had been. Adam groaned with pleasure, eyes just about rolling back in his head.

Rosie seemed amused, watching him stuff his face as she ate her own sandwich a lot more neatly... though the way she licked a stray droplet of melted butter off her thumb made his whole body perk up and take notice.

"Best breakfast anyone's made me in years," he said when he'd finished. "Thank you."

"You're welcome." She looked a bit bashful. "I'm pretty sure you're a much better cook than I am, but I do make a mean breakfast, if I say so myself. Get some eggs in and I'll do even better next time."

"There's going to be a next time?" He moved closer, reaching out to put his hands on her hips.

She stilled, looking up at him. "I... would like there to be a next time. You?"

"Very much so." He leaned down to place a gentle kiss on her lips, deepening it when her arms snaked up around his neck. "Not ready for this time to be over, to be honest. Do you have to work today?"

"Yes... but it's still early. I'm not in a shocking rush." Grinning, she pulled him down for another kiss, trying to tilt her hips up against his, but she was too short to get any sort of good contact.

Adam lifted her easily to the counter, stepping in between her spread knees. Now they were in contact, through only thin layers of clothing since he wore only running shorts and she was wearing one of his T-shirts with, he discovered, nothing at all underneath. The T-shirt was like a dress on her, falling to mid-thigh, and he really should have noticed just how damn sexy she looked in it before, he thought as his questing fingers pushed it up and off over her head, but he'd been too distracted by the smell of the cooking bacon. Which probably said terrible things about him as a human being, that food could take precedence even temporarily over a woman as gorgeous as Rosie.

At least she didn't seem to mind that he hadn't noticed her sexy dishevelment immediately. She'd probably appreciated the opportunity to eat her own breakfast without being pounced on, actually. And now she was reaching to the end of the counter, to the purse she'd left there last night, scrabbling in it and pulling out a small box of condoms with a triumphant grin.

Which meant he didn't need to carry her off to the bedroom to ravish her again, which was good, because he could barely think of anything beyond how utterly gorgeous she was, stark naked on his kitchen counter with the early morning sun slanting through the window behind her playing over her soft curves.

He spared only a moment to think a mental apology and a silent promise to disinfect the counter later to the house's owner before reaching for Rosie.

***

Rosie was five minutes into her walk back to the resort when she admitted to herself that she should have got over her embarrassment and accepted Adam's offer of a lift. Indeed, he'd tried to insist, but she found herself suddenly unable to look him in the eye, getting a bit sniffy and telling him he needed to go take a shower. He got a slightly stricken look on his face, sniffed at his own armpit, and headed for the bathroom hastily, calling over his shoulder;

"I really will give you a lift back, Rosie - just give me a few minutes!"

Instead of waiting, she got dressed, scribbled a quick *Sorry, have to get to work* note on a sticky note from a pad in her purse, and left it in the middle of the bed, the bright pink unmissable on the muted grey sheets.

Now she was trudging along the track, mentally cursing her own stupid stubbornness. It was going to take at least twenty minutes to walk back, her shoes were already killing her, and it was ridiculously hot already. She didn't even have a hat or sunscreen on, which meant she was going to arrive back turning an unattractive shade of pink, too.

"Idiot," she muttered to herself. "Stupid, stubborn idiot."

The electric golf carts made almost no sound, so she jumped when one suddenly hummed up beside her.

This is going to be embarrassing. She didn't want to look Adam in the eye after running out on him.

"Walk of shame, hon?" a cheerful voice said, and Rosie started, her head snapping around.

"Nessa!" She almost gasped with relief to see her bartender friend.

"Need a ride?"

"Oh God, yes please!"

Nessa looked fresh and pretty in a white cotton sundress, her long black hair in its dozens of tiny braids almost down to her waist. She put the golf cart back into gear as soon as Rosie was seated, humming on down the track towards the resort.

"Why are you up and about so early?" Rosie asked. Nessa lived with her fiancé, the resort's billionaire owner Jace Hunter, at his private villa. Although she didn't need to work, she enjoyed still doing a few shifts a week at the poolside bar at the main resort, usually in the afternoons.

"Supply run," Nessa said cheerfully. "We're just about out of milk, and Jace is a bit of an arsehole until he's had his third cappuccino of the morning."

Rosie laughed, relaxing back into the seat.

"So, is it a walk of shame?" Nessa pressed gently. "Gotta say that looks like a last-night kind of dress..."

"Ugh." Rosie covered her face with her hands. "I feel skanky," she muttered into them. "Even though it was a really good night and he's a really nice guy. Morning afters are just so awkward."

"Always," Nessa commiserated. "Uh. Not to be nosy, except I'm totally being nosy, but who...? I'm wracking my brain trying to think of who's resident in any of those villas who might be remotely your type."

Obviously she hadn't met Adam yet, because he was every red-blooded woman's type, at least to Rosie's way of thinking.

"Adam Gillespie," she said. "He's staying at Tad O'Dell's villa."

"You like him." Nessa tilted her head slightly, studying Rosie briefly before she returned her gaze to the track. "You're practically glowing, and not just because you've been walking in the sun. Morning-after embarrassment is all very well, hon, but I hope you didn't just run out on him."

Rosie winced slightly. Nessa was much too perceptive. "Not exactly," she equivocated. "I left a note."

"Rosie!"

"It's not going anywhere, no matter how much I like him!" she defended herself. "He doesn't live here. It's just a fling."

She could hear the wistfulness in her own voice, so it was hardly a surprise that Nessa picked up on it. Her friend cast her a disbelieving look as she pulled the golf cart into the small parking area beside the resort's main service doors.

"You know what," Nessa said, "even if it is just a fling, that doesn't mean you have to actively sabotage it before it's run its course. Seize the day, hon. You never know how things might turn out."

Rosie just didn't know what to say to that. Nessa was the same age as she was, but sometimes seemed a hundred years older in experience, with the wisdom she came out with. On the other hand, Nessa was engaged to a literal billionaire, a man she'd originally had a 'fling' with, and it had somehow developed into love. So maybe she was onto something.

After all, Rosie had already concluded that she couldn't stay on Sunfish. And Adam was going to be living in Sydney, he'd mentioned that he planned to head there next while he worked out exactly what he was going to with his life, since he had a friend running an MMA gym there who'd invited him to come and teach some advanced students. So maybe if Rosie could find a job in Sydney... maybe she and Adam might have a chance after all.

"Thanks for the ride," she said aloud, hopping out of the golf cart. "I gotta run. Need a shower and change before I go to work."

"Call him and say you're sorry you ran out on him!" was Nessa's parting shot as Rosie scurried away.

She would. Well, she'd text him, when she got a minute. And the other thing she was going to do today was call the headhunter agency with offices in Brisbane and Sydney, she often used to find experienced new staff for the resort. Tell her contact there that she herself was looking for a new position, preferably in Sydney, and ask what they might have for her.

Chapter Twelve

Adam set out straight away once he realised Rosie was gone, but he didn't find her on the track back to the resort, and had to assume she'd either taken a shortcut he didn't know about or hitched a ride. He was debating going to the front desk and asking where he might find her - and guessing they wouldn't tell him, not to mention start gossiping about Rosie behind her back - when his phone pinged in his pocket.

Hey, I'm sorry I ran out on you. Felt suddenly awkward - not your fault - but I really did have to get to work. Dinner tonight? The Asian fusion bar does takeout. I can bring some over to your place?

He didn't think twice before texting back. *I'd love that. I'll see you when you're ready.*

Feeling at somewhat of a loose end, and not understanding why - he'd been perfectly content in solitude until Rosie crashed into his life - Adam spent the day wandering around the island, exploring. It was a beautiful place, and not difficult at all to see why Rosie loved it so much. He visited the marine biology centre and watched with fascination as one of the staff experts gave a stingray feeding demonstration to a group of riveted resort guests. Eating lunch in a sandwich bar in the main resort, he wandered on and came across a stunning pool, quiet in the early afternoon heat. There was a bar beside the pool with a swim-up area on one side and open seating on the other, a single customer sitting on a stool chatting with the bartender the only other people in sight.

A cool drink would be pretty good, Adam thought, and headed over to take one of the other stools at the bar. The other customer, a fair-haired man of around his own age, glanced over with a welcoming nod. Adam nodded back, seeing the flare of recognition in the other man's eyes and bracing himself to be social, but the blond just nodded and looked back at his drink.

He's oddly familiar. Where have I seen him before? The guy wasn't part of the MMA world, Adam was pretty sure; maybe he was an actor or something?

"What can I get you?" The bartender had moved in front of him; a pretty Black woman with waist-length hair in tight braids, she flashed him a bright smile as she spoke with a distinct English accent.

"Something long and cool - virgin, please."

The guy on the other bar stool laughed into his drink, and the bartender shook her head, chuckling like it was an in-joke between the two of them. "Virgin fruit punch coming right up. Jace, stop it, you'll give the man a complex."

And with that, Adam suddenly placed the guy. "You're Jace Hunter," he said, surprised. It wasn't every day you sat down next to a billionaire, after all.

"Guilty as charged, and you're Adam Gillespie." Jace didn't offer a hand to shake, but he did lift his glass in salute. "Didn't realise we had a sports superstar as a resort guest."

"I'm staying at a friend's villa, not at the resort," Adam said, picking up the glass the bartender set in front of him and nodding his thanks.

"Welcome to Sunfish, then," the bartender said.

"Let me introduce you - this is my fiancée, Nessa," Jace said.

"Pleased to meet you," Adam said, and then the penny dropped. "Wait a minute. You own this place, don't you?"

"For my sins." Jace's smile was crooked.

Nessa laughed. "Don't let him fool you. He bloody loves Sunfish."

"Can't imagine why," Adam said dryly, letting his gaze rove around the idyllic scenery. "Such a hardship, waking up to a view like this every day. Such suffering. Must be dreadful for you."

"It really is," Jace said, laughing. "Retirement absolutely sucks."

"Retirement?" The word piqued Adam's interest. He was pretty sure Jace was around his own age, maybe even younger.

"Of a sort. More a change of lanes, really. When Dad and I sold our majority interests in Hunter Enterprises, I kept Sunfish as part of the deal. I don't interfere with the day-to-day running of the place, but the bigger strategic plans - well, there's plenty to keep me busy there. Like this." Jace pushed a large sheet of paper down the bar towards Adam, and he glanced down, tilting his head curiously as he realised it was a map, showing a cluster of islands.

"What am I looking at?"

"This is Sunfish, here." Jace tapped a finger on one of the islands, roughly in the centre of the cluster. "Up here is Hamilton, which is our nearest airport, though about fifty percent of our guests come in off the mainland, along this route." He traced a dotted line which ran off to the left of the map.

"Right." Adam nodded.

"These three islands immediately to the south of us are locally known as Chapel's Folly. A businessman called Charlie Chapel bought them about a decade ago, wanted to turn them into the premier resorts on the Reef. He built a fancy golf course first on West Chapel, spent a shedload of money on that and some premium resort facilities on Little Chapel, and broke ground for a runway on Big Chapel which would have set the Chapel group up as a genuine rival to Hamilton Island, and benefited Sunfish hugely too, I should point out. Unfortunately, he ran out of money before he finished it, the resort was losing money hand over fist due to mismanagement, and for the last three years the whole place has been almost completely abandoned, except for yachties using the anchorage facilities at Big Chapel Island to avoid paying fees elsewhere."

"They look pretty close," Adam said when Jace fell silent, studying the map.

"Oh, they are. In fact, if you lean out to your left there and look to the south, you'll see West Chapel. It's ten minutes by boat from our marina."

"And you're thinking about buying it?" Adam guessed astutely.

"Lock, stock and barrel," Nessa confirmed. "Charlie Chapel's run afoul of the state government on some of his other ventures and needs to raise some quick cash. He's selling the islands off cheap."

"But not just anyone can buy them," Jace pointed out. "They're actually on a long leasehold and the state government have to approve intended usage. If I presented a plan to finish the runway, re-open the golf course, invest in finishing it all off..." He trailed off, fingertip tracing a slow loop around the cluster of islands. Sunfish was close enough to make the four islands almost a diamond shape, Adam thought. "It could be huge, but it's a heck of a big project."

Nessa snorted. "You'd enjoy the challenge, admit it."

"I would. And I'm probably the only person with enough interest in this to take it on, who wouldn't have to take out a bunch of risky loans to pull it off. I just don't know about West Chapel." Jace tapped a finger on the western island again, a crescent-shaped sweep. "The golf course wouldn't take that much to re-open, but the rest..." He sighed, brow furrowing. "What the hell was Charlie Chapel thinking?"

"The rest of what?" Intrigued now, Adam hunched closer. "What's on West Chapel?"

"What isn't? There's an Olympic-sized swimming pool, for starters, with a fully-equipped diving pool and hydrotherapy pools. A state-of-the-art medical facility, with a couple dozen treatment suites. Indoor courts for basketball, tennis, squash..."

Adam blinked, and as Jace kept talking, the idea came to him in a blinding flash of inspiration. "It's a sports training and rehab facility," he said.

"Say what?" Jace looked up, arrested.

"I just spent six weeks in a place very much like that, except without the spectacular weather and scenery and not as many facilities. Full of elite athletes recovering from surgery, rehabbing from various injuries and prepping for major tournaments under the watchful eye of specialist sports doctors and physiotherapists."

"Bloody hell, that's perfect," Nessa said when Jace didn't speak. "That must have been what Chapel intended, but he never got it open. Shit, I bet you could actually get the state government on board with that, Jace. Maybe even the Australian Institute of Sport."

"I dunno," Jace said doubtfully. "It'd need a lot of specialist medical staff, wouldn't it?"

"Maybe not as many as you'd think," Adam said. "If you're aiming it at the very, *very* elite level, a lot of those guys actually have personal support staff they'd travel with, physiotherapists and the like. Yes, you'd need at least a couple of top physios, an elite sports nutritionist maybe. If you could get the AIS on board, they'd probably send a couple of conditioning coaches up here. Make it a joint venture facility and you'd have plenty of custom, believe me. Hell, with a 50-metre pool, you might well get them holding training camps up here before major tournaments. Like a holiday but without actually taking a holiday from training..."

"Would you like to come take a look?" Jace said suddenly.

"Me?" Adam blinked.

"I showed you this on impulse, but you obviously know what you're talking about, and I doubt there's anyone else on the island who has direct experience of what professional-level training and sports rehab facilities should actually look like. I could fly in an expensive expert, and I probably will... but since you're here, why not come take a look and tell me what you think?"

Why not? Adam shrugged. "Sure. When?"

"We could go now. Plenty of daylight and I have my own boat. Nessa can send out a search party if we're not back before dark, won't you, darling?"

"Of course." Nessa had been listening to them with obvious amusement, leaning on the bar as they chatted. She shook her head at Jace as he leaned over the bar to kiss her. "Only you could have an expert just wander in and sit down next to you as you're mulling over a problem."

"I'm not an expert," Adam disclaimed hastily.

"Probably the closest thing to it within a couple hundred miles." Jace's smile was easy. "Don't stress, I'm not gonna make a billion-dollar decision based on your say-so alone."

"Is it really gonna cost a billion dollars?" Adam asked hesitantly as he walked alongside Jace towards the boat dock. "Because holy shit. I thought having a couple million in the bank meant I was seriously rich."

"It does. And no - probably not a billion. Maybe half a billion." Jace chuckled at the look on Adam's face. "It's a very big chunk of what I've been left with after the Hunter Enterprises sale, but it's money which has pretty much been sitting in the bank while I figure out what to do with my life. I've given a fair bit away to some major foundations, and I'll give away a lot more, but... a project like this could create so many jobs, make a huge difference to the local economy."

"It could also change Sunfish beyond all recognition," Adam pointed out.

"Which is definitely a part of why I'm hesitant. We've created something special here, and I don't want to risk losing that particular magic which makes Sunfish so much more than just another resort."

"It does have a magical atmosphere," Adam agreed. "Your staff are incredibly happy, for a start, and I don't think it's just because you pay them well." He was thinking of Rosie, of course, at her obvious distress at the mere idea of having to leave. "It's home, for them."

"That's right." They'd reached the dock, and Jace gestured Adam to a handsome white motor launch tied up at the end. It was only about a twenty-footer, pretty modest considering what Jace's money could have bought him, but Adam didn't comment. Only a few minutes in the young billionaire's company and he'd already figured out Jace Hunter was uncomfortable with his wealth, considering it a responsibility to be shouldered rather than glorying in the indulgences it could bring him.

"Done much boating?" Jace asked.

"Not since I was a kid, fishing and dodging crocs on a tinny in Darwin Harbour," Adam admitted, but he could manage to cast off a line, unwinding the one Jace pointed to as Jace fired up the engines. Within a minute they were pulling smoothly away, the engines a low roar as the launch cut smoothly through the small waves just riffling the blue-green surface of the Coral Sea.

They had to circle around the southern end of Sunfish to go across to West Chapel, but it was still only a ten-minute journey. Adam braced his feet and stood beside Jace at the wheel, enjoying the ocean breeze, the salt spray whipping lightly across the deck as the boat heeled over slightly to port.

The dock at West Chapel Island was solid concrete, designed for large boats to tie up beside, and three years of neglect had done little but cause some seaweed to be washed up on it from high tides. The island seemed almost asleep, rather than abandoned, Adam thought as he and Jace walked among the buildings being rapidly overtaken by the tropical grounds, like an enchanted land with a spell of sleep cast on it. He almost laughed at himself for the whimsy.

"That's the pool," Jace pointed out. "It was never filled. Shouldn't be any structural issues. That might actually be the easiest thing to bring up to a completed status."

Most of the buildings were completed and locked up, but some were unglazed, meaning the two men could walk right in and look around.

"This would be a fantastic boxing gym," Adam said thoughtfully as they examined a high-ceilinged room, nothing but bare concrete right now and dead and rotting vegetation on the floor.

"The accommodation here isn't set up like standard resort rooms, which didn't make sense to me at first, but it does now I'm looking at it as a rehab facility. Two and three bedroom apartments, with larger kitchens than usual for holiday apartments, a hot tub on each apartment balcony." Jace pointed straight up. "Up above the sports facilities."

"Wouldn't make sense for regular holiday guests because of noise," Adam agreed. "Is all the accommodation like that?"

"No, there's some luxury stuff as well, lining the closer fairways on the golf course. That's the only part which really saw any use; the course was in operation for a couple of years, and most of the clientele stayed right here. We brought people over from Sunfish, as well. It was quite a drawcard. Honestly, even just getting that back open, I reckon would be worth it. Do you golf?"

"Never learned." Adam shook his head. "Might be something I take up in retirement, once the elbow's settled down, anyway."

"I enjoy a game, but I've never really had the time to play much." Leaving the building via one of the unglazed windows, Jace led Adam up a broad, paved path with weeds sprouting thickly from the cracks until they arrived at a spectacular building which was obviously the golf clubhouse. Set on what Adam rather thought was one of the island's highest points, the clubhouse commanded absolutely stunning views, or would when the golf course wasn't massively overgrown, anyway. They leaned on a rotting wooden verandah outside what was obviously a large restaurant dining room and looked out across the fairways.

"This could be incredible," Adam said. "I've never seen a facility like it. You'll have every elite athlete in the world who has to do physical rehab wanting to come here."

"It does seem purpose-built for it," Jace agreed. He'd asked a lot of questions as they wandered around, listening intently to Adam's answers. "I reckon... six months from breaking ground, I could have the golf course operational. Bring the rest on in phases, depending on how much work each facility needs. The airport's gonna take the longest, unfortunately, but by the time I have that done, we'd be fully operational. Running at max capacity."

"You look like you've already made a decision."

"If I don't do it, somebody else will. The airport makes it too attractive a proposition to turn down. But if I pass up the opportunity and somebody else takes it on, and makes a mess of it, Sunfish is at risk."

"Some retirement," Adam said after a few minutes of contemplative silence, and Jace started to laugh.

"Eh. What can I say. I like a challenge."

Adam nodded, feeling something like envy. The Chapel Islands project would be a challenge which could last a lifetime. Hell, he'd start visiting the resort himself, once it was open. He did fancy taking up golf.

"You interested?" Jace asked, and Adam looked at him in confusion.

"In what, sorry?"

"Investing." Jace grinned at him. "I'd rather not have it be *all* my own money. I'll be looking for investors. Give you a chance to get in on the ground floor."

"Maybe have a say in what you do with the place?"

Jace's eyebrows rose. "Well, I'll mostly be looking for silent investors, I admit. I'm control freak enough to want to do things my way. That said... you've got the kind of expertise which could make you very useful... as an employee."

"Are you offering me a job?" It was the last thing Adam had expected, but as he looked around, suddenly it was the only thing he could imagine wanting to do.

"Absolutely. We can work out the exact job title and your responsibilities later, along with a salary you're worth, but I'm willing to say here and now I want you on board."

"Yes." He didn't have to think about it. Didn't even particularly care how much he got paid. He wanted to be a part of this, wanted to be included in Jace Hunter's vision, to make his own mark here in this beautiful part of the world. Offering his hand, he smiled broadly when Jace clasped it. "You got yourself a new employee."

"We've got a lot of planning to do," Jace warned. "Could be a year or two of contracts and environmental studies and negotiating with the state government before anyone gets to even pick up a shovel or a paintbrush, much less getting the place open for business."

"Good. It'll give me time to do research on other facilities who'll be our competition," Adam pointed out. "I'll leave the construction and all that to you, because that's your area of expertise; mine is going to be convincing the pro sports world this is *the* place to be for rehab and training." Turning to look at the incredible view again, he grinned broadly, suddenly energised by the challenge ahead. "Gotta say, the location will make it a hard sell, but I'll do my best."

Jace's laughter echoed over the overgrown fairways, startling a pair of tropical birds flying overhead; they swooped and arched away with loud, protesting shrieks at the interlopers in their domain as Adam and Jace turned to head back to the boat.

Chapter Thirteen

"Of course I can find you something!" the cheerful voice trilled in Rosie's ear. "Sydney? Easy! I can name half a dozen of the big hotels who'd be delighted to have you... that's if you want to stay in hospitality? You've got the experience to handle a big staff. Several companies spring to mind where you could potentially step up a level from where you are now..."

"Give me the options in hospitality first," Rosie said.

"Sure, sure. What about sports? I heard a rumour one of the rugby league teams might be after someone... smaller staff but bigger pay."

On the verge of saying she didn't care about the pay, Rosie caught herself. Sydney was a seriously expensive city to live in, and unlike Sunfish, she was unlikely to have board and lodging as an included benefit with her new job.

"Just send me what you have to look over, Carole," she said. "And, uh... I haven't handed in my notice yet, so if you could keep this between the two of us for a little while, I'd appreciate it."

"Of course! Just between us. Although I might start lining up a list of replacement candidates for you, since I know Luke will be calling me as soon as you let him know."

That made it feel suddenly alarmingly final. Ending the call, Rosie clutched at the edge of her desk, seeking stability as she felt briefly dizzy. Was she really doing this? Really leaving Sunfish?

"Hey, boss." Nadiya rattled her nails against Rosie's office doorframe. "I'm going on a coffee run. Want some?"

"Yes, please," Rosie said gratefully. It was well on into the afternoon and she was starting to feel the effects of a night with not a lot of sleep, not to mention a distinct ache in her thighs beginning to make itself known. Not only that but it had been a busy day, lunch had been a sandwich quickly bolted down at her desk, and now, at just before four o'clock, she was starting to flag.

Nadiya set the coffee cup on her desk a few minutes later and Rosie mumbled a grateful thanks, eyes on her screen as she sorted a stack of incoming resumes in her email.

"I've no idea what we're even looking for here," she muttered. "How do you pick the best qualified doctor when you're not a doctor?"

"Applicants for the GP position?" Nadiya queried.

"Yep." With four hundred permanent resident staff and anywhere up to two thousand guests on the island at any one time, there were always medical needs which had to be seen to. They had three nurses who rotated on a 24-hour roster, but they'd been having to helicopter in a doctor from Hamilton Island - or a guest out to the mainland - on an almost daily basis recently, and it was just getting too expensive. The higher-ups had decided it was time to get a permanent doctor in residence.

"I think I'm just going to forward all the ones that seem actually qualified to Luke and dump the problem in his lap," Rosie concluded, taking a sip of her coffee and sighing with pleasure. "How do I decide between the surgeon in her sixties who wants to retire to a quiet life after thirty years in emergency medicine at the Royal Melbourne, or the young guy who's only been qualified five years but has spent all of them in war zones with the Red Cross?"

"I'd pick the young guy," Nadiya said cheerfully.

"Because the older woman might retire completely in a couple years and leave us to do it all over again? That feels super ageist."

"No, because the young guy might be hot."

"Nadiya!" Rosie laughed, though, as Nadiya had obviously meant her to. "That never even occurred to me!"

"Which is why you're in charge of this department, not me." Nadiya grinned at her. "I agree with you, though. You're not qualified to pick the most suitable candidate any more than I am. Forward them all to Luke and let him decide who to interview. And then take the rest of the afternoon off and go for a swim in the pool or a massage or something; you look tired and way too tense."

"Tempting," Rosie said, but she could see her inbox icon blinking again; Carole had sent through some of the job roles in Sydney which might suit her. "I'm just going to look through these first..."

"Your funeral," Nadiya replied cheerfully. "I've cleared my desk, unless you have anything else for me?"

"No, we're good if you dealt with all those backpacker applications," Rosie said, and Nadiya nodded. "Thanks, then, go enjoy your afternoon. Got plans?"

"A swim and a drink at the pool bar, I reckon. Laters!" Nadiya departed with a cheerful waggle of her fingers, leaving Rosie alone in the quiet office, looking at a job description for a human resources manager for a major Sydney sports stadium.

At five o'clock she quit reading through job listings, still undecided about which, if any, she might want to put her name forward for. Maybe she shouldn't be limiting herself to Sydney.

Maybe I should talk to Adam tonight, find out if he really does plan to settle there. If he'd be interested in seeing me again, if he does. Or I'm taking a major step and committing myself to this for no good reason at all.

Closing down her computer and locking up the office behind her, she headed to her cabin for a welcome shower. Jill wasn't around, for which Rosie felt guiltily grateful. She really wasn't in the mood for the sort of interrogation Jill would undoubtedly dish out.

She'd sent Adam the link to the Asian restaurant's menu earlier, asking what he'd like, but he didn't reply until she was towelling herself dry and trying to decide what to wear.

Sorry, been out on a boat trip.

Sounds like fun. What would you like to eat? I'll order it now and be at yours in about 30, she sent back.

He sent back a list of dishes long enough to make her laugh out loud; it would feed her and any six of her girlfriends. Maybe Adam planned to have leftovers for lunch and dinner tomorrow... or maybe he was just hungry.

***

Adam found himself yawning as he showered, scrubbing the salt spray from his skin. The wind had picked up as Jace piloted the boat back, sheeting spray over them both as the boat sliced through the waves. It had been invigorating, but left him feeling slightly gritty and sticky when he eventually made it back to the villa, hoping he'd have time for a shower before Rosie arrived, though he'd left the front door propped ajar just in case she did arrive while he was washing up. He didn't want to leave her waiting outside in the mosquito-ridden darkness.

As it happened, he was just pulling a clean shirt over his head when he heard the crunch of wheels on gravel, and a slight squealing of brakes, which made him raise his brows. He hadn't even realised you *could* make the brakes on a golf cart squeal.

He arrived at the front door in time to pull it wide for her, leaning down to press a welcoming kiss to the corner of her mouth and relieve her of the large paper sack she was carrying.

"Hey, beautiful." She looked tired, he thought with a pang of guilt; since he was basically retired, and the whole island lent itself to a permanent holiday feeling, it was hard to make himself remember that Rosie was working a full-time job.

Adam was smart enough to know that you should never tell a woman she looked tired, though, so instead he asked "Busy day?" as they walked through to the kitchen together.

"Ugh," she said, flopping into a chair, so he took that as a yes.

"Wine?"

"Oh, please!"

He grinned and reached for plates and cutlery, setting them on the table and indicating she should serve herself while he poured her a glass of wine and grabbed a non-alcoholic beer from the fridge for himself.

The food was excellent. Rosie had only added one dish to the list he'd sent her, but sampled everything he'd ordered, laughingly saying she was boring normally and always ordered the same thing; it was nice to get to try some of the other things on the menu.

She finished eating before he did, of course, and sat gazing out of the window a little wistfully. Looking around, Adam realised she was admiring the villa's pool, lit up blue in the dark night.

"Fancy a swim?" he asked.

"I wouldn't mind, but I don't have a swimsuit."

"The pool's not overlooked." He gave her a challenging grin. "I'll skinny-dip if you will."

Rosie never even hesitated, just kicked off her shoes and discarded the rest of her clothes on the way out the door, executing a surprisingly good racing dive into the pool with her laughter hanging in the air behind her. Adam was left scrambling to strip his own clothes off and catch her up.

She swam like a fish, fluid and graceful in the water, a fast smooth crawl he couldn't come close to keeping up with. He had to wait for her to do a tumble-turn at the other end and meet her on the way back; she swam right into his arms, laughing at his surprised face.

"I swam competitively all through high school. Wasn't fast enough to compete at state level, but it kept me fit."

"Still does, I reckon." His hands skimmed down over her hips and thighs, thick with muscle.

"I don't have the time for it these days. The ninety-minute sessions four or five days a week are long in the past, I'm afraid. I'd die if I tried to do swim that long now, don't have the stamina for it!"

"You've got plenty of stamina for my purposes," Adam said with a wicked grin, and Rosie laughed, hooking her legs around his waist.

"Gotta keep up with you somehow!"

She was warm and soft and willing in his arms, and all he wanted was to thrust inside her then and there, but he didn't have a condom on, couldn't get one in the water either. So instead he curved a hand under her thigh and reached to stroke the heated cleft between her thighs, finding her nub and tweaking it, again and again until she cried out, her head tipping back, hair floating on the water as her nails scraped on his shoulders.

***

"Now *that,*" Rosie said on a soft sigh, "makes up for a long and tiring day."

Adam chuckled, a soft rumble vibrating through his big frame. He nuzzled her neck, before lifting her a little higher in the water and pressing kisses down her breasts. "Glad I could help you out."

"You definitely did, but we should probably get out of this water so I can help *you* out."

"I'm good," he disclaimed, but she could feel his cock nudging eagerly at her thigh, hoping to get in on the action. "You're tired."

"Not that tired… though you'll need to make the most of the next hour, because I do need to get a good night's sleep in. There's a big conference starting tomorrow and it'll be all hands on deck right through the weekend." She felt the need to apologise in advance. "I doubt I'll be able to get away much."

"It's fine." He walked towards the edge of the pool carrying her with him easily, though Rosie supposed she weighed a lot less in the water. Not that he seemed to have any issues with her weight out of it, that said. "Uh. Incidentally. Talking of the weekend. What day it it?"

She laughed, but she knew how easy it was to lose track in the island's laid-back, holiday atmosphere. For Adam, every day must feel very much the same. "It's Wednesday."

"Gotcha." He lifted her to sit on the pool edge, put his own hands down and pushed up, lifting himself out. She stared unabashed at the magnificent ripple of muscles across his chest and shoulders, the thick swell of his biceps, the corded power of his forearms.

"You are so cut," she sighed happily. "This feels like I'm in some fantastical dream. Like I've fallen into a Hallmark movie."

"Nah." His grin was roguish as he stooped to scoop her up in his arms. "This is a lot more R-rated than anything they'd show."

Very true, Rosie thought as he carried her inside, but it didn't feel like a sleazy porno either. A tastefully expensive Netflix adaptation of a romance novel? She laughed at her own musings as he laid her down on the bed; a moment later she realised her hair was wet and reared up, almost headbutting him in the face as he leaned over her.

"My hair's wet, with pool water! I'll have to wash it or it'll make the pillows foul - afterwards," she clarified as she saw his face fall. Reaching up, she pushed on his shoulder playfully. "Lie down. I'll go on top."

"Oh hell yes please," Adam said enthusiastically. He reached for the nightstand before rolling to his back, holding up the foil packet with a questioning glance.

Rosie plucked it from his fingers. "I got you," she said, tearing the foil open. He was erect and ready, cock thick and standing almost straight up from the nest of dark curls at his groin. She curled her hand around it for a few teasing tugs, swiping her thumb over the drop of pre-cum beading at the tip. She grinned when he groaned aloud.

"Need something?"

"Tease," Adam muttered thickly.

"It doesn't count if I follow through, does it?" She smiled down at him, feeling bold and wild, more so than she'd ever felt in bed with a man. Adam made her feel that way, she thought, free to do anything, say anything, without fear he'd laugh at her or put her down for it.

He groaned again, biting hard on his lower lip as she rolled the condom on, his hands coming up to reach for her breasts as she moved to straddle his hips, squeezing and tugging at her nipples.

Rosie's breath caught at the sensations, the insistent tug low in her groin almost a surprise, so soon after she'd come in the pool. She was already hungry for more, greedy for Adam, for the sensations he seemed to evoke in her so easily.

"God, yes," Adam muttered as she grasped his cock and sank slowly down on it, taking her time, hips rocking gently. He didn't try to thrust up, letting her set the pace at which she took him. "Fuck, Rosie, you feel so good."

"You too," she told him, her voice thin and breathy as she sank deeper, internal muscles stretching and clenching exquisitely. "Oh, *Adam*!"

"That's it, angel," he encouraged her, cupping her breasts and rearing up to kiss them, wrapping an arm around her lower back and lifting up to meet her as she finally took all of him.

The room was filled with the sounds of their lovemaking, soft gasps and cries from her, deeper groans from Adam, the slap of wet, heated flesh, the bedframe creaking with protest as Adam took over the rhythm and increased it to an almost frenetic speed. Rosie's screams of pleasure and Adam's triumphant shout.

Afterwards, Rosie very nearly collapsed atop him. It was only her own face buried in her wet, salty hair that convinced her to get up and stagger to the bathroom to take a shower, and she was far too exhausted afterwards to dry it properly, just wrapping it in a towel and toppling into bed with a vague mumble of apology.

She was barely aware of Adam leaning in and kissing her brow gently, drawing the top sheet up over her.

"Sleep, angel. I promise I won't wake you until morning."

"Your turn to make breakfast," she mumbled into the pillow, and heard him laugh quietly.

"You got it. Go to sleep."

Chapter Fourteen

Rosie woke warm and comfortable, sunlight falling across the bed, but not at the kind of angle which meant she'd slept alarmingly late. She blinked around a little blearily, finding her phone and handbag set on the nightstand by the bed, a sticky note propped up against the bag.

Gone to get breakfast, was written in a blocky script. *Please don't vanish before I get back.*

"As long as you don't take too long," Rosie murmured, but checking her phone she discovered she had a good hour before she needed to leave. And since she'd brought fresh clothes for the day, she wouldn't have to rush back to her own cabin, either.

Sitting up, she grimaced as the towel she'd wrapped her hair in to sleep fell away. She was probably going to have to spend at least ten minutes dealing with her hair, but since she'd brought detangler and a comb, at least she had the tools to do so.

She was sitting out by the pool drinking her first cup of coffee and combing her hair when Adam returned. He popped his head outside to ask "How are you for time - can I have a quick shower before we eat, or do you need to eat now? I've got croissants."

"Plenty of time," Rosie said cheerfully. "Go wash, you sweaty beast."

Not that he wasn't absolutely delicious when sweaty, she thought privately, watching him through the windows as he deposited his backpack in the kitchen before heading for the bathroom. Sweaty was a very good look on him... but he definitely smelled better post-shower.

Smiling at her thoughts, she got up to go and refresh her coffee cup and investigate the backpack, discovering a large paper bag full of warm croissants inside. She found butter and jam in the fridge, honey in the pantry, and decided to set the table while her coffee brewed.

Singing from the shower made her twitch with surprise. Obviously Adam liked to sing while he washed, and wasn't self-conscious about it, even though he had an absolutely terrible singing voice, a fact which made Rosie giggle as she listened to him thoroughly butchering what she *thought* was meant to be Maroon 5's *Moves Like Jagger*.

She was still snickering to herself when he came out, wearing loose board shorts and towelling his hair dry.

"What's so funny?" Adam checked, accepting the coffee she offered with a grateful smile.

"You might have moves like Jagger but you definitely haven't got the voice," Rosie teased.

"You're not wrong." Adam gave her a rueful smile, but then he shrugged. "I've known since childhood I had a tin ear. I decided it wasn't going to stop me enjoying music. You can't let what other people think of you dictate what you enjoy. Dance like nobody's watching and sing like nobody's listening, right?"

"That's not the whole quote," Rosie said without stopping to think.

Adam cocked a brow at her. "It's a quote? I've only ever seen it on like, hand-painted inspirational signs at craft markets."

"It's Mark Twain, I think." She felt awkward now, but couldn't exactly back down. "Dance like nobody's watching, love like you've never been hurt, sing like nobody's listening, live like it's heaven on earth."

"Love like you've never been hurt," Adam said softly, his dark eyes on her face. "I've been lucky that way, so far. Maybe that's why the rest comes easier."

"I can't say I've ever truly had my heart broken," Rosie admitted. "I've been let down a fair few times... usually when I've built something up in my own mind to be far more than it really is. Like that morning we met and I was in pieces because I'd sold myself a fairytale that was never real."

"You've still been hurt, though. Which makes you cautious."

"It does." She looked down at the croissant crumbs on her plate, nudging one around with a finger. "I called a friend who runs a head-hunter agency yesterday. Specialises in hospitality sector jobs," she said, her voice quiet. "I realised, after the other day, that if I truly do want to find any kind of stable relationship, that I need to go somewhere there's an actual dating pool. Stop waiting for something to fall in my lap. It means leaving Sunfish, obviously, which will break my heart, but... I asked if she could maybe look for something which would suit me in Sydney."

"Why Sydney?" he asked, a certain tension coming to his voice, and she didn't quite have the courage to look up to meet his eyes. "You could work anywhere. Why there, specifically?"

"Because you'd said you might be there." She dared to peek up at him. "I thought... I know we barely know each other, it's only been a few days, but I feel like this could maybe go somewhere, *if* we have a chance to find out. If we were in the same city, at least we might have a shot. We could try. If you wanted."

"I want, Rosie." His big hand came out and covered hers, his broad smile breaking out, white teeth flashing. "But you don't have to leave Sunfish."

"You can't imagine how many long-distance relationships I've seen fail," Rosie started, but he was shaking his head at her, grin widening.

"I didn't get round to telling you about my boat trip yesterday, did I? I met Jace Hunter and he took me over to the Chapel Islands. He's going to buy them and redevelop them... and West Chapel is going to be a huge, state of the art sports rehab and training facility. He's asked me to come on board and work for him, help get it off the ground."

Rosie's jaw dropped. Rumours had been flying for a while about Chapel's Folly, about Charlie Chapel putting the islands on the market. Nessa had let a few hints drop that Jace had been looking at the project, but wasn't sure what to do about West Chapel and the half-finished development there.

"Of *course*," she said wonderingly. "That explains all those facilities."

"It's a huge project, and it won't get off the ground for a little while yet. I'm going to have to do some travelling, check out other facilities." He squeezed on her hand. "Recruit and train a lot of staff... for which I'll need a personnel manager very much in my corner."

"Oh," Rosie almost whispered it, hardly able to comprehend what Adam was telling her. "You'd be living here?"

"Probably on West Chapel, eventually, anyway. But it's only ten minutes from here by boat, and Jace says there'll be boat shuttles every half hour, moving guests around the four islands. We don't have to live together unless you want to, but it definitely needn't be a long-distance relationship."

I won't have to leave Sunfish. Hope flooded Rosie, along with an intense relief that she hadn't got very far into job-hunting yet and hadn't even hinted to anyone but Jill that she'd planned to leave. "You said you have to do some travelling?" she queried, still a little cautious.

"Research. Probably a week or two a month for the next few months, at least until Jace is able to get the golf course back into operation. But as far as I'm concerned, Rosie, Sunfish is going to be my home base. I'll be back. And when I'm here... I want to be with you. I want to see where this goes too." He raised his free hand to cup her cheek, stroking the soft curls of her hair tumbling at the side of her jaw. "I really like you, Rosie. I think you're right - maybe we could have a shot."

Still she hesitated, frightened even to dream. "Are we... exclusive?"

"You're worrying I'll be, what, finding a different girl to sleep with everywhere I go on my research trips?" He didn't laugh, taking her concerns seriously. "I'm not interested in that. If I had been, I'd have taken opportunities which were offered when I was on the MMA circuit. Monogamy's my style... I've just been looking for the right woman. And I think I found her."

A lump welled in Rosie's throat. She almost launched herself out of her chair and onto Adam's lap. His arms closed around her, his lips meeting hers in an extremely satisfying kiss - one which only ended when Rosie remembered she still had to get to work.

Epilogue

Eight months later

"Knock, knock."

Rosie looked up from the stack of printed resumes on her desk with a slight frown, wondering who was darkening her office door so late in the afternoon. A delighted smile dawned at once, though, as she saw Adam leaning on the doorframe.

"You're back!" Jumping to her feet, she hurried around the desk and leaped into his arms; he laughed and caught her, raining kisses on her face. "You're early," she mumbled against his lips. "Didn't expect you until tomorrow."

"The advantage of working for a billionaire with his own private jet; when you're finished, you can just leave without having to wait for scheduled flights."

"Colorado was good, then?" He'd been gone almost three weeks this time, visiting high-altitude training and rehab centres in the US. Rosie had missed him quite desperately, even though they'd talked daily. Burying her face in his neck, she breathed in his warm, heady, masculine scent.

"Yes, but with the golf course re-opening next week, I need to be here. Construction's ramping up on the rest of the facility and it's time to start looking for staff."

"You're going to be staying a while this time, then?" Rosie asked hopefully. Adam had been so busy, he'd been lucky to spend a total of one week out of every month on Sunfish. They'd made it work, but she was looking forward to getting to spend a lot more time with him.

"No more travelling for a while," Adam agreed. "My apartment's ready over on West Chapel for me to move into, and I wondered... if you'd maybe like to move over there too? I talked to Luke and he said now the boat shuttles will be starting up, it's no problem for you to commute over here, and that's if you actually need to be here, you can have a computer set up over there with a virtual office, we've got stacks of office space..."

"Are you asking me to move in with you, or just to share your office?" Rosie teased.

"Both?" He kissed her again, for long enough she almost forgot what she'd been asking, losing herself in the delicious heat of him. Forgetting where they were long enough to start unbuttoning his shirt, too, at least until Nadiya rattled her knuckles against the open door and scurried off laughing.

Blushing, Rosie buried her face in Adam's shirtfront.

He kissed the top of her head. "Come on, it's knocking-off time anyway. Let's get you out of here. Go somewhere you can finish that thought." He gestured to the half-unbuttoned shirt, grinning broadly.

He was still ostensibly living in Tad O'Dell's villa, even though he hadn't been around much, but that was much too far away from Rosie's liking, even though it would only be a few minutes drive in the golf cart.

Instead, she grabbed his hand and almost towed him through the staff quarters to her cabin, passing a laughing Jill who waved and called hello to Adam on the way. It had been a huge relief to Rosie that Jill and Adam got on really well; Jill could be prickly and outspoken and didn't always get on well with everyone, but the pair had clicked straight away and knowing that her best friend liked and approved of her boyfriend was just one more thing reassuring Rosie that this time around, she'd lucked into something good.

"Oh hey, you're back," Luke said as they hurried past him, almost jogging.

Adam waved cheerfully. "I'll catch up with you tomorrow," he called.

"No rush!" Luke yelled after him, a laugh in his voice too.

"I'm pretty sure everyone knows we're rushing off to have sex," Rosie said as she finally slammed the door of her bedroom behind him, "and a few months ago I'd have been embarrassed about that, but now, frankly, I'm just smug."

Adam was already peeling off his shirt, kicking his boots off and throwing himself on the bed. "I'm going to apologise in advance for passing out from jet lag. We've probably got an hour before it catches up with me and I conk out for twelve hours."

"Let's make the most of the hour, then." Rosie's own clothes were flying every which way as she threw them aside, and then they were toppling onto the bed together, laughing, hands and mouths all over each other.

***

"Did you mean it?"

"Hm?" Adam blinked his eyes open a little groggily. A bit more than an hour had passed, and the jet lag really was catching up with him. Rosie was lying half on him, head resting on his chest, her soft warm weight and sweet scent comforting as he drifted off. She'd lifted her head to look at him now, though, and he forced himself to focus. "Mean what?"

"About moving in with you."

She looked suddenly vulnerable, and he tightened his arms around her. She'd come a long way in getting past the worst of her insecurities, but something was obviously making her doubt herself again.

"Yes," he said. "Of course I want you to move in with me. I want to wake up with you every morning, fall asleep beside you every night. Hopefully, the worst of the travelling is done, for a while at least."

"I'm okay with you going away, as long as I know you're coming back."

"I'll always come back." He reached for her lips, to claim another kiss. "So what do you say, my love? I know you don't want to leave Sunfish, but West Chapel's only ten minutes away..."

She giggled, the sound pure joy and her eyes alight with it. "Yes. Yes, I'd love to live with you."

And one day soon, Adam thought, he'd pull out the ring he'd found in a gorgeous boutique jewellery store in Aspen and ask Rosie to take the next step with him. Because he was very sure living with her wasn't going to be enough. He wanted Rosie to be his wife, and when the time was right, he'd propose and hope she said yes.

A year ago, with his career over, he'd been lost and directionless, but Sunfish Island had not only given him a whole new career and purpose, it had brought him to Rosie, and that was the greater gift. Hugging her close, he pressed his face into the softness of her hair, breathing in her sweet scent with a sigh of pure contentment as he drifted off to sleep.

~ The End ~

I hope you enjoyed Rosie and Adam's story!

*Read on to enjoy **Crop It Like It's Hot**, where resort photographer Gemma finds her own path to true love in the next book in the Island Escapes series!*

Crop It Like It's Hot

Island Escapes Book 6

Caitlyn Lynch

SHENANIGANS PRESS

shenanigans press.com/EN

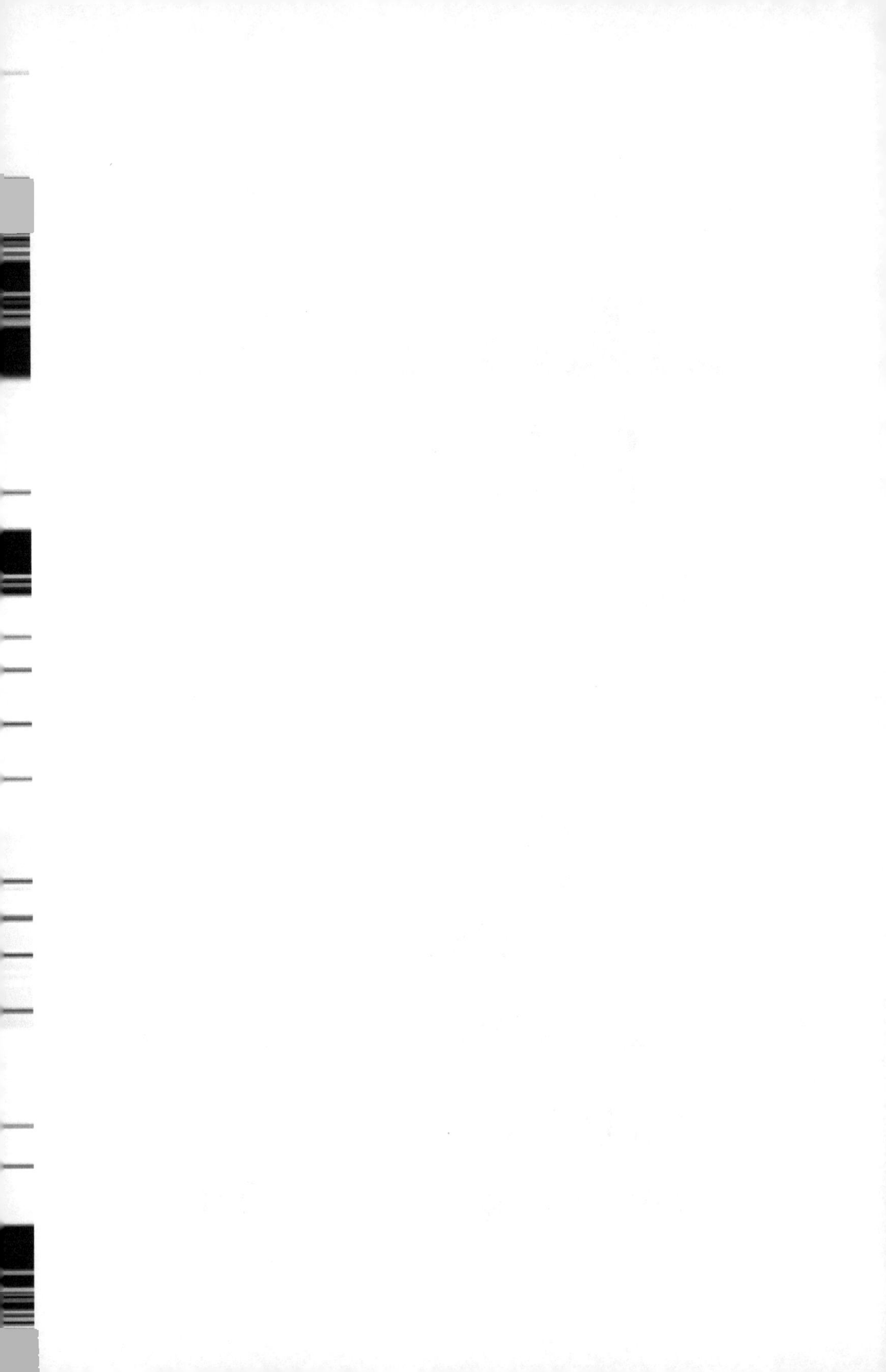

Contents

Author's Note

Crop It Like It's Hot is set in early 2020, and the COVID-19 pandemic features strongly as a plotline due to border closures occurring around the world at that time affecting the tourism operations of the resort.

Chapter 1

"Hold that pose! Keep looking at her just like that!"

The camera shutter clicked repeatedly as Gemma snapped off shot after shot, perfectly capturing the adoring way the handsome groom stared at his radiantly beautiful bride. Late afternoon sun fell dappled through the palm trees fringing the beach, lighting up the pair in a soft glow.

"I think my heels have sunk in the sand," the bride shrieked, before cackling raucously, and the moment was lost. Gemma lowered the camera, pleased with the perfection of the shots she'd just caught.

"Didn't anyone tell you stilettos aren't a good idea if you're getting married on a beach?" She offered a hand to help the bride out, since the groom had stepped away to light a cigarette and chat with his best man, apparently losing interest. Well, it wasn't Gemma's job to care about the status of their relationship, only to capture the illusion of perfection on their wedding day, here on beautiful, tropical Sunfish Island, jewel of the Great Barrier Reef.

"Yeah, but Kevin's a foot taller than me, gotta make up the difference somehow, haven't I?" The bride accepted her aid, staggered to sit down on a lounger a a few feet away. "God. My feet are killing me."

"If you'd like to take the shoes off, I could take a few nice solo shots of you," Gemma suggested. "We'll only have this light for a few more minutes; the sun sets fast here in the tropics."

The bride brightened. "That's good. And then we can go and get some dinner; I'm bloody starving! Kevin, be a love, go and order me a large cocktail, will you? One of those mango daiquiris like we had last night."

Looking relieved to be let off the hook, Kevin and his buddy fled, and the bride sighed and eased off her shoes.

"Hold them in your hand for a second," Gemma suggested. "They're so pretty, why not have a photo with them in it?"

"You're full of good ideas!" The bride beamed at her. "They're Prada. Cost nearly as much as the dress."

Fifteen minutes later, the light fading fast and another eighty shots saved on Gemma's memory card, they headed back up the beach and towards the restaurant where the reception was being held. This was one of the bigger weddings Gemma had seen at Sunfish; nearly a hundred guests had flown in from all over Australia to be present, and most of them right now seemed to be propping up the bar having pre-dinner drinks.

Which was why Gemma thought it was disappointing not a single one of them - not the mother of the bride, not the maid of honour, none of the five other bridesmaids - came to check in with the bride and see if she needed anything.

And how it came to be Gemma who had to squeeze into the bathroom with her and hold her immense meringue of a dress over her head so the poor woman could take a pee.

Such glamour, Gemma thought wryly. *Much fairytale*. She couldn't even remember this woman's name, embarrassingly enough - she was pretty good normally but she had photographed a wedding every single day this week and they were starting to blur together. *Cassie*, she thought. *It might be Cassie.* And here she was holding the woman's dress above her head.

"Thanks, love!" The toilet flushed, Cassie shuffled forward a bit, and Gemma let the dress drop. "Could you help me put my shoes back on?"

"Of course." Gemma consoled herself with the thought of the hefty paycheck she was already guaranteed for this shoot, and that was with just the minimum agreed contract terms. There were lots of add-ons the couple might well ask for once they saw how stunning the photos were going to turn out. The bride's father was a wealthy man and nothing was too much for his darling daughter.

"There you are, Casey!" the father boomed as they re-emerged into the restaurant. "Still looking pretty as a picture!"

Casey, Gemma thought. *That's it*. She lifted the camera on instinct and snapped a candid shot of the bride and her father sharing a hug. Glancing down at the image on her camera's rear screen, she smiled. It was a really good photo. She suspected the proud papa was going to want one of those for himself, blown up in a nice frame to put on his desk at work or his wall at home. She'd make sure to email him a proof copy.

For the first time that day, Gemma got a few minutes to relax as the wedding party sipped their drinks and made their way to their seats in the restaurant. She took a seat at the bar and nodded at the bartender, who nodded back and poured her a large sparkling water over ice.

"Cheers, Joey. I need this."

"Good-looking couple," Joey said laconically. She was Swedish, a backpacker travelling around Australia picking up bar work every now and then to top up her funds. Classically pretty, tall and blonde with two thick braids reaching past her shoulders, she'd been on Sunfish two months now and probably wouldn't stay much longer, which was a shame. Gemma liked her a lot. "Pity about the groom."

"What about the groom?" Gemma took a long slug of her drink.

"They've been staying here a week and every night he's sent her off to bed and then tried to hit on me." Joey arched a golden brow. "Not my idea of a great start to a marriage."

"Oh, dear." Gemma glanced across at the top table. "Well. Maybe he was just hopeful of a last fling before tying the knot?"

"You're such a romantic. I suppose that comes of being a wedding photographer. You only see the fairytale bit. Not the aftermath."

"And being a bartender, you do?"

"Every night." Joey gave her a wink and moved off down the bar to attend to a guest.

Gemma sighed, took another sip of the room, and looked at the bridal party again, with a slightly more jaundiced eye. *Maybe I am a romantic*, she thought. *Who doesn't want to believe in fairytales, though?*

A man crossing the room caught her eye, and she turned her head slightly to watch him. Dressed in dark trousers, open-necked shirt and a silvery waistcoat, he walked with a slight limp, which was what had attracted her attention, and he also didn't appear to be going to any of the tables to take a seat. Instead, he moved to the dance floor at the side of the room, skirted the polished wooden surface, and took a seat at the piano, reaching to make a brief adjustment to the microphone set atop it before starting to play and, a moment later, to sing.

Thinking he was a wedding guest, Gemma half-rose to her feet to go over and stop him, before spotting a shadowy figure at the control panel just beyond the dance floor. The microphone was live, too. Obviously the musician was expected.

He was good, too, she realised, as he performed an excellent rendition of Bruno Mars' *Marry You*.

"They must have paid a bit to fly this guy in," she commented as Joey came back to stand in front of her. "He's a pro."

"Didn't you meet him yet? He's *our* pro. Hired to perform for guests five nights a week in the Dolphin Lounge, available to book for weddings."

"Oh!" Gemma shot another look at the pianist, startled. She'd been too busy lately to catch up on the in-gossip amongst resort staff, obviously. Because this man would definitely have been the cause of gossip. He was tall, lean and dark-haired, and from what she could see, quite good-looking, with sharp cheekbones and an aquiline nose, a short growth of designer stubble lightly fuzzing his jaw. "No, I didn't. How long has he been here?"

"A couple of weeks!" Joey laughed at her, refilling her glass without waiting for Gemma to ask.

"I really have been too busy to catch up on gossip, haven't I? What's the deets?"

Joey shrugged. "Don't know. He's not my type."

"Too male to catch your interest?" Gemma teased, knowing Joey's tastes tended female for the most part.

"Exactly." Joey tipped her a wink, before suddenly stiffening to attention. "Good evening, Mr Collyer. Can I get you anything?"

Gemma glanced to her other side, finding the resort's general manager, Luke Collyer, just slipping onto the barstool there.

"A ginger ale would be nice. Good evening, Gemma. How's the shoot going?"

"Very well, thanks. The usual difficulties with a group this size." Gemma shrugged. She was more than used to wrangling large parties, and this one had the blessing of only including a very small number of young children, who were always a spanner in the works.

"Good." Luke took a sip of his drink, eyes scanning the room. The waitstaff were beginning to come out from the kitchen, plates in hand to serve the appetizers, smooth and efficient as they moved swiftly about the room. "It all looks under control, though I'll check in with the kitchen if I need to. Stock all good behind the bar, Joey?"

"Yes, sir," the bartender said politely.

"Excellent. Josh sounds good, hm?" He glanced at Gemma.

"Is that the new guy's name? I haven't met him yet."

"Really? He's good; we're lucky to have him. Actually, would you do me a favour? I'd like to get a few shots of him playing, maybe a short bit of video to put on Instagram, and we need a new headshot for the website. Grab a couple tonight and email them through to me, please?"

"Of course." Gemma shrugged. It was easy enough; she'd have plenty of time over the next half hour while the guests were eating. A videographer was recording the speeches, so she only needed to take a few shots to catch each speaker. The busy part of her day was all but done.

Rooting in the bag strapped around her waist for a spare memory card, she swapped it into her camera as Luke finished his drink, nodded a farewell and headed for the kitchens to check in with the catering staff. No time like the present, Gemma thought, and headed across the room towards Josh.

He saw her coming, mid-song, with her camera raised, and gave her such a ferocious scowl she froze. A sharp shake of his head and she lowered the camera, wondering what on earth his problem was. Fine, she'd wait until the end of the song, introduce herself and explain Luke's instructions.

The last thing she expected him to do was lean away from the microphone during the piano outro to the song and hiss "No photographs!" at her.

Chapter 2

He wasn't supposed to take a break yet, but the photographer was standing right there, arms folded beneath the heavy camera hanging from her neck, her toe all but tapping on the floor as she obviously waited to speak with him. Josh finished the song, acknowledged the polite smattering of applause, and stood up, taking a few steps away into the darkened corner by the piano, wanting to be far enough clear the microphone wouldn't pick up their conversation.

The photographer followed him. A pretty, slender young woman with dark hair cut in a short, gamine crop, her neck looked almost too slender to support the weight of that heavy Nikon. She wore a simple black dress and flat black sandals, obviously designed to make her fade into the background and fit into any social situation, but the way the stretchy dress fitted to the curves of her waist and hips was enough to make any red-blooded man look twice. Josh snatched his gaze away and focussed on her face.

"No photos," he said, at the same moment as she said;

"Hi, I'm Gemma."

"Josh," he muttered, feeling ungracious as he accepted the hand she held out.

"I'm the resort photographer..."

"Couldn't have guessed."

Delicate eyebrows arched at his sarcasm. She scanned his face, and he deliberately turned his head a little further. Hiding the scars that marred his right cheek deeper in the shadows.

"Mr Collyer asked me to take some photographs of you," she said bluntly, cutting to the chase. "A headshot for the resort website, and some video to put on Instagram. I'm sure you're aware this is normal and part of the job. As a customer-facing staff member, you'd have signed a social media release form."

"I did," he agreed, "but I have a special clause in mine which states I need to be given advance notice when photographs are going to be taken. So that I can prepare for them."

"Prepare for them?" Her brows went up even further. "In what way?"

Her disbelief rubbed him the wrong way, and deliberately, he jerked his head around, almost shoving his scars in her face. "So that I can put makeup on to cover these!"

He expected her to recoil, but she didn't, just looked at him thoughtfully, tilting her head slightly, before stepping to her right and looking again. "I can shoot you without showing them. They're barely visible straight on, and not at all looking from this side of your face. Which is where I'd want to shoot from, considering the light in here."

Wind taken slightly out of his sails, he stared at her. She gave him a small smile before adding "Of course, if you're insistent, I'll just email Luke and tell him I'll get them to him tomorrow. Can we arrange a time tomorrow when you can get your makeup on and let me shoot?"

He felt stupid now, and rude. "No... no, tonight's okay. If you can just make sure..." he lifted his right hand, touched his scarred cheek, feeling the ridges, the skin rough in some spots, smooth and shiny in others, all of it still feeling subtly wrong under his fingertips.

"Even if I accidentally catch some of your scarring - which I won't - please trust that my Photoshop magic can make sure nobody would have the faintest idea," she promised.

"Thanks," Josh muttered, feeling even worse. She was really sweet, and he'd just been an unbearable curmudgeon. "I better get back to it. I've got quite a playlist to get through."

"Is there any song in particular you'd like me to record for the Instagram video? Something you think you perform great and the audience will love?"

"*The Way You Look Tonight* always goes over well," he said after a moment's thought. "It's next but one on my playlist."

"Fantastic. I'll take a few stills during the next song, record that one, then leave you in peace for the night. Oh, and if you want to see the final images before I let anyone else look at them, stop by my office in the morning."

Okay, she was bending over backwards to make him feel comfortable now, and he had to say something. "Sorry I was grumpy," he said, with an awkward tip of his head.

"Don't apologise. I didn't know about your contract condition. I do now and I promise I'll always consult with you before including you in any shots."

Josh felt about five centimetres tall as he headed back to the piano, but he had to pull himself together. He was vaguely aware of Gemma moving about, choosing her angles as he started to play a Savage Garden song and then, as usual, managed to lose himself in the music and forget she was there.

***

Gemma couldn't help but be curious about how Josh had gotten those awful scars, but she vowed as she carefully positioned herself to take the video that she would never, ever ask him, since he was obviously so sensitive about them. They looked like burn scars; maybe he'd been in a fire. His cheek looked almost melted, the scars running down to disappear beneath his collar, and she wondered how far down they went. Maybe they were the cause of his limp, too, she thought, recalling the way he'd crossed the floor.

He could really sing. His voice absolutely soared, powerful as he hit some high notes in the Savage Garden track, and the applause when he finished was enthusiastic. Maybe he'd been a professional stage performer somewhere, maybe even on a track to pop stardom, and then an accident had left him with a scarred face and a career that was dead in the water.

Ordering herself to stop speculating, Gemma focussed on capturing Josh's performance. The beautiful old Sinatra song would play very well to their audience, even the younger crowd who hung out on Instagram; she'd see if Josh would allow it on Facebook and maybe even a permanent upload to the resort website, too. He would be quite a draw, and she could definitely see him getting booked out with nearly as many weddings as she was.

***

Josh didn't bother stopping by her office in the morning, and Gemma told herself sternly that she didn't mind. It was good that he trusted her to keep her word and not allow his scars to show. She sent several shots through to Luke, uploaded the video to Instagram, and then recalled that she needed to get Josh's permission to put it on Facebook as well. She'd need to go track him down. Grabbing the phone, she called the personnel office and explained what she needed; they gave her the number of his cabin in the staff section of the resort and she grabbed up a tablet to take with her to show him the video on, as well as her trusty Nikon. She'd feel naked going anywhere without it.

Her phone chirped as she headed out the door, the chime indicated an incoming Whatsapp call. Glancing at the screen, she broke out in a broad grin as she saw her friend's Philly's face.

"Hey, lovely! Where are you today?"

"Scotland." Obviously in a hotel somewhere; or more likely, knowing Philly, a quaint little guest house or bed-and-breakfast she'd discovered. Philly was a travel blogger and she loved nothing more than going off the beaten track, discovering hidden treasures often known only by locals and sharing them with her followers. "How's the land of permanent sunshine?"

"Sunny, of course!" Laughing, Gemma exited the building, heading down one of the paths into the staff section of the resort. "See?" she panned her phone camera so Philly would get a nice view of the bright morning sunshine falling over the hibiscus trees blooming nearby. "Although I think we're due a storm this afternoon, which hopefully will hold off until after today's wedding has concluded... we're in the beach chapel again."

"I was thinking of you today, saw a couple getting married in a gorgeous ruined castle." Philly giggled. "He was wearing a kilt! Very Scottish. I got a couple of cute pics."

"Sounds lovely! Are you in Scotland long? Where are you off to next?"

"Possibly home. This situation with the coronavirus has a lot of people here nervous. Talk of border closures. I'd rather be home in Melbourne if that happens."

"You really think it will?" Startled, Gemma stopped walking. "It's that serious?" She didn't keep up with the news much; the outside world rarely seemed to impinge on life on Sunfish, but border closures definitely would. The tourism trade would suffer enormously; more than half their guests at any given time were international visitors.

"I think maybe. People here are definitely worried." Philly pulled a face. "I don't want to wait too long and get stuck somewhere, running out of money. At least back home I can move into the granny flat at Mum's place, you know?"

"Well, if you get a chance..." Gemma was about to invite Philly to come and visit her on Sunfish when suddenly, a collision with a solid form sent her falling back on her butt and her phone flying from her hand.

"Sorry, sorry!" It was Josh, she discovered as she looked up. He pushed sunglasses up on top of his head and leaned over her, face the picture of concern. "Are you okay? Did I hurt you? Don't get up, you should check for broken bones..."

"I landed in the flowerbed, it's soft," Gemma said a little crossly, shoving herself to her feet. "Where'd my phone go?" She could hear Philly yelling her name.

"Here it is." Josh scooped it out of the flowers. "Hi, sorry I interrupted your conversation." He smiled at the screen. "I knocked Gemma over. She's just dusting dirt off her butt."

Philly burst into giggles, and even at a distance from the screen, Gemma could hear the flirtatious note in Philly's voice.

"I'm sure Gemma doesn't mind too much! And who are you, handsome? You weren't there when I swung by Sunfish a year ago, I'd have remembered you."

"Joshua Gaddrick. Josh. I'm new here. Lounge singer." He smiled at the phone. He kept his face angled slightly to the screen, Gemma saw, and at the phone's resolution, Philly wouldn't be able to see his scars. "And you are?"

"Philly, travel blogger extraordinaire. Gemma and I went to uni together and she decided to settle down and photograph the same scenery every day with a different couple in front of it. I got itchy feet. Done much travelling?"

Josh's face got that odd, closed look to it again. "Some," he said, a bit shortly. "Not many places where anyone would actually want to go. I was in the army."

"As a lounge singer?" Philly said, that teasing, flirtatious note still in her voice.

Feeling inexplicably jealous, Gemma reached out and gently plucked the phone out of Josh's hand. "Stop flirting with him, Philly, you're a couple of continents too far away. Go find some cute Scotsman to hit on. I gotta go."

"You go." Philly waggled her eyebrows suggestively, chin resting on her hand. "Don't waste time on me when he's right there."

"Oh, shut up." Despite her irritation, and a thread of embarrassment winding its way in as Josh just stood there and watched Philly basically encouraging Gemma to flirt with him, Gemma smiled. Philly was irrepressible, and there was a reason - many reasons - their friendship had survived the years and miles between them. "Catch you soon. Take care, and let me know if you do decide to come home."

"Will do!" Philly blew her a kiss before the screen went black.

Chapter 3

Gemma looked up to find Josh watching her, hands thrust in the pockets of his long cargo pants. Long pants was an oddity here during the daytime, especially among the staff who generally wore the resort's uniform of turquoise polo shirt and khaki shorts, and she wondered again how far down his scars went.

"Sorry again," he said abruptly. "For knocking you over, and interrupting your call."

"It's all right. It was a social call anyway, not work." She shrugged. "I was just on my way to see you."

"So was I. On my way to see you, I mean. Not to approve the photos," he hastened to add when she must have looked suddenly a bit panic-stricken. "It's after noon, and you said in the morning. Luke forwarded them to me and asked which one I wanted on the website. I picked one, but I wanted to say thank you. For being so considerate last night. And so nice when I was rude. The photos are very good."

"Oh." Warmth inexplicably suffused Gemma. But then, she was standing right in the blazing sun; that must be it. "Well. Thanks. Fine."

Why can't I speak in sentences of more than one word? He's not THAT good-looking.

"What did you want to see me about?"

"Right!" she startled. Held out her tablet towards him. "I put the video on Instagram. Wanted to get your approval for Facebook and the website too. Maybe a clip on TikTok?"

"Why not Youtube too?" he said, deadpan, as he took the tablet from her.

"The resort doesn't have a channel... oh, you were kidding."

"I don't do social media at all, but you seem to be right on top of it." He tapped at the screen, angling it in the bright sunlight. "Can't really see it. Can we go indoors somewhere?"

Gemma glanced about. They were only a short distance from the staff canteen, and it was in the midst of the lunch hour. She pointed. "Want to come and get lunch, or have you eaten?"

"Lunch sounds good." He handed her the tablet back and fell into step beside her.

She really had been missing a lot, working so hard, Gemma realised, as they entered the canteen and several people greeted Josh cheerfully. They all obviously knew him already. Josh didn't show any inclination to join anyone in particular, though, grabbing a tray and leading her to a vacant table once they'd both selected some food.

"So how come I didn't meet you until last night?" he asked as they seated themselves. "You never seem to eat in here."

"I do," she defended herself, "but... it's usually just an early breakfast before I bolt off to get started on the candid shots of the bride for whatever wedding is on that day. And then lunch is usually on the run, and dinner a plate on the bar during the evening reception."

"Every day?" He arched a brow at her.

"Technically, I'm only supposed to work five days a week, and if the wedding party has their own photographer, I'm off. But the resort does weddings seven days a week, and the part-timer who comes over from Airlie Beach to shoot some of them had a baby three weeks ago, and nobody's brought their own photographer recently." She spread her hands. "The resort's not in the business of saying no to people who are shelling out a lot of money to host their wedding here. A photographer is part of the package."

"So you're getting paid plenty of overtime?"

"Sure."

"Doesn't do much good if you've no time to even spend it!"

"True," Gemma conceded. She *had* been working too hard, she thought. Maybe she'd talk to Luke about the resort finding someone else to do part-time shoots. Most wedding photographers only worked weekends, often having to take other jobs during the week to make ends meet; she was sure they could find someone who'd love a couple of days' work during the week. "Maybe I've been letting them take advantage of me a bit."

"People will if you let them. Don't let anyone walk all over you." His gaze was far away briefly, before it snapped back to hers. He put his fork down. "Anyway. This video?"

"Right here." She brought it up on her tablet, handed him an earpod so he could listen without having to blast the speaker.

"Looks good," Josh said finally, handing the earpod back. "Sure. Upload it wherever you like."

"Thank you." Accepting the tablet as he slid it back over the table, she glanced down and did a double-take. "Whoa."

"What?"

"Those stats!" She tapped on the Instagram post, staring at the numbers. "That's... a lot. People really like you." The comments were extremely complimentary, too, remarking on Josh's beautiful voice.

"Huh." He leaned over to look, his face - and his scarred cheek - close beside hers. "Cool."

His smile was pleased... and surprised, she thought. She couldn't resist probing lightly. "So where were you before this? You seemed surprised by everyone praising you last night, too."

"Like I said to your friend. I was in the army." His hand came up to touch his cheek, an unconscious movement, she thought. "My mother was the musician in the family. A professional opera singer. She taught me to play, was kind of disappointed when I wasn't really into classical music. I wasn't able to pursue music as a career, so I joined the army."

Surely there were other options? Gemma wondered, but didn't say anything as he continued.

"No pianos in Afghanistan, but I had a guitar in the barracks. I used to play and sing for my squad. Got offered a slot with the Army Band, travelling around, entertaining the troops. Did that for a couple years. Better than getting shot at." He gave her a wry smile. "Learned a lot from the other performers, too. Then one day we were in convoy, returning to Kandahar. IED blew the truck off the road."

"I'm so sorry," she said inadequately.

"I was the lucky one. All the others died except me and the girl next to me; she lost both legs below the thigh. I dragged her out and we hid under the shelter of the burning truck, from the snipers trying to pick us off, until reinforcements arrived." His hand was fully covering his cheek now, fingers pressing at skin she suspected had no sensation in it. "Wasn't until they got me back to base that I discovered I'd lost half my own foot. The burns on my face hurt so much I hadn't noticed."

"That's terrible." Instinctively, she reached out, put her hand over his free one, clenched into a fist on the table. "So you were invalided out?"

"Yep. I've still got a heel but the rest of my foot is a prosthetic. I could have stayed in, the Army Band is one of the few places where you could carry on with a disability like that, but I was pretty sure I wouldn't be able to get back into a truck again and head back out." He shook his head. "I still have nightmares about that day."

"Of course you do." Gemma couldn't even imagine the horror of it. "So... you came home?" she prompted gently when he went quiet.

"Yeah, they gave me a good payout, of course. Quite a lot of rehab later I decided I was going to try and make a go of singing for my supper. Did a couple of stints on cruise ships, then the job here came up." He shrugged. "I was surprised to get it, frankly. Didn't think I'd have enough experience, but the manager said he liked my audition tapes and he thought I'd fit in well with the crew here. Who all seem very nice, I must say."

Gemma could see exactly what Luke had meant. Josh fit right in with the crew of Sunfish, most of whom were aged in their twenties and thirties. She'd barely known the previous lounge singer, a perfectly charming gentleman in his sixties who'd nevertheless kept very much to himself.

"I'm sure you'll do great here," she said, still unsure what to say after the revelations he'd just dumped on her. And she'd thought he'd be unwilling to talk about what had caused his scars!

"I don't know why I just told you all that." Josh looked a bit bemused himself. "Sorry. I normally just say I was injured in the army. I guess it's because you seemed really interested in how I got into music."

"I am really interested." Her hand was still resting on his on the table, the fist which had now unclenched. "I think you're really talented. I was wondering if you'd maybe been a budding pop star or something and decided you couldn't be on camera any more after an accident."

"Ha. No." He dropped his hand from his cheek finally. "I'm self-conscious about them, but not because I'm used to being on camera. I just... my fiancée dumped me when I got home. Made me kind of paranoid."

Gemma's jaw dropped. "No. What a bitch," she said, outraged.

Josh laughed, a full-throated belly laugh. "Don't hold back. Say what you think, huh?"

"She was! What a terrible thing to do. It's not like you were, I don't know, unable to give her children any more. That might be a deal breaker, I suppose, if she was set on having kids. But just because of some scars? Bitch!"

Josh was looking at her warmly, and then he turned his hand under hers and squeezed her fingers gently. "Thanks, Gemma. That means a lot."

Chapter 4

Although Gemma stopped in to see Luke a couple of days later and mentioned to him the possibility of finding another wedding photographer to take on at least a couple of gigs a week, Luke seemed deeply preoccupied when she spoke to him and only mumbled something vague, not at all like his usually attentive self.

"Is there a problem?" she asked curiously, and Luke grimaced.

"This virus thing. We've already lost a lot of bookings from China, with the flight restrictions starting. I think it's going to get worse before it gets better."

"Do you think Australia will close all borders?" She fumbled for a chair, sat down. Trying to imagine the effect on the tourism industry. On the resort.

"Yes, but I'm wondering if it won't be even worse than that. Maybe state borders too. Tom Hanks and his wife have just tested positive on the Gold Coast; with celebrities affected, this thing's about to get a lot higher profile." He shook his head, his attention on his computer screen. "I think we're about to find out what it's like to live in interesting times, Gemma. I'll look into what you asked, but right now... I suspect our wedding bookings are about to drop way off."

Rumours were flying among the staff, too. Everyone was watching the news and discussing it in dire tones. The resort already seemed emptier, quieter. And then, a week later, the news broke. Australia was closing its borders to all international travellers except for Australians returning home.

The following day, the news they had all dreaded was delivered. The resort was closing down until further notice. All tourists would be returning home immediately. Staff who wanted to leave should do so as soon as possible; anyone who had nowhere else to go would be allowed to stay, but restrictions would be implemented on even small gatherings. They couldn't even all gather to eat in the staff canteen. The buffets were closed and meals had to be prepared on individual plates, collected and taken back to their rooms to eat.

Gemma's mother called, asked if she wanted to go home to Brisbane, but Gemma could hear the hope in her mother's voice that she'd decline. Gemma had never gotten on well with her mother's boyfriend - the man was a sleaze - and she shuddered at the thought of spending who knew how long trapped under the same roof with the man. She declined, grateful for the opportunity to stay on Sunfish. There were no weddings and no work, but the government's JobKeeper scheme meant she'd be getting a decent base rate of pay, more than sufficient to cover the cheap staff rate of room and board for however long it took. She had a comfortable room, a roof over her head, a whole island to walk on with its stunning rainforest interior and beautiful beaches, even friends to talk to… even if it was at a distance, on adjacent verandahs outside their cabins, or via their phone cameras on Whatsapp.

They were two weeks into lockdown when she discovered Josh was still on Sunfish too, as she saw him coming out of the canteen one day as she was about to go in to pick up her lunch.

"Oh, hey," she said, startled. "Didn't realise you were still here."

He smiled, a little wryly. "Nowhere else to go, I'm afraid. I'm not eligible for Jobkeeper since I've only been here about five minutes, but living here's a lot cheaper than it would be anywhere else."

Probably true, she supposed; renting an apartment anywhere would cost more, and then he'd have to pay for food and utilities too. "Want to go for a walk together sometime?" she offered on impulse. "Suitably socially distanced, of course!"

"Of course," he agreed. "Though I'm pretty confident the protocols put in place are going to keep the virus off Sunfish."

She was too, but still, she wasn't about to do anything stupid. "I like to go out fairly early," she said, "even though the heat's eased off. Eight thirty tomorrow?"

"Sounds good," he agreed, and they arranged a place to meet up before he headed off with his tray and Gemma went to collect her own lunch.

***

Josh wondered at the surge of excitement causing butterflies in his stomach. Yes, he acknowledged he was a little starved for company, reduced to calling occasional greetings to friends on their verandahs as he passed, but it was silly to feel like a teenage boy getting asked on a date by a girl he liked. Gemma was just being friendly, he tried to tell himself. She was probably starved for conversation too. She seemed to be quite the social butterfly; before everything shut down, he'd seen her at the weddings they both worked, always laughing and on easy terms with the brides in particular, obviously with a natural skill at befriending everyone.

He still couldn't believe how easily he'd opened up and told her about his experience in Afghanistan. She'd listened with a look of empathy - not sympathy, not pity - as he'd spilled his guts. He'd even told her about the nightmares, the ones that still sometimes woke him in a cold sweat, teeth chattering and his numb cheek burning with remembered pain.

Was he interested in Gemma? In any kind of relationship? It had been two years since Alice broke his heart and his spirit, walking away from the hospital leaving her engagement ring on his bedside table. And he hadn't been totally celibate in that time, since there'd been plenty of opportunities on the cruise ships where he'd been working, ones which he'd availed himself of a time or two, but with a mutual understanding that it was just sex. Just blowing off steam, relieving tension, whatever you wanted to call it, but just sex with no emotional attachment.

Gemma, he didn't feel like that was even possible. He already liked her too much. If there was any possibility of anything with Gemma - if she was even interested - it wasn't going to be casual. Not on his part, anyway, which meant he needed to be cautious. She might well be bored and looking for a fling, and the last thing he needed was to get his heart broken again.

***

"Well, going for a walk sounds like as close as you can actually get to an in-person date," Philly pointed out, chin on her hands as she peered out of the screen. "He's very cute, Gemma. I can think of far worse people to be locked up with!"

"How's lockdown treating you?" Gemma asked sympathetically.

"Could be worse." Philly grimaced. "I'm not eligible for Jobkeeper so I have to do something to keep from starving. Or having to fall back on sponging off the parents, anyway. I've taken a couple of jobs organising collections of digital photos; it's pretty interesting, actually."

"I've been doing some of that myself. Catching up on the backlog!" Gemma admitted. "Found lots of non-wedding shots I've taken of the island, and of friends here. It's been nice to share them and reminisce."

"That's what photos are for, after all. Memories." Philly smiled. "Well, I hope you enjoy your *walk*." She put a teasing emphasis on the word.

"I will. And if I hear of anyone who needs digital collections organised and curated, I'll send them your way," Gemma promised.

"Love ya, honey." Philly blew her a kiss.

"Love you too," Gemma said to the blank screen, before heaving a sigh. The time on her hands in lockdown had at least afforded her the chance to catch up properly with Philly, hearing all about some of the incredible places her friend had been these last few years. It didn't make Gemma wistful for travel, though. She'd done that; she and Philly had spent the first year after they graduated university travelling together. Philly had adored every moment of it; Gemma had spent most of the time recovering from one sort of travel sickness after another. They'd had some fun times, though.

Flicking through old photo albums, she smiled reminiscently at the wild splashes of colour which had been a massive wedding they'd ended up being invited to in Delhi; astonishingly, despite hundreds of wedding guests, there had been no official photographer. Gemma and Philly had taken thousands of photos between them and were paid handsomely by the bride's family for the job.

Gemma thought it was then she'd decided she wanted to be a wedding photographer exclusively. She'd left Philly to travel intrepidly on alone and come home; set up a small business doing wedding shoots on a shoestring and slowly built up a name for herself, even while she did midweek portrait and glamour shoots and hated every moment of them. Seeing an advert for the job on Sunfish Island, realising she'd never have to photograph anything but weddings again, had honestly been a dream come true.

It was time to head out for her not-really-a-date walk with Josh. Slathering sunscreen on quickly, Gemma grabbed her hat and headed out, only realising once she got out that clouds were massing thickly on the horizon.

"We might have to make it a quick walk," she said as she walked up beside Josh, waiting for her outside the resort's closed reception area. "Those clouds don't look pretty."

"I thought it tended to be afternoon storms up here in the tropics?" he asked as they set off.

"In the summer, yes. Winter they can blow up any time of the day. You're a southerner, then?"

"Geelong in Victoria, originally." His eyes were smiling as he glanced across at her. "Is it that obvious?"

"At least you're wearing a hat." She nodded at it. "But yes, the weather patterns are a bit different up here in the tropics. I'm from Brisbane but my grandmother lived in Cairns: I used to spend holidays with her, so I'm used to the weather up here. The cyclones are when things get ugly. They usually evacuate the island, if there's enough warning."

"How long have you been on Sunfish?" Josh asked curiously. He matched her pace comfortably, despite his limp; Gemma didn't feel like she needed to slow down for him, and she suspected he'd either tell her or just slow down and let her deal with it if he needed to.

"Four years. Only the one major cyclone during that time; we've been reasonably lucky. There was a big one about a decade ago, did a lot of damage. After that was when most of the resort was built. The owners poured a lot of money into it."

"The cabins we live in used to be guest cabins, isn't that right? Cory mentioned it."

"Apparently, yes. Which is why they're quite large and a lot nicer than staff cabins most places on the Reef!"

"A lot bigger than I had on the cruise ships," he noted. "A shared room with bunk beds and a tiny porthole barely above the waterline!"

Gemma shuddered at the thought. She avoided leaving Sunfish if at all possible because of her travel sickness. A cruise ship, and tight, enclosed spaces below deck, sounded like a nightmare.

"I've got friends on cruise ships," she said. "Which ones were you on?"

They didn't seem to have any friends in common, but the conversation flowed on easily, Josh making her laugh with his stories of trying to play the piano and sing during a storm at sea which had tossed the massive cruise liner about like a toy boat.

"When I looked up and realised I was playing to an empty lounge, I quit mid-song!" he concluded the story.

"I wouldn't have even got out on stage." Gemma laughed helplessly. "I've always had shocking travel sickness. Can't even ride in the back seat of a car for more than about ten minutes."

"You live on an island; you have to take a boat to get anywhere!" He looked at her curiously.

"But I don't actually have to go anywhere. I hadn't left the island for months before lockdown." She had to think about it. "Last time was before Christmas. I took the boat over to Hamilton Island and flew down to Brisbane to visit my mother for a couple of days. Anything I can't get here on the island, I just mail-order."

"Huh." Josh fell silent, obviously thinking about what she'd said. "You know," he said finally, "it's weird, I hadn't really noticed, but I have absolutely no urge to go anywhere either. Everything we need is right here, isn't it?"

"We literally live in paradise." Gemma spread her arms wide, then winced as the first fat raindrop bounced off her hand. "Uh-oh. Quick, get to shelter!" She ran for the beach gazebo, a large permanent structure with large timber pillars at the corners and a palm-frond thatched roof. Lounge chairs were stacked in the middle with tarps strapped down over them, but there was enough room for Gemma and Josh to huddle away from the rain, now pelting down in a torrent of thick, soaking drops.

Chapter 5

Josh shook his head, rubbing the water from his face. He hadn't quite been able to keep up with Gemma as she ran from the rain, had gotten caught as it started to really belt down. He'd forgotten what tropical rain could be like; visibility was down to just a few metres as the water fell in torrential sheets.

"It won't last long. Maybe ten or fifteen minutes." Gemma had pulled out her phone, was looking at the rain radar live tracking. Clambering up to perch on one of the stacks of covered loungers, she rested her chin in her hands and gazed pensively out at the rain.

Impulsively, Josh started humming, and then launched a capella into Creedence Clearwater Revival's classic *Have You Ever Seen The Rain*, drumming his fingers against the stack of chairs beside him to keep the beat.

Gemma applauded when he finished, and he bowed to her, grinning. "It'd sound better if I had my guitar."

"Sounded fantastic anyway. A classic." She smiled, a soft look on her face. "My dad loved all that classic old rock. Takes me back to riding in his old ute with him, driving up to the pier at Redcliffe to go fishing."

"Mine too!" He laughed with delight. "Only it was on the way to fish off the Warrnambool pier. And he tended a bit to old country, rather than straight rock. CCR hit in both genres, really."

"Dad quite liked country too. John Denver was one of his favourites. He used to sing *Take Me Home, Country Roads*... even though he'd never been a country boy by any stretch of the imagination."

"I get that one requested a lot, by plenty of people who've definitely never been to West Virginia."

"Tell me." Gemma tilted her head. "If it's up to you - what do you like to sing? What's your favourite song?"

"I don't have one." It was an easy answer. "But if you're asking what I sing for preference... my own original songs."

She sat up straighter, eyes wide. "You write songs too? But that's so cool! What sort of music?"

Already feeling awkward at having made the admission, he shrugged a little bashfully. "Soft rock kind of thing. I flatter myself I'm somewhere between Rob Thomas and Lewis Capaldi."

"Oh my god, I love both of them!" She paused, obviously taking in his expression. "I'd love to hear some of your music, when and if you're ready to share it."

"I'll think about it," he mumbled, a bit sheepishly.

"And even if you don't want to play your own music... I just had an idea. Obviously we can't all crowd into the lounge to listen to you, but maybe you could bring out your guitar and do a little outdoor concert for the staff who are still living here? We could socially distance on the lawns, make sure we're all far enough apart and far enough from you..."

He liked the idea, a lot. Thought it might provide some much-needed morale, but he knew he'd have to check with Luke, get permission to do it and make sure they weren't breaching any regulations.

"I'll look into it," he promised Gemma, who clapped her hands happily.

"It'll be so good to hear some live music!"

Luke loved the idea, when Josh approached him. Made the arrangements, got permission for up to thirty staff to attend the outdoor mini-concert and had a couple of groundskeepers set out chairs, at what looked like a hilariously wide distance from each other.

Josh honestly didn't think anyone apart from maybe Gemma would turn up, but the virtual 'tickets' Luke put out were snapped up within minutes, and every seat was full when he walked out on the lawn with his guitar, plugging it in and waving to his audience.

"Everyone hear me?" he checked. "You're all so far away. I feel like I'm playing in a stadium but it's nearly empty!"

"We'll make enough noise for a stadium crowd!" Gemma called from a seat in the second row, and everyone promptly started hooting and cheering, making Josh laugh.

"Save it for if you like the performance!" He looked down at the tablet he'd set on the music stand before him. "Now I said everyone who came could request one song, but I don't guarantee to play it... and I can tell you now, whoever thinks I can match Mariah Carey's high notes is dreaming!"

Laughter greeted his joke, and he strummed a chord. "I do a decent Adam Levine if you I say so myself, though, so Olivia? Where are you? Cory wants me to dedicate *Girl Like You* to you."

He ran through a playlist of songs, enjoying himself as he got to perform for the people he'd really only just begun to call friends. Working down the list of requests, he smiled as he saw *Take Me Home, Country Roads* on there, and decided to leave it for last.

"This one's for my new soul sister," he said as he began to gently strum the first chords, "and in memory of our daggy dads, who raised us on old rock and country music."

He was sure he saw Gemma wipe tears away as he sang the aching lyrics, pouring his heart into them, and she leaped to her feet as he finished, applauding as hard as she could smack her hands together. He laughed and gave her a thumbs-up. "And just for you, Gemma," he said impulsively into the microphone, "here's one of my original songs. It's called *I'll Be Gone Tomorrow.*"

Faces were rapt in the soft darkness, lit only by fairy lights strung in the trees above and a few torches flaring to one side of the lawn, as he played the song he'd written in the hospital while learning to walk again on half a foot. It had come from deep inside, a scream from his soul, and he knew in his heart it was easily the best thing he'd ever written.

The applause as he let the last chords die away startled him; it seemed too loud to come from just thirty pairs of hands. He hadn't been able to look at any of them while he was playing, unable to face what they might think of his original music. It was Gemma's face he sought now, and her expression was a mixture of amazement and delight as she stood on her chair and blew a deafening wolf-whistle through her fingers, making him laugh aloud in relief.

She'd liked it.

They'd all liked it.

He wasn't kidding himself; he really could write songs.

And it was at that moment Josh let a tiny splinter of the hope he'd been keeping buried for so long surface.

Maybe he really did have a future in music that wasn't just playing other people's songs.

***

Josh was only mildly surprised to receive an email from Luke requesting a Zoom call the following morning. With only thirty seats available at the 'concert' and with how much those who attended had obviously enjoyed themselves, he fully expected to be asked to repeat the evening so others could have the opportunity. While well down on their usual complement of staff when the resort was open, there were still more than three hundred staff members living on Sunfish, between the marine biology centre, which had never closed down, and the construction workers commuting daily to the massive works on the three nearby Chapel Islands which the resort's owner had recently purchased. Honestly, he wouldn't mind doing a nightly concert, just to keep himself in practice, especially if they didn't mind him trying out his original songs on them.

He was halfway through telling Luke that when the resort manager held his hand up, laughing slightly.

"That's very much appreciated, and I'll certainly take you up on it. We'll get a piano moved into the covered gazebo over there too, so you can choose what instrument you want to play. But what I actually wanted to ask was if you'd consider letting us film you. That one clip Gemma put up on Facebook and Instagram is still getting quite a bit of response, even several weeks later. A live mini-concert could be a great way to engage with the resort's fans who are wishing they could be here. Show them some love and what they can hope to see when they get back."

Josh paused, his hand creeping up unconsciously to his scarred cheek. Still shots were one thing, even video to be broadcast later; it could be edited, cut, touched up. A livestream was something else.

Luke watched him with knowing eyes, just waiting.

"Would Gemma film it?" Josh asked eventually.

"She'd direct, if that's all right with you. The videographer we normally use lives in Airlie and commutes over, so we can't use them at the moment, but we do have cameras. You can work with Gemma to get them set up where you want, and recruit whoever you choose to operate them. Gemma and Olivia will handle the social media streams when it goes live; there will likely be a lot of comments and chatter."

"Did you already ask them?"

"Olivia came to me with the idea; it's literally her job, you realise, as marketing manager. We can't advertise at the moment because we can't take bookings, but it's crucial for us to stay engaged. To make people want to come here, especially because I foresee international travel is going to be out of the question for some time, probably more than a year unless I'm very wrong. We need to engage with Australians, make them want to holiday at home."

Josh nodded, fully understanding what Luke was getting at. Social media engagement was one of the few free methods of advertising they had available to them, and word of mouth was priceless. He knew the team at the marine biology centre had been providing lots of stunning marine life photos, and Gemma had been doing her best with shots of the beautiful island landscape, but something like a live mini-concert, with real-time interaction, would be invaluable.

"Did you ask Gemma?" he checked again.

"I thought I'd check with you first." Luke tilted his head, smile growing curious, and Josh realised he'd asked about Gemma twice in five minutes.

He could feel the blush rising up his neck.

"I'm fine with it," he said quickly. "Whenever you want. I presume you'll want a few days notice so you can let people know it's happening, so I'd definitely like to do nightly shows for the staff - just so I can rehearse!"

"No worries. I'm looking forward to taking one in myself. Olivia said you're amazing, and that we're not paying you enough. Which brings me to another point... since you're actually back working, we can put you back on the payroll."

Josh shrugged. "I'm not worried about it. I've been here rent free for the last few weeks, I'm happy to sing for my supper."

Luke stared at him. "We don't want you to have to live off your savings. You told me you got a decent payout from the army, but still..."

Josh shook his head. "It's not a problem, Luke. I don't broadcast it about, but I'm financially independent. My family's wealthy. My grandfather set up a trust. I'm never going to be on the breadline."

"Oh." Obviously startled, Luke regrouped quickly. "Nevertheless. Despite the loss of cashflow, Sunfish is doing fine. We're owned by a billionaire, remember. We can afford to put you back on the payroll, I promise."

"Whatever." Josh didn't feel like he was really doing enough to earn the comfortable living he was getting on Sunfish, but Luke was right... Sunfish Island was literally owned outright by Jace Hunter, and even though Jace had recently taken on the enormous Chapel Islands redevelopment program and was building an airport, a golf course, a huge sports training and rehab centre, and another entire resort on the islands, he wasn't even going to notice the tiny drop in the swimming pool which would be Josh's salary.

"I'll let you coordinate with Gemma and Olivia, then," Luke said. "And I'm looking forward to hearing you."

Chapter 6

"Ready?"

It was a soft question from Gemma. Josh took a deep breath, flexed his fingers briefly, and nodded. They'd completed the soundcheck a few minutes before, he'd checked the makeup covering his scars - even though they'd positioned the two cameras carefully to avoid focussing on them - and it was a couple of minutes to the start time they'd declared and promoted heavily.

Olivia had spouted numbers about followers who'd expressed interest, but they'd gone right over Josh's head as he started to develop a sudden and extremely surprising case of stage fright, in the hours before the concert. He'd played to thousands with the Army Band, but this, with a potential future audience of far more who he couldn't even interact with, was inexplicably much more unnerving.

"Let's do it." He flashed a slightly shaky smile at Gemma, though he could barely see her behind the bright spotlight shining on him.

"You're going to be amazing, Josh," was her reply, which made his smile firm up and become more real and natural, before she stepped back and called "Three, two, one... rolling!"

He waited, holding still. Listening for her voice in the tiny earbud he was wearing.

"All live. You're up," she said.

"Hey, folks!" He smiled into the camera, launching into the short introductory speech he'd written with Olivia. "My friends and I at Sunfish Island are missing you all desperately, hope we can see you again in person soon, but in the meantime, I'd like to share a few songs with you. We've had some requests, and since I plan to do this again next week, you can submit some more..." he gave them the website address to submit requests, before lowering his hands to the piano keyboard. "Gonna start off with some Billy Joel for you," he said, "the *Piano Man* is in the house!"

***

Gemma barely had time to breathe. She was directing, switching occasionally between the two cameras, one fixed and one being manned by Cory, Olivia's boyfriend who was moving it in slow gentle sweeps according to her instructions, and also keeping half an eye on the social media streams.

"I underestimated this, oh my god, I need more help," Olivia hissed beside her, fingers flying on her laptop. "I can't handle both the Instagram and the Facebook!"

A couple steps and Gemma grabbed the arm of her friend Jill, sitting in the back row of the crowd. "Need your help," she hissed, and Jill rose and came with her quietly, taking in Olivia's predicament at a glance and taking over one of the two laptops Olivia had in front of her.

Comments were scrolling at a dizzying pace, Gemma could see.

"Is that right?" she leaned over Olivia's shoulder twenty minutes in, touched a figure at the bottom of her screen. "Five thousand viewers live on the stream?"

"Yup." Olivia's fingers danced over the keyboard. "Better not tell Josh. He's doing tremendous. Don't want to put him off."

Josh did seem to have relaxed, Gemma thought, losing himself in the music. He'd taken a brief break from the piano, picking up his guitar to play a few songs.

"You're doing amazing," she touched the icon to switch on his earbud as he played a soft outro. "Going to play one of your originals?"

She saw his throat work as he swallowed, and he shook his head infinitesimally. *Not tonight*, she interpreted. "No worries," she said quietly, not letting the disappointment she felt show in her tone. "Everyone's loving what you're doing. Keep up the good work."

***

Josh was drenched in sweat by the time he finished his last song and farewelled his audience, both the few present and the few hundred he guessed were watching live. He sagged against the piano with relief as Gemma walked past Cory's camera, grinning at him.

"All the streams are down, Josh. Well done, that was amazing!"

"Ugh." He closed the lid over the piano keys with hands that were shaking slightly. "I'm wrecked."

"You did great." She put her hand on his shoulder, smiling directly into his eyes.

It was the first physical contact he'd had with anyone in weeks, and that was why, Josh told himself, he found himself swaying towards her, desperate for more of her touch. He was just starved of it. They all were.

"I need a drink," he blurted out.

"You've earned one. Did you order dinner? I could pick it up and bring it to your cabin, if you want to go and have a drink. And maybe a shower."

She was being tactful; she'd obviously noticed how sweaty he was. Josh nodded, trying not to look like a desperate fool as she took her hand off his shoulder.

"Thank you, I'd appreciate that. And, uh, if you want... maybe stay and eat your own dinner with me? I've got a bottle of wine, and it's no fun celebrating alone."

"I'd like that." She ducked her head slightly, before lifting it again and giving him a shy smile. "I'd like that a lot."

***

I acted like a silly groupie, Gemma admonished herself as she almost bolted away from Josh, her face flaming. "Get it together, Gemma!" she said aloud to herself, almost shrieking as she rounded the corner and just missed running into Jill.

"You know what they say about talking to yourself, right?" Jill danced aside neatly, saving her dinner tray from toppling.

"Thanks for helping out tonight!" Gemma called after her.

"You're welcome," Jill called back cheerfully.

Collecting the two dinner trays, Gemma carefully balanced hers on top of Josh's and headed back to his cabin. He stepped out onto the verandah as she arrived, looking clean and refreshed in a white shirt and loose tan cotton pants, running shoes on his feet and his hair spiky with water.

"Hey, thanks." Josh reached to take the top tray, putting it on the table.

"That one's mine."

"Gotcha." He moved around to the other side of the table, getting out of the way as she put her own burden down. "Oh, wait, I forgot the wine!"

He looked almost nervous, Gemma thought, as he stumbled past her and back inside, returning a couple of moments later with two glasses, and a bottle of wine.

"Give me a moment, I need to go digging in the kitchen drawers for a corkscrew..."

"It's a screw top," she pointed out, and he looked down at the bottle and frowned before starting to laugh.

"So it is!" He sank into his chair, still chuckling, and opened the bottle with a firm twist of his wrist, reaching to pour some into her glass.

"Thanks." She sniffed appreciatively. "Merlot?"

"Pinot noir." He poured a glass for himself, lifted the glass and offered it in a toast. "To a successful livestream."

Chinking her glass against his, Gemma took a sip and waited until he'd set his glass down before she asked. "Did Olivia tell you the viewing figures?"

He shook his head, taking the plate cover off his dinner and leaning down to inhale the fragrant steam rising off the food. "No, she was still responding to comments, I think."

"We topped out at almost five and a half thousand."

Josh froze, fork poised above his plate, staring at her wide-eyed. "I'm sorry, what?"

She snickered at his deer-in-the-headlights expression. "I'm not yanking your chain, I promise. I had to recruit Jill because Olivia couldn't keep up with moderating all the comments. If we do it again, we'll need a whole response desk set up."

He looked shell-shocked, but he scooped up some of the satay chicken and rice on his plate and took a bite, shaking his head slowly.

Amused at his reaction, Gemma tucked into her own dinner. Josh must have been used to playing in front of good-sized crowds with the Army Band, she thought, and he hadn't seemed bothered about a crowd of over a hundred at some of the weddings she'd seen him play at on the island. Maybe he was just surprised by the sheer number of people who'd tuned in for the virtual concert.

"Olivia's going to be at you for a repeat performance, you know," she said finally, setting her fork down on her empty plate. "Probably weekly, at least."

"I'm okay with that. Got to sing for my supper." Josh glanced at her wryly, picking up his wine glass and sitting back in his seat. "I'm pretty much just squatting here uselessly unless I can entertain someone."

"I feel like that without any weddings to photograph." Gemma made a face. "Soon. I hope. The state government are making noises about maybe opening things up in a small way soon, and because overseas travel isn't happening for the immediate future... and big weddings I think will be off the table for a while too... we're hoping that people may opt for a small destination wedding here. We've been fielding a lot of inquiries, but we can't take any bookings right now."

***

Gemma lit up when she was talking about weddings, Josh noticed, her eyes sparkling and her wide mouth curving up in an infectious grin. He studied her covertly as he poured more wine for both of them. Her dark brown hair had been clipped in a gamine pixie cut when they'd first met, but she hadn't had it cut while they were in lockdown and it was growing out fluffy, starting to curl over her ears and at the nape of her neck. He felt a fierce impulse to run his fingers into it, twist a silky curl around his finger.

Sit your ass down, Josh. Rein it in. Slow down.

"You really, really like weddings, huh?"

Talking about weddings really didn't feel like slowing things down. But it was obviously a topic which mattered to Gemma, and he wanted to understand why, what it was about weddings that made her light up like that, because he really, really didn't get it.

"I love weddings!" She took another sip of wine, smiled at him over the rim of the glass. "My friend Philly doesn't get how I can photograph the same scenery with a different couple in front of it every day, as she puts it. But the scenery is just the frame. It's the love story I'm there to capture. The bridal couple's own personal fairytale."

"But considering the divorce rate... is it really all that realistic?" Josh wrinkled his nose.

"Cynic," Gemma accused. "I mean, I get why. With your fiancée pulling that absolute bitch move on you. Oh. Sorry." She looked into her wine glass, made a little *oh yikes* face. "Haven't had alcohol in a while. Apparently it's removing my verbal filters."

He laughed, charmed by her honesty. "No, it's fine. She did pull an absolute bitch move on me, but I'll be honest. I was cynical about weddings already. Both my parents are serial remarriers. Mum's on husband number four and Dad's on wife number six."

"Whaaat?" Gemma nearly dropped her glass. "Wow. Were you... I don't know how to phrase this tactfully. The product of the first marriage for either or both of them?"0..

"Yes." He grimaced. "First marriage for both. I'm the oldest son. They called it quits when I was five and both of them had remarried within a year. I've got a bunch of half and step-siblings, and I'm not close to any of them."

"That is... I don't know what to say. What a strange family situation." She paused, as though considering whether to tell him something. "My dad died when I was twelve, but until then my parents were so in love."

"I'm so sorry about your dad." He could see the pain still in her face from it. "That's a really tough age to lose a parent."

"I got through it okay." She shrugged, trying for nonchalance and missing by quite a lot, he thought. "My mother did it tough. Got hooked on prescription antidepressants for a few years, and then a couple of crappy boyfriends messed her up further. She was trying to recreate what she had with Dad and it's never happened."

"I'm pretty sure neither of my parents even know what they're looking for," Josh said dryly. "That said... my current stepfather's lasted nine years. He's a pretty good sort, I'm hoping Mum manages to hold onto him."

Gemma wrinkled her nose. "I wish my mother would dump her current boyfriend. He's the reason I stayed here through lockdown instead of going home to Brisbane."

Josh raised his glass to her sympathetically. "Yeah. Even though my current stepfather is all right, there's no way I was going home to live in their basement."

"So glad we could stay here!" Gemma leaned over and clinked her glass gently against his.

"Amen to that." He leaned back in his seat, kicked his feet up to rest on the verandah railing and sighed theatrically. "It's a tough life in tropical paradise."

Gemma giggled softly, matching his relaxed posture. "Company's not too bad, either."

Startled, he looked across at her, but she'd leaned her head against the back of her chair and closed her eyes.

If she'd been sitting next to him, he might have tried to kiss her at that moment, but he'd have to get up and move around the table, and he might have hugely misinterpreted her comment. They were friends, Josh told himself; Gemma was a grown woman and surely capable of letting him know if she was interested in anything more.

"There are certainly worse places to ride out a pandemic," he murmured, looking out into the darkness. Listening to the crickets chirping, the warm wind sighing softly in the palms. Music playing from someone's stereo not too far away a reminder that they weren't the only two people in the resort, despite the absence of guests.

"I should get out of here," Gemma sighed, making Josh jump.

He'd slipped into a relaxed reverie, a kind of contended zen state, just listening to the night sounds and enjoying her quiet company. He glanced across at her as she drained her wineglass and set it down.

"Thanks for the wine. I'll drop these back at the kitchen," she said, efficiently stacking their trays.

"Thank you for having dinner with me. I enjoyed your company," he replied honestly.

It was hard to tell in the low light, but he thought maybe she blushed, a little, before she flashed him a quick smile.

"Good night, Josh. You were awesome this evening."

He was blushing too, but he was pretty sure she didn't see it as she walked away.

Chapter 7

"So the resort is reopening as of next Saturday," Luke said, grinning as just about everyone on the video conference channel started cheering. "Limited occupancy, every space will have a maximum person capacity with no more than 20 people per section, hand sanitizing stations everywhere. No buffets in the restaurants."

"Do we have bookings?" It was Jill, the guest relations manager, who asked.

"We're reopening bookings as of tonight. Rosie is working on what staff we need to call back in and getting them back... most of them are within the state which simplifies things. We'll be quiet for a while, especially with no overseas or interstate guests, but Sunfish Island is back in business!"

Details were sketchy for a few days after that, but the state government quickly put out some guidelines on weddings being restricted to 20 attendees, with no dancing, and a little to Gemma's surprise, the resort began getting wedding bookings immediately. It seemed couples were finding it easier to whittle guest lists down if they were going for a destination wedding. And then they were booking huge photography packages so that they could share with the family and friends who weren't able to attend.

With no dancing allowed, everyone was requesting a musician rather than a DJ, which meant Josh was booked to do just about every wedding too... and people were asking for him by name anyway. They'd been doing a live virtual concert twice a week since the first one and the audiences were growing each time.

Things weren't quite back up to the seven days a week Gemma had been working before the shutdown, but she was definitely enjoying being back to work.

And seeing the joy and relief of couples managing to celebrate their marriages despite everything going on around them lifted her spirits immeasurably.

"That sounded amazing," Gemma said as Josh joined her outside the reception centre on a mid-set break. "I hadn't heard you sing Tom Petty before."

"*Free Fallin*'s a classic." He took a seat on the low wall beside her, sipping from the bottle of water he'd brought outside with him. "The groom requested it. Don't think the bride had ever heard it before." He slid a sideways glance at Gemma, cocked a cynical brow. "What odds are you giving on this being a lasting marriage?"

"Don't be like that," Gemma scolded gently, though privately she too had thought that the sixty-year-old groom and twenty-three-year-old bride seemed rather mismatched. "He absolutely adores her, you can see it in the photos."

"And she absolutely adores his place in the Top 100 Richest Australians list?"

"Stop it!" She whacked him gently on the shoulder. "She's really sweet."

"I'm judging him a lot harder than her. You don't get to be that rich without exploiting a lot of people. I just hope he continues to treat her like she hung the moon and doesn't start feeling like she's just a pretty ornament he's purchased."

"Wow," Gemma said when she got her breath back. "That sounds like you're talking from experience."

"I've seen my father repeat the cycle too many times to count. He's on wife number six, remember, and there've been quite a few girlfriends who didn't make it to the altar, as well. Stood up to him, or refused to sign his prenup, or... anything which set off his dictatorial personality, really."

"What does your father do?" she asked, curious.

"Trash." He grinned at her confused look. "He owns the largest rubbish collection concern in Australia. Contracts with state governments and urban councils all over the country. There's a lot of money in rubbish... or getting rid of it for people, anyway. The problem is that he treats people like they're disposable too. Interchangeable. Replaceable."

There was genuine rancour in Josh's tone, and Gemma wondered just what his father had done to make Josh resent him so much. "Was it your mother he treated like that... or you?" she asked gently.

"Oh, both of us. Mum was just the first in a long string of trophy wives. I was his eldest son, but when I didn't grow up just like him, he washed his hands of me and turned his attention to my siblings. He's spent years pitting them against each other to determine which one is 'worthy' of being his heir."

"That's horrible!"

"You're telling me. We haven't spoken since the day he told me he wouldn't put up a cent for me to study at university... if I wasn't going to study either accountancy or law. Didn't think anything else would be of any use, if I was going to take over the business." Josh drained the last of his water. "I basically joined the military to spite him. Cost me half my foot, but I've got no regrets about not dancing to his tune."

Gemma kept forgetting about Josh's foot. He always wore trousers and long-sleeved shirts, covering the majority of his scars, and he walked smoothly unless he was tired or on rough ground, with no sign of a limp. Something she suspected took a lot of effort and practice. He pushed off the wall now and offered a hand to help her up.

"Back to the grind?"

"Sure." She accepted his hand, smiled up at him as she got to her feet. They wound up standing close, chest to chest, and something in Josh's eyes made Gemma catch her breath. For a long moment they just stared at each other.

"Is this something, Gemma?" His voice was very soft.

"Maybe," she whispered back.

He didn't let go of her hand, his thumb stroking the back of it gently. Gemma trembled as a tingle raced through her entire body from that light contact.

Someone called her name from inside the function room, and she twitched, pulling back from Josh as though she'd been scalded. A flush rose to her cheeks.

"Later?" he asked quietly.

"Later," she agreed, reaching for her camera bag. They were both on the clock right now; it wasn't the time for... whatever that had suddenly, unexpectedly turned into. She couldn't stop thinking about it for the rest of the evening, though. The way his eyes had darkened as he looked into hers.

She liked Josh. And if she was going to be completely honest with herself, she'd been nursing a bit of a crush on him since, well, not quite the first time they met when he was rude and grumpy, but definitely the second, when he'd apologised so graciously and turned out to be really quite nice. She just didn't think he reciprocated her interest. And if he did... was her serious, or was he just looking for a fling? Everything he'd said to her seemed to indicate he didn't believe in love or other fairytales, as he'd probably put it, but something deep inside Gemma cried out in protest.

"I just don't want to believe it, but I think I'm kidding myself," she muttered under her breath, circling the room looking for photo opportunities. Without dancing, she was restricted, and the guests were starting to tend towards drunk and messy, so she was probably about done for the night anyway.

"On the other hand, would a fling be so bad?"

"Flings are never bad, gorgeous," a voice behind her slurred, and she sighed, turned around and prepared to deflect the best man, who'd been attempting to flirt with her all day. Now drunk, he was even less inclined to take no for an answer, but she dealt with him firmly, eventually siccing Terry and Jerome, the resort's wedding planners, on him. They gave him short shrift and had him escorted off to his room to sleep it off, leaving Gemma to breathe a sigh of relief and go to speak to the bride and groom, explaining that since the night was winding up she'd be finishing up.

"You've been wonderful. Could I give you a hug?" The bride had obviously had a little too much champagne and was a bit teary. Gemma put her camera down on the table for a moment and permitted the embrace.

"You look beautiful, and I hope you've had a wonderful day," she said warmly.

"It's been tremendous. So glad we decided to have our wedding here." The groom spoke up unexpectedly. "We'd planned a big wedding in Sydney originally, 400 guests, but I think this has made you happier in the end, hasn't it Kerri my love?"

Kerri nodded tearfully. "The stress of the big wedding was too much. This has been so much nicer. Just the really close people who really love us."

"You know I'd have done whatever you wanted, but honestly this suited me much better." The groom smiled wryly, and Gemma thought privately that despite his grey hair and wrinkles, he was still a good-looking man. She could see what Kerri saw in him. Especially since he was looking at Kerri as though she hung the moon.

"Be looking at your email in about two weeks," Gemma said in parting, "I'll send the first proofs through for your approval!"

She was in the habit of stopping by her office to ensure all photos from the day were safely backed up to her cloud storage before she called it a night. She could still hear the piano playing as she left there and walked back to her cabin, wondered what time Josh would finish up. Whether he would knock on her door later.

***

Josh was booked to play until midnight, but thankfully the bride and groom decided to call it a night about an hour before that, and the small wedding party quickly broke up. He waited until the last guest had left and still finished the song he was playing, even though he was only singing to the cleanup crew, hard at work clearing the tables. A couple of them paused in their work to give him a quick round of applause, and he grinned, rising to his feet to give them a quick bow.

"You've been a wonderful audience, Sunfish, thank you and good night!"

Laughter and cheerful thanks followed him as he shoved the tablet he used to bring up the music he needed to read into his satchel and slung it over his shoulder, picking up another bottle of water on his way out.

He had to walk past Gemma's cabin to get to his, and he found his steps slowing. Her light was on, even though she'd left the wedding party an hour ago and he'd have thought she would be asleep by now.

Was she waiting up for him?

That moment earlier had been... unexpected. Josh couldn't say he hadn't had thoughts about kissing Gemma before - that night when they'd eaten dinner on his verandah, especially. But tonight was the first time he'd thought she might be considering kissing him back.

He stood irresolute on the path outside Gemma's cabin for several minutes. Should he knock? Or just leave things for now, try to catch up with her tomorrow sometime? There was no wedding booked tomorrow, so they might actually get a little time to talk. Or do other things.

Now he'd started thinking about kissing Gemma, he couldn't stop. Couldn't stop thinking about taking her face between his hands, looking into those deep blue eyes, running his fingers into her dark hair. He bet it would be soft; he knew it smelled good, having caught a sneaky sniff a time or two when she'd stood close beside him. Coconut and apricot.

"Are you going to stand there all night?"

Josh jumped and let out a sound he would definitely not describe as an unmanly squeak. Gemma was standing just inside the screen door to her cabin, watching him.

"I was..." he started, and then trailed off.

"Dithering?" She slid the screen door open and stepped out onto her verandah, closing the door behind her to keep the bugs out. She leaned on the rail and looked down at him.

"Wondering if I'd be welcome if I knocked on your door."

"Depends what you'd be expecting."

"Just the pleasure of your company." He tried for a winning smile, and she laughed.

"Take a load off." She gestured, and he saw that instead of two chairs and a table like he had outside his cabin, she had a two-person swing seat instead. She sat down, swinging her legs up and resting her feet against the verandah rail.

Josh wasted no time dumping his satchel by the door and taking a seat beside her. He groaned with pleasure as she reached down into a cooler on the floor and pulled out two beer bottles, offering him one.

"Oh, wow. Bless you. I needed this."

"I've noticed you never drink while you're performing, but I know you do like a beer."

"Mm hm." He was too busy removing the screw cap and taking the first long, cold gulp. "Ahhh."

Gemma laughed, opening her own beer and taking a sip. They had to sit close on the narrow swing, shoulder to shoulder and hip to hip, their legs touching all the way down their thighs. Josh put his feet up on the rail beside Gemma's, taking a moment to ensure both his heels were firmly grounded against the rail. She looked at his feet, in his usual plain black boots, next to her slender bare ones, but said nothing.

They sipped their beer in comfortable silence for a while, listening to the crickets chirping and the breeze rustling softly in the palms.

"So," Josh said eventually. "That was a thing. Earlier."

"A thing?"

He felt, rather than saw, her tilt her head to look at him. He kept looking out into the dark night.

"It was a thing I'd been thinking about for a while. About you, I mean. That was the first time I had an impression you might be thinking about it too."

She laughed. He chanced a quick look at her. Amusement was reflected all over that pretty, piquant face, and he wanted very badly to kiss her.

"You're really doing a thorough job of beating around that bush, Josh. Do you want to kiss me, or not?"

"Oh hell yes," he said fervently, and she leaned in closer, her eyes drifting closed, in very clear invitation.

Gemma's lips were warm and soft under his, her body yielding against his. Josh kept a tight grip on himself, ordering himself sternly to keep his head, not to grab and take and ravage as his instincts were screaming at him to.

Fingertips sank into his shoulder muscles and Josh pulled back, breathing rapidly, assuming she was pushing him off. Instead, Gemma made a small impatient sound, hooking a hand around the back of his neck and pulling his mouth back to hers.

Chapter 8

"I should go," Josh said quietly at last, pulling back, though only far enough to lean his brow against hers.

"Should you?" Gemma teased gently. She felt rather than saw his smile, felt the warmth of his breath as he tilted his head to kiss her again.

"What are we doing, here?" he asked, finally pulling back to look at her properly. "I value our friendship, Gemma, and the last thing I want to do is fuck it up by misinterpreting things. Is this just friends with benefits, or are you interested in something a bit more serious?"

She didn't know how to answer, didn't know what he expected. Was there a right or wrong answer?

"Do we have to define it right now?" she asked cautiously.

"No." His lips quirked in a smile. "I just want to make sure you're not thinking with your libido, and you're not going to wake up in the morning full of regrets."

"Okay, you might be right about my libido being in charge right now," she admitted with a laugh. "I like you, Josh, as a friend and maybe a lot more, and I don't want to ruin our friendship either."

He pulled back slightly, regret in his gaze, and she grabbed for his hand.

"With that said, I'm not much for regretting my decisions in the cold light of day. I think we're both mature enough to deal with whatever changes this might bring to our friendship."

"Do you?" It was a blunt question. "Because I know myself pretty well, Gemma, and I know if we do this, there are certain things that I'm not going to be able to manage well."

"Like?" She raised a brow.

"Jealousy. It's a pretty unattractive trait and God knows I've tried to stamp it out of myself, but it's likely to rear its ugly head every now and then. Not if you're just interacting with other guys, but if I think you're romantically interested in someone else, I doubt I'd handle that well."

She appreciated his honesty, so she gave him some in return. "You're the only guy I've been romantically interested in, as you put it, in quite some time."

Josh got a pleased little smile at that, not quite a smirk, but she elbowed him gently in the ribs anyway.

"Let's agree this, then," she suggested. "While we're doing... whatever it is that we're not specifically naming just yet... we're not doing anything with anyone else which would be the kind of thing we'd do if we had any romantic interest in that person."

Josh's chuckle was low and deep. "A lot of double-talk to say can we be exclusive?"

"Exclusive friends with benefits sounds like an oxymoron, but yes. I can see myself getting jealous if you're flirting with other women all over the place."

"I promise not to," he said solemnly, picking up her hand and kissing the back of it.

"Even when they're draping themselves over your piano and shoving their boobs in your face like groupies at a BTS concert?"

He burst out laughing at that. "I mean, if I was in BTS maybe that would happen. But I can't say it ever has. I'm not the kind of performer who gets girls' knickers thrown at me."

She had to laugh too. "But if you did?"

Josh wrinkled his nose in distaste, and Gemma collapsed laughing across his chest.

"Alright, alright."

"Come on. You know it's against resort rules to get involved with guests anyway. And you're the only woman here who's caught my eye, Gemma. I just didn't think, until tonight, it was reciprocated."

"It was," she whispered, leaning up to kiss him, and then she pushed back, scrambling a little awkwardly to her feet, and offered her hand. "Coming in?"

"Yes, please." He accepted her hand to get out of the swing seat, following her inside her cabin.

***

Josh wasn't entirely sure what he'd expected from Gemma's bedroom, but it seemed to fit perfectly with what he knew of her; painted plain white like his own, it was nevertheless full of personal touches, from a colourful rag rug on the floor to a gorgeous selection of photos framed and hanging in artfully arranged groupings on the wall. Predictably, they were all wedding-themed, but there wasn't a bride or groom among them; instead they were pictures of wedding cakes, table decorations, confetti artlessly scattered across a bleached wooden floor, a horseshoe trimmed with lace hanging against a lattice background with the blue ocean out of focus in the distance.

Tempted to stop and admire the images, which were obviously Gemma's work and presumably something she took a lot of pride in, Josh nevertheless recognised that now probably wasn't the time. Gemma hadn't invited him here to look at her photographs. And considering she was now unbuttoning her shirt while smiling up at him, suddenly he was a lot less interested in the photographs anyway.

She was small, and slight, and her breasts weren't more than a handful, but to Josh she was utterly beautiful, and he drank in the sight of her like a desperately thirsty man finding water in the desert. She wore a pretty, lacy pale pink bra which didn't seem quite Gemma, somehow, and he wondered if she'd put it on for him. Decided he was extremely flattered if she had.

Music was playing quietly in the room, a soft steady thrum just at the lower range of his hearing. He recognised the distinctive beat, smiled in appreciation. INXS' Devil Inside; was Gemma channelling her inner devil to seduce him? He was more than willing.

"Take your shirt off," she requested, her dark blue eyes glinting with emotions he didn't know her well enough to put a name to. Lust, he thought. Which was certainly reciprocated. He was a little startled to find his hands were shaking slightly as he fumbled at his buttons.

Gemma came closer, reached up to help push the shirt off his shoulders, gazing into his eyes. She licked her lips, seemed about to say something, then bit her lower lip and dropped her gaze.

"What is it?" Josh asked quietly, lowering his hands to put them on her waist gently. "You can back out any time you want, okay? I'm not gonna be mad."

"It's not that." She obviously steeled herself, glanced up and gave him a wry little half-smile. "I'm all in. I'm just afraid I'm going to do something stupid and awkward when I see your foot and make you feel uncomfortable."

"You've not made me feel uncomfortable yet," he pointed out. "And you saw my scars the first time we met."

She reached up to touch his scarred cheek, her fingertips feather-light as they traced down, over the puckered, rippled skin on his neck. Across his shoulder, his pectoral muscles, down to his abs.

"The scarring's less here," she murmured quietly. "I thought they'd have worked harder on repairing your face, for cosmetic reasons?"

"Combat uniform protected my torso surprisingly well. The materials it's made of are designed to be pretty fireproof."

"Right." Her fingers drifted lower, to his belt.

"It's okay if you do think my foot's ugly," he said quietly. "I certainly bloody do."

Her eyes flicked back up, and he read astonishment in them.

"What, I'm not allowed to hate my own disability? Believe me, if I could go into an experimental lab and get a new foot grown back tomorrow, I absolutely would. But it's not an option, so I wear a prosthesis and keep it covered up so I don't have to look at it too much myself." He shrugged. "As long as you don't run screaming we're good."

"I feel like the emotion I'm most likely to feel is pity, and you wouldn't like that."

She was so honest, and he bloody adored that about her.

"I've felt plenty of self-pity over it. I can take a bit of pity from you, if it comes to it, but I think empathy's more your speed. Are you going to undo that?"

A smile touched her lips, and she set to undoing his belt.

"Actually, hold that thought, or I'm going to end up hobbled with my pants around my ankles. Let me take my boots off. And my prosthesis."

She didn't hesitate. Just took a seat beside him on the bed and watched while he bent over to unzip his boots. Easing them off, he took off his right sock, then his left, and it wasn't until the sock was completely off that anything looked at all out of the ordinary.

***

Gemma found herself fascinated watching Josh matter-of-factly removing the prosthesis from his foot. He still had a heel, as he'd noted, but the front part of his foot was completely missing, a white seam across the skin showing where the surgeons had cleanly amputated it.

"Huh. It really doesn't look that strange at all." Curious, she looked at his foot, as he leaned back on the bed, watching her, obviously waiting for her reaction. It was smoother than she expected, the single white seam across it the only visible scar. "Do you get phantom pain?"

"Not much any more. I did for the first few months after." He grimaced. "The worst is when I dream. It's still there in my dreams."

"Oh, that would be really crap," she said with instant, instinctive sympathy.

"It really is." He pushed himself back up the bed, bracing strong forearms on the mattress, until he was leaning against her pillows. "You know what's not crap? Being here, with you looking like that, Gemma."

She ducked her head, a little shy.

He crooked a finger at her. "Come up here. I want to kiss you some more."

Scars and partially missing foot or no, he was still one of the most attractive men she'd ever known, and lying on her bed like that, solidly muscled chest exposed, belt undone, he looked entirely delicious. Gemma got up on her hands and knees and crawled up the bed towards him, she hoped in a sexy rather than awkward way, and was rewarded by his appreciative grin. He patted his stomach suggestively and she threw a leg over to straddle him, leaning forward to kiss him again.

Josh's hands were warm, his fingertips callused from playing his guitar, as he stroked lightly over her skin. He fumbled for a moment with her bra, making Gemma smile against his lips, but eventually managed to unsnap it and pull it away, letting her breasts spill free into his hands. Not that there was much to spill, but he didn't seem to mind, making enthusiastic, hungry noises against her mouth as he cupped them in his strong hands, thumbs brushing over nipples getting harder by the second.

She had to pull back to gasp for breath when he squeezed lightly, and he grinned at her reaction.

"Okay?" he checked quietly.

"If you stop now I'm going to be really cross," she told him breathlessly, which made him laugh. He let go, though, dropping his hands from her breasts. Gemma let out a grumpy noise. "What the..."

But he was putting his hands on her waist, urging her a little further up his body, and then bending her forward, until one nipple brushed his lips.

"Okay, that's a good enough reason to stop," she said magnanimously. "I'll allow it."

"Damn, you make me laugh," he murmured against her breast, tongue darting between words to tease the puckered tip. And then he was too busy to talk, licking and sucking on her nipple while deft fingers stroked the other, driving her nearly mad with want. She sank one hand into his hair and gripped, holding him to her, while the other braced her against the headboard.

Gemma lost track of time. Josh seemed unhurried, tireless, determined to have her at fever pitch before he did anything else. She was sure she was making deeply ungraceful noises, breathy pants and moans, gasps of his name as he dragged his teeth over her skin. A needy sob as he finally shifted her off him, easing her down to her back on the mattress.

"Off?" he queried, fingers tweaking at the waistband of her shorts.

"Now!" she demanded desperately.

"I got you." There was a laugh in his voice, but only heat in his gaze as he looked down at her. He undid the button and Gemma grabbed at her shorts, shoving them down hastily and kicking them off, discarding her knickers along with them. Too aroused to even think about being shy or cautious now.

"Damn," Josh breathed softly, taking in her body with a long, sweeping gaze. "You are so bloody beautiful, Gemma. Look at you. Perfection."

She didn't think so. She was too boyish, narrow-hipped and small-breasted. Under Josh's appreciative stare, though, she felt womanly for the first time in her adult life, really. She stretched, arching luxuriantly against the pillows, thrusting her breasts upwards, and was gratified to hear him groan.

"Condoms," he rasped, "because I don't know how much control I've got."

"Oh. Here." She reached for the nightstand, fumbled the drawer open. Felt blindly around inside for the box she'd bought at the resort shop a few days ago, resolutely avoiding the cashier's avidly curious glance. It was definitely easier to hide red cheeks when you were wearing a face mask, at least!

"Got them." Josh took the box from her, stripped off the cellophane and extracted a packet. "Here. Hold onto it for me for a few minutes." He pressed it into her palm. "Got something I need to do first."

She thought he meant a bathroom visit. Realised he had something else in mind when he eased back down the bed and nudged her thighs apart, shifting to lie in between them.

Gemma could feel her thighs starting to quiver, and he hadn't even touched her yet. She wanted to scream when he took his time, pausing to part her labia gently with his thumbs, blow cool air lightly over her clit before his tongue flicked once, so gently she should have barely been able to feel it - except she was already so sensitive even that light touch hit her like a bolt of lightning. A desperate, guttural sound erupted from her throat and she arched up, grabbing at his head, running her fingers into his hair again and gripping tight.

Josh laughed against her, a low rumble which made her shudder with need, and then he stopped teasing and got to work driving her right out of her mind.

"Oh yes. Oh my god." Gemma thrashed her head left and right, mindless with want, as his lips and tongue teased her clit, dragging her rapidly up to the precipice. Sweat beaded at her hairline, tingles raced up and down her spine, and then he slid a finger deep and crooked it.

Chapter 9

Gemma bucked up against Josh, wordless wails of pleasure spilling from her lips, her dark blue eyes blank. He could feel her walls clenching against his finger as she came, her body quivering, breath stuttering, until she collapsed bonelessly back against the pillows, her fingers finally unclenching from his hair.

He tried another gentle lick, but she stiffened, and he backed off. She was too sensitive right this moment. He could wait. Gently he kissed his way back up across her stomach, pausing to spend several minutes loving on each breast. Her hands came up to stroke his shoulders and she made a greedy little sound when he nibbled at her throat.

"Condom," she mumbled, eyes closed.

"You sure? I can wait, it's fine..."

"Now," she demanded.

Josh chuckled quietly, obediently ripping open the foil packet. Gemma's directness was just one of the many things he adored about her. "Whatever you want, beautiful," he assured her, nudging her knees further apart and lifting himself between them. His missing foot didn't impair his ability to kneel, though he had to make sure his right foot was properly braced lest he wobble off balance.

Gemma lifted her knees instinctively to bracket his hips, the movement putting the tip of his sheathed cock right where it needed to be, gliding easily into the heated, wet cavern of her pussy. She sucked in a soft breath, nibbling on her lower lip, hands clenching in the sheet beneath her as her hips rocked to urge him deeper.

"Too good." Josh groaned it against the softness of her throat, fighting to slow himself, not to just slam deep and take what he wanted without regard to her pleasure. "Too much."

"Not enough!" She hooked her ankles together behind his back, bucking up against him.

"Gemma," he almost pleaded it, but she was blind and deaf, near-wild with passion, letting go of the sheet and clutching at him frantically.

"Please!" she almost shouted, and he gave in, giving her what she wanted with a deep, almost rough thrust. "Oh, yes!"

She was perfection. Sheer, utter perfection, matching his pace and urgency, letting him know exactly how much she was enjoying herself with wordless cries of pleasure and blunt nails raking his shoulders, until he could take no more and released with a desperate groan, back bowing as the pleasure ripped through him.

Gemma hadn't quite got to the peak with him, Josh registered distantly, and he rolled to his back, taking her with him. "Sit up on me," he whispered to her, slipping his hand in between them, urging her to ride him as he circled his fingertips over her slippery, soaking bud.

He was softening, but clearly there was still enough stimulus for Gemma as she moaned and quaked in the throes of another orgasm before flopping to collapse on his chest with a deeply pleasured sigh.

"Okay?" Josh checked after a couple of minutes in which she didn't even move beyond breathing.

"Ummmm." She rubbed her nose on his chest, then let out a quiet chuckle. "I should probably have warned you. I have a shocking tendency to just fall straight to sleep after sex. Especially after spectacular orgasms like that."

He couldn't keep the grin off his face. "You can fall asleep. I don't mind, I don't feel the need to rehash and critique my performance."

"Oh." She lifted her head, squinted at him in the soft light. "I detect the slightest hint of bitter memories. Bitch queen fiancée strikes again?"

The laugh rumbled up out of his chest, and he felt an odd sort of lightness settle on him. "Maybe."

"Forget her. She was trying to hurt you and she knew exactly how." Gemma rolled off him with a soft sigh, reached her hand back to brush lightly over his chest as she sat up. "I have no complaints. Only compliments."

Josh couldn't keep the smile off his face. He watched Gemma slip off the bed and amble to the bathroom, completely unconcerned about being naked in front of him. Comfortable in her own skin.

"Do you want me to go?" he asked as she returned, still naked and unbothered about it, and slipped back into bed.

"Not unless you want to." Gemma looked slightly surprised. "Or unless you get night terrors and are going to try and strangle me in your sleep?" She gave him a little smile, but he sensed it wasn't entirely a joke on her part. And considering his history, it was a perfectly reasonable question to ask.

"No night terrors." He shook his head, moving to sit up against the pillows. "Nor do I snore."

"I mutter in my sleep sometimes. Or so Philly always used to tell me." She flopped face-first onto the bed beside him, before turning her head to give him a cheeky grin. "And I'm a cover hog."

"In this hot weather? You're welcome to them!"

They were both laughing as Josh got out of bed. He felt a little self-conscious as he made his way to the bathroom, knowing that without his prosthesis and shoe his limp was much more evident, but considering Gemma hadn't reacted unfavourably when looking directly at his foot, he wasn't too worried about limping in front of her.

She was asleep when he returned, sprawled bonelessly but somehow still elegant, one slim arm flung up beside her head, the other lying lax across her stomach.

Switching off the light, Josh eased into bed beside her, trying to move carefully and not wake her up. It had been a long day for her, he presumed, with the wedding preparations kicking off early, and the party running late.

Gemma made a soft little sound in her sleep and he froze, but then she rolled onto her side, the arm across her stomach fumbling lightly at him until it came to rest on his chest. She snuggled up closer, cheek pressing against his shoulder, a contented smile on her lips.

Tentatively, Josh put his own hand over Gemma's. It felt so right lying here with her, so incredibly natural. He had to put that down to Gemma herself and her unaffected, straightforward attitude. She was entirely unflappable - a trait she'd have cultivated for her work, he supposed. To be calm and still when brides were losing their cool and panicking would be a gift.

He drifted off to sleep with a smile on his own face, Gemma's breath soft and warm against his shoulder, her small hand captured snugly against his heart.

***

"Gem?"

Someone was knocking on her screen door. Gemma forced bleary eyes open. Found herself looking at the very fine view of Josh's naked chest. She admired it vaguely for several moments.

"Gemma! Are you here?"

"Bloody hell," she mumbled under her breath, sitting up and scrabbling for a sheet to swathe over a still-sleeping Josh, preserving his modesty at least, before grabbing a long T-shirt off the chest by the bed and pulling it on. "Yes, I'm here. What is it?" She half-staggered to the door, trying to keep her voice down, and stepped outside, blinking in the bright morning light. "What time is it?"

"After nine." Olivia folded her arms and smirked, taking in Gemma's dishevelled appearance with an amused stare. "Not like you to sleep in. Up late, were you?"

"Bugger off, would you? There's no wedding today so it's my day off. I'm allowed a lie-in!"

"Sure you are. Don't suppose you've seen Josh, by any chance?" Olivia flicked a glance at the screen door, which Gemma had firmly closed behind her. "He's not in his room."

"I might have done." Gemma felt oddly defensive, though she hadn't done anything wrong. "What of it?"

"Luke needs to see him soonest."

"Why?"

"Nothing bad." Olivia gave her a maddening, mysterious smile. "It's a meeting Josh is going to want to go to sooner rather than later. So if you do happen to see him, maybe pass the message on."

"Will do." Gemma liked Olivia, she really did, but it was hard sometimes not to feel inferior when confronted by just how gorgeous the other woman was, and just how well put together she always looked. None of the women on Sunfish wore much makeup because it was just too hot, but somehow Olivia managed to look absolutely flawless with nothing more than lip gloss and a touch of mascara. Even her thick, glossy curls were behaving themselves beautifully, despite the humidity.

"See you later. Enjoy your lie in." Olivia gave her another secretive little smile before leaving, and Gemma went back inside, hoping Olivia wouldn't gossip.

"Who am I kidding," Gemma muttered to herself. "Somebody probably saw us last night." Or somebody would see Josh leaving in full daylight this morning. Gossip travelled at the speed of light on Sunfish, she sometimes thought.

"Wassup," Josh mumbled sleepily as she crawled back into bed beside him.

"Olivia was looking for you."

"Oh." He seemed to come to instant alertness, his eyes popping wide open. "Ah. Here?"

"Educated guess on her part, I'm thinking. I neither confirmed nor denied anything."

"What did she want?" He pushed himself to sit upright against the pillows.

Gemma tried not to stare too greedily, but it was difficult; he looked absolutely delicious sitting in her bed, the morning sunshine slanting through the window to cast him in a soft glow. She could barely even see his scars. "Luke wants to see you about something. Olivia was being cryptic, but she implied you'd want to hurry up. It's nothing bad, though. I think."

"Huh." He frowned, reached for the nightstand where he'd left his phone. "Oh. It's flat."

"Use my charger." She fished down beside the bed and came up with the cable end.

Josh plugged it in, put the phone back down and grinned at her. “Well. Since Olivia didn’t actually find me, and it didn’t sound like it’s all that urgent, and you’re looking particularly beautiful this morning...”

Gemma blushed, flattered. Josh reached out, trailing his fingers lightly down her cheek.

“You did say you wouldn’t regret it in the morning... but if you don’t want to repeat the performance, that’s okay too.”

He looked hopeful, though, and Gemma smiled at him.

“Definitely no regrets. And if you’re serious about being in no hurry... I reckon Luke can wait a bit longer.”

"I can’t imagine what could be so important it couldn’t wait... for this,” he said, before leaning over to kiss her again.

Chapter 10

Josh was very nearly skipping as he made his way to Luke's office, almost an hour later, after a quick stop at his room to put on clean clothes. He needed a shower, but a few quick sprays of deodorant should ensure he didn't smell too bad until he could grab one.

"Hey Sarah," he said to the assistant who sat at the desk in the outer office. "Got a message that Luke wanted to see me?"

"Sure, go on in." She barely glanced up from her typing. "He'll probably welcome the break from wading through the latest round of updated operating restrictions."

Josh winced in sympathy, moving towards Luke's open office door and popping his head into the office. "Hey. Heard you wanted a break from some horror paperwork?"

"Oh god, yes, please come in." Luke jumped up from his desk with alacrity, obviously relieved to escape whatever was on his computer screen which had been making him tear at his hair. He gestured to Josh to take one of the comfortable chairs over by the window and joined him, slumping into the chair with a weary sigh.

"Bad?" Josh asked sympathetically.

"Every morning I wake up, log onto the news sites and brace for the bad news," Luke said baldly. "And then I look at my email and it's more bad news. There's just no end in sight."

"I'm sorry," Josh offered, not sure what else he could say. "If there's anything I can help with..."

"Thank you, but all the staff are already doing so much. You've made a big difference, with your concerts. Which is what I need to talk to you about."

"I've got one scheduled for the day after tomorrow... unless there's a late change?"

"No, not at all." Luke smiled genuinely at him, some of the worry lines on his face relaxing a little. "For once, one of the messages in my inbox was good news, and it's for you. The last live concert you did, four days ago... you performed one of your original songs."

Josh stiffened a little, surprised. "Yes," he said, a little hesitantly.

"*Never Mine*, is that the title? Turns out it's gone a little bit viral. More than a little."

He honestly didn't know what to do with that information. He'd played the song, a wistful ballad he'd written recently, on a whim.

"Right," he said slowly.

"Got a lot of comments on social media saying things like, the girl he's written that about doesn't know a good thing when she sees one." Luke's eyes crinkled at the corners as he smiled. "You're certainly popular with our female audience."

Josh didn't know where to put himself. He shrugged uncomfortably.

Luke took pity on him and got to the point. "Anyway, someone shared it with Myst, and she shared it on her Instagram account yesterday evening."

It took Josh a few seconds to process what Luke had just said. He blinked several times. "What? I'm sorry. Myst. As in, the Myst?"

"The pop star, yes." Luke appeared to be enjoying himself immensely, his eyes twinkling as he leaned back in his chair. "She's a friend of the resort. Shot a music video here a couple of years ago - that duet she did with B-Rex, which got her big break in the US market? Anyway, she bought a house here last year. Doesn't get here as often as she'd like, but when she does, we make sure she has absolute privacy, which she appreciates, obviously."

That made perfect sense. Sunfish Island was a paradise. Josh couldn't imagine why anyone with millions of dollars at their disposal wouldn't want to own a holiday home here. What was not computing in his brain was that Myst had not only watched him sing, she'd shared a video of him - performing an original song, no less! - to what had to be an audience of millions.

"How many?" he said, a little incoherently, but Luke obviously understood.

"Myst has nearly eight million followers; your video has been viewed more than half a million times. In fourteen hours."

"Whaaaaa."

Luke snickered quietly behind his hand. "I should have had a camera running. Your face is classic."

"Pardon me for being a bit shell-shocked." Josh managed a sensible sentence eventually. "I don't quite know what to do with this information."

"Understandable." Luke gave him a paternal smile. "However, that's not all. Even before she saw the response you got once she reposted your video, Myst sent me an email. She likes *Never Mine* very much, and she's interested in the song's potential, either with you as a performer or her, with you credited as the songwriter. Or potentially a duet."

"Excuse me," Josh said faintly, and had to lean down to put his head between his knees, as he was suddenly feeling incredibly dizzy. "Did you just say that Myst is interested in my song?" he said, staring at the floor. Wondering if he'd somehow stumbled through the mirror into a parallel dimension where good things happened to people like him. Gemma last night, this today... it felt like some sort of impossible dream.

"She's invited you to fly to Brisbane. She's in the studio right now recording her new album. Wants you to come in and talk, maybe she can help you out laying down a production track. She's got her band there, of course..."

Luke kept talking, saying something about Myst's manager also having emailed him expressing interest in signing Josh as an artist, but Josh couldn't take any more in.

"When?" he asked.

"As soon as you can, I think." Luke shrugged. "Yes, it's not particularly convenient for us, but I'm certainly not going to stand in the way of an opportunity like this for you. And there's no lockdown right now, so I'd say go. If you get locked down in Brisbane for a while, well... it's not the end of the world. Go. I'm sure Sarah can get you on a flight this afternoon. Hey, Sarah!" he called towards the door, and his assistant appeared with an inquiring look. "Get Josh on a flight to Brisbane this afternoon, will you?"

"You got it." She disappeared.

"You'd better go pack a few things," Luke said cheerfully, "Sarah will text you your flight details."

"Flight out of Hamilton Island at ten past four!" Sarah called. "You'll need to get the one o'clock boat transfer!"

That gave him a couple of hours to get a few things together... and see Gemma. God, he needed to see Gemma, to explain what was happening and why he was running out on her literally within a day of them getting together. He winced just thinking about the conversation, but if he didn't find her and explain before he left, she'd never forgive him, for sure, and he didn't want to risk losing her.

***

Gemma hadn't felt like staying in bed, once Josh finally left, so she took a shower, dressed and headed for her office. Might as well get a start on editing the proofs from yesterday's wedding, so she sat down at her desk and powered up her computer. She'd uploaded all her shots to the cloud yesterday even while she was taking them - her camera had Bluetooth - and now planned to do a preliminary run through to take out any bad shots to start with, before curating a selection of the best ones to share with the clients. Once they'd chosen which ones they wanted, she'd do some further editing before providing the high-resolution final images and some prints.

Checking the contract - yes, as she'd thought, they'd prepaid for 100 shots with the options for further add-ons - she set to work, humming softly under her breath as she picked out and deleted every shot where someone had blinked or had a weird expression on their face.

Her phone, lying beside the keyboard, chirped with an incoming text message. From Josh, she saw as she picked it up.

Where are u? Need to talk to u, urgent.

My office, she texted back, wondering what on earth could be so urgent. Unless he really had been fired, though she couldn't imagine what for... no, Olivia had hinted it was good news.

Josh's face didn't look like good news when he entered her office, though. He looked worried and bemused, as he grabbed one of the chairs she had in there for clients to sit and look through images, and brought it closer to her desk.

"So," he said, "something really weird has happened, and I don't quite believe it still, but I have to fly to Brisbane this afternoon..."

Gemma listened in astonishment as he explained, stumbling a little over his words. He was in shock, she thought, seeing his pupils slightly dilated, and who wouldn't be? He'd just done the equivalent of winning the lottery, for an unknown musician.

And even though her stomach was twisting itself in knots at the realisation that he was leaving and there was a pretty high probability he wouldn't be coming back, she forced herself to smile happily and say "That's amazing, Josh! How wonderful for you!"

"You're okay with me going?" He stared at her, and she wondered what he wanted her to say. She wasn't going to cry and beg him not to go, even though a part of her wanted to do just that. It wouldn't be fair to him, and in asking him to choose between a dream opportunity like this and her, Gemma was pretty sure she was going to come out the loser. She would never see him again.

But if she let him go, if she told him she believed in him, well... she'd probably never see him again anyway. They'd be parting on a good note, though, and if things didn't work out and he came back, there wouldn't be acrimony between them because of a bad parting.

So she bit on her tongue for a couple of seconds, until she was sure her voice wasn't going to waver as she spoke, and said "Look, I'm not going to lie. The timing could be better. But it's not like we're in a serious, committed relationship, is it?"

"No, I suppose not." He looked like he wanted to say more, but he didn't, so she carried on after a moment.

"This is an amazing opportunity and I think you'd forever be kicking yourself if you didn't go. I wouldn't want you to live with regrets of what might have been. Go. You deserve this. You'll knock their socks off."

He reached out to touch her hand, his voice soft and deep as he said "I wish we'd had more time, Gemma."

"Me, too." She leaned in to brush her lips against his. "It was fun while it lasted - and I'll always be your friend, Josh. No matter what."

"Thank you," he whispered against her lips, and they kissed once, long and slow, before he pulled back with a regretful look. "I have to go. I need to pack a bag and get down to the dock to make that boat."

"Hey," she said as he rose and headed for the door, and he looked back at her with an inquiring smile. "When you're rich and famous, you can buy a holiday home here and come back and see us."

"My first big purchase. I promise." He flashed her a grin, and then the door closed behind him and he was gone.

Gemma waited a couple of minutes, until she was quite sure he wasn't coming back, before letting her face drop into her hands. Her breathing came faster, painful, gulping breaths, as the tears began to trickle down her cheeks, and she rocked back and forth in the chair.

One night. Is one night of happiness all I'm going to get?

One goddamn night!

It had been perfect. Utterly perfect, and waking up beside Josh had been like a beautiful dream coming true; she'd dared to imagine a rose-tinted future for the two of them, together... only to have it all snatched away inside a single hour.

Sitting alone in her quiet office, she cried her lonely heart out, for the first time in many years unable to face her work. Looking at wedding photos of a happy couple was quite simply beyond her right now.

All she could do was let her grief out and hope that by tomorrow, she'd be able to do her job again without breaking down completely.

***

Myst was smaller than Josh had expected, was his first thought on meeting the pop star. She was slight and willowy, which gave the impression on film that she was quite tall, but the top of her head barely reached his chin. She also had a surprisingly dirty laugh, a wicked sense of humour and a work ethic that would put anyone to shame.

She made him feel comfortable inside five minutes, despite Josh feeling extremely star-struck, shoving a cup into his hand and telling him to help himself to tea or coffee.

"I have a gift for you," he said. "I was just about to get onto the boat when one of the chefs came running up to me and shoved a package into my hand; they'd heard I was coming to see you."

"Carlo? Or Suzannah?" Myst took the package eagerly, laughing when she opened it up to reveal a beautifully packaged bakery box full of biscuits. "God, I love those two so much. These biscuits were the only thing I could stomach for about a month while I was pregnant with my daughter. They're really good. Want one with your coffee?"

Feeling instantly put at ease by her cheerful, down-to-earth friendliness, Josh accepted a biscuit and took a seat.

"Now, this song of yours," Myst said after she'd eaten a couple of biscuits, humming with pleasure at the taste, "I love the sentiment and the melody, but there's at least one line where the words don't quite scan, and I think you could improve it out of sight if you take it up a major third..."

Josh listened intently. He was proud of the song, but the opportunity to work on improving it with a musician of Myst's calibre wasn't to be passed up. She encouraged him over to the piano in the corner and he played around with the melody as she suggested, astonished by how much better it sounded with just that one simple change.

"Tell me where the song came from," Myst requested, leaning on the piano as she scribbled lyrics in a notebook. "It feels like it's very personal to you."

Josh fought down a blush. "I wrote it about a girl I had a huge crush on," he admitted. "She's one of those people who really has her life together. She's found the thing she loves doing and she's good at it, and she's just... happy, you know? And I felt at the time like a square peg trying to fit into a round hole, and certainly that a girl like her would never look at a misfit like me."

"You sound like you don't feel that way any more?" Myst gave him a curious glance.

"Well, turns out I might have a chance with her after all. Maybe. One day." He changed the subject quickly. "So tell me... I thought you wrote all your own music?"

"Most of it," she said with a shrug, "but I'm not precious about it. I've worked with other songwriters, much like I am with you right now. I like to put my own spin on things even if the song's been written entirely by someone else. Speaking of which. What else have you written?"

Her enthusiasm was so contagious, it was impossible to deny her anything. Josh found himself playing another song for her almost before he knew it.

"You've got genuine talent," Myst said as he played the closing notes, "as both a performer and a songwriter. I'd absolutely love to work with you, Josh. You could be a star, if you want it."

That was the million-dollar question, of course, and the one which occupied Josh's mind all day, and into the evening. He'd planned to get a hotel room but Myst wouldn't hear of it, insisting he come home with her, where Josh met her amiable husband, Australian rugby captain George, and her adorable fifteen-month-old daughter Seren. They were all friendly, easy company, living much more simply than he might have expected considering the level of fame and success both Myst and George enjoyed, but they were obviously incredibly happy and very much in love.

Lying in bed in a comfortable guest room late that night, Josh stared at the ceiling, wakeful, unable to stop thinking about the night before, with Gemma's words to him that morning running around and around in his brain.

I wouldn't want you to live with regrets of what might have been.

"That's the problem," he said out loud, keeping his voice low to avoid disturbing Myst and her family. "I think I already am."

Chapter 11

Six weeks later

"You okay, Gemma?"

"Hm?" Gemma lifted her head from where she'd been resting it in her hands, elbows leaning on the bar.

Olivia was sitting beside her, gazing at her sympathetically. "You've been much quieter than usual lately. Not your usual cheerful self, even at weddings. I was wondering how you're doing."

"Just feeling a bit tired and run down." Gemma shrugged, forcing a smile. "Been working too hard. But since Luke found a part-timer to come over from Airlie a couple times a week, at least I can have days off now and then. Let him cover the smaller weddings. And help me out with the bigger ones."

"We were thinking maybe you should actually take a break."

"We? You've been talking to Luke," Gemma realised. "Why are you talking to me, and not Rosie?" She named the resort's Personnel Manager.

"Because if Rosie does it, it's official and she has to do things like order you off the island for a break. If I do it, it's as a friend and you can arrange things in your own time. But Luke told me to pass it on... if you haven't made arrangements to take leave within the next month, he will hand it on to Rosie."

"Fair enough," Gemma said slowly, understanding that her friends were apparently genuinely concerned about her. She didn't think it was all that serious - she knew she was just having a bit of a mope, really, feeling down in the doldrums since Josh left. She'd get over it eventually. "Actually off the island kind of leave?"

"Knowing how much you hate travelling, I don't think Luke will enforce that. Especially since we could get plunged into lockdown again any time and you might get stuck!" Olivia grinned at her.

"Gotcha. All right, I'll rearrange my schedule to take some proper days off and go lie by the pool and drink cocktails. Does that work?"

"Don't want to see your camera in your hand at all," Olivia warned. "And you can lock up your office and give me the key."

"Good grief, you're serious!" Gemma shook her head in disbelief. "Fine. I promise. I'll even go off the island... for a day trip, at least. I really do need to go do some clothes shopping, so I'll go to Airlie one day."

"Good. And talking of cocktails." Olivia gestured to the bartender. "I could really go for a margarita right about now... and there's Jill coming in. Want to share a pitcher with us?"

"Why the hell not." Drowning her sorrows sounded like an awesome idea, even if somewhere in the back of her mind, Gemma knew she was going to end up drunkenly babbling about Josh breaking her heart. It'd feel good to get it out, maybe. She'd been bottling everything up and it wasn't good for her. "I'm done for today, and I'm not working until tomorrow evening. Bring on the drinks!"

***

"And this is why I don't drink much." The ceiling was bloody well spinning. Gemma closed her eyes and groaned, but it was no use. She'd woken up because she needed the bathroom, and her bladder was being insistent about its urgent requirement to be emptied. She was going to have to manage to stagger the few steps to the bathroom and hope she didn't need to throw up by the time she got there.

Falling back into bed a few minutes later, Gemma pulled the pillow over her head and groaned. The sunlight spilling in around the edges of her blinds was way too bright.

But she did feel marginally better after downing most of a glass of water in the bathroom, and the room had stopped spinning, at least.

"So it appears drinking away heartbreak doesn't work," she said aloud finally, pulling the pillow off her face. "And pretending it's not happening hasn't exactly gone well either, so it's time for Plan C."

The only problem was, she had no idea what Plan C might consist of. Taking some time off work was apparently compulsory in the near future, but she suspected all it would achieve was giving her more free time to mope around and feel sorry for herself and miss Josh.

"Unless," Gemma said suddenly, sitting up and immediately regretting it. She clutched at her head with a small moan. But now the idea was in her head, she couldn't shake it... what if she used her time off to go down to Brisbane and see if she could meet up with Josh? He'd sent her the occasional text enthusing about how nice Myst was and how much she was helping him out. Gemma hadn't even been able to bring herself to reply. She'd left the messages on Read. She was sure if she texted him back, though, he'd make time to see her.

Wouldn't he? They were friends first before they were lovers, and he'd seemed to want to hold onto that friendship, so surely, if she mentioned that she was going to be in Brisbane for a few days, he'd want to catch up?

"And then what?" Gemma asked herself, scaldingly honest as always.

Then what indeed. Josh wasn't going to take one look at her and declare he couldn't live without her. Even if he did, she didn't want to live in Brisbane, or any other big city, and she couldn't ask him to give up his dream to live a quiet life here with her. Their dreams weren't compatible, and that meant no matter how heartbreaking it felt, neither were their futures.

Going to Brisbane would be reopening an already painful wound. She had to stop letting herself hope, had to let Josh and her wistful dreams of a future for the two of them go.

Tears slid from the corners of Gemma's eyes and trickled into the pillow as she stared at the ceiling, trying to order herself to forget Josh and failing miserably.

A knock at her cabin door startled her. "Just a minute!" she called, drying her eyes hastily on the sheet before scrambling out of bed and grabbing the nearest item of clothing which came to hand, a loose cotton dress. Pulling it over to her head, she stumbled to the screen door, pulled back the curtain covering it, and gaped at the impossibility of who was standing on her verandah.

***

"Hey." Josh waggled his fingers in a small wave.

Gemma looked like she'd just woken up, her hair ruffled, the thin cotton dress hanging shapelessly around her. She was paler than usual, her eyes tired. She was staring at him as though she didn't quite believe the evidence of her own eyes.

"I'm really here, I promise. Sorry I didn't tell you I was coming."

"Josh." She wobbled slightly on her feet, putting a hand out to steady herself on the doorframe, and suddenly concerned she might faint, he instinctively reached out towards her.

"Are you all right? I didn't mean to give you a shock..."

She gave him a wry smile. "I'm a little bit hung over, to be honest. Got on the cocktails with the girls last night for the first time in a while." She clicked the lock on the screen door and slid it open. "How are you? You look good."

"Doing great, thanks." He felt suddenly awkward, face to face with her at last, though he'd been mentally rehearsing what he wanted to say for weeks now. "You?"

"Doing fine." She crossed her arms over her chest.

"You didn't answer my texts," he blurted, which was not at all what he'd wanted to say, but it had been on his mind for a while.

Gemma sighed heavily, walked out and flopped down into the swing seat on the verandah.

Josh hesitated a moment before following, sitting down beside her.

"I didn't know what to say to you," she said finally, not looking at him, but staring out into the gardens. "I know you said you wanted to be friends, and we were friends first, but after we slept together... well, I found myself wanting more, and I couldn't have it, and being friends wasn't enough."

Her voice was trembling, and Josh realised to his horror that she was on the verge of tears. He grabbed for her hand, squeezing it tenderly.

"It wasn't enough for me either," he said huskily. "It was never enough."

"But I couldn't ask you to stay." She bit down hard on her lower lip, before looking up at him through glassy eyes. "It wasn't fair, and you'd have resented me and it would have broken us anyway."

"I know." He twisted at the waist to face her more fully, lifting his free hand to her cheek. "I had to go. You were right, that I'd always have had regrets if I didn't. But it didn't take me long to realise that I was living with much bigger regrets at not giving us a real chance."

"What... what are you saying?" she whispered.

"I made myself stick it out and give it a shot. Myst was terrific, I can't say enough nice things about her. Introduced me to a heap of influential people and even invited me to play a gig with her, since live gigs are back on again and she's doing some small shows to warm up for a proper tour. And I learned so much about myself... I learned, particularly, that I'm not like her. You can see her feed off the energy of the crowd; she absolutely loves performing, being on stage."

"Don't you?" Gemma's brow furrowed.

"No. I love the music. Performing to a crowd is a job, and the bigger the crowd, the tougher the job. Myst doesn't see it like that. She gets so excited, she can't wait to go out there and perform... whereas I can't wait for it to be over. Hiding my scars and my missing foot, because I don't want people to see the real me. The bigger the crowd, the harder that is to do. It's impossible when you start doing big stage shows and TV performances with cameras everywhere."

"Huh." Gemma seemed to think it over, before saying tentatively "So... you don't actually want to be a rock star?"

"No. We all have dreams of that sort of thing, don't we, especially as kids, but it didn't take me long to realise I'd actually hate it."

***

"Like the brides who half-kill themselves organising a huge wedding and then get overwhelmed on the day and realise they'd have much preferred a smaller, intimate affair." Gemma has seen so many brides burst into tears at just that realisation. Had talked a few of them out of the bathroom, too.

"Exactly like that!" Josh looked relieved that she understood.

"So... what's your plan?" She could hardly believe it, but she was starting to hope, a small kernel of warmth growing in her chest.

"I'm going to write songs, play them to live audiences here and work on refining them, and send them as demo tapes to Myst's manager, who's taking me on as a client. He's going to forward them to record companies and see if they can sell them. I've already licensed *Never Mine* to Myst." Josh grinned. "Ten thousand dollars, songwriting credit, a generous share in royalties... and the promise that we can use her holiday house here whenever she's not going to be here herself."

"You're going to stay?" She stared at him in dawning delight.

"I'm going to stay. Everything I've ever wanted is right here, Gemma." His hand stroked lightly along her jaw. "I don't want or need fame or fortune, though it seems a bit of fortune is determined to come my way anyway, and I won't turn it down."

Tears were running down her face in earnest now, and she couldn't stop them. She flung her arms around his neck, setting the swing seat to creaking dangerously.

Josh hugged her back tightly, pressing kisses on her hair. "I'm so sorry I left you," he whispered.

"No, no." She shook her head fiercely. "I'm glad you left. Because you came back. Which means it must be real, don't you see? Haven't you ever heard that saying about if you love something, set it free... and if it comes back, it's yours forever?"

"Does that mean I'm yours forever now?" He pulled back a little, smiled down at her. "Because I think I'm good with that."

"Yes." She was laughing through joyous tears as she pulled his head down and plastered her lips to his. "Yes!"

~ The End ~

Read on to enjoy ***Better In Practice****, when the island's new resident doctor falls for shy massage therapist Shae!*

Better In Practice

Island Escapes Book 7

Caitlyn Lynch

SHENANIGANS PRESS

shenanigans press.com/EN

Contents

Chapter One

Shae Everly looked up as the door opened, a smile spreading across her face when she saw her client Mina Hartley walk in to her spa treatment room. Mina had been in every day for the last week, and Shae had come to really like the other woman. Shae waved her over. "Right on time as always. How was the beach?"

Mina sighed, sliding into the chair across from Shae. "Gorgeous, but Mark had to work again. We only have a few more days on the island and he's spent most of our holiday on conference calls." She shook her head. "I don't know how much more of this I can take."

Shae's heart ached for her. Mina deserved so much better. "I'm really sorry to hear that."

"Thanks." Mina smiled weakly. "But enough about me. How's the new guy you've been seeing?"

Heat rose in Shae's cheeks. She hadn't told Mina the truth—that there was no new guy. She'd made up the story to seem less pathetic. "You know, it didn't work out."

"What?" Mina gasped. "Why not? He seemed perfect for you."

Shae cleared her throat, avoiding Mina's gaze. Time for the facial. "Okay, why don't you get settled on the table? We'll start with a deep cleanse and exfoliation."

Mina's eyes narrowed, but she didn't push further. She lay back on the table and closed her eyes.

Shae busied herself gathering supplies, the familiar motions soothing her frayed nerves. She soaked two washcloths in a bowl of warm water, wringing out the excess. "This is a new aloe vera cleanser," she said, gently wiping Mina's face. "It will deeply hydrate and brighten your skin."

The tension eased from Mina's forehead as Shae massaged the cleanser in. Shae breathed a quiet sigh of relief, grateful the scrutiny had passed. She wasn't ready to admit the truth, not even to her closest friends: that she was tired of waiting for the right man and wanted to take charge of her own happiness.

Shae rinsed away the cleanser and patted Mina's face dry. Whatever the future held, she knew one thing for certain—Sunfish island, and the friends she'd made here, were home. She smiled, dipping her fingers into a jar of exfoliant. "Now, close your eyes and relax. I'm going to make you glow."

When she rinsed away the exfoliant, Mina's skin was soft and smooth. Shae patted on a hydrating serum and said, "Your skin looks great. Keep up a good moisturizing routine and you'll be glowing in no time."

Mina opened one eye. "You're not getting off that easily. Spill—what's really going on with you?"

Shae busied herself preparing a honey almond mask. She should have known Mina wouldn't give up so easily. With a sigh, she said, "I've been thinking about what you said, about not waiting around for some man. You're right, I don't need that. I have a good life here, and maybe it's time I start appreciating what I have instead of wishing for what I don't."

"Exactly," Mina said. "You're amazing, and any man would be lucky to have you. But you don't need a man. Do what makes you happy."

Shae smiled, feeling lighter than she had in weeks. "Yeah. I think it's time I start doing that." Mina was right—it was time she started living for herself.

***

Shae cleaned up the treatment room, humming softly under her breath as she worked. She felt lighter and more optimistic than she had in a long time. Mina's advice had struck a chord, and Shae realized how much she'd been limiting herself.

She peeked in on Mina, who was relaxing on the table. "How are you doing in there?"

"Wonderful," Mina said. "This mask is heavenly. You're a miracle worker."

Shae laughed. "Glad I could help. Take your time—no rush."

She returned to the front desk, glancing around the spa. This place had become her home over the last few years. She loved her job and the clients she saw every day. There was no need to wish her life away waiting for some fantasy of the perfect relationship. She already had so much to appreciate right here.

A text from her friend Lucy popped up on her phone: *Drinks and dinner tomorrow night? The girls are all getting together down at the beach!*

Shae smiled, tapping out a reply: *Sounds perfect. See you there!*

She set down her phone, humming again. Looked like the start of a new chapter in her life. One filled with new beginnings, new adventures, and a determination to live fully. Her heart swelled with excitement at all the possibilities stretching out before her. The future had never seemed so bright.

Shae tidied up the treatment room once Mina had left, wiping down the countertops and tables while the calming spa music played. Lavender and eucalyptus scents wafted through the air, instantly relaxing her.

In the next room over, she could hear the gentle hiss of the steam room. One of her colleagues, Jenna, was providing a detoxifying mud wrap for a client. Shae peeked in, smiling at the sight of the woman coated in green mud and cucumber slices over her eyes, clearly blissed out.

Another perfect day at the spa, Shae thought. She couldn't imagine being anywhere else.

***

The next morning, Shae arrived at the spa to find Mina waiting in the lobby, clutching a cup of coffee. Dark circles hung under her eyes, and her blonde hair was pulled back in a messy bun.

Shae smiled warmly. "Good morning, Mina. How are you today?"

Mina gave a weak smile. "I didn't sleep much last night. Tom and I had another fight." She sighed, staring into her coffee. "I don't know what to do anymore."

"I'm sorry to hear that." Shae guided Mina to her treatment room, helping her onto the bed. "Do you want to talk about it?" Shae listened as Mina described yet another argument with her husband, her fears of their marriage crumbling into pieces.

Mina wiped her eyes. "I'm sorry for unloading all of this on you."

Shae said gently, "Communication and compromise are so important. Have you thought about relationship counseling?"

"I don't know. Maybe. I'm sorry, I'm such a mess today..."

"Don't apologize." Shae patted her arm. "I'm always here to listen."

She began the facial treatment, applying creams and serums to soothe Mina's stressed skin. Slowly, Mina relaxed under her ministrations. By the end of the session, her eyes were clear and a soft smile graced her lips.

"Thank you," Mina said. "I feel like a new woman. And you know what, I'm going to tell Tom that if he doesn't agree to come to relationship counselling and start listening when I talk, I'm done with this marriage. I'm sick of being taken for granted."

"I think that's a great idea." Shae felt a surge of satisfaction, knowing she had provided comfort and maybe helped Mina out a little. Interacting with clients and easing their troubles, even in small ways, gave her a sense of purpose. She loved being able to make a difference in people's lives, bringing them joy through her work. It was these moments that made her job truly fulfilling.

***

When her shift ended, Shae walked along the beach at sunset. The blindingly white sand was soft under her feet and a warm breeze rustled through her hair. The resort glowed with golden light as the sun dipped lower in the sky.

She smiled at the vivid colors, breathing in the fresh sea air. The rolling breakers stretched to the horizon, as endless and constant as her love for this island. She stood watching the sunset fade into dusky twilight, at peace in the place she called home.

“Yoohoo, Shae!” a loud voice hollered, and she turned and grinned. Her friend Lucy stood at the top of the beach in front of the cabana regularly used for weddings, waving both arms.

“Hey!” Shae waved back, and made her way up the beach to join her friends. Several of them were sitting on plastic chairs, plates of food and glasses of wine on their laps. “Oh, this looks yummy. Was I supposed to bring a plate?”

“No!” Lucy laughed, pulling her into a quick hug before nudging her towards an empty chair. “Suzannah brought leftovers from a huge wedding buffet. Tuck in, there's loads!”

Suzannah, the beautiful redheaded French chef who ran the resort's Michelin-starred restaurant along with her husband Carlo, looked up from her own plate and grinned. “And nothing has strawberries in, I promise.”

Shae smiled back, amazed at how Suzannah seemed to remember absolutely everything about everyone's dietary requirements. Shae wasn't even seriously allergic to strawberries - they just gave her itchy hives, but she preferred to avoid them even so.

“Wine?” Olivia, the resort's marketing manager, offered a glass. “Nessa raided Jace's wine cellar again, so we have the good stuff.”

“I'll have a glass of that rosé then, please,” Shae said, browsing the selection of platters on the table and selecting a few different things to eat. She wasn't sure what half of it was, but it wouldn't matter; literally everything Suzannah cooked would be a feast for the taste buds.

“Hey.” Lucy nudged her as she sat down with her plate and glass. “A little birdy told me a rumour about you. That there's a new man in your life?”

“Ah.” Shae paused mid-sip. “I hate to tell you this, but your little birdy was misled. I invented a boyfriend to appease a nosy client, and then had to dump the imaginary man just as fast when she hassled me to meet him.”

Laughter rose up, and Shae smiled, not at all embarrassed. She trusted these women, close friends who would honestly love to see her happy in a relationship, but would support her no matter what. “Who would I be dating anyway?”

she asked jokingly. "There's just nobody exciting and single. No cute new staff members coming in, Rosie?" She looked at the resort's personnel manager.

"Not lately, though the new doctor arrives tomorrow," Rosie said.

"Another retiree looking to spend his last few useful years relaxing in paradise seeing five patients a day? I'm not looking for a sugar daddy," Shae joked.

"Not a retiree this time. He's in his thirties." Rosie smiled secretively, as though she knew something none of them did. "And he's cute."

"Can't see a doctor that young sticking around, he'll be bored in a few weeks, surely!" Lucy exclaimed.

"You forget - we're about to open the sports rehab facility on the neighbouring island. Dr. McArthur has an interest in sports medicine. We'll have plenty to keep him busy."

Sunfish Island had been in the throes of a major expansion for the last few years; the resort's billionaire owner, Jace Hunter, had purchased three neighbouring islands, one with an unfinished airstrip and the other with an abandoned golf course and a half-built sports rehabilitation centre. He'd spent a great deal of money and effort finishing everything off to a world-class standard. The airstrip had opened a few weeks before, and Sunfish had been booked to capacity ever since. The sports rehab facility and golf course grand opening was only a few weeks away. Rosie's husband Adam, a former world champion MMA fighter, was the general manager.

Content to listen as her friends discussed the new facilities and the resort expansion, gossiped and laughed, Shae relaxed in her chair and let her mind drift. The new doctor would just be the first of quite a few new arrivals, with sports physiotherapists and golf pros due any day to start work at the new facility. She felt a curious sense of anticipation.

Maybe she really would meet someone new. Maybe her time was coming, maybe love really could be just around the corner.

And if it wasn't? Well, she had a good life here, Shae reminded herself, taking another sip of her wine and looking around at her friends, laughing and talking, faces animated in the soft glow of the fairy lights strung over the gazebo. She was happy, fulfilled in her career. She didn't need a man to complete her.

Chapter Two

Tylin McArthur sighed and pinched the bridge of his nose as the man next to him droned on about the inferiority of the female sex.

"Women simply can't grasp complex ideas like men can. Their brains are wired differently, you see." Derek leaned back in his seat, clearly pleased with his profound insight.

Tylin glanced at his neighbour out of the corner of his eye. What a pompous jerk. He tried to tune out the endless stream of nonsense but it was no use. Each absurd claim grated on his nerves like nails on a chalkboard.

"If your woman idolises any other man - an actor, a musician, follows them on Instagram or whatever - she doesn't really love you. Once a woman loves you, you become the only male in her world."

Tylin snapped. "That's utter rubbish."

Derek blinked, nonplussed. "I beg your pardon?"

"Your theory. It's ridiculous and deeply offensive." Tylin gave Derek a withering look.

Derek's eyes narrowed. "And what makes you such an expert?"

Tylin smiled without humor. "I'm a doctor."

"Is that so?" Derek's tone dripped with condescension. Clearly he didn't believe a word of it.

Tylin gritted his teeth. This was going to be a long flight.

"Do you at least agree, men have a biological imperative to spread their seed?"

Tylin took a deep breath and counted to ten, trying to calm his frayed nerves. Getting into an argument would do no good and likely only make things worse.

Especially since he was resort staff - even if he hadn't technically started work yet - and this fool next to him was a paying guest.

After a moment, Derek scoffed. "Cat got your tongue, doctor?"

Tylin fixed him with a cool stare. "There's no point in debating this further. You have your views and I have mine."

"My views are based on facts, not feelings."

"Your so-called facts are biased and deeply flawed, and no doubt sourced from highly dubious sources rather than respected medical journals. I'm not going to engage with your nonsense any longer."

"Because you have no logical counterargument." Derek's smug grin returned. "I win."

Tylin gritted his teeth and said nothing. There was no winning against willful ignorance.

Several tense minutes passed before Derek spoke again. "So, what brings you to Sunfish Island... *doctor*?" The mocking lilt in his voice set Tylin's teeth on edge.

He considered not answering but remained polite. Barely. "I've taken a position at the medical clinic."

"Ah, I see." Derek eyed him shrewdly. "And do you make a habit of confronting strangers with opposing views?"

"Only when their views are harmful and promote discrimination."

Derek barked out a laugh. "You must confront a lot of people then."

Tylin said nothing. There was no point in further discussion. He gazed out the window at the clouds, silently counting the minutes until they landed and he could escape this infuriating man. It was going to be a long flight indeed. Sighing, he pulled out his book and earbuds from his carry-on bag. If there was any chance of surviving this flight with his temper intact, it was by tuning out Derek completely.

He slid his earbuds into his ears, selected a playlist of classical music, and opened his book. The words on the page blurred as the first strains of Vivaldi's Four Seasons filled his head.

After several minutes, he dared a glance at Derek from the corner of his eye. The man was engrossed in paperwork, pen scratching across the page, and blessedly silent.

Tylin released a breath and felt the tension ease from his shoulders. Perhaps the rest of the flight wouldn't be so trying after all.

He lost himself in the pages of his book, the drama and intrigue of the mystery temporarily banishing all thoughts of his annoying seatmate.

An insistent poke to his arm jerked Tylin from the story. He looked up to find Derek peering at him expectantly. With a sigh, he removed an earbud. "Yes?"

"I never asked why you were heading to Sunfish Island." Derek leaned back in his seat, steepling his fingers.

"I told you. I've taken a position at the medical clinic there."

Derek waved a dismissive hand. "Yes, yes, but why Sunfish Island? It's rather out of the way, isn't it?"

Tylin shrugged, impatience rising again. "Location wasn't a priority."

"I see." A smug smile curved Derek's lips. "As it happens, I'm not heading there for work."

Tylin remained silent, not caring to know Derek's personal reasons for travel.

"I'm going to win back the woman I should have married." Derek glanced at him, eyes glinting with triumph. "My ex-fiancée lives on Sunfish Island."

Tylin's gaze sharpened on Derek's face. So the poor woman lived on Sunfish Island, did she? His fingers tightened around the book in his hands. He wanted to ask why exactly the engagement had ended, but sensed Derek would only lie about it, not wanting to acknowledge he might have been even the slightest bit at fault.

Tylin tucked his book into the seat pocket and regarded Derek seriously. "I know we've only just met, but I am a doctor. If you need someone to talk to about relationships or emotional health, I'm happy to listen and provide guidance."

While he spoke the offer, his thoughts churned. If he kept in contact with Derek, he might be able to intervene should the man's behavior become unacceptable. Tylin wouldn't stand by and watch an innocent woman suffer emotional abuse. The offer wasn't for Derek's benefit. If the ex-fiancée lived on Sunfish, that meant she was staff - and that meant her well-being was Tylin's responsibility.

Derek's eyebrows rose in surprise. "That's, er, very kind of you." He smiled, though it didn't reach his eyes. "But I won't be needing counseling. Once she sees me, she'll realize we're meant to be together. I simply need to remind her of what she's missing. We broke up three years ago and I know she's still single; she's obviously never gotten over me."

Tylin resisted the urge to roll his eyes. The man's arrogance and delusion knew no bounds. "The offer stands should you change your mind," he said evenly.

Derek's smile faded, and he studied Tylin with a calculating gaze. "You're serious, aren't you? You really would listen and, what was it, provide guidance?"

Tylin nodded. "I'm a doctor. Helping others is what I do."

"Hmm." Derek looked away, watching the clouds drift by the plane window. After a long moment, he sighed. "Perhaps we could continue our discussion over drinks, once we've both settled into the island. It's good to have a professional ear, even if one doesn't think they need it."

"Of course." Tylin kept his expression neutral, though triumph flickered in his chest. He'd gotten a foot in the door. Now to make sure Derek didn't slam it shut.

Fortunately, Derek then turned back to his paperwork, freeing Tylin to put his earbud back in and dive back into his novel. He was just turning the final page as the plane came in to land, smiling to himself at his good timing as he packed the book away.

Derek, however, sighed and muttered as he put his things away, obviously disappointed not to complete his work. Turning to Tylin as the seat belt light dinged off for the final time, he offered his hand. "I appreciate your generosity in offering your help, Dr. McArthur. It seems I may have misjudged you upon our first meeting."

Tylin smiled and shook Derek's hand. "And I you, Mr. Langston. I'm always happy to help however I can."

"Please, call me Derek." He stood, grabbing his carry-on bag from the overhead bin. "I'll be in touch about meeting for those drinks. It was a pleasure speaking with you."

"The pleasure was mine." The lie very nearly burned Tylin's tongue.

Derek nodded and made his way up the aisle as other passengers began to stir.

Tylin waited for the aisle to clear before standing and stretching his arms overhead. Perhaps Sunfish Island would prove more interesting than he'd first anticipated.

***

Tylin squinted at the resort map in his hands, the bright sun glinting off the glossy paper. He'd been wandering the staff-only area behind the main resort building for ten minutes now, completely lost.

He scratched his head and turned the map upside down again. None of the little landmarks matched up to anything he saw around him. Just rows of identical staff lodgings and mysterious unlabeled buildings. Sighing, he folded up the useless map and shoved it in his pocket. *I'll just have to ask someone for help.*

As he turned the corner, he collided with a young woman exiting one of the cabins. "Oh! I'm so sorry, excuse me," Tylin said, reaching out to steady the woman.

She brushed back a strand of dark, wavy hair and gave him a searching look with striking green eyes. "You're not supposed to be back here," she said in a quiet but firm voice. "This is a staff-only area."

"I'm terribly sorry. I seem to be a bit lost." Tylin gave her a helpless smile. "I was looking for cabin twelve? Where the new doctor is staying?"

The woman's expression softened slightly. "Yes, the staff cabins don't have numbers on the outside."

"Ah, that explains it then." Tylin chuckled, a bit embarrassed. "I'm afraid my map isn't very helpful. Could you point me in the right direction?"

"I'll walk you over. I'm headed that way." She gestured for him to follow. "I'm Shae, by the way."

"Tylin. Thank you, I really appreciate it." He fell in step beside her. "Are you staff here?"

Shae nodded. "I work at the spa."

"Well it's a pleasure to meet you, Shae." Tylin smiled warmly. "I think I'll be relying on the other staff quite a bit until I get my bearings around this place."

Shae looked at him curiously. "Are you the new doctor?"

"Guilty as charged."

She pointed towards a distant cluster of buildings. "Cabin twelve is the third one in that row. And the staff canteen is behind that big palm tree, when you're hungry. There's food available twenty-four seven, though limited choice outside scheduled mealtimes."

"Good to know, thank you again." Tylin paused. "Hopefully I'll be seeing you around, Shae."

The corner of Shae's mouth turned up ever so slightly. "Take care, Tylin." She gave him a small wave before walking away.

Tylin watched her go, intrigued by her quiet grace and those striking green eyes. With a shake of his head, he set off towards the lobby and his cabin, thoughts lingering on the mysterious Shae.

Tylin wandered the winding paths of the resort later that afternoon, hopelessly lost again. The tropical foliage and charming villas all looked the same. A helpful landscaper had pointed him to the medical centre earlier, but now he couldn't find his way back.

Just then, he heard hurried footsteps behind him. He turned to see Shae jogging to catch up.

"We have to stop meeting like this," she said with a playful smile. Her green eyes danced with amusement.

Tylin grinned sheepishly. "I know, I'm sorry. This place is like a maze."

Shae laughed, a light melodic sound. "Here, let me walk you back. I'm off work now anyway."

Tylin studied her profile as she led the way, appreciating her natural beauty.

"Thanks again for rescuing me," he said. "I'd probably wander the jungle all night without your help."

"It's no problem," Shae replied. "I'm happy to be your guide."

"Well I appreciate it. And the company." He smiled warmly.

Shae met his eyes briefly before looking away. Was that a hint of blush on her cheeks?

They continued chatting lightly about the island and the resort. Tylin felt completely at ease with her, captivated by her quick wit and quiet charm.

Too soon they arrived at his cabin. "Home sweet home," Shae said.

"Thanks to you."

Shae turned to leave, her long dark hair swaying gently as she walked away. Tylin watched her go, admiring her graceful movements. Though they had only just met, he felt drawn to her kind spirit and air of mystery.

As she reached the end of the path, Shae glanced back over her shoulder. Her green eyes met Tylin's, and for a moment they shared a look of mutual interest and intrigue.

Tylin raised his hand in a small wave. "See you around," he called.

Shae smiled softly. "See you," she replied, her voice carrying on the warm breeze.

Then she disappeared into the trees, leaving Tylin's heart beating just a little faster. He couldn't stop thinking about the beguiling young woman who had so unexpectedly come into his life.

Though their encounter had been brief, Tylin sensed there was more to Shae than met the eye. Beneath her calm exterior, he detected a well of untold stories and hidden depths. He found himself wanting to unravel the mystery of this island siren.

As Tylin entered his cabin, he replayed their meeting in his mind. The way Shae had challenged him at first when she caught him wandering the staff area, only to quickly soften when she realized he was lost. Her emerald eyes flashing with mirth as she teased him. The brush of her hand against his arm as she led the way.

***

Shae let out a deep breath as she returned to her own small cabin after leaving Tylin. Their encounter, though brief, had left her unexpectedly flustered.

Usually so composed around new arrivals to the island, something about Tylin's warm smile and gentle demeanor had caught her off guard. She found herself thinking about the crinkle in his eyes when he laughed and the soothing timbre of his voice. He was as handsome as Rosie had teased, tall, with dark brown hair and eyes. He was darkly tanned and seemed unbothered by the hot, humid weather, not sweating in the slightest - unlike her! She winced as she caught a glimpse of her flushed face in the mirror. She looked thoroughly hot and bothered, quite unlike the cool, calm demeanour she tried to project at the spa.

As she tidied up her cabin, Shae's mind kept drifting back to Tylin. She sensed in him a kindred spirit - someone who understood restraint and solitude. Yet there was an openness about him that drew her in.

Shae shook her head, trying to regain her focus. What was it about this newcomer that had made such an impression on her guarded heart? She barely knew him.

Still, she realized with a small smile, she was looking forward to their next encounter. If Tylin intended to stay on the island for awhile, their paths were bound to cross again.

Shae found herself unexpectedly hoping they would. There was more to Tylin than his charming exterior - she wanted the chance to discover the depths beneath.

For now, she would tuck away the memory of their meeting like a seashell, turning it over in her mind and waiting for the tide to bring them back together again.

Chapter Three

Tylin looked around the bustling staff canteen, filled with chattering employees and the sweet aroma of lemongrass and coconut. His stomach rumbled, reminding him he hadn't eaten since the crack of dawn this morning.

"Hey Tylin, over here!" A waving hand caught his attention, and he smiled gratefully at the familiar face. Rosie, the staff manager who had welcomed him to the island that morning, was waving him over to a table with one vacant seat. He accepted the seat with grace, smiling politely as Rosie introduced him to the others sitting with her.

A flash of emerald caught his eye. Shae glided into the canteen, her a soft cotton dress swishing around slender calves, the golden light of the setting sun slanting through the windows at the side of the room making her almost glow. Her long dark hair was swept over one shoulder, revealing the elegant arch of her neck. She moved with effortless grace, her gaze lowering demurely, plush lips curving in a soft smile as friends called out greetings.

Tylin's breath caught in his throat. She was beautiful, almost ethereal. He watched, transfixed, as she collected a plate of food and settled at a table in the corner with two other women. Her movements were efficient, reserved.

"You want to get a plate, Tylin?" Rosie asked the question twice before it registered with him.

"Oh, uh, yes. Thanks." He got to his feet awkwardly, catching the corner of the table with his toe and almost upsetting it, to the yelps and good-natured joshing of the others seated there. Apologising, he made his way to the buffet, trying and failing to keep his eyes off the beautiful woman seated on the other side of the room.

Tylin finished his meal and accepted Rosie's invitation to join the others in the staff bar solely because he could see Shae had already gone over and ordered a glass of wine. Leaning against the bar, swirling the ice cubes in his glass, he knew he should mingle, make the rounds and introduce himself properly. But he only had eyes for the dark-haired woman in the corner. Her beauty was subtle, unassuming. Yet it drew him like a magnet.

He watched as she laughed lightly at something her friend said. The sound sent a spark through him. He wanted to make her laugh like that. Hear her say his name.

"You should go talk to her."

Tylin turned to see the bartender grinning at him knowingly. He chuckled, rubbing his neck. "That obvious, huh?"

The bartender shrugged. "She's gorgeous. Who wouldn't be interested? But you'll never know if you don't shoot your shot."

Heart pounding, Tylin set his glass down with a decisive clink. It was time to be bold.

***

Shae tensed as she saw him approaching out of the corner of her eye. Her friend Aria nudged her leg under the table.

"Breathe, girl. The hot doctor's coming over."

Shae pressed her lips together. She would not make a fool of herself. But as he stopped before her table, she couldn't help the shy smile that crept across her face.

"Mind if I join you?"

His voice was warm honey. She nodded wordlessly. As he sat, their eyes met again, and the rest of the room faded away. Shae was only dimly aware of Aria giggling and making herself scarce.

Shae's breath caught as Tylin's bright blue eyes locked onto hers. His gaze was direct, and it made her pulse quicken.

"I hope you're finding everything to your liking so far at the resort?" she asked.

"I am," he said. "Especially the company."

Heat rose in her cheeks. She wasn't used to such direct flattery. But she found she didn't mind it coming from him.

"Sunfish Island is known for its natural beauty," she said. "I could show you some hidden coves and waterfalls, if you'd like."

His eyes lit up. "I'd love that."

Their conversation flowed easily after that. She learned of his work overseas and his passion for helping others. He coaxed gentle smiles from her as they spoke late into the evening, the rest of the room forgotten.

As the party wound down, Tylin helped Shae to her feet. His touch lingered a moment too long on the small of her back.

"I hope this won't be the last I see of you," he murmured.

Shae flushed. "No, it won't."

"Well. Good night, then." He glanced around, and Shae suddenly become conscious that there were curious eyes on them.

She'd monopolised the new doctor all evening, and clearly the two of them were the hot new gossip topic. She winced inwardly as she caught Rosie's laughing gaze.

She'd been about to ask Tylin if he knew the way back to his cabin or if he was likely to get lost again, but there was no way she was walking out with him into the darkness. She'd never hear the end of it.

"Good night," she said, her voice coming out a little squeaky. "I'll see you around."

"You certainly will." He gave her that warm smile again, the one that felt like basking in sunshine, and Shae felt her stomach turn over.

Shae closed the door to her bungalow a few minutes later, leaning against it as she tried to process the whirlwind of emotions she was feeling.

On the one hand, Tylin intrigued her. He was charming, intelligent, and seemed genuinely interested in getting to know her. The attraction between them was undeniable, like two magnets being slowly drawn together.

But she also felt uneasy. After her last relationship ended so painfully, she had sworn off romance. She was wary of letting someone new into her heart, fearful they would only hurt her again. She'd literally been jilted at the altar, when her former fiancé decided he didn't want to be married. Not to her, anyway. He'd married someone else just a few months later. That kind of rejection took a lot of getting over.

Could she trust Tylin not to break her heart? He seemed kind, but looks could be deceiving. Was she ready to make herself vulnerable again?

With a sigh, she pushed off from the door and moved to sit on the edge of her bed. She thought back over the evening, replaying their conversations and interactions. His smile made her stomach flutter. The touch of his hand on hers had sent tingles up her arm.

Despite her reservations, she wanted to see him again. There was something about him that made her feel alive in a way she hadn't felt in years. She wanted to get to know him better.

Shae knew the risks. But sometimes you had to take a leap of faith. She would proceed cautiously, but she wouldn't let fear hold her back any longer. For the first time in a long while, she felt a spark of hope.

***

Shae stared down at the dish of fruit and yogurt in front of her, absentmindedly taking small mouthfuls as she tried to ignore the playful jabs from her friends.

"Come on, give us the details!" Olivia said, leaning forward across the table. "We all saw Dr. McDreamy making eyes at you last night."

"He couldn't take his eyes off you," Gemma added with a wink.

Shae felt her cheeks flush but tried to brush it off. "Oh stop, he was just being friendly."

"Friendly? Honey, that man was captivated," Lucy said.

Shae shrugged, keeping her eyes on her breakfast. The truth was, she hadn't been able to stop thinking about Tylin, had slept badly because she kept remembering the warmth in his blue eyes. The way he had looked at her so intensely, like he was peering into her soul. It stirred up feelings in her she thought she had locked away.

Her friends continued their lively chatter and speculation, but Shae only half-listened, lost in her own thoughts. She had to be cautious, despite the flutter of excitement Tylin sparked in her. The last thing she needed was her friends' well-intentioned matchmaking. No, she would take her time with this. Get to know him first.

Still, she couldn't deny her smile as she thought of seeing him again.

"You know, if you wanted an excuse to see Dr. McDreamy again, all you'd have to do is come down with a little something," Lucy said playfully. "A nasty cough maybe, that needs some special attention."

Shae rolled her eyes, but couldn't help the smile tugging at her lips.

"Ooh, or terrible migraines!" Gemma chimed in. "I'm sure he gives excellent head massages."

The three of them dissolved into giggles as they invented more imaginary ailments, each one more absurd than the last. Shae laughed along, enjoying the silliness and camaraderie of her friends.

But eventually she held up a hand. "Alright, that's enough," she said, though her tone was light. "I appreciate what you're all trying to do, but I'd rather get to know Tylin in my own time."

She gave them a pointed look when Lucy started to protest.

"I'm serious," Shae said gently. "This is new for me. I don't want to be rushed into anything."

Her friends exchanged glances, then nodded.

"We're just excited for you," Olivia said. "It's been awhile since we've seen that sparkle in your eye."

Shae smiled softly. "I know. And I love you all for caring. But for now, let's just take it one day at a time."

With that settled, the conversation moved on to a new topic. But in the back of her mind, Shae felt a new sense of anticipation. However slowly, she was ready to open her heart again.

Shae arrived at the spa to start work for the day a little before noon, humming softly to herself. She couldn't remember the last time she felt this lightness in her step.

As she pushed through the front doors, the new receptionist Aria glanced up from the reception desk and beamed.

"Shae! You have a visitor," she said in a singsong voice, pointing towards the sitting area.

Shae followed her gaze, then froze. There, flipping idly through a magazine, was Derek. Her ex-fiancé.

He looked up and his face split into a wide grin. "Shae," he said warmly, standing up. "There's my beautiful girl."

Shae stood rooted to the spot, shock crashing over her in waves. She hadn't seen or spoken to Derek in over a year, not since she'd broken off their engagement and moved to the island.

What was he doing here? How had he even found her? Her mind raced, but she couldn't form any words.

Derek didn't seem bothered by her stunned silence. He stepped towards her, arms open. "What, no hello for your favourite guy?" he asked with an easy smile.

Shae took an instinctive step back, her eyes darting around the room. This couldn't be happening. Not now, when she'd finally started to feel free.

Shae took a deep breath, trying to steady her nerves. She couldn't let Derek rattle her, not after how far she'd come.

"What are you doing here?" she asked evenly.

Derek's grin didn't falter. "I wanted to see you, of course. It's been too long." He moved closer, lowering his voice. "You're as gorgeous as ever. This island air agrees with you."

Shae crossed her arms, unwilling to be swayed by his familiar charm. "How did you find me?"

"Oh, you know me. I'm nothing if not persistent." Derek reached out to brush a strand of hair from her face.

Shae recoiled from his touch, anger rising hotly in her chest. She thought of everything she'd confided, all the ways he'd made her feel small. Never again.

"You need to leave," she said sharply.

Derek blinked in surprise. "Come on, Shae. Don't be like that." His voice took on a wheedling tone. "We have so much history together."

Shae shook her head. "The past is done. I've moved on."

She thought of her friends, her community on the island. And Tylin - kind, gentle Tylin who looked at her like she held the answers to every question. This life belonged to her now, and she was absolutely not going to let Derek ruin it for her.

Derek's expression hardened. "Don't throw away what we had over some stupid spat. I'm not giving up on us."

Shae met his gaze unflinchingly. "There is no *us*. Not anymore. Not since you decided you didn't want to be married to me." She took a deep breath. "I've moved on. Now please, leave me in peace."

For a long moment, Derek just stared at her. Then his mouth twisted in a scowl. "You'll regret this," he hissed.

He turned on his heel and stormed out, slamming the door behind him.

Shae let out a shaky breath, reaching out to steady herself on the reception desk.

"Shae?" Aria said in a small voice. "Who was... was that not a friend of yours? I'm so sorry, he said he wanted to surprise you."

"It's all right." Shae managed a smile for the new girl. Aria had only been at the resort a few days, could not possibly know Shae's history.

"Yoohoo, Shae!" Mina Hartley came in through the spa's main doors, smiling broadly, and Shae somehow dredged up a professional demeanour.

"Mina, how lovely to see you. What do you have booked in today?"

"A seaweed wrap and a hot stone massage." Mina beamed, obviously in a much better mood than the last time Shae had seen her. Setting aside her troubles, Shae led her client through to the treatment room.

"You seem happy, Mina," she noted as she set out everything she would need for Mina's treatments. "Did you talk with Tom?"

"I did! And you won't believe it. He's apologised for everything... it turns out all the phone calls, he's actually been negotiating to sell the company and the sale is going through!" Mina was absolutely beaming. "For an amazing price... he'll never have to work again. He has to work for the new owner for three months and then he's promised to take me to Europe!"

"Oh Mina, I'm so happy for you. How wonderful." Shae truly meant it. Mina was so sweet, and obviously loved her husband. They deserved to be happy. "Now, come and lie down and let me get started on this wrap for you."

She needed to keep busy, to lose herself in work. If she thought about what Derek being on the island could mean for her, she might start screaming and not be able to stop.

Chapter Four

Tylin stepped out of the medical centre for a breath of fresh air, rolling up the sleeves of his shirt and loosening his tie as a warm breeze rustled the palm fronds overhead. It seemed ridiculous to wear formal clothes to work on a tropical island; maybe he'd talk with the boss about an alternative. Maybe one of those resort polo shirts he'd seen other staff members wearing.

A flash of movement caught his eye—a young woman bursting through the spa doors and stumbling down the path, clutching at her face as her shoulders shook.

Concern flooded him. In a few quick strides he reached her, gently grasping her elbow. "Are you all right?"

She whipped around, hazel eyes swimming behind a veil of tears. "I'm so sorry," she sputtered. "I didn't mean to—I've ruined everything!"

He steadied her with a hand on her shoulder. "It's okay. Take a deep breath."

She sucked in a shuddering gasp. "I'm Aria, the new receptionist. This guy came in and wanted to surprise one of our therapists - he seemed so charming and I thought it would be all right, but it turns out he's her ex and Shae was obviously really upset to see him!"

Tylin's stomach dropped. Shae.

"I should have double-checked first," Aria said miserably. "I feel awful. It's only my second day!"

"Mistakes happen." He gave her shoulder a gentle squeeze, despite the unease winding through him. Shae's ex was here, and she was upset. He needed to make sure she was all right.

"You're the new doctor, aren't you? I saw you last night."

"That's right, which means your welfare is my responsibility. So I want you to stop worrying about this, Aria - you didn't do anything wrong and you're not going to get into trouble. It's not your fault the guest lied to you." Tylin spoke firmly, holding Aria's gaze, and after a few moments she nodded timidly, obviously accepting his reassurance.

"Do you think I should talk to Shae?" Aria asked, eyes wide and earnest. "Apologize again?"

"No, let me." He managed a reassuring smile. "I'm sure she'll understand it was an accident. Why don't you take a break? Splash some water on your face and try to relax."

"Are you sure? Shae was doing a seaweed wrap on a client, she'll be in the back room while the client relaxes."

"I'll smooth things over. You take a few minutes."

As Aria retreated with a grateful nod, Tylin took a steadying breath. Time to figure out why Shae's past had suddenly shown up to haunt her. And figure out if the unexpected ex was who he feared - the creepy Derek, with his horrible misogynistic theories on the inferiority of women, and his determination to win back his ex-fiancée. It couldn't be a coincidence.

His stomach knotted, a sour taste flooding his mouth. Derek had seemed harmless enough, if overly smug—but everything he'd said painted the picture of a man unwilling to accept rejection. A man determined to reclaim what he saw as his.

He found Shae in the break room, staring out the window with her arms wrapped tight around her middle. At the sound of the door closing behind him, she glanced over her shoulder, eyes rimmed in red.

His chest ached at the sight. "Are you okay?"

She blinked rapidly and looked away. "I'm fine."

"Shae." He moved closer, keeping his voice gentle. "Talk to me."

Her shoulders hunched. "It's nothing. Just—memories I'd rather forget."

"Is it Derek?" At her flinch, he pressed on. "Aria told me your ex unpleasantly surprised you. Strangely enough, I was seated next to a guy on the flight up here who was absolutely desperate to win back his ex."

She scrubbed a hand over her face, smearing what was left of her makeup. "I thought I was over this. Past it. But the second I saw him..."

Shae trailed off, gaze fixed on some point in the distance only she could see. Tylin stayed quiet, giving her space to gather her thoughts, even as scenarios played through his mind. What had Derek done to hurt her so badly?

After a long moment, she sucked in an unsteady breath. "He was manipulative. Controlling. I didn't even have the words to understand what he did to me until after it was over - he gaslighted me into being absolutely dependent on him, but then right before we were due to get married, he got cold feet. I found out afterwards he'd told several friends he was having second thoughts, but he waited until we were actually standing at the altar before announcing that actually, he didn't want to marry me."

Tylin's hands curled into fists as anger ignited in his chest. No wonder she struggled to trust people. "I'm sorry you went through that."

She offered a wan smile. "I survived. It just caught me off guard today, seeing him again."

"If he gives you any trouble, I'll—"

"No." She placed a hand on his arm, a brief touch that still made his pulse jump. "Don't do anything rash. He's not worth it."

"But you are," he said softly.

Shae's eyes widened, a flush staining her cheeks as she stared up at him. His heart pounded, nerves and longing swirling together in a heady mix. He hadn't meant to blurt that out, but the depth of his feelings refused to stay contained any longer.

She wet her lips, a flicker of something like wonder in her gaze. "Tylin, I—"

The break room door banged open, startling them apart. Aria popped her head in, relief breaking across her face when she saw them.

"Dr McArthur, thank goodness you're here! There's been an accident at the dock. A boating mishap—they need medical assistance right away."

Tylin straightened, pulse shifting into overdrive for an entirely different reason. "I'll grab my kit." Duty first, personal matters later. He smiled at Shae, hoping to reassure her. "We'll continue this conversation soon."

She nodded, tucking a strand of hair behind her ear as color still stained her cheeks. "Be careful."

He brushed his fingers over her hand, a fleeting promise. "Always." Then he turned and hurried after Aria, thoughts of Shae filling his mind.

***

Aria stuck with Tylin as he raced through the grounds to the dock, and he was glad of the extra pair of hands and her calm demeanour as he patched up the young man who'd slipped unloading supplies off a boat and taken a nasty fall, breaking his arm and hitting his head. A helicopter was already on the way to evacuate him, summoned by the efficient boat captain's radio, and Tylin was able to hand over to the helicopter paramedics for the short flight to the mainland hospital with confidence.

“Thank you for your help,” he said to Aria as he picked up his medical bag.

“You're welcome!” A blush stained her cheeks. “I'm only working as the spa receptionist for the summer - I'm going to college in the autumn to study nursing.”

“You'll be very good,” he praised. “You're steady in a crisis. Good instincts.”

“Thank you, Doctor!” She fell into step beside him as he started back to the clinic.

“Can I ask you a question?” Aria asked as they neared the end of the path.

“Of course.” Tylin smiled down at her. She was a decent kid, he thought. Doing her best.

“Was Shae all right?” Aria bit her lip. “And is she mad at me?”

“She’s not mad at you at all, don’t worry about that. And I think she will be all right as long as that creep keeps his distance.” Just thinking about Derek having the gall to approach Shae after what he’d done to her made Tylin’s blood boil. “Can you do something for me, Aria? If you see Derek hanging about the spa, or indeed anywhere near Shae, come get me right away." His hands curled into fists, jaw clenching. However charming his exterior, Derek represented a threat—and Tylin would do whatever it took to keep Shae safe.

"I can do that. Just promise me you'll avoid direct confrontation," Aria said, catching his arm. "Violence will only make the situation worse."

Tylin grimaced. She had a point. As much as he itched to lay into the bastard, it wouldn't actually solve anything.

"You're right," he said. "But I won't stand by if he's harassing her. I'll get security involved and have him removed from the island if necessary."

"That would probably be the best thing for all concerned!"

He nodded, shooting her a grateful look. It was a comfort knowing there were people around willing to help and support them. "Thank you. I’ve got a couple of patients to see this afternoon and two telehealth appointments, but I’ll come get Shae when she finishes work and walk her back to her cabin. Make sure Derek doesn’t have a chance to catch her alone and harass her."

"Good luck," Aria said. "And remember—avoid violence unless absolutely necessary."

"I will." Tylin strode off before she could say anything else, determination steeling his nerves. He wasn’t going to let Derek make a nuisance of himself.

***

Tylin’s last appointment dragged on longer than he expected, one of the gardeners showing him a number of spots Tylin was concerned might be skin cancers. He took his time, wanting to give his patient his full attention, though in the back of his mind there was the awareness that Shae would be finishing work. Hopefully she might be running a few minutes late too.

By the time he closed up the medical centre for the evening, the spa was empty, dim and quiet in the fading evening light filtering through high windows. No sign of Shae. His pulse picked up as he hurried along the path that led back to the staff area of the resort.

Empty.

Panic clawed at his throat, strangling his breath. Where was she? Had Derek already—

No. He refused to consider the possibility. Shae was fine. He would find her.

Tylin broke into a jog as he let himself in through the staff gate, heading for Shae's cabin. *Please let her be there. Please—*

A glimpse of movement up ahead caught his eye. A familiar figure sitting on the front step of a cabin, head bowed. His heart nearly burst from his chest at the sight of her.

Shae. Safe and unharmed, as far as he could tell. The panic receded, relief flooding in to replace it. He slowed to a walk as he approached, not wanting to startle her.

"Shae?"

Her head jerked up at the sound of her name. Green eyes wide, she stared at him for a beat before recognition set in. She stood, dusting off the back of her black work pants.

"Tylin. Hi." A faint smile curved her lips, though it didn't quite reach her eyes. "What are you doing here?"

"Looking for you." He stopped in front of her, hands sliding into his pockets to resist the urge to pull her into his arms. "I was worried when I couldn't find you at the spa."

"Oh." Her gaze dropped, a faint blush staining her cheeks. "I'm fine. Just needed some air after..." She trailed off with a shrug.

After her run-in with Derek, she meant. Anger simmered in his gut at the thought, but he kept his tone gentle. "I understand this has been difficult for you. If there's anything I can do to help..."

Shae peered up at him through her lashes, expression softening. "You're sweet to offer. But really, I'm okay now." She smiled, small but genuine this time. "It was just...a shock, seeing him again. But it'll be fine."

"If you're sure." He didn't quite believe her bravado, but wouldn't push. "I'm here if you need me, though. For anything."

"I know." She stepped closer, going up on her toes to brush a kiss over his cheek. "Thank you, Tylin. It means a lot."

Warmth flooded his face, heart stuttering at the casual intimacy. He cleared his throat, fighting to regain some semblance of composure. "You're, um, you're welcome."

Shae's lips twitched, eyes gleaming with mirth at his reaction. Mercifully, she didn't comment, instead stepping back to her cabin door. "Goodnight, Tylin."

"Goodnight, Shae."

He waited until she was safely inside before turning to head back, tension easing from his shoulders. Shae was okay. And if Derek caused any more trouble, Tylin would be there to make sure he regretted it.

Tylin made his way back to his own cabin, mind whirling. He couldn't shake the unease that had settled in his gut, or the anger simmering beneath at Derek's gall. What kind of man ambushed his ex-fiancée like that, with no thought for how it might affect her?

If he was honest, jealousy had flared hot and bright at the thought of Derek trying to get back together with Shae. Tylin clenched his jaw against the surge of possessiveness, dragging in a sharp breath. He had no claim over Shae, as much as he might wish for one. She was free to see whomever she chose.

Still, he couldn't ignore the instinctive need to protect her, to shield her from harm. And Derek had already proven what a mistake it had been for Shae to trust him once before. Tylin wouldn't stand by and watch her get hurt again.

By the time he made it to his cabin, determination had crystallized in his mind. He wouldn't pressure Shae or make her feel smothered, but he would keep a close eye out. For any sign of Derek causing trouble. And if he had to step in...

Tylin settled onto the edge of his bed with a sigh, scrubbing both hands over his face. What a mess. When he'd taken this job, all he'd wanted was a quiet life helping people and enjoying the peaceful island setting. Now here he was, tangled up in drama and heartache that wasn't even his own.

He should have known things wouldn't be that simple. Life had a way of derailing even the best laid plans.

With a rueful shake of his head, Tylin stood to ready for bed. At least in the morning, things might look brighter. He could only hope the rest of his time on Sunfish Island wouldn't be quite so complicated. But deep down, even as he tried to convince himself otherwise, he had a feeling this was only the beginning.

Chapter Five

Shae was scrubbing the last of the massage oil residue from the treatment room counter when her phone buzzed again. Derek.

"Oh, give it up already," Shae muttered under her breath. Eleven calls today alone. It was getting ridiculous.

The spa phone rang, and Shae rushed over to answer it, since Aria had left a few minutes ago.

"Sunfish Island Resort Spa, this is Shae speaking, how may I help you?"

"Ah, Shae, my petal, it's so good to hear your voice," purred the unmistakable tenor of Derek Langston.

Shae rolled her eyes, clenching the phone tighter. "What do you want, Derek?"

"You, of course. I want to see you again, Shae. Let me book a massage—"

"I'm afraid my schedule is entirely full," Shae said briskly. "Now if you'll excuse me, I have to finish closing up."

She quickly hung up before he could respond.

Just then, the front door chimed as someone entered the spa reception area. Shae froze. She hadn't locked the front door yet. Please don't let it be...

"Knock knock," called Derek, strolling casually up to the counter, hands in his pockets. "Did you miss me?"

Shae groaned internally. This was not happening.

"We're closed," she said shortly, moving behind the counter to put space between them. "You need to leave."

"Not even a 'hello' for your favorite ex-fiancé?" Derek spread his arms wide. "I'm hurt."

"Goodbye, Derek."

Shae marched to the front door and held it open pointedly. Derek sighed and walked over.

"I'm not giving up on us, Shae," he said firmly, pausing in the doorway. "You'll see."

With that, he was gone. Shae slammed the door, flipped the sign to 'Closed' and sagged against the wall, willing her frustration to dissipate. This was not part of her plan when she came to work at Sunfish Island; it was supposed to be far enough away that he'd never bother her again. Taking a deep breath, she finished closing up the spa. She couldn't wait to get back to her cozy cabin, pour a glass of wine, and try to forget this unpleasant encounter.

As she locked the front door and headed down the path in the gathering dusk, she heard footsteps behind her.

"Shae! Wait up!"

She cringed, knowing that voice all too well. Derek jogged up beside her, slightly out of breath.

"I was hoping we could talk," he said.

Shae quickened her pace. "There's nothing to talk about."

"Oh, come on." Derek easily kept up with his long strides. "Don't you miss us?"

Shae whirled around to face him. "Let me make this clear. *We* are over. I have moved on and want nothing more to do with you."

Derek held up his hands. "Whoa, no need to get upset. I just think we ended things too quickly. We were so good together."

"Good together?" Shae gave a hollow laugh. "You mean when you ignored me for weeks on end while you were on business trips? Or when you brushed off my interests because they didn't fit your definition of cultured? Or how about when you blamed me for your own mistakes? Or maybe - and I'm just spitballing what the issue might be here - when you left me at the altar and married someone else?"

Derek blinked, seemingly caught off guard.

"Are you even divorced from Kellie?"

"Well... it's not finalised yet," he admitted.

Shaking her head in disgust, Shae turned her back on him and started walking. "I put up with your self-centered behavior for far too long. I won't make that mistake again. Please respect my wishes and leave me alone."

She continued walking, back rigid, heading for the locked gate that would admit her to the staff area, where Derek couldn't follow. After a moment, she heard Derek's retreating footsteps behind her.

Shae let out a shaky breath, willing her inner turmoil to settle. She had finally stood up to him. Now hopefully he would get the message and she could move on for good.

Hurrying back to her cabin, Shae struggled to rein in her emotions and not break down where anyone might see her. The confrontation had shaken her more than she cared to admit. She thought she had moved past all this, but seeing Derek again brought it rushing back - the insecurities, the nagging self-doubt.

No. She gave herself a firm mental shake. She refused to second guess anymore. What's done was done. Time to close that chapter for good.

Shae was so lost in thought that she nearly collided with a solid form as she rounded a bend in the trail. Strong hands grasped her shoulders, steadying her.

"Whoa there," said a familiar voice.

Shae glanced up to see Tylin's concerned blue eyes searching her face. Heat rushed to her cheeks.

"Sorry, I didn't see you there," she mumbled, taking a hasty step back.

Tylin studied her a moment, his brow furrowing. "Is everything okay? You seem...upset."

"What? Oh, no I'm fine," Shae said quickly, forcing a smile. "Just, you know, distracted."

Tylin didn't look convinced. He crossed his arms, head tilted. "Want to try that again?"

Shae bit her lip. She didn't want to burden him with her problems. But something about his steady presence made the words come tumbling out.

"It's my ex," she admitted with a sigh. "He showed up out of the blue wanting to get back together. I told him no, but it brought up a lot of old feelings..."

She trailed off, dropping her gaze. Tylin stepped closer and put a hand on her shoulder.

"I'm sorry you're dealing with that," he said gently. "But it sounds like you handled it with courage and grace."

Shae glanced up, blinking back sudden tears. His quiet faith in her was like a soothing balm, easing the rawness left by her confrontation with Derek.

She managed a real smile. "Thank you. I needed to hear that."

Tylin smiled back, giving her shoulder a supportive squeeze before letting his hand drop. "Anytime. I'm always here if you need to talk more."

Shae nodded, the lingering warmth of his touch chasing away the last of her doubts. She held Tylin's gaze, the air between them suddenly electric. Neither moved, suspended in the moment. Then, before she could second guess herself, Shae rose on her toes and pressed her lips to his in a soft, searching kiss.

Tylin tensed in surprise before his arms came up to pull her close. He returned the kiss, gentle at first, then building in passion. Shae's hands slid up his chest to twine around his neck. The length of their bodies pressed together, fitting like two long separated pieces.

Shae's thoughts scattered, overwhelmed by sensation. The solid strength of him, his woodsy scent, the scratch of his stubble against her skin. She lost herself in Tylin, leaving behind all her doubts and fears.

Too soon Tylin slowed the kiss, pulling back just enough to meet her eyes. His own reflected a riotous mix of emotions - desire, affection, concern.

"Shae..." he started, a little breathless.

She laid a finger over his lips. "I know. We should talk." Her cheeks heated, suddenly shy. "But not yet. Just...just hold me a little longer?"

His expression softened. Wordlessly he gathered her close once more, tucking her head beneath his chin. They stood entwined under the stars, the rest of the world fading away.

Shae closed her eyes, letting the steady beat of Tylin's heart soothe her. She felt safe here, wrapped in his arms. It was an unfamiliar sensation; she couldn't remember the last time someone made her feel this protected.

With Derek, she'd always been on edge, braced for the next criticism or put-down. His arms had never been a refuge, only a trap.

But Tylin... he was different. Kind. Patient. He didn't push or demand anything from her. He seemed to understand her in a way no one else ever had.

Shae sighed, nuzzling against his chest. She wished they could stay like this forever, suspended in this tender bubble. But the real world still waited beyond.

"We should talk," Tylin murmured again, voicing her own thoughts.

Reluctantly Shae drew back to meet his gaze. His eyes brimmed with care and something more, something deeper that made her heart skip.

"I know," she said. "I just...I don't know where to start."

Tylin brushed a strand of hair from her face. "How about we start with how you're feeling right now?"

Shae considered. A smile teased her lips. "Warm. Safe. And maybe a little reckless." She quirked a brow at him. "You?"

Tylin chuckled. "About the same." He paused. "But also concerned. I don't want to make things harder for you."

Shae nodded slowly. "I know. With Derek back..." She shivered. Just saying his name conjured shadows of the past.

Tylin's jaw tightened. "Has he tried to contact you again?"

"Yes. I've been ignoring him, but..." She bit her lip. "I'm worried he won't give up easily."

Tylin smoothed a hand over her hair. "You're not alone, Shae. I'm here for you, whatever happens next."

She searched his face, reading the sincerity in his eyes. And for the first time, she truly believed it. She wasn't alone anymore.

Shae let out a shaky breath, allowing herself a moment of vulnerability. "I'm scared of what he might do. He has this...hold over me still. Even after all this time."

Tylin's expression softened with understanding. He took her hands in his. "I know it's not easy facing the ghosts of your past. But you're stronger now. You don't need to let him control you anymore."

Shae blinked back tears, gripping his hands like a lifeline. "I want to believe that. I'm trying to believe it." She exhaled slowly. "I just need a little more time to sort through this. Figure out what I really want."

"Of course," Tylin said gently. "Take all the time you need. I'll be here when you're ready."

Shae smiled, reaching up to caress his cheek. In that moment, she could imagine a future with this kind, steadfast man who saw her for who she was. But the fantasy wavered as Derek's shadow fell over them once more.

"Thank you for understanding," she whispered. "I should get back. We both have a lot to think about."

Tylin nodded, his eyes full of wordless care. He pulled her close, placing a parting kiss on her forehead before letting her go and wishing her a good night.

As Shae walked back to her cabin alone, she felt buoyed by possibility, yet weighted by the past. The road ahead remained uncertain, but she moved forward with cautious hope.

***

Shae stared down at the bouquet of roses on her desk, her stomach churning. She didn't need to read the card to know they were from Derek. He'd been sending gifts and showing up unannounced ever since he arrived on the island. She tossed the roses in the trash just as Tylin walked in.

"Another gift from your admirer?" he asked, nodding towards the trash.

Shae sighed, tucking a strand of hair behind her ear. "I wish he'd take a hint. I've told Derek it's over between us, but he won't stop pursuing me."

Tylin leaned against the wall, his brow furrowed in concern. "Have you told him clearly to back off?"

"Multiple times, but he doesn't listen. Just keeps spouting some nonsense about his 'Theory of Women'." Shae rolled her eyes. "According to him, playing hard to get is just part of the chase."

"That's ridiculous," Tylin scoffed. "You need to be firm with him. Make it clear his behavior is unacceptable."

Shae bit her lip. "I don't want to be cruel. We were together a long time. Part of me doesn't want to hurt him."

Tylin stepped closer, his blue eyes earnest. "I understand, but you shouldn't have to put up with harassment. What can I do to help?"

Shae smiled softly, touched by his support. "Just having someone on my side makes a difference. Maybe you could help distract him sometimes? Keep him occupied?"

"Consider it done," Tylin said. "We'll figure this out together."

Shae nodded, feeling a swell of gratitude. With Tylin's help, maybe she could get through to Derek once and for all.

Tylin and Shae made their way down to the staff canteen, weaving between tables filled with chattering staffers until they reached a corner booth. Sliding into the plush seats, they were greeted by the beaming faces of Lucy and Bryce.

"Hey you two!" Lucy chirped, her wavy blonde hair bouncing as she gave them an enthusiastic wave. Though petite, the marine biologist's vibrant energy filled any room she entered.

"Glad you could make it," Bryce added with a crooked grin, his blond hair artfully tousled from a morning spent diving. The resort's handsome dive master was Lucy's partner both in life and in pranks.

Shae smiled as she settled in across from her closest friend on the island. If anyone could help with her Derek dilemma, it was these two.

"I filled Lucy and Bryce in on the situation with Derek," Tylin explained, his jaw tightening. "I thought they might have some ideas on how to keep him occupied and away from you, Shae."

Lucy nodded, her expression growing serious. "Don't worry, we've got your back. We'll make sure that sleazebag doesn't bother you anymore."

"Maybe we could trick him into doing something embarrassing," Bryce suggested, a mischievous glint in his eye. "Like pants him in front of the guests or put itching powder in his shorts."

Lucy swatted his arm. "Bryce! We want to distract Derek, not traumatize him. Or get sacked!"

"It was just a thought," Bryce muttered.

"Let's try more positive methods first," Tylin said diplomatically. "Ideas that engage Derek in activities he enjoys, so he doesn't have time to pester Shae."

The group spent the next hour brainstorming, suggesting everything from signing Derek up for sailing lessons to involving him in the resort's volleyball tournament. Though Derek's unwanted attention frustrated them, they were determined to respect his feelings while firmly maintaining Shae's boundaries. With their help, Shae felt a spark of hope that she could finally regain control of her situation.

Tylin clapped his hands together. "Alright, I think we've got a solid plan here. Lucy and Bryce, you two will be in charge of getting Derek interested in the sailing lessons and volleyball tournament. Make it seem like his ideas so he feels included."

Lucy nodded eagerly. "We can be very persuasive when we want to be."

Bryce rubbed his hands together with glee. "This is going to be fun!"

Shae smiled gratefully at her friends. Their enthusiasm gave her courage.

Tylin continued, "The sailing lessons start tomorrow at 9am sharp. Bryce, you'll invite Derek to be your sailing partner since you need someone with 'experience' to show you the ropes." Bryce snorted at the nautical pun but gave a thumbs up.

"And Lucy, you'll convince Derek that entering the volleyball tournament is the perfect way for a stud like him to impress the ladies," Tylin said with a wry smile.

Lucy tossed her hair back. "Please, I could sell ice to an Eskimo. Derek won't know what hit him."

"Great!" Tylin said. "Now let's synchronize our schedules to make sure someone is always keeping Derek occupied..."

As they headed out to put the plan in motion, Shae felt a rush of gratitude for her friends. With their support, she knew she could handle Derek. This was one obstacle she wouldn't face alone.

***

The next morning, Derek was lounging by the pool when Bryce sauntered up.

"Yo Derek! You ready for those sailing lessons today?" Bryce asked with an easy grin.

Derek peered over his sunglasses, annoyance flickering across his face. "Sailing lessons? What are you talking about?"

"Aw c'mon man, I heard you're the best sailor on the island! You gotta show me your skills so I can impress the ladies," Bryce said.

Derek sat up, puffing out his chest. "Well, I am an excellent sailor. But I've got plans to see Shae today."

Bryce waved his hand dismissively. "Shae's busy at the spa all day. But think of all the hot girls who'll be watching us sail!"

Derek pondered this, his ego winning out. "Alright, one lesson I suppose. But just know, my time is valuable."

Bryce grinned. "You're the man! Let's get sailing!" He clapped Derek on the back and steered him towards the marina before he could change his mind.

After the sailing lesson, Lucy found Derek at the tiki bar. "Derek! I need you on my volleyball team. Those other guys don't stand a chance against your athletic prowess!" she gushed.

Derek sat taller. "Well I am an excellent volleyball player." He glanced around. "But shouldn't I go find Shae?"

"Forget Shae, she's missing out! Come prove your skills on the court and we'll destroy the competition," Lucy said.

Derek flexed his biceps. "Well if it's for the sake of good sportsmanship, count me in." Lucy laughed and pulled him towards the volleyball nets.

And so it went all day, with various friends diverting Derek to activities across the resort. Though resistant at first, Derek's ego made it impossible to turn down opportunities to show off.

Meanwhile, Shae enjoyed a rare day of peace knowing Derek was occupied. She smiled watching him try paddleboarding, knowing her friends had her back.

She met Tylin for lunch on the resort's scenic poolside restaurant. The ocean breeze lifted her hair as she smiled across the table at him.

"I can't thank you enough for everything you and our friends have done," Shae said. "It's been such a relief having a Derek-free day."

Tylin smiled warmly. "Of course, I just want you to feel comfortable here. We'll keep him occupied as long as we need to."

Shae nodded, picking at her salad. "I almost feel bad, monopolizing everyone's time like this."

"Nonsense," Tylin replied. "We're happy to help. All that matters is you feel safe."

Shae met his earnest gaze. In that moment, she felt truly cared for, like she deserved the kindness being shown to her. It was a new feeling, but one she wanted to hold onto.

After lunch, Shae and Tylin took a stroll along the beach. The sun shone down as laughter echoed from the distant volleyball games. For the first time in a long while, Shae felt at peace. There were still challenges ahead, but she had an entire island of friends ready to face them with her.

"Shae! Tylin!" Lucy called out as she jogged across the sand to meet them.

"We've got a bit of a situation," she said, catching her breath. "Derek slipped away while we were setting up the scavenger hunt. Bryce is out looking for him now."

Shae felt her shoulders tense. After such a nice afternoon, of course Derek would find a way to ruin it.

Tylin placed a reassuring hand on her back. "It's okay, we planned for this. Bryce will track him down and we'll keep him busy again."

"I know, I just thought we had more time," Shae said quietly.

"Hey, don't worry about a thing," Lucy said. "We've totally got this covered. In fact, I have an idea..."

She whispered something to Tylin that made him chuckle.

"That just might work," he said. "Let's round up the others and put the plan in motion."

Lucy grinned and gave Shae a wink. "This is going to be fun."

Despite her anxiety, Shae had to smile. Her friends' enthusiasm was contagious. With their help, Derek didn't stand a chance.

Chapter Six

The path from the resort to the staff area was dark and deserted, lit only by dim solar lights planted into the ground intermittently. Shae walked quickly, her heart thudding in her chest. She just knew Derek was out there, watching and waiting to pounce like a tiger stalking its prey.

Shae shook her head, scolding herself for the ridiculous thought. She was being paranoid. Derek wasn't actually following her or hiding in the shadows.

Was he?

She picked up her pace, her flats slapping against the pavement. The sooner she got home, the better.

Shae glanced back again, scanning the darkness for any signs of movement. When she turned forward once more, she gasped. A dark figure stood directly in front of her, blocking the path.

"Miss me?" Derek asked, flashing that smug grin of his.

Shae's stomach twisted into knots. She should have known he would show up when she least expected it. He always had a knack for knowing exactly when she was most vulnerable. She gritted her teeth, steeling herself against the effect of that grin.

"Go away, Derek." Her voice came out stronger than she felt. "I have nothing to say to you."

"Now is that any way to greet your fiancé?" Derek tutted. "After all we've been through, I'd expect at least a hug."

Shae's hands balled into fists at her sides. "You're not my fiancé. We're through, remember? You married someone else?"

"I don't remember that at all." Derek took a step toward her. Shae resisted the urge to step back. She refused to give him the satisfaction. "In fact, I think you're just playing hard to get."

"I'm not playing any games." Shae glared at him. "We're over. Now leave me alone before I call the police and have you arrested for stalking me."

Derek's smug expression didn't waver. "You can deny it all you want, Shae, but you and I both know we're meant to be together. I'm not giving up on you that easily."

"Yes, you are." Shae strode past him, shoving his shoulder as she went by. Her heart pounded with each step as she walked away, waiting for the sound of his footsteps behind her.

But the footsteps never came.

Shae quickened her pace, not daring to look back until she reached the gate to the staff area. When she finally did glance over her shoulder, the path was empty. Derek had actually listened for once.

She leaned back against the wall, drawing in a shuddering breath. Her hands were still clenched into fists, her nails biting into her palms. She forced herself to relax, one finger at a time, and took another deep breath.

Derek was gone. For now, at least. But she knew this wasn't over. He would be back, as persistent as ever, refusing to accept that their relationship was finished. As much as she hated to admit it, Derek's surprise appearance had shaken her more than she cared to show.

A familiar ache bloomed in her chest, born from the ashes of what she and Derek once had. Before everything fell apart. Before his lies and selfishness tore them apart, piece by piece, until there was nothing left to salvage, she had honestly believed he was her soul mate. The one she was destined to spend her life with, have children with, grow old with. She had wanted that with every piece of her heart and soul, wanted the stability she'd never had as a child, when her mother bounced from man to man after her father died when Shae was small.

Shae closed her eyes, willing the ache to fade. She had come to Sunfish Island to escape the ghosts of her past, to find a new beginning. She didn't want to dwell on what was gone. She wanted to look forward, to a future filled with light and laughter and love.

If only it was that easy. If only she could silence the doubts that whispered she might never find that kind of true, forever love.

With a sigh, Shae pushed off from the gate and continued down the path. Somewhere here, Tylin was waiting for her. He'd promised to wait, until she was ready.

Waiting, but for how long? She shook off the thought and quickened her pace once more. Now wasn't the time to ponder relationships or the state of her love life. Now was the time to escape the shadows, to surround herself with light and pretend everything was going to be okay.

Even if she didn't quite believe it herself.

***

Shae spotted Tylin and Aria just inside the staff canteen as she approached, hungry for her dinner and weary to the bone. Her steps faltered for a moment, stomach twisting into knots, but she shook off the feeling.

Derek's threats were empty. He couldn't make her do anything. The past couldn't hurt her anymore.

Tylin glanced up as Shae entered, his face creasing into a relieved smile. "There you are. We were getting worried."

"Everything okay?" Aria asked, brow furrowing. "You look a little shaken up."

Shae waved away their concern, pulse skipping as Tylin took a step towards her. "I'm fine. Just had to take care of something."

His hand brushed against hers, a fleeting warmth that set her skin tingling. "Do you want to talk about it?"

"Not right now." Her gaze dropped to their hands, barely an inch apart. So close and yet not quite touching.

Tylin's fingers twitched, as though he longed to take her hand in his, to offer comfort and chase away the shadows lingering in her eyes.

Shae's breath caught, heart clenching with longing of her own. How she wished to lose herself in the strength and safety of his embrace, to leave the past behind and build a future together, free of doubts and fears.

If only she could be sure the shadows wouldn't follow.

She blinked, startled to realize Tylin and Aria were standing side by side, hands clasped between them. Her stomach twisted anew, sharp and painful, as the old fears rose once more.

Fears she couldn't escape no matter how hard she tried.

Tylin glanced over with a small, confused frown, as though sensing the change in her mood. His hand remained empty at his side, not holding Aria's as Shae had thought for one heart-stopping moment.

She shook her head and forced a smile, hating herself for doubting him even now. "Sorry. Long day."

Tylin's frown deepened, gaze searching hers, but he didn't press for answers she wasn't ready to give.

Instead he smiled, slow and sweet, and held out his hand in silent invitation.

This time, Shae didn't hesitate. She slipped her hand into his, pulse racing, heart soaring at the warmth and strength in his grasp. She glanced up to find him watching her, eyes crinkled at the corners with his smile.

"Better?" he asked softly.

She ducked her head, cheeks warming, but couldn't contain her own smile. "Getting there."

Aria fell into step beside her as they headed for the line up at the buffet, looping an arm through hers. "You work too hard, Shae. When are you going to learn to relax and enjoy life?"

"I do relax," Shae protested with a laugh.

"Liar." Aria gave her arm a gentle squeeze. "You've been wound tighter than a spring ever since I met you. I'm starting to worry you'll snap if you don't unwind soon."

Tylin's thumb rubbed a slow circle over the back of Shae's hand. "Perhaps a picnic on the beach this weekend? We could pack a picnic basket, find a secluded cove, and spend the day relaxing in the sun."

Shae bit her lip, torn between longing for the escape and time alone with Tylin, and the fear of being vulnerable with someone she was still learning to trust.

Aria nudged her with her hip. "A day at the beach sounds perfect. You should go." Her voice dropped to a conspiratorial whisper. "Besides, I happen to know Tylin looks amazing without a shirt."

Heat flooded Shae's cheeks as Tylin threw back his head with a laugh, eyes dancing with mirth. "You'll get me into trouble, Aria."

"Just trying to help speed things along," Aria said airily. She released Shae's arm and skipped ahead, casting a playful wink over her shoulder. "Let me know if you need help packing that picnic basket!"

Shae groaned, covering her face with her free hand. "I'm so sorry. She has no filter."

"Don't apologize." Tylin gently grasped her wrist, pulling her hand away to meet her gaze. "She means well. And she does have a point, you know." His lips curved into a teasing smile. "I do look rather nice without a shirt."

Shae swatted his arm, torn between embarrassment and laughter. "You're impossible."

"And yet you haven't said no to the picnic," he pointed out, blue eyes gleaming.

"I haven't said yes either," she retorted, though the thought was growing more appealing by the second.

"Not yet." Tylin grinned. "But the night is still young."

Chapter Seven

It hadn't taken much for Tylin to convince Shae to join him on the picnic, and they scheduled it for Saturday, two days away. Busy with work, Shae barely had time to think about anything other than relief that Derek seemed to have quit bothering her. She'd had a bad moment when she arrived at the spa to find a bunch of flowers on the desk for her, but they turned out to be from Mina, as a thank-you to Shae for all her advice.

Shae hummed softly to herself as she dressed for the picnic. She didn't think much about what she wore on a daily basis, mainly because she was usually in either work clothes or in casual shorts and shirt, but she wanted to make an effort to look nice today. She was pretty sure this was actually a date, her first proper date with Tylin, and her stomach squirmed with butterflies just thinking about it. Examining herself in the mirror, she smoothed her hands down the skirt of her dress, a soft white cotton printed with tiny blue and yellow flowers that fell just past her knees. She'd left her dark hair loose for once, out of its normal no-nonsense braid, and the dark waves tumbled about her shoulders.

"Don't you look lovely!" Lucy happened to be walking past as Shae came out of her cabin, paused to look her up and down. "Go get 'em, tiger!"

"Oh, hush." Shae blushed. "It's just a picnic."

She was a few minutes early, she saw as she glanced at her phone, but she didn't suppose it mattered. Tylin had said he would pick up the picnic and meet her at the beach, so she headed down the path that would lead her to the quiet cove the staff usually used, being off the beaten track for resort guests.

She was halfway down the track, humming softly to herself as she walked, when movement between the palm trees off to the left caught her eye. Turning her head, she smiled as she spotted Tylin and Aria talking together, was just raising her arm to wave and call out, when something stopped her. They were standing so close to each other, looking into each other's faces, and unbidden, the memory of what she thought she'd seen the previous evening came back to her. Had they been holding hands? She'd thought it impossible at the time, but now... even as she watched, Aria reached up, put her arms around Tylin's neck and her face up to kiss him.

At the angle Shae watched, she couldn't see if Aria kissed his mouth or his cheek, it only lasted a second or two but either way, Tylin certainly didn't push her off. He hugged her back, a broad smile on his face.

Jealousy and hurt swirled in the pit of Shae's stomach. She wanted to believe his interest in her was real. That he saw something beyond the scars of her past. But how could she ever measure up to someone like Aria, carefree and vivacious, who seemed able to lift Tylin's mood with a single smile?

Shae shook her head, brushing away the sting of tears. She was being ridiculous. Tylin had given no indication his affection for her wasn't genuine, and Aria only wanted the best for them both. Surely she was misinterpreting what she was seeing, as Aria stepped back from Tylin and they both laughed.

Even so, doubts persisted. Whispers of not being good enough, of finding her heart broken into pieces once more. She yearned to take a chance on Tylin, to open up and let him in, but the risk felt too great.

With a weary sigh, Shae turned and headed back the way she'd come. The beach could wait for another day. Right now, she needed the solace of her little cabin, a place to gather her thoughts and steel her resolve. She wouldn't be swayed by smoldering blue eyes or teasing smiles, no matter how they made her pulse race. Not until she was certain she wouldn't end up losing herself again. She'd text Tylin when she got safely back to her cabin, tell him she wasn't feeling well and couldn't make their picnic. Maybe he'd ask Aria instead, she thought miserably.

Shae glanced over her shoulder for one last look at Tylin. He'd turned away from Aria and was looking in her direction. The concern etched into his expression made her falter in her steps.

In that moment, she wanted nothing more than to run to him. To wrap her arms around his neck and feel the warmth of his embrace, losing herself in the tenderness of his kiss.

With an ache in her chest, Shae turned away. Some risks were too great, even for a chance at love. She could only hope that in time, the heart she had guarded for so long would be ready to try again.

***

Tylin froze as he met Shae's gaze, only briefly before she turned and walked away, heading towards her cabin rather than to their rendezvous point at the beach. His stomach twisted into knots as his heart hammered against his ribs.

"Tylin?" Aria leaned back, peering up at him with concern etching lines across her brow. "What's wrong?"

He raked a hand through his hair, pacing in a tight circle. "She saw us. Shae saw us hugging and now she's going to think—"

"What? No, you don't mean—" Aria's eyes widened with dawning horror. "She didn't see us kissing, did she?"

"No, no kissing. Just hugging." He shook his head. "But she's so insecure already and if she thinks I have feelings for you then—"

"You need to go after her. Now." Aria gave him a little shove toward the path. "Explain it was just a friendly hug. Tell her you only have eyes for her."

Tylin peered down the empty path, his chest tight. But Shae was already gone.

He sighed. Time for damage control.

"Shae! Wait!"

He caught up at her back at her cabin, sitting on the steps outside with her face buried in her hands. She didn't look up as he stopped before her, and he sighed. She'd definitely seen him and Aria, and she had massively misinterpreted their interaction, just as he'd feared. Tylin dropped down beside her, reaching out a tentative hand. "Shae, listen to me."

She flinched away. "Go away."

"Not until you hear the truth." He scooted closer, keeping his voice soft. "Aria was thanking me for writing her a recommendation to nursing school. That's all the hug was. I don't have feelings for her."

Shae lifted her head, eyes red and glassy. "Really?"

"Really. She impulsively hugged me and kissed my cheek, and it wasn't until I saw you watching that I realised how that could have looked. I shouldn't even have let her get that close." He met her gaze steadily, willing her to believe him. To have faith in him. "You're the one I want, Shae. Only you."

A fragile hope flickered in the depths of her eyes. "Do you mean that?"

"With all my heart." He reached out again, slowly, giving her time to pull away. When she didn't, he took her hands in his and brought them to his lips. "You're the one for me, Shae Everly. I haven't been able to think about any other woman since the moment I laid eyes on you."

A smile trembled on her lips as fresh tears welled in her eyes. She threw her arms around his neck and held him close.

"I'm stupidly head over heels for you too, you foolish man."

Relief flooded Tylin's chest as he enveloped her in his embrace, breathing in her sweet scent.

Shae cried into his shoulder, trembling against him. Her gasps for air came in hiccuping sobs as she clutched at his shirt.

Tylin stroked her hair, his heart aching at the sight of her distress. "Shh, it's okay. Everything's okay now."

How could he have been so stupid? He should have known how it would appear, embracing Aria like that where anyone could see. Shae's fragile trust in him was still new and delicate, and he'd very nearly shattered it.

He sighed, tightening his arms around her. "I'm sorry for hurting you. Will you forgive me?"

Shae nodded against his chest, her tears soaking through his shirt.

"Then let's have our picnic." He tipped her chin up, wiping away her tears with his thumb. "I've got it right here." He shrugged off the backpack he was wearing. "I'd just picked it up when I ran into Aria. We don't have to go to the beach. We can have it right here if you like... where you feel safe."

A flicker of hope lit her eyes. "You mean that?"

"Of course I do. I want you to feel comfortable, Shae. And I just want to be with you. I don't care where."

A watery smile curved her lips. "I'd like that."

Relief washed over him. He stood, drawing her up with him, and she slipped her hand into his and led him into her cabin.

They sat at the tiny table on her verandah and ate sandwiches and cake, drinking lemonade and just talking. Tylin talked about his time in Africa with Doctors Without Borders and how he had loved every minute of it - until his aid convoy was captured by a Somali warlord and he'd spent six months as basically a slave, saved from a terrible fate only by his medical skills being useful to his captors.

"So that's why you wanted a quiet life on Sunfish Island," Shae murmured, shocked to the core by his story. "We'd wondered why such a young doctor would want what's basically a retirement position!"

"I had enough excitement in Somalia to last me about five lifetimes. General practice was always what I wanted to do anyway, but a practice in suburbia somewhere felt a bit too stifling. This?" He gestured around them, at the endless blue sky, the palm trees whispering in the afternoon breeze, the sea just glimpsed in the distance. "This is literal paradise. Who could feel stifled here?"

"I know what you mean." Shae leaned her chin on her hand, gazed out at the view. "I've been here almost three years now, and I can't imagine ever getting tired of this place."

They talked all afternoon, sharing stories about their lives with each, the events that had made them into the people sitting here now, growing closer and more accepting of each other the longer they talked.

At sunset, Tylin invited Shae to go for a walk down to the beach, and she accepted, slipping her hand into his. They walked down to the cove and stood in peaceful silence watching the sunset paint the sky in incredible, almost neon colours.

"I've never seen sunsets like here," Shae murmured, leaning back against Tylin's chest. He wrapped his arms around her, pressing his face into her hair and breathing in her scent.

"Incredible," he murmured quietly.

They wandered behind a thick copse of trees, seeking privacy in the growing darkness. Once secluded, Tylin pulled Shae into his arms again, cradling her head against his chest.

Shae relaxed into him with a sigh, her hands sliding around his waist. The tension eased from her body by slow degrees as he held her, his cheek resting atop her hair.

After a time, she tilted her face up to his. He brushed his lips over hers, a feather-soft caress. "Thank you for giving me another chance."

"I think you're worth it," she said, a wry twist to her mouth. "I think... I might be falling on love with you." Her lashes fell to cover her eyes as she revealed herself to him, hiding her vulnerability.

Joy swelled within him at her words. "I know for sure I love you, Shae. More than I can say."

Her lips curved into a tremulous smile. "Prove it."

"However you want." He tipped her chin up, covering her mouth in a slow, deep kiss.

Shae melted against him with a quiet moan, her fingers spearing into his hair. The kiss gentled, becoming a leisurely exploration of lips and tongues. A sweet ache started low in his belly, but he kept the kiss unhurried, focused on the simple pleasure of being close to her again.

When they finally parted, her eyes were heavy-lidded and a becoming flush stained her cheeks.

"Was that enough proof for you?" he asked, a teasing lilt to his voice.

"For now." A mischievous dimple appeared in her cheek. "But you have a way to go yet to make up for earlier."

Relief and joy bubbled up inside him, escaping in a soft laugh. "Well then, I'd best get started."

He kissed her again, long and slow, and when he lifted his head, he said softly; "Will you come back to my cabin? To sleep, nothing more, not yet. I just... want to hold you."

She nodded, absolute trust in her eyes. "I'd really like that."

They walked hand in hand back to his cabin - which Tylin had only suggested because he knew it had a bigger bed than Shae's. Hers was a standard double, and he was tall; he didn't love sleeping with his feet hanging over the end. She looked at his king-size and laughed, understanding without his having to say the words why. Borrowing a T-shirt of his to sleep in, she used the bathroom briefly and then came to his bed, curling up in his arms without the slightest hesitation.

He wanted more. Of course, he wanted more, his body was practically screaming at him, but Shae wasn't ready, was still learning to trust him, so he carefully kept his hips angled away from her and did nothing more than hold her until she fell asleep, her breathing slowing and her body going limp against him.

Tylin held Shae close, relishing the feel of her in his arms. His heart swelled with affection for this complicated, captivating woman. She brought so much joy and meaning to his life, more than he'd ever dreamed of finding.

With a quiet sigh, he tightened his hold on Shae. She nuzzled closer against him, her even breaths warm against his neck. Peace and purpose settled over him as he gazed down at her sleeping form. Here, holding the woman he loved, was exactly where he wanted to be. The rest of the world could wait. All that mattered was Shae, and keeping her safe in his arms.

Chapter Eight

The morning sun filtered through the curtains, casting a warm glow over the room as Shae stirred reluctantly from his sleep. She was still snuggled into Tylin's arms, and he woke as she sifted her position.

"Morning," Tylin mumbled, rubbing his eyes.

"Morning." She smiled at him, a little shy, but after last night, confident that she wasn't making a mistake trusting him. He'd been a perfect gentleman even with her sleeping in his bed.

At that moment, there was a knock on the door, followed by an impeccably polite, yet somewhat tense voice. "Tylin, Shae? It's Luke Collyer. We need to talk."

"The boss," Shae mouthed, knowing her eyes would be round with shock. Why was Luke here? Tylin looked as confused as she did.

"Give us a minute, Luke," Shae called apprehensively. She and Tylin couldn't get into trouble for sleeping together, as relationships between staff members weren't in any way prohibited, so there must be some other reason Luke was looking for them at this early hour. His grave tone indicated it was nothing good.

Luke stood outside the door, his short, neatly trimmed blond hair perfectly coiffed and his dark brown eyes glinting with a hint of trepidation. He rarely wore a tie on the island, but his white shirt was crisply pressed, his formal grey pants and black shoes setting him apart as management from the more casual resort staff wear. He exuded an air of calm professionalism, his hands clasped firmly behind his back.

"Good morning, and I'm sorry to disturb the two of you so early. I want you both to know that I'm here to help. But we need to address the allegations made against you, Tylin."

"Allegations?" Tylin stared at Luke, and then at Shae, his expression showing his utter confusion. "What are you talking about?"

"Yesterday evening," Luke explained, his voice steady and calm, "Derek Langston came to me with some serious accusations. He claims that you offered him counselling and advice in a medical capacity regarding his relationship with Shae, only to then commence a relationship with her yourself. The last part of which, well," Luke gestured towards them, his smile apologetic, "is obviously indisputable. I'd like to hear your side of the rest of the story."

Shae laughed, a short, sharp sound, and she held up a hand to stop Tylin from speaking. "First of all, Luke, I'd like you to hear my side of the story."

"I'm here to listen," Luke returned, and gestured to the small couch and two chairs on the other side of the room. "How about we sit down?"

"I'll make coffee," Tylin muttered, giving Shae's hand a supportive squeeze. "You fill Luke in."

"I certainly will. I was on the verge of making a complaint against Derek myself, Luke," Shae began. "A police report, for stalking. He literally left me at the altar three years ago and married someone else, and I hadn't seen him again until a few days ago when he turned up and started acting like nothing had happened, insisting that he and I belonged together."

"He sounds like a massive jerk, frankly," Luke said with a sympathetic smile. "And I'll absolutely support you if you do want to put in a police report, but he has put his complaints about Tylin in writing and informed me that he plans to forward it to the Medical Board."

"Who does he think he is?" Tylin clenched his fists, rage obviously simmering beneath the surface, and Shae got up and went to him.

"Apparently, Derek's had it in for you since you arrived on the island," Luke said, his brows furrowed. "He saw you as a threat to his chances with Shae. Is there any truth to his allegation that you offered him counselling?"

"Yes and no. We were on the same flight up here and he spent the entire flight talking about himself and this ghastly misogynistic Theory of Women he has, and insisting he was here to win his fiancée back. Frankly, once I realised she had to be on staff here, I felt a responsibility to safeguard her from the jerk." Tylin gave Shae a small smile. "However... I'd already met and fallen for Shae before I realised she was his intended victim. And yes, I did offer Derek my advice - though I didn't use the word counselling - but, he hasn't sought me out and we haven't spoken since arriving on the island."

"Clearly he's seen us together, though," Shae said angrily. "Derek has always been manipulative, but this... this is beyond anything I could have ever imagined. He's trying to ruin your career, Tylin!"

"Seems like he's trying to ruin my life, too," Tylin muttered darkly. "But why? All because of some petty jealousy?"

"Unfortunately, yes." Luke sighed, rubbing a hand across his brow. "It's not just jealousy, though. From what I've gathered, Derek sees you as someone who swooped in and stole his chance at happiness. He's convinced himself that if he can discredit you, Shae will come running back to him."

"Ugh, that's sickening," Shae groaned. "Tylin, I'm so sorry. I never thought he would go this far. I really thought he'd given up after I made it clear to him the other night that I would never go back to him."

"Hey," Tylin reached out and gently touched her arm, offering her a small smile. "This isn't your fault. We'll get through this, together."

"Right." She nodded determinedly, taking a deep breath. "So, what do we do now?"

"First, we need to gather evidence to refute Derek's claims and clear your name," Luke suggested, getting up from the couch. "I'll ask Derek when and where this alleged counselling occurred. I doubt he realises just how much video surveillance we actually have all over the resort. If he can't give me a specific time and place, it won't go well for him."

"And I'm going to make that police report for stalking," Shae said firmly. "Because I can give you specific times and places... and I've got witnesses. Aria saw him harassing me in the spa reception, and he turned up there again after closing one evening... and waited for me in the dark on the path outside."

"Excellent." Luke's smile broadened. "I'll have that footage pulled and compiled, and confront him with it. We can provide it to the Medical Board as evidence if he does go through with reporting you, Tylin. I'm pretty sure they'll understand his motives and dismiss the whole thing as nonsense."

"Do you need me to do anything?" Tylin asked. "I don't like having my reputation called into question this way."

"Carry on as you have been doing." Luke nodded to him. "You haven't been here long, but I'm already hearing good things about your bedside manner. Be prepared, though. If Derek walks into the medical office, make sure he stays in the reception area - there are no cameras in the doctor's office for patient privacy reasons. We want any interaction between the two of you on video."

"Understood." Tylin nodded.

"And Shae? Don't go anywhere alone. Think witnesses. Always." Luke's expression turned a little grave as he looked at her. "When it becomes apparent Derek isn't going to get his way, he might escalate. I don't want you in danger."

"I'm not afraid of him. He talks a big game, but he's physically a coward," Shae said, her chin high and her tone resolute. "Derek might have started this fight, but we're going to finish it."

*

Tylin clenched his fists in anger, his nails digging into the palms of his hands. He couldn't believe Derek would stoop so low as to concoct these false allegations out of jealousy. He was relieved Luke was being so supportive - he supposed that while Luke barely knew him, he had known Shae for three years and would have no doubts about her honesty and integrity.

“Don’t worry, Tylin,” Shae said quietly, turning to him as Luke left them. “You haven’t seen how supportive the staff community is here. Luke knows now that Derek’s allegations are all nonsense; he won’t allow your reputation to be smeared.”

"Thank you," Tylin said quietly, touched by her unwavering support. "I truly appreciate everything you're doing to help me."

"Of course," she replied, offering him a small, determined smile. "We're in this together, remember? It’s my fault this is happening to you at all."

“It’s not your fault,” he disagreed immediately. “How can it be your fault that Derek is such a massive jerk? Like I told Luke, I wanted to keep an eye on him because it was obvious his ex was staff here and that made her well-being my priority, no matter who she turned out to be. It’s just a coincidence that it happens to be you.”

Shae smiled a little teasingly, reaching up to put her arms around his neck. “So you’d have offered the same support even if the ex had turned out to be someone else? Say... Aria?”

“The same emotional support, yes,” Tylin agreed, his arms sliding about her waist. “Definitely without the kissing, though. I knew long before I found out you were Derek’s ex, you were the only woman on this island I intended to be kissing.”

“Better get on with it then,” she whispered against his lips, and he didn’t hesitate another second before obeying.

“Do you have to be anywhere this morning?” Shae asked between kisses.

“Well,” Tylin tore himself away long enough to look at his phone. “As the only doctor on the island I’m technically always on call, but... I don’t have any actual patients scheduled until nine. You?”

“Working the noon to eight shift today.” She grinned up at him. “So that’s almost two hours before either of us have to be anywhere. Maybe we could make use of the bed again... for something more than sleeping, this time?”

His breath caught. “Are you asking...?”

For answer, she put her hands to the hem of the dress she’d put back on for Luke’s visit, pulled it all the way up and swept the dress off over her head.

Tylin's eyes widened in appreciation as she stood before him in just her underwear. He couldn't help but stare at her flawless curves and toned physique. Shae was stunning, and right then all he could do was stare.

"Is that a yes?" Shae asked, a playful smirk on her lips as she tossed the dress aside.

He didn't reply, instead, he pulled her into his arms and kissed her deeply before lifting her onto the bed, their lips still locked together. He couldn't resist exploring her body with his hands, running them over her smooth skin as he kissed her neck and trailed his lips down to her chest.

Shae moaned in pleasure, arching her back as he continued to kiss and caress her. Tylin couldn't believe how incredible she felt in his arms. It was like they were meant to be together, like they fit together perfectly in every way.

Shae was the first to break their kiss, gasping as Tylin's lips moved over her nipple.

"You have the softest skin," he murmured as his lips teased and his tongue swirled around her pert nipple. "I could kiss you all day."

"I don't mind if you do," she replied, reaching down to run her hands through his short hair. "You're really good at this."

Tylin chuckled, his lips moving down to her navel. He wasn't sure what he was good at, but he did know he loved every minute of it. Shae's hands stroked through his hair as his lips and tongue traced over her stomach, his hands caressing the backs of her thighs.

"I think I'm getting tired of seeing you in just your underwear," he said, his hands moving to the waistband of her underwear.

Tylin pulled her panties down over her legs, licking his lips in anticipation. Shae's curves were perfect and he couldn't wait to see her naked.

Shae raised her hips, allowing Tylin to pull her underwear off. When she was finally completely naked, he threw the remaining garments to the floor and gazed at her.

She was so beautiful.

"You're staring," Shae said with a smirk. "Are you really this eager to get me naked?"

"I can't take my eyes off you," he replied honestly, moving up the bed to lie beside her. "You're gorgeous."

She ran her fingers through his hair again, a sly smile on her lips. "I think I need to return the compliment. Stand up."

His heart pounding in anticipation, Tylin stood and removed his pajama pants. Shae didn't waste a second before her hands were all over him, stroking up and down his thighs, his chest, his stomach. Her touch was light, but it sent shivers through his body.

"You feel so good," she whispered, her hands exploring his body, her eyes fixed on his.

"You too," he murmured, fighting to keep his voice even. "Where shall I touch you, angel?"

"Anywhere," she whispered, her eyes hooded as she slid up the bed so she was lying beneath him. "I'm all yours."

"I hope so," he replied, his voice thick and his cock twitching as he gazed down at her. "Because right now I'm going to make you feel absolutely incredible."

Tylin leaned down to kiss her, his lips lingering on hers as he supported his weight on one arm. His free hand went to her breast, caressing her soft skin.

Shae moaned in pleasure, her fingers lacing through his hair as she kissed him back. Tylin could feel himself becoming harder, his cock pressing against her as she writhed beneath him.

He began to kiss his way down her neck, moving to her breasts as he teased her nipple between his thumb and forefinger. When he moved lower, kissing over her stomach, Shae made a sound like a whimper.

"Please," she begged him, her hands gripping his shoulders. "Tylin, I want you."

"I know," he replied, a smile tugging at his lips as he kissed his way down her body. "I'm getting there."

"I want you inside me," she continued, her tone pleading and hungry.

"I will be," he reassured her, his lips hot against her skin as he kissed his way over her hip.

When Shae whimpered again, Tylin took pity on her and pressed his lips to her clit. Shae cried out in pleasure, her fingers tightening in his hair. He teased her clit with his lips and tongue, exploring, finding out what she liked.

"Tylin!" she gasped, her head thrashing on the pillow.

He could feel her body tensing, her back arching as she moaned his name. Tylin ravished her pussy with his mouth, his tongue tracing sensual patterns over her clit as his fingers teased and stroked her inner thighs.

Shae's cries grew louder as her body arched off the bed. He could feel her hips undulating beneath him as her orgasm overtook her.

"Tylin," she panted, her eyes glazed as she gazed up at him. "Oh god, that was incredible."

"Glad you enjoyed it," he replied, his chest heaving as he looked down at her. "Now, where were we?"

"I think you were about to fuck me," she replied with a cheeky smile as she sat up.

Tylin didn't argue with that. Tender, passionate lovemaking was all well and good, but he wanted more. He wanted to fuck Shae until they both couldn't take it anymore.

Tylin moved to the side of the bed and pulled her into his arms. He kissed her deeply as his hand moved between her thighs. As his fingers found her wet slit, she moaned into his mouth and began to kiss him back even more passionately.

Tylin was almost shuddering with desire. He loved the way Shae felt beneath his hands, the way her pussy was so wet for him.

He wanted to be inside her.

As if reading his mind, Shae pulled away from the kiss and pushed Tylin back onto the bed. He gave her a questioning look, but she just winked at him and straddled his waist. Tylin shuddered as she slowly lowered herself onto his cock, his hands moving to her waist to support her.

He couldn't believe how incredible it felt, to finally be inside her. It was the most amazing thing he'd ever experienced.

Tylin was driven almost mad with lust as Shae began to move, her hips rocking slowly as she rode his cock. She moved slowly at first, her hands resting on his chest as she gyrated her hips against him. As he moved his hands to her waist, she began to move faster, her body moving as Tylin thrust gently into her.

"Shae," he moaned, his hands moving to her hips as he thrust harder into her. She moaned in pleasure, her head thrown back as she rocked her hips against him.

"Harder," she murmured, her head falling forward as she rocked her hips against him. He gripped her hips tightly as he thrust into her, his body moving against hers with every motion.

He felt his orgasm building, his balls twitching as his cock throbbed inside her.

"Yes," Shae hissed, her hands running up over her breasts as she arched her back.

Tylin watched her throw her head backwards, loving the way her body began to tremble with the force of her orgasm. Shae cried out in pleasure, tightening around his cock as she rode her orgasm to the end.

"That's it," he groaned, his hands gripping her hips as he thrust into her again and again. "Come for me, angel, come for me!"

She cried out again, her body shaking violently against him as her hips jerked rhythmically.

When she was finished, Shae's breathing was ragged and her cheeks were flushed. Tylin pulled her down onto his chest, kissing her temple as he held her close to him.

"Fuck," he groaned. "That was amazing."

"It was," she murmured, with a satisfied smile.

"Come here," he said, pulling her up his body so she was lying on his chest. "My turn."

Shae giggled as he rolled her onto her back and climbed on top of her. He took her hands in his and pinned them above her head, kissing her hard as he slowly eased his cock deep inside her.

"Tylin," she moaned, her hips bucking against him.

"Come on," he said, thrusting into her. "Come for me again."

Shae threw her head back, her back arching as her fingers tightened around his. Her body began to shake almost immediately, her hips bucking against him as her orgasm began to overtake her.

"Tylin," she gasped, her eyes locked on his.

"Yes," he hissed, pumping into her harder and harder. "Come for me."

Shae cried out in release, her back arching and her thighs squeezing his hips as her orgasm overtook her. Tylin groaned as he came hard, his body shuddering as he came deep inside her.

He felt like he was going to pass out before he even began to come down from his orgasm.

Finally, Tylin collapsed against her, his head on her chest, heaving for breath. Shae's fingers moved through his hair and down his back, stroking gently.

"Fuck," he groaned, his body still twitching with the aftershocks of pleasure. "I need to clean up."

"Hmm," she murmured, her fingers tracing over his skin in random patterns. "Don't leave me for too long."

When he'd cleaned up, Tylin returned to the bedroom to find Shae still lying in his bed. She smiled at him as he crawled onto the bed next to her, her warm body pressing up against his.

They didn't have much time, but he pulled her close, nuzzling his face into her neck, closing his eyes in bliss.

"Thank you," he whispered against her skin, felt her arms tighten around him.

"Thank you," she replied softly. "I needed that. Needed you."

They lay curled together, murmuring soft endearments until Tylin's alarm sounded, and he groaned.

"I have to go to work. I'm sorry."

"Don't be." She stretched like a satisfied cat, smiling up at him as he got out of bed. "I have to work too, just later. Meet me for a late dinner when I'm done for the night?"

"Love to." He couldn't resist swooping down for one more kiss, which threatened to linger until he tore himself away and almost flung himself in the shower, turning it on cold with a yelp.

It was the only way he was going to make it out of there without making love to Shae again.

Chapter Nine

Shae's hands stilled on the last bottle of lavender massage oil as the spa's front door chimed. She glanced at the wall clock—a quarter past eight already. The other girls had just a few minutes ago, and she was looking forward to locking up and going to meet Tylin for dinner. Just thinking about his smile made her stomach flutter.

The door chimed again—an insistent, impatient sound. With a sigh, Shae capped the bottle and stepped out to the front.

"I'm sorry, but we're cl—" The words died in her throat. Derek stood in the entryway, one hand still on the door handle.

Shae's heart kicked into overdrive. She consciously relaxed her grip on the oil bottle, not wanting to betray her anxiety. The security cameras were running. She couldn't afford to lose her composure.

"Get out," she said evenly.

Derek's mouth quirked. "Now, is that any way to greet your fiancé?"

"I'm not your fiancée. I haven't been for over a year, not since you made it abundantly clear you only see me as a possession."

He blinked at her, nonplussed. She'd always known the truth about him, but it had taken ending their engagement to finally find her voice. To stand up for herself.

"Shae, baby, don't be like that. I love you. I made a mistake, I want another chance."

She shook her head, a wry twist to her lips. "You don't love me, Derek. You love controlling me. I'm not an ornament for you to play with when you're bored. I'm a person, with my own thoughts and desires, and I will never be with a man who can't respect that."

"You can't mean that," he scoffed. "This is about that doctor, isn't it?"

"No, it's about you," Shae corrected. She crossed her arms. "I know what you tried to do to Tylin. Threatening to send that bogus complaint to the medical board? Despicable."

"I was just looking out for you, babe." Derek spread his hands innocently. "Can't blame a guy for worrying."

"I can blame you for being a manipulative snake." Shae's voice hardened. "The only person I need protection from is you." Shae pointed at the door. "Now get out of my spa and off this island. Don't ever contact me again."

"Babe," Derek began, clearly not having listened to a word she'd just said, "you're being emotional..."

Just as Shae was about to repeat her demand for Derek to leave, the spa door burst open and Luke strode in, followed closely by Tylin. Shae's heart leaped at the sight of them; she had never been so relieved in her life.

"Shae, are you alright?" Tylin asked, his eyes scanning her face for any signs of distress. His concern was palpable, a comforting balm on her frayed nerves.

"Tylin!" Shae exclaimed, her voice wavering slightly, betraying her relief. "Yes, I'm fine. Luke, thank you for coming."

"Of course," Luke replied, his eyes fixed on Derek with an intensity that made the hairs on the back of Shae's neck stand up. "I've been watching the security cameras and saw him heading this way. I grabbed Tylin and came right over."

"Appreciate it," Tylin said, taking a step toward Derek, his sandy blond hair catching the dimmed spa lights. "Now, Derek, we need to talk about your behavior." He crossed his arms, shoulder muscles bunching and showing off his broad-shouldered frame, his blue eyes narrowing as he stared Derek down.

"Talk about my behavior?" Derek scoffed, attempting to maintain his cool facade. "What about yours, Dr. McArthur?"

"Enough!" Tylin raised his hand, silencing Derek. "This isn't about me. This is about you, and the way you treat Shae and other women like her." He stepped closer, his voice low and steady. "You think you can manipulate and control people to get what you want, but you're wrong. You're only hurting those around you, and it needs to stop."

Derek opened his mouth to respond, but the look on Tylin's face stopped him cold. Shae could see the gears turning in Derek's mind, struggling to find a way to deflect the blame from himself. But for once, his slick charm seemed to have failed him.

Shae watched as Tylin's words settled over Derek like a heavy weight, and she couldn't help but feel a surge of pride for the man who had come to her rescue. Her heart swelled with gratitude, not just for his support in that moment, but for the countless ways he had shown her kindness and respect since they'd met. He was the antithesis of Derek, and she knew without a doubt that she had made the right decision in refusing her ex-fiancé's advances.

"Luke," Shae said softly, turning to the resort manager. "Thank you for being here, for watching out for me."

"Anytime, Shae," Luke replied with a reassuring nod. "You're part of our Sunfish Island family, and we look out for our own."

Derek finally found his voice, a defensive sneer creeping onto his face. "You don't know what you're talking about, McArthur. Shae and I have history; we belong together. I'm just trying to protect her from people like you."

"Protect her?" Tylin scoffed, shaking his head in disbelief. "You've been stalking her, harassing her, and making her life miserable. That's not protection, Derek. That's obsession."

"Enough!" Luke interjected firmly, stepping between the two men. "Derek, it's clear that your complaint against Tylin is baseless. You have no evidence, and your actions are only causing more harm than good. However, Shae here has more than enough evidence for a restraining order against you, considering how you've behaved."

Shae watched as the realization of the situation he was in dawned on Derek's face, his smug grin faltering. She felt a mixture of relief and trepidation, knowing that this confrontation might finally put an end to Derek's relentless pursuit.

"Restraining order?" Derek repeated, swallowing hard as he glanced nervously between Luke, Tylin, and Shae. "Now, now, let's not get ahead of ourselves. I was just... concerned. For Shae."

"Concerned?" Shae asked incredulously, crossing her arms over her chest. "Is that what you call it? Because it feels more like harassment and stalking to me."

"Exactly," Tylin chimed in, nodding in agreement. "Your so-called concern is nothing but thinly veiled manipulation. It's time for you to leave, Derek."

As she observed Derek's reaction, Shae marveled at the solidarity she felt with Tylin and Luke. It was true – they were a family here on Sunfish Island, and families protected each other. In that moment, she felt more at home than ever before.

Shae took a deep breath, steeling herself for what she needed to do. "Here's the deal," she said firmly. "I won't file a restraining order against you, as long as you agree to two conditions."

Derek's eyes narrowed. "What conditions?"

"First, you withdraw your complaint against Tylin and do not submit it to the medical board."

Derek scowled. "And why should I do that?"

Shae met his gaze levelly. "Because it's based on lies and jealousy. Tylin doesn't deserve to have his reputation damaged because of your pettiness."

Derek flushed. "It's not petty to report misconduct—"

"Except there was no misconduct," Shae cut him off sharply. "Tylin has been nothing but professional. You're just trying to get back at him for being with me."

Derek fell silent, caught out.

"My second condition," Shae continued. "You leave Sunfish Island tonight and never attempt to contact me again. Your presence here is toxic. It's time for you to go."

"You expect me to just walk away forever?" Derek demanded in disbelief.

"Yes," Shae said simply. "Those are my terms."

"You can't be serious, Shae. You're throwing me out? Just like that?"

"Dead serious," Shae confirmed, her resolve unwavering. She had spent too long letting Derek control her life, and it was time to take it back.

"Shae's right, Derek," Luke added, crossing his arms over his chest. "This island is a community, a family. And we protect each other."

"Exactly," Tylin chimed in, his blue eyes meeting Derek's defiantly. "If you truly care about Shae, you'll respect her wishes."

Shae could see in Derek's eyes that he was struggling to process what was happening. He looked from her to Tylin, then to Luke, and back to her again, as if trying to find any hint of doubt or uncertainty. But all he found was a united front, three people who were ready to stand together against him.

"Fine," Derek finally spat, his voice bitter with disbelief. "I'll go. But don't expect me to come crawling back when you change your mind, Shae."

"Trust me, Derek," Shae responded coolly, her heart aching with both relief and sadness. "I won't."

As he turned to leave, Shae felt a comforting hand on her shoulder. She looked up to see Tylin's reassuring smile and Luke's nod of approval.

With a heavy sigh, Derek shoved open the spa's glass door, letting it slam shut behind him. The sound echoed through the room like a gunshot, punctuating the end of an era. Shae watched his retreating figure with mixed emotions, relief and sadness warring within her.

"Good riddance," Luke muttered as he glanced at the security cameras, making sure Derek was truly leaving the premises. "You were very brave standing up to him like that, Shae. I'll follow him to make sure he doesn't pull any more tricks. And I promise... he'll be off the island on the first boat in the morning, or I'll call my friends at the police station and have them over here before lunchtime. Put the wind up him that you'll make good on getting that restraining order."

“Oh, I absolutely will,” Shae said firmly. “You can count on it.”

"Thanks, Luke," Tylin said gratefully, clapping a hand on the resort manager's shoulder. "We appreciate your backing us up."

"Of course," Luke replied, flashing them both a reassuring smile before heading out after Derek.

As soon as the door closed behind him, Tylin turned to Shae, his blue eyes searching her face for any sign of distress. She could see the concern etched in the lines of his forehead, but there was something else there too—a flicker of admiration that made her heart swell.

"Are you okay, Shae?" Tylin asked softly, stepping closer to her.

Shae nodded, swallowing the lump in her throat. "I am now," she admitted, her voice barely above a whisper. "Thank you, Tylin. For everything."

"Hey, we're in this together," he reminded her, his smile gentle and warm. "And I meant what I said earlier. I'll always be here for you, no matter what."

The sincerity in his gaze was enough to bring tears to Shae's eyes. She'd never had anyone stand up for her like that, let alone someone as kind and caring as Tylin. Suddenly, all the pent-up emotions from the confrontation with Derek came flooding over her, and she found herself collapsing into Tylin's arms.

"Hey, hey, it's okay," Tylin murmured, wrapping her in a tight embrace. "You're safe now. We've got your back."

Shae clung to him, letting the warmth of his presence seep into her very bones. She took solace in the steady rhythm of his heartbeat against her cheek, the gentle rise and fall of his chest beneath her hands. It was a reminder that she wasn't alone—that she had people who cared about her and would fight for her happiness.

"Thank you," she whispered again, her voice muffled against Tylin's shirt. "I don't know what I would have done without you."

"You were amazing," Tylin murmured against her hair. "The way you stood up to him...you're so strong, Shae."

She shook her head against his chest. "I couldn't have done it without you and Luke."

Tylin gently tilted her chin up so their eyes met. "Yes, you could have," he said firmly. "You've always had that strength in you. I'm just glad I could help set it free."

Shae smiled up at him, her heart full. With Derek gone, it felt like they could finally move forward together without his toxic presence looming over them. The future seemed bright again.

Hand in hand, they left the spa behind them, ready to face whatever the future held—together.

~ *The End* ~

I hope you've enjoyed reading the Island Escapes series! Turn the page to find out about my other books, and don't forget to sign up for the Shenanigans Press newsletter to stay advised of all new releases!

Also By Caitlyn Lynch

THE MCKENZIE LEGACY SERIES
Trust The Process
Breaking Barriers
Level Ground
Written In The Stars
Ridgewater Christmas
RESCUE RANGERS SERIES

Ranger's Rescue

Ranger's Homecoming

Ranger's Mission

Ranger's Blood
ISLAND ESCAPES SERIES

Finding Cory

The Reluctant Billionaire

Her Fake Island Wedding

Slow Simmer

Fighting Fate

Crop It Like It's Hot

Better In Practice
OTHER BOOKS

Star Rucked Lovers

If Wishes Were Horses – An Irish Romance

Caitlyn also writes historical romance as Catherine Bilson and paranormal romance/urban fantasy as Caryssa Cole.
Find out more information at shenaniganspress.com

Sign up to the Shenanigans Press newsletter to find out about our latest new releases!

www.ingramcontent.com/pod-product-compliance
Lightning Source LLC
Chambersburg PA
CBHW030348310726
48979CB00001B/226

* 9 7 8 1 9 2 3 1 9 5 1 4 1 *